The Luna City Compendium #3

Containing: Luna City Lucky Seven, Luna City Behind the 8-Ball, And Luna City Number 9, Number 9, Number 9 In One Complete Volume

By
Celia Hayes
& Jeanne Hayden

San Antonio, 2020

ISBN-13 978-0-9897821-7-3
ISBN-10 0-9897821-7-4

Cover design by Alex of 3iii Graphics

Printed in the United States of America by Lightening Source, Int'l. and distributed by Ingram.

Geron & Associates
A Division of Watercress Press.
2020

Dedications and Acknowledgments

Thank you to the readers who love the series, and demanded a further chronicle of events, lives, and loves in Luna City. To my family, friends and the memory of those who have gone before. *Semper Fidelis!*

Jeanne Hayden

The Luna City series is dedicated with affection to those residents of Texas small towns who have not only welcomed us over the past half-dozen years of doing book events and markets, but who have also served as an inspiration by telling stories which are woven into this continuing chronicle: Fredericksburg, Boerne, Bulverde, Beeville, Goliad, Gonzalez, Comfort, Richmond, Junction, San Saba and Harper, Giddings, Llano and Lockhart, Richmond, New Braunfels and Kerrville. Thank you all for your continuing inspiration. Special thanks are due again to Larry H. for expert advice on the cooking, classic French kitchen-management, and catering aspects of this and the previous Luna City chronicles, and gratitude to J. "Pouncer" Melcher, of Lancaster, Texas for attentive beta reading and extensive suggestions, and to the late Professor John Igo, of San Antonio, who read an early version of the first Luna City Chronicle and encouraged us to continue with the tale.

Celia Hayes,

San Antonio, 2020

Contents

Luna City & Environs

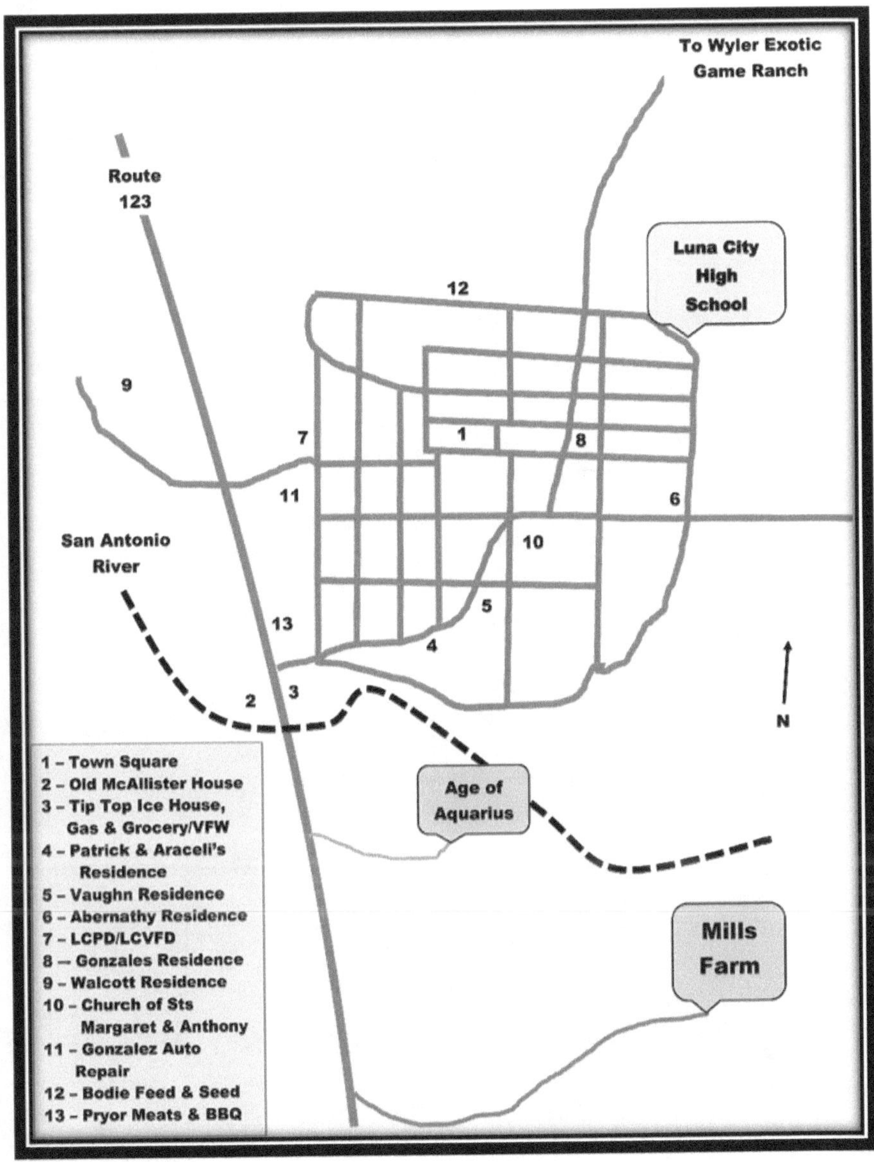

Luna City Town Square

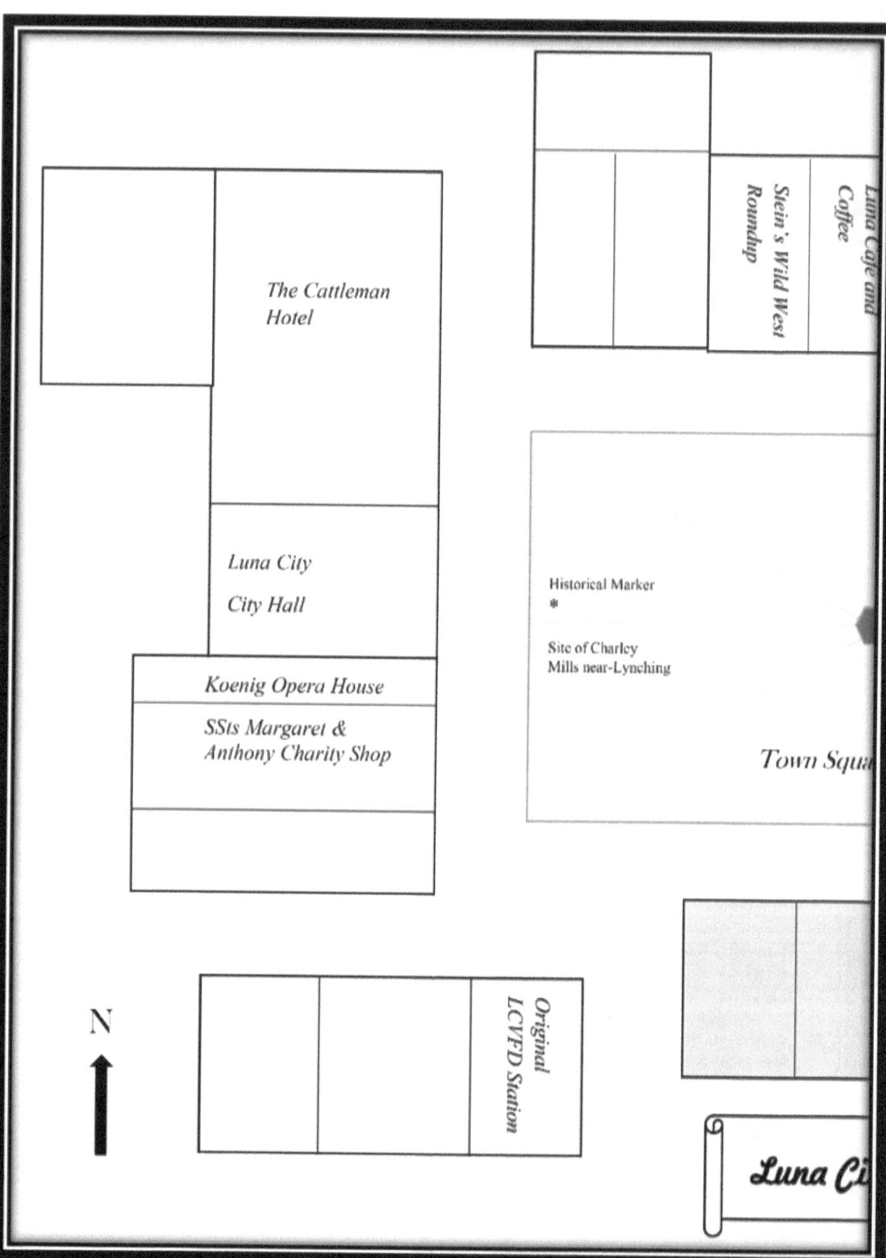

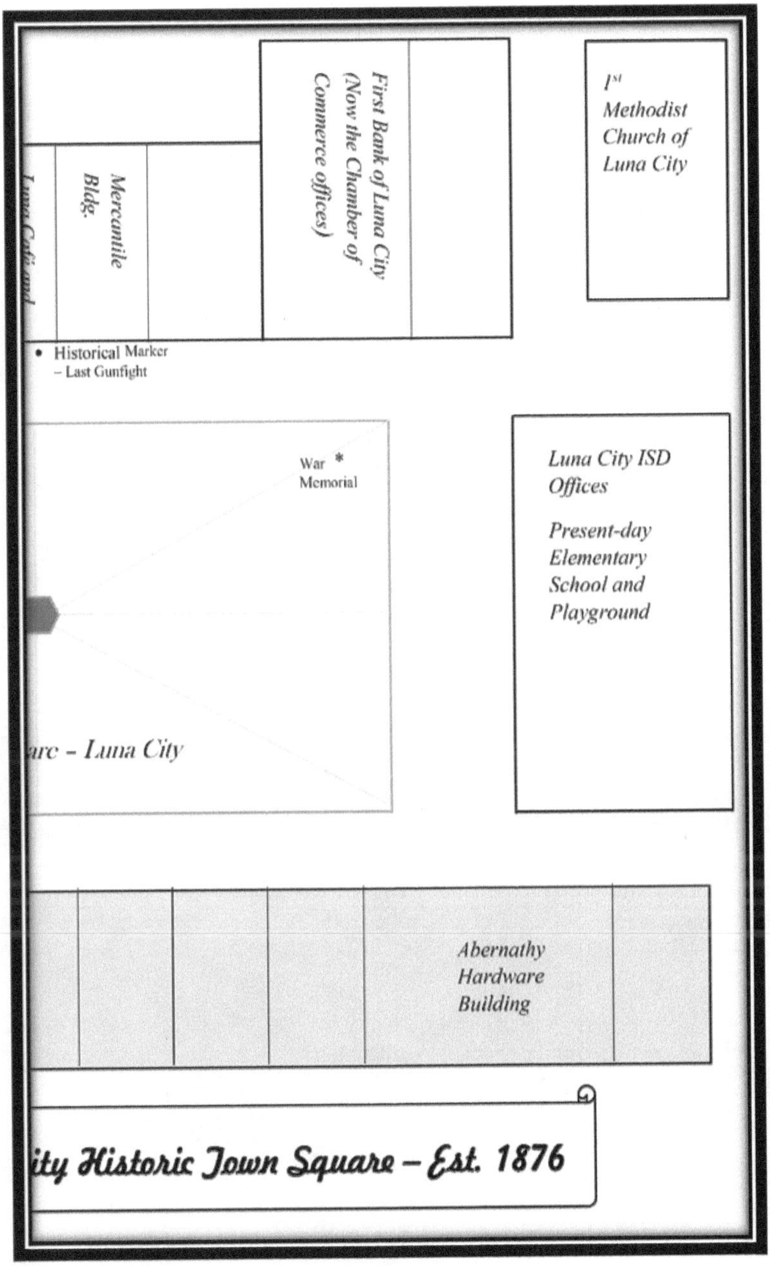

First Bank of Luna City (Now the Chamber of Commerce offices)

1st Methodist Church of Luna City

Luna Café and

Mercantile Bldg.

• Historical Marker – Last Gunfight

War * Memorial

Luna City ISD Offices

Present-day Elementary School and Playground

are – Luna City

Abernathy Hardware Building

ity Historic Town Square – Est. 1876

Cast of Characters

(An asterisk marks those who are deceased)

Richard Astor-Hall *(Ricardo to his friends in Luna City, Rich Hall in his previous life)*	A former celebrity chef, who through a chain of circumstances, finished up in Luna City, managing the Luna City Café and doing the occasional catering event.
Martin Abernathy	Widower, father of Jess, mayor of Luna City, hereditary owner of Abernathy Hardware.
Jessica "Jess" Abernathy Vaughn	Daughter of Martin, qualified CPA, Air Force Reservist, champion barrel-racer, newly-married to Joe Vaughn.
Benny Cordova	The devious and ninja-skilled general manager of Mills Farm.
Samantha "Sammi" Colquhoun	Sometime actress, media personality, and ex-girlfriend of Richard.
Lucien "Lew" Dubois	Director of Marketing for the corporation which owns Mills Farm.
James Wyler "J.W." Ellis*	Grandson of Doc Stephen Wyler, once boyfriend to Jess Abernathy, best friend of Chris

	Mayall.
Dwight David "Music Man" Garrett	Coach of the Mighty Fighting Moths and band music master.
Alberto "Berto" Gonzales	Student and part-time limo driver, younger brother of Araceli Gonzalez, friend of Richard, and grandson of *Abuelita* Adeliza Gonzalez.
Sylvester Gonzales	Gaming geek, computer nerd, USMC veteran.
Roman Gonzales	Construction contractor.
Roman "Romeo" Gonzales	Cousin of Berto and Araceli, former oilfield worker, currently top male model, married to Susannah Wyatt, no longer an unwitting focus for strange and unearthly energies.
Adeliza "Abuelita" Gonzalez	The revered and feared matriarch of the Gonzales/Gonzalez clan, dedicated Food Channel watcher, and Richard's biggest fan.
Araceli Gonzales-Gonzalez	Older sister of Berto, married to Patrico, mother of Angelika and Mateo, manager, assistant cook, head waitress at the Luna Café & Coffee.

Patrico "Pat" Gonzalez	Husband to Araceli, drives a tanker truck for an oil company in the Eagle Ford Shale Oil Field.
Hernando "Nando" Gonzalez*	Korean War fighter ace, local hero, for whom the high school gymnasium is named.
Judith "Judy" Stillwell Grant	With her husband Sefton, the owner of the Age of Aquarius Campground and Goat Farm, the last two holdouts of a 1960s commune.
Sefton Grant	Husband of Judy, landlord of Richard.
Brianna "Bree" Grant	Youngest grandchild of Judy and Sefton, willful and intelligent, former apprentice at the Café.
Katherine "Kate" Heisel	Gonzales cousin, reporter for the *Karnesville Weekly Beacon*, significant other to Richard.
David Chung MacNamara	Personal assistant to Collin Wyler, master of the financial universe.
Lucas "Luc" Massie	New chef at the Café, drummer in a local band known as OPM.

Christopher "Chris" Mayall	Manager, Tip-Top Icehouse, Gas & Grocery, bartender at the VFW, disabled Navy veteran, volunteer medic for the Luna City VFD, best friend of J.W. Ellis, and friend of Richard.
Allen Lee Mayne	Former pro football player, Food Network star, host of roving restaurant show *A La Carte With Quartermayne.*
Leticia "Miss Letty" McAllister	Oldest person in Luna City, WWII Red Cross service, kindergarten teacher, friend to Chris Mayall.
Douglas McAllister, Phd *	Miss Letty's older brother, professor of history, and author of *The History of Luna City.*
Phillip Noel-Barrett	Actor, media personality, romantic rival and frenemy of Richard.
Ozymandias-King-of-Kings "Ozzie"	Richard's one-eyed cat, mascot for his cooking-for-kids blog "Captain Kitten's Kitchen."
Xavier Gunnison Penn	Unsuccessful international treasure-hunter.

Andrew Pryor	Oilfield geologist, headquartered in Karnesville, owner of small BBQ restaurant.
Patricia Wyler Pryor	Granddaughter of Dr. Stephen Wyler and Miss Alice, wife of Andrew Pryor, HS girlfriend of Joe Vaughn.
Georg Stein	Native of Germany, a retired corporate lawyer, passionate reenactor, owner of Stein's Wild West Round-up, married to Annise.
Annise Stein	Co-owner of Stein's Wild West Round-up.
Joseph "Joe" Vaughn	Army veteran, local football hero, chief of the Luna City Police Department, married to Jess Abernathy.
Joseph James Vaughn, Jr.	Infant son of Joe Vaughn and Jess Abernathy-Vaughn.
Harry Vaughn	Great-uncle of Joe Vaughn, retired federal marshal, and former police chief in a small town in Alaska.

Clovis Walcott, (Colonel, USAR/Ret.) Retired US Army Reservist, currently consulting engineer, keen reenactor.

Sook "Isabel" Walcott Wife of Clovis, socially ambitious, and the tiger-mother from Hell.

Jeremy "Jerry" Walcott Oldest child of Clovis and Sook, a student nurse and family care-giver.

Robbie Walcott Younger son of Clovis and Sook, bright and wildly curious, part-time cook at the Café.

Belle Walcott Daughter of Clovis and Sook, student at the Julliard School of Music.

Susannah Wyatt-Gonzales Former regional manager, at VPI, sexually stalked Richard, got over it and married Romeo Gonzales.

Collin Wyler Son of Doc Wyler and Miz Alice, father of Patricia, international financier, serial husband, and treasure-hunting enthusiast.

Stephen "Doc" Wyler Owner of the Wyler Exotic Game Ranch, a qualified veterinarian, part-owner of the Café and second-oldest resident. Father of

Collin, grandfather of Patricia Pryor and J.W. Ellis.

Marigold Amy Yasbeck A student, and semi-girlfriend of Berto, formerly known as the child actress Amy Butler.

Luna City Lucky 7

The Path of True Love

"Richard, I need you to promise on anything you hold to be holy and good in your life, that you will not facilitate any surreptitious meetings between the Walcott girl and that tattooed freak of yours in the Café!" Doc Wyler looked over his copy of the *Beeville Bee-Picayune* newspaper with an expression on his age-leathered face which suggested that he had but one surviving nerve, and someone the size of Hulk Hogan was standing on it with both feet shod in hobnailed boots.

Richard sighed, and pushed up the sleeve of his chef's jacket. It was a temperate spring Monday morning, the first business day after the grand opening of Mills Farm's newest attraction, the 1912 Boathouse. Which for him had been a glittering culinary triumph, until the ghastly moment that he and Sook Walcott had surprised Sook's daughter Belle and Richard's junior cook embracing each other in the tiny prep kitchen on the water-side level of the boat house. Belle Walcott and Luc Massie in full passionate grapple, clothing madly disarrayed and exploring each other's tonsils; nope, there was no way that scene could be excused as *'just good friends and a casual, affectionate kiss'*. Not that Sook Walcott allowed anyone involved the opportunity to embellish a bald and unconvincing narrative with a single shred of corroborative detail in the interests of artistic verisimilitude.

Fortunately, the event had been almost over. An audience for the resulting histrionics and spectacular exit by Sook and her offspring was a relatively small one, for all that Sook's furious lecture to her daughter had ranged the length and breadth of Mills Farm between the Boathouse and the entrance gate, where the Walcott's blinged-out SUV was parked. For this small blessing Richard was grateful. Young Robbie had been relatively stoic, manly in his vintage USMC garb, and so had Belle, though the latter had given a pretty good impression of Joan of Arc being marched to the unlit pyre and stake by her outraged parent.

"You been getting hourly calls from *la Walcott?* I finally had to turn off my phone on Sunday morning, and damned if the wretched woman didn't drive over to the Age late that afternoon and chew on me personally. It was embarrassing; I was in the middle of fixing *steak au poivre* for Kate. A celebratory supper, don't you know? All for naught, as the steak turned well-done, while I was distracted."

"A tragedy, I am sure," Doc Wyler snarled, wolfishly.

Richard replied. "It was, damn the luck – a waste of a prime bit of steak! From one of your cows, by the way, and Andy Pryor cut and trimmed it for me to special order. Ruined by that wretched woman, banging on the door of the Airstream and screaming abuse at me through the screen window!"

"Sorry about all that," Doc Wyler was abashed. "About the steak. I'll make it up to you, son. Your lady-friend didn't get put off by the performance, I hope."

"Miss Kate Heisel has a high tolerance for screaming drama, fortunately," Richard answered. "She was more amused than horrified. She was even taking notes."

Doc took up his newspaper again. "It's a darned good thing the girl is going back to that fancy-ass music school in another week. You'll only have to stand guard over your freaky pal until next Sunday. Son, I want your word of honor, that you will not assist him in arranging a meeting between him and the Walcott girl anywhere near the Café. I as much promised Mrs. Walcott that much, just to get her to stop harassing the house at all hours. He's a starving musician in a busted-flat band, and she is a girl with a bright future head of her, less'n he drags her down."

Richard straightened his posture into something resembling attention to orders. "Honor bright, Doc. I will not assist Luc in any kind of assignation, romantic or otherwise with Belle Walcott. However – if between them they should manage such a meeting without my knowledge or assistance, I simply do not see how I might be held responsible."

"Trust me, Mrs. Walcott will find a way," Doc grunted. "At least, your boy is under your eye every day at work in the kitchen. And when he is not…"

"He is upstairs at his flat in the Mercantile, practicing on his drum-kit," Richard replied. "Behind a well-locked door. As anyone with upstairs windows which open into the Square can attest. Saturday night, she tried standing out in the street in front of the Mercantile, screaming up at the windows. Fortunately, Chief Vaughn came along in his official capacity and read Sook the riot act. The Steins have already complained to me – in a fairly nice way, for Germans – and that ghastly Mason woman who is overseeing the redecoration of the Cattleman had also made pointed mention." Richard snickered. "All part of the small-town ambiance experience at full-strength, I told her. You can't help it, I said; you will live cheek by jowl in small apartments, or tiny cottages, and what your neighbors do, you can't help being made aware of, in every detail. She should put up with what I endure at the Age, on those occasions when the campground is overrun. At any rate, when I told her that, she made a face like she had discovered a live slug in her *salad nicoise.* An obnoxious woman; I can't think why Lew left her in charge of the final touches on the Cattleman."

"The man had family obligations," Doc Wyler acknowledged. "Fiftieth wedding anniversary and he had already promised to be there, as soon as he had his project for those bastards at VPI launched and well-out to sea. Mind you, I think he had expected to have the last touches to the hotel well in hand by this time. Can't change hotel and river cruise reservations made a year ago. Though I suppose one can, if you are royalty, or rich enough."

"Lew is too much of a gentleman to disarrange any of his well-announced plans," Richard answered. "The man is well-recognizant of the pain that it causes, cascading all the way down. A gentleman of the first water. I imagine that Her Majesty feels much the same about a last-minute disarrangement to her published schedule."

"More to the point, he could not disappoint Mrs. Dubois," Doc Wyler grunted. "I suspect that she would have ways of making her unhappiness known. Miz Alice could always turn the knife in a most ladylike way when she was on the outs with me."

"Still, I wish that he had not left the Mason woman in charge," Richard lamented. "But I suppose that the board of directors approved room designs from that pretentious bag of bones and silicone. The ground floor rooms at the Cattleman are exquisite. At least she cannot do too much to alter them, at this late date."

"Ah – reminds me of something," Doc laid down his newspaper again. "Damn near forgot, until you mentioned the Cattleman public rooms. My son Collie; you remember him, of course. Played a round of golf with you and I and Walcott, just before Christmas a year ago. Well, he is blowing in for a visit, sometime over the summer. Wants to introduce me to the soon-to-be next Mrs. Collin Wyler."

And soon after that to be the former Mrs. Collin Wyler, Richard thought, but had the belated sense of tact not to say aloud. The sequential wives of the much-wed international finance magnate and father of Patricia Wyler Pryor were the topic of horrified amusement in Luna City. Not anywhere within Patricia's hearing, for Lunaites were generally an understanding lot, even if Patricia had on the odd occasion been humorous regarding her fathers' penchant for increasingly younger and more exotic women.

"He tells me that this one wants to be married here, for some damn-fool reason," Doc Wyler continued. "Ah, well. Likely he'll have changed his mind about marrying her by then. He usually does." Doc shook his head, sadly. "You'd think that one woman – her habits, likes and dislikes, funny moods – is more than enough for a man to learn to handle. Who is fool enough to go out and start all over with another one, every six months or so? This one is one of his old girlfriends, though. Name escapes me for the moment. An actress, I believe. Not Joan Collins, but someone whose name reminds me of her. Anyway, if the wedding is still on when Collie does visit, I'll talk to you then about catering. I'd frankly rather have all the fuss and upset someplace other than the ranch."

"I'd be happy to work up something for a happy event," Richard answered. "Just let me know where, and how many guests."

"Good," Doc picked up his paper, indicating that business was concluded, and Richard escaped to his kitchen, where Araceli, Beatriz and Blanca, the junior waitresses, were wrapping up the breakfast rush. Luc Massie, the Café's junior cook and target of Doc Wyler's breakfast ire and Sook Walcott's unappeasable fury, was beginning preparation of tomorrow's batch of the Café's signature cinnamon rolls, rolling out a long rectangle of sweet-roll dough on the lightly-floured worktable surface. The vast Wolff oven would be ready to accommodate the finished breakfast rolls in another hour or so, when the vast beef pot-roast, and pork butt roast intended for today's luncheon entrée would be done.

Richard regarded this scene of culinary chaos, aware that everyone glanced up as he came back to the kitchen; wordless and wary. They bent to their assigned labors with renewed vigor almost instantly, which he viewed with approval and satisfaction. His kitchen moved as a well-lubricated machine, no matter how deeply the stickiness of love gummed up the gears; Araceli and the girls all neat in their old-fashioned pastel dresses and crisply starched aprons, for they worked the front of the house. Luc – spectacularly tatted, pierced to a fair-the-well, with a crest of magenta-dyed hair adorning his otherwise shaved skull … Richard preferred that Luc exercise his considerable talents at the grill station well out of sight of customers.

"I've just been speaking to Doc Wyler," Richard raised his voice slightly. "Who is, as I am certain you are all aware, the majority owner of this enterprise, and therefore our employer. He brought to my attention the fact that Mrs. Sook Walcott is extremely unhappy that one of my subordinates – that would be you, Luc – has formed a *mésalliance* with Miss Isabelle Walcott. Hardly necessary, as I was already well aware of the matter.” He added, upon correctly interpreting expressions of bafflement from Luc, Beatriz and Blanca, “*Mésalliance*; that means an unsuitable and damaging relationship. Doc Wyler has asked me to ensure that there should be no such *liaison* on these premises; especially a private meeting in the week remaining before Miss Walcott returns to New York. I have given my word on this, as Doc has assured Mrs. Walcott. I would ask you to do the same.”

Beatriz and Blanca, Araceli’s pretty, dark-haired, Gonzalez/Gonzales cousins, looked like sisters. And now their faces both had the same expression; obdurate and scowling. They were friends, contemporaries and former classmates of Belle Walcott at Luna City High School. Catering their joint quinceanera had been the job which cemented Richard’s welcome among the clan, over and above Abuelita’s enduring fan worship.

“It’s not right, Chef,” Beatriz spoke first. “They’re really seriously in love and they’re both of age.”

Luc was looking down at the pastry dough on the tabletop. “’S not against the law, Chef,” he mumbled. “She’s nineteen, and I’m twenty-five.”

“Pat and I married when we were eighteen,” Araceli pointed out, and Richard scowled at her. *Thanks for not backing him up on this!*

“Very true,” Richard agreed, keeping his voice level with an effort. “Old enough to know your own minds. But I would remind you that the undeniably charming Miss Walcott is still under the authority of her parents, and they are paying a not-inconsiderable sum for her continuing musical education; an education, which if completed, is supposed to guarantee her a continuing and remunerative career in music. I would advise you not to imperil that future, no matter what unwise impulse your gonads urge upon you. There is more at stake than scratching a sexual itch."

"'Got a career in music," Luc answered mutinously.

Richard snorted. "Really? With OPM, whatever that stands for this month? One or two nights a week, playing in low-rent bars and nightclubs and passing the hat among the audience does not count as viable career in music, my lad. No reflection on your talent and the other members of OPM, but you are likelier to make a viable living as a cook than as their drummer. The fact remains that neither of your sources of income are sufficient to support Miss Walcott in a manner likely to lead to a happy family life. Be reasonable. Keep your flies zipped, your hands off Miss Walcott's bosoms or any other body parts for the duration of this week, and keep Mrs. Walcott and Doc Wyler from landing on all of our necks! Are we agreed on this? A strict no-nookie policy in the Café regarding Luc and Miss Walcott?" Richard fixed each one of his subordinates with the trademarked ferocious glare which played such a pivotal role in his previous career as a celebrity chef and purveyor of spectacular public tantrums. He was mildly gratified to see that Luc nodded assent – reluctantly, but then Luc was not one of those suited to easy relations with others of his species. First Beatriz, then Blanca replied, "Yes, Chef," their faces set in identical expressions of sullen reluctance.

Araceli, privileged as senior waitress and acting general manager, ventured an additional objection, "Chef, I don't …"

"A word in private," Richard indicated the back door with a jerk of his head. Araceli followed him in silence; the back door fell shut behind them. The mid-morning sun beat down on the crumbling pavement at the back of the Café, a space broken only by the presence of several large wheelie bins, and a pair of large raised planting beds in which Richard cultivated a variety of fresh herbs. Araceli planted her arms akimbo on her hips.

"I don't think you have any right to ask us to do that, Chef," she said in reasonable tones, provoking a scowl from Richard. "They're both of age. Sook Walcott has no business sticking her nose in. The woman is the worst kind of control freak."

"No argument on that score from me," Richard folded his arms. *No, he did not want trouble in his kitchen, no matter what form it arrived in.* "But the fact is that she will make our lives hell and make Doc Wyler's life – maybe Miss Letty's life for extra-good measure – hell as well, just on general principles. Don't forget that they own this place and pay us to work in it. At this point, maybe we should all be grateful that she didn't demand that they fire Luc outright."

"They wouldn't ..." Araceli ventured, and from the sudden uncertainty in her expression, Richard guessed that the possibility of such a demand had not occurred to her.

"No, I don't think they would," Richard replied, already relenting. Luc was not his cuppa, but he was a damned good cook. His command of the grill station was without peer and beyond reproach; an ornament to the Café's growing local reputation for caviar cuisine at a canned tuna-fish price. And he could readily imagine Belle Walcott as Rapunzel, locked in the highest tower of the Walcott mansion by her infuriated and infuriating parent. "But I wouldn't put it past Madame Walcott to have demanded it, right off the bat. Look, Araceli – I have given my word that we won't connive at Luc and Belle Walcott meeting any time here in the Café. Let's just leave it at that. Whatever happens between them, it cannot happen in the Café. I want to make certain that the staff of the Café have plausible deniability if something does come of it all. Luc seems pretty laid back about the whole matter." Richard had not noted any change in Luc's attitude or bearing since being caught in all but the ultimate act, but then, Luc was one of those sullen and withdrawn types anyway.

Araceli glared at Richard, planting her hands on her hips. "He's suffering, Chef, but keeping it inside. The big kid adores her, and she him. How could you not see that?"

"Pardon me for not having been gifted with the ability to create windows to see into men's souls," Richard answered. "As I see it, not my business anyway, to proctor Luc's associations when he is not working at the Café. However, it is my business when he is. Yours' as well, since you are in a management position. All that I ask is that we all take care during this week that whatever course Luc and Miss Walcott take regarding their mutual attraction, they keep any sexual consummation of it far, far from the Café. Or else the Wrath of Sook will roll downhill upon us all."

"Got it, Chef," Araceli nodded in reluctant acknowledgment. "I still think Sook is being perfectly awful about all this, though."

"It's not like Luc is the answer to every mother's prayer for her darling girl," Richard sprang ahead to open the door for her, a last battered standard of gentlemanly conduct which still remained in him. "Suppose that you walked in on your own little Angelika, well, grown to eighteen or nineteen – your sweet, innocent darling Angelica – all but doing the nasty with a bloke like Luc? How would you feel, as a mother? Answer honestly."

"Me?" Araceli smiled, dangerously. "They'd never find his body."

News Story History Today Magazine

By – Staff Writer

The Italian Ministry of Art and Antiques today announced the discovery of a previously unknown portrait by the Renaissance master Leonardo da Vinci. The subject of the portrait is thought by experts to be of Sister Giovanna Silvio y Gonzaga, contemplating a reliquary containing a tooth of the favorite horse belonging to St. Gigobertus of Bethany, an obscure late medieval saint said to be the patron saint of innkeepers and post-riders. The portrait hung for several centuries in a dark corner of the refectory in the convent of the Sisters of St. Lucia-in-Brolo in Milan, Italy. Recently taken down for cleaning following conversion of the ancient convent to a luxury boutique hotel, experts tentatively attributed the painting – in oils on a walnut panel – to da Vinci during the time that the artist was in the service of Ludovico Sforza, the Duke of Milan. Convent records note the date of vows for Sister Giovanna, a natural daughter by one of his several mistresses of Cardinal Pedro Gonzaga, and the gift of the reliquary presented to the convent. The silver-gilt reliquary, said to have been designed and assembled in the workshop of Benevento Cellini, was richly adorned with precious stones surrounding a small image under crystal of the Virgin Mary seated on the back of a horse with the baby Jesus in her lap. It appears to have been lost sometime in the 16th century. This painting is be one of the few images actually showing the reliquary, although it was described in detail by Vasari in his *Lives of the Most Excellent Painters, Sculptors, and Architects*.

9-11 Aftermath

The acres of collapsed office towers in New York were still burning, when Jessica Abernathy took the telephone call from her boyfriend.

"I'm done with this university sh*t," Jamie announced.

"You're in your senior year!" Jess protested. "You'll graduate next June, won't you? You're throwing that all away, Jamie!" She was twenty-two and looking forward to graduating in the spring. She had the Reserve obligation, but that was a doddle, according to her ROTC advisor.

"No, actually not," Jamie admitted, sheepishly. "I flunked a couple of classes last year. And I missed out on a couple of classes that I needed anyway. I don't think I'm cut out for Higher Ed, Jess.

Dad will be glad to be off the hook for tuition. I'm gonna withdraw."

Jess, staggered by this information, was taking his call on the phone in her student apartment, the cost of which she shared with three other students. In the silence at her end, Jamie continued, in that obdurate tone of voice which Jess knew that his mind was made up, and not all the force in the universe could move him from that decision.

"What are you gonna do, then?" She asked, finally.

"Enlist in the Marines," Jamie replied. Upon Jess's inarticulate exclamation of dismay and disbelief, he added, "Already done, Jess. I swore into the inactive reserve on Monday. I'm just waiting on a call from my recruiter, letting me know when to report for Basic Training."

"Jamie … what will your parents say?" Jess finally got out the words. Jamie replied, with insouciance which barely clothed his own bravado. "I dunno; but like I said, Dad will be glad to be off the hook. Hell, I only went to college because everyone said I ought to. I'll bet Grand-pop and Miz Alice will be thrilled to pieces. They're all sorts of patriotic, ya know."

"I'm sure they will," Jess answered, after a long moment. This was all an upset to those plans they had, half-voiced, half merely assumed. The Marines went places, dangerous places, joyously looking for trouble and finding it all too often. But Jamie sounded jaunty, relieved.

"Hey – sorry, Jess, love ya, I hafta go."

WWI Veteran Laid to Rest

From the Karnesville Weekly Beacon – Katherine Heisel, Staff Writer

A brief memorial service was held Saturday at the First Methodist Church of Luna City, to honor LCpl. Michael Delaney Walters, USMC, late of Marlton, New Jersey. LCpl. Walters was a survivor of the horrific WWI battle for Belleau Wood, and badly wounded in later fighting along the Asine-Marne front. Disabled, with a disfiguring facial scar, and eventually homeless, he lived for a brief time in a makeshift encampment on the outskirts of Luna City in 1935, before succumbing to exposure during severe winter weather early in 1936. His presence in Luna City gave rise to the local legend of the 'Scar-Faced Tramp.' His remains were discovered last fall during the early stages of construction of expanded recreational facilities at Mills Farm. Over subsequent months, he was identified through painstaking efforts by members of Luna City's VFW post and Allen Lee Mayne, host of the popular Food Network series *Ala Carte with Quartermayne.*

Following the service, conducted by the Reverend Peter Dawkins, senior minister at First Methodist, LCpl. Walters was interred with full military honors in the Luna City Municipal Cemetery, in a procession led by members of the Luna City Volunteer Fire Department, and representatives of the Luna City Police Department and an honor guard of the Karnes Company Historical Reenactors group. The Mighty Fighting Moths Marching Band performed the Marine Corps Hymn, and other suitable selections, including the hymn, "Eternal Father, Strong to Save," and the "Washington Post March."

Chief among the mourners were the family of Mavis Harrison, of Toledo, Ohio, LCpl. Walter's grand-niece. Costs for burial, and a memorial headstone were met by funds raised by local Boy Scout Robert A. Walcott as his Eagle Scout project, and a donation of services by the owners of Rhodes Funeral Home, of Karnesville.

That Ever-Fixed Mark

With that promise, extracted however grudgingly from the distaff members of the Café staff and from Luc himself, Richard was content. He managed to hide from himself a realization that all he had gotten was an assurance that whatever Luc and Belle managed as their heartbreaking last meeting until the summer holidays *(and he utterly refused to contemplate that incipient and looming quandary, since it was three months in future and remote as far as day-to-day went)* wouldn't happen at the Café, and such an assignation would not involve him.

He was to the point of assuming that everything would go back to normal when Robbie Walcott appeared to work the weekend shift on a bright Saturday, driving the battered old Volvo sedan which was the main ride of the younger Walcotts, accompanied by Bree

Grant, granddaughter of Sefton and Judy, who ran the Age of Aquarius Campground and Goat Farm. Bree, seventeen and charmingly the image of her grandmother at that age, chirped a cheerful greeting at him, while she tied a kitchen apron around her waist, netted her long hair and went to work at once, prepping garnishes for the Saturday brunch and thereafter the weekend crowd. Robbie also donned an apron and went to work. He too was seventeen, with the sloe-dark eyes and black hair inherited from his mother. Fortunately, as Richard viewed it, he had also inherited the four-square physique and equable nature of his father.

Richard, who had trained both Bree and Robbie as kitchen apprentices over the previous summer in the exacting manner of the traditional French kitchen system, was secretly relieved to see them both. Reliable, dependable, not overly-burdened with temperament; a pair of honest young souls, who would cheerfully do as he ordered in the kitchen, no matter if it sounded fantastical at first – and, he was certain, were too young and innocent to go about sexually exploring boundaries with each other or anyone else.

He did note that Robbie held a quiet conversation with Luc, as the latter scraped down the grill, midway through breakfast. Robbie spoke, Luc replied briefly, but did not seem especially moved. Richard felt obliged to take an interest; Robbie was Belle's younger brother, and who knows what kind of role he would play in whatever subterfuge might develop.

He took the opportunity when he and Robbie reviewed the fresh produce waiting for the lunch hour in the walk-in cooler.

"What were you telling Luc about, just now?" Best take the bull by the horns. "Yes, the large carrots – they're good for nothing but a mash of carrots and turnips. And as for the potatoes – boiled, and then plated with melted butter and a sprinkle of fresh parsley."

"I told him that Belle was fine," Robbie couldn't have sounded more innocent, regarding Richard with a wide-eyed gaze. "She has to be back in New York for her first class on Tuesday morning. Mom's going to drive her to the airport for her flight on Monday evening."

"You didn't have a message from your sister to Luc?" Richard asked, suspiciously.

"There's no sense in that, Chef," Robbie explained patiently, as if Richard was complete imbecile. "Belle an' Luc have been text-messaging all week. Mom took away Belle's iPhone, but Belle found Dad's old one in his study and Sylvester Gonzales cloned all her social media accounts on it. I thought of that," Robbie added, sounding slightly smug. "Sylvester's way-cool. He coached me on all that Marine knowledge, when I was asking for contributions at the Boathouse opening. Dude's a super computer genius!"

"Er … so Luc and your sister are not communicating through notes smuggled by their friends?" Richard hoped that he did not sound quite as boggled as he felt. He was supposed to be the grownup, here.

It wounded his ego no end, when Robbie answered, "Oh, jeeze, Chef! How old-school do you think we are, 'round here? Yeah, Mom went a little ballistic …" which Richard thought was a mild understatement of Sook Walcott's half-mile long lecture and tantrum of the previous Saturday, and the subsequent sequestration of Belle in the palatial Walcott manse. Only it seemed that such sequestration was not quite as complete as Mrs. Sook had assumed. Richard wrenched his thoughts back to his original purpose.

"Look, Robbie; on my word of honor, the future of the Café, and by extension the employment of everyone currently working in it, an oath has been demanded of me and which I have given as a gentleman, for whatever that is worth in this degraded age – that a *tete-a-tete* involving your sister and Luc not have anything to do with the Café. Your dear mother has made her feelings known …" Richard winced. Robbie, to his credit, had a sympathetic expression on his juvenile countenance. "At top decibels and in several venues – including my own residence! The owners of the Café have made it a condition – a condition on which all of our futures in this enterprise depend – that we do nothing to facilitate any meeting between your sister and Luc in this place. They have been quite definite on that point. I know; your sister and Luc are deeply in love, or something that looks to them a lot like love, and the course of which if true never does run smooth, blah-blah-blah … but as you care for the Café, your future employment in it, and for those of us who work here, do not bring the wrath of your mother down on us all. Don't even give her an excuse. I've already been through hell this week where she is concerned."

"Yeah, I guess Mom can seem pretty overwhelming," Robbie hefted up the bin of potatoes, with a large bag of oversized carrots on top another of rather woody and over-aged turnips, cheerfully insouciant about risking the Wrath of Sook. Richard could only think that proximity and constant exposure must have inured her son to the horror. "But Mom means well, you see. Jerry says that Mom is just hyper-driven, above and beyond the normal requirements for a Mom. You know that she had it pretty grim, growing up in Korea, back in the day? Yeah, the next thing to living in a cardboard box in the gutter, to hear Mom tell it. She clawed her way out of that, got herself an education, a decent job, finally – sheer stubborn guts. She doesn't want any of us to even think of slacking off, because we could wind up back in the gutter like that.

"Jerry says," Robbie mused thoughtfully, "That Mom knows damn-well what Luc's life is like. Living in dumps, always struggling for the next dime, putting up with a ration of crap because you are poor, and have no options. Yeah, Mom thinks about <u>that</u> kind of life for Belle, and she just goes frigging ape-shit."

"I wish that there was some kind of happy medium," Richard sighed, considering what he knew of Luc's previous life; parents uninvolved to the point of being rather like a turtle or a frog; laying the fertilized egg and wandering away to let nature take its course. Not for the first time, he considered how fortunate he had been in his own parental units. "A medium between being uninvolved, and over-involved. Ah well; tell your sister not to involve the Café, all right? Start peeling these, at once. Being old and tough, they'll have to cook for longer than usual. Do them in broth, throw in some sugar to sweeten the dratted things. Butter just before you mash 'em…"

"Sure thing, Chef!" Robbie's enthusiasm was almost exhausting. And Richard felt even older and wearier when he added, in a speculative tone of voice. "Hey Chef? Do you think I should get my eyebrow pierced, like Luc?"

Utterly appalled at the suggestion, Richard found his voice. "Why on earth would you ever want to do such a thing? A stud – why don't you go all the way and get a tattoo, as well?"

"I could take out the stud, or change it to a ring," Robbie answered, with all the sweet reasonableness of a seventeen-year-old, "Luc can't take off a tattoo if he wanted … well, he could, but it costs a bit …"

"I'm not entirely in favor of either!" Richard snapped. "And why the hell any sensible young chap would look to Luc to set an example of gentlemanly fashion is beyond me!"

"You gotta admit, Chef; he's like a whole catalog of options," Robbie shifted the bins of root vegetables to one arm and opened the door of the cooler with his free hand, continuing with undiminished enthusiasm. "Piercings, tattoos, dye jobs … he even has the logo for OPM shaved in one side of his head!"

"Mark my words, young chap," Richard warned, ominously, feeling some despair that Robbie might just go ahead and do something stupid anyway. "Following transient fashion is a guarantee to look a perfect idiot when people look at old pictures of you in twenty or thirty years. If you don't want to be giggled at by your children, then stick to the classics. Nothing trendy, nothing flashy … and definitely nothing involving body modification. Besides," Richard added. "Your mother would have words to say about that!"

"I know," Robbie was the very picture of innocence. "But if I did it … it would make Luc look more normal. Wouldn't it, Chef?"

"No," Richard lowered his voice so that Luc, across the kitchen at the griddle station, could not hear. "I'm afraid that nothing will ever make Luc appear normal. Least of all to your mother.

Having had the final word, Richard left Robbie peeling root veg and took refuge in the pleasure of the Café in the luncheon rush.

All was humming along as planned, with a pleasing influx of customers, many of them non-Lunaites, venturing into the back country to partake of the weekly Market Day, to absorb the scenic splendors of the turn-of-the-last century architecture of Town Square, and the newly-renovated public rooms of the Cattleman Hotel. The only fly in his personal ointment – and it was a very small fly, hardly the size of a tiny gnat – was the fear that someone among the visitors might yet recognize him as the erstwhile Bad Boy Chef, Rich Hall, star of various internationally-broadcast cooking shows, the tabloid headlines, and a few *(yet devastatingly humiliating)* amateur videos on YouTube.

Having shaved off the romantic stubble sometime after arrival in Luna City, ditched the trademark black-and-red bandanna for a professional chef's toque, and let his dark black-brown hair grow out to a medium-shaggy length, Richard was certain that he looked … well, somewhat like Gonzales/Gonzalez kin, at least to the casual eye of visitors. He had it on the received authority of Araceli that her grandmother, Abuelita Adeliza, the absolute ruler of the whole tangled clan, firmly believed that he resembled her late husband, Jesus Gonzalez – hence the enduring fanship of Adeliza "Ari" Gonzalez, she who was also his inadvertent *entrée* into Luna City society – that part of it which counted.

* * *

"Hey, Chef," Bree Grant came up to Richard Saturday afternoon, after the luncheon rush, as he was finalizing the dinner prix-fixe menu, writing it out on the chalkboard which would be posted just outside the Café doors as was the fashion in Europe. Bree nervously fiddled with her apron ties, but also simmered with suppressed excitement. At seventeen, she was the charming and fully-clothed image of Judy, her grandmother and titular owner of the Age of Aquarius Campground and Goat Farm; nearly as willful, but fortunately more driven by an urge for academic excellence than by every crackpot New-Age-ism going. "On Monday afternoon, I'm gonna fix a big supper for Gramps and G-Nan and all our friends … vegan, but everything good that I've learned. You and Miss Heisel wanna come? Everyone from the Café is gonna be there, except Blanca. She and her boyfriend already got tickets for *Ant-Man and the Wasp* at the multiplex in San Antonio. It's casual, you know how Gramps and G-Nan are; but they're even gonna put on clothes. Please say that you can come, Chef!"

It was enormously hard to resist Bree: Richard presumed that it had been just as hard for Judy Grant's contemporaries to resist her, back in the day.

"I'd be happy to," Richard found himself saying and mildly chagrined to find himself doing so. Dammit, Monday was his and Kate's private together time, although all that meant in practice was that he fixed a light supper for her, and they ate it together and then sat outside, chastely watching twilight fall, and the Grant's goat herd frolicking in the meadow opposite. "I'm certain Miss Heisel will be happy to accompany us …" *and if the fare on offer is too awful*, Richard added privately, *we'll make our excuses and I'll fix something edible*. Bree beamed; such a picture of happiness that Richard felt a brief pang of guilt. After all, he had been training Bree all last summer, in the classical French method of cuisine; surely most of his lessons should have stuck, even if Judy Grant had to be the most inept, appalling cook on the face of the earth outside of a British boarding school kitchen.

Keeping the wheels of the kitchen turning left Richard very little time or energy during the weekend, now that the Café offered supper service Tuesdays through Sunday evenings. Even with a limited menu and having Luc as the junior cook covering the breakfast hours, and Robbie on weekends and holidays – it was still a grind, since Richard felt obliged to spend most of his waking hours at the Café. Yet he still found it a most satisfactory existence, his third year of living and working in Luna City. If living well was vengeance against enemies, living a busy and fulfilled existence, at peace with himself and the world, was the very best revenge of all. Sook Walcott made no more sudden appearances at the Café or in Town Square. Miss Letty, Doc Wyler, Jess and Joe appeared as was their fashion every morning; Richard could only assume that the unappeasable fury of Sook had been appeased, or if not appeased, at least tempered. Perhaps her husband had come home from overseeing that huge Dubai project, and talked her down from whatever high ledge of unthinking hysteria she had chosen to roost upon. Maybe he had only made a very long phone call. Richard reposed enormous trust in Clovis Walcott's powers of reason and logic, although how he came to marry such an unbridled fire-cat for temperament was anyone's guess. Perhaps it was a case of opposites attracting.

"You want to go up to the Straw Castle for supper tomorrow? We've been invited. By Bree." Richard called Kate on Sunday afternoon, during a pause in supper service. Just to make belatedly certain that Kate was OK about risking the possibility of exposure to Judy Grants' signature Lentil Surprise casserole, a dish which had launched a thousand cases of acute culinary revulsion.

"Sure!" Kate answered. "I like the Grants! Bree is a sweetie, and Sefton is an absolute riot. And their new straw house is so cool!" Across the miles, Richard could hear Kate's rapturous sigh, even over the clatter of … well, whatever it was, in the background. He was of the vague impression that actual printing of the *Karnesville Weekly Beacon* had been farmed out to a lithographic print shop in San Antonio's industrial district. Perhaps she was there, overseeing the print run.

"All right then" Richard managed to conceal his relief. "Tomorrow then, the usual time. We can just walk over, when we have the energy. Bree says it's pretty much a free-range buffet. Come when you feel like it, sample what you like."

"Liberty Hall, then," Kate replied.

Richard could feel the warmth of her regard across the miles. *What a wonderful and literate girl,* he thought. And that he was just barely worthy of her. She could have shopped him out to the tabloids, at any time in the past two years – and yet, she had not.

His mild Kate of Kate Hall. A potted plant, a cat, a best girl … maybe he wasn't so much of a shit of a person at all.

Monday – his one day, his holiday – turned out to be one of those achingly beautiful spring days. A perfect pale-blue sky overhead was artistically embellished with fluffy cotton-wool clouds which Turner would have given his left nut to paint. A mild temperature rendered the air conditioner in the Airstream surplus to needs. Richard slept in, but only to mid-morning, until Ozzie the Cat began mewing querulously for his brekkie and freedom to roam circumspectly in the open air. *(Which freedom Ozzie was not allowed after dark. The local coyotes, according to Sefton Grant's grim analysis, were cunning, bold, and hungry. Most free-range cats did not survive long in the neighborhood of the Age, being that it was far outside the habitat of town itself.)*

In due time, a dozen automobiles and pickup trucks bumped along the unpaved track which gave access from Route 123 to the Age, and arrayed themselves in random fashion in the gravel-strewn expanse which served as visitor parking to the Straw Castle. The first-comers nose-edged into the shade of those oak trees which surrounded the Straw Castle. All those vehicles were familiar to Richard since he saw them nearly every day; the little red coupe which belonged to Chris at the Tip-Top, Jess Abernathy-Vaughn's yellow Jeep Wrangler, the aging and battered Volvo sedan driven by the younger Walcotts, Roman Gonzalez' builders' pickup truck *(accessorized with two ladders and a portable generator)*, and half a dozen others.

Finally, he spotted Kate's little recent-model VW, poking a leisurely and careful way along the ruts and potholes into the Age – conditions which made obedience to the speed limit mandatory, for those who valued their suspension systems. The little Bug pulled aside from the main driveway, and ventured across the lumpy meadow, punctuated with crumbling stretches of concrete marking the hardstands for RVs and trailers, coming to a stop just aft of the Airstream.

"Hey, you!" Kate Heisel emerged from the driver side, prim and immaculate as always in her work skirt-suit, and flat-heeled pumps, topped with the oversized tan trench coat whose bulging pockets carried all of her professional gear. "Hey, Ozzie! Got some prime catnip for you, kitten! Fresh from Abuelita's patch of gourmet catnip, just for you!" She and Richard exchanged a chaste social kiss. "How was your week, Rich? Oh, I want to sit with my feet up and hear about your week, before we go traipsing off to Sefton and Judy's! Can we have about twenty minutes before being social to other people? You would not believe the week I have had!"

"Tell me about yours, and we can watch Ozzie coking himself to the gills on 'nip," Richard replied. "I've already poured you one. Shall we sit inside, or out?"

"Bliss!" Kate twinkled at him, those amazing blue-green beryl eyes sparkling. "Outside, please. I don't want to miss anything of this lovely day." No, Kate was not conventionally beautiful, falling as she did on that part of the Gonzales/Gonzalez female spectrum of 'healthy, young and attractively intelligent.' Roundish face, dark hair, which contrasted with amazing blue-green eyes, the color of beryl gems, which must have come from the Heisel genetic inheritance. In his old celebrity days, Richard would have barely given her a glance, unless of course, he was substance-addled to the eyeballs and desperate. He brought out a filled glass for each, filled with Sefton Grant's home vintage, to find Kate dribbling out some slightly wilted sprigs of greenery for Ozzie's benefit from out of the pockets of her oversized trench-coat. His temporarily-silly, one-eyed brindled cat was rolling around on the paved concrete blocks at their feet, among the scattered greenery, already lost to chemically-inspired transports of happiness.

"If you don't tell your cat about the perils of nip, who will tell them?" Richard settled into the other lawn chair in his patio, and raised his glass in a toast to Kate, his lovely Kate of Kate Hall.

"Hey, is there any law here in Texas against getting a buzz on?" Kate answered, and settled back into her chair. The two of them sat in blissful silence for some long minutes, until Kate continued. "Thanks – I so needed this! What a week! The opening of the Boathouse and stables; I did four stories alone for this week's paper, and every single pic in the print issue is one that I took! I'm thinking of renegotiating my contract, you know. I'm a reporter, the photog bit is just an extra. Is it true that Lew and his wife have gone off to do a tour of France on a houseboat? I tried to get a look-in with that Georgina Mason, about how she is finishing up the renew on the Cattleman, but all she did was give me the stink-eye and tell me to call the VPI public affairs office. What a bitch – especially after Lew has been such an absolute prince about interviews. This will not end well for VPI, I can say that much. And …then, Sook Walcott throwing a max quantity of crazy, all over Mills Farm, and then bringing it here personally. She hasn't been back here since last week, has she?"

"No; I think that soberer heads got to her in time," Richard replied. He lived through the week for these blissful moments keeping company with Kate. "In time to prevent her from sinking social relations with every person and enterprise in Luna City. The woman fuels herself on fury. God knows how her children have emerged relatively sane."

"She's not that bad," Kate remarked, generous and tolerant, unconsciously channeling Richard's judgment. "I've met worse. You have to admit that Luc is hardly the answer to any mothers' prayer when it comes to a date for the only beloved daughter. For Sook, only a rich young, teetotaling tech millionaire would be good enough for poor Belle. The single thing Luc has going for him is that he can cook."

"That," Richard agreed. Which was all that he had going for himself, as well, but it seemed to satisfy Kate. She was happy enough to eat what he cooked for her, and mercifully, had never criticized him for a lack of ambition with regard to any other career. "Another refill before we go up to the Grants?"

"Better not," Kate shook her head. "I haven't eaten since breakfast, so I hope to heck the food is good."

"I am assured that Bree did all the cooking," Richard answered.

"I guess we'd better go while there is still some left," Kate agreed.

She gathered up Ozzie, now limp in catnip-delirium and left him to sleep it off in the Airstream, while they strolled up the hill toward the Amazing Straw Castle, tall and proud in a ring of gnarled old-growth oaks which crowned a low rise in a gentle bend of the river.

The roof – a weathered old tin grain-bin roof – caught the afternoon sunlight, turning the color of lightly-tarnished silver. Half the tall tower was a mostly blank wall, broken with a few small, deep-set windows, but the other half, looking out to the east and north, over the river and the distant view of the Wyler Ranch meadows and pastures, was a bank of glass picture windows, most of them salvaged from various renovation projects by Roman Gonzalez. Those windows were shaded and sheltered by the roof overhang at the top, and a half-circle of pergola, which ran out to the foot-print edge of the original Age. The first Age of Aquarius home place, the residence of Judy and Sefton, had been an immense yurt; a dim and rather smelly place, as dark and disorderly as the replacement was tidy, light-filled, and comfortable. Between young Berto Gonzales's essay into home design, Clovis Walcott's engineering skill, Roman Gonzalez' scrounging – plus the volunteered skills of half Luna City – they had come up with a most aesthetically pleasing replacement for the old yurt. Using the precepts of straw-bale construction and his own not-inconsiderable talents for scrounging and wood-working, Sefton Grant had even built a couple of small outlying cottages in the stand of oaks; guest quarters for when members of the old commune assembled, Richard supposed.

Now chairs and benches of every description filled the pergola, and the terrace slightly below it. The sliding doors stood open; people passed in and out, bearing plates of food – which must be good, Richard assumed, from cheerful expressions on their faces, and the way they were tucking into it all – vegetarian or not. Everywhere was laughter, a happy burble of conversation, music floating from a boom-box perched about halfway up the spiral staircase leading to the upper level.

Bree, flushed and smiling with triumph, waved to them from the kitchen as he and Kate walked through the opened front door – a massive, hand-carved thing, specially donated by one of the Grants' old friends.

"Hey, Chef! Good to see you – you know everyone else, I guess! Come on in and help yourself! It all came out super-fantastic! You taught us so much last summer! Grampy is so pleased, you know he doesn't have to drive all the way to Karnesville for his … umm, you-know-what-fix! And," her voice lowered to a confidential whisper. "I think I have found every notebook and card-file where G-Nan's recipe for lentil-barf was written down and torn the pages out. You know, nuke it from orbit, just to make certain. And I don't think she has noticed!"

Robbie Walcott emerged from the small but utilitarian kitchen, an empty platter in his hands. "Hey, hi, Chef! Isn't this great? Bree, they ate all of the roast-corn frittata; you want me to make another one?"

The small table which normally served as the supper table, and the work counter in the kitchen were covered with dishes, casseroles, pans and bowls. Richard cast a professional glance over it and had to admit to being impressed. Not bad, for vegetarian, and prepared by a pair of teenagers, working in a small domestic kitchen.

"Sure," Bree agreed. "It'll be ready in just a bit. I invited all of the regulars who are friends with G-Nan and Grampy – and they're having so much fun! I don't think we'll run out, though – I fixed a lot!" *(The apron tied over her jeans and OPM tee shirt bore mute witness to this, being generously splashed with oil, tomato sauce and other miscellaneous ingredients.)*

"Good!" Kate, who was just as adventurously omnivorous as Richard, eyed the various offerings with happy anticipation. "It all looks wonderful, Bree. And I am hungry!"

"Help yourself," Bree gestured expansively. "Most everyone is sitting outside."

Obediently, Richard and Kate filled their plates from the buffet selections star-scattered through the kitchen and on the dinette table; not as much of a grim chore as Richard feared. Under his tutelage, Bree had developed a keen understanding that vegetarian did not have to mean tasteless, fiber-rich and unappetizing. The bounty of the Grants' thriving truck garden was all on display, as well as the results of Bree's mostly successful experiments with soft goat-milk cheeses. Pilaf, salads, breadsticks, loaves and biscuits, cheese quiches …

"One might very well not miss meat, for a meal or two," Kate remarked.

Richard growled, "Apostate! Backslider! You would, eventually. No *steak au poivre*, no chicken marsala, no …oh, good afternoon, Mrs. Grant!" he added, as Judy appeared in the nearest of the open doorways out onto the pergola; a round-faced woman with madly-curling grayish hair hanging down her back in a wild mane. She was dressed in a shapeless druid robe of handwoven fabric *(wholly organic, natural and likely handwoven of threads woven by Judy herself, if Richard knew anything about Judy, and after three years, he did)*, a robe embroidered with arcane symbols and dotted with little roundels of mirror and sparkling sequins.

"Richard and Katie! So marvelous of you to come and share today!" Judy beamed on them both impartially. She was a sweet, but slightly featherheaded woman, of adamantine will and imperishable enthusiasm for every crackpot New Age belief around, and devoted to the welfare of animals of every description. Besides the goats and a row of beehives, the Age of Aquarius was home to a substantial flock of chickens, a spectacular peafowl with a very loud voice, a snow-white llama named Azúcar, a good assortment of cats both tame and semi-feral, four large dogs of indeterminant breed, including one of a simply humongous breed, and the latter's two best friends, a small pony *(slightly smaller in comparison to the enormous dog)* and a tiny white bantam-hen. Those last three went everywhere together, having arrived on the wings of a catastrophic flood more than a year ago and consigned ever since to the care of the Grants, for no one had ever claimed the oddly-assorted trio when the flooded river resumed normal level. Even now, dog, pony and hen lurked with Azúcar, just beyond the rickety makeshift fence keeping the larger quadrupeds out of the close-in demesne, glumly waiting for the party to end and their little world at the Age to return to normal … or as near to normal as it ever was.

Richard looked around the open-air party on the pergola-shaded terrace; an oddly familiar gathering of people in a not-familiar place. Kate drifted away, momentarily, talking to Berto Gonzales, who was sitting with Roman Gonzalez in a corner together – admiring the look of the tower over plates of gourmet veggie fare. Belle Walcott sat a little apart, with Beatriz; Beatriz was talking animatedly, while Belle looked off into the distance. Richard wondered if she were waiting for … *no, she couldn't be waiting for Luc, could she?* Belle didn't appear to have taken any particular trouble with her attire or makeup, that Richard could see, although her shoes were thick-soled trainers, quite suitable for running away, especially from Sook.

"I thought that her mother was keeping Belle Walcott at home, until the moment she delivers her to the airport tomorrow," Richard observed, in a low voice. "It is splendid of you to have invited her, Mrs. Judy. I'd go mad, locked up in that dismal pile of a house."

Judy beamed and whispered confidentially, "Actually, Sook thinks she is spending the afternoon with Beatriz at the movies in San Antonio. I know that Sook has forbidden her to associate with poor Luc … but really! True and honest love cannot be denied. Thwarting the practice of the sex-magick between the spiritually attuned is … well, almost a crime against humanity!"

"I don't want to know any more," Richard answered, shuddering. "I gave my word that the Café would not be involved in any resolution of their affair, on pain of Sook throwing another scene. It's bad for business, bad for my nerves, too. Besides … he's not exactly what the old biddies would call a catch!"

"He's an old soul." Judy insisted. Richard inwardly cringed. "And they are in love! Truly, madly, deeply! Besides, this is the Age of Aquarius, not the Café! If Luc shows up here – guided by the spirit of pure devotion, and they want to slip away and work the magick in private – well, so they shall!"

"I don't want to know about it, in that case," Richard answered, horrified. "I advise most strongly against that. But if you wish to risk the Wrath of Sook…"

"Nothing shall stand in the way of expressing their truest desires," Judy insisted, and Richard, despairing, decided there was nothing more to be gained in this conversation. On Judy's head should properly fall any consequences. He wished he could be absolutely certain that such repercussions would fall there exclusively. Mercifully, Kate appeared at his elbow.

"Miss Letty's over there in the shade; about the last person I would expect to be here."

"Bree did say that she had invited all the regulars," Richard nodded toward Judy, who had already begun to drift away. Miss Letty McAllister; that was a bit of a surprise. Richard supposed that she had arrived with Chris Mayall. He followed Kate to where Miss Letty sat, as if a queen at serene rule over her court, in an upright chair padded with several cushions, in the most shaded corner of the pergola.

"Miss Letty!" Richard made his obeisance, cheered by her august presence. If Patricia Pryor was the uncrowned junior queen of Luna City, Miss Letty was the senior; an austere and stern autocrat, the oldest resident by four months, the ultimate repository of civic memory. Miss Letty, Richard was certain, knew where all the social and metaphorical bodies were buried; in some cases, may have been instrumental in putting them there. Miss Letty nodded, all royal dignity, even to the point of sporting a regal matching hat, handbag and gloves. She appeared somewhat distracted from talking to Jess Abernathy-Vaughn sitting opposite, whose infant was essaying the fine art of standing uncertainly, balanced on wobbly, fat little pins. Little Joe balanced himself against the edge of a low table, before sitting abruptly on his diapered behind.

"Richard – Katherine," Miss Letty acknowledged their presence. "I am so glad to see you. Brianna was so very anxious that you should be here. She has accomplished so much with this supper buffet; a credit to your apprenticeship program in the Café! I would not nearly been so confident of my abilities in the kitchen when I was her age; perhaps I might have ventured a fancy cake and only with my mother's help."

"It all looks wonderful, Miss Letty," Kate exclaimed. "Richard told me about Bree's supper, and I could hardly wait." That wasn't quite how she had responded, but then Kate was genuinely fascinated by people, and interested – among many other things – in Richard's long-term cooking and food-appreciation project, including the blog and video series that she had set up, starring Ozzie as Captain Kitten, the Kid's Kitchen Cook.

Now Kate set her loaded plate down and crouched until she was at eye-level with Little Joe. "Hi there, Big Boy! Jess, I can hardly believe he is practically walking; championship season for the Moths in sixteen years, for certain. He'll be talking, next, I'm sure; what a handful for you."

"Gooo-gush!" Little Joe replied, drooling slightly, and revealing two whole small lower teeth. Obviously, Kate was one of his favorite people.

Jess sighed. "Yes, especially when he gets a little brother or sister…" At that exact moment, Little Joe wobbled and sat down more than extra-heavily on his well-padded bottom, and instantly began to wail, distracting everyone from Jess' words. "It never fails," Jess added, scooping up her offspring, assessing his welfare, and administering brisk comfort practically in the same moment. "There, there, punkin: there's nothing wrong with you. If there's no blood, I don't want to see any tears."

Richard winced – crying babies; one of those things he could not stand. At least, when he took his turn at baby-minding with Little Joe late in the previous year, he had not had to put up with much fussing.

"Kate; let's find a place where we can sit down," he suggested, hastily.

Kate dropped a light kiss on the top of Little Joe's fuzzy infant head, saying, "Bye-bye, little one – see you around!"

Richard, with another respectful nod toward Miss Letty, led Kate toward a rustic bench at the edge of the pergola terrace, one of which was at the moment, two-thirds unoccupied. Harry Vaughn sat on the occupied end. Richard was surprised. He would have thought that Harry, as near to a fire-eating law-n-order reactionary old fogie as ever there was, wouldn't be caught dead visiting a place which the old-timers still called 'Hippie Hollow' and partaking of their hospitality.

"Mr. Vaughn," Richard ventured tentatively, "May we join you? You know Miss Kate, of course – Kate Heisel?"

"'Course I do," Harry grunted. "I'm old, not dead. Miss Kate, darlin', you are a breath of fresh air. I been interviewed for her paper I don't know how many times. Take a load off, have a seat. The grub's not bad, I have to say."

"It's prepared by two of my apprentices," Richard retorted. "Of course, it would be … superlative. I wouldn't have it any other way."

"Good to know," Harry didn't sound any more conciliatory. Deep in the innermost recesses of his heart, Richard deeply feared

Harry; an aging, judgmental, uncompromising god, with a craggy weathered face and a truly impressive old-fashioned soup-strainer mustache. Harry had on one memorable occasion, threatened to beat Richard around the head and shoulders with an oar unless he belted up and did his duty as a gentleman. That Richard had obliged, and they had succeeded wildly in a mad mission to rescue a family of women and children from a location just out of sight of this place … Richard did not like to dwell on that memory. Especially as necessity dictated that Harry got all the public credit for the rescue. "I came with Jess and the munchkin. Joe's still on duty."

Ah; that explained it all. Richard and Kate sat on the bench and ate, between desultory rounds of light conversation, mostly to do with either Richard explaining what was in some particular dish – Harry had never heard of quinoa, or feta cheese – or Harry expounding on recent doings of the local criminal underclass, or what he called 'the dirtbag element.' The conversation drifted on, touching on the renovation work being done at the old Cattleman Hotel. With the 1912 Boathouse and Stables being finished, Richard had assumed that faster progress would be made on restoring three floors of guest suites to a glory approximating that achieved by the public rooms. Judging by the numbers of workmen's battered and equipment loaded vehicles hogging all parking places at the western end of Town Square and slopping over as far as Stein's Wild West Round-up and the Café, such a consummation had not been achieved.

"I'll have to ask Roman what is holding up completion," Richard ventured. He meant it idly, as a means of having a topic of conversation. "Your pal Dubois kept such a tight hold, when it came to getting things done."

"He's a tiger for the work, that man," Harry grunted. "Leads from the front, knows everyone's name, gets the job done under budget and before the deadline. Castle Mountain; what a place! Usta take hunting parties there, from my li'l place in Talkeetna. Repeat client; got the full courtesy treatment for my folks, every time. Me and Lew go a long way back." He shot Richard a severe look from underneath his beetling brows. "Can't help thinking that his notion of going on vacation just at this time was a good idea. That Mason floozy is about fifteen kinds of bad news, or my experience of woman-kind is seriously maladjusted."

"Apparently, she is well-thought of by VPI's higher-ups," Richard answered, fully aware that Kate was listening. And that Harry's judgment of woman-kind was finely-honed through experience. Experience with women … women like Richard's Aunt Moira, she of the interesting self-defense skills and many travels to foreign and violent lands. Only his sure and certain knowledge that Kate was not one of the professional scribbling fraternity given to rush into print or on-line with a breathlessly urgent, yet unproven flight of fantasy kept him from guarding his tongue and opinions. "I suppose that he was overruled by higher management. It happens, you know. A pity; I can't help seeing disaster looming!"

"Disaster looming?" Kate remarked. Although she had been listening attentively, and eating from her plate of vegetarian selections, she had also been looking out over the territory below the hill which the Amazing Straw Castle crowned and adorned. "Speaking of disaster, is that Luc? I don't think there is anyone else in Karnes County who rides a red motor scooter."

"Oh, my god," Richard closed his eyes, shuddering. "It is." No one could mistake the red scooter – or the rider of it, once he dismounted and took off his helmet, just short of the Amazing Straw Castle. While there may have been other young residents of Luna City with a more resplendent collection of tattoos, Luc was the only one additionally sporting a multi-colored Mohawk, modified earlobes and facial piercings. And Belle, who stood up as soon as the little red scooter came into sight, walked out to meet him halfway up to the Castle.

Harry Vaughn shook his head, sadly, and observed, "Hard to believe, he paid someone to make him look like a circus sideshow freak."

"Love is blind," Kate observed. "And occasionally tone-deaf as well."

"I suppose I had better do something about this," Richard sighed.

"I don't see why you should," Kate pointed out. "You only promised that they wouldn't meet at the Café."

"But he works for the Café," Richard set aside his own almost-empty plate. "And everyone, to include Sook, will hold me responsible. I'd like to be able to look them all in the eye and honestly say that I tried."

"Good luck with that, sport," Harry didn't sound as if he held any brief for Richard's success.

Two others at the party were already converging on the embracing couple; Judy Grant in her flowing robe, twittering welcomes … and surprisingly, Miss Letty, leaning magisterially on her heavy cane.

"Dear children," Judy exclaimed. "Merry meet, merry part and merry meet again! Welcome to our abode, the temple of happiness and everlasting joy – a refuge for the weary!"

"Isabelle, Lucas." Miss Letty nodded formally. "I expect that you have much to say to each other."

"I am certain that they do!" Judy burbled. "Belle is leaving tonight! This is their only chance to be together; together in body as they are in soul, to work the magick. There is a special place that I have blessed and purified! There is nothing more holy and powerful than the sex-magick!"

Ah, thought Richard; t*he Age doubles as a New-Age blessed knocking shop. That's what the little cottages were for; fornication in decent privacy, rather than around the bonfire on mid-summer eve. Nice to know.* Meanwhile, he noted that Luc and Belle both appeared mildly horrified. Miss Letty cleared her throat.

"Judith, I am certain that the children appreciate your consideration. And that …" Miss Letty appeared to have some trouble getting out the phrase. "The magick, as you say it … is undeniably powerful. Which is why it is hedged around with rules and proscriptions, in the minds of decent people; rules which rightfully should be universally taught and upheld." She bent a severe glance upon Luc and Belle, yet a look not lacking in sympathy. "More than anything, I believe Isabelle and Lucas need such an understanding, lest they rush into a situation which may be cause for later regrets. I have always been of a mind that careful chaperonage is a useful social good. Richard, would you be so kind as to join me in that duty? Isabelle, Lucas … there is a lovely small stone ledge just at the riverside, some small distance from here; as if nature herself conspired to carve out the perfect place to watch the river. I would suggest that the two of you go sit on it and contemplate nature and quietly discuss your future. And just on the bank above, Sefton has placed a very comfortable-looking bench, where Richard and I will sit, ensuring your privacy and that certain proprieties will be observed."

"Yes, Miss Letty," Luc answered. Richard noted that he had gotten to the point of looking his interlocutor in the face; some kind of social adaption had been taking place. Belle took his hand. Perhaps she had been responsible in part for this breakthrough.

"Yes, Miss Letty," Belle echoed. Richard took Miss Letty's arm in his, and the two of them followed Belle and Luc, across the terrace and down along the riverbank, from which vantage the burble of conversation among Sefton and Judy's guests on the terrace above was reduced to an agreeable hum, on about the same level as the buzzing of the ever-present cicadas. Yes, the stone ledge was there, just above the pebbly small beach at the edge of deep green water.

"We shall sit here, Richard," Miss Letty commanded. The bench was one of those rough, rustic things formed of unpeeled cedar logs and branches; Sefton's handiwork. "And keep an eye on the children. For the sake of propriety."

"And that we can swear truthfully to Sook Walcott that nothing took place which would stain the cheek of an innocent maiden with a blush," Richard replied. Miss Letty settled upon the bench with a sigh of relief. Richard wondered momentarily that the energies of a nonagenarian had been overtaxed, but the aged lady in question favored him with a wintery smile.

"That," She agreed. "And to Stephen, as well. My word is my bond, you know."

"Indeed." Richard looked down at the stone ledge. Belle and Luc had settled themselves upon it – and he noted that they sat close – but in the fashion which suggested friendship, rather than any inclination to explore the bounds of sex-magick. He wondered if Miss Letty had ever entertained venturing into such an exploration for herself, and quashed that mental question almost at once.

He and Miss Letty were just out of hearing whatever Belle and Luc had to say to each other, as they sat side by side on the stone ledge. The two lovers faced the sweep of river trickling past in a sweep of clear-brown-green water. They held hands at first, but midway through the conversation, Luc put his arm around Belle, and she leaned her head on his shoulder. In contrast to the frenzied embrace of the previous week – the observing of which had blown any pretense of 'just friends' all to hell – this encounter seemed, so far, to be tame to the point of tedium.

"What do you think they are on about?" Richard's curiosity overcame him, along with a degree of discomfort at sitting in silence.

"I believe that they are going to come to some kind of agreement," Miss Letty replied. "Of what kind, I cannot say, of course. They may choose to go their separate ways or continue their romantic attachment in an appropriate manner at long-distance. I think the latter. Sook Walcott will not like this, of course."

"It is difficult contemplating anything which she herself has not willed into existence pleasing that woman," Richard said, and Miss Letty nodded agreement.

"One learns so much from a lifetime of observation," she said. "Some people are motivated by being forbidden to do something. Some have the capacity for making sensible and mature decisions when the necessity for making such decisions is thrust upon them and the responsibility for the outcome of such decisions rest wholly upon themselves. Thoughtful self-interest, I call it. To my mind it bodes well that Lucas and Isabelle did not choose to indulge their carnal desires, when Judith offered them every opportunity. I do believe they love each other, in that sweet old-fashioned way which demands putting the welfare and happiness of the loved one above ones' own. *Love is not love, which alters when it alteration finds, or bends with the remover to remove*," Miss Letty quoted. "They will do the right thing."

"*It is an ever-fixed mark*," Richard capped the quote. "*That looks on tempests and is never shaken; It is the star to every wandering bark, whose worth's unknown, although his height be taken.*"

"Indeed," Miss Letty favored him with another wintery smile. "I sometimes forget, Richard; you have been educated in the strict old-fashioned way. So very reassuring."

Out along the river, a single kayak drifted past, paddled by a single enthusiast; the opening of the Boathouse had brought many such to Mills Farm; some as far as Luna City. From Kate's conversations, as well as those with Lew Dubois, Richard knew that more such excursionists would appear, especially when renovations to the old Cattleman Hotel were complete. Which was … he made a mental note to ask Roman Gonzalez about that. The parking situation at the western end of Town Square was a continuing annoyance; how could he transform the Café into the premier fine dining experience when potential diners had to park off the Square and walk some distance in the withering summer heat?

Miss Letty jolted him from that contemplation, observing, "Lucas and Isabelle have come to a resolution, I think." She struggled to rise from the bench, leaning heavily on her cane, and Richard took her other elbow. "Thank you, Richard." She bent her magisterial regard upon Luc and Belle, who approached, still holding hands. "Well?"

To Richard's mild astonishment, Luc spoke first. "We're still serious, Miss Letty. But we're gonna wait. We agreed. It's only right."

Belle nodded in quiet agreement, and before Richard's gaze, she and Luc kissed, a quiet, undemonstrative kiss, like that of adults long habituated to each other. "Text me when you're back in New York, 'kay?" Luc said.

Belle laid a gentle hand on his cheek. "I'll do that, *caro-mia.* 'Bye. See you in the summer." She kissed him again, and then was gone, walking up the riverbank toward the Straw Castle terrace, and Luc nodded somberly to Miss Letty and Richard and vanished in the same direction. By the time that Richard assisted Miss Letty back to the gathering on the shaded terrace, both were gone, the red Vespa sending up a brief smoke-trail of dust as it vanished beyond the campground. Blanca and Belle were already making their departure and there was Kate, his wonderful, bonny, companionable and undemanding Kate, waving to him, across the terrace.

"So. Sorted?" Richard said to Miss Letty, as she settled onto that sheltered, comfortable chair. "The star-crossed lovers, I mean. They were da – they were very good about it all."

"Of course," Miss Letty favored him with another one of those wintery smiles. "Isabelle was in one of my First Aid classes at the school a few terms ago. One of those who vomited in the segment regarding emergency childbirth, if I remember correctly. So important, I think – that children learn about consequences, you see. So that they may make wholly informed life decisions. Thank you, Richard. I think we may depend on Lucas and Isabelle behaving as mature adults."

"I hope that we can count on her ma-ma doing the same," Richard replied, and nodding courteously, made his return to Kate.

Spring Newsletter

Spring 2018 Newsletter

Luna City Chamber of Commerce

5 North Town Square, Suite 4

Check out our Facebook Page

The traditional Mills Farm Easter Egg hunt, which has been held every year on Easter Saturday since 1978 on the lawn and gardens below the Old Tyme Dance Hall will be held this year in the landscaped area to the north and east of the newly-completed 1912 Boathouse. This new space is larger and more open, affording expanded opportunities for those aged 12 and below to hunt for eggs, including five special Golden Eggs. Tickets for entry to this special event are available at the Mills Farm Country Store, and at the gate on March 31.

The Spa Comes to Town

With the recent addition of the 1912 Boathouse and Stables to Mills Farm, the Chamber of Commerce anticipates an increased number of visitors to Luna City over weekends and holidays, especially around Town Square, and to the renovated small boat landing along the east riverbank between the VFW and Gonzalez Auto Body. There will be regular Mills Farm shuttle-bus traffic in town, and on Rte. 123 whenever kayak excursions are scheduled. Although renovations of the historic Cattleman Hotel are not yet completed, Mr. Lew Dubois, marketing manager for Venue Properties International, anticipates an increased number of Mills Farm guests taking advantage of the opportunity to experience good old Texas country hospitality, and to visit many of our locally-owned and operated establishments around Town Square, such as Luna Café & Coffee, Artisans@The Mercantile, Stein's Wild West Roundup, Abernathy Hardware, and the St. Margaret and Anthony Parish Thrift store, located in the historic Fire Station building.

Luna City, Texas – Home of the Mighty Fighting Moths

Upcoming Events

January 20

A memorial service for LCpl Michael Walters, USMC will be held at 10 AM at First Methodist of Luna City. Interment to follow at the city cemetery.

February 14

The Valentine's Day Sweetheart Hop will be held at Mills Farm's Olde Tyme Dance Hall beginning at 6 PM. The popular Karnesville conjunto band *Los Maldonados* will be featured.

May 26

Memorial Day pot-luck at the Luna City VFW Post, beginning at 4 PM.

Grand Reopening of The Cattleman Hotel Postponed

Due to unanticipated delays in completing renovations, the grand reopening scheduled for Easter Week is delayed until mid-summer.

Page 1 of 2

Luna City ISD News

Spring Break Senior Trip

Permission slips for those intending to participate in the Spring Break Senior Trip to Dallas-Fort Worth must be turned in to the LCHS administrative office no later than Friday, March 16. Payment for the trip, to cover chartered bus and hotel stay, is also due at that time. The bus will depart from the LCHS Nando Gonzalez Memorial Gym at 9 AM on Monday, March 25, and return on Saturday, March 31.

Elementary School Cooking Class

Richard from the Café has volunteered to teach an after-school grade-school-appropriate cooking class on Monday afternoons from 1:00-2:00. Simple preparations which do not involve contact with hot surfaces and sharp implements will be taught to interested students on a weekly basis. Captain Kitten, the Magical Cooking Cat will make scheduled appearances. Permission slips to attend this class, noting any possible food allergies must be signed and turned into the LC Elementary School administrative offices, first floor at 1 Town Square, before participants are admitted to the class.

Junior Class Project

Luna City HS Class of 2019 will hold a car wash every Saturday in April in the parking lot of the Tip-Top Ice House Gas and Grocery from 9 AM to 3 PM to raise funds for the establishment and maintenance of three chemical porta-potties, to be installed beneath the Moth Field bleachers in time for the Moths Homecoming Game next fall. This will augment the current restroom in the Mighty Fighting Moths Fieldhouse, which are inadequate for public events, and replace those rented facilities unfortunately destroyed in a massive and spectacular fireworks explosion during the Moths Homecoming Game in 2015.

Community Marketplace

Easter Smoked Ham

Order your whole or half hickory or mesquite smoked ham for Easter supper from Pryor's Meats & BBQ no later than March 14thth for delivery to your home or business. A limited number of smoked pork tenderloins are also available. Call and order today!

From Chief Vaughn, Luna City PD

There has been a rash of after-dark tress-passing, particularly around Mills Farm. The antique Farmall tractor belonging to Mills Farm was taken for a brief and illicit joyride several weekends ago and retrieved after being abandoned in the parking lot in back of the Tip Top Ice House, Gas and Grocery. Jaimie Gonzalez of the Rincon de las Robles Ranch reports that someone or something has been regularly spooking the horses in the ranch pasture adjoining properties on the south-eastern edge of Luna City. Chief Vaughn would like to remind teenage pranksters that in certain cases, their juvenile records may officially be sealed, but the grapevine telegraph is forever.

Luna Café and Coffee Serving Supper!

Luna Café and Coffee now offers an evening meal, Tuesday through Sunday evenings, until 9 PM, with takeout available. Consult the menu posted weekly at the Café for the daily lunch and dinner specials.

Luna City, Texas – Home of the Mighty Fighting Moths

Page 2 of 2

The History of the Gonzales-Gonzalez Land Grant

The land upon which the small town of Luna City was formally established was originally part of a Spanish land grant to Don Diego Manuel Hernando Ruiz y Gonzalez *(or Gonzales)* and his sons Augusto *(the eldest and eventual heir)* and Tomas. Correct spelling of the family name is a matter of uncertainty. Handwriting on the original records of the grant is difficult to read, and within a generation or two Don Diego Manuel's descendants were spelling their surname with either an 's' or a 'z' interchangeably. The grant, consisting of a league and a labor of land *(that is about four and a half thousand acres)* was officially recorded in 1769, although there is evidence for the family to have established a residence and begun raising stock in the area from the 1720s on.

The first Don Diego Manuel was a trusted officer in his youth, serving under the command of Jose de Escandon, the first governor of Nueva Santander, a colony stretching along the Gulf Coast between Tampico, Mexico and into present-day Texas as far as the San Antonio. The Gonzalez/Gonzales family originated in Gijon, Cantabria; and connected to the Escandon family through social and kinship networks. The Gonzalez/Gonzales family name is an alternate spelling of Gonzaga; the Gonzalez/Gonzales of Gijon are thought by historians to be descended from the notorious Cardinal Pedro Gonzaga – a dissolute but able administrator, and ally of the equally notorious Borgia family two centuries previously.

In any case, the grant – known in most records as Rincon de los Robles, or Oak Corner – continued in its original incarnation and acreage for a century after being officially recorded. Taking its name from a grove of particularly fine oak trees, many of which still stand throughout Luna City, the Gonzalez/Gonzales clan ran cattle, horses, sheep and goats on various tracts, establishing several small herding camps for their employees. One such camp was excavated in the early 1970s just inside the present-day main gate of the Wyler Lazy-W Exotic Game Ranch; a two-room adobe structure, half bunk-house and half-stables. Although of interest to social historians, nothing much besides a few coins, pottery shards and bottle fragments was found in the course of the excavation. A historical marker was placed on the site in 1975, as this is the oldest known permanent building of any kind in or near Luna City.

Meanwhile, location of the main residence for the Gonzalez/Gonzales clan is uncertain, although certain outbuildings on the present-day ranch headquarters of Rincon de los Robles hint at a very early date of construction. The Gonzalez/Gonzales family prospered in a mild way; both Augusto and Tomas are recorded as having fathered eighteen and twenty-three children, respectively, through several marriages or other, less official arrangements. Most of these offspring are known to have lived to adulthood, although due to a rather casual attitude to record-keeping, only the main line of descent from oldest son to oldest son can be ascertained with precision. An inclination toward very large families, with frequent use of the same names, marriage within the extended clan and informal adoption over three centuries complicates any attempt to make sense of the Gonzalez/Gonzales family tree. The majority of Augusto and Tomas' descendants still live in and around Luna City.

Proud Tejano patriots during the Texas War for Independence, at least three members of the Gonzalez/Gonzales clan of Rincon de los Robles on the San Antonio River served with Captain Juan Sequin during Sam Houston's retreat into east Texas in 1836 and fought at the Battle of San Jacinto. Alas, having served with valor in the war did not spare local Tejanos from later suspicion and political disenfranchisement on the part of the mainly Anglo establishment. Although having no interest in and taking little part in the Civil War, a mere fifteen years later, the hardships brought about by that war and the collapse of the Confederacy, took a toll on Rincon de los Robles. In 1867, a large portion of the grant remaining was sold for hard cash by Don Anselmo Gonzales, *(in direct line the great-great-great grandson of Don Diego Manuel Hernando Ruiz y Gonzalez or Gonzales)* to Captain Herbert Kling Wyler, CSA. During the War, Captain Wyler *(a native of Kentucky)* had been posted to Texas. He was involved in moving Confederate cotton to Brownsville and thence over the border to the Mexican port of Baghdad, from where it was shipped to Europe. In consequence, Captain Wyler, unlike many of his Confederate compatriots, emerged prosperous from the conflict, and turned his considerable energies into building up his own ranch property.

The infusion of cash into the much-diminished Rincon de los Robles Ranch was not wasted on Don Anselmo, or on his son, Don Antonio, who inherited Rincon de los Robles in his turn and turned his attention to breeding and raising prize-winning merino sheep and angora goats. It should be noted that Don Anselmo had cannily held on to the lushest pasturage adjoining the river and most of the oak woods which gave the ranch its name. Don Antonio, who trained originally in law, eventually became one of Texas' leading authorities on parasites afflicting angora goats. It is Don Antonio who fought the last officially recorded duel on the streets of Luna City. A historical marker on Town Square marks the place.

In 1884-5, Captain Wyler developed an interest in making a third fortune, upon realizing that the best route for a proposed railway connecting San Antonio with Aransas Pass lay across a portion of his vast properties in Karnes County. He proposed forming a corporation to establish a model town at the point where the old road between San Antonio and the coast to Don Antonio, still the second-largest landowner in the district. Don Antonio agreed but being no fool and having little reason to trust Captain Wyler *(who had a long-established reputation as a man of great determination and very few moral scruples)* made his contribution to the corporation with a few acres on the northern border of Rincon de los Robles for the town site rather than from his bank balance. Don Antonio made it a condition that as few of the standing oaks be felled as possible. Captain Wyler attracted the interest and investment of other parties, before abruptly withdrawing support for the railway, with half the town plots already sold and construction completed, when his adored younger daughter Bessie suddenly eloped with a handsome train engineer. Local historians are in accordance, in agreeing that out of all the investors in the corporation to found Luna City, only Don Antonio escaped financially undamaged from the debacle.

The Rincon de los Robles grant exists to this day, as a ranch under the management of Don Antonio's son, Don Jaimie. His granddaughter, Mindy Gonzalez-Ramirez, is currently conducting research on the existing ranch headquarters buildings, to determine which, if any of them, pre-date the mid-19th century.

Memorial Day - 2018

Jess Abernathy-Vaughn, being of that pale tint of skin which burned and freckled rather than tanned, lounged under the shade of a dark and ultra-violet-ray protective umbrella, planted at a rakish angle, deep into the beach sand at the Gulf-shore side of Galveston Island. She was also slathered with the highest over-the-counter SPF-level sunscreen available. In spite of not being a fan of sunbathing until one looked more like a leather saddlebag, she was truly enjoying this holiday. A second honeymoon, everyone called it, now that she and Joe had been legally wed for more than a year. Their son was almost ten months old, well-able to withstand the baby-sitting ministrations of his great-grandparents, living in the high-ceilinged apartment on the second floor of the ancestral hardware store on Main Square. She watched Joe – as fit and muscular as a classical Greek bronze of an athlete – mastering the use of a boogie-board in the indifferent surf with the same single-minded attention that he brought to every enterprise which took his interest. It killed Joe to not be the best at anything, so he applied himself relentlessly; football, soldiering, law-enforcement – and of late, to fatherhood.

Jess was glad that she had been able to arrange all this; she and Joe needed that vacation.

"Your grandmother has been longing to get her hands on our boy," Joe agreed when Jess first tentatively broached the question of a holiday in the sun, surf and sand. That was the evening in Spring Break week, and he had just come home from a tedious day of upholding the law in Luna City, and on the stretch of Route 123 which adjoined the municipality. "Let's do it, Babe – go back for a weekend, and try and recall the people that we were before becoming a life-support-system for the rug-rat. I'm trying my best to be patient until the day that we can throw the ol' pigskin around, but I need a break, too."

Jess sighed. "I can hardly wait until he can cook! Richard swears that he will start teaching him to make a lovely proper mayonnaise as soon as he knows how to handle a whisk."

"When will that be?" Joe spun his white work Stetson onto the old-fashioned coat-and-hat-rack which stood by the front door of the old cottage on Oak Street. He collapsed with a sigh onto the overstuffed sectional sofa – an overstuffed and sprawling thing which took up altogether too much space in the old-fashioned front room, but which was too comfortable to give up entirely. Jess dropped their cooing offspring onto Joe's mid-section and he yelped, "Ooof! What have you been feeding him, Babe – bricks?"

"Growing boy," Jess replied, with a remarkable lack of feeling. "You entertain the Soup-Monster for a while I fix supper – tell him mad tales of all the dirtbags you have arrested, and all the speeders you have ticketed. I've been talking to him all day about the necessity for retaining receipts for cash business expenses. Among other topics of note." *(Soup-Monster was her nickname for her son, taken from Marsupial Monster, from the early days when she carried him in a baby-sling across her chest.)*

"Sounds deathly dull," Joe replied. Jess answered with heavy sarcasm as she opened the deep-freeze unit in a corner of the kitchen.

"Attention to such minutia pays the bills for our incredibly lavish personal lifestyle!" she called in reply, smiling at the hearty horse-laugh from the other room. It pleased and satisfied her to know that she could make Joe laugh. He was wrapped too tight, sometimes; too earnest, too serious entirely. Now, Jamie – she had always been able to make Jamie laugh.

Yes, that pan of frozen lasagna … and a mixed salad to go with, once the lasagna was warmed and bubbling in the oven. Say an hour or so; Jess was also tired; a full day of seeing to her various clients in Luna City, Karnesville and Beeville, driving hither and yon, with Little Joe uncomplaining in his car seat. He was a good baby, for all that. But now and again she really missed the days when she and Joe went out for burgers or pizza as impulse took them or drove into San Antonio for a meal at one of the Riverwalk restaurants. Oh, for a table on one of the outside terraces, overlooking the river, the lights that twinkled like fireflies in those monumental cypress trees lining the artfully-channelized river! Live music spilled from one of the other places, and she and Joe people-watched in the twilight, and swifts and grackles swooped into their night roosts. All that without the labor of hauling the Soup-Monster and the heavy freight of his impedimenta; the diaper bag, the stroller, the baby-car-seat and all that along with them.

A weekend of leisure in Galveston would be just the ticket. Jess covered the lasagna with tinfoil, turned the oven to 350 and went to join her menfolk, just as Little Joe grinned at his father, an open and uninhibited grin which revealed all of two new baby teeth in his lower jaw. Jess's heart turned over in her chest. The child looked so like Joe, it was uncanny, even to his tiny nose, which gave a hint of the ancestral Vaughn beakiness. A miracle, the blending of her blood, flesh and bones with Joe's, yet, Little Joe was his own person, even at the age of eight months! A whole, new, original, and miraculous little person … again, Jess thanked with her whole heart for Miss Letty's wise advice.

"Supper is served in about fifty minutes," she said, as he settled onto the sectional next to Joe. "Give me twenty minutes, I'll feed the Soup-Monster and put him down to sleep, so that we can have supper in peace."

"Sounds like a plan," Joe replied. "The weekend thing; let's go for it, Babe. We need a break, some R-and-R, you know. Be good for the Monster to learn how to wind the grands around his little finger."

"Share the blessings," Jess leaned her head against Joe's substantial shoulder, the one with the uniform patch embroidered with the city logo of the Luna City Police Department sewn upon it. Another brief moment of pure contentment; Gram and Grumpy had insisted that such in retrospect would be considered the happiest times of their lives.

"We'll be happy to have a baby in the house, once again!" Martha Abernathy exclaimed, when Jess had ventured the casual boat of her suggestion; that she and Joe spend a luxurious weekend at a Galveston resort destination onto the tranquil sea of familial relations over the Memorial Day holiday weekend. "Do make the reservations, Jess! You need to take a break now and again! It's good for a marriage, to make a little time for yourself and your man. Don't trouble yourself in the least, worrying about Little Joe!"

Now she watched Joe abandon the mild surf, the boogie-board under his arm, striding up through the receding surf, which cast a brief swath of lacy bubbles across the white sand. He collapsed with a brief grunt onto the spread beach towel at her side. Jess spared a covert and concerned glance at him. She'd bet anything his knees were giving him hell again. Good thing she had packed a bottle of extra-strength Motrin. She would mildly suggest that he take a few before they went out for dinner, and hope that he would take the suggestion.

"How's the water?" She asked.

Joe chuckled. "Salty and wet, Babe."

"It's the ocean, it goes without saying."

Joe lay back in the shade with a sigh. "Thought about where to go for dinner? I've an appetite for fish tacos. That place on Seawall with the two big-ass balconies overlooking the Gulf would suit me fine. OK with you?"

"Perfect," Jess agreed. "A bit noisy, but we can go early… it's an anniversary for us, you know. We can celebrate."

"Oh?" Joe raised an eyebrow.

Jess grinned. "The first time we seriously kissed … and umm. Other stuff."

"Oh, that." Joe chuckled, reminiscently. "After the Memorial Day pig roast at the V, you had too much to think, and I walked you home? Yeah, I remember." The grin widened into an expression of outright lewd reminiscence. "Hoo, boy – do I remember, Babe! I was so damned glad you didn't punch me in the nuts when I made my move!"

"Joseph P. Vaughn, you are no gentleman!" Jess exclaimed with an attempt at a Scarlett O'Hara exaggerated Southern accent and swatted at her husband with her discarded tee-shirt top. Which launched a good quantity of sand at him but he just chuckled again and lay back on his spread beach towel.

"No regrets though, Babe?" he said.

Jess shook her head. "No regrets, Joe."

* * *

Jess's thoughts went back to that particular Memorial Day – six years ago to the day. She was back in Luna City at that time in her life, aged thirty-three, having resigned from the big-city corporate CPA practice and hung out her own shingle in Karnes County. She was living in her childhood home amid a strange mixture of old family furniture overlaid with those of her own books, knick-knacks and souvenirs acquired in a peripatetic decade of living in dorms, quarters and rented apartments. Martin had moved into a second-floor apartment in the stately old Abernathy Hardware building on Town Square, claiming that he no longer wanted to cope with mowing the fairly substantial lawn, although both she and Martin both knew very well that this was to keep a better eye on her grandparents; both still spry and in possession of the full original ration of marbles, but not getting any younger. Jess taking over the house meant that it was still in the family. Her potentially-champion barrel-racing horse – dear Sweet-Pea – could live in the shed and corral enclosure which once had housed Stinker, her first horse. Among the first things Jess did upon moving back home to Luna City in the spring of 2012 was arrange with one of the Gonzalezes to come around with his combine-size riding mower once a week, in exchange for her doing his business income tax returns.

She had quickly built up her business client base, helped immeasurably that even people who didn't know her right away were reassured, recognizing that she was one of the Luna City Abernathy Hardware kinfolk; a known quantity, right from the bat. Folk in Karnes County were inclined to proffer trust in her fitness and integrity – even more upon hearing through the county-wide grapevine that she had taken over financial management of Doc Wyler's varied business affairs; his scattering of smaller properties like the Café and the Tip-Top, as well as the Wyler Ranch. She had work sufficient to keep her busy for all the working days. She also had the benefit of coming home every night to sleep in a familiar place and eat breakfast in the sunny little banquette off the kitchen. No more of staying in some impersonal hotel suite and partaking of an uninspired breakfast buffet which came free with it, while CNN blared the morning news rotation on a wide-screen television mounted on a blandly-decorated wall.

When she tired of her own cooking, or something frozen and warmed-up, she could always walk over to the Abernathy Hardware building and have supper with Pop and the Grands. Gram had often chided her about her lack of social life at this stage of her life.

"I'm busy, Gram," Jess repeated patiently. "Seriously, all I have the energy to go most nights is come over for supper here. And if I really want to walk on the wild side, Joe Vaughn and I go out to the Whattaburger in Karnesville."

"Joe Vaughn?" Gram had perked up immediately. "Such a nice young man! You should encourage him. You two have so much in common, and you do make a lovely couple together."

Jess rolled her eyes and protested. “Gram, you’re positively Victorian! Joe and I are just friends. Barely friends at that and all that we have in common is that he wrote me a traffic ticket last year, and we went to the same schools in Luna City! Three years apart and he was dating Princess Patty Wyler the Queen-of-Homecoming-Cheerleader all that time, too.”

“Don’t give me any sass, young lady,” Gram had a touch of disciplinary frost in her frown. You two have supper dates? In my day, that counted as a young man and woman courting. Really, Jess – be serious.”

“I am,” Jess replied. In that spring of 2012, she was certain in her own mind that was all there was to the occasional drives to Karnesville, and the chaste return, after wolfing burgers and fries in the spartan dining area of the Whattaburger franchise. Joe – for it was his truck that conveyed them hence – confessed to a dislike of smelling the old odors of food in his main ride, and so they consumed their burgers, fries and whatever on the Whattaburger premises. Like Jess, Joe had returned to his ancestral domicile.

“Gram, we’re just friends! We go out for fast food now and again, when we aren’t too tired after work. There’s nothing more than that. Don’t go picking out your Gram-of-the-bride dress on that account, OK?”

“Yes, darling, whatever you say,” Gram had conceded, upon intercepting a stern and wordless visual reprimand from both her husband and Martin, Jess’s father.

After a moment, Martin said only, “Joe’s a solid guy. Now that he’s proved himself on the police force, we’re considering offering him the chief position. He was an MP in the Army, and he’s been taking a bunch of police management courses at night to catch up. Chuy Gonzales wants to retire at the end of the year. Joe’s a shoo-in for the job, if I’m reading the city council all right. Jessy-Belle, you know your own mind. Don't let anyone rush you into a hasty decision."

"Thanks, Pops," Jess had responded, with mild sarcasm, and turned her mind toward Gram's chicken a-la-king casserole. This dainty was made with a can of cream of whatever soup. As a small child, Jess had loved it. She regarded the glutinous mess on her plate, a lumpy concoction of overcooked noodles, shredded chicken without much flavor remaining, and peas gone the dark olive color of an Army blanket. She wished that she had decided to go out with Joe instead, when he had asked her, that very afternoon.

He had stopped her, flashing lights on the Luna City PD patrol car, even though she had been crawling around the margin of Town Square, at a speed well below the posted limit. Joe – alpha-male swagger already well-established, and his substantial khaki sleeve adorned with Luna City Police Department PD sergeant's stripes – had come up to the driver-side door of her little yellow Jeep Wrangler and ventured, "Hey, Jess, wanna go honky-tonking in Victoria tonight? There's a live band at KB's on the Cuero Highway. We can eat BBQ on the patio under the stars. Wanna go?"

She had been exhausted and brain-dead from a day at Doc Wyler's town office, and said no, not tonight.

Joe had shrugged, saying, "Not a problem. See you on Sunday, then?"

"What's happening on Sunday?" she had asked.

Joe shrugged again. "Memorial Day at the V – the VFW post. Andy Pryor is spotting us a whole dressed pig for a pit-roast, starting on Saturday. The eating starts at four on Sunday, but the drinking commences at mid-afternoon. I'd … I'd really like it, if you came with me."

"I'll be there," Jess answered, her mouth had begun to water at the thought of a Pryor-provided pig roast.

The Pryors at that point had only just opened their occasional restaurant and food truck. On pain of death, Jess would never confess her ironical and inward amusement at seeing Patricia Wyler Pryor – in her mind, Princess Patty, the other half of the Golden Couple of Luna City HS, serving up BBQ sandwiches, a sauce-smeared apron over her doubtlessly high-end outfit, her hands gloved in those hygienic blue food-safety gloves, dealing out sandwiches from a food truck. How low were the high-school high-and-mighty fallen! Jess felt slightly ashamed of this unworthy emotion. Then and now, Patricia had never been anything less than cordial to the slight, bespectacled horse-mad tomboy that Jess had been, or to the polished professional that she was now, trusted to attending to the Wyler Ranch business affairs. Jess supposed that Patricia knew very well how things had stood between Jess, and Patricia's younger cousin Jamie …

Jamie. Jess put the yellow Wrangler into gear and drove away, wondering if she were quite up to Memorial Day at the V. It meant dealing with the memories of Jamie, memories still lively, vivid and in color.

That was the day for remembering; even more so than Day of the Dead. Memorial Day was for those lost in war, from Abuelita Adeliza Gonzales-Gonzalez' sailor brother Manny *(at Pearl Harbor)*, a score of other Gonzaleses and Gonzalezes on battlefields as far-spread as Salerno, St. Lo, Guadalcanal, a Japanese prisoner-of-war camp on Luzon Island, at Pusan and An Loc. There was an Abernathy second cousin a casualty on Omaha Beach, and Campbell Bodie *(a great-uncle of the Bodie feed-mill family)* in a flash-attack on the Legation Quarter during the Boxer War in China. There was even a woman, Miss Letty's childhood friend,

Henrietta Keyes – an Army nurse at Anzio. All of them existed safely in the past, in tinted sepia-photographs, casualties in wars long consigned to the history books. Part of the past, the bloodlessly-remembered and honored dead. Jamie was still real, living, a voice and a thousand small memories in Jess's mind. A war in color, even if it was the dun-color of desert dust and a harsh blue sky arched overall.

Never mind. She would have to go. Jamie would have wanted that – Jess taking his place, to sit under the cypress trees out in back of the V, drinking beer and swapping outrageously humorous yarns with the older veterans. And Joe – certainly his memories were in color, too.

"If it makes you feel any better, Gram," Jess had said, moved a forkful of chicken a la king from one side of her plate to the other, "I've agreed to go to the VFW pig-roast next week with Joe Vaughn – are you satisfied?"

"Yes, dear," Gram would only say. "I'm sure you will have a good time. He is such a nice young man."

Memorial Day at the V - 2012

Jess Abernathy walked toward the V that late afternoon on that memorable Memorial Day, six years previously. This was a matter of a couple of blocks along Oak Street, a narrow street which meandered along the southern edge of Luna City, and eventually raveled out into an unpaved ranch road on the far side of Route 123, beyond the old McAllister place. Jess strolled along the shaded margin of Oak Street, wondering vaguely how early she could make her excuses and leave without causing offense. When she came up on Araceli and Pat's place, she slowed her pace. Pat was doing BBQ. The massive unit that was Pat's pride, joy and fond hobby was sending up an enticingly scented thread of smoke. In the front yard, her best friend Araceli's small daughter was playing in the small inflatable pool, attended by their watchful mother, as a small sprinkler unit played back and forth on a patch of emerald-green lawn.

Jess and Araceli had been inseparable best friends since the third grade, for reasons that Jess could never quite articulate or comprehend. Anglo, privileged, single-minded and earnest, intensely focused … and Hispanic, cheerfully working-class, with a haphazard attitude toward everything but home, family, and eventually her part-time job at the Luna Café and Coffee. They had shared clothes, sleep-overs, tips on dating prospects and makeup since practically forever. Jess had been one of Araceli's court at her *quinceanera*, and a bridesmaid at her wedding, a bare three years later. Araceli, in turn, had schooled Jess in the subtle art of applying makeup, and was the first to clue her in about the necessity of shaving her legs and armpits at the age of fourteen or so, or else risk being called 'tarantula-woman' by the viciously-inclined among their male and female peers. Araceli's kin, even Abuelita Adeliza, appeared in a body to cheer Jess on at rodeo events. Jess was grateful for being scooped into the outer fringes of an affectionate and cohesive family, even if only in a peripheral manner. The dynastic ambitions of the Abernathy clan had descended, undiluted as they were unspoken, onto her. Really – there was only her. A burden spared for Araceli, being only one among a multitude of the younger of her clan.

Araceli waved to her and rose from her perch on the front steps to the brief porch of the double-wide. Jess waited for Araceli at the low fence which guarded the yard around the aged, but well-maintained trailer. Araceli had a diet Sprite soft-drink can in her hand, her infant son Mateo balanced expertly on her hip.

"Hey, Jess! Guess you're off to the V! Pat is PO'ed; here he has a whole brisket, and hardly anyone to eat it. Just about everyone's off to the V, 'cause of Memorial Day, and the pig roast."

"Yeah," Jess replied, somewhat regretfully. She would really have rather been at Araceli's. There were no deep undercurrents at Araceli's. "Joe Vaughn asked me, so I gotta go. Sorry, 'Celi."

"Never mind; the leftovers go in the deep-freeze, and they'll be awesome," Araceli replied, and shifted Mateo to a more comfortable position. "Pat works so many night shifts, I swear that he loses track of the days. Joe Vaughn, OK?" Araceli got the same identically-calculating expression her face as Martha Abernathy did, at the mention of Joe. "Wow, Jess. Awesome. And he's really a nice guy, in spite of being a total Nazi about speed limits. Which is OK with me, you know. It fries me, when drivers go flying down this street. What about Angelika, and Tio Jaimie's old Bassett hound? I hate speeders. Where do you have to be in such an all-fired hurry that you can't take care and be there half a minute late to the stop sign?"

"I have no idea," Jess sighed. She had half a mind at this moment to forget about the V tonight and invite herself to Araceli's instead. "Pops says that Joe Vaughn is a shoo-in to be the next police chief, and Gram wants me to throw myself at him. A good prospect, she says. We make a nice couple, she says."

"You do, actually," Araceli replied, with a long considering look at her best friend. "Besides being a nice guy with a good job, I'm pretty sure he would be amazing in bed."

"Why do you say that!" Jess demanded, indignantly, already beginning to blush. She was blushing even deeper, as Araceli expanded on this topic, in luxurious *(not to mention near-pornographic)* detail.

"Index fingers," Araceli finally finished up. "Dead give-away that he has substantial other parts. And been around long enough to know the best ways of using it. I'd be the last to encourage messing around outside the bounds of marriage vows, Jess, but I don't think you'd be really be doing wrong, not if you go to Confession afterwards. You're only human, and there are worse things to be tempted into. Promise me you'll give him a whirl." She gave Jess a very severe look and hesitated before adding. "He likes you, girlfriend. And Jamie's been gone for what … eight years, now? Time enough to close that book and move on. It would do you good, you know. Do both of you good, actually."

"I loved Jamie," Jess protested. "We were soulmates, from the time we were just kids and he spent the summers here. You can't just tell me to just move on, like it was a bad date with someone I just met!"

"Yeah?" Araceli had the same stern look as her grandmother did, laying down the law and an uncomfortable truth to the clan. "Jamie's not coming back, girlfriend. Not ever. Don't spend the whole rest of your life tied to a ghost." And Araceli used a very blunt word. "Do it with the living, Jess. There's a future there. Move on and grow the hell up."

"Thank you," Jess was stung. "Does Pat know you talk dirty like that?"

"Yeah," Un-stung, Araceli grinned. "He likes it. It's our little secret." Her expression went sober. "Look, I don't want to hurt your feelings, but we've been friends forever, too. You're back in Luna City, you haven't hooked up with some nice guy in all that time you were working in the big city. As good as your little CPA practice is, I'll bet it'll be a long time before you run into as solid as Joe. You don't necessarily <u>have</u> to go to bed with him. Just give yourself and him a chance. I'll drink on it," Araceli lifted up the can of Sprite, and hitched up Mateo again. "Will you? Promise to give him an even chance? I'll drink to that, if you will. I promise – no spit in this."

"I'll do that," Jess promised, more to content Araceli than anything else. She solemnly drank from the can of diet Sprite after her friend. "Promise onna drink, 'Celi."

"So do I," Araceli swigged again from the can, and then regarded her friend. "OK, then; what are you waiting for. Go get 'em."

Jess walked on, mildly revolted at the sick-sweet taste of lukewarm Sprite. She had never liked the taste of artificially-sweetened sodas. Per her oath to Araceli, she resolved to be cordial to Joe Vaughn, since this was an occasion which marginally-qualified as a date. Not cordial to the point of anything that would shock Gram, or Pops, though, she assured herself. Just before Oak Street, the sidewalk ended in a crumble of concrete. A path beaten through the dirt by the feet of pedestrians, horses, and bicyclists led through a scattered copse of young trees toward the riverbank and the sand-pink building which housed the Luna City chapter of the VFW.

Jess walked silently along the last bit. This was where she and Jamie had ridden to buy Moon Pies at the icehouse; she on Stinker, the Birthday Horse, and Jamie on whatever he chose from the Wyler stables. This path was clogged with memories for Jess, childhood memories of summertime hours in Stinker's worn saddle, exploring the paths and byways around Luna City and the meandering river, sneaking around the margins of Mills Farms, of Jamie repeating tales of Old Charley Mills' treasure of gold hidden somewhere about the place. They had trespassed surreptitiously onto the golf course a couple of times, Jamie being certain that the treasure was somewhere around the eleventh hole on the golf course. They had been chased off on one occasion by Mills Farm security that last time. Jess had been so frightened at the prospect of being arrested – *the ultimate humiliation!* – that she prevailed on Jamie to never do that again.

Childhood. Another country. A country to which your passport has been revoked, and in which you may never walk again.

This wandering path also led to the back of the VFW – that open space at the back of the old temporary classroom building, where a bank of windows overlooked a concrete patio, a couple of rusty BBQ units made from 55-gallon drums cut in half, some weathered plank picnic tables, and a lumpy stretch of grass meadow sloping down to the riverbank. The amiable crowd at the V spilled out from the creaky sand-pink building, and the smoke from the BBQ, and the pit where the pig awaited its final apotheosis – made a sweet, meat-tinged incense. Jess walked past the gathered revelers, some of them as gray and weathered as Gram and Grumpy, exchanging cheerful greetings with those who were her clients and some whom she hoped would be her clients.

There was Benny Cordova from Mills Farm; Benny had no need of her financial services *(he came under the Mills Farm encompassing management umbrella, as a long-time medium-level local employee.)* In the long-distant past, he had been drafted into the Army, serving a blameless and uneventful military career of a mere two years duration, managing an MWR facility in Germany. He sat at one of the tables with a Gonzalez cousin; Sylvester, the youngest son of Jesus-of-the-Garage, dapper in chinos and a vintage Hawaiian shirt. She knew him only slightly, as he was nearly a decade younger, barely in elementary school when she went away to college and a job in the city. He had a steno notebook laid out in the table in front of him, into which he was scribbling a desultory note.

"Hey, Jess – how's it going?" Sylvester asked. "Come have a beer with us, an' tell me about what you can do for me, if I set up my own little computer consulting business here in Luna City. Uncle Roman says you have your own office now."

"At present, housed in a briefcase and a laptop in the back of my car," Jess replied, and fished in her pocket for her wallet with a couple of business cards tucked into the cash. She had not expected to be trolling for business at the V this evening, but she thanked her fortunate stars that one of her small-business mentors had emphasized the importance of always having a card handy. "I think small, and nimble. The phone number is my cellphone, which is always with me. Call me if you have questions, day or night. No, not actually night, not after seven; I have to sleep sometime."

"I like that," Sylvester replied, appearing somewhat cheerier, as he tucked away Jess's card in the colorful front shirt-pocket. "But somehow, I think my clients will be calling me any ol' time their computer is acting up."

"What kind of business are you thinking of starting up?" Jess asked, genuinely curious. Sylvester was one of a clan with profitable enterprises built into their bones and blood. Nothing like getting in on the ground floor.

"Computer consulting, maintenance, training," Sylvester waved an airy hand. "Security, specialty coding; anything to do with bits and bytes. Anything the Geek Squad can do, I can do better and more efficiently for a local clientele."

Jess snorted. "And without a long commute from the city. Sounds like an interesting business plan, but I hope your ride can stand the mileage. You'll be racking up miles and miles, and wear on your tires, doing in-home client calls. I speak from experience, just so you know."

"Already counted into the mix," Sylvester replied in a jaunty tone of voice. "Poppa says he has me covered."

"Tell him to invoice you at the full price," Jess advised. "For repairs and maintenance. It's a legitimate expense, for tax purposes."

"Hey, thanks," Momentarily distracted, Sylvester scribbled a note onto his notebook. "You've been a help already."

"My pleasure," Jess replied, and drifted on. She could already see her father – a brief hitch in the Navy, courtesy of the Vietnam-era draft – sitting at the other table with Doc Wyler, wizened and irascible as always. "Hey, Pops. Hi, Doc."

"Jessy-bell," her father beamed, and Doc Wyler half-turned to squint up at her.

"Hey, young lady," the aged veterinarian moved his battered medical bag from the bench next to him. "Come sit with the old fogies for a spell, so we can look at ya, and remember what it is to be young."

"Charmer," Jess grinned. "Sorry, but I have to find Joe, first. Dance with the one who brought me, you know. Although Joe doesn't dance, I guess. But he did ask me tonight."

"He's inside," Pops exchanged a weighted look with Doc. Jess inwardly sighed. But this was Pops, and Doc. Both of them loved and respected her, so she supposed that she could forgive them for an unseemly interest in her personal life.

She strolled around the end of the VFW building; an aging, temporary structure transported by dint of building-moving technology provided by Roman Gonzalez's construction firm from the high school campus some years previously when the new extension made it extraneous to needs. It was still very obviously an old classroom; shaped like a Monopoly hotel-piece, with a shallow pitched roof. The bank of windows across one long wall looked out on the concrete slab where the picnic tables and the BBQ grills stood, the tree-dotted meadow and the riverbank beyond. There were a pair of doors on either end of the opposite side, which faced into the extended and crumbled parking lot of the Tip-Top at some distance. Jess sighed a very small, resigned sigh, and went to meet her assumed fate – er, date – for the evening.

He was inside, leaning against the bar, such as it was. What it was: OK-grade plywood, slightly singed with a welding-torch for texture and color, and then finished with layers and layers of shiny industrial-strength lacquer. There were military-created dives the world across, Jess had found in her Air Force Reserve hitch, such little social hubs created in odd locations wherever soldiers, sailors, airmen, and Marines gathered and were wont to set aside in a gathering place. There should have been a formal designation for the various styles of GI scratch-made décor, Jess always thought; something to add to the categories of "GSA Tacky," "Issue Danish Moderne" and "HQ Palatial." She had once seen such a hang-out boasting a chandelier adorned with rows of the little metal can-openers that used to be packed with C-rat and boxed aircrew meals.

"Hey," Joe unpropped himself from the bar and grinned down at her. "You made it! Want a beer? You're just in time. Andy is about to open the pit and serve up pig. Say, in about twenty minutes."

Jess covertly surveyed him. Yes, as good-looking as ever, still lean and athletic, a physique which the tan Luna City PD uniform showed off to perfection.

"Sure," Jess replied. "It's a date. And I'm hungry."

"Good." And Joe grinned all over his face, open and guileless. "Buy you a beer to go with. Two beers, Chris – my tab," he added to the guy tending bar. "Dos Equis, to keep it classy.

"Sure thing," Chris Mayall brought a pair of dark bottles from the aged refrigerator which stood behind the bar, popped and tops and set out a pair of heavy glass mugs. Chris had a prosthetic leg; you'd never know, since he didn't limp at all. "Miss Jess – you doin' OK?"

"Fine," Jess replied, hoping she didn't sound curt. It was awkward with Chris, although she had never talked about it, most of all never with Chris. She knew that he had been Jamie's good friend, the medic in his Marine unit, adopted sight unseen by Luna City after Jamie wrote to his grandmother, Miss Alice. *'He has no real family, and never gets any letters or care packages when the rest of us get mail,'* Jamie had written. When Chris was horrifically injured and lost his leg below the knee in the IED detonation near Fallujah that killed Jamie, he was visited in hospital in San Antonio by Miss Alice and Miss Letty McAllister. For some reason known only to Doc Wyler and his abiding sense of noblesse oblige, when Chris got out of hospital and released from the Navy, Doc Wyler hired him to manage the Tip-Top. Miss Letty rented him a tiny apartment over the garage at the old McAllister place. Jess didn't know anything about the ins and outs of how that came about; a Detroit ghetto orphan on a military disability coming to roost in a tiny South Texas town. She had been busy with her own Reserve tour and then with the consulting CPA work. But when she came home for good, six months ago, there was Chris, lean and cappuccino-colored, managing the Tip-Top and tending bar at the V, as much a fixture as if he had been there since forever. It didn't make much sense to Jess; but then, this was Luna City. She was still afraid that if she began to talk about Jamie to Chris, she would uncork a flood of raw grief that would have her screaming and crying, and not able to stop. Jess found that unacceptable, and so she had avoided anything but strictly formal conversation with Chris, mostly to do with business at the Tip-Top.

Now Joe grinned and said, “Jess-girl, have you been breaking any speed limits, lately?”

“You would know if I had,” Jess replied, smartly.

Joe’s grin broadened. “I can’t be everywhere, Babe,” he drawled.

Across the bar, Chris grinned as well. “Damn, the po-po ain’t everywhere? I am so f**king disappointed in y’all. As oppressors in the hood, you honkies are a complete f**king failure.”

“We’re hicks from the sticks, ya hood-rat,” Joe shot back. “We got some standards when it comes to enforcing the law. Not to mention, a better class of citizens. But thanks for the morale boost, Squid; I’ll go polish up my jackboots.”

Joe continued enlarging on the civic shortcomings of Chris’ geographic point of origin, and Chris reposted with a stinging commentary on the shortcomings of rural Texas. Jess closed her eyes, briefly. Yeah, there were civilians of a more sheltered sort who would dissolve into a ball of quivering jelly at hearing some of the terms with which Joe and Chris were needling each other.

This went on, until Andy Pryor put his head around the door, saying, “Hey, y’all, supper is served! Get some before it’s all gone!”

Chris wiped his hands on his bar-towel, observing to no one in particular. “Pit-roast pig? Haji don’t know what they’re missing!”

“All the more for the rest of us infidels,” Joe tossed back the rest of his beer. “Want another, Babe?”

“Yeah, sure,” Jess replied, and Chris grinned and set up three. They walked out together, Jess with her final beer and mug in hand, Joe walking companionably half a step behind, one hand resting proprietarily in the small of her back, as if escorting her to the dance floor. It was easy with Joe, she thought. He made no demands on her at this point, other than amiable companionship, and shared memories of a childhood lived in the same small town. The simple gesture marked … well, something new, and it made Jess mildly uneasy.

2012: Jessica Memorious

The buffet table was set up, adjacent to the opened pit where the whole roasted pig had met his final apotheosis the afternoon before; stuffed with onions, applies, peppers and assorted spices, swathed in layers of aluminum foil and a shroud of chicken wire, and temporarily interred in a pit of coals, to gently roast overnight, and emerge succulent and flavorful. Pig roast was not the only item on the menu for Luna City's VFW Memorial Day BBQ; those members – and most usually their wives – had provided a bounty of casseroles, Crock-pots and restaurant-service sized pans of hot and cold side dishes, salads, cakes, and puddings. Most had scorned to provide store-made, although there was a pile of commercial sliced bread stacked up next to the pan of shredded sliced pig, and the crock-pot of Pryor's special BBQ sauce. It was commonly acknowledged that nothing quite set off a proper country pit-roast pig like a wad of plain sliced Butterkrust™ sliced bread, sopping up the juices and the fiery red sauce that was a Pryor specialty – although Anna-Maria De Luca Gonzales, whose recipe for genuine

Italian meatballs had been the keynote feature of the parish church of Saints Margaret & Anthony yearly spaghetti and meatball feed for nearly half a century had stoutly insisted on bringing a basket of sourdough boules, whose recipe she had been perfecting for nearly as long. *(Anna-Maria's opinions on the qualities of American commercial bread need – no, can not – be repeated here, first for the terms of vituperative abuse in three languages with which they were couched and secondly for the length of comment, which was encyclopedic.).*

Joe, Jess and Chris joined at the end of the line, which already went halfway around the paved area.

"Do you know if Miss Letty made her special bread pudding with bourbon sauce again this year?" Joe asked, as the line inched toward the bountiful table.

"Oh, man – bread pudding and bourbon sauce, N'Alins-style?" Chris made a sort of moan. "Does she make it with raisin bread? This is my first year at this. I just couldn't face Memorial Day here, until last year. Maw-maw who raised me, she made it with raisin bread. Swear to God there was nothing more heavenly than Maw-Maw's bread pudding."

"Don't know about it being New Orleans-style," Jess answered, "But yes; Miss Letty's bread pudding is legendary. She doesn't make it, every year. Most years she brings banana pudding, instead, rather than heat up her kitchen, baking bread pudding."

"Banana pudding is OK by me," Joe remarked, in the line behind Jess. "I'm a guy with simple tastes. Nothing more simple than vanilla wafers, sliced bananas, Coolwhip, and pudding mix…"

Simultaneously, Jess and Chris groaned, and informed Joe that he was an uncouth being, lacking appreciation of the finer things in life, while Joe defended his taste in those simple commercial confections which had informed his childhood in lively fashion.

The head of the line inched closer to the feast of good things which was the buffet table. Jess ventured a question of Chris;

"Can you get your grandmothers' recipe? I'll bet that it's pretty close to Miss Letty's."

"Naw," Chris replied. "She's … she passed away when I was twelve. The place where we lived was a rental. The landlord threw all her stuff onto the sidewalk the week after the funeral. I was in foster-care by then. All that I had was what the care worker let me pack."

"Damn, that's cold, Squid," Joe's reaction was heartfelt, totally unstudied. Jess murmured something conventional in sympathy, and the line inched forward again. "Around here that kinda shit would so not happen. Not if the neighbors and kin had anything to say about it."

Chris merely shrugged. "Yeah, well, different time, different place. I guess some of the neighbors grabbed what they wanted of Maw-Maw's trash an' traps before the city garbage collectors came around. I had what I wanted most, at the time. Wish I had thought of her little box of recipes, though. Leastways, I had the photo album, with pictures of my Mom and all, when she was a lil' girl, and the book of stories that Maw-Maw usta read to me."

Jess thought of the house where she lived, the apartments over Abernathy Hardware, of all the mementos contained therein; the furniture, the books, those bits and bobs and scraps of a settled life, accumulated over a century and more of blameless middle-class residency. None of this had ever been in danger of being cast out onto an unfeeling sidewalk, for the municipal authorities to carry away in a trash truck, after neighborhood scavengers had picked them over. And then of the many-galleried Wyler Ranch headquarters, and the little hunting cabin down by the lake on the Wyler property, that place which Jamie loved … Chris had been

Jamie's best friend, or so Jamie had written to her. *"A great, solid guy. A medic, but he hangs with the toughest. Comes from where he was brought up, Jess. You'd like him, I'll reckon. Sharp as a tack, and just the guy you want at your back. Gramps would look down his nose a bit and make a crack about uppity coloreds but a credit to his race – Gramps' generation and all being what it was – but I believe he'd like our Squid medic on first introduction. Ambitious and focused! All the things that I'm not!"*

Jess blinked back an incipient tear and ordered those tear ducts to behave themselves. This was not the time. Or maybe it was. Memorial Day and all. The portion of line containing Joe, Jess and Chris finally approached the stack of paper plates, napkins and plastic forks, spoons and knives piled up at the end of the table. Just beyond those were a pair of large aluminum pans, piled high with roughly-carved pit-roasted pork, sending up a mouth-watering aroma. The food was set out along two tables set together, everyone helping themselves, as was customary.

"An offering by fire of pleasing odor to the Lord," Chris remarked. "Maw-Maw always said, when the roast got scorched. Says so in Leviticus, Maw-Maw said."

"Oh, yeah?" Joe replied, as he helped himself to a lovely, steaming helping of BBQ, and slathered it with a dip from the crock-pot of Pryor's special fiery-sauce. "I always like the one about beer being proof of His love and wish to make us happy."

Chris snorted, in a manner which could have been taken for disparaging. Jess did not think so, having considerable familiarity through her own Reserve deployments with male-to-male japes. She took a small portion of BBQ, a mere tablespoon of fiery-sauce, knowing well that the stuff – being composed of ingredients which included macerated ghost peppers – was the nearest thing to vegetarian napalm in existence. She followed along behind Chris and Joe, listening with amused toleration to their exchange of remarks. It was kind of restful, that Joe was not expecting her to make any contribution to the conversation.

For she was remembering Jamie's final words to her in a hasty email sent from an MWR-sponsored internet café at a forward operating base in Iraq, in the spring of 2004. *Hey – sorry, Jess, love ya, I hafta go.*

A week later, his name flashed across the local TV evening news: Lance Corporal James Wyler Ellis, USMC, a crawl accompanying a severe countenance in an official USMC picture, Jamie in dress-blues and white cover, trying to look fierce and martial for the camera; a cheerful ghost haunting Jess, a stab at the heart whenever she came home to Luna City, and walked in the places that she had walked with him, ridden their horses. The telephone call from her father.

Jessy-belle, I've just gotten off the line from Doc. I'm afraid I have bad news…

Half-lost in memories, Jess moved through the evening in mechanical fashion, nibbling at the pulled pork – which was indeed as delicious as anything ever produced from the Pryor's boutique little business – and conversing with the other veterans. She had another Dos Equis, possibly another, maybe one more after that, danced with lackluster enthusiasm with Joe, to country dance music from a portable stereo perched in one of the opened windows, while twilight fell, and shadows lengthened across the glade, painting long stripes toward the riverbank. She and Joe returned to the table at the edge of the concrete patio to see Miss Letty McAllister being shown reverently to a seat by a hovering Chris Mayall. Miss Letty stowed her walking stick *(which she barely used, save for aesthetic effect)* against the bench and regarded Jess and Joe with the piercing regard which recalled Jess to her first day of kindergarten. Yes,

Miss Letty had that powerful effect, having taught kindergarten and first grade in Luna City for nearly forty years. No one among the long-time residents *(unless their parents had sent them to the private Catholic academy of St. Scholastica's in Karnesville)* would have escaped Miss Letty's assured and assessing gaze, or the experience of her velvet-glove-clad iron-core authority.

"Joseph, Jessica," Miss Letty greeted them with a regal nod. "How very pleasant to see the two of you here, this evening. It's a first time for you both, isn't it?" Miss Letty – formal to every jot and tittle of strictures contained in the old etiquette books, never called anyone by a shortening of their first name, when she unbent sufficiently to address them by their family name predicated with Miss or Master. Jess struggled to repress an urge to say, "Yes, ma'am," and failed in that utterly.

"Yes, Ma'am – Miss Letty. Joe asked me … and I thought … well, since I have come back to Luna City, I might as well," Jess stammered, taken out of herself, her memories and Miss Letty's basilisk regard. "It's Memorial Day, after all. And I'm a veteran, too."

"You are, indeed," Miss Letty's severe regard thawed marginally. "One of the very few women at this post. Aside from Beatrice Gonzalez (she was a nurse in Vietnam, you know, and now lives in Houston) you and I may be the only women in Luna City who are members of the V in our own right."

"I try and hold up the honor," Jess blurted, and then wished that she had said anything else. She was afraid that she had drunk too many Dos Equis; in danger of embarrassing herself in front of Joe, but mostly in front of Miss Letty.

"Jessica deployed to Kuwait, in support of the operation to free Iraq from Saddam Hussein," Miss Letty explained, in an aside to Chris. "With the Air Force … the personnel office, wasn't it, dear?"

"Rear echelon," Chris noted with a nod of wry understanding, and lifted his own drink in mock salute.

"If there was a personnel classification more in the rear with the gear than the one I was in," Jess replied, with some asperity, "Then I would have liked to know about it. And y'all at the pointy end of the spear did like getting paid on time, your letters from home, and hot showers and a hot meal at the end of a spell at a forward post, *n'est ce pas*?"

Both Joe and Chris chuckled appreciatively.

Joe raised his own beer. "*Touché*, Jess. To the ladies, Squid – and all the fine-feathered fobbits, as well. They also serve who also … do necessary stuff in support."

Jess opened her mouth, a smart-ass retort on the tip of her tongue, but intercepted a warning glance from Miss Letty, and swallowed the retort unvoiced. Joe grinned at her, a wry grin of understanding and appreciation, and her mood was unaccountably lifted. He was truly such a nice guy, against all the odds and expectations. His attentions were a sweet flattery to the bespectacled and dreamy nerd girl that she had been in high school, when he was the Moths varsity football hero. Back then, she could hardly imagine being intimate friends with any male but Jamie, who wasn't really of Luna City. He just spent summers there, with his grandparents, Doc Wyler and Miss Alice. Jess's mind went wandering down memorious paths again, as Chris and Joe went to fetch them all another round, Miss Letty decorously requesting a soft drink. When the two men had vanished around the corner of the sand-pink building, Miss Letty looked at Jess with a particularly keen gaze.

"Jessica – are you all right?"

"Fine," Jess replied. "Just thinking about old friends."

Miss Letty didn't look as if she believed her but was too tactful to remark upon that disbelief. "I am so pleased that you have returned to Luna City and settled down. You know – my own financial interests, and those of the Wyler family – are so depend on a trustworthy advisor. Stephen has spoken very highly of your abilities, so of course I will be pleased to entrust overseeing my own small holdings to you. My brother looked after all of those so well …" Miss Letty ventured a small and mournful sigh. "Since he passed away last year, I have been rather at a loss, thinking of whom I might entrust seeing to all those forms and declarations for tax purposes…"

Jess looked at Miss Letty thinking, *'Oh, bull-crap, Miss Letty – you've never been at a loss in your life!'* Aloud, she only said, "Let me know of a time convenient to you, Miss Letty. I'll come and take a look. I'll be glad to take you on as a client. I'll bring a copy of my standard services contract and answer any questions that you might have."

"Very good, my dear," Miss Letty replied. "I will be at home receiving visitors on Thursdays. My teaching day at the school is Wednesday. You did know, I am still teaching? It is the First Aid segment of the survival course for the high school sophomores and juniors. I do believe they find the course most useful."

"I am certain that they do," Jess replied. Miss Letty's portion of the course included a graphic section on emergency childbirth, a prospect which usually so horrified male and female attendees that most of them left the classroom silently swearing never to experiment with sex, ever. "I will stop by around …" Jess swiftly consulted her cellphone for her schedule for Thursday. Yes – she could squeeze in a stop at the old McAllister House between her late morning and early afternoon client visits. "11:30, Miss Letty, if that is good for you."

"Perfect," Miss Letty beamed. "That is about the time that I have luncheon. I shall fix something for you, Jessica, if you wish to share."

"Thank you," Jess replied, with a small stifled sigh. "Don't go to any trouble, though." She hoped that Miss Letty would not go to any trouble – least of all, to prepare something like Gram's awful casserole of the other evening. At that moment Joe and Chris reappeared, bearing bottles – cold bottles, sweating condensation in a small damp ring when they were set down.

"The man of the hour, bearing ice-cold beverages!" Joe exclaimed. "Thanks, Squid – next round is on me!"

With a smile, Chris deftly popped tops and dispensed said beverages all around. Jess resigned herself to having to pay attention and be sociable, still wishing that she could draw a line under the evening and walk home.

And then, memories and the present all collided, with catastrophic effect.

Chris remarked, "Miss Jess, you must have been acquainted with my buddy, J. W. You know – Doc's grandson? He was from Houston, but he spent summers here. J.W. would have loved this; pig roast and all. I left a beer for him on the remembrance table." Chris shook his head, sadly. "Man, do I miss that guy! The solidest buddy a guy could have."

Jess felt as if she had taken a fall from horseback, had the breath knocked out of her, so thoroughly that she could hardly speak. All her self-control this evening had been for naught, all her rigid command of memories and tear ducts shattered in an instant.

"He … I … we … I'm sorry, I have to go now!" she stammered, and then lost her voice entirely. The tears she had been able to hold back all evening threatened to spill over, as a tidal-wave of grief threatened to carry all before it. It was so unfair! She raged inwardly; Why! Why was Jamie dead and gone, her beloved, and so dear to his parents, his grandparents and friends! Unfair, unjust, and God was so cruel to have ruled so arbitrarily!

Now Miss Letty, with a look of concern on her aged countenance was saying something to Chris and Joe, something that Jess was too overwrought to comprehend. But Chris had a stricken expression on his own face, and Joe was leaving his beer, rising from the table, and taking Jess's elbow.

"I'd better see you home, Jess. You look like you've had too much to think."

Jess was too choked with emotion to do anything more than nod. She let Joe lead her away, abandoning the new drinks, walking away through the grove of spindly trees in back of the V, too overcome to do anything more than nod to those which they passed on their way out. Those members and guests were mostly too busy eating, drinking and dancing to pay much attention at all. They reached Oak Street before Jess recovered her composure and her voice.

"Thanks, Joe … for seeing me home. I really shouldn't have come. I'm still not … OK."

"No prob," Joe replied, tersely. "Yeah, sometimes it gets to ya." He was silent after that for some time; she sneaked a sideways look at him, as they walked along the crumbling sidewalk. A grim and brooding as ever a Heathcliff there was. Oddly, Jess was reassured by this; Joe had memories of lost friends, too, but the discretion not to talk about them, even after a good few beers. A male tendency, Jess presumed. On this evening, her own grief was enough to bear, not take on the burden of another. They passed Joe's grandparents' place, the charming small cottage where he lived now, and kept faultlessly maintained, as if still under military regs. They walked on, past Araceli and Pat's place. Lights were on within the double-wide against the slow-falling early-summer dusk, and the streetlight at the corner winked on as they passed. A figure moved in the largest window; Jess thought it might be Araceli, calling in Angelika for bath and bedtime by tapping on the glass.

"I thought it would get easier," Jess said. "Everyone says that time is the great healer. Everyone says that I should get out more, that I ought to date more. That I ought to date you. But then I get smacked in the face with something that reminds me of him, and it's as bad as when Pops first told me. When does it get better, Joe? Can you tell me that much? You and Pat were a thing, and then she dumped you to marry Andy Pryor. How long did that just keep bugging the hell out of you?"

Joe shrugged, wordlessly. After a moment, he replied. "Well … we'd been friends for a long time. Still were friends, even then. We came around to seeing that we wanted different things out of life. Not as harsh as … nothing left to know if it would ever have worked out, like you and Jamie. Pat and I just went separate ways." He was silent for a little way longer, before adding, "Not to say that it wasn't a bummer when I was first back in Luna, seeing Pat and her boys, working the food truck with Andy. Man, I couldn't help thinking – that could have been mine! Why didn't I put up more of a fight? But then it just wasn't anything that mattered all that much to me, not for a while, and especially once you came back to town."

Jess, sunk in misery, didn't think she had heard that last bit right. They had reached the stretch of crumbling sidewalk in front of the Abernathy place – a nondescript post-war bungalow of no particular charm or distinguishing features, other than the bed of daylilies and lantana in front of it, carved out of a sweep of lawn.

"I … this is home," Jess said, when Joe paused by the mailbox, surrounded by a tall planting of white, purple and pink cosmos. "I guess we'd better say good-night. Thanks for walking me home."

She went on tip-toe, intending to offer only the briefest, most perfunctory kiss, but as she did so, his arms went around her – gentle, strong, supportive, and she was swamped by emotion. First, how lovely it was to be held close against the solidity of a male body. Jess' inner being cried out against the loneliness of the last eight years, as he returned the kiss. A long, long moment, and a tiny flame of desire flickered in Jess, flickered, and grew strong.

"Jess, babe – do you want me to stay?" Joe murmured, and Jess' last inhibition was lost.

"Yes," she answered. "I don't want to be alone tonight."

Anything to blot out the misery and grief.

"So, you had a nice time last night?" Araceli remarked the next morning, bringing a glass of orange juice and a cinnamon roll to Jess's table at the Café. It was still cool in the mornings, and Jess relished the unobstructed view of the Square, the cool shade under the towering oaks, and the pale dome of the bandstand rising up through them as if to punctuate the vista of green leaves. She was breakfasting later than her customary hour – being that she often met clients at the Café.

"The pig roast was fantastic," Jess answered. "And Miss Letty brought her special bread pudding, but I was too full for dessert."

"And afterwards?" Araceli lowered her voice to a confidential murmur. "You and Joe? Was it as good as I said it would be?"

"I don't know what you are talking about," Jess could feel herself beginning to blush. Araceli chuckled knowingly. Araceli knew Jess' blushes of old.

"Su-r-r-r-re you do, girlfriend. I saw you and Joe go past our place, just about a quarter to nine. Pat and I sat outside for another couple hours after I put the kids to bed, but we never saw Joe walking back alone from your place to his. 'Fess up – was he as good in the sack as I said he would be?"

Jess, blushing even more furiously, nodded and Araceli looked conspiratorial. "The morning rush is over; I'll take my break. Let me some coffee for us and you can tell me all about it. Don't leave out a single detail."

"It was … lovely," Jess brought herself to speak. "No awkward fumbling. He spent the whole night. Brought me coffee in the morning. So sweet – I have this little one-cup maker that most people can't figure out without the instructions in hand. But he brought me a cup this morning, first thing. He had to be at work and said he had barely enough time to walk home, shower and change." Jess sighed. Being unfaithful to Jamie, even the memory of Jamie had not been such a wrench as she dreaded. "He took the time to be sweet and considerate."

"Every single detail," Araceli commanded over her shoulder as she went to fetch her own coffee. The old-fashioned spring-bell over the front door chimed, as the door opened. Jess giggled, still blushing.

No; she would not enliven Araceli's day with every single detail of last night, just enough to reassure Araceli, that everything was good between her and Joe. Better than good – promising, even. Which she had not expected in the least, when she was first roused from a deep post-coital drowse, sometime around midnight by a drag at the bedsheets and the mattress quaking slightly under her.

Oh, he's going to leave, she thought, with some mild regret. Well, never mind then. Wham, bam, thank you ma'am.

Joe slid stealthily from the bed and padded silently around the foot. The light in the living room was still switched on. Jess, feigning sleep, assumed Joe was gathering up his shoes and items of clothing, scattered hither and yon between the front door and the bedroom, and preparing to make an equally stealthy exit. What on earth would she say to him, the next time they encountered each other around Luna City? Or would it be best to just pretend that absolutely nothing had happened?

She could hear him moving around, now in the front room. There came the snick of the front door lock shooting home. No, Joe was still within the house – walking out to the kitchen, to judge from the faint creaking of the wooden floor, the scuffle of his bare feet. The back door opened and shut. Jess presumed that he was trying to be subtle and go out through the back door. But Joe came padding back through the house. He paused in the bedroom doorway, and Jess peeked at him through half-closed eyes as he stood there; watchful, wary, as if he stood sentry looking out into the darkness on the other side of the wall that he guarded. The light fell at his side as he turned, making him a sharp silhouette, only his tats distinct – the elaborate "Death from Above" on his arm, and the other one on his chest, which she had never noted until this very evening when he shed his shirt.

The light flicked off, and Jess opened her eyes all the way. He was moving in the darkness, returning to bed. She felt the mattress shake a little, the shuffle of bedclothes as he lay beside her again. She was touched to the heart, when he carefully rearranged the light bedclothes to cover her shoulders again.

"I thought you were leaving," Jess affected a sleepy murmur, turning to face him in the darkness.

"I said I would stay," Joe replied, reasonably. "I was just turning off the light and making sure the doors were secure. I know this is Luna City, but you really ought to lock the doors at night."

"I have no concerns," Jess replied, arranging herself more comfortably against him. "We have a fantastically efficient police department." That drew a rather lewd chuckle from Joe and Jess blushed in the darkness.

"Always on top of things?" His arms went around her.

"Oh, stop it!" Jess answered. "No, not that. But I'm glad. I'm glad that you didn't go, just now. It wasn't easy for me. I kept thinking about Jamie, missing him so awfully. Sometimes it seems to me like he died just yesterday, and I can't even think straight for grief. Shouldn't it get easier with time, Joe? When does it get easier to bear?"

"I dunno," Joe answered. "You asked me that before, and I didn't know then, either. You just keep on, even when you think you're done in. Pick up your ruck and stagger on, Jess. You got friends that will help, and you gotta be there for them." In the darkness between them, Jess put her hand on his chest, on the tattoo inked over his heart; a wreath, encompassing a date, 4 October '93 and five names: – *Smith – Cavaco – Joyce – Kowalewski – Ruiz.* She felt the beat of his heart, and when he breathed in, and out, finally confessing. "I didn't want to spend the night alone, either, Jess."

"Understand," Jess sighed, leaning her head against Joe's shoulder, secure in the circle of his arms. As if he were still standing guard. "Your friends. Mogadishu. I didn't know you were there, until someone said something to me, years afterwards."

"Mog," Joe pulled her closer against him. "Filthy place; the asshole of earth, I'll swear. When God decides to give the world an enema, that's where He'll stick in the nozzle. Not a doubt in my mind. I'll give it to the skinnies, though; they're game when it comes to a straight-up all-in fight, which is better than I can say for most of the Talibs, or the Iraqis, even." She felt him kiss the top of her head, as they lay, close together. "I was shaking like a leaf, when it was over – when we got back, mostly safe and all, after fighting our way back through Mog. God, what an awful, wrecked place. My first deployment, too. Once we rotated home from that hellhole, I got the tat to cover up where I had Pat's name inked in.

Over my heart, for Chrissake. I was a sentimental jerk when I was nineteen!"

"Comes with the territory," Jess consoled him. It felt so… Jess couldn't find any other words than 'comforting' to describe how she felt at that moment. Comfortable, comforting, pleasingly exhausted … and content, feeling Joe's heartbeat against hers.

Pick up the ruck and stagger on.

No, Jess would never tell this to Araceli. Nor how she had leaned against the kitchen sink, after Joe had gone, regarding dawn in pale colors over the back of the Abernathy house, mist rising from the river, and from the tall grass. Her agile barrel-racing horse, dear nimble Sweet-Pea, hung her head over the bars of the small corral, waiting expectantly for her morning ration of affection and horse-appropriate treats.

"Sorry, Jamie," Jess said to the kitchen window. "Love you – I have to go."

Searching for The Fabulous Gonzaga Reliquary

From – Treasure-Hunters: The Internet Magazine

Well-known international treasure-hunter Xavier Gunnison Penn is off to the United States on another search for a historic missing treasure, his first since the abortive attempt more than a year ago to find the late-19th century Mills Treasure Hoard; a fabulous collection of gold coins and ingots taken in a train robbery by the notorious Bent Cactus gang in 1892, and thought to be concealed somewhere on a Texas homestead by one of the gang's ring-leaders.

Once funded by international finance magnate Collin Wyler, Gunnison Penn has been independently financing his own searches for various treasures since the 1970s, with sales of a series of books outlining his experiences. Often controversial, Gunnison Penn is still one of the grand old men of treasure-hunting, having five decades of experience under his belt, since being part of an excavation of the Oak Island Money pit as a teenager. This time, Penn is on a quest for an entirely new and relatively obscure treasure, the existence of which has only been verified in the sketchiest records, unearthed by the tireless efforts of Penn himself.

He first became aware of the existence of the fabulous jeweled Gonzaga Reliquary when its likeness was noted as part of a hitherto unknown da Vinci painting, discovered upon restoration work earlier this year done as part of converting a historic convent in the city of Milan into an upscale boutique hotel. The painting, which was hung for more than four centuries in a dark corner of the convent refectory, is claimed to be of Sister Giovanna Silvio y Gonzaga, in prayer before the reliquary, which is thought by Penn himself to have been designed and executed by the polymath goldsmith, poet and soldier Benevento Cellini earlier in the century. This reliquary, of gold, set with jewels and enamel, containing a tooth of the horse owned by St. Gigobertus of Bethany, which carried the Holy Mother and Child to Egypt, was a treasure of the noble Spanish family of Gonzaga, of Gijon in the duchy of Cantabria. The most famous scion of the Gonzaga clan was Cardinal Pedro Gonzaga, famed for being almost as venial and ambitious as his contemporary Cardinal Rodrigo Borgia, later Pope Alexander VI. The subject of the da Vinci painting, Sister Giovanna, was one of Cardinal Gonzaga's numerous illegitimate offspring by several mistresses. Penn, as well as other a few other historians who have considered the matter, speculate that the reliquary was – not to put too fine a point upon it – a bribe on the part of Cardinal Gonzaga to the convent to admit his daughter into their sisterhood. Approximately ten years later, when it became obvious that vows of obedience, chastity, and poverty had not taken serious hold, Sister Giovanna withdrew from the convent – and it is assumed by Penn that the reliquary went with her. From that point, the whereabouts and even the existence of the reliquary are unknown, although Penn theorizes that both woman and reliquary returned to the Gonzaga ancestral estates in Cantabria.

From research conducted by Penn in archives in Madrid and in Mexico City, Penn believes the priceless artifact was brought to the New World by descendants of the Gonzaga family, who took up a grant in the Spanish colony of Nueva Santander. Penn plans to conduct further research over the summer.

Staggering On With The Ruck

A bare three weeks after their return from their seaside holiday in Galveston, Jess returned from a day on the road and in the Café, tending to her various clients, and burdened with more than just the carrier with her tiny son and the heavy bag of baby impedimenta which accompanied him everywhere. Joe's house – her house! <u>their</u> house was cool and welcoming, a refuge from the relentless summer heat, which beat down upon South Texas like a red-hot hammer on a scorching anvil. Jess felt briefly faint in the sudden coolness. It was ten to five on a Thursday. Joe would be home soon, and she had news for him.

Until then, Jess nagged herself into going through the motions.

Put Little Joe in his swing – the one with the falling weight which rocked the seat back and forth for fifteen minutes or so. Fifteen minutes or so of blessed peace from a fussing infant. Empty the diaper bag of empty bottles and those filled diapers which had been filled in places where she had not been able to put them in an appropriate receptacle. Restock with fresh diapers and a couple of changes of onsies for the next day, throw the soiled into the washing machine out in what once had been the covered back porch (now enclosed to make a combination laundry and mud room) and start a load of wash.

As she walked back through the kitchen, Jess felt suddenly exhausted; her head swam, and she sagged into the nearest chair.

To think about fixing supper, when all she really wanted to do was to lie down and sleep, blessed sleep for hours and hours and hours! What to fix for supper for herself and Joe after a long and busy day, and soon the Soup-Monster would be hungry also, and then his bath-time … it never ended. Would never end. Jess felt as if she was on an enormous treadmill, climbing steadily as the wheel turned. Her whole existence was an epic of exhaustion. The brief holiday on the island seemed to have been an age ago.

Against the humming air conditioning unit and that of the washing machine tuning up, and the regular creak of Little Joe's swing, she didn't hear the crunch of tires on the gravel drive outside.

Nothing, not until the screen door, then the main door sung open and shut.

Joe came in through the back porch and into the kitchen, asking,

"Hey, Babe – how was your day?" Cheerful exuberance turned instantly to concern, as soon as he saw her slumped there at the dinette table. "Babe … what's the matter? You look wiped out."

"I'm pregnant!" Jess wailed.

"Yeah? Good thing we know what causes that," Joe answered, and pulled her up into his arms. "Babe – it's ok," he added, as Jess hiccupped, caught halfway between tears and laughter. "So … the weekend in Galveston wasn't wasted," he said to the top of her head.

"Little Joe won't even be out of diapers!" she moaned. "And now we're starting all over again! Another baby! And I'm so tired, Joe! How are we gonna manage?"

"We pick up the ruck and stagger on together," Joe said, and Jess sobbed against his shirtfront for a brief moment, while his badge pressed against her cheek, a hard metal star-shape. "Look, Babe. It's cool. The Soup-Monster will have a playmate. We'd love another kid, right? We already got all the baby stuff on hand, so points for efficiency, OK?"

"But I'm so tired!" Jess wailed. "It's past five, and I haven't even started supper…"

"Don't worry about it," Joe admonished her. "Go and lie down for a bit. Look, let me call the Café for some take-out for supper, and I'll have Milo or Pete swing by and deliver it. I'll take care of Soup-Monster. Nothing to worry about, Babe. We got this all squared away, working together, OK?"

"Sure, Joe," Jess said, and leaned into his embrace for just a moment longer.

Working together, staggering on with the ruck – yes, that was what it took to be a family in Luna City.

The Cattleman Matter

"Roman, a question of a professional nature, if I may," Richard cleared his throat and tentatively addressed one of his most loyal Café clients, the week following Bree Grant's vegetarian hospitality at the Age, as he delivered personally the traditional mixed grill English breakfast to an assortment of Roman's senior workmen. Roman himself sat alone at one of the smaller tables. The full English brekkie – eggs, sausage, bacon, beans, and toast had become insanely popular among the hardest-working clientele at the Café, almost as soon as Richard had introduced it. "How bloody long is the work going to continue on redecorating the guest rooms? I am told that all the basic reconstruction was accomplished; that it was only a matter of … paint and draperies and décor, once the basic stuff was done."

It had long been at the back of his mind to ask why the renovation work at the Cattleman Hotel still seemed to be dragging on, and on, and on. Lew Dubois, the local face of the corporation which had taken on the long-term project of the once-splendid, but sadly-aged Cattleman Hotel *(formerly the Grand Palazzo Vittorio)* with a written-in-stone arrangement to see to the renovation of the place in exchange for a long-term lease with Venue Properties International, had gone off on his long-planned European vacation to celebrate his fiftieth wedding anniversary with his tolerant, yet long-suffering spouse. Which was fine with the denizens of Luna City, and as far as Richard knew, with the local management of VPI at Mills Farm. Lew was a fine, public-spirited, and conscientious man. What wasn't so fine was that in his going off to France on a family vacation, he had left his all-but-finished hotel renovation project in the hands of an arrogant and supremely tactless woman. It had now been a month since Lew had departed. Whether Georgina Mason possessed any actual talent for the task which Lew Dubois had left to her was a matter of conjecture. Increasingly, the judgment of the regulars at the Café was not just 'no' but 'hell, no!' based on general principles and brief encounters with her in various places around Luna City, to include the Café, the Tip-Top and Mills Farm. The professional response of Roman Gonzalez was a matter on which the cognoscenti waited, with increasing impatience.

Now, Roman looked at the lavishly-piled plate of hard-working-mans' breakfast and sighed. "I just don't know, Ricardo. I just don't know. When Lew left, I would have said the end of the month, according to his deadline reflected in our contract. All that was really left to do on most of the rooms was the painting. Couple of bathrooms on the top floor needed tiling, and practically all the rooms had to have new light and plumbing fixtures installed. Re-install all the historic old fixtures from the dining room and ballroom that were supposed to be re-wired by Lucifer Lights in San Antonio. Hang the curtains and move in the furniture and the day-core, that's all what Mizz Mason was supposed to boss. Bob's your uncle, right? But no … You got an hour to waste, while I bend your ear?"

"Let me get myself a cuppa, and you can give me the abridged version," Richard answered. From Richard's own admittedly limited experience, Roman Gonzalez was the most efficient builder in Texas, possibly on earth. His projects, Richard knew from personal experience and observation, routinely came in under budget and ahead of time. He and a scratch crew of his employees and cousins had – on a moment's notice and in a bare two or three hours – rendered the old Airstream serviceable and comfortable on the notable occasion of Richard moving into it. Roman and a volunteer crew of charitable and skilled citizens had also completed the Amazing Straw Castle almost in a single weekend. And the 1912 Boathouse and Stable complex was a monument in itself to his professional expertise. Yes, the Cattleman guest rooms were three floors worth – but weren't hotel suites pretty much of a muchness? Apparently, Georgina Mason wasn't entirely tuned in to that concept … which soon became clear. And also clear that Roman was starting to worry. When Roman became worried – that was cause for deep concern among lesser mortals.

"She's starting changing things," Roman had made a good dent in his breakfast fry-up. Richard silently topped up Roman's mug from the coffee carafe he had brought from the kitchen. "Lots of things. Look, Ricardo; I'm used to working with clients. Badda-bing-badda-bam; want it this way, layout like this, tile here, paint this color there, doorway here, window there. Easy-peasy. They tell me what they want, I put it all in the proposal down to the inch and penny, we sign the contract – my guys and I go to work … and bam. It's done. Client is happy, 'lessn he – or she isn't satisfied right away, then we touch up, in accordance with the contract. Client approves the job, makes the final payment plus unforeseen extras. I don't make a living through having to dance like a puppet for someone who doesn't know what she wants and changes her damn mind every twenty-four hours!"

"Well, is she at least paying you for the annoyance of constantly changing requirements?" Richard waited courteously for Roman to inhale more of his eggs, borracho beans, and fried tomato-and-mushroom combo.

"So far," Roman answered, with his mouth full. "I turn in the invoices to her on Friday for work done, as soon as my guys post their time-sheets. I have a check from VPI delivered by overnight messenger on Monday afternoon at the latest. The trouble is – by Monday, it starts all over again."

"What does?" Richard waited for Roman to crunch through the fried bread.

"The changes," Roman – normally an easy-tempered tolerant man – sounded as if he was crunching small pebbles, along with the crisp, hot bread. "It's oh … we need to go back and replace and re-site THIS fixture, THAT switch … no, no, no – that color is just so WRONG in the light of the setting sun, it won't do at all for the ambiance I am trying to create. My drywall and paint guys are fit to be tied, I tell ya. Repaint the entire suite, she tells me … and I want glass tile for THIS bathroom, tile the exact color of lightly-cooked fresh shrimp … and … I have changed my mind. I KNOW it's the color that you had specially mixed for this project, but it JUST doesn't work! Can't you grasp the unique vision, Mr. Gonzalez! And I say … they won't take it back at full price, Mizz Mason, and she looks at me, and says, very snippily, 'then it's your loss, is it not?' and I …" Roman fetched up a deep, sad sigh from the depths of his soul. "I'm not sure what to do about her, Ricardo. I've never worked with an artiste before. This last week, we spent most of our time ripping out and re-doing all the work we finished over the two weeks before. AND that glass tile costs four-five times as much as ceramic, and don't wear nearly as well. This place may be a luxury hotel, but ya think VPI would be realistic about maintenance."

"It sounds like bloody hell," Richard sympathized. Roman nodded. "It is. Ya know," he added plaintively. "The worst thing is that nothing is ever completed. That's soul-destroying, I tell ya. Nothing is ever finished, signed off on, the client satisfied. My guys are fit to be tied, already. I thought we did good on all these other VPI jobs, but at the rate this one is going, I don't ever wanna sign a contract to do work for them again. It ain't worth the grief."

"It sounds as if Mrs. Mason is the source of the problems," Richard sympathized. "The fly in the ointment, as it were."

"The cockroach in your margarita, more like," Roman scraped up the last few bites of his breakfast and retrieved his Thermos from the chair beside him. "Doing the breast-stroke and bitching ya out because it doesn't like the flavor. Can you top this up for me, Ricardo? I gotta get moving."

"So, what are you going to do?" Richard emptied the rest of the carafe into the Thermos.

Roman sighed. "Finish the damned job. Didn't mean to unload on ya, Ricardo. As long as we're getting paid, it's all good. At least I'm getting the worth outta 'Nacio and Reuben. They're the only guys who can put up with her. I just wish the woman would look at a suite or so, and say, 'ok, good, I'll sign off on this.' I just wish Lew was coming back soon!"

"As far as I know, they were going to spend three months in France," Richard replied. "Another month and a half to go. I would think that in the case of a dire emergency, someone at VPI, or even at Mills Farm would know how to reach him. Benny Cordova, perhaps."

Roman was already shaking his head. "I got Benny's number, but I don't wanna break in on a man's vacation until it IS a dire emergency."

Richard put the matter of the Cattleman out of mind; none of his direct concern anyway. He had been looking forward to increased patronage for the Café from having the Cattleman opening to guests, and perhaps the occasional special catering undertaking for him, in the Cattleman's beautifully-ornamented dining room. It had been his understanding that maybe by mid-summer? Nothing had been written in stone, but still…

On Wednesday morning of that week, there were just as many battered utility vehicles parked down at the western side of Town Square. Richard, accustomed to the preferences of the regular customers had begun the full English fry-up for him as soon as he saw Roman's truck pull into a parking space. Araceli delivered it to Roman's table, and returned, saying,

"Chef, Uncle Roman looks as if he wants to unload. The joint is jumping, and Luc's got the grill station humming. You wanna take five, bring the man some coffee?"

"Why me?" Richard asked, with some suspicion. "And don't roll your eyes at me like that – I'm not a complete numpty, you know."

"I'd have to know what a complete numpty is," Araceli shot back, "But yeah, whatever it is, you probably aren't one. Go and talk to the man."

"Right." Richard sighed and took up a mug and a full carafe. "But I can't let him sob on my shoulder for too long, you know. We do food, not personal counseling."

"You'd be surprised. The two often go hand-in-hand." Araceli scooped up two plated hot omelets still sizzling from the grill and a basket of just-warmed cinnamon rolls and vanished with them into the dining room. His duty clear, Richard followed. Really, he thought – should he just start unloading his woes on his customers, willy-nilly? Kate was his sympathetic outlet; he had already fixed a bounteous supper for her on Monday evening. And Kate had thought that everything was at last going swimmingly with the Cattleman. But in response to Araceli's bluntly expressed hint, he made a show of meandering through the dining room, exchanging casual greetings with other customers. "Hey, Chef! G'morning, Chef! Great to see ya – how they hangin', Chef?" *("Where they should be," he replied to that last, which unaccountably gave a fit of giggles to Beatriz, who was taking orders at the stammtisch from Jess Abernathy-Vaughn and Sylvester Gonzales. The latter two appeared as if they might be holding a breakfast-business-meeting, with Little Joe snoring away in the high-chair next to the table.)*

"Brought you a top-up, from my special coffee-stash," Richard said, as he sat down opposite Roman, who displayed a countenance of stone. Richard administered a dose of blessed caffeine to Roman's near-empty mug and filled up his own. "The one I keep for my special customers."

Roman laughed, hollowly. Richard added, "All my customers are special. OK, so the ones who come down from the City on weekends, and ooooh and ahhh over the Town Square, and DEMAND of me to know when that pathetic little craft shop in the Mercantile will be open, and tip like misers … they get the last reheated dregs from the urn. No skin off mine … no matter how it is hanging. What's with the Cattleman project, now? You look as though you had a tale to tell."

"I don't know what to think, now," Roman admitted, although he tucked into his breakfast with the same enthusiasm that a man does, at least a man who has been doing heavy physical work in the open air – work of the sort which used to be the lot of most human males before the Industrial Age. "We went through the same old goat-rope with Mizz Mason last week. I set two of my most useless guys, 'Nacio and Reuben to do the work; no use in tying up my best on shit that will have to be re-done anyway. She had the usual major cow and demanded that practically everything be re-done, I turned in my bill … and then …"

"No check?" Richard ventured, and Roman nodded, "No check from VPI," he said. "Me, I'm fit to be tied! I got other projects lined up. Thank God I can send my reliable, trustworthy guys to work on them. Small stuff, but that's what pays the bills around here, ya know? It's a coup to get work for a place like VPI, but as it looks – not worth the … which reminds me. I gotta tell Conchita to add the PITA fee, from every job for VPI from now on."

"The PITA fee?" Richard inquired delicately.

Roman scowled. "The extra fee – for being a pain in the ass, over and above the 10% for bills paid not on the dot. It's a little something I add to the bill for clients who have been a major …"

"Pain in the arse," Richard agreed. "A wonderful concept. A veritable stroke of genius. Wish that I could only copy it here at the Café."

"I got 'Nacio and Reuben, too," Roman agreed, with a deep sigh. "A little extra, over and above. They're not actually bad workmen … just not able to focus on finishing stuff. I figure they're a good match for Mizz Mason. She can't finish stuff, either."

Richard ran his mind over what he recalled from early mornings in the Café, when Roman and his various crews met for an early brekkie and a fill-up of his Thermos.

"I can't bring them to mind," he said. "Do they frequent the Café with you on a regular basis?"

"Yeah." Roman chuckled coarsely. "Any venue when someone else is buying. 'Nacio is tall and skinny, thinks he's an unrecognized genius, Reuben is short and fat, and believes that he's God's gift to the construction trade. The older guys call them 'Mutt and Jeff', after that old comic strip. They're Gonzalez kin by marriage. Man, I hate to think that a good Gonzalez girl would even begin to think that 'Nacio or Reuben's dad was good father materiel, looking at how those two dufuses turned out. Talk about beer goggles!"

"Ah, yes; I can picture those two gentlemen now," Richard ventured. "Did you mention the lack of remuneration to Mrs. Mason?"

"I did," Roman scowled. "Yesterday. And she was actually very decent and apologetic about it all. Problems at the head office, she said. And she wrote out a check on her business account – hers', not VPI's. Which – I thought was a little odd, but not out of line. All square, you'd think? I deposited that check last night, and first thing today, I get a call from Conchita in the office. She got a call. From the bank. That sucker bounced. Insufficient funds."

"That's … not a good thing," Richard ventured. Roman glared at him. "Thank you, Captain Obvious. Of course, it's not. I came here to try and calm down before I roar into the Cattleman and ask that pain-in-the-ass woman what the hell?"

"It probably will be a good idea to calm down, first." Richard agreed, and Beatriz set down his breakfast plate.

"Thanks, girl … hey, sorry for snapping at you, Ricardo. Not your fault at all. But I can't help thinking that there is something hinky going on with this job. I just hope that whatever it might be doesn't carry criminal charges. We've always been open, above-board, no short-cuts taken, no shady practices. Saves trouble in the long run, you know?" Roman looked honestly baffled. "You heard any kinda gossip in the Café about the Cattleman work?"

Richard wracked his recent memory. "I was last inside the place, talking to Lew about the Boathouse opening," He said slowly. "The public rooms were magnificent, by the way. Your chaps did a splendid job. The only thing missing in the dining room – and the ballroom too … that was the light fixtures. Lew said something about how they were original Lalique glass. I'm looking forward no end to seeing them installed, finally."

Roman stared at him, in bafflement. "Ok, are those lights something special? I know Lew had a bug about them. They got delivered from San Antonio two weeks ago. About twenty big-ass crates stacked up on the loading dock. The guys were pissed over how much room they took, and what a bear it was, moving them into the ballroom."

"Lalique glass," Richard took a deep breath. "Genuine, certified, early 20th century Lalique. The very top-of the line ceiling fixture currently retails at more than ninety-thousand of your dollars – that's for a new one. I had a mad moment when I was planning my London restaurant, back in the day and made some exploratory phone calls. New; available by special order only. I decided they were too rich for my blood, although I did experience a pang or two. For an authentic, hundred-year old chandelier fresh from the mitts of Rene Lalique and the old boys at his glass factory in France … and there were how many of them?"

"Eighteen," Roman was pale under his working-man's outdoor tan. "Jeez, Ricardo. I had no idea. Twelve in the ballroom, six in the dining room. Not something you can pick up at Home Depot, then?"

"No," and Richard felt the skin on the back of his neck grow cold, although it might just have been the down-draft from the air conditioning vent over the table where he and Roman sat. "A bloody fortune in glass fixtures, mate. Sitting in crates in an empty building. Tell me; were they properly installed?"

"I … think so," Now Roman looked positively rattled. "Anyway, the crates were off the dock and into the ballroom. Mizz Mason was complaining about it. Couple days later, they were gone. The work in the dining room was done. Ya know; the switches are flipped, and the lights come on."

"But … are those the right fixtures?" Richard mused, and observed Roman turning even more pale, as pale as someone who had spent decades under cloudy English skies.

"Aw, jeez." Roman had picked up his fork, ready to tuck into breakfast. Now he set it down again. "They gotta be," he said, as if trying to convince himself. "They better be. My company sure as hell can't take a twenty million dollar hit, if we managed to lose valuable city property in the course of renovations."

"Look," Richard advised, cognizant of how Araceli had just insisted that therapeutic counseling was on offer at the Café, as well as good food. "I didn't mean to suggest anything untoward had happened. I was just thinking out loud. I'll bet it's been years since anyone noticed the light fixtures; the place was only open once a year, for god's sake."

"I thought we were just renovating an old dump of a hotel," Roman began tucking into breakfast, although Richard didn't think his words had reassured the other man. "I just saw a bunch of dusty old glass and polished nickel chandeliers. Nice enough, not to my personal taste, though. It was Lew's notion to restore them, rather than spring for something antique-looking, but more modern, with more light bulbs. Now that you tell me what they were worth, I understand. I can't even recall what they looked like, once they were taken down. Do you?"

Richard shook his head. "I met with Lew to plan the menu for the Boathouse opening, maybe six or seven weeks ago. He gave me a tour of the ballroom and dining room then, but the lights had already been taken down for repair. I only had his word for it that they were Lalique, anyway."

"Here's what we do," Roman obviously had been thinking as he ate. "I'll go over to the hotel as soon as I'm done and confirm that the fixtures in the ballroom and dining room are the same ones that came in crates from Lucifer Lights and sat in the ballroom for a week. My main electrical guy is on a job in Beeville today; he'd have done the install with his guys. If his answer is 'yeah, sure thing, boss' – then I got nothing to worry about. But if not … I gotta think about this, Ricardo. I don't wanna start casting stones."

"Is there anything I can do?" Richard offered, almost without thinking. He owed the whole Gonzalez clan, owed more than he might ever be able to repay, and now he felt vaguely guilty for even having brought up the value of the fixtures as well as the possibility of them being missing.

"Yeah," Roman forked up the last bit of egg, and replied with his mouth full. "Miss Letty and the Historical Association – they have – or they used to have a whole bunch of picture postcards an' stuff, showing how they place used to look. She showed them to Lew an' me at the start. I think Lew had copies of it all for his files. Miss Letty said it would give us a notion of what the place looked like in its glory days. Can you ask her for any of them that show the original lights, in case I come back with the wrong answer to my question?"

"Certainly," Richard promised, as Roman pushed back his chair. He was already on his cellphone, as he went out the door.

Roman's return, not ten minutes later, was even more abrupt than his departure. He strode into the kitchen, with his cellphone in one hand, and under his other arm, part of a cardboard box. His expression was thunderous. Richard's heart sank right down to the level of his trainers.

"I take it that the answer to your question was not satisfactory?" he ventured and Roman waved the cardboard at him. Richard saw that it was part of a good-sized carton, with "Luminous Lighting" and a color illustration of a chrome chandelier lavishly hung with clear glass crystals printed on it.

"I didn't have to ask it," Roman answered. "This and seventeen other boxes were on top of the dumpster. All new; Lowe's has 'em for two-three thou each retail, but contractors and decorators get them for a discount, especially in bulk."

"Even at full retail, that's a fraction of what the originals would be worth," Richard articulated his thoughts without thinking of the effect.

Roman swore, viciously, at length, and in Spanish. Finally, he calmed sufficiently to return to English. "I will find out who organized this … and I will kick their asses so hard their ancestors will feel the pain. And I have to find out where those crates with the originals finished up at. I can't let this pass, Ricardo. Whoever did this – they stole from us! From Luna City, and under my watch." He reverted to vituperative Spanish again, and Richard was reminded of how Sylvester Gonzalez, computer genius and internet spook extraordinaire, had reacted upon reading the script for that benighted movie project, two summers previous. Yes, Sylvester had been livid with rage … *Sylvester*!

"I have a thought," Richard said, hardly daring to break into Roman's monologue of non-specific abuse. "Your nephew, Sylvester, is he still meeting with Miss – Mrs. Abernathy-Vaughn?"

"I just brought him his order," Araceli was an interested spectator to this exchange. "Roman, what's going on?"

"Special counseling," Richard answered. "You explain. I have to speak with Sylvester. I think he may be able to assist."

"Yeah," Sylvester replied, with his mouth full of breakfast. "I can do that … sure. I did the FB page for the Historical Society. I got all the scans of those old postcards. They're archived. I can bring them up right now."

He opened his laptop, and conducted some mysterious passes through … oh, Richard didn't even begin to comprehend the processes whereby a Master of the Internet performed the magic; one-handed, and with his other holding a half-eaten orange-pecan breakfast bun. "Here ya go," he added, and turned the opened laptop so that Richard could view and thumb-through the picture gallery; a series of pastel-tinted and sepia studies of the exterior and various rooms of the Grand Hotel Vittoria, Luna City, Texas. At the other end of the *stammtisch*, both Georg and Annice Stein watched with polite interest.

Oh, shit. Just what he feared; the hanging chandeliers in the postcard views of the ballroom, and dining room were nothing like the picture on the carton which Roman has found in the dumpster. It must have shown in his expression, for Jess Abernathy-Vaughn looked across the table at him, with sudden and close attention.

"Is something the matter, Richard?" she asked. Richard could no more have lied to her, than to her husband, or to Miss Letty.

"There is," Richard drew in a deep breath. "And I'm afraid it's serious. I need to have Roman look at these pictures. And then it may be a matter for Joe. And for your father, the Lord Mayor of Luna City." Jess was already thumbing through the contact list on her cellphone. After exchanging a few words on it with her husband, she looked around the table.

"Joe wants us all to come over to the police station right now – no, not to be booked or anything. He and Milo want to talk to anyone who might be able to shed any light on this. And no, he was not being humorous. Even you, Richard."

"Right," Richard sighed. "I think the official term for this is 'Assisting the police with their enquiries.' Allow me to let Araceli know. Thank god the morning rush is nearly over," he added, wondering why the Steins were also joining the party. Oh – their place was nearest the Cattleman.

Verre and Veritas

"So," said Joe, not fifteen minutes later, looming vastly in his crisp tan summer uniform over the gathering. "We've verified the existence of eighteen extremely high-value vintage chandeliers, property of Luna City and the Historical Association and established the fact that they are, indeed, unaccounted for. Is that a fair assessment, ladies and gentle-grunts?" Joe's right-hand man, Sgt. Milo Grigoryev sat next to him with his note-taking book open. His uncle, Harry Vaughn, the retired federal marshal seemed to have been called to assist in the enquiries. Little Joe, on the other hand, had been deposited with his doting maternal great-grandparents, in the apartment over the venerable Abernathy Hardware store. Jess' father Martin, the mayor of Luna City was also squeezed into the circle around the table. He and Milo, with Sylvester, Roman, Richard, Jess and the Steins had gathered around the table in the police station break room, the only space large enough to accommodate everyone. Sylvester's laptop sat open in the center of the circle, showing the historic pictures of the Cattleman. Richard looked across the table at Milo and repressed a small shudder. How did a guy who was the spitting image of Joseph Stalin, even down to the cockroach mustache ever come to be a sergeant of the constabulary in a little South Texas town like Luna City? Milo had one thing over old Uncle Joe; he was a genuinely jovial and amiable person; not a political psychopath. Still, the resemblance was damned unsettling.

Roman took his cellphone down from his ear and nodded.

"That was the guys at Lucifer Lights. They confirmed that yes, the eighteen fixtures they handled for Lew were the genuine antique deal. They're sending us a copy of their write-up and bill, plus a memo outlining how they packed and returned them by secure shipment. The crates came back here, that's for sure. I'll have to talk to 'Nacio and Reuben to confirm – but they were there until a couple weeks ago. And that was a big-ass pile of crates. Whoever took them would need a big trailer and horse them out of the building without anyone noticing."

"Who had access to the Cattleman, during the day," Joe was busy making notes, along with Milo. "I am assuming the place was locked up at night. I <u>can</u> assume that?" He added with a sharp look at Roman, who nodded slowly.

"At night, sure. My guys left a lot of their high-value tools and shit there, rather than lug it back and forth. During the day? Jeez, Joe – who the hell didn't? My guys, my sub-contractors, Mizz Mason, every Tom, Dick and Harry delivering supplies and furniture. The place was like an intercity bus station, everyone coming and going. I'll get the time-sheets from Conchita, that'll narrow down the list of my guys who were working at the Cattleman during the time that the crates were there."

"We observed nothing untoward at night during that time," Georg Stein put in, and Milo nodded agreement. Richard was not sure how the Steins had become a part of this, although if Joe didn't have any objections, neither had he. But the building which housed Stein's Wild West Round-up overlooked Town Square, cat-cornered from the Cattleman. The window in their living room offered a fine view of the alley which gave onto the back of the Cattleman. "Anni and I were often awake to all hours, and with the weather so fair, we kept our windows open."

"Not so much as a possum stirring, after ten or eleven most nights in Luna City," Milo Grigoryev consulted his own notes. "How long do you figure it would have taken to load up a truck? A couple of hours, even with a bunch of guys, working fast; you'd still think someone would have noticed!"

"Gotta be someone working inside," Sylvester put in. He frowned at his laptop. "Someone who knew just what was in those boxes."

"That's just the point," Richard felt obliged to speak up. In his experience, there had been no more painfully honest group of sentient beings in the universe than those residents of Luna City, although Sefton Grant's decades-long pretense of being a vegetarian might have been the most outstanding exception. "No one had any notion of just how highly valuable they were, or even knew <u>what</u> they were, except Lew Dubois and I. And I only had Lew's word for it that the old lights were genuine Lalique. Roman says that everyone assumed they were just … lights; lights to be reinstalled as part of the job. A bit of value, but no more than just about anything else being installed."

Martin Abernathy winced, visibly. "The city council also had no notion of how valuable they were," he added. "Else we would have sold them ourselves to fund a renovation."

"A good point," Roman agreed. "I had no idea until Ricardo told me. I damn-near had a heart attack on the spot." His face suddenly went introspective. "I just thought; hey, the client wants them re-wired and polished, broken glass bits repaired, it means a lot to him, and he's footing the bill on behalf of VPI – so what the heck? Sentimental value, ya know."

"Sentimental value counts for very little on a cost sheet," Jess put in. "Actual, monetary value is another kettle of fish. Someone had a notion, someone saw to removing them. And where are they now?"

"On the unseen market for stolen art," Joe grunted, grim and depressed as a super-hero whose arch-enemy has just made a daring escape.

Milo flipped his notebook closed, and added, "Not necessarily. How often do we find the stolen items at the nearest shady pawnshop, Joe?"

"True, that," Joe admitted. "Your average thief around here is usually just a lazy dirtbag with poor impulse control and no ability to plan ahead. But swiping the chandeliers took some organization, or at least, a big-ass truck, a strong back and a couple of hours. And they aren't something you can unload at the pawnshop for pennies on the dollar."

"A dealer in rare *objects d'arte*," Georg Stein said, as if it were the most obvious answer. "A dealer prepared to not examine closely the provenance and accept only the assurances of the seller. The slice of commission for the eventual sale, you see. There are, alas, many such. And even more who are merely trusting. So much of the business depends upon trust, you see. The very best, most respectable auctioneers will not comprehend that an agent known to them would dare to present them with stolen goods! It is simply incomprehensible to those of the highest caliber that their good name might be abused by vulgar thievery. They deal in art, in the finer things. They might be worldly, in some respects – but in their minds, they dwell in a rarified world, far above a pawnshop which is merely a … what is the word; a field barrier for the dishonest."

The rest of the table regarded him with mild bafflement, until Milo Grigoryev said, "Ah, a fence, I think you mean. A fence."

There was a short, depressed silence around the table. Richard did not dare voice what he was thinking. Who among those who had intimate dealings with the renovation of the old hotel knew, absolutely, what a platinum mine lay in the old, little-regarded light fixtures? Only Lew. He shoved that thought aside, No; surely not Lew. Harry Vaughn's countenance was already reddening. Milo saved him the trouble and the incipient guilt of voicing that suspicion.

"I hate to say it, but to my mind, Mr. Dubois would be first on my list of suspects. I mean; he is the only one who knew from the get-go how valuable the missing items were."

"The man is currently on a vay-cay in France," Richard pointed out, feeling obliged to defend Lew, since he had been the first to raise the possibility, even if only in his mind. Surely the proper law-enforcement professionals must have gotten to that point even more rapidly than he himself had. "He is a well-compensated, highly-respected executive with a sterling reputation! What need would he have, that he could risk it all?"

"For a twenty-million-dollar payoff, most guys would risk a hell of a lot more," Sylvester pointed out. Joe, his voice heavy with weary cynicism, added, "Besides having knowledge of the value, he had knowledge of the layout of the Cattleman, the work schedule – he could have set it up with an inside man beforehand, giving himself the best possible alibi."

Harry Vaughn's knotted fist hit the table with a crash. "I won't countenance accusing a man who isn't here to defend himself!" He snapped. "A man I have known for twenty years, whose honesty and good character was a byword!"

"So was Bernie Madoffs'," Joe pointed out. "Until it wasn't. And lots of people trusted him with their money. Until they couldn't. I don't like the thought any more than you do, Uncle, but I'm not gonna let old friendship blind me to the possibilities. Who else do we have on the list of potential suspects, Milo?"

"Well," Milo looked uneasily between Joe, Harry, and Roman. "We do have our old pals, Ignacio Gomez and Reuben Sifuentes …"

Both Roman and Joe exchanged a meaningful look and a weary sigh, while the others present looked slightly baffled. Joe explained, for their benefit. "'Nacio and Reuben barely rise to the level of petty larceny. That would be an unachievable career ambition for the pair of them, even assuming they had the energy to pursue it. They might, if no one was watching, boost a few unconsidered trifles and insist indignantly when they were caught – that they were only taking them into protective custody. You know, to keep them from being stolen by some other dirtbag. All with an expression of injured innocence, and protestations of how they are so unfairly prosecuted …"

Roman shook his head, regretfully. "Yeah, the two of them together don't have the capacity to light a fifteen-watt bulb, but they might just be dumb enough to get suckered into participating in something like this – but it would never have been their idea."

"Cat's paws," Uncle Harry supplied. "Perfect cats' paws, for someone with the ability to think and plan ahead."

"Which doesn't put Mr. Dubois out of the picture," Milo answered, which earned him a deep and threatening growl from

Uncle Harry, not unlike that of a bear just out of hibernation. Meanwhile, Sylvester and the Steins were huddling over Sylvester's laptop. They were across the table from Richard, so that he couldn't see what they were doing, only that all three were totally absorbed. He was just about to ask Joe and Milo if they had any more questions specifically for him – since he had a Café to run, when Sylvester grinned, triumphantly.

"Bingo! I think we found 'em! Take a look at this, Joe!"

"Found 'em! The lights? Where?" chorused Joe, Martin and Harry nearly in unison, and Sylvester's grin widened. "Behold the power of the fully-engaged internet!" He named a notable and world-renowned auction house. "They're at their Houston location, all eighteen of them, to be sold separately or as a job lot. Can't be any others; the pictures and the age of the items are an exact match, and the provenance … *'from a renovated historic hotel in South Texas, professionally restored to working condition,'*" he read from the description, and turned around the laptop so that everyone present could confirm.

"They got a contact number anywhere on that page?" Joe had already brought out his own cellphone. As Sylvester read out the area code and the numbers, Joe punched them in, while everyone else listened, hardly daring to breath.

"Good morning … who am I speaking with? Yes … thanks. Someone in charge, please. This is Joseph Vaughn, chief of police, Luna City. About your … *(what's the lot number, Sylvester ... thanks.)* Lot number 8, that would be the collection of vintage Lalique glass and nickel chandeliers. I'll wait until you're with me. Yes … those are the items. Look, I'm sorry to have to tell you this, but … they are rightfully the property of the city. Yes, the City of Luna City, the owner of the Cattleman Hotel. The person who … yes, I'll hold for your supervisor." Joe held the cellphone a little apart from his mouth, explaining, "Whoops, look like I have rattled the cage a bit. Being kicked upstairs!"

"Keep drilling until you hit a vein of intelligence," Uncle Harry grunted, and Joe replied, "You don't have to teach me how to suck eggs, 'kay? All right," he added, into the cellphone. "Who is this? Nice to talk to you; Joseph Vaughn, Chief, Luna City PD. Sorry, gotta break it to ya, those Lalique items are stolen – or at least, the perp—person who provided them to you was not the legitimate owner and had no right or permission to put them on the market. Clear with me, so far? Yeah, I can provide this in writing, no problem; Fax or overnight FedEx, whatever your choice. Still with me? Look; understand, unless those items are withdrawn from the market in the next half-hour, you will be hearing from Luna City's Legal Department and the State of Texas' Attorney General's office … *(Hey, Martin, do we even have a Legal Department?)* Consider this your notice that any sale will be … OK, good. Nice to speak to you – sorry to have to put damper on your business. Say, while I have you on the line, can you give me the name of the person who put them up … yeah, don't put me through the trouble of filing an injunction to get that name. Just consider this a law enforcement matter. Yeah, I'll wait." Joe took the phone away from his ear again. "They're looking it up. Jeez, I like it when people are agreeable to answering questions, straight off the bat. Saves us ever so much trouble."

"Who?" Uncle Harry looked alert; so did Martin. "Who is the jack-leg who ripped off the city?"

"Who is the a-hole who left my company to hold the bag?" Roman demanded. Of all of those present, Richard decided after careful consideration that he would fear the wrath of the construction-firm Gonzalezes over and above any other. After all, they owned earthmovers and cement mixers. And there was a lot of empty land, here and there around Luna City. The Gonzaleses and the Gonzalezes probably knew a lot of places to stash a body where it might never be found. Even if Joe and Milo took it into their heads to search for it.

Joe was listening on the telephone for quite some time. Finally, he said, "Right. Thank you for your time. Absolutely certain …. I see. I'll send you the official notification in writing. And someone will be in touch with you regarding secure return shipping of the chandeliers. A pleasure…" He put his cellphone down and looked around the table. "I think we're at the point where I need to speak to Lew – French vay-cay or no. Or better yet, his higher-up at VPI."

"Surely, he …" Richard protested.

Uncle Harry growled, "I'd have staked my life on it; Lew Dubois would never have…"

"Not Lew," Joe said, tiredly. "Georgina Mason. She's the one who sent the lights to Houston to sell. She had local help here in Luna City, probably from Nacio and Reuben, but she was known as a decorator in Houston, old pals with everyone on the high-end arts and collectibles scene. The possibility didn't even occur to them that she wasn't the rightful agent for selling those fixtures."

"That *puta*! Yeah, I see it now! She was running over budget on the decoration through all her demands for changes! Yeah, and she stiffed me on the last payment too, so add my complaint to whatever list you got going, Joe!" Roman swore vituperatively in Spanish. Richard was glad that he only understood a few of the more common terms of personal abuse. Joe added. "Is she at the Cattleman today?"

"Yeah, she'd be there today. If not, then where she's staying at Mills Farm."

"Ysidro's on speeder patrol today," Joe looked around the table. "Milo – I want you to meet him at the Cattleman and invite

Mizz Mason nicely to come along to the station. Let her call her lawyer, if she wants, but the cuffs won't be required unless she gets obstreperous. Thanks for coming out, people. Couldn't have solved it all so quickly without y'all, but we can take it from here."

That was obviously their dismissal. Much as Richard would have liked to see the obnoxious Georgina perp-walked into the station, it looked as if they were all going to be deprived of the pleasure. Roman offered him a ride back to the Café – yes, he had work to do. Let Joe and Martin take care of administering law and justice.

In the Offices of the Karnesville Weekly Beacon

"Kate! Get in here and enlighten me as to what in the blue blazes was going on with this masonry expert and that old hotel in Luna City!" Acey McClain bellowed from his editorial office, which occupied the front corner of the second floor of the venerable Karnesville Weekly Beacon, the newspaper voice of Karnesville and environs as far as Kenedy and Beeville. "Arrested on charges of grand theft and … what – fraud? What in hell does that have to do with renovations! I can't make head or tale from Rita's message."

(Rita was the near-to-retirement secretary receptionist at the Beacon, whose notes taken of telephone calls to the newspaper were a source of bafflement to all not accustomed to deciphering the most illegible handwriting in Karnes County – and this from a woman who had matriculated from St. Scholastica's back in the

day, under the tutelage of nuns unsparing in their use of the disciplinary ruler and usually unerring in their aim with it.)

"Sure, Chief!" Kate Heisel, chipper as a squirrel with a whole wealth of nuts stashed away for that inevitable slow news day, called from the other side of the Beacon's near-empty newsroom. This was a high-ceilinged space, as were most work places before the advent of air conditioning, haphazardly filled with battered metal military surplus desks and filing cabinets, presided over by an old-fashioned Regulator clock and a stuffed moose head, which surveyed the organized chaos below with a disapproving eye. Kate, trim in a primly-cut skirt suit, settled onto the guest chair before Acey McClain's desk and opened one of her slim-line reporter notebooks. "It wasn't a masonry expert, by the way. It's a name – Georgina Mason. It was wild, so Cousin Araceli told me. Mason came dashing out of the Cattleman, and charged into the Café, just as the morning breakfast rush was winding down, screeching that it was all an unfortunate misunderstanding; she couldn't possibly be under arrest, didn't everyone understand, she was an artist, doing what she had to do! Araceli said it was amazing, how fast that woman could run in four-inch heels! Must be a natural gift, or something. Then Sgt. Grigoryev came barreling in after her, and she ran out through the kitchen, and Officer Gonzalez tackled her as she went out the back door … wow! Araceli said she wished that he had intercepted that well when he played for the Moths Varsity … it was all an incredible scene! She kept screaming about police brutality, and then Uncle Roman appeared out of nowhere, and began yelling about how she had left him and his guys to hold the bag and bounce checks all over the place … it was wild, Chief, I tell ya!"

"Pictures or it didn't happen," Acey said, somewhat depressingly.

Kate beamed. “It happened, all right, Chief. Three different Café customers got it on their cellphones. I isolated the best frames from the video they sent me. Isn’t it great, how many times ordinary people can cover the news, when stuff happens right in front of them?”

“Big Brother is always watching,” Acey intoned, sounding rather less than enthusiastic. “So, what happened then? What had the Mason woman stolen? Is she still in the county lock-up, wearing an orange jumpsuit?”

“Alas, no,” Kate sighed. “Out on bail. Her husband is a VPI executive, so I guess he can afford a good lawyer. No one minds all that much, since they were able to get back the all Lalique fixtures. ‘Cept Uncle Roman is still pretty pissed over how he nearly got left holding the bag.”

“Back it up, Katie, and start from the top; this Mason frail swiped some glassware?” Acey McClain squeezed the bridge of his nose, as if his sinuses ached. “Klepto, is she?”

Kate concealed a small and patient sigh. “Twenty million dollars’ worth of antique light fixtures, originals and meant to be reinstalled in the Cattleman. The renovations ran behind schedule, mostly because she kept changing things. She already blew Lew Dubois’ original budget out of the water and needed money from someplace, so she sent the fixtures to an auction house buddy, and had Roman’s crew install some modern chandeliers, and hoped that in all the confusion that no one would notice. Bad idea; Uncle Roman said that Richard at the Café passed a remark one morning that started him thinking, and it all unraveled from there. Someone would have noticed, when Lew Dubois came back for the grand opening. That’s still on, you know.”

“Is it?” Acey McClain brightened. “Well, that’s something. Will the Mason frail serve hard time, you think?”

"Nah," Kate shook her head; she and Acey united in cynicism. "Suspended sentence, and a couple of months community service – the woman has influential friends, you know, and she's an artist, who just got carried away … yeah, I can write her lawyer's final defense speech for her in my head already. But at least the Cattleman opening is back on track, that's for sure." She flipped through another page in her notebook. "Looking to open officially at mid-summer and start off with a high-society wedding in the ballroom; show-business and economic royalty." Kate flipped her notebook closed, having sufficiently refreshed her memory. "I'd commit … well, I'd commit <u>something</u> just to have the look at the pre-nup <u>and</u> the guest list!"

"Anyone I know?" Acey's career as an old-style big-name newspaper reporter had peaked somewhere in the early 1970s and had been sliding gently downhill ever since. His stint as part-owner and editor of the Beacon was more in the nature of a working retirement; agreeable enough, but sometimes he did hanker for the splashy days of a 40-point headline, above the fold in a nationally-distributed daily, with his name and 'exclusive!' attached.

"Collin Wyler, and one of his old girlfriends," Kate replied. "A sometime actress, slightly past her prime: Samantha Colquhoun, keen to give the wheel of matrimony another whirl and collect some of that sweet, sweet alimony cash. I was told that back in his gay bachelor days, she is alleged to have dated Prince Andrew."

"Oh, her!" Acey snickered, in a way that in anyone else would have been described as being bitchy. "Not just slightly past her prime, Kate. Likely she can barely see it in the rearview mirror. Usually, she just shacks up, and then skedaddles six months later. Left more rubber on the asphalt than the jets taking off at Atlanta International. Still, though … is she going to go with the white dress and lacy veil?"

"Likely," Kate agreed. "Since the word is that the whole thing will be veddy, veddy traditional. That all, Acey? I got an interview with an art expert in Beeville in thirty minutes."

"Sure thing, doll-face," Acey turned back to his computer, the operation of which he was still somewhat uncertain. "Art expert? Care to share with the class?"

"Still working on it. Background."

"Elucidate." *(Acey was a long-time aficionado of the Readers' Digest feature 'It Pays to Expand Your Word Power.')*

Kate hesitated, her keen news-seeking mind already romping hither and yon, and in several different directions. Such was her adamantine concentration, that she could keep mental track of any number of conversations, or threads of possible leads into the potentially newspaper-story payoff.

"There's some talk here and there on the internet, in some of the out-of-the-way fora," she ventured cautiously, at last. *(Acey gave her mental credit for using the proper term for more than one forum. He was <u>that</u> old-school when it came to grammar.)* "About a missing Renaissance artwork… no, not a painting. Remember that kerfuffle late last year, about a hitherto unknown da Vinci being discovered at an old convent in Milan? It was the reliquary in the painting, never mind if it was a genuine da Vinci or not. The reliquary itself went missing within a decade or two of the year of it being painted. And the talk is that somehow, that reliquary finished up here in Karnes County. A buried treasure … or a not-so-buried treasure. It's just curious, and may come to nothing, Chief – but I thought I'd look into it."

"Have at it," Acey waved in a dismissive manner. "But don't burn up too much work time on it, Kate. We got a paper to run."

"Sure, Chief," Kate replied, and made her escape.

Grand Reopening of the Historic Cattleman Hotel!

From the Karnesville Weekly Beacon

By Staff Writer Katherine Heisel

The grand old hotel which has dominated the western side of Luna City's historic Town Square for over a hundred years formally reopens for business on Thursday afternoon, June 21st. The hotel, which was leased more than a year ago by Venue Properties, International as part of expanding the recreational activities offered by their local destination resort, Mills Farm, was originally expected to reopen in April, after undergoing extensive renovations, but the project is back on track, helmed by VPI's experienced director of marketing, Lucian "Lew" Dubois.

Mr. Dubois, previously the manager of VPI's flagship property, the Chateau Venasque, in France's Provence, and then of the Castle Mountain resort in Banff, Canada, initially tasked with overseeing a proposed water park project as an addition to Mills Farm, instead conceived and promoted the idea of a more sensitive, and low-key resort featuring a more authentic South Texas outdoors experience; hunting, horseback trekking, and kayak excursions along the San Antonio River. Rather than expanding guest accommodations at Mills Farm and diluting the exclusive boutique flavor of the limited number of individual cottages available, as well as disrupting the easy-going atmosphere of the high-end resort establishment with new construction, Mr. Dubois proposed a long-term lease of the Cattleman Hotel. Owned jointly by Luna City, and the Luna City Historical Association, the hotel – with the exception of four suites available through on-line B&B listings – had been closed since the 1970s. In return for generous terms, Mr. Dubois proposed that VPI renovate the public rooms; the bar, restaurant, and ballroom, as well as the remaining disused rooms at their expense. The results of that epochal agreement between VPI and the Town Council will be on display over the weekend.

The Cattleman Hotel, originally the Grand Palazzo Vittoria Hotel, was built in 1885, with every then-modern convenience and no expense spared by an Italian hotelier and entrepreneur, Signor Alfredo Vittorio di Barreca. Under his management the hotel prospered for much of the remaining 19th century and well into the 20th, when ownership and management fell to the Bodie family of Luna City. The Grand Palazzo/Cattleman began as a destination for those desirous of spending winters in a more temperate climate, then to regional travelers, and a venue for local celebrations of note. Signor di Barreca spared no expense when he built the hotel – and now those glories have been fully restored, to delight another generation of visitors. Each of the guest rooms and suites have been individually decorated, to reflect the original Belle Epoque aesthetic, but all with fully-modern conveniences, and every possible luxury.

The formal ribbon-cutting will be held at 2 PM, at the front entrance on West Town Square. Mr. Dubois and Mayor Abernathy will share the honors. Visitors are invited to partake of refreshments in the dining room, and in the splendid 19th century bar. The formal hotel ballroom will not be open until Sunday afternoon, as it has been reserved for a private event.

From Out of the Past

"So, everything is on-point for the Cattleman to open at mid-summer, now?" Araceli ventured, during a lull in the breakfast rush, a bare two weeks after the spectacular resolution of what Richard was calling, sardonically, "L' affair Mason."

"Indeed," Richard answered, raising his voice slightly over the sound of the television set in the corner. Tradition dictated that the morning news talk variety show be on, although the exact program was a matter of dispute – mostly according to the tastes of the regulars at the stammtisch, which ran heavily in favor of the local morning show out of a local affiliate in San Antonio. Just at that moment, a bubbly blond hostess in a painfully-short dress revealing pipe-stem legs rather like those of a stork was interviewing an associate professor of art history from … somewhere? A local uni, no doubt. What that had to do with the blurry still insert of a painting was a mystery to Richard. "What's all that in aid of?" he asked, gesturing with his thumb at the TV screen.

"The question of that found da Vinci painting," Araceli replied. "Do you think it's genuine?"

"Certainly not. The great Leonardo wouldn't have painted a portrait of a girl with a face like a boiled suet-pudding," Richard replied. "If he did, he would have made her look a lot better than that!"

"She looks very healthy," Araceli stoutly defended the girl in the disputed painting, now shown in a quick close-up, who did, alas, look rather lard-pale and with such round cheeks and heavy jawline that her lips and eyes practically disappeared. "And rather like our Aunt Conchita, when she was young. You know, Auntie Conchita who does housekeeping for Doc Wyler? Not Uncle Roman's wife Conchita – Beatrix's mother, but Auntie Conchita, Uncle Jaimie's half-sister. You remember her, I think. And it could be that there is a connection. They say that the name Gonzalez comes from the Gonzaga family back in the day. Well, now that the Cattleman is going to reopen on time, Auntie Conchita wants to meet with you sometime next week to see about the wedding buffet and all that."

"She's getting married? Bit late in the day for that," Richard observed. "But who are we to scorn true love and all that?"

"Not her wedding," Araceli shot him one of her trademark withering glares. "Collin Wylers'. His next future ex-Mrs. Wyler wants to be married here, at mid-summer, with all the bells and whistles, and Doc says he is too gosh-darned old to deal with the fuss, so he handed it all to Conchita and Jess to make the arrangements, and commit to the Cattleman, if at all possible. Auntie Conchita sent me a text message; she is going to meet with Collin Wyler's personal assistant, and the party manager at the

Cattleman, at 2 PM next Tuesday, and can we come with some wedding cake designs and our usual sample menu, so that we can get something tentative pounded out by the time Collin and his next ex arrive the week before the wedding."

"Nothing like leaving it to the last minute," Richard grunted, and then got caught up in the secondary breakfast rush; the one which took hold when the school-day began, after all those customers who had early-morning jobs to get to had dined and dashed. The secondary rush was comprised of those mothers of school-children, and of business owners who did not actually have to be anywhere until nine or ten of a morning. Fortunately, most of those merely required cinnamon or orange-pecan buns, Café-made and baked, still warm and aromatic from the oven, and endless cups of coffee.

The meeting request went totally out of his mind; the press of daily work that that effect on him. Sufficient unto the day were the tasks thereof, and in most work-days he could only think about a week ahead on matters to do with the Café. And in the interim between Araceli's conversation with him, and the appointment at the Cattleman, he was distracted by the curious behavior of an occasional new customer.

This was a heavy-set and not-quite elderly gent, with straggling long hair, but a clipped beard, given to wearing heavily-tinted glasses of an antique rimless design, and a slightly-motheaten pork-pie hat pulled down over his forehead. He appeared when the Café was usually crowded, furtively requesting a take-out order in hoarse whisper. He would wait for it to be prepared, pay in cash and scuttle away, vanishing among the trees on Town Square. Richard wondered if he was staying in a burrow underneath the bandstand, or something. There was something distinctly badgerlike about him, after all.

"Singular chap," Richard observed, on the sixth or seventh day that the odd little man had appeared, and then disappeared with his plastic bag overflowing with Styrofoam take-out boxes. "Any idea where he is staying? As far as I know, the Cattleman isn't open for paying guests, yet, although I suppose he could be a hotel reviewer or a travel writer going incognito."

"He's staying in one of the B&B rooms over the old fire station," Araceli replied. "Doesn't have a kitchenette, so he has to eat out."

"Not terribly sociable, I must say," Richard nodded. "Still; all kinds to make a world. Are we on for today, to confab with the Walcott party about the wedding? I made up a portfolio, since I suppose we will be doing this kind of thing fairly often, now. I also did some sketches of wedding cakes, purely in the nature of suggesting my capabilities in that area."

"Today at two," Araceli replied. "With Auntie Conchita, and Collin Wyler's personal assistant. His name is Chung McNamara. I've already exchanged some text messages with him. He seems … well, focused. I think it will go well."

"I have yet to see any of our events go absolutely without a hang-up," Richard conceded, "But in this case, I also will hope for the best."

At the appointed hour, Richard and Araceli gathered up the portfolio which listed a wide range of buffet or plated servings which could readily be prepared and provided, and the sketchbook in which Richard had limned some fanciful designs for wedding cakes; everything from the severe, plain white version, topped with a pair of sugar swans whose arched necks formed a heart, to a riotously colorful six-tier production adorned with garlands of sugar fruits and flowers, and small panels along the sides featuring small portraits of the happy couple and scenes of places significant to them.

"A little over the top, I think," Araceli commented with a sniff, and Richard tucked away the sketch, replying, "Collin Wyler is a kind of over-the-top chap, and I suppose that his lady-love will have no hesitation about going along."

"Was it you who told me that the next Mrs. Wyler is English?" Araceli ventured. "Oh, look – there's that weird little man again! I wish that I could think of who he reminds me of. I could swear that I've seen him somewhere before, but then there are so many people who come to the Café…"

Richard searched his memory. "Yes, I believe she is English. Doc Wyler said as much. One of my suggestions is that the cake … or at least, one of the layers be the traditional English wedding cake, which is what you know as fruitcake."

"That would be interesting," Araceli ventured. They crossed the corner of the square, where the Cattleman's spanking-clean and exuberantly-ornamented façade presided over that end of Town Square, now divested of the scaffolding and tarpaulins which had veiled it for nearly a year. Richard noted the more obvious absence of construction vehicles, and battered pickup trucks clogging the parking along that side.

"I approve of the plantings," he said, noting the monumental urns with carefully-maintained topiary sculptures in them. "Are they supposed to be walruses, or longhorns?"

"No idea," Araceli replied, as they passed through the old-fashioned revolving door, into the splendors of the revived lobby. Bianca Gonzalez – one of Araceli's tribe of younger cousins – looked up from the computer terminal; the only jarring technological note at the fabulously Art Nouveau reception desk.

"Hi, Chef, hi, 'Celi! They're waiting for you in the dining room. Go ahead in."

"Hey, girl, you got that promotion!" Araceli beamed approval.

Bianca grinned, triumphantly. "They want me to start running through the protocols, now that I cut my teeth at Mills Farm," she replied. "Benny recommended me, and Mr. Dubois approved. And I got a raise, too!" Now Richard recalled; she had been a cousin of the honorees at his first catered do for the united Gonzalez-Gonzales clan, during his first year in Luna City, a slightly older Gonzalez maiden in a pale lavender dress. Beatriz and Blanca were hardworking waitresses at the Café now.

"Congratulations," he said, and Bianca smiled, the sudden heartbreaking smile of a momentarily uncertain young woman.

"Thanks, Chef!" she said, and then professional assurance slipped over her like a force-field once more. "Sorry. I simply have to get this glitch straightened out before we check in the first guests. And I don't want to bother Sylvester again. Go on; you'll be late."

The fabulous *quinceanera*; that formal marking of the moment when a young woman passes from being a girl into an adult, was now two – or was it three – years in the past. This realization made him feel momentarily old. Bianca, only a year or so older than her cousins, known as the "battling Bs" for their energetic participation on the Moths cheerleading squad, now looked stunningly, effortlessly and agelessly chic, in an elegant black dress and understated jewelry; the very perfect gentle concierge. Time was rippling past, all too swiftly, like the river in one of its unaccustomed floods.

The double doors to the formal dining room stood open. His and Araceli's footsteps made only the most silent of footfalls on the carpet, as they crossed the lobby and into the Cattleman's opulently ornate dining room.

"Oh, Chef – this will be the most gorgeous place to have a meal in the whole of the county!" Araceli whispered, in awe. This was the first time that she had ventured into the Cattleman since completion of the renovations – although she might have ventured in once or twice, in the dim and distant past, when the old hotel was in its dusty, neglected state. "Are those the Lalique fixtures that there was so much fuss about?"

"Yes; the very ones," Richard whispered back. "Good on Roman for getting them returned and installed, so expeditiously!"

They were within earshot of the table where two women and a young man awaited them – obviously with some impatience. The older of the two women was Conchita, the housekeeper at the Wyler manse; sixty-ish and heavy-set; jeans and a t-shirt bearing the Lazy-W logo of the Wyler Exotic Game Ranch displayed across her matronly chest. Richard couldn't place the second, at first; artfully dark-haired and still slender in spite of being roughly the same vintage, and then the penny dropped with a clang like the gong which always opened the scrolling titles in those old Rank Organization movies.

"Mrs. Dubois!" he exclaimed. "How marvelous to see you again! We thought that you would still be in France, you and Lew, enjoying your well-earned summer holiday!"

"Oh, call me Anne," Lew's wife allowed him to kiss her upraised hand. "Yes, we thought we would be too. But with this awful imbroglio over the redecoration, Lew just could not stay away. This project means so much to him, and with this …" her eyes slid toward the third of the trio, who had stood to meet them. "Well, anyway – it's all nearly sorted now. Lew and Harry and the rest of the VPI board thought that I might as well take on overseeing the last few details here, since I have had so much more real-world experience in hotel management than poor Georgina.

Chung, this is Richard Astor-Hall, who is an absolute miracle-worker when it comes to catering, and Miss …"

"Araceli Gonzales, sous-cook and kitchen manager," Araceli supplied, promptly.

The young man, who must be Collin Wyler's personal assistant, was a slim and smooth-faced character with distinctly Oriental features and jet-black hair, turned out in an immaculately cut white linen suit and a silk old-school tie. Well, that was one way to beat the summer heat in Texas.

Now he put out his own hand, and said, in a disconcertingly flat Australian drawl, "G'day; pleased to meetcha. David Chung McNamara; most blokes call me Chung. Ya know Gonz and Dub, I see. Let's get straight to the point: three hundred guests, here on Mid-summer Day. What can you do in the way of a buffet supper? Cost no object, of course, but something to make it memorable for the guests." The accent jarred so comprehensively with Chung's Eurasian appearance, Richard was momentarily boggled. Even after years of globe-trotting, he took a lot of boggling.

"Short of setting up an artificial river down the center of the table and letting the guests mine for jeweled trinkets in it with silver trowels," Richard answered, recalling an account of a splendidly vulgar Belle Epoque banquet where something like that had been essayed by the host. It sounded as if Chung were in the habit of shortening peoples' surnames; must be an Australian thing. He feared that Chung would inevitably shorten his own name to "Azz."

Chung gave a rather knowing chuckle. "Mr. Wye just might like that, you know, but it is supposed to be a wedding supper, not a treasure hunt. Think cash, flash, and splash. I'm supposed to brief Mr. Wye in about twenty minutes by conference call, and he'll either give the go-ahead or ask for more suggestions on the spot. He doesn't let the grass grow, you will have seen."

"No, I guess not," Richard opened his portfolio of optional menus, and Araceli took out her notebook and ever-ready pen. "I've met him, just the once. Impressive, but I thought the bride would want to have some input into her own wedding."

"Mr. Wye is taking it all in hand," Chung agreed, taking out his own iPhone, as they gathered around the table, although Conchita did snort rather skeptically. "Since he is paying the bills, his fiancée is agreeable to leaving it all to him."

Conchita snorted again, by which Richard assumed that the domestic establishment at the Wyler Ranch were not particularly impressed with the next prospective Mrs. Wyler junior, but were doing their bit in the spirit of glum acceptance of Collin Wyler's oft-demonstrated preference for loving, marrying, and leaving a sequence of nubile and attractive women. If he were a betting man and one without any compunction regarding his fellow humans, Richard would have set up a pool on how long this marriage would last. For a good long time, he had been that kind of man; heartless and superior, observing tragedy and misfortune with a coldly detached eye. But now that he had been settled in Luna City, it was hard to maintain that kind of superior 'master of the universe' detachment. A long time ago, in his schooldays, one of the masters had quoted the old axiom about the boys throwing stones at the frogs; the boys did it in jest, but the frogs died in earnest. Now he had lived among the frogs long enough to know that their woes and hurts mattered.

"I believe that because the Wyler family fortune was so signally founded on cattle ranching, that the main course should be beef; I have previously prepared Beef Wellington for a private banquet, to great acclaim. We can also offer tournedos Rossini – that is rounds of beef fillet topped with foie gras, or fillet of beef Richelieu served with stuffed mushroom caps and braised lettuce, or tournedos Henri VI – rounds of beef fillet topped with artichoke bottoms filled with sauce béarnaise. I have attached a list of vegetable dishes suitable to accompany. If we begin with hors d'ouvres, our kitchen can prepare a wide array of enticing nibbles for guests. As for the soup course …"

Richard dilated at some length on a selection of delicate broths and consumes, finally adding, "I would suggest any two from this list. As for the fish course – perhaps *galette de crabe* with a light mustard sauce. For the salads; a light and simple concoction of spring greens with a blood-orange vinaigrette of my own devising. As for the wedding cake itself," Richard wound up the last ends of the discussion and opened his notebook of sketches. "I have a couple of proposed designs; there's the classical four-tier round cake, with smooth rolled fondant and small nosegays of sugar roses and tulips tied with ribbon, topped by a pair of white sugar swans. We can do this in white, or with flowers tinted to any color scheme, from pure white, through pastel to vivid, and in a quantity sufficient to serve 300 hundred guests – if not in the main display cake, then in additional cakes already cut and plated in the kitchen. We can make the basic cake in whatever flavor is preferred, although my inclination, since I know that the bride is English, is for the traditional English wedding fruitcake. It really depends on what the guests will expect, of course. I am not averse to making the smallest layer in fruitcake and the rest in something which the guests may savor. Has the … umm, happy couple settled on a general color scheme?"

"Black, gold and white has been suggested," Anne Dubois interjected, and Chung nodded. "Thanks, Dub for reminding me of it. Black, gold and white, with a vivid accent color … perhaps deep rose or dark red. London to a brick on it – that would be ace! The décor of the ballroom itself would readily lend itself to that."

"This design – elegant and slightly futuristic," Richard turned the page of his sketchbook. "May suit very well with that in mind; the lowest layer in black fondant, with geometric shapes in gold foil, the next layer in dark gray with a monochrome photo effect, the third layer in white with a gold stipple effect, and the top layer pure white fondant with a garland of contrasting roses twining from top to bottom."

Chung nodded, and brought out his iPhone. "Let me take a quick snap of that one, and the first. What next?"

Richard turned over another page. "Now this one – also four layers; not round, but square and elevated on classical pillars at the corners. Each side of every layer is adorned with oval or square plaques in Wedgewood style; the colors of the plaques depends on the predominant color chosen by the happy couple, and depict significant armorial bearings, initials, or classical motifs."

"Very elegant, I think," Anne Dubois said, and Conchita nodded.

"Look nice with the Wyler brand on them, though. Silhouette of the HQ house, and a coupla longhorns – pretty fine. The personal touch."

"On to the next one," Richard turned the page again. "Six layers of cake in graduated pairs, each pair separated by pillars and a wealth of flowers filling the space. The topmost level is also crowned with a bouquet of sugar-paste flowers. This one I visualize in pale cream-color frosting, with the edge of each layer trimmed in an edging of fondant lace and the flowers in various pale tints to coordinate with the décor."

Chung snapped another quick picture with his iPhone and waited courteously for Richard to turn another page.

"That all ya got?" he asked when no more designs were forthcoming, and Richard sighed. "All that I have at this time, Mr.

McNamara. I am supremely confident of my talent and my staff's abilities to deliver any one of these to the event and I am perfectly open to considering any other designs which the happy couple would like me to duplicate. But I have always advised clients that they are paying me to exercise my considerable expertise and professional judgment in such matters as this, and it is most unwise to disregard it in favor of their own half-baked notion."

"Understood, mate," Chung flashed a wry smile, as he was thumbing through his contacts list and selecting a number from it. "OK, I'm calling Mr. Wye. I've already sent him the snaps … it's mid-evening in London … G'day, Mr. Wyler! Chung here, with Gonz and Dub at the Cattleman, and Richard, and his assistant from from the Café… Going to put my phone on the speaker mode so that we can all have a good chin-wag." Chung nodded, and set his iPhone in the center of the table. "He can year ya fine, just be sure and speak up." Chung nodded to the others at the table and continued in a voice slightly louder than before. "Yes, we've been going over Richard's proposed menu. You got my text messages – then whattya reckon? Yes … yes … the tournedos Rossini and the crab mousse? Big bikkies, but yeah, thought you'd be stoked. What about the cake, then – has Miss Cole had a dekko? That six-tier job is a real corker, that is."

"She hasn't, yet," the voice at the other end of the line replied – yes, Collin Wyler, serial monogamist and financial ruler of the known world. "Sorry, old man. Out with her lady friends, so the decision on the cake will have to wait on her return … and a confab with all her friends; no idea on how long that will take. Sorry about this. Richard – so good to know that you are in on this. The old man says that you're a better cook than a golfer; I trust you and Anne with the arrangements, regardless. Just a couple of things to clear up, if you don't mind taking the time?" The voice on the other end was crisp, decisive. Yes, Doc Wyler's son would be all that; not a man with patience when it came to be flannelling about. He expected from his underlings and hirelings what he expected for himself, which was well-informed but swift decision-making. Richard waited, more or less in patience, as Collin reviewed the suggested menu, approving most of what had been suggested – which was gratifying. And time-economical. Richard thought of the hours – and hours – and hours that had been burned on a pyre sorting out the Gonzalez-Gonzales quinceanera. So far, he had not spent a fraction of his time on this one event, although likely he and the Café team would spend hours more on the eventual prep. And as for the wedding cake; he would be burning the midnight oil on that one, and no mistake. The sugar flowers alone … He wrenched his thoughts back to the present, in time to hear Chung say,

"All right, blokes – and blokesses, anything to add?"

"No," Richard replied, when his turn came. "Just let me know about the cake design, and the flavor of the cake itself. I will absolutely have to have that settled by … the first week in June to allow the time to complete the thing. There'll be no quibbling with that, Mr. Wyler – if you want our best for this project, I must have the time in which to produce it in a way that will do you, your intended, and your guests proud."

"Sure thing, Richard," Over the tinny iPhone and god-knows-how-many time zones, Collin Wyler sounded proud and decisive – rather like the Doc, if truth be told. "Chung; send me the contract as soon as you have it in hand. My sig is assured. Thanks, Richard; your hard work is appreciated. So is yours, Anne. I have your bank numbers – so, expect payment on the dot."

"Our thanks for the business in return," Richard said. "Anything else for yourself and Miss … Cole, is it?"

"Colquhoun," came the reply, and Richard felt a sudden bloom of cold sweat. "Samantha Colquhoun. You might know of her; did a few TV series a while back, gets into the tabs a lot and she's real tight with the Kardashians, but a real down to earth person, once you get to know her."

"I'm sure she is," Richard said, "Since you are marrying her." He was aware of Conchita Gonzalez' carefully blank expression, and Araceli, suddenly alert and looking from Chung's phone to his own face. "I … erm. Look forward to … erm, working with you both."

"Same here," Collin Wyler's tinny voice exuded confidence and enthusiasm. "Is this everything, Chung?"

"Sorted," Chung looked around the table. "Any questions, cobbers? No, then. I'll print up the contracts and bring them round for the proper signatures. G'night, Mr. Wyler."

"It's been grand seeing you again, Anne … Mrs. Dubois," Richard excused himself with alacrity from the meeting. "We'll be in touch, sorting out the details when we're closer to the day. Basically, I see this as the same operation as we did for the Boathouse – all the work in our own kitchen and kite it over to yours for last-minute prep serving … all right. Grand. Must be going, have a Café to supervise."

To Richard's great unspoken relief, Araceli kept her mouth closed until they were safely out the front door and away from anyone likely to take an interest.

"That Sammi, who was your – ahem, is now marrying Collin Wyler," she announced, as they strolled. "Well, this is going to be interesting, Chef, I must say; interesting as in a twenty-car pile-up on the I-35."

"I had no idea," Richard protested. "And it's not as if I was her one and only. She's probably gone through half the English

Football League by now, as well as the fling with Pip Noel-Barrett. God, I'm buggered. As soon as she lays eyes on me, she'll shop me to the tabloids. Everything about my life here will be an open book. Screaming headlines. You all won't be able to walk out the kitchen door without being bombarded with a bunch of sweaty news-proles with cameras and microphones. And nice, long shiny knives, all ready to slip into my back."

"You can't know that," Araceli said, bracingly, but Richard refused to be solaced or reassured.

"Oh, yes, she will," he retorted. "Sammi is the most purely self-centered, thoughtless, conniving tart outside the pages of a Mills & Boon romance. And now we're committed to catering her wedding! Jesus, should I just leave town now, or wait until I am door-stopped by the press!"

"You can't leave town," Araceli repeated, patiently. "And don't take His name in vain, Chef. Look – you're just the caterer. So we're committed to her wedding cake, but you don't actually have to meet with her, do you? Luc and I can cover anything at the Café, and that Mr. McNamara is doing everything at his end." Araceli warmed to the subject. "She need never actually lay eyes on you. And besides," she squinted thoughtfully. "You really look pretty different from when you first got here. And from when you used to be on the Food Channel. Much less scruffy, and thinner. All that bike riding is good for you. I'll bet that if any of your old friends saw you across a crowded kitchen, they wouldn't think anything of it. Just don't talk, Chef. As long as you keep your mouth shut, they'll think you're from around here … I've just had the most brilliant idea, Chef!" Araceli's face brightened with inspiration.

Richard sighed. "I'm afraid to ask."

"You know how Abuelita always said you reminded her of Abuelo Jesus? What if you pretended to not speak English? You look Hispanic enough, you know. When your old GF comes to town, you stay in the kitchen and pretend not to understand English!"

"You have gone completely out of your mind," Richard finally brought himself to say.

Araceli shook her head. "All you have to do is look blank and say, *'no habla Ingles,'* to anyone who looks like they might recognize you! Most everyone calls you Ricardo anyway – just play along with them. You're Chef Ricardo from … from Jalisco, and you don't speak English."

"Barthelona," Richard insisted, still depressed. "I'd much rather be Manuel from Barthelona and say '*que*? A lot. That's a joke, Araceli. A joke. It would never work."

"Must be an English thing," Araceli replied, insisting, "You mean Barcelona … It would so work! It would! You just wait and see. I'll explain to everyone at the Café… Oh, look – there's our weird little customer with the take-out menu fetish."

They approached Café, as the odd little man in the tinted glasses and moth-nibbled pork-pie was just at that moment coming out through the Café door, laden with his usual bag of takeaway in clamshell covers. They were, in fact coming almost nose to nose with him, as blundered across the broad sidewalk set with tables and chairs in the shade of the green awning, blinded momentarily by the glare of the harsh afternoon sunlight slanting into Town Square.

"Pardon me," Richard said, almost automatically, as the man dodged as adeptly as an offside defense player.

"No trouble, I'm sure," the odd little man snapped, and something about him drew Richard's swift attention, as the customer in the pork-pie chapeau scurried across the road, cutting through the stand of trees in his hurry to return to his lair.

Richard stared after him – and yes, that was the second penny of the day, dropping with a clang which outdid the first.

"Oh f**k me running," he exclaimed, ignoring Araceli's half-spoken reproof. "Him! That man! I recognize him how! It's Gunnison Penn, the dodgy treasure-hunter!"

"And dog-meat if Joe and Doc catch up to him," Araceli scowled. "What is his game, I wonder? Is he still after the Mills Treasure?"

"He's not supposed to be anywhere near the Café, or me," Richard's frustration with life, and how events and certain people were conspiring to wreak havoc with it, suddenly took flame. He took hold of Araceli's arm, and pulled her after him. "He's not supposed to harass you, either! Come on – I want this blighter sorted, right now!"

He hurried across the road, dodging a fortunately slow-moving battered blue pickup truck, whose driver beeped the horn at them in an irritated-sounding way. "Hurry up, Araceli – he's getting away!"

They hurried across the Square, a blessed patch of green shade defending against the already harsh summer rays. The figure of Gunnison Penn scuttled ahead of them, putting on a burst of speed when he glanced over his shoulder and spotted them in pursuit. He was still looking over his shoulder when he stepped off the curb on the far side of the Square – and collided full-on with the slow-moving pickup truck circling Town Square; a thud as of something heavy against a metal fender, a sharp cry from Penn, and an indignant shout from the driver as he laid onto his horn and his brakes.

Araceli cried out, "Oh my god! Is he hurt?"

"No, I don't think so; not of he can yell that much abuse at the driver," Richard replied, and he and Araceli broke into a run.

The driver of the pickup – a youngish Hispanic man in dirt-stained boots and worn work clothing had set the parking brake and gotten out of his truck. It looked like Gunnison Penn was getting as good as he was giving, as the young man shouted,

"Look, you crazy *pendejo*, could ya at least look where the hell you are going!"

"I was crossing the street!" Gunnison Penn yelled back. "Pedestrians have the right of way!"

"Not when there's no crosswalk they don't!" the young man retorted, and that was when Araceli and Richard panted up to them.

"I want this man arrested!" the tone of Gunnison Penn's voice attained a hysterical scream, "He meant to assassinate me!"

The driver shouted, "Assassinate! Like, yeah – not my fault, *pendejo*! You weren't looking where you were going and stepped out right in front of me! Lucky I was minding the speed limit…!"

"Hi, 'Nando," Araceli stepped out into the roadway. "Yeah, you were – I saw everything, and so did Chef Ricardo."

A cousin – one of the unlimited Gonzalez-Gonzales constellations of cousins; Richard might well have known. One could not throw a brick in any direction in Luna City without hitting half a dozen Gonzaleses and Gonzalezes. Meanwhile, the incensed treasure-hunter drew a deep breath. Before he could let it out, Richard stepped up.

"Penn! Why the bleeding <u>hell</u> are you stalking the Café! Don't tell me any porkies, you right bastard! I know who you are, and why you're here, and I'm not going to put up with it for a moment longer! That injunction forbidding you to come within fifty feet of me, the Gonzales house and the Café had no bloody expiration date! What are you up to, coming back to Luna City again! You know bloody well – since you read the bleeding newspapers – that Collin Wyler is getting married here next month, and if you want to have your guts seconded for his garters, then be my sodding guest – just leave me and the Café out of it! I'm sick of you, your insane treasure quests, your… your harassment of my friends, myself and my place of work! I hope that sodding llama gave you lingering and painful disease! Get the hell away from here, and never come back!"

Richard went on, for a good few minutes, verging into French when he could think of no terms sufficiently vile in English, and when he came up for air in the midst of his diatribe, he noted that both Araceli and Nando Gonzalez/Gonzales were observing him silently; in the case of young Nando, in his dirty work clothes, with something of awe, while Gunnison Penn, for it was indeed him, just opened and closed his mouth gasping like a landed fish.

When Richard had run out of verbally-abusive steam, Araceli commented only, "What my boss just said, Mr. Penn, and double."

Cousin Nando shook his head and added in tones of deep admiration, "Nice what an education can add when it comes to a good ass-chewing. Me, I'm in awe. We're cool, Chef, and I dig your coffee."

"Thank you," Richard made a brief nod of acknowledgment, just as Luna City's police department cruiser pulled in behind Nando Gonzales's halted pickup. Joe Vaughn himself emerged from the drivers' side door, stalking along with his usual exaggerated wariness.

"Afternoon, gentle-grunts," he drawled. "Araceli, Ricardo … what seems to be the problem here? Don't answer all at once, y'all."

"He ran out in the road without looking, and I bumped him a little," Nando Gonzales explained, "But I was under the limit, Joe –

he never even looked! And he wasn't knocked down! He ran into my truck! Look – there's a new dent in the fender! And Chef an 'Celi saw the whole thing, anyway."

"This … this cretin is Gunnison Penn," Richard snarled. "That Canadian treasure-hunting idiot; the one whose friends with their cameras door-stopped me on a Sunday evening, the year that the Grant place burned down."

"I remember," Joe cleared his throat, regarding Gunnison Penn with his customary air of mild menace, before addressing that unhappy man directly. "Mr. Penn, you should remember that the order taken out against you did not expire. You were enjoined to stay away from the Café, and from attempting contact with Chef Richard, and with any members of Patricio Gonzales' family. Do you have anything to say for yourself, or are you going to refer all questions to your legal representative?"

"No!" Gunnison Penn stammered. To Richard's puzzlement the man seemed utterly transformed from the arrogant, demanding Canadian jerk-wad who had managed to offend and alienate practically everyone in Luna City, even the superhumanly tolerant Grants. "No; it's of vital importance that I continue my research! I know that I was supposed to stay away from the Café, but there is nowhere else to eat. I simply had to come back to Luna City … but incognito. Because of the treasure, you see."

"Some cog, some nito," Joe replied, depressingly unimpressed. "Look, Mr. Penn – best come clean. No one has a sense of humor about you and the Mills Treasure at all, and if you're back in town again because of the Wyler wedding, then let me be the first to tell ya in that case that your ass is grass and Doc Wyler will be the lawnmower!"

"No, not the Mills Treasure!" Gunnison Penn yelped, wringing his hands in agitation. "But a greater, more important artistic treasure! The Gonzaga Reliquary!"

"The what?" Nando's jaw dropped as Richard and Joe exchanged baffled looks.

Gunnison Penn babbled on. "The fabulous jeweled reliquary – immortalized in the da Vinci painting! The one they found this year in a convent in Milan, of Sister Giovanna Silvio y Gonzaga! She was a natural daughter of Cardinal Gonzaga, you see, dedicated to the religious life at a tender age … and fifteen years later the reliquary vanished! Completely vanished … but there are clues, of course! Clues which I have unearthed and …"

Behind Gunnison Penn's back, Araceli made the silent gesture of circling an index finger around her temple – the ancient non-verbal signifier of *'a multitude of bats having taken up residence in the belfry tower.'* Gunnison Pen babbled on, his audience riveted with horrified curiosity, including Nando, who if Richard's judgment was anything to go by, was increasingly fascinated. This was almost a given, with a young sprout like Nando, who possibly had never encountered flamboyant full-frontal delusion, and was therefore the likeliest to be fully drawn into a mental landscape of treasure-hunts and mysterious oracles, even given his initial reaction.

Men wanted to believe, Richard knew. They wanted to believe in the most extraordinary things, like being able to walk with a metal-detector across a plowed field and discover a fortune in Bronze age or Roman gold. It looked to him as if young Nando had already been bitten by the treasure-searching bug. Pity – as he looked otherwise like a rather sane young man. Another pity he hadn't been exceeding the speed limit by just a titch around the Square, otherwise he would have rendered Gunnison Penn completely unconscious and spared everyone the trouble of listening to him. Would have been a pity about Nando's driving record, though. From the stories that Richard had overheard, there was a kind of historic record for stunningly incompetent driving by a Gonzalez ancestor of the same name …

"What kind of clues," Joe, being one of these brutal realists, cut ruthlessly into the stream of babble from Penn. "Seriously; Gonzaga is not the same surname of Gonzalez."

"But a lingual cognate!" Gunnison Penn insisted, fully-embarked on the flood of his enthusiasm. "And from the historical records in Northern Spain – indeed, the Gonzalez family is lineally-related to the late medieval-Gonzagas; I have proved it through geometric logic – the Gonzaga Reliquary was taken back from the convent in the year 1503, when Sister Giovanna gave birth to a son, and departed the convent!"

"I take it that the vows of chastity and devotion were a bridge too far," Richard murmured. "These modern girls; such a crushing disappointment!"

Araceli shoved an expertly-aimed elbow into his ribs and muttered, "Chef, that was seriously against Church teachings!"

"Don't blame me for the Renaissance papacy!" Richard muttered back. "Me, I was raised in the good old C of E tradition – Anglican to you Yanks."

"A heresy based on Henry VIII's gonads!" Araceli replied. Meanwhile, Gunnison Penn rabbited on.

"The will dated 1793! A copy in the civil archives in Mexico City! The will of Don Diego Manuel Hernando Ruiz y Gonzalez, of Gijon in Cantabria, and of the Rincon de los Robles in the colony of Nueva Santander!" Now Gunnison Penn was in full, hyper-dramatic flood, as if he were in the midst of one of his overwrought internet videos. "Among those items bequeathed to his family – see, I have it here, a copy! Of course, it's in archaic Spanish! But among those items of value disposed of in the will to his nearest is … here, let me read it to you."

"Must you?" Joe Vaughn murmured, but Gunnison Penn swept that mild objection aside.

"It's here, in contemporary documentation!" the enraged treasure-hunter insisted, waving a much-folded scrap of paper, before adding, in milder tones. "I must put on my reading glasses… it says – as I interpret it … *'custody of the ancient jeweled reliquary of St. Gigobertus of Bethany, which is the treasure of our family.'* Here – this is a picture of it, taken from the painting! *'This precious memento of Our Blessed Savior's journey is adorned with a representation of the Holy Infant in the arms of his Holy Mother and set with precious stones ... it is to be held in the custody of my dear son Augusto, to be taken to our holdings in the remote parts of Nueva Santander, so that it may serve as a guide and guardian of our lives and fortunes'*… you see!" Gunnison Pen cried, in an excess of enthusiasm. "The reliquary was to be taken here! To this place – and being so precious, it must still be here!"

"Naw, I don't think so," Young Nando shook his head, quite understandably skeptical. "That jeweled thingummy in the painting? I've never seen anything like that around the old Rincon."

"It… looks kind of familiar, I have to say," Araceli ventured, looking at the printed picture which Penn Gunnison was waving before them. "I could swear I have seen something like this before."

"You will see dozens of reliquaries just like it, in any vendor of religious memorabilia in a catalog," Joe pointed out, and then addressed Gunnison Penn directly. "But if you wanna hunt for it here in Luna City, be my guest, pal. Just don't make a pain in the butt for every fool that you button-hole and talk at them until they are deaf." Joe took off his mirrored sunglasses and directed an especially severe look at the unfortunate treasure-hunter. "Don't let me hear any complaints. I mean it, Penn. You're already in my dirtbag book for harassing my pal Richard. Don't make me put another black mark against your record."

Young Nando had been looking over the papers which Gunnison Penn had been brandishing, and now he spoke up. "You know – you ought to come over to the Rincon. My sister Mindy is going through all the old family papers, and she was bitching me out because I don't have the time to help her out."

"Family papers?" Gunnison Penn sounded like he was a man lost in the desert, suddenly discovering an oasis. "What kind of family papers?"

Nando shrugged: "All kinds. Great-grandfather Antonio, and his father, Don Anselmo; they never threw anything away. Receipts, account books, letters – you name it. Tossed them into a trunk, and when it was packed tight, lock the lid down, and stash it in the old smokehouse shed. Mindy wants to prove that the Rincon headquarters house was even older than the McAllister place. She wants a historical marker for the Rincon. I mean, the family settled here a couple hundred years ago. It's only fair."

"I'd be … that would be a fascinating survey…" Gunnison Penn replied. "I would be honored to assist in such a task. Especially if there is some mention of the reliquary. There must be, of course! Since it was directed to be brought here in Don Diego's last will and testament…"

"If it was," Richard muttered, under his breath. Gunnison Penn and Nando paid no attention; they were exchanging telephone numbers.

"Well, that's that, gentle-grunts," Joe closed up his notebook, nodding to them all. "Let me know if I can be any further help to y'all. See ya, Penn – or not, as the case may be."

"Well, that's sorted," Richard remarked to Araceli as they walked away. "One less thing to give me aggro over."

"Now, all you have to worry about is hiding from the old girlfriend," Araceli agreed. "And … is that Mr. McNamara?"

Indeed, it was that gentleman, beaming jovially from ear to ear, as he spied them, walking across Town Square. He waited for them on the sidewalk in front of the Café.

"Azz!" he called, when he was within earshot, and Richard winced. "Glad I caught you! No time like the present! Miss Cole called me just now; the black and gold number for the cake; black and gold, with the flower garland in deep rose-color, shading to white. And the cake – the traditional English thing, Miss Cole specified. I thought you'd want to know at once; you said the work involved would be considerable."

"It will be," Richard wondered exactly how popular English wedding fruitcake would be, among the guests. Then he consoled himself; the wedding cake was not something to be eaten by guests. It was a showy centerpiece, an object to decorate the venue, and hint, very broadly, at the wealth of those celebrating the wedding, and the expertise of the pastry chef. "Thanks for letting us know so promptly, Mr. McNamara."

"Oh, just call me Chung," Another blinding smile, as he waved in a deprecating manner. "Everyone does. OK, if I bring around the contract tomorrow? Dub is still sorting out the office at the hotel; printer not hooked up yet."

"No problem," Richard answered, feeling that he was telling himself and everyone else a bit fat porkie. As far as his eye could see – only problems, the biggest of which would be staying out of the way of Sammi Colquhoun.

The Gift

Tuesday, early afternoons was the time that Jess Abernathy-Vaughn held the brief meeting with Richard at the Café to review the previous weeks' financials. These meetings had moved from mid-morning, and gradually became more and more perfunctory as business at the Café expanded, and to the mild astonishment of Jess herself, began to turn a profit which fell into a fluctuating zone somewhere between 'barely marginal' and 'satisfactory,' even with the payroll and additional penalties involved with additional staff, in the form of Luc and the Battling Bs. Jess viewed these developments with pride and trepidation, mainly as she had quietly encouraged Doc Wyler and Miss Letty to take such radical steps.

"No way would I ever advise someone wanting to make a fortune to start up a restaurant," Jess remarked on that particular day, and Richard nodded, glumly. Jess wondered briefly what

Richard appeared so distracted about. Café business was otherwise booming.

"No, it's more of a fame, fortune, and feeding people," He replied. "On the other hand – people always want good food… it's just that it's a constant struggle to provide it at a cost that the public will judge to be fair. You know that the margins are always thin, and most people who go into full-frontal food service are as mad as hatters…"

"I've gathered that," Jess observed dryly, just as Luc emerged from the kitchen, blinking absently, like something strange, and tatted, fresh from a long stretch of hibernation or suspended animation.

"Is there something the matter in the kitchen?" Richard asked, a slight edge in his voice, as Luc merely stood there, staring blankly at the tables, as if he had forgotten their purpose.

"No … nothing," Luc replied. "I was just thinking."

"It must have been painful," Richard answered. Jess snickered into her glass of unsweetened iced tea. "You'd probably best not do it again."

"On it, Chef," Luc replied. "Oh, I just remembered. The cake layers are done. That raisin-wedding-cake thing."

"Why didn't you say so!" Richard exclaimed and bolted from his seat.

"I took them out of the oven," Luc said, to Richard's back, and Jess rolled her eyes, thinking that yes, nothing could more have proved Richard's point about the madness of food service in general than that brief exchange. But Luc's expression briefly cleared as his distracted gaze wandered toward Jess.

"Oh – Hi, Mizz Vaughn. Mizz Letty doin' OK?"

"Yeah, she is," Jess replied, cautiously. Good heavens, Luc had made some progress toward a social manner. "How are you doing?"

"Fine," Luc replied. "Hey – business doing good?"

"Very well, I think," Jess answered. Luc nodded, as if mildly pleased at this revelation. Then he wandered back toward the kitchen, just as the old-fashioned bell over the front door jingled – that sweet, silvery, old-fashioned jingle. The door at Abernathy Hardware had the same old-style bell over it as well. Likely, they had come from the same place, decades before Jess was even born.

"Hi, Jess!" It was Patricia Pryor – Princess Patty, as Jess had always called her, in her own mind. "I'm glad I caught you! I saw your jeep outside! Look, I have something for you, but I don't have it with me now! Are you going to be at home later? I can bring it by."

"Sure, after about 4:30." Jess sneaked a peek at her schedule, cruelly mapped out on her cellphone. "Is it bigger than a breadbox?"

"Nothing like that," Patricia's smile was brilliant, unforced. "Just something I found, when we were sorting out the guest rooms at the ranch, for Daddy's latest wedding. A little thing, really – but I thought of you and Joe, immediately, and I want you to have it for the baby. See you around five, then!"

Just then, Richard came out of the kitchen, scowling; a dark expression which lightened by several degrees when he caught sight of Patricia. Jess repressed a small sigh. Patricia; gorgeous, accomplished, blond and rich, by way of being Doc Wyler's beloved granddaughter, had that effect on practically the entire world. Jess had always thought that unfair but then, she had married Joe Vaughn, who was Patricia's high school flame, so perhaps she herself possessed a charm or two. Still, Patricia had always made her feel inadequate, merely by existing.

"Hi, Richard!" Patricia exclaimed. "We got your order for beef tenderloins for Daddy's wedding supper at the Cattleman. Andy and the boys will deliver them next week, if that's OK."

"Prime beef, nothing less than choice," Richard said, with relief.

"For one of our best customers, nothing less," Patricia agreed with a twinkle. "We'll give you a call when it's ready for delivery." Her cellphone, deep in the depths of her Birkin handbag, burbled merrily, and she added. "Must fly – see you at about five, Jess."

"See you," Jess answered, without enthusiasm, and began closing up the folder for the Café. Little Joe peacefully slept in his stroller seat. "Nothing more for this week, Rich, unless you have any questions."

"None at all," Richard answered, sounding abstracted. "See you next week."

Her paid work wrapped up for the day, Jess took herself and Little Joe home – a matter of a mere few blocks. She would have walked, pushing Little Joe's stroller, with her briefcase and the diaper bag slung into the carrier, but she had begun feeling that pregnancy-fueled weariness again, in a major way. Six more months to go, she told herself, as she carried Little Joe into the house, the bag and her briefcase slung over her other arm.

A prerequisite for motherhood is the ability to juggle.

She popped him into his swing, and looked around the living room, thinking, *'Yeah, you might not be able to eat off the floor in our house, but guaranteed nothing will take a chomp out of your ankle when you walk through the place.'* Thank god for Joe and his neat-nick inclinations, plus long years of bachelor housekeeping! Jess felt a rush of sudden affection for her husband. He was a much more persnickety housekeeper than she was. Of late, he had rather been going overboard with the dusting, scrubbing, and vacuuming, wishing as he said, to spare her in her 'delicate condition.' 'Delicate my ass,' Jess replied, but she was grateful anyways, and quietly thanked her lucky stars for Joe's consideration. And that he was pretty fanatical about laundry, as well.

"Ready for company!" she said to Little Joe, who grinned, drooling only slightly. He had already cut two tiny bottom teeth. From the way in which he continued to gnaw on teething biscuits and on Jess's breasts, he was likely to start cutting the top teeth any time now.

Jess brought in the jar of sun-tea, which had been sitting on the back-porch step since she had set it to brew at midday. Yep – plenty of ice in the refrigerator freezer. A bowl of lemons and limes on the counter. Ready for company, on a summer day in Texas. Jess did hope that Patricia wouldn't stay for very long. She had to get supper on, for Joe would be home soon, off-duty at the dot of 5PM.

At ten minutes to that hour, she heard a car pulling up in Oak Street in front of the house. Two minutes later, a polite knocking at the door. Jess peeked through one of the tiny diamond-shaped windows set in the door; yes, indeed, Princess Patty, with a silvery gray pasteboard department store gift box tied with matching silver ribbons under her arm. Jess opened the door, hoping in her heart of hearts that Patricia wouldn't stay for very long. She was tired, and still had to make a gesture of starting supper, or at the very least, warming one of the casseroles in the freezer. And Joe would be home soon.

"Hi," Patricia said, "Don't mind me, I won't stay long. I have to supervise supper for Andy and the boys. But when I found this, I thought of you and Joe at once."

"Would you like some sun-tea?" Jess asked. "Do come in and sit down for a moment, at least."

"I'd love it!" Patricia beamed at her. "Bless you – I am totally parched. This summer is going to be brutal, I can tell already. Well; more brutal than usual. Thank god for Willis Carrier and his wonderful invention!"

"Iced tea, coming up" Jess said, as Patricia set her Birkin bag, and the gift box on the coffee table, and went down on her knees before the swing.

"He is such a darling!" Patricia cooed. "And growing so fast! I was afraid that Anson was going to be an absolute dwarf, you know. He didn't get his growth until he was thirteen or fourteen and then … my god, what happened to my little baby boy! He shot up six inches, practically overnight, and now he has to shave! I can hardly believe that, let me tell you!"

Jess went into the kitchen; hearing Patricia talk to her son; mercifully not that fatuous infant-babble which some people thought was appropriate to address children. Patricia was telling Little Joe about his football prospects, and that he would be breaking the hearts of little girls all across Karnes County before he was very much older. When she emerged from the kitchen, carrying two tall glasses, clinking with ice and a lemon wedge perched uncertainly on the edge of each, Patricia rose effortlessly from her position on the floor.

She must really work at the yoga, or something, Jess thought.

"He's teething now, isn't he?" Patricia accepted the glass of tea and sank onto the overstuffed sofa. "I can tell by the drool … you know, teething is so handy! A little bit of cranky, a slight temperature, a more than usually-messy diaper! Nothing to worry about, the baby is just teething!"

"Not handy when he bites on my boobs," Jess observed.

Patricia grinned. "There is that," she agreed. "Well, you are stacking your kids close together – and that is tiring, I know. But spacing them out – I don't know if that is any less …"

"Exhausting," Jess agreed. Somehow, against all the odds, and that long history – she was warming to Patricia. Naturally; anyone who admired Little Joe automatically had a good mark against their name in her books. "So, what is it that you found, that you thought I should have?"

"Open it," Patricia pushed the box across the coffee table toward her. Now Jess noted that it was a Nieman-Marcus box, and that it was unaccountably slightly worn, the ribbons a little crushed. As if it had been sitting, wrapped on a shelf for a long time. "It was something that Miss Alice must have bought, and then held onto. You know – for me, just in case any of my babies were girls. But all three of them turned out to be boys. You remember Miss Alice's gift closet, of course. Her stash of appropriate presents, no matter what the occasion? How that woman loved to shop!"

Jess set aside her iced tea, and untied the silver ribbons, taking off the top of the box. Yes, it had the Nieman-Marcus logo in elegant script, a single repetition. The contents were swathed lovingly in Nieman-Marcus tissue paper. Jess lifted them out, one by one; a baby dress of finest white cotton lawn and delicate lace, smocked elaborately across the neckline in pink thread, a ruffled bonnet in the same fabric and design. A tiny knitted pink cardigan sweater in an ornate pattern, and matching booties completed the infant ensemble.

"They're beautiful!" Jess breathed, awed by the craft, the sheer quality of the little dress and sweater. Patricia waved dismissively.

"And also sized six months. You can practically watch them grow out of that in a day and a half! But I thought that you should have them, Jess. I'd rather that the first of my friends to have a girl have this now this very minute, rather than wait until Anson and the boys marry and propagate. I want to see someone get the enjoyment out dressing a little girl in a darling little outfit like this!"

"But you aren't entirely past having more children," Jess ventured. Patricia was only four years older than Jess, and the youngest of her boys was still in elementary school. Patricia waved a dismissive hand.

"There were some … complications with delivering Andy, and my OB said … best not risk it again. Oh, don't look like that, Jess – it's no big tragedy to us. I'm quite happy with our family as it is, and anyway, if we really wanted another child we could always go to China or someplace and adopt. It was Miss Alice who had her heart so set on me having a daughter and she would be as pleased as punch for you, if you were the one to get the good out of this."

"Thank you, then," Jess was honestly touched. Miss Alice, Doc Wyler's late wife, had been famous for the elegance of her attire. When Jess must assume proper professional office drag, the memory of Miss Alice was the vision which guided her on those now mercifully rare occasions; impeccably turned out, every hair in place, every accessory coordinating perfectly, adorned with tastefully-understated jewelry … Jess could still hear Miss Alice dispensing advice; *'Put together your outfit completely – and then look in the mirror and take off a single piece of jewelry.'* Now Jess said, "Miss Alice's gift closet was amazing. She always had the most perfect thing to give as presents."

"Whenever she visited Houston," Patricia agreed, "She spent simply <u>days</u> in Neiman-Marcus. She knew all the salesladies by their first names, and they all adored her. Sometimes she would start advising other customers; she was so commanding, everyone assumed she was one of the regular staff!" Patricia sighed, a deep and nostalgic sigh. "I so miss that woman! She would have had such a ball with Pop's latest wedding! This is the first time he has ever brought his intended home to the ranch for the festivities. I err, Jess." Patricia looked as if she was reviewing old memories. "I think Daddy's first wife came to the Lazy-W a couple of times. My mom did, but she hated the place."

"I thought your mom was his first wife," Jess mused, honestly puzzled – and for nearly the first time in her life, feeling something of genuine interest in Patricia's life. Somehow, Princess Patty had been deposited with her grandparents, early on, to be raised by them in Luna City. Jess had never wondered particularly about how that came about, merely assuming Patricia's mother must have been infamously incapable of raising a child, and her father infamously uninterested in the task. She herself had the advantage of a pair of conscientious parents, right up until the year when her mother died, wasted by fast-moving cancer, and then she had Pops, all to her self.

Patricia shook her head. "No, Mom was his second. No one ever talked to me about Daddy's first wife. A secretary, or something. She was killed in an auto wreck; if you ask me, that all happened before he could get bored and move on. Rather like Henry VIII and Jane Seymour, I always thought. After that? I have the most gruesome collection of bridesmaid and attendant dresses you can imagine!"

"Truly?" Jess sipped deeply of her own iced tea. This interchange was turning out to be more agreeable than she expected. Really; had she been so proud and prejudiced when it came to Patricia, all these years? "I had some really awful ones. The worst was four-tiered ashes-of-roses ruffled number that made me look like a Sears bedspread. I burned it in Pop's BBQ pit the next time I was home."

"Screw the damage to the ozone layer!" Patricia raised her glass in a mock toast. "Some dresses are too horrible to continue existence on this mortal plane. I shipped the most awful ones to a thrift store, but I never considered the heinous aesthetic damage they might do in the secondary market. I was young. Forgive me, for I have inadvertently sinned!"

"Never mind," Jess consoled her. "You weren't thinking straight. Overwhelmed by the awfulness of it all. Dragooned over and over, into dancing attendance on the next Mrs. Wyler…Sorry for all that," Jess added in what she considered to be a handsome apology, and Patricia laughed.

"Over and long done with, Jess. I always came back here, to Miss Alice and Doc. They were cool about it all. Exasperated, but always cool. Daddy's a special case, I have to admit." She squinted into her iced tea glass. "Special – that's him, all right. Pity; some of his wives I really think I could have liked, but those were the ones whom he ditched the soonest. Can I have a refill, Jess? It's so hot outside, now. I need to <u>completely</u> rehydrate before heading home to the madness. Daddy's latest wedding has turned everything upside down… but there's no truth in the rumor that one of the bridesmaids will be a Kardashian. Honestly, I don't know where that one got started. Likely the bride herself. I know it for a fact that Susannah Wyatt is the matron of honor, this time around. Isn't that precious? She and Roman just announced the birth of their own babies. Twin boys, can you imagine?"

"Good lord," Jess collected the nearly empty glasses and went with them to the kitchen. "I wonder that she has the energy. Two at a time would absolutely kill me."

"I understand they did it with a surrogate mother," Patricia raised her voice. "Which to my mind takes all the fun out of it at the start!"

Jess laughed, returning to the living room with a full glass in either hand, to find Patricia cooing at Little Joe, "Oh, you wouldn't kill your mommy! Such a sweet innocent little face! Honestly, Jess; he is the image of Joe! One of those things that I found this week was a picture of Miss Letty's kindergarten class back in the day. And there is Joe, looking just like this little man! I should make you a scan of that picture, just to prove it!"

"There probably is a copy of it, somewhere," Jess handed the refreshed glass to Patricia, who accepted it with an expression of gratitude, and sank half of it in a gulp. It was hot outside; the hottest time of the day. "But probably buried in an album at his parent's place in San Antonio. Do send it to me, Pat – I'd love to have a copy of my own."

"I will," Patricia smiled, comfortably. And then she hesitated for a bare moment, before plunging on. "He's so happy with you, Jess. Content. I'm glad. You know, we were always friends, Joe and I. But being friends really means one must be honest with each other. I know that it must look to everyone – especially to you – as if I was brutal about breaking up when we did. But it was something that wasn't going to work, not in the long run. And I have Andy and the boys, and now you have Joe and … well, it really worked out for the best. Sometimes that's hard to see, living day by day…but it did work out."

"Yes, it has," Jess replied. She smiled at Patricia, an unforced and natural smile. Outside the house, she heard the familiar crunch of the gravel drive under the wheels of Joe's car. *Yes, right on time.* "And thank you for the little outfit. If I don't have a daughter this time around, I'll save it for the next. And if I don't – than it will go to the next of my friends who does."

"Grand!" Patricia exclaimed. "I think that you will, actually. Something that Miss Letty said to me… Is that Joe? I'd better go, now. Anson is starting supper for us; do you know, he was in Richard's cooking class at school? Roast chicken with vegetables.

Anson says he has it all under control, but you know … best linger helpfully in the background, just in case."

"I know," Jess replied, her heart lightened. "Moms never quit. I'm certain it will be a fantastic supper. Richard is a good teacher; cruelly demanding, sometimes, but it means that the kids pay attention, like they do with a stern coach. Thanks again, Pat."

"You're welcome, sweetie," Patricia tossed off the last of her iced tea. "See you around … Hi, Joe! Must run – it's that time. How's crime waving in Luna City?"

"Got it sorted," Joe sent his white Stetson spinning onto the hat-rack. Although he had a smile for Patricia, Jess saw that his gaze went immediately toward her, then to Little Joe, who wriggled in ecstatic joy and reached up his arms to his father.

"Don't get up, I'll see myself out," Patricia set down the iced tea glass and gathered up her handbag and car keys. "Wish me luck with the wedding! So grateful that Lew and Anne are such a help, getting the Cattleman organized. Daddy's current assistant, Mr. McNamara, is a treasure! He's taken on all the Daddy-and-Sammi-wrangling on his own shoulders. We're so grateful, but still, it's all rather…"

"A chore," Jess supplied, as Joe lifted his son out of the swing and over his own head. Little Joe crowed in delight. Patricia lingered with her hand on the doorknob.

"A blessing," she added, and then let herself out. Joe tucked his son under his arm, as if he were a small and lively football, and collapsed with a mild groan onto the sofa next to Jess.

"Your knees?" Jess said only. "Motrin on the rocks?"

"Yeah," Joe replied. "What was Pat here for?"

"She had a gift for the baby," Jess said.

And went to get the bottle of Motrin.

History of the Borgfeld-McAllister House

The best-documented, oldest and still-in-use structure in or near Luna City is the historic Borgfeld-McAllister House, which stands in manicured grounds just to the east of Route 123 and the bridge over which it crosses the San Antonio River. Once a general store, saloon and boarding house serving traffic between San Antonio and the coast, it has been a private residence since 1885.

There is inconclusive evidence in the historical documents of a simple two-pen log cabin on the in the 1840s, as that was the point where a heavily-traveled road between San Antonio and those early settlements on the Gulf Coast crossed the San Antonio River. Scanty records suggest the presence of a small trading post and saloon at that point. Both cattle and freight moved up and down that road during the time that Texas was a colony of Spain and then of Mexico, but it was not until the 1850s that there was any more permanent dwelling constructed on that site which would later become Luna City.

Hermann Borgfeld, a stonemason from the Duchy of Bavaria arrived in the aftermath of the failed 1848 revolution, under the auspices of the equally-doomed Adelsverein, a philanthropic consortium of princes and nobles which recruited German farmers and craftsmen to settle a grant in frontier Texas. The Adelsverein – or to use the expanded title of the society, "The Society for the Protection of German Immigrants in Texas" began with the best and most optimistic of motives and ended in bankruptcy in the space of a decade, having over-promised and underestimated the costs of providing all that they had so glibly assured prospective settlers to their land grant in Texas. Hermann Borgfeld, who if anything was a shrewd and observant character, noted the hapless disorganization prevalent in Adelsverein operations at their port of entry, Karlshaven on the coast of Matagorda Bay *(later to become Indianola, the briefly-reigning Queen City of the Gulf Coast)*. He decided, with his five sons and two daughters *(all unmarried)*, to bail on Adelsverein promises of land in the Germanic beachhead established in settlements like Fredericksburg and New Braunfels, in favor of his own native wit and energy, halfway through the slogging journey between Karlshaven and New Braunfels. The story, handed down through descendants of the Borgfeld family, is that at the mid-point in their journey from the coast to New Braunfels in the company of a Verein-led wagon train of hopeful settlers, the Borgfeld family were handed their evening meal rations of cornmeal and preserved salt-beef, and utterly rebelled at what their patriarch viewed as nasty, inedible and moldy.

"We're done with the Verein," vowed Hermann Borgfeld, "We can do better, and we will!"

The following morning, the Borgfeld clan abandoned the Verein convoy, taking their few goods, chattels and tools with them, and took up residence on the banks of the San Antonio River, determined to seek their fortunes, independent of corporate sponsorship. Family lore has it that they traded Mrs. Borgfeld's second-best set of linen sheets and a stout iron cooking pot for possession of a portion of land and a decrepit log cabin on the banks of the San Antonio River. Transfer of the property was recorded in the records of the then-county seat at Goliad – the first official records of Borgfeld presence at the place in Karnes County where present-day Route 123 crosses the San Antonio River.

The road was a moderately well-traveled one, and the Borgfeld family swiftly adapted: the paterfamilias was a skilled stonemason, his oldest son a blacksmith, the second oldest had apprenticed to a glass-blower, back in Germany, and the third son apprenticed to a baker. The Borgfeld women were all superlative cooks, and within a short time they were operating a profitable business providing to the various needs of hungry travelers. Editor, travel writer, and landscape designer Frederick Law Olmsted left a vivid description of the Borgfeld's hospitality in his 1855 account of a horseback travel through Texas. While their various enterprises were maintained under canvas awnings set up among a small grove of oak trees, he gave them generous credit for superlative cooking and generous old-world hospitality. Olmsted noted that the foundations of a fine stone house had already been laid out in the year of his visit. Over the following years the house was completed; two stories tall, with porches and galleries front and back, with a separate summer kitchen. The forge sat at some distance from the house, on the site of the present-day Tip-Top Ice House, Gas and Grocery; the Tip-Top, in fact, gradually took over an increasing share of business as automobiles replaced horse and ox-team transport in the 1920s.

The stone building served as saloon/restaurant and boarding house, as well as the Borgfeld's family home until 1885, when it was sold by Herman Borgfeld's heirs, in the belief that the enterprise would be soon be superseded by the proposed railway. The house was purchased by Arthur Wells McAllister, surveyor, architect, and ardent backer of Luna City as a profitable real estate venture. He oversaw extensive renovations and creation of extensive landscaped grounds, since the house served as sales office and temporary headquarters for the Luna City Development Corporation, as well as a home for his family. The Texas Historical Commission placed a marker in front of the house on the centennial anniversary of the founding on Luna City in 1985. The house is still the residence of Leticia McAllister, Arthur Wells McAllister's granddaughter.

Those Wedding Bell Blues

As Richard expected, the sheer creative and logistical challenge of catering the event managed to blur the reality – that this was for the faithless, heartless, celebrity-addled Sammi, otherwise known as Samantha Colquhoun, she of the Page-3 notoriety, and subsequent fame for being famous. Richard searched his mind, as he combined towering quantities of dried raisins – both ordinary and golden, with dried currants, and the orange peel that young Brianna was industriously scraping off a bale of fresh oranges. The perfume wafted through the kitchen like a dusky incense, doing enticingly fragrant battle against that of ripe molasses, vanilla extract, cinnamon and cloves.

"So – basically, a dark gingerbread raisin cake," Bree ventured, and Richard nodded.

"Exactly; with the additional benefit of being practically as indestructible as the legendary fruitcake. One can make the cake layers far in advance of the blessed date. And the sugar-paste flowers as well," he mused. "It's just as well that the cake is more for show than for eating … although the cake itself will be delectable at any age, like a fine wine or an enticing woman."

"I'll reduce the recipe by about a hundred percent and make it up for G-Nan and Grandpa," Bree bent her head *(suitably sanitary-netted)* over her task. "I'll bet they will like it. You wouldn't mind if I – if we – started making them for sale? Along with G-Nan's soaps and things, for the holidays? In small batches, I mean. I wouldn't want to steal business from the Café," she added hastily. "Not if you plan on selling it along with the cinnamon buns…"

"Just don't stick a sugar flower on it," Richard advised. "Someone could easily break a tooth. Speaking of which; we will need an acre of flowers and foliage for this bloody cake. Do you mind working on those with me? Gum-paste sugar flowers – it's an arty sort of specialty, you'll enjoy learning to do, I believe, since you have a taste for that finicky detailing of garnishes and things. I have a full set of the required tools and molds. The wretched things take all kinds of time to dry, once constructed, and then they are so fragile that likely a lot of them will be lost in assembling the bloody cake …"

"Sure, Chef!" Bree beamed, so sunny and agreeable that Richard was cheered. This was his new life – his mission, as Katie so often said, to teach the fine culinary arts to those who were enthusiastic about learning and practicing them. And the decoration of cakes seemed to be one of those trendy arts among bored wives these days, if what Katie had told him about Insta-something-or-other-gram. "This is going to be a big thing, isn't it, Chef? The Wyler wedding, and the Cattleman reopening … and at the mid-summer solstice, too! G-Nan and Gramps are over the moon with how many guests have made reservations at the Age. G-Nan is planning the most splendid *Litha* celebration ever! That's the summer solstice celebration. This is gonna put Luna City on the map, isn't it?"

"In a good way, we sincerely hope," Richard replied. Katie had picked up an internet rumor that a Kardashian was going to be a bridesmaid. "Umm … Bree. Don't forget that if an aggressive someone with a notebook and a camera asks about me; I'm Ricardo from Jalisco and I don't understand English."

"Sure, Chef," Bree replied, the air of fond indulgence almost palpable. In previous days Richard might have cringed in humiliation, but now Bree and Robbie, Araceli and Luc, and the waitresses were his tribe, his people in the restaurant trade. Beyond that small circle, there was the larger one, of those residents of Luna City; all of them, in their eccentric human glory, his customers and friends, those whom he lived among, whom he looked after in providing food, and who looked after him in so many human and caring ways. This was armor against whatever the fates had in store for him – the media fates heading toward Luna City with the object of covering the fabulous Wyler wedding, like the *Titanic* and the iceberg. With the luck that had not been granted that hapless steamship, he hoped – when he thought about it at all – that he could dodge that particular fate. Richard had shoved that possibility away into that part of his mind labeled 'tomorrow.' Or as Joe Vaughn was apt to say, with a cynical chortle, *'Napalm that bridge when we come to it, OK?'*

In another week, the Age of Aquarius Campground and Goat Farm would begin to fill up; fill up not just with the Old Aquarians, a group of moderately-aged and otherwise respectable but sentimental former Communards to whose presence he had become accustomed over the last few years, but travelers drawn by curiosity. Travelers who could not afford the eye-bleeding prices at Mills Farm, or for a room at the now-equally eye-bleeding Cattleman. Many of those guests at the latter were doubtless guests for the Wyler wedding … but those drawn by vulgar curiosity would, by default and relative lack of funds, come to roost at the Age – and that would include the scribbling fraternity.

Much as he hated the thought of disrupting his routine – he might have to make other arrangements, in defense of his own continued sanity, and privacy.

At the first opportunity, in an interval of folding together wedding cake batter, he stepped to the bare little garden patch at the back of the Café. This space was enlivened only by the bare concrete loading dock, a number of wheelie bins, and a patch of crumbling macadam ornamented only by a couple of raised planting beds full of herbs – those herbs with which he seasoned those special dishes at the Café, and in which he suspected that Ozzie sometimes favored for a bask and nap in the sunshine. He dialed Chris's cellphone.

"Chris at the Tip-Top; speak to me, Ricardo," Chris answered before the second ring. Richard could picture Chris, lean and dark, manager of the mini-market and gas station out at the edge of Luna City on the main road between San Antonio and the coast.

"I need a place to hide out over the summer solstice and the Cattleman opening," Richard stated, baldly. "The news-ghouls are gathering. Can Ozzie and I hide out at your place for a week or so? I promise I will be a good guest, and Ozzie will shit in the appropriate pan for the duration."

"Sure," Chris chuckled. Richard could picture him, likely at the cash register, or at a break from restocking the shelves at the Tip-Top; restocking water, and packaged displays of commercially-manufactured snacks. The small shelf of fresh and locally-baked goodies from the Café featured highly in a prominent place on the cash-stand. "You and your one-eyed mini-tiger are welcome, any time."

"Thanks," Richard hoped that his gratitude was manifest over the telephone. Chris's apartment, situated as it was over the garage/coach-house behind the Historic Old McAllister home, was a short bicycle-distance from the Café. The apartment was a commodious one, in comparison to the Airstream. Very likely he and Chris would hardly be in it at the same time, save perhaps to sleep. "I'll bring over Ozzie's potty and a bag of food. He's good with being indoors at night, but during the day, he'll hang out at the Café as he always does."

"No problem, Ricardo, just let me know when to expect you."

"Probably Tuesday, after work," Richard sighed. "The old Communards are already gathering. And did you know that mad berk of a treasure-hunter is back in town?"

"Yeah, I heard, straight from Joe," Chris chuckled, indulgently. "But at least he is hunting for something else than the Mills Treasure. Apparently, he has given up on that one, and is obsessing over some religious piece of furniture associated with the Rincon Ranch Gonzaleses."

"Good to know," Richard was relieved to hear this. Gunnison Penn had continued his habit of skulking unconvincingly into the Café and ordering take-out once daily. That was all that the Canadian treasure-hunter had done to bring himself otherwise to Richard's attention. Some of the regulars had taken to greeting him – *Hey, Penn, how ya doing? Found the Gonzales Reliquary yet?*

This must play merry hob with Penn's illusions of being undercover. "At least he won't be in my hair, at this tense time. I have a huge catering project to manage, and I must give it my full attention!"

"Good for you, pal," Chris' chuckle was rich, and lewd. "And dodging your old GF, the bride? Give that some attention too, old pal."

Richard vented his frank opinion on that matter, whereupon Chris laughed outright, and answered, "Hey, got a delivery truck just pulling in. Good luck with Sammi the Freak, OK? And your other old flame, Susannah the Bunny-boiler! See ya Tuesday, Rich. Wish my love life was as entertaining as yours, but Miss Letty would have a fit, and likely throw my ass out for having no morals."

"She'd never," Richard replied, "The old dear depends on you far too much. See you Tuesday after work,"

"I'll put a pizza in the oven for ya," Chris replied, chuckling coarsely when Richard told him exactly what he could do with that pizza.

"I'm timing it just right," he confessed to Katie, the following Monday evening. Kate – his lovely, undemanding, Ozzie-loving Kate – lounged on the banquete with her feet up, and Ozzie in her lap. She had slipped off her shoes and hung her suit jacket in the Airstream's miniscule wardrobe. Richard was only mildly distracted by how the blouse under it clung flatteringly to her neat, but unspectacular figure. "The Aquarius is filling up. There were a pair of berks with Aussie accents and suspiciously large cameras who pulled in this afternoon, in a rented RV. They're here for the Wyler wedding, or perhaps the Cattleman opening. I'm staying at Chris Mayalls' digs until it's all over."

"I don't think you have anything to worry about from them, or from any other media," Kate said, patiently. "It's been a couple of years since …"

"Yeah – well, some poor blameless sod working at a grocery store just got himself spread all over the international media because he got recognized by some customers as a bit player yonks ago on a TV sit-com," Richard answered, on edge. This topic made him nervous. "I cannot take that risk, my Kate of Kate Hall. We've talked about this before."

"We have," Kate agreed comfortably. "And I said before, I'll say again, and I'll say it again when you bring it up tomorrow – I don't believe that you have anything to worry about, but you're the one who'll be up the proverbial creek if I am wrong about outside interest in your previous life. So … we'll have our usual Monday night a week hence?"

"If not, I'll let you know," Richard replied. He lifted the lid on the saucepan containing their supper for the evening, now blissfully bubbling away, gave it a careful stir and turned down the heat.

"What is that?" Kate inhaled the blissful odor and even Ozzie – slumbering in her lap, overcome with affection and an overdose of catnip from Abuelita Adeliza's garden – roused himself to sniff appreciatively. "It smells absolutely heavenly!"

"*Bœuf bourguignon*," Richard answered. "I could think of no better use for the scraps and trimmings of the finest choice beef fillets from Pryor's, than to make a hearty stew from them; to nourish you, my dearest Kate, and for Ozymandias-King-of-Kings, who will dine luxuriously on the leftovers …"

"Waste not, want not," Kate twinkled companionably. With that, Richard was assured that all, for the brief moment, was well in his world. Tomorrow began an exile from those home comforts to which he was best accustomed, and a time where he would have no leisure to contemplate that lack: the home-stretch of preparation for the Wyler wedding. Which – considering the notable guest list, the high quality which Richard required, the fact that most of the final prep should be performed in a huge and newly-renovated restaurant kitchen *(which Lew Dubois had personally assured him would be up to the task, and the additional Cattleman wait-staff)* the additional challenge of having to hide in the nearest men's bog at the threat of an appearance by Sammi or Susannah paled in comparison.

* * *

"All looks to be good to go," Richard assured Lew on the Wednesday before the madness was supposed to begin. He had transported the wedding cake layers and a garden of sugar flowers and foliage, on one of the rolling catering carts which he had begun to make so much use of. The walk-in cooler in the Cattleman kitchen was several times the size of that in the Café, which relieved his mind no end. Lew's attention to detail extended to matters back of the house; not always the case when it came to the hospitality industry, Richard knew.

"The kitchen is even more splendid than I thought possible. A wedding banquet for three hundred guests will be a snap." Lew – his usual casually-clad in self, disreputable work-shirt and Dickies trousers, looked like one of the workmen finishing off last-minute touches on the back-of-house. He nodded companionably.

"Good, *mon vieux*," he replied, leaning in a casual manner against the edge of the nearest prep table. The Cattleman renovations were at last compete, down to the final detail. "I have no need to remind you – how important this event will be? Not only the grand opening itself – but the Wyler wedding. It is a matter most *intéressant* to yourself, of course," Lew added. "But for the future of this expanded enterprise – a matter for us all. I do believe that I owe you great thanks," Lew added. "For noting the matter of the glass chandeliers. Your keen observation of a seemingly minor matter is appreciated, as well as your perspicuity in mentioning your observations to the right person is deeply appreciated; perhaps VPI as a corporation will not have taken note of the debt owed to you, but I have. It spared me, indeed spared us all a disaster most comprehensive. You have a … what is the phrase – a deep well of gratitude with me, which will not soon run dry."

"Luna City makes mad partners of us all," Richard answered, and Lew Dubois grinned like a schoolboy.

"So it does," he replied, "Anne and I have so much enjoyed this project – so close to my heart! Even when we return to Houston, rest assured that I will be returning here often."

"Good to know," Richard replied, quite honestly reassured. "I must say – we are no end relieved that you will be on hand again for the do this weekend. I'll be able to fully-concentrate on the kitchen…"

"No bloodied armadillos, I can assure you, *mon vieux*," Lew promised, and Richard laughed uncomfortably, recalling a near-disaster at a previous catering event; naturally at the Walcott's, where disaster often attended. Lew unpropped himself from the worktop, indicating in a subtle fashion that the casual interview was done. "Let me know if anything I can do to assist you, *mon cher Richard.* Anything within my power – just say the word."

"There is one thing," Richard ventured, thinking of a favor, hesitating a trifle and then thinking – *oh hell, go for it*. "I … umm … had a rather high-flying life, before I arrived here. And in it, Sammi Colquhoun – soon-to-be Mrs. Collin Wyler – and I were a couple. Ages ago," he added rather hastily. "In my life before. An old life, Lew. One which I have no interest in reviving, in any way.

But now my old flame is getting married in this hotel, and I committed to catering the wedding, and constructing the cake without knowing that she was the bride. You can see that it put me in an awkward position."

"Ah," Lew Dubois chuckled, a worldly, knowing chuckle. "An unenviable position, *mon vieux*. I perceive that your heart is not broken by this happenstance?"

"Not the least," Richard retorted. "I wish her husband the best of bloody good British luck to him. He is paying me so generously that I wouldn't care if he were bigamously marrying my mother, but I don't want it spread about, or for the bride to know of my contribution to her big day."

"You wish to be modest and retiring?" Lew asked, looking much amused.

"Indeed," Richard answered. "If anyone asks; I am Ricardo from Jalisco, and I don't speak English. Araceli can handle any interface with the public, or the bride and her coterie of friends. But it would be embarrassing and possibly be comprehensively and personally damaging to me, if the new Mrs. Wyler …"

"Say no more, Ricardo from Jalisco!" Lew chuckled again. "Should the new Mrs. Wyler inquire, I shall be discretion itself. My promise on it, my dear old friend."

That sorted, Richard made the proper arrangements to move temporarily to Chris' bachelor quarters, in back of the old McAllister residence. He packed a small gym-bag on Tuesday morning, locked the door of the Airstream – not that there was anything of much value inside, but he hated the thought of uninvited strangers invading his personal space, and strapped the bag onto the bicycle. He pedaled away with Ozzie riding as usual in the crate bungee-corded to the back, as the sun rose above the shady fringe of oak trees which lined the unpaved drive into the Age of Aquarius. He waved to Sefton Grant resplendent in tattered shorts and cowboy boots, already out scattering food for the goats. The morning already gave a strong hint to the days' heat; yes, this summer would likely be a hot one. Summers in Texas, he was already dismally aware, were hellishly hot. How human beings had lived in comfort there before the development of air conditioning was an ongoing mystery to him, although he supposed that houses with tall ceilings, tall windows on all sides and deep overhanging verandahs must have had something to do with it.

He meant to drop off the bag with Chris at the Tip-Top, rather than port it into town with him. As he came up on the Tip-Top, though, he saw that there were a number of automobiles parked out front. Not that this was unusual, but two of them were shiny black town cars of the sort which Tony Gonzalez had for hire through his limousine service. Richard coasted to a stop in the parking area where the pavement gave way to gravel and contemplated the Tip-Top warily. Well, no time like the present. Collin Wyler wasn't due to arrive with his new bride for another day or so. This lot must be guests; very important ones, by the appearance of the hire cars. Surely not among the reporting fraternity – they could hardly afford such luxury.

"As you were, Ozzie," Richard commanded Ozymandias, who had proved to be almost dog-like in his obedience, within reason, to certain commands. Ozzie crouched within the plastic milk crate, and licked a paw, with deliberate feline indifference. Richard took the bag with his clothing in it and approached the entrance to the Tip-Top; a double door, like that of an old-time Western saloon, even to a sign which advised that horses could not go beyond the low porch which wrapped the front of the ramshackle structure.

Richard shoved the door open, and then thought to himself in screaming all-caps, *"Oh, f**k no!"*

The Tip-Top had customers. And one of them was Sammi. Yes, he knew Sammi; he'd know that view of her from across a crowded room anywhere; slender, tall, still and always artfully blond. That was Collin Wyler, standing next to her, as Chris rang them up at the cash-stand. Richard caught Chris's eye and momentary curiosity, which brought Sammi's head turning around, from where she stood.

Every fiber within him urged immediate retreat-retreat-retreat with a sound like the *aaa-oogah* of the dive alarm in all those old movies about wartime submarine service. Richard, being a sensible man, obeyed the wisdom of those fibers. As the door fell closed, he distinctly heard Sammi saying, "Was … wait, Collie – who was that?"

And Chris replying, deft and smooth as if he did this all the time, "No idea; looked like one of the guys from the Café. They change staff so much, I never remember their names…"

If Collin Wyler had any reply, Richard didn't linger. He slung the gym-bag with his clothing for the week over the mountain bike's handlebars and took off, pedaling in a fury, as if all the fiends in hell pursued, which wasn't far off the mark, given Sammi's penchant for spectacular tantrums when thwarted in any particular way. Or even when she just felt the need for emotional exercise.

What a difference from Kate; his lovely, even-tempered, reasonable Kate. Richard gave an extra burst of speed along the road which led by back-ways into the heart of Luna City, and for a brief time, contemplated the ways in which his life had changed – and so much for the better – since he had arrived in Luna City.

Yes, let Collin Wyler have the joy of matrimony with Sammi, he concluded, as he skimmed around the corner and into the indifferently-paved back yard at the Café. *Just let him get through this wedding.*

"I just saw ..." he began saying to Araceli, as he came in through the back door. Araceli, her notepad in one hand, coffee carafe in the other, cut him off.

"Collin and his glam bride? Yeah, they came in this morning. Auntie Conchita called me from the ranch first thing. They'll have an easy day today, getting over jet-lag, but tomorrow afternoon, SHE wants to look over the wedding cake and the venue."

"I will consider myself warned," Richard sighed. "So I'll work on assembling the cake today with Bree. Anything else? Will the Cattleman ballroom be ready for the big day?"

"If Anne and Chung have to haul chairs and iron tablecloths themselves, it will be," Araceli assured him. She vanished into the dining room, as the bell over the door jingled merrily. Richard saw that Luc and Robbie Walcott had the grill and fry station well in hand. School was done for the year; Robbie again was working full-time at the Café, and appearing to enjoy himself immensely, while Sook and Belle were away. It looked as of the elements for half a dozen good English breakfasts were sizzling happily away, and the scent of bacon and good sausage filled the air. All was in its proper place, all right with the world. All he needed do for the next six days was to duck being in the presence of soon-to-be Mrs. Wyler. In that, he had the help of friends. Lots of friends.

Now, he looked around at his kitchen crew with satisfaction: the lads at the grill, and Bree working the sauté station with the assurance of an old pro, the Battling Bs – Blanca and Beatriz – coming and going briskly with the orders. All was right with his world, in this place.

"Look, chaps ... Bree and all. I've got a bit of a favor to ask of you all..."

"Araceli already told us," Bree expertly folded together the cheese and mushroom omelet simmering and congealing in the pan before her. "If outsiders come to the Café, you're Ricardo, the Chef from Barthelona."

"Jalisco," Richard corrected her with a sigh. "Ricardo from Jalisco. And I don't speak English."

Luc frowned with the effort of thought. "But you do, Chef."

Richard sighed again. "Yes, I do – but not to strangers. People not from Luna City – for the next week."

Luc struggled with this concept; the concept won, handily. "How come?"

"Because his old GF is the bride," Beatriz explained, with a show of patience, as Bree plated the omelet, and added a side of cut fruit, and a little cup of house-made fresh salsa. "And because he used to be famous, and now he doesn't want anyone to recognize him and start bagging on him because of who he used to be." Beatriz took the plate from Bree's hands and sashayed away with it. Luc still looked baffled. Blanca sighed, and took up the cause of explaining to Luc.

"We just pretend that Richard is someone else, while all the strangers are in town, 'kay?"

"OK," Luc replied, still dubious. "Is she pretty? Your old girlfriend?"

"More like well-polished," Richard began to say, just as Araceli returned to refill her carafe and tray, overhearing this interchange.

"Yeah, she's pretty, if you like the Barbie doll, fish-face look. She's about five-ten, skinny as a rail, but with enormous breasts. Hey, size-nothing women do not naturally sprout tits the size of cantaloupes, you know? I'm betting they're not hers."

"Of course, they are hers!" Richard shot back. "She paid for them, after all. Or someone paid for them! If I remember Sammi, she was a flipping genius at getting susceptible blokes to pay for stuff that she wanted. If she ever goes into politics … Jesus, what a thought!" He got a scowl from Araceli, as she collected three full English breakfast orders from the grill.

"All I paid for was her flat reno," he added to Araceli's back, as she ferried her tray out front. "In the time that we were a couple. And some other small expenses. I am of the opinion that I got off lucky, at that; considering that what I forked out to the trendy decorator at the time would have paid for this place, freehold and all, about twice over."

"Were they real?" That was Luc, industriously slapping more bacon and sausage links on the grill. "Her breasts?"

"As near as I could tell," Richard replied, somewhat jolted by Luc even considering that aspect of the opposite sex. Luc raised his head, from his contemplation of the sizzling meats.

"The real ones feel different, you know."

"Thank you, I did not realize that," Richard fetched his jaw from somewhere about floor level. *Luc – knowing what a real female breast felt like?* Maybe his social development was farther along than everyone assumed, even if Belle Walcott and her mother were off in Dubai, visiting Clovis for the summer – now at the mid-point of the fabulously huge development project which had taken him there.

Fortunately, no further comment on the subject of female breasts, natural and artificial seemed to be required and the bell over the door of the Café chimed yet again.

The Fabulous Wedding!

People Magazine – May 25, 2018 (English Edition)

The spring wedding of Megan Markle and Prince Harry at Windsor Castle, a gala affair attended by a star-studded guest list, is unmistakably the wedding of 2018 – but the upcoming nuptials for international financier Collin Wyler and actress-model-lifestyle guru Samantha "Sammi" Colquhoun are definitely running a close second when it comes to uber-magnificent weddings!

The much-married Wyler and his fiancée claimed in a recent exclusive interview with our top lifestyle expert that this time it's for keeps. "Sammi" Colquhoun, still glamorous and shapely after three decades in the public eye, has been famed previously for her appearances in a wide range of movies and television programs, as well as the number and variety of her male companions, ranging from Prince Andrew, to actor Phillip Noel-Barrett and celebrity chef Rich Hall, among others. Her charm is infinite, and never stales – or so claim a wide circle of her fans and admirers.

"It is like a new start for the both of us," she confided, in that wide-ranging interview. "After so long a time, and so many false starts – we're ready to make a permanent commitment; you know, the deep peace of the marriage bed after the hurly-burly of the chaise lounge. I believe that we really have love, this time – after so many false starts for us both! We have such confidence in the future that we have decided to go all-out! Collie—you know, that is the intimate pet-name which his nearest and dearest have for him – he is taking care of everything! Such devotion; like Romeo and Juliet, except for the messy dying part in a tomb, of course! I have the loveliest dress, from Alexander McQueen's top designer – you know, they did the Duchess of Cambridge's dress – but for me, they did something much more suitable for an older bride such as myself. Not that her dress wasn't perfect, but so plain – and mine is absolutely a top secret until The Day!"

We asked about the venue for the wedding, which until this very week has been a top secret to the happy couples' closest friends, who were sent elaborate invitations which contained a date and time, but no address, and only a number to call, where Collin Wyler's staff would make the appropriate reservations, and inform the invitees on the day when they needed to travel. Yet Sammi was happy to confide in us.

"Collie's home, of course! We wanted to keep it a surprise for everyone! It's in Texas, can you imagine? I would have been pleased with a wedding at Skibo Castle – you know, that was where Madonna married Guy Ritchie! I was a guest then – oh, it was so romantic, and Collie is a member of the Carnegie Club, of course it would have been perfect … but he insisted on being married at his father's ranch! Such a sentimental darling, and he assured me that there aren't muddy streets with those tumbleweeds rolling through them, and gunfights every morning and afternoon. And the husband of my dearest American chum grew up there – you know Susannah Wyatt-Gonzales, who is my matron of honor? Suze and her husband tell me it's all quite ordinary and civilized, but quaint beyond belief! Imagine – there is no Harvey Nichols in Luna City! But Collie has his heart set on a wedding there. I have seen the pictures of the estate – it's quite palatial!"

"A cattle ranch? Indeed?" our interviewer inquired. "Like Dallas, that old television series?"

"Not a bit of it!" Sammi insisted. "It <u>is</u> a cattle ranch, but the old house is this magnificent Southern plantation mansion that Collie says was copied from some old pile in Louisiana, with columns all the way around, and landscaped gardens that are to die for! Collie's mother designed the formal gardens simply ages ago, and they are the very picture of magnificence! The pictures that Collie showed me are every bit as fine as any English garden. We're going to be married in the garden, before all of our friends, standing before this marvelous rustic pavilion all overgrown with roses … and since it is not an English summer, we can be certain of the weather! And then we will have a supper and a ball at this wonderful old-fashioned hotel in town, which has just reopened after years! Most of our guests are staying there – Collie has reserved all the guest rooms for our party, so of course we can simply dance the night away."

Our interviewer and staff wish Sammi and her husband-to-be the very best on their special day, which will be June 21th, Mid-summer Day in the Americas.

Guest Quarters

Not to put a fine point upon it, the stay in Chris' flat over the old garage and stable at the McAllister place promised to be mildly enjoyable. The flat was roomy – several degrees roomier than the Airstream; one large sitting room with a gallery kitchen in one corner, several bedrooms and a full bath, complete with a monumental claw-footed iron tub. It had once housed the family which had comprised the McAllister household domestic staff, back in the day when ordinary middle-class families had domestic staff. Windows, at both back and front of the narrow structure, gave on a view of Miss Letty's spectacular gardens and a low woodland beyond, all at their best until the late summer heat turned all to mildly crispy. Although there was the distant noise of traffic on the main road – but Richard was accustomed to the hum and honkings of vehicular traffic. So was Chris.

"I really feel at home, when I hear the crunch of fenders, and the sounds of sirens," Chris had assured him once.

"Got a frozen pizza ready to start warming in the oven," Chris said, when Richard and Ozzie arrived. Chris himself "The good kind; I added extra mushrooms and cheese. Set a spell, Ricardo. You look beat. Wanna beer?"

"I thought you'd never ask."

Chris waved a careless hand from where he lounged in an overstuffed chair, before the sixteen-light window looking toward the west and a sky from which the color was swiftly fading to a blue the color of Chris' jeans. "Help yourself, man. Top shelf in the fridge but if you prefer it warm, there's a six-pack in the cupboard to the left. We'll chow down in about half an hour. I'll hit the sack early, but if you wanna watch TV, it's all yours. Don't worry about waking me up in the morning; I like get in a good few miles in the morning when it's cooler, before I get to the Tip-Top."

"A good lager is best chilled," Richard sniffed; finding his own bottle, he settled into the other, slightly less battered chair. Meanwhile, Ozzie – Ozymandias-King-of-Kings – made a leisurely patrol of his new perimeter as twilight fell on that Tuesday evening. Outside, a few moths orbited in the glow of the lights over the stair landing. "Thanks for this hospitality. I scarpered just in the nick of time this morning at the Tip-Top. Did they buy your story that I was just a working sod from the Café?"

"Gotta be situationally-aware at all times," Chris agreed. "Yeah, I think they did, although I don't know that your old girlfriend bought it entirely. She looked kinda skeptical, and Collin gave me a look. The man is sharp, but he had his back turned toward the door the whole time. Ya got that going for ya; he's met you before, hasn't he?"

"Yeah, I played a round of golf with Clovis and Doc and him, a while back."

"He'll know you again, then," Chris scowled, deep in thought. "I guess you'll be dodging them both. Good luck with that, pal."

"The planning is already done," Richard sank about a third of his lager. "He deputized all that to Chung McNamara, who is almost insanely competent. Araceli actually penned her name on the contract, so I'm in the clear. Me, I can slink off to the kitchen until it's all over, knowing that the both Collin and Sammi will have no earthly reason to come looking for me, when they have the wedding and hob-nobbing with all their guests to attend to."

"If you say so," Chris finished the last of his bottle, and got up from his chair. "I'm gonna start the pizza now. You want another?"

"When I finish this," Richard answered, and contemplated the twilight garden below the window. "The cake is all done – good lord, what a monstrosity. We were working on it this afternoon, young Bree and I. Anne Dubois had a call from Sammi, wanting to see it. I'll be safely out of the way, of course. Young Bree will have the honor and credit for being on hand for the royal visit, of course. Only fair, as she did most of those flowers. A sharp child, and a dab hand with the sugar paste."

Chris padded back from the refrigerator with a beer bottle in each hand. "Here ya go, save me a trip. So, three days to the wedding. Whaddya gonna do until then?"

"Work like a …. Umm, fiend," Richard replied, hastily editing what it was that he was going to work like as the comparison was about to depart his lips. "First in the Café kitchen, doing all the prep. And then – transport everything to the Cattleman, for the final day. It's a gorgeous kitchen – Lew's chaps did everything up brown, but it's still … everything in the Café kitchen is exactly where I know it is. I could cook a six-course meal there blind-folded. But on tomorrow, we transfer operations to the Cattleman for the final push. What with their staff, and the general hurly-burly of an event like this, I can count absolutely on being lost in the scrum. Have you ever seen the back of the house, with an event for three hundred guests going on, all to be served at once? Controlled chaos, my friend; controlled chaos. The bride and groom will be too damn busy at front and center to invade the kitchen at that time, and any of the gossip-grubbing fraternity who try it are likely to be trampled in the rush. And … we have sharp knives, hot burners and very heavy pans and plates at hand to repel all boarders." He chuckled, nastily. "The damage that can be done with a hot *crème brûlée* salamander … I'll leave that to your imagination, of course."

Chris shuddered. "I already know what burned human flesh smells like, thanks. Can we talk about something else, while I still have an appetite?"

"Of course!" Richard waved the empty lager bottle, airily. "Forgive that I spoke so casually. But I'll be fine, once I get through the next couple of days. The payment for this one job will make it so worth all the agony. When I departed London for these climes, so many years ago … my bank accounts there were pillaged mercilessly by various parties after the crash of my restaurant endeavor. It will be a relief to me to have a bulging personal account once again … So – any truth to the rumor that one of the bridesmaids will be a Kardashian?"

Chris leered, in a most lubricious manner. "Nope – worse luck. Me being me … I might have an excellent chance at tapping some of that! But my ambitions are more modest, these days. There are some fine-looking women hanging around the local marathon scene; I'll stick to what might be within my grasp. And if she has amazing skills, I will so count myself lucky."

"Lucky if they don't call you a chauvinist pig," Richard contemplated his second lager, mildly depressed as to mood. There were indeed splendid women in Luna City; Chris' misfortune was that just about all of them were already married, well-beyond the age of serious consideration, or well below it. He himself had Kate, at least; as far as he knew, Chris had nothing but his job at the Tip-Top, and his schedule of marathons.

"I'll take that chance," Chris replied. "Pizza will be done in twenty minutes or so – soon enough for ya? I even got a can of tuna for your little buddy. If he catches a mouse or two over the next week, I can see my way clear to offering him a can every evening as a reward."

"Make it a small can," Richard warned. "Tuna gives him gas. If he burps or farts after eating it, that'll clear the room."

"I'll take my chances," Chris popped the cap on his beer, and held it up in a mock toast, in Richard's direction. "To you, pal – good luck, fair skies and following seas." He stretched and yawned, hugely.

"Thanks for the hospitality," Richard went on a quick mental search for his manners and located them belatedly. "Couldn't have endured this week without having a bolt-hole like this."

"Hey, us adopted sons of Luna City got to stick together," Chris waved his beer bottle as if it meant a small consideration. "Your secrets are safe with me, pal."

"Appreciated." Richard lifted his own bottle, just as Ozzie finished his patrol, and leaped silently onto the arm of the chair.

Yes – he had friends in Luna City.

The Wyler Wedding Party

On the pre-dawn morrow, Richard flung a leg over the saddle of his bicycle. Ozzie, somewhat unusually, declined to accompany him, obviously finding the prospects of a mouse-hunt in the old stables-and-mews-flat a more enticing prospect than his usual haunts at the back of the Café.

"Your choice, chum," Richard said, as he pedaled away. He looked over his shoulder, seeing Ozzie trotting purposefully into the lower level, where one of the big doors had been left half-open – the garage which had once housed a couple of horses, and then the late Professor McAllister's 1949 Plymouth sedan, before Miss Letty had sold the vehicle to an aficionado of vintage automobiles. Doubtless, the mouse-hunting potential in an ancient stable was off the charts.

Mouse-hunting – at this moment, he felt considerable sympathy for the mice. He was a mouse himself, wary, whiskers all-atwitch. The cats of the media weren't hunting him specifically, he knew. But they were here in Luna City, and if they were baffled of their main prey …Their eyes, their pitiless lenses could not fall upon him! He must be wary, swift, elusive over the following days, just like those mice escaping Ozzie. Araceli had already showed him the issue of *People Magazine*, containing the interview with Sammi on one of the back pages – that feckless wench! Richard swore silently to himself when he read it, lest Araceli be offended. The kitchen was his refuge, the bustle of preparation there a camouflage. There he could do the necessary work, and the work necessary for the grand event at the Cattleman eventually took over, blotting out all those lesser concerns. No matter that Sammi, self-centered, career-oriented, faithless Sammi, was going to be married with all flamboyant ceremony on Thursday, Mid-summer, *Litho*-Day, or that her new mark – er, her husband – Collin Wyler, the International Economic Master of the Universe was footing the bill. This was his calling, his duty. His mission? Food, of the finest possible level of creation, a smooth presentation of the same, an eventless event … and of course the substantial paycheck from the client. Richard reckoned that eventually, some of the parties left hanging in the Carême debacle might come calling for their pound of flesh and economic losses. Better be able to have something in funds to throw them, in that eventuality, in the form of his share of the profits from the Wyler event, and from other special events at the Cattleman. For all he knew, what he had left behind in his English accounts had been ravaged in the manner of the Vandals of old, which was why he had never drawn on them, in settling into his new life. There was much to be said for hard and somewhat well-paid work, a minimal social life and no expensive hobbies, he thought, as he pedaled through the scattered streets of Luna City. He came up on Town Square, lighted as if of a town of old, with a bare handful of gas lamps, casting a mellow golden light against the dark oak boughs. *(The bulbs in the old standards were of the expensive golden flickering sort, which gave the illusion of antiquity. The Town Council had voted willingly for this extra expense to the city budget, both because many of the members of the Council had social media accounts which stressed the scenic appeal of Town Square, and because a few, to include Mayor Martin Abernathy, lived in or rented out apartments over the shops in the Square, and the scenic aspect of the old flickering lamps was a part of the aesthetic appeal.)*

As he crossed past the façade of the Cattleman, looming over the eastern side of Town Square, he spotted a pair of vans parked under the shelter of the trees opposite – each with a satellite dish mounted on their roofs, and the sides adorned with the logos of two different television stations. *The game's afoot, Watson!* There was another van with the logo of a very upscale florist parked in front of the Cattleman, and two men in overalls bringing in box after box on industrial dollies. Even as he pedaled away, diving into the safety of a side street leading around to the back of that rank of storefronts which included the Café, yet another television van joined the first pair.

A more than excellent excuse to stay buried in the kitchen.

"We'll handle the Café up through the lunch rush," Richard directed his people – Beatriz and Blanca, Araceli and Bree, Robbie and Luc, the last two blinking in the bright lights as they came in through the back door. "And then – Robbie, you'll handle the prix-fixe supper selection with Beatriz and Blanca, while all other hands fall-too at the Cattleman. Close up the Café and join us at seven. I don't think we'll have too many customers tonight. Everyone will be at the Cattleman, either at the banquet, or in the restaurant." He looked around at his kitchen and front-house staff, feeling absurdly like he was about to blow a whistle and lead them over the top into No-Man's Land. "Pace yourselves, ladies and gentles. It's going to be a long, hard day. The official ribbon-cutting for the Cattleman is at two PM sharp. Likely we'll be packing in customers until then. Afterwards; who knows?"

"On it, Chef!" Robbie answered, irrepressibly cheerful, and echoed by the others. "We can do it!"

Ah, the resilience of youth, Richard thought sourly to himself. It was so unfair that all that energy was wasted on youth – when he could have used a heaping ration of it himself.

"I expect nothing less," he said, just as the bell over the Café door chimed. Araceli caught up the newly-filled carafe, saying, "It's Roman and his guys – full English for four."

"On it," Luc fired up the griddle and Richard advised again,

"Pace yourselves!"

Plunged into the maelstrom of work – that of the ordinary day, and that of the special banquet, Richard did emerge for air, very briefly during the afternoon, after transferring operations to the cavernous kitchen of the refurbished hotel.

"It's so large!" Bree exclaimed, twirling like a ballerina, with her arms spread out. "We could do a simply humongous banquet in here! Twice the size of the Wyler wedding supper!"

"Indeed," Richard agreed. "The regular dining room staff will be assisting us tonight, as the Cattleman restaurant proper will not officially open for meal service until tomorrow morning, and only for serving guests. Still, we will have our work cut out for us – and in a kitchen we are barely familiar with …it's a challenge," he added almost to himself. "One is only truly, ultimately comfortable, working in a space which one knows intimately. Still – we have accomplished all the prep-work…"

"'Allo, cher!" That was Lew Dubois, unexpectedly dapper in formal evening garb, an archaic bow-tie crowning his pleated shirtfront. "Over the first hurdle, are we not? And now ready for the home-stretch in this magnificent race!"

"Lew!" Richard exclaimed. "Is all ready and waiting for the event tonight? Madame Dubois has been so very helpful – I know that I should regret that her splendid French vacation was cut short, but I am so very relieved that both of you are back in harness, as it were. This whole project is of such importance – the bungling of that dreadful Mason woman might have damaged it beyond all repair!"

"Thank you, cher!" Lew beamed upon them all impartially. "I should thank you once more for retrieving the *fixtures Lalique*! If not for your casual remark to M'seur Roman Gonzalez, then the theft of the lights might have gone unnoticed, or at too late for us to retrieve them! Come and admire them; yes, my dear Richard and your wonderful staff! Take a moment to revel in the splendor, now that the ballroom and the dining room are properly adorned!"

"May as well," Richard agreed, since it was at the point where he and his kitchen brigade could take a few moments away from kitchen labors to see the venue where triumph awaited. With a small flourish, Lew bowed and led the way, out from the swinging double doors between the kitchen and the old dining room.

"Oh, how very nice!" Araceli breathed, followed by a murmur of appreciative agreement by the other Café staff. They had only seen it empty, unadorned. Now it was very nice – more than that, it was splendid, on a most royal level; a vista of ice-white tablecloths, precisely-arranged chairs of an antique and pleasing design, and flowers in silver vases and epergnes, white, pink and dark red roses and trailing stems of white jasmine which lent their faint scent enticingly to the atmosphere. The wedding cake towered over the long serving table, the garland of sugar flowers wound around the layers and crowning the topmost layer – the intended cynosure of all eyes, once the room filled with guests awaiting the presence of the bride and groom. The prized chandeliers hung overhead, each a vision of glittering ice-etched glass leaves and gleaming silver branches casting a warm glow.

"This is absolutely splendid," Richard tried to keep as much envy as possible from his voice. Yes, Carême was like this, on that evening when his entire world crashed into flames. "I can hardly believe that such a place as this can exist in Luna City. You are to be congratulated for your vision, Lew, and for being able to carry it out against the odds."

Lew spread his hands in a deprecating gesture. "I cannot justly claim all credit, cher. I had the assistance of many who shared in this grand achievement. Now – through here, you will see a private passage between the dining room and into the ballroom. The restrooms are through there, should any guests inquire. We shall go through the lobby…"

Again, the murmurs of awe and admiration from Richard's staff: the lobby had been one of the first of the public rooms renovated. It had also been one of the least decayed, so that its appearance was not so much changed as it was primped and polished to best effect. Bianca Gonzalez looked across from the check-in desk and smiled, cutting short an intense conversation with Chung McNamara, who leaned elegantly against the carved Art Nouveau splendors of said desk.

"Hi, Lew – everything is ready for Mr. Wyler's first guests! Mr. McNamara wanted to be here to great them as they arrived from the airport."

"Good!" Lew beamed impartially upon them both. "The formal ribbon-cutting is in fifteen minutes – but behold now the ballroom! The piece de resistance!"

He led the troop across the lobby, to where the double doors to the ballroom stood open. Even Bree, not often at a loss for words, was struck speechless.

Araceli only whispered, "Oh … My! I so wish that Pat and I could have had our wedding reception here!"

The ballroom presented an even grander spectacle than the dining room, adorned with even more flowers, garlands of roses, swags of roses, lilies, jasmine and greenery between each pillar surrounding the room. The small stage, outfitted now for the musicians who would play for dancing later in the evening, was also a bower of roses and ferns. An army of small, spindly chairs lined the walls, chairs upholstered with ivory and dark red brocade which matched the stage curtains. All was in readiness for the grand moment, a wedding ball in the old-fashioned style; lively music, skirts swirling across the polished golden-parquet dance floor, gentlemen bowing over their partners' elegantly gloved hands, champagne flowing like spring-water. Richard moistened his lips.

"There are movie directors who would kill to film a sequence in this place," he observed, and Araceli snorted.

"The last one who tried that got his jaw broken in two places!" She sighed, in mild regret. "All right, kids – for us, our job today is just beginning. Let's get to it, enough of the ooing and ahhing. We'll have dozens of more chances, now that the Cattleman is opening for business again."

With that, Richard and his crew got back to work.

He purposefully buried himself in that work, drawing the clamor, heat, the purposeful hustle of the kitchen around him as a kind of armor, absorbed in the moment, relishing the wordless teamwork that made producing three hundred meals, plating and serving them all at once seem like something accomplished by magic. A few words of direction, a blast of heat from the opened oven as he removed the pans of beef tenderloins to rest on the worktable, tented with aluminum foil, swift hands wielding serving tongs, a towel wiping away a spill of sauce, a grin from Robbie as he ladled out consume into an endless array of soup bowls and Bee scattered garnishes on each as the waitresses carried away filled trays with the practiced grace of ballet dancers, weaving and bending through the kitchen, returning for another full tray.

His crew were on top of their game; Luc, Robbie, Bree and himself. The regular Cattleman front of the house staff were on-point as well. He thought he recognized some of them. Gonzales and Gonzalez sons and daughters, cousins and sisters; swift, silent, adept! His heart sang within him, knowing that with this event, Luna City might yet be one of those minor stars in the culinary firmament – outwardly modest, yet delighting the palates of the discriminating and appreciative. His vision of a country Carême was still a possibility. With Lew's luxury boutique hotel, and the occasional special project such as this … really, if he had not been so dedicated to the Café and grateful to Doc Wyler and Miss Letty, and fearful of exposure in the international tabloids, he would have seriously considered Lew's offer to be the resident chef in the Cattleman's restaurant. Having all the glories of this establishment at his command was a heady thought.

Which, with some small effort, he put aside that luscious temptation. That way led again into celebrity hell. A man must know his limitations, to quote from one of those movies which Chris was watching the other night when Richard returned from work.

Speaking of limitations … mid-evening, the wedding supper in full swing in the Cattleman dining room, and his staff were in the pause after serving up the main course and side accompaniments. His bladder demanded attendance and relief.

"Personal break," he muttered to Araceli. "Back in a sec."

"Take five, relax, and breathe, Chef," she replied. "The nearest bathroom is off the corridor to the ballroom. We're OK for the moment."

Richard took her immediate advice and looked around the vast kitchen. Yes – the frantic, yet controlled rush had slacked off. From the faint sound of music wafting in from the live band in the ballroom, the dancing was set to begin; any time now, as soon as the ritual of cutting the cake was done. Richard couldn't imagine whatever ritual was involved in this case. Was Collin Wyler going to slice the cake with a metal-detector? That would … well, it would be an interesting spectacle for Sammi, if even technologically possible.

He came out of the male-designated bathroom, considerably relieved as to bladder and mood, just at the very moment that a woman – a tall and artificially-lovely blonde woman, a woman arrayed in an elaborate ivory-satin gown – emerged from the Ladies'.

"Rich!" she exclaimed, with delight. "You're here! A little bird told me that you would be – and there you are!"

(To be continued – of course!)

Luna City Behind the 8 Ball

Brief Encounters

"Rich!" the willowy blonde woman in a superbly-cut ivory satin gown exclaimed, in delight. "You're here! A little bird told me that you would be – and there you are!"

Richard nearly jumped from his own skin – all too familiar, that voice, adorned with the plummy accents of an expensively-educated woman from the Home Counties. He turned, just barely able to affect an expression of mild puzzlement; a veil behind which he was thinking furiously. Samantha. Samantha Colquhoun, the former Page-3 girl now better known as Sammi, famous for being famous, presently famous for being the latest in a long string of Mrs. Collin Wylers. One of Rich's own and most notorious … companions. Live-in lovers. Regular escorts. Whatever the current euphemism was. Of one thing he desired more in the world, it was to never, ever encounter her again, in any guise and name.

"Que?" he stammered, recalling in a rush Araceli's suggestion that he pretend to be … no, not Manuel from Barcelona, but … yes, that was it. Ricardo from Jalisco, and … "*No habla Ingles…*" he offered, seeing the faint flicker of doubt cloud Sammi's perfectly made-up countenance. Almost there! He searched his mind for any phrases in Spanish he might throw into the mix. "*Limpie sus pies…Levántate y brilla!*" he gabbled. Yes, that should do the trick; commanding mottoes worked into those little wool work-rugs created by Abuelita Adeliza, the doyenne and ultimate ruler of the whole entwined network of Gonzalezes and Gonzaleses in Luna City. If Abuelita's queenly power had any juice at all…

Sammi's perfect, pale and heart-shaped face was clouded with doubt.

"But you're not Rich?" she ventured. Richard shrugged elaborately.

"*Que?*" he replied again, hoping that a) he wasn't overdoing it, and b) that Sammi did not retain any memory of watching Fawlty Towers, even if she had appeared once on the series as a guest with three lines of dialog. "*Levántate y brilla!*" The strains of a Lehar waltz drifted in from the ballroom, accompanied by laughter, and the gentle clinking of expensive crystal and silverware. It sounded as if the dancing was well underway. Behind Richard, another door – the door into the kitchen – opened and closed with an almost silent pneumatic breath. To his enormous unspoken relief, Araceli appeared, almost silent in her thick-soled trainers. He shook his head, shrugged again, and repeated, "*Limpie sues pies…*"

Sammi's gaze went from Richard, to his assistant chef and sometime Café manager – who, bless her, was insanely quick on the uptake.

"Chef, te buscan en la cocina!" Araceli commanded, adding in deliberately slow, carefully enunciated English. "They need you in the kitchen, Chef."

"Gracias," Richard mumbled, thereby completely exhausting his Spanish vocabulary, as Araceli assumed command of the situation.

"He's from Jalisco; he doesn't understand much English," she added, by way of apology to Sammi. "Just enough to cook. Good thing that we all 'round here speak Spanish anyway. Is there something I can help you with, Mrs. Wyler? Is everything OK out front?"

"Yes," Sammi still sounded theatrically baffled. She lifted a manicured hand to her expertly Botoxed and un-furrowed brow, brushing back a wisp of blond hair, which had been quite content, thank you, to languish where it had been combed back into a perfect Grace Kelly knot under a pearl and platinum tiara. "But … he looks so like an old chum of mine, at a distance. From England, you know. I was so certain…"

"No, this is Ricardo from Jalisco," Araceli replied, giving Richard a surreptitious nudge from her sharp and expert elbow. "Been with us for … I don't know how many years now. And he's never learned much English. Seriously, we think he must be a bit retarded, or something but he's a darned good pastry cook. The cinnamon rolls of his at the Café are to die for. Seriously." Araceli shot a barbed look at Richard, who gratefully took the hint, although not going so far as to tug, serf-like, at his nonexistent forelock; a mere deferential nod sufficed before he set his steps kitchenwards. Although as he did so, he overheard Araceli ask, with a gratifying show of customer-relations concern,

"Is everything satisfactory, Mrs. Wyler? The Cattleman reopened officially just this afternoon, and this is our first big event in this venue. You should let us know about any problems you have seen – if we can't fix it tonight, at least we can take note for the next wedding…"

"No," Richard heard over his shoulder, as Sammi sighed in rapture. "It's all been perfect, the loveliest wedding dream come to life that I have ever had. Our cake was a marvel – so much what my … friend would have done for me. I so believed that it was his secret gift. We broke up – under the most tragic of circumstances – but we are still perfect good friends, you know!"

"Our catering team does excellent work," Araceli replied, and then the door to the kitchen closed behind Richard. He heaved a sigh of profound relief, leaning his back upon the doorjamb.

God, that had been a close one, he thought, and then; *Do I really look that different now, that Sammi could be convinced I was Ricardo from Jalisco? Well, she was always as thick as a plank, and nearsighted as well, but you'd think that she wouldn't have been fooled so readily, when it came to a man she had been intimate with on every level for two years and some… Do I really look that different?*

A moment later, Araceli burst through the kitchen door, exclaiming, "Whew – that was a close one, Chef! Aren't you glad that I thought of the Ricardo-from-Jalisco dodge! What were the chances that she would catch you, coming out of the men's restroom! Though, I think she bought it, hook, line and sinker."

"Alas, Miss Colquhoun-that-was, was never known for the power of her intellect," Richard admitted. "In fact, rather the reverse."

Araceli barked a short laugh. "Beats me what you ever saw in that *puta*, Ricardo; you're a smart man. From what Abuelita says, she had her claws into you real good – guys, you think with your …"

"Sammi had amazing skills in other ways," Richard answered, annoyed at this late date over how devotedly Abuelita Adeliza had followed his once-magnificent career as an international celebrity chef. "And you just now termed me as 'a bit retarded'! Pray, what is the merit in that bit of calumny?"

"You had just told her, in Spanish, to 'wipe her feet,' Araceli replied.

"You have a point … set and match," Richard yielded ungracefully. "Do I really look that different now, from when I was on all those ghastly cooking shows?"

Araceli shot him another one of those basilisk-looks. "You do, at that, Chef. You're thinner, and fit as all get-out, from riding that bicycle back and forth. Clean-shaven, rather than that designer stubble – I swear, it made you look like the cover of a romance novel. And tanned – about as dark as Patrick, instead of looking like sunshine would make you curl up and burst into flames like a vampire. You look like a whole different person. Not Rich Hall anymore – just Ricardo. You're much better off here, Chef. And much better off with Katie. Is it OK if we let the staff have dinner, now that the wedding cake has been plated and sent out?"

"Yeah, perfect," Richard agreed – and yes, now that it was mid-evening, and all was done but the final run-through of the small dessert plates upon which the magnificent five-tiered wedding cake had been served – his staff could settle down to their own meal. The back-stage offices of the Cattleman included a spartan room suitable for a staff dining-space, or conference room; two long tables with lots of chairs, all depressingly modern, in contrast to the Belle Epoque splendors on display at the front of the house. Still – gratitude was owed, and he brought it all to bear, when he said, "Thank you, Araceli – all this couldn't have been possible without your help."

"I'll add that to my bill," Araceli replied.

No, he could never get the last word with her.

The kitchen was calming down; only the one pearl-diver on staff was still at work, processing the last of dinner plates and wine glasses, and a full tray of small dessert plates, adorned with the crumbs and frosting from the grand wedding cake. Richard helped himself to a smidge of beef tornedos Rossini, a few boiled baby potatoes, crab mousse, and some salad, and carried his plate into the staff room, where he found – to his mild astonishment – Lew Dubois, tucking into his own supper with considerable gusto.

The chief local manager of Mills Farm, and one of the managing directors of the parent company, clad in formal black evening gear and splendidly-knotted black silk necktie, was notorious for turning up in working gear and turning his hand to any task going, generally the grubbier and more menial the better. An experienced manager of VPI's various high-end international resort properties, Lew was single-handedly responsible for the miraculous renovation and revival of the Cattleman Hotel. This was the man who was also responsible for Mills Farm not turning into some ghastly modern water-park at the bidding of the multinational corporation who was the second (or possibly the third-biggest) land-owner and employer in the area. It was only expected that he would now eating with the behind-the-scenes restaurant staff. Richard had to hand it to him; the man knew how to lead from the front, his craggy-late-middle-aged countenance at decided odds with the elegance of his evening attire.

"H'lo, Lew," Richard said, as he set his own plate down at the next place at the unadorned utility table. "I take it that everything is going well? My old ex-girlfriend, the bride – she is content? She spoke with Araceli just now, and says that everything was lovely, a wedding dream come true. You have heard nothing otherwise? From Mr. Wyler, or Mr. McNamara?"

"No, cher Richard," Lew replied, a-beam with contentment. "The arrangements for the ballroom were of the perfection that my dear wife and I require of our staff to achieve, new as many of them are to this place. The supper … sublime. Not even in France – our beautiful France – could this splendid meal of yours be equaled! Your skills in the kitchen have not rusticated in the slightest. For that we are grateful."

"I have my brief moments," Richard mumbled, feeling the usual English embarrassment at being fulsomely complimented. He regarded his plate – yes, his staff at the Café had outdone themselves, in the manner which he had come to expect. Obviously, Lew had come to expect the same. Everything perfect; perfectly seasoned, perfectly cooked, expertly and attractively-plated; this was what he expected, had always expected. Animals eat – but humans dine. There was a galaxy of difference between those two concepts.

"Are you reconsidering my offer, cher Richard?" Lew ventured, after a pleasant moment in which the two of them forked in tornedos Rossini and crab mousse. "My offer to be the chef-in-residence, to command this establishment in every detail…"

"No," Richard replied. Yes, Lew had dangled that temptation before him several times … And yes, the prospect was alluring; managing chef of an upscale resort, and the show-piece being their destination restaurant … but this was Texas. This was Luna City, Texas. Richard had arrived there in a drunken, broken-down, almost catatonic state. In a handshake deal with the small-town owners of the Café on the following morning, he had been offered a second chance. Miss Letty and Doc Wyler had been honest and fair-dealing with him, away and beyond what he deserved. A second chance at life, the universe and everything, and it had all – so far – turned out well. He had since fled any passing brush at revived celebrity with the alacrity of a hemophiliac dodging a date with a thirsty vampire, and would continue to do so, against temptations offered by VPI, or any other dark Mephistopheles. "You may as well stop asking me, Lew. I haven't changed my stance on that; yes, the occasional special event, on the same footing as my other catering clients."

"There is no harm in asking, yet one more time," Lew grinned, utterly unoffended. "Having worked this evening in the splendid new Cattleman, I thought that you might be considering your options anew."

"No offense taken, Lew. You're in business, just like I am."

"True, mon vieux," Lew replied, and they consumed the rest of their meal in companionable silence – a silence not shared by the others at the table, who came and went as their scattered duties allowed. It didn't escape Richard's notice – alerted by the flint-hard gaze of Araceli – that Bianca of the Clan Gonzalez, now a desk clerk/concierge at the Cattleman, came in with the dapper Chung McNamara, now Clovis Wyler's multi-skilled Australian-Chinese personal assistant. They were sharing what appeared to be a staff tête-à-tête over their supper plates at the end of the other table. Richard regarded this spectacle with a certain degree of distaste. In his bitter experience romantic attachments between staff members, or staff and outsiders were fraught with potential for disaster, especially of the correspondents had no sense of discretion or responsibility. Here in Luna City, it was the attachment between Luc Massie, assistant chef and sometime musician, and Belle, the daughter of Sook and Clovis Walcott. And he often wondered about the exact nature of the friendship between his two teenage apprentices, Robbie Walcott and Bree Grant. In his previous life, the unrequited affections of an assistant chef for some top-tier society bint had spelled unmitigated disaster at the calamity-ridden launch of his all-star London restaurant, Carême.

"Young love," Richard nudged Lew and directed the latters' attention towards the young couple with a jerk of his chin. "Hope it doesn't mean you'll be looking for a new concierge, tout suite."

"I think not," Lew replied, with serene unconcern. "Our Mademoiselle Bianca is a most level-headed young lady – and while M'sieur McNamara is a gentleman of the most charming and exotic, I do not believe either party will be tempted into … a situation and a relationship which will excite the frenzy of the romantically imaginative."

"Your word to God's ear," Richard thought that Bianca and Chung certainly looked chummy enough. Bianca, elegant and understated in black with a discrete strand of pearls around her neck, and hair done up in an Aubrey Hepburn roll on the top of her head was certainly attractive enough for a second look from any man possessed of a libido. And Araceli was scowling – not a good sign. There were altogether too many sharp knives in this kitchen, and in the Café and quite enough professional cooking gear of a construction sufficiently heavy to constitute a deadly weapon when wielded by a determined hand.

"Not to be concerned, mon vieux," Lew scraped up the last of the gravy from his plate with a scrap of bread and consulted his expensively discreet wristwatch. "This triumph for you and your staff is complete – the hour has come for you all to wend your way home … and you will forgive me for having made that journey most comfortable. And added some personal tokens of appreciation, from my wife and myself, on behalf of Venue Properties. I took it upon myself," Lew added. "Your people should wrap up their duties here in the kitchen and be out in front of the hotel at ten precisely … that is, in twenty-one minutes. Your carriage awaits at that hour."

"What have you …" Richard demanded, and Lew grinned.

"It is a surprise. At my expense. Enjoy, cher."

Their work being all but done, and those of his staff primarily finishing their own evening meal, it took only half that time for Richard to pass the word to his all-but-exhausted staff. Even Robbie and Bree – young and superhumanly energetic – were stifling yawns, as they put off their work aprons and collected their outer garments and handbags from the Cattleman's office, or from around the corner at the Café. There was no need to whistle for Ozzie, better known as Ozymandias-King-of-Kings, for he had chosen to spend this long day mouse-hunting in the old stables/garage at the McAllister place. Richard, in attempting to hide out from any media interest in the grand Wyler-Colquhoun wedding, had bunked in with Chris for the duration. And in any case, he could walk to work in the morning, as it was only a matter of a few blocks.

The moon sailed over the trees in Town Square, a great silver orb attended by a few faint wisps of cloud, bathing the sleeping Square in pallid moonlight, the evening itself still cooling from the heat of summer; it was, Richard thought, like a warm summer day in the Bickley of his childhood. Sounds of music and laughter in the hotel ballroom echoed pleasantly in the building behind them, as Richard, with Luc, Araceli, the B's, Robbie and Bree waited under the archaic glass awning over the massive double door entrance to the Cattleman, where they were joined by Bianca.

"Mr. D. said I should go with y'all, since my shift is done," she explained, although that did not explain the hovering Chung McNamara, who alternated checking his iPhone with speaking in a flirtatious undertone to Bianca. He was the only male among them still seeming fresh and un-smirched by hours of messy labor in a hot kitchen, dapper in his bespoke tailored linen suit, Still, he had likely been in attendance on his employer for even longer than the others had been at their work. Around the perimeter of the Square, golden lamplight flickered in the antique street globes which adorned the streets which delineated it. A few lighted windows in second- and third-floor windows overlooked the quiet Square; there were people still awake. Across the road, directly in front of the hotel, a big hole had been excavated, to accommodate a magnificent cypress tree, which stood like a princess attended by a court of oak trees – all part of the renovations, apparently.

"It was nice of Lew to send us home in taxis at his expense," Araceli ventured. "Saves me the walk." She sighed, deep and heartfelt. "I swear, I think I have walked a marathon, today … but it was all worth it. The Café is on the map, for sure! I'd work an event here at the Cattleman any time. We did good here today, Chef – even better than at the Boathouse."

"And all without Sook Walcott screaming at us," Richard nodded, as a pair of headlights appeared at the corner, flaring large and bright, masking the vehicle which they heralded. "It's ten – I hope that's our taxi. Lew was very exact about the time."

The lights adorned an enormous, royal black extended limousine – a vehicle so extended that it nearly rivaled the smallest and oldest of the Luna City ISD school busses. This splendid automobile pulled grandly to a stop before the doors of the Cattleman, and Araceli observed,

"Oh, that's one of Uncle Tony's. Handles like a beast, and slurps gas as if there were no peak oil, but the customers love it for big weddings and proms. Mr. Walcott must have ordered it for their getaway…"

"Oh, shit," Richard said, and then Berto Gonzales emerged from the driver-side; comically-innocent Berto in driver-livery, with a nametag over his left pocket, opening the passenger-side doors with a flourish.

"Hi, 'Celi, Ricardo – I'm your driver for this evening. Mr. Dubois said to take a couple of rounds around the Square, take some time to unwind, before delivering you all home. There's champagne in the 'fridge, so help yourselves … and, um … he and Mrs. Dubois left a gift basket for each of you, with your names on them, by way of thanks for making the opening event at the new Cattleman such a success. So, um …"

"Champagne!" Bianca squealed. She kissed Chung – on his cheek with enthusiasm which must have given him some pleasure, yet with a brevity which kept Araceli from permanently marking him with whatever kitchen implements might come to hand, even if she had to run back into the Cattleman to fetch them. "'Bye – see you tomorrow, OK? Mr. Dubois is so good to work for; now you see why we all love him to bits!"

"Take us home, Berto," Richard commanded, as they all scrambled in through the doors which Berto had ceremoniously opened for them. Inside was a faint whiff of alcohol-from-the-past emanating from the upholstery, rather like that of a well-frequented drinking establishment. Richard found an empty place on the bench which ran the length of the extended-length-lux limo – not expecting very much else. Just a ride home, back to Chris' apartment over the old garage/stables at the McAllister place. Anything more was a bonus unlooked for and unexpected.

"This is yours, Chef!" Bianca exclaimed, having somehow declared herself the doyenne of the corporate generosity genie. She dropped a basket into his lap—OK, it was one of those cardboard two-bottle-packs. Richard hefted one of the bottles which Bianca had passed to him.

French cognac, of discretely fine vintage and origin, yet not of the vulgarly-tasteless variety, served up in expensive crystal or any other packaging intended to relieve the vulgar rich of their ill-gotten gains. Richard approved, whole-heartedly. He had always known that Lew was a man of taste and discretion. Good liquor spoke for itself, not needing any such additional adornment. This gift would be metered out with a careful eye – only on the most special occasion, and for the most appreciative guests. He cradled the two-pack in his arms and leaned back against the comfortable, yet faintly-funky-smelling limo upholstery. He was exhausted and content with a day and a job well done – and this token of appreciation to garnish it all? Yes, the end of a very good day. It did briefly occur to him that Sammi might even have recognized him, in the back of a limo, drinking champagne, instead of lurking in the service corridor of the Cattleman Hotel.

It sounded as if everyone else was equally content – Lew and Mrs. Dubois must have hit the sweet spot when it came to gifts for the staff. Araceli was tying a silk scarf over her head and laughing with the Battling Bees, and Bianca – the scarf looked, to Richard's experienced eye, like a genuine vintage Hermes. The other girls were exclaiming over their own gifts – handbags and scarves from an upscale and quality atelier. Luc was admiring a set of fine chef's knives in a fancy presentation case. Ah, yes – life was good. Very good, indeed.

A royally-slow circuit of Town Square – twice, perhaps thrice, allowing all to appreciate their gifts at least as much as the glasses of champagne which Bianca dispensed to them all – and Berto announced bashfully as the grand limousine slushed to a halt in front of the Mercantile Building.

"All right – Luc first, then 'Celi, the girls, and then Ricardo an' Bree at the Age, then I'll deliver Robbie … 'kay?"

"Just drop me off at the Tip -Top," Richard interjected. "I'm staying for a while at Chris' place, until the uproar from this wedding dies down."

"Right, Ricardo!" Berto rendered an unexpectedly snappy salute. Richard sighed, and leaned back against the funky but comfortable upholstery.

No, not long now. The champagne was a good thought, on Lew's part. What a night! What an event – and Richard and his people had come through it unscathed. Better yet, dripping with garlands of accolades and rewards.

And tomorrow – back to the Café for breakfast service.

He thought he might have dozed off for some minutes out of sheer exhaustion and release of tension from a long, busy and nerve-wracking day, for the next he knew, Berto was opening the door of the nearly empty limo, saying, "G'night, Ricardo. You're OK from here?"

"Perfectly," Richard answered, carefully hugging his gift pack to his chest. "G'night, all – thanks for the ride, Berto. If you see him before I do, tell Lew he is a prince among men and convey to him my undying gratitude."

Berto had pulled the limousine around to the graveled expanse behind the old McAllister house, where was parked Chris Mayall's little red coupe by the old and presently empty coach-house/garage/mews. No lights showed in the house itself. Miss Letty had probably retired to her righteous slumber hours ago. But the vintage industrial porch light at the top of the stairs – the stairs which gave unto the apartment over the transport-storage unit – shown bright, as bright as a good deed in a cold, cold world. Rags of pale grey fog crept in from the distant riverbank – the porch light was surrounded by a nimbus of tiny water droplets and attentive moths. Richard wilted slightly in the sudden muggy warmth, after the pleasant air-conditioned fug inside the old limo.

"I will that, Ricardo," Berto replied and threw the limo door closed with a practiced degree of force which argued that the old beast possessed certain crotchets, to which Berto was perfectly accustomed.

"Thanks again." Richard said again, as Berto crunched around the gravel towards the driver door.

"No prob," Berto said, over his shoulder. "See you later, uh? It was a good night for y'all, wasn't it?"

"Perfect." Richard was already climbing the stairs, as the extended limo ground away, bearing the last two of his staff – Robbie and Bree – away to their respective homes and righteous and presumably chaste slumbers.

There was a faint shifting and blue-white light glowing in the garage apartment windows – likely the television. So Chris was still awake – most unusual. Like Richard, Chris was an early bird. Either he was working out for his next marathon run or getting ready for an early day at the Tip-Top, signing for deliveries.

The door was not locked. Richard had come to realize that doors were almost never locked in Luna City. It was that kind of place. He let himself in. The apartment over the McAllister garage was a small one – two bedrooms, a single spartan bath, and a tiny galley kitchen appended to the main living room. The whole place was comfortably if shabbily furnished with solid old mis-matching pieces of furniture seconded from the main house – a bachelor establishment, although Richard was given to understand that in the dim and distant past it had housed a large family of domestics employed by the McAllister family. Now it only housed Chris, the war-disabled Navy corpsman whose connection to Luna City was a familial thing, mostly to do with a service-related friendship with Doc Wyler's grandson, and the protective care of Miss Letty, long a volunteer with the Red Cross. Chris, a man of color (coffee with lots of cream in it), was casually attired in baggy pajama trousers and a singlet, lounging in a battered lounge chair with Ozymandius-King-of-Kings in his lap.

"Hey, man," Chris drawled, upon hearing the door open and shut. "'Bout time you got home. Ozzie-cat here was getting freaky. How did it go? The do at the Cattleman. A blinding success?"

"In every way," Richard replied, shedding his coat and tossing it in the general direction of the coat-rack by the door, as Ozzie roused himself and hopped down from Chris' lap. "It was … it exceeded my dreams. And Lew Dubois is ecstatic over the success of his hotel launch. He presented me with some excellent French cognac, as a gesture of his esteem and approval … and sent us all home in a hired limousine by way of rewarding my staff. I'd offer you a drink from it, but I'm knackered from a day of labor, and a bit squiffy from the champagne which came with the ride."

"Not to worry," Chris yawned, levering himself from the lounge chair by easy stages, favoring the amputated leg augmented by the latest in prosthetics. "Got an early day tomorrow. I just stayed up to hear of your adventures. Did you manage to escape the notice of your freaky ex-girlfriend? The latest of several, I might take note of?"

"Mostly," Richard allowed, as Ozzie seated himself at Richard's feet – assuming the posture of an ancient Egyptian cat-god statuette, and fixing Richard with an accusing glare from his one good eye.

"Mrooow!" Ozzie remarked with special cold command emphasis, which well those passions Richard read. Meaning: It was late, where had Richard been, his (Ozzie's that is) personal cat-schedule was just wrecked and Richard would be lucky to find a dead mouse on his pillow, since Ozzie's attempts to teach Richard to hunt feline-properly and he was simply the dumbest human-servitor ever to be taken on by a cat.

"Yeah, she spotted me, but I think that she thinks now I am Ricardo from Jalisco, and I don't understand English. Araceli and I spun her that song and dance. She's not the sharpest knife in the block, so I think that she bought it. Anyway, I'm home free now, and about to drop dead from exhaustion."

"Cosmic," Chris yawned. "Tell me more about it in the morning. G'night, Ricardo."

"Good night," Richard replied, as he toddled towards the other small bedroom, sternly shepherded by his feline familiar.

A culinary triumph – and another splendid day in Luna City. Although come to think on it, just about every day was a splendid one in Luna City.

Obituary: Vaughn, Phillip G.

Phillip G. Vaughn, Junior, formerly the city manager of Karnesville, and three times elected to the Texas State Legislature representing Karnes County, died on Saturday, 23 September, 2018 in San Antonio following a long illness. Mr. Vaughn, 74, was the son of Phillip G. Vaughn, Senior, and Mary Bodie Vaughn, of Luna City. He graduated from Luna City High School in 1962, and attended the University of Texas in Austin, where he studied history and public administration. Upon graduation, he served two years in the US Army, fulfilling his draft obligation. In June, 1969, he married Myrna Everett in the First Methodist Church of Luna City, where they subsequently made their home. Phillip Vaughn was employed as a manager by various firms in Beeville, Victoria, and Karnesville. Developing an interest in politics, he was elected to Luna City's town council in the early 1970s, followed by four terms in the State Legislature. A public-spirited citizen, upon defeat for a fifth term, Phillip Vaughn was offered a position on the board of trustees for San Antonio's Incarnate Word University, where he served until increasing ill-health forced him to retire from public life in 1996.

Phillip Vaughn is survived by his wife, Myrna, son, Joseph P. Vaughn of Luna City, daughter-in-law Jessica Abernathy-Vaughn, and a grandson, Joseph James Vaughn. A memorial service will be held at Croker Methodist Church in San Antonio on Wednesday, September 27, at 11 AM. Interment will be at the Texas State Cemetery in Austin. In lieu of flowers, friends and admirers are asked to donate to the University of Texas M.D. Anderson Cancer Center.

En Residence

"Roman, my old and rare," Richard ventured on a morning, a week past the triumph of the Cattleman grand reopening, and the equally grand Wyler wedding. "Last night, as I was wending my weary way homewards, I noticed that some of your splendid chaps were unloading a quantity of … I presume it all was building materials? Yes, in front of that charming small villa, just around the corner from the old fire station house. Vulgar curiosity commands me to inquire; are renovations underway? Is this in the service of a new owner, who might yet become a habitué of this establishment? Or is it being fitted out as a B & B? Either way – it's a winner for me."

It was early morning at the Café; Roman Gonzalez, the working owner and supervisor of a not insubstantial and significant local construction company, was tucking into his customary full English – customary on those days when he had a full day of heavy labor on his schedule. Now, he looked up from his heaping plate of sausage, bacon, fried egg, tomato and mushroom, baked borracho beans, and toast, and replied,

"Not much gets past you, Ricardo. Yeah, that's the old Everett house. Owner decided to come back to Luna for family reasons. It's been a rental for about twenty years and ya know how renters can beat up a place. Whole refit of the bathrooms and kitchen, repaint inside and out, and re-finish the floors. New windows, too. Nice bit of change – my guys can do it in their sleep."

"Everett…" Richard ran a brief mental scan of the names of Lunaites in his mental Rolodex and came up dry. "The name is familiar, but I can't quite place it."

Roman grinned. Only later did Richard note the lack of mirth. "Local notables, Ricardo. Miss Alice, Doc Wyler's wife? She was an Everett. So was Old Charley Mills, on his mothers' side. This Everett is Myrna Vaughn, by her married name."

"Vaughn?" Richard ventured. "Any relation to Chief …"

"His mother," Roman replied, and forked in another mouthful of beans, assisted with a side of fried toast. "And she's a real pistol."

"Oh?" Richard hinted in a manner intended to invite further confidence. Roman did not rise to the bait, instead folded the last slice of toast around the lone rasher of bacon and wolfed it in two bites.

"Gotta run, Ricardo," Roman added, around that last mouthful, reaching for his Thermos. "Fill 'er up, long day ahead."

"This Mrs. Senior Vaughn: I take it you mean she is…"

"What I said – a real pistol. Ask around, you'll get the idea." Roman departed, leaving Richard frustrated and with his curiosity roused. He sought further enlightenment from Araceli, although the Café was in the middle of the breakfast rush.

"I hear that Mrs. Myrna Vaughn – she who brought forth our illustrious chief of police into the world – is returning to Luna City after a long hiatus," Richard ventured, hoping that his chief waitress and manager would prove to be a font of information, or at least, amusing gossip. "Is this in aid of Joe and Jess's pending new sprout on the familial tree?"

"Yeah. That and Joe's dad passed away last month. You do remember about that? The obituary was on the second page of the Beacon, and the flag in front of Town Hall was at half-staff for a week. And you did notice that Jess and Joe went to San Antonio for the funeral?"

"Come to think on it, so I did," Richard admitted. With the press of work in the Café kitchen, all having to do with anything outside of that often fled from his concern and memory within hours of his having encountered them. "And so now the widowed Mrs. Vaughn is moving back to town. Roman told me that his crew is renovating that charming little Spanish colonial revival cottage around the corner from Town Square. He would only say that she is somewhat of a character."

Araceli giggled. "Yeah, Joe's Mom is a law unto herself. Look, I only knew her at a remove. The Vaughns lived here when Joe was a kid in school so I can't say I knew her all that well. But she coached the girls' field hockey team back then – even did a bit, coaching other sports, as a volunteer concerned parent, you understand. She and Miss Letty went head-to-head over leadership of the Historical Society about the time that I started high school; that's when she and Joe's dad …" and Araceli hastily crossed herself, "Decided to move to Victoria, and then to Austin when the Legislature was in session. Oh, she *told* everyone it was because of Mr. Vaughn being elected to the Lege but everyone really knew that it was because Miss Letty had slapped her down, good and hard, when she tried to throw her weight around with the Historical Society. Miss Letty does not put up with people trying to do dirt to Luna City. And Doc Wyler backed her up, when it came to VPI, when they established Mills Farm."

"Something to do with the Cattleman Hotel, wasn't it?" Richard ventured, and Araceli nodded. The bell over the main door chimed sweetly again, and Araceli shot off in obedience to hospitality's command.

Upon her return, Araceli enlightened him briefly. "Really, Chef – I don't know all of the gory details. I was just in high school at the time and Joe was a senior. It made all the difference in the world. We might as well have been on different planets. You might want to talk to Miss Letty about that. She was there and she would know."

"Indeed," Richard agreed. "I suspect that what the old dear doesn't know about Luna City, past and present, would fit into a thimble."

He took the opportunity of approaching Miss Letty during the mid-morning lull, when the press of those with jobs to get to thinned out. Miss Letty, who breakfasted regularly at the Café, occupied her usual place at the largest table nearest the Café's wide front window – that table which Georg Stein jokingly called the *'stammtisch'* – the regular patron's table. The oldest person in Luna City, Miss Letty was arrayed beautifully in a print rayon shirt dress, and carrying a handbag which matched her hat, perfectly. Miss Letty was perhaps the last woman in Karnes County who never left her house without wearing a hat.

"Miss Letty, I've been told that Mrs. Myrna Vaughn will be moving back to town, very shortly, and I hope to see her here in the Café as a regular customer. I've been given to understand that she is … umm, a woman of decidedly strong character. I do not want to inadvertently finish up in her bad books. Araceli said that you have known her for a long time. Do you have any advice for me, in appealing to Mrs. Vaughn's better nature?"

Miss Letty favored Richard with a wintery smile.

"Cousin Myrna has many fine qualities, as a woman, but even her dearest friends must admit that a sense of tact is not among them."

"And are you one of her dearest friends, Miss Letty?" Richard ventured. Miss Letty's expression went from wintery to glacial.

"I cannot honestly say that I am, but I have known her since she was a child after the War, as she is the cousin of my very dear late friend Miss Alice, as well as a distant connection of my own family, on my mother's side. She was some twenty years younger than Alice and I. It was often in my mind that Myrna both envied and resented us in equal measure – so much older and accomplished, you see. And Alice was quite lovely, almost a movie star beauty. Myrna … Poor Myrna; a handsome woman in her way as an adult, but *such* an awkward teenager. She excelled at sports," Miss Letty allowed. "Really, I think it was most healthy for her. She had ambitions to compete in the Olympics at one time, but life has a way of interfering with plans … Good morning, Stephen," Miss Letty looked beyond Richard, as the silver shop bell hanging from the Café's outer door jingled sweetly.

Doc Wyler merely grunted in reply; he was always uncommunicative before his required coffee ration was administered. Miss Letty, undeterred by reason of long familiarity, continued. "Richard was asking about Myrna Vaughn, since she will soon take up residence in Luna City after a long hiatus. He was naturally curious."

Doc Wyler grunted again and shot Richard a piercing glance. "Woman's a menace, pure and simple. It was her bungling bullheadedness that brought those VPI bastards to town in the first place."

"She was one of the primary heirs to what was left of the Mills acres," Miss Letty interjected. "Which were of no earthly use to anyone."

"Bull-pucky," Doc Wyler accepted a cup of coffee from the hovering Araceli. "Land is always of use. After all, it's not something the Good Lord is making any more of, is there?"

"Be fair, Stephen; she had every right to entertain any good offer for her share of that land," Miss Letty said in a placating manner. "And to use her influence with the other heirs."

"She bulldozed them, plain and simple." Doc glared. "Dratted, bull-headed, bossy woman. They agreed to sell their share of the inheritance just to stop her hounding them and get some peace and quiet – and that's the truth of it. But that's not the worst of it, not by a long chalk. Tell Richard here how she tried to broker a deal with those bastards over the Cattleman."

"Must we?" Miss Letty sighed deeply. "It's old history."

"Do tell," Richard urged. "Tell me all; for it is not old history to me. I wish to avoid putting a foot wrong with regard to a local Boudicca."

Miss Letty snorted – it sounded like an attempt to stifle a chuckle. Doc Wyler merely looked puzzled. Miss Letty sighed again.

"It's a very sore point, Richard. Myrna was active at that time in the Luna City Historical Society. It is a matter of record that she was viewed as a person of influence with regard to local matters. I believe she had her eye on a position as president of the Society. As it was, she was the recording secretary. The life of a wife to a man with a comfortable income and some political ambition is … and was … insufficient for an energetic woman with a sense of purpose and a disinclination to minister solely to the home sphere. Myrna had only the one child, you see. I think it might have been different, had she and Phillip been blessed with half a dozen or so; a meet challenge to her considerable organizational energies. Instead, they were turned to the management of civic affairs." Miss Letty – as stalwart an old bird as any of Richard's Gran's wartime Land Girl comrades – was grim in judgement.

"She poked her nose in any damn place where it wasn't welcomed or wanted," Doc Wyler sounded inclined to wax explanatory. He had mellowed slightly after sinking half a mug of the Café's finest coffee, leavened with cream. *(This against the advice of his general physician, but Doc was ninety-six and still going strong, fueled by good genes and all-around irascibility, and what the hell did a grandson of an old Texas A&M buddy barely old enough to set up a medical practice know about diets, when Doc had been practicing veterinary medicine for three times as long? Doc Wyler was of the opinion that if consuming vast quantities of coffee with real cream straight from the cow, bacon, good rare steaks from his own cattle, and an evening mint julep or two hadn't killed him over the previous seven decades, likely he would last for another couple of years.)*

"Myrna was the person who broached the possibility of VPI purchasing the Cattleman outright in – what was the year, Stephen? 1974?" Miss Letty seemed ready to expand on exactly why Mrs. Myrna Everett Vaughn's name was mud in local repute. Richard waited, in breathless anticipation.

"Yeah – that was the year." Doc held up his drained-to-the dregs coffee mug. Without a word spoken, Araceli flew from across the dining area to refill it from that bountiful carafe in one hand, adding that dollop of pure dairy cream from the pitcher in her other – that cream which was the signature accompaniment to Richard's splendid Café coffee. "She was the one who let those VPI bastards know – or at least, allowed them to think – that they could purchase the building entire from the Historical Association, rip it down, cart the building in stages out to their place, and re-assemble it – of course, no one knew about that angle until later. They were bent on offering a night in a historic Texas hotel, ghosts and all, for a pittance! Ripping the heart out of my town – our town, dammit! My grandfather wouldn't have stood for that, and neither did I, once word got around."

"I still think that sending notice to VPI's marketing director, challenging him to a duel in Town Square was a little excessive, Stephen," Miss Letty murmured. She sounded placating. It was obvious that she had a lifetime of experience in ameliorating Doc Wyler's homicidal impulses. "I am certain that dear Myrna didn't intend …"

"The road to hell is paved with good intentions," Doc snarled. "I blame her for those bastards at VPI even getting a toe-hold in Karnes County, with their lah-de-dah 'experience the past beautifully' pile of bull-pucky. I've shoveled enough of it in my time, I know the smell well enough, when I run across it again … thank you, darlin'," he added to the hovering Araceli. "As I was saying …"

"I hadn't heard any of this," Richard, despite himself, was fascinated. Someone getting the better of Doc Wyler, whose personal wealth was only exceeded by his business acumen and careful nurture of ancient grudges? Myrna Everett Vaughn must be a formidable woman, indeed.

"You wouldn't have," Doc Wyler snapped. "This all happened before you were a gleam in your daddy's eye."

"Strictly local lore," Miss Letty murmured. "And in England, you would never have heard anything of our little entanglements, anyway. Stephen, dear – this is of little interest …"

"But it is, it is," Richard insisted. "Chief Vaughn and his good lady honor me with their friendship, no less than your good selves…"

"I smell that bull-pucky again, son," Doc had perfected a perfectly ferocious glare, over eight decades. "Don't push your luck."

"I wouldn't presume," Richard hastily retrenched. "But it is my duty and obligation – as manager of this enterprise – to remain as neutral as I may, in a clash of determined personalities. I must have a … map of the minefield, as it were. To prevent inadvertent offense to either party."

"Quite sensible," Miss Letty nodded, magisterially. "And the best of luck to you in that enterprise. The trouble is that dear Myrna is … at the best of times, a difficult, and opinionated woman." Left tactfully unsaid was that Stephen Wyler was also a difficult and opinionated man – and that was showing his good side. "As nearly as we in the Historical Society can determine …"

"They near as dammit offered a bribe," Doc fumed. "And Myrna Vaughn was their Western Union delivery girl! Oh, she tried to make it all sweet and pretty, but the stench was all over that offer of a donation … and then when they tendered another offer to me privately … well, it's been a long time since a Wyler was offered a packet of cash under the table …"

At least a century and three-quarters, Richard estimated silently. Thanks to any number of conversations with Kate on the topic of local history, he was aware that well-informed opinion held that Doc Wyler's grandfather, Captain (late CSA) Herbert Kling Wyler had been morally elastic on the means by which his initial fortune was acquired during the mid-19th century unpleasantness. *Something to do with the smuggling of cotton over the border to Mexico during the Civil War to circumvent the blockade of the South, Kate surmised. Captain H.K. Wyler had been an officer overseeing elements of that process. "Opportunities for him to acquire illicit boodle by the basketful must have been as plentiful as bluebonnets in a Texas spring," was how Kate put it.*

"I'm certain that dear Myrna did not wholly realize how VPI's offer could be so construed at our end," Miss Letty seemed intent on being the peacemaker. "But there it was; so tactless. So blatant… overt. The members of the Historical Society were outraged, of course. And the officers – that is, Stephen and I, and Don Jaimie – were furious. It was a gesture of contempt, we all felt; that VPI's management then seemed to think that we might be bought off so readily."

"Like cheap whores," Doc Wyler obviously was still simmering over the four-decade old insult, and Miss Letty frowned in arctic disapproval of his language.

"How did Mrs. Vaughn further blot her copybook, with regard to VPI and their initial offer to the Historical Society?" Richard was genuinely eager to know, and Miss Letty sighed.

"She took it on herself as recording secretary to propose new elections for officers, and put up herself as the new president of the Historical Society …"

"A confounded coup d'état was what it amounted to," Doc Wyler grunted. "And she proceeded it by sending around a letter to all the members accusing the existing officers – Don Jaimie, Letty and myself of mishandling funds, and other inappropriate conduct, with regard to VPI's offer."

"The row among the membership must have been of epic proportions," Richard observed sagely, and Miss Letty nodded.

"It all but tore the Historical Society apart. Because of course Myrna did have friends and adherents among them. But Miss Alice was stung to the heart, that her own kin should take up arms, metaphorically speaking, against her husband. All that most everyone knew at that particular point was that VPI wished to purchase the building – no one knew about their plans to disassemble it and move it. That came as a bombshell – not just to the Historical Society, but to Luna City as a whole."

"Those crafty VPI bastards had kept their plans secret," Doc Wyler was as grim in rendering a verdict as any judge donning the black cap of condemnation. "It was as if they knew that we wouldn't stand for it, and wanted to go at it sideways, with Myrna Vaughn as their cat's paw, on the off-chance that they would get what they wanted."

"I don't believe that Myrna knew of their plans for the Cattleman beforehand," Miss Letty murmured, and Doc Wyler fixed her with that that trademarked glare – to which Miss Letty, thanks to decades of exposure, appeared mainly to be immune.

To steer the discussion back into the channel most useful to him, Richard interjected, "So – then how did you discover their … ultimate destructive intention, if I might ask – without broaching the State Secrets Act, or whatever there is here which administers that kind of thing?"

"I have my ways, son," Doc Wyler replied. "I was tipped wise, through a friend of a friend of a friend, who just happened to have a seat on the VPI board of directors, and privy to company reports."

"I take it that the revelation of this spot of intelligence must have some highly interesting results among your association, and the town at large," Richard ventured, and Doc Wyler nodded grimly.

"A nuclear detonation wouldn't have had quite the devasting effect, metaphorically speaking," Miss Letty mused, with serene detachment. "Dear Myrna was censured by a majority of the members of the society – a spontaneous action taken entirely on the part of the members, without any suggestion or encouragement from Stephen, Don Jaimie or myself."

"You colonials are a bloody-minded, independent lot," Richard agreed, earning another wintery smile from Miss Letty. "Disinclined to follow the lead of their betters. No good will come of this recalcitrant attitude in the long run, mark my words."

"Part of our happy, inconsequent charm," Miss Letty agreed. "And we have rubbed along most agreeably over the past two hundred and fifty years, so there must be something positive said for an independently-inclined mind. In any case – in the aftermath of this revelation, Myrna was … not to put too fine upon it – socially shunned. Such a sentence means much in a town like Luna City. The embarrassment was so horrific that very shortly thereafter, she and her husband moved from Luna City, although Joseph chose to stay with his grandparents to complete his schooling here. He was already a good football prospect, and a youth well-thought of." Miss Letty fetched up a deep sigh from the bottom of her weary soul. "No one wished to hold the failings of his mother against him, after all. Not when it comes to the Moths and a chance at regional championships. This is a small town, after all."

"So … has Mrs. Vaughn-the-elder permanently blotted her social copybook for all time, then?" Richard asked, still considering the potential minefield laid out before him, knowing that these two might be his only means of providing the means of walking unharmed through it. Miss Letty tilted her head in considering fashion and after a moment, answered,

"No, perhaps not. Joseph is respected in his office of chief of police, and Jessica is held in the highest consideration of by all. It has, after all, been many years since the original damaging faux pas. The fact that Mr. Dubois has been an exemplary partner in his dealings with the City… we in the Historical Society have nothing to complain of, in our dealings with VPI. In fact, we are drawn to laud him as a model of what ought to be in the dealings with civil authority…" Miss Letty paused, in regretful consideration. "It would have spared us all so much grief, if VPI had been honest and above-board in their dealings with us from the very first. But alas – we do not live in a perfect world. And it is in my mind that most – at least, among the Methodist ladies – would be inclined to forgive Myrna for what must have been an unconsidered impulse. It is the Christian thing, to forgive sins. In the loss of Phillip this last year, after so many years of failing health… it's quite understandable that she would want to return to Luna City, finding refuge in the bosom of her family, especially as now that it is to be increased…"

"Err … wot?" Richard had lost that train of thought, and Miss Letty smiled, in mild apology.

"Oh, I suppose that was not generally known yet. Joseph and Jessica are expecting again. It is a good thing, I have always believed, to have siblings so close in age. That way, they can be playmates and companions. My brother and I had a bare sixteen months between us, and we were practically inseparable: Douglas and I, together with Stephen…"

"Good times, Letty," Doc Wyler's expression was uncharacteristically mellow. "Good times. Remember when they used to call us 'the three Musketeers'?"

"Indeed," Miss Letty sighed, reminiscently. "We were such terrors, the three of us … and our own little D'Artagnon, Artie Vaughn. That was Harry Vaughn's older brother, you know," she added in a parenthetical manner to Richard. "Josephs' grandfather. He was a full year younger than we were – but so terribly persistent. And mischievous! All the trouble that we got into, rescuing Artie from his own folly in trying to follow us."

"Scrawny and loud, like a baby bird," Doc Wyler grunted, as he emptied the last of his coffee mug and collected up his aged leather medical bag. "Full of bright ideas. That was Artie. I still miss the little sprout. He had the most original ideas for making mischief, back when we were kidlets. That he lived to the age that he did is proof positive of the existence of a Divine Providence. Got to go, calves to castrate and brand … Richard, you want a full harvest of fries for your next Café menu specialty?"

"I believe that I shall pass on that kind offer," Richard replied, with a mild shudder. Larousse had no suggestions for dealing with that kind of bounty.

Doc Wyler grinned; a humorless grin reminiscent of a wolf, observing, "Son, take my word on it, there's nothing better than a good fry-up of Rocky Mountain oysters for putting lead in a man's pencil!" He took his leave on that note, leaving Richard muttering to himself,

"What an original name for that kind of organ meat…"

Miss Letty make her own departure shortly thereafter, leaving Richard to muse on the historic entanglements of families and friends in Luna City. *Really; Eastenders had nothing on this*!

When next he emerged from the kitchen, on the downside of the morning rush, it was to see Martin Abernathy sitting alone at the regulars' table.

"Good morning, Mayor Abernathy," Richard greeted him. "You're late today – Doc Wyler and the Steins have been, breakfasted and gone. May I have Araceli bring you your usual?"

"Sure, Ricardo," Martin answered, with a slight cough. "The usual – but skip the coffee. My doctor says I should cut back on the caffeine. Makes the old ticker go into overtime."

"Damn," Richard replied. "Life is hardly worth living, without alcohol, caffeine, chocolate and bacon."

"Yeah," Martin sighed. "The doctors say you'll live longer without them all, but I think that it just <u>seems</u> longer."

"You seem … a trifle under the weather," Richard ventured, in accordance with Araceli's firm conviction that the Café ought to offer sympathetic understanding to personal woes, in additional to outstanding cuisine. Martin looked grey and ill, so much in contrast to his usual brisk and businesslike demeanor. "Is that something you want to talk about? I understand that Mrs. Myrna Vaughn is returning to Luna City to live. And that Joe and Jess are expecting an addition to the family…"

"Word does get around," Martin agreed, with a sharp and understanding expression, which proved as fleeting as his briefly cheerful mood. "At the Café, of course – that, and at training sessions with the VFD. They used to call it the grapevine."

"The 'bush telegraph,'" Richard agreed, feeling some sympathetic twinges for Martin, who was about the age of his own father – and who now was appearing distinctly seedy, slumped in his chair at the *stammtisch.* "Is Mrs. Myrna Vaughn all that much of a trial to humanity as some have been suggesting? A woman who can best be appreciated at a distance of several leagues?"

"No, Myrna's OK," Martin replied, adding with the air of someone confessing a small sin. "I always rather liked her – knew her since I don't know when. Forever – Miss Letty's kindergarten and First Grade class, I believe. Smart, driven. Ambitious. Never say die. Hasn't got an ounce of tact in her, which is why Phillip never went farther than the State Lege. He might have been

Governor, otherwise. Congressman, even. But Myrna's a good woman, when you come right down to it. She's your friend? She's your friend to the last instant and last drop of blood. I'm pretty certain that Phillip only lived as long as he did with his health issues because Myrna stood at the door and defied the Dark Angel."

"A formidable woman," Richard acknowledged. Really, Luna City seemed to breed them, like dragons' teeth, sown in fertile soil, and springing fully-armed out of it. Martin nodded in agreement.

"Our Texas ladies. Formidable, all right."

"And this one is your kin by marriage?" Richard hinted, for Martin still appeared unwell. "Is that something that you consider a good? I mean – Jess is a formidable woman in her own right. In my experience, such a one cannot endure another formidable female in a room, since they tend to be hellishly jealous of any potential rival. It must make family suppers rather fraught. Two strong women, face to face, though they come from the ends of … well, Luna City, anyway."

"Well, there was that moment," Martin agreed. "At the dead spread … umm – the funeral luncheon, after the ceremonies for Phillip. When Jess told Myrna that she and Joe were expecting again. Intending to be comforting, Jess said. And Myrna said that every family needs a good brood mare."

"Good lord," Richard was appalled. "And what did Jess hit her mother-in-law with?"

"A tray of Costco mini-quiches," Martin sighed. "Almost. But one of Myrna's San Antonio friends got ahold of her, and burbled into her ear what good news that was in her time of grief and reflection, and Joe put his arm around Jess and reminded of her about what a caution his mother was, and it was all smoothed over. Jess was only seriously pissed for about two minutes." Martin raised his gaze to meet Richards'. "I know; you'd think that with only the one son, Myrna would be the mother-in-law from hell. She would be possessive, and sabotage whoever Joe chose to marry, no matter *who* he married, but the instant Joe and Jess formally tied the knot, Myrna all but adopted Jess as her daughter in blood. Though," Martin added, with a weary sigh. "The tact thing. It's a foreign country to Myrna. What comes to her mind is coming out of her mouth a millisecond later."

"A trial," Richard sympathized. "Nonetheless, I am grateful for the advanced war … word about the Dowager Mrs. Vaughn."

"Forewarned is fore-armed," Martin agreed, just as Araceli arrived with his regular breakfast order.

Back in the kitchen, she observed to Richard, "He doesn't look well at all, Ricardo – did you tell him he ought to see a doctor?"

"I believe that he is under care of competent medical authority," Richard answered. He agreed with Araceli, much as he was reluctant to concede it. Martin did look rather grey around the gills, and foregoing the Café's famous coffee? Whatever the medical issue was – Richard could only hope that Martins' doctors were competent and understanding.

And soon he would have to meet Myrna Vaughn – a formidable woman. Richard was still in two minds about how he would handle another one of Luna City's women. The ones that he knew already were enough.

Continuing the Search for The Fabulous Gonzaga Reliquary

From – Treasure-Hunters: The Internet Magazine

Famed international treasure hunter, Xavier Gunnison-Penn continues his exhaustive search for the long-lost Gonzaga Reliquary. Thought to have been created in the 16th century in the workshop of Benvenuto Cellini, the Reliquary was memorialized in a recently rediscovered painting attributed to Leonardo da Vinci. The painting was found during renovations of an old convent in Milan, where the fabulous jeweled reliquary briefly adorned the chapel, before it passed back into possession of the family who had originally donated it – the Gonzagas of Gijon, in the province of Cantabria, Northern Spain, whose' family name later metamorphosed into Gonzalez, or Gonzales, probably about the time that they emigrated to Spanish possessions in the New World.

Gunnison-Penn – famous for embarking on a long series of unsuccessful quests for various long-lost treasures – claims to have discovered evidence of the presence of the Gonzaga Reliquary in the Spanish colonial archives in Mexico City. Penn says that a will, written by one Don Diego Manuel Hernando Ruiz y Gonzalez (or Gonzales) late in the 1700s mentioned the Gonzaga Reliquary. Don Diego Hernando was granted vast holdings in what was called Nueva Santander, which stretched along the Gulf Coast from Tampico, Mexico, into present-day Texas as far as San Antonio. Don Diego's two sons inherited that property, which extending from the banks of the San Antonio River where it runs through present-day Karnes County. The will specifically mentioned the

Reliquary as a great treasure of the family, and stipulated that it be taken to that holding, presumably to inspire the community that gathered around Don Diego's establishment. The remnant of that Spanish-era grant is still a working ranch, the Rincon de los Robles (or Oak Corner), so called for the stands of magnificent, centuries-old oak trees along the banks of the river. The ranch is maintained by the direct descendant of Don Diego's oldest son, "Don" Jaimie Gonzalez, and his family. Xavier Gunnison-Penn was invited by the family, to assist in reviewing the copious historic archives held by the family over the decades since establishment of the Rincon de los Robles.

The archives are unexpectedly copious, says Penn: the current owners' father, grandfather and great-grandfather were serious about their business and exacting in their record-keeping. Everything was saved and stored away. The archives, claims Penn, were stored in a series of metal-lined trunks, cases and cannisters – each one sealed as it was filled and packed tight to the lid, and stored away in a ranch outbuilding. They encompass everything from personal letters, legal and business correspondence, to extraneous materiel received through the post as it existed over a century. This, claims Dr. Miranda "Mindy" Ramirez-Gonzalez, who teaches history at Trinity University in San Antonio is a rich treasure-trove of documents relating to an historic Texas Hispanic-owned property, as they have never been examined since the day that they were packed away, years and decades ago. Doctor Ramirez-Gonzalez is confident of discovering fresh insights into the history of native Hispanics in Texas through her exploration of the family archive.

It's been a painstaking and exhausting labor, says Gunnison-Penn, although his enthusiasm is undimmed after months of reviewing the Gonzalez/Gonzales archives. He claims that he has found a single promising reference to the Gonzaga Reliquary, in a personal letter received in response to an undated letter composed and dispatched sometime during the American Civil War. The letter was from an unknown correspondent in Mexico City to an addressee at Rincon de los Robles. Such correspondence was severely frowned upon by the authorities in charge of Confederate-governed Texas at that time and might have drawn a death penalty for treasonous correspondence for the recipient of the letter in question. The letter, written in haste, to judge from the scribbled handwriting, directed the recipient to hide "the supreme treasure of our family" in a secure location. The nature of the treasure, and the location of it's hiding place is in nowise suggested – but Gunnison-Penn is certain that it refers to the Reliquary.

Further intelligence regarding the Gonzaga Reliquary resides on what further may be discovered in the Gonzales/Gonzales family archives.

1932 - Indians, Cowboys and Outlaws

"Where are you going today, Letty?" Mama asked, on one Monday mid-morning after breakfast. It was the second week of the summer vacation. "You and Douglas?" Sunlight poured golden into the covered back porch of the McAllister house. The bees danced among the hollyhocks and delphiniums in the flower borders which curved around the grand old stone house. Around the side, beyond the carefully tended sweep of lawn, the dust settled silently back in the wake of a Ford truck, which had rattled past the McAllister house, heavily laden with a load of vegetables for a market in San Antonio.

"Out to play," Letty answered. "At our fort, with Stephen. Maybe Retta, if she is finished with her piano lesson by then." *(Retta was Letty's best friend, after Stephen – Henrietta Keyes, somber and bookish like Letty. Retta lived on her father and mothers' small ranch west of Luna City and wanted to be a nurse when she grew up.)*

"Just be back by suppertime," Mama replied, looking up from sorting the household laundry from several baskets. Monday was washing-day; not such a chore as it had been once, since the McAllister's boasted a patent washing machine, complete with a mechanical wringer which Letty was absolutely forbidden to touch because it was dangerous. It could mash your fingers to splinters in moments. "Did you finish your chores, then?"

"Yes, Mama," Letty had. She was conscientious about chores, even at the age of eight. Eggs gathered from the flock of hens kept in back, scraps and cracked corn put out for them and the garden weeded. In the house, her bed was made tidily, the breakfast dishes cleared from the table. Douglas – her eleven-year-old brother – had finished his own daily chore, of splitting wood for the kitchen stove and hauling water from the well to water the garden. Douglas was very strong for his age – almost twelve and handled a small splitting maul and wedges with skill, slivering quarters of wood into smaller portions for the stove. "Can we make sandwiches to take for our lunch?"

"A day of it?" Mama smiled. "Of course – there's some ham in the icebox, but don't take it all. Your father will want his lunch as well. And there is some lemon cake from Sunday supper; you may have two small slices of that – oh, take a piece for Stephen as well. Just leave enough for your father."

"Yes, Mama!" Letty wrapped her arms around her mothers' comfortable middle for an exuberant and brief embrace. She ran up to her room on the second floor of the old stone McAllister house to change into her play clothes; a worn middy-blouse and a pair of her brothers' outgrown knee-britches, her feet thrust into canvas tennis shoes, also outgrown by Douglas and boasting holes by Letty's littlest toes. She didn't mind that. When they played around the fort, she would kick off the shoes and go barefoot. It was summer, after all. Summer was for bare feet, although Mama would sigh and say that being barefoot all summer was a sign of being poor and trashy. McAllisters were proper. They always had shoes, even if times were hard in Luna City. She and Douglas would have new shoes when school started, in August. For now, they went barefoot. When Letty absolutely had to wear shoes in summer, she wore her brothers' old pair or crammed her feet into the Sunday shoes that she had new for Easter … and now which pinched dreadfully, but would have to last until spring, when Mama and Papa bought them all new Sunday best and good shoes.

That done, she raced downstairs again, and into the kitchen. Outside on the back porch, she heard the regular thump-thump-thump of the mechanical washing machine. Letty knew that having electricity in the McAllister house, and most of the better homes in Luna City was a sign of advance and prosperity. In the old days, doing laundry by hand took all the day and all the time and labor on the part of the women in the household … that is, if they did not sent it out, and who knows where it really went and what was done to it?

Letty quickly assembled sandwiches; she was deft with slicing bread and carving off thin slivers of ham in order to leave enough for Papa. Mama let her handle the biggest kitchen knife, at least. She wrapped the sandwiches in brown paper and cut three portions of cake – alike wrapping that in paper – just as her brother Douglas thundered down the staircase and erupted into the kitchen like a small and erratic storm. He had his.22 rifle slung, soldier-like over one shoulder, and a metal water canteen over the other. The canteen was a metal Army-surplus one; practically Douglas' proudest possession.

"Ready, Letty?" he demanded, bouncing from one foot to another. "We gotta go to town first."

"What for?" Letty wrapped the sandwiches and cake in a large calico handkerchief and tied the opposite corners in knots.

Douglas puffed out his chest with pride. "I earned two dollars in tips for Mr. Dobie Shaw at the Tip-Top last week – helping people clean their windows and top up their radiators. I'm keeping out fifteen cents for ice cream … an' some candy, but the rest I'm gonna put in my savings account."

"A whole two dollars – and people just gave it to you, like that?"

"'cause I was helpful, Letty," Douglas explained.

"I wish people would give me money for being helpful," Letty ventured, somewhat wistfully. Their father had taken them into the Luna City Savings and Loan the previous year, and ceremoniously presented them to the Chief Teller, saying that they were old enough to open bank accounts of their own. To save for their education, their father said, although Douglas had confessed that he would rather save up for a fancy wind-up phonograph. *Much, much later, Letty would realize that their father had – most sensibly – chosen to demonstrate his own faith in the solidity of the Luna City Savings and Loan in this fashion. After all, the McAllisters were among Luna City's leading families; Grandfather Arthur Wells McAllister was one of the founders. (For all the good it did – the Luna City S&L closed for good a year later.)*

"You have your Christmas and birthday present money," Douglas consoled her. "When you are ten, maybe you can run errands and help at the Tip-Top."

This was true, but Letty still wished that she had as much as fifteen cents to spend on ice cream and penny-candy. But she and Douglas were fortunate in having bicycles of their own. Times might be hard for many people, even in Luna City – and Letty knew very well that the McAllisters were fortunate indeed, even if her bicycle was an old boys' bicycle and slightly rusted along the frame. She followed her brother, crossing the dusty main road which ran between San Antonio – the big city, far to the north, and Aransas Pass, down on the Gulf Coast, baking in the mid-morning sun. Beyond the shabby weathered Tip-Top Ice House with the range of gasoline pumps out in front, the road into Luna City wandered past a meadows and stands of trees, eventually past houses with smaller and smaller gardens as they approached Town Square, marked at one end with the gleaming façade of the grand Cattleman Hotel, and the white columns and pediment of the Luna City Public School at the other. This was a familiar passage for Letty: during the school term, she and Douglas went this way twice daily and back – to school, home for lunch, back to school and finally home again.

Town Square basked in the mid-summer sunshine, although the massive stands of oak trees cast pools of cool shade under their branches. Some of the oaks were so large that three children holding hands could not reach all the way around them. By the old Fire Station, she and Douglas drew abreast of a friend – or perhaps more accurately, a sort of friend. One who was determined on his part to be their friend, or at least be in association with them.

"'Lo, Artie," Douglas rested his feet on the ground, and Letty followed suit. Artie Vaughn was yet a year and a half younger than

Letty; a skinny boy tall for his age, with a nose way too big for his narrow face and dark hair which grew every which way, like an untidy haystack. "Got stuck with minding the baby again?"

Artie – barefoot under the faded denim overalls which were his only garment – nodded in agreement. He had his little brother Harry in a battered wooden wagon. Harry was five but likewise big for his age. Harry had the same beak of a nose and unkempt black hair; like Artie, shorn by an inexpert hand armed with a bowl and a pair of shears. Artie and Harry's father was employed by Luna City's tiny force of police officers. This was out of desperate necessity, as the Vaughn's small ranch near Beeville had been lost to foreclosure. The fifteen dollars a month paid by the city was what kept Artie's family from abject poverty – that and the kindness of neighbors and the extensive vegetable garden in back of the tidy frame bungalow on Oak Street, where Artie's mothers' family lived, and which the Vaughn family now shared..

"Until Mama gets done with the shopping. Harry is too big an' ornery to take with her. You going out to the Fort with Stephen?" Artie's countenance reflected eagerness and a pathetic longing to be included in the afternoon. Letty sighed. Now they would have to invite him. Artie was like a burr that couldn't be shaken off.

"Yeah," Douglas replied. "Look, if you wanna come out to the Fort, you gotta know the password. For today, the challenge is 'Montcalm' and the password is 'Wolfe.' Otherwise you're an enemy spy and we won't let you in." *(Douglas loved history.)*

"'Montcalm' and 'Wolfe'!" Artie exclaimed, beaming with happiness. "It's the bees' knees, Douglas! I won't forget!"

"See you," Douglas didn't sound enthused, to any degree. Artie was a trial to Douglas, Stephen and Letty, a trial only alleviated by his free access to father's collection of tattered *True Detective Magazines* (*Vaughn, Senior purchased them for the professional articles, so he claimed)*, and Artie's own imagination, which tended in the direction of flamboyantly creative. Artie was unfortunately burdened by the damp and dampening presence of his baby brother, as he was frequently tasked with looking after the younger Vaughn. *("It's not really fair," Douglas confessed to his sister when the Vaughns first moved to Luna City two years previously. "Artie's a good egg – but really ... having to play with a kid who isn't even out of diapers? It's just not fair, Letty! He's not* <u>*our*</u> *baby brother!" "At least we can pretend that he is a Comanche sentry," Letty consoled her brother. "Or set him down and say that he is first base.")*

Douglas pushed off, and Letty followed; she liked riding her bicycle, even if it was an old and battered one. With it, she had the freedom of Luna City, the winged freedom of a bird to come and go without trudging in her hand-me-down, holey-toed shoes in the dust. They emerged into Town Square, at the edge of that sculpted grove of ancient trees, hemmed in by the facades of the various buildings which framed the Square with their ornate pediments, their banks of windows, their white-painted columns and discrete statuary. It was a busy place on a Monday, with automobiles and trucks putt-putting their decorous way, amid the horse- and mule-pulled wagons. Even in the midst of hard times, Luna City displayed a mild prosperity. The Luna City Savings and Loan had quite recovered from a midnight raid several years previous by the notorious Newton Gang to rob the antiquated vault. Their fruitless attempt to blow the vault's door had only succeeded in shattering every window in the place and awaking just about everyone who lived above the shop premises in Town Square. The windows were new, but there were still several divots in the brickwork left from gunfire – not all of it from the Newton Gang.

"I'll be a minute," Douglas said, as he leaned his own bicycle against the pillar nearest to the door. Letty sat down on the tallest step, next to her own bicycle, and contemplated the view of Town Square from there, and felt the familiar throb of pride and belonging. This was her place, bone of her bone, blood of her blood, as deep in the soil as the roots of the oak trees reached. She was a part of it, it was a part of her, and she loved it fiercely, even the awkward parts, like Artie and his tag-along baby brother. There was no other place in the world where she wanted to live.

Along the Square, sporadic traffic came and went: Letty's attention was briefly drawn towards one motor-car. A flashy new sedan, shiny black with a racing chrome greyhound on the hood, and not one that she recognized. Although a fair number of strange motor-cars passed by the Tip-Top every day, most which came into Luna City itself were driven by owners who were well-known. She watched with interest as it idled along the Square, came to a halt, and two men emerged from it, along with an elegantly attired young woman. The lady was tiny, hardly taller than Letty herself. And she had red hair, combed under a modish hat of pale grey felt, trimmed with a ruffle of veil and a darker grey felt flower. Letty regarded the hat with pure envy: it looked like something a movie star would wear. The men were young and dressed in suits which Letty instinctively understood to be spiffy and a bit vulgar, not like Poppa's plain dark Sunday suit. Letty noticed them all particularly because they looked toward the Savings and Loan building, and it seemed they were conferring together for some moments. And then they got into the motor-car, and it puttered away. Douglas emerged from the Savings and Loan, with a satisfied expression, his hands in his pockets.

"It's getting hot, Letty. Ready for some ice cream?"

"Sure!" Letty replied, for it *was* quite warm at near-to-noon, sitting on the steps waiting for Douglas. They walked their bicycles the short distance down the sidewalk to the Mercantile Building – the one which announced its name in white glazed bricks along the elaborate façade. Their father rented the street-level shop premise to an ice cream parlor, and the small apartment above to the family which managed the parlor. There were several small divots in the brickwork surrounding the storefront window of the ice cream parlor – again from an exchange of gunfire; this time between Don Antonio Gonzalez of the Rancho Encino de los Robles, and a man with a grudge against his family – but all that had happened before Letty was born, although Poppa frequently pointed out the small damage to the front wall of his property and often thanked providence that he hadn't had to demand that Don Antonio to pay for replacing an expensive plate glass window.

Douglas and Letty left their bicycles leaning against the nearest lamppost; the ice cream parlor was relatively cool, with a ceiling fan lazily stirring the air – and perhaps the merchandise itself lent a suggestion of cold to the place. Douglas chose chocolate, Letty strawberry ice cream, a single scoop packed into a crisp sugar cone, and five cents worth of hard candy chosen from the short display of candies presided over by the beaming shop-keeper. Douglas resolutely paid for it all, although Papa's tenant insisted at first that they take nothing for the candy.

"It would have saved you a nickel," Letty pointed out, as they retrieved their bicycles, and Douglas looked stern. "He has a business, Letty. It would be wrong to take advantage, just because Poppa owns the building? He wouldn't have given Artie or Stephen a discount … well, maybe he would have given it to Stephen. But it would still be shady. McAllisters do not do shady business, Letty. We do open and above-board."

"Yes, we do," Letty agreed, and they pedaled away towards the edge of town, towards where the river scribbled a blue and deep gouge into the landscape to the south of Luna City. Tall trees, thirsty poplar, cypress, sycamore and oak lined the banks, in places with their roots revealed by erosion. Small footpaths and deer-trails threaded stands of native cane and thickets of wild plums and persimmons, blackberry tangles and swags of mustang grapes handing in festoons. It was too late for blackberries, too early for plums, grapes and persimmons. Douglas and Letty skirted the old Sheffield place, and the decaying range of outbuildings, which once had been intended to be a resort, with a hot-water well rumored to have curative properties. But the resort never really took off, and the main house had burned and never been rebuilt because of hard times. The deepest pool in the river was at the bend by the Sheffield place. That was where everyone went for a swim, at the height of summer. Letty knew it well, and that it was the older kids who favored it most.

The Fort – the hideout, club-house and refuge of hers and Douglas's friends was some way past the swimming hole and the Sheffield place; they were all quite certain that none but a select circle knew of it, for they had built it themselves the summer before, and added it over the winter.

Just up-river from boundary to the ramshackle Mills place, the river spread and widened; a shallow flood-plain, floored in gravel and sand, where all the wrack from previous years' floods accumulated - tree branches, lengths of cane and other trash. An oak with gnarled branches, branches which ran almost perpendicular to the ground held a tenacious position there. And that was where Douglas, Stephen and Letty had collected up lengths of cane, lengths of scrap plank, and straight branches, and brought them to lean from ground to branch, to form a kind of layered driftwood teepee, eight or ten feet in irregular diameter. This was "The Fort" – not entirely weatherproof, but sheltered against the wind and weather, and furnished with some small comforts. The most notable of those comforts included a moldering buffalo robe which cushioned the larger part of the space within, and an ancient camp-stove – a metal tray on legs, in which they could kindle a small fire, and a couple of tin pots, plates and mugs – most of which were the measuring cups given out by the flour-milling companies.

As Douglas and Letty walked their bikes around the last bend in the river, towards the clump of trees that sheltered the Fort, they saw that Stephen Wyler was already there. A cowpony from the Wyler ranch stable browsed morosely on the sparse tufts of grass which had found purchase on the sandy soil of the river bottom, tied loosely by the reins to another tree limb. Stephen himself, wiry and whip-smart, sat on the edge of the riverbank, his legs dangling over the edge, with his own.22 at his side.

"You're just in time, Captain!" he commented, as he slid down in a rush of dust and pebbles. "We got word from HQ; we're to attack the German trench in Sector 22 in an hour."

"I thought it was going to be the Comanche winter camp today," Letty was disappointed. She much preferred stalking the Comanches, to storming the German's trench.

"That's no fun," Stephen answered.

"Maybe we be G-men hunting for robbers," Douglas suggested. "You know, like the Newton brothers, or the Barker gang. Public enemy number one!"

Letty considered this. Yes, not as boring as storming a German trench and pretending to fight imaginary soldiers. "There were some strangers in the Square today, while you were inside the Savings & Loan. They kept looking up at the building and talking.

Two young men in spiffy duds and a lady with red hair and a fancy hat."

"Gangsters and their moll, for sure," Douglas nodded. "What did they do then, Letty?"

"They talked for a bit, and then they got into the car and drove away. It looked as if they were studying the building and seeing how many people were around."

"What kind of car?" Stephen looked as if he had already come around to considering hunting for gangsters.

"A shiny black touring car. It had a silver running greyhound on the front. It looked pretty new."

"A Lincoln," Douglas took especial note of cars – their makers and their styles, because of helping at the Tip-Top. "They must have been passing through; no one around Luna City drives a black Lincoln like that. We should wait for Artie. He knows everything there is to know about gangsters."

"Oh, him!" Stephen looked deflated. "Is he coming, too?"

"Yeah," Douglas answered, with a sigh. "We gave him the password for today and all."

"Rats," Stephen kicked the toe of his boot at the sandy ground. "He's a pain, always dragging his little brother along…"

"We ought to wait a bit for him anyway," Douglas insisted. "He'll know enough to make it all interesting. Anyway, I bought some candy at the ice cream parlor. I made two dollars in tips this week, and Mama said that I might treat Letty and my friends with a bit of it."

"Well, that's all right, then," Stephen yielded with little grace. "So where do we go, hunting for gangsters and robbers?"

"The Mills place would be a good start," Douglas mused, as he followed Stephen into the Fort, bowing halfway to the ground in order to make it through the low doorway. Inside was still cool from the shade, and faintly musty-smelling from the old buffalo robe. "I heard tell that Old Man Mills was a gangster himself, in the old days. The Bent Cactus gang, the Dalton gang and all. Everyone says that that Old Man Mills brought home the loot from all their robberies and hid it somewhere."

"Old Man Mills has been a likker bootlegger from a long time back, too," Stephen agreed. In the shade of the Fort, his eyes were as big and dark as those blackberries which grew on the field-side hedges and wastelands. "And he got some big ol' pet alligators in a pond out at his place. They say that he threw the dead bodies of his gang that he double-crossed to the alligators to eat. That way there'd be no evidence."

Now Douglas shook his head. "He doesn't neither, Stephen; his alligators aren't big enough."

"Bet you they are," Stephen insisted. "We ought to just scout around and take a look!"

Letty shivered, as if a cold draft had blown suddenly down her neck. Old Man Mills was a bogeyman to them: an old, cranky and unkept man with an evil reputation. He didn't much dare show his face in town anymore, so Letty had only seen him above half a dozen times. He had a wife, although Mama had a very sour expression on her face, whenever she might encounter Mrs. Mills about town. Mrs. Mills was a smooth-faced, black-haired woman, considerably younger than Old Man Mills. She spoke Spanish but was as pale-complected as any Anglo in Luna City, and she drove an old green-painted Ford truck with the authority and skill of a man, on frequent and mysterious errands. Most folks assumed she was making deliveries of Old Man Mills' illicit liquor.

"That woman is no better than she ought to be!" Letty had heard Mama fume to Poppa, once, when Mama thought that Letty and Douglas were out of hearing, after encountering Mrs. Mills in the doorway to Abernathy Hardware. It sounded like Mrs. Mills was indeed a gangster moll, Letty thought, upon reconsideration. Just like the pretty red-headed lady with the modish hat and a black Lincoln touring car. Her ruminations on this and Douglas and Stephen's discussion of how they should go about surreptitiously visiting the Mills place were interrupted by a shout from outside.

"Hey – anybody there!"

"It's Artie," Douglas peered through a gap in the planks and poles which made up the Fort. Cupping his hands around his mouth, he shouted back. "Halt! Who goes there?"

"It's Artie! Jeeze, you guys!"

"Montcalm!" Douglas bellowed. "Remember; that's the challenge! Now give the password, you stupe!"

"Oh," Artie was close enough to the Fort to not have to shout. "Wolfe! Izzat what you meant me to say, to get in?"

"Yeah," Douglas sounded exasperated, as Artie scrambled into the Fort, exclaiming in his excitement, "Hey, guys – you'll never guess what just happened at the Tip-Top!"

"It was robbed by a bunch of gangsters!" Stephen ventured, in flippant tones, and Artie's face fell.

"How did you know that?"

"I was just funning you!" Stephen's face fell, in turn. "It was a joke! Someone really has held up the Tip-Top?"

Both Letty and Douglas regarded Artie, mildly horrified. The McAllister house was across the road from the Tip-Top. They passed by it every day, and Douglas routinely hung around there on weekends and after school, running errands. Artie looked a bit deflated.

"Naw … not really. But Mr. Shaw thought they looked real dangerous. There was this brand-new shiny black Lincoln outside at the pumps, filling up when he looked through the window … and he told my Pop that he thought he saw one of the men take a shotgun out of the back and hide it under his jacket, and the woman – she had red hair – was getting into the driver's seat as the two men came inside to pay for the gas. Mr. Shaw put his own shotgun on the counter next to the cash register, and he was watching the two men as they came in the door, one by one. He told Pop that when they saw that *he* was watching them real close, and he had his shotgun handy … well, they looked *real* nervous. The two men looked at each other, and the first one shook his head, an' came an' paid for the gas, and they both walked out together. Mr. Shaw, he called Pop on the telephone and said he was sure they had been planning to stick up the Tip-Top, an' he was pretty certain they were wanted men, they acted so suspicious."

"I'm sure it was the same as I saw at the Savings and Loan," Letty said, with a sinking feeling at the pit of her stomach. "There was a girl with red hair, too. They were looking at the building. Mr. Shaw was right to call on the law. I'm sure they were up to no good at all."

"You saw them?" Artie breathed, electric with excitement. "They were casing the joint, for sure, Letty. That's what they call it, when they're planning to rob a place."

"Did Mr. Shaw say where they drove off to?" Douglas asked. Artie nodded.

"He says the car went south, towards Beeville." He sighed, a short and disappointed sigh. "They could be anywhere by now, with good hideout. Bet they are real notorious, like Alvin Karpis an' the Barker gang. Public enemy number one!"

Another call from outside the Fort; this time a girl's voice, courteous and tentative. Letty poked her head out through the low opening.

"Hi, Retta – we're all inside." As Retta scrambled inside, nearly on hands and knees, Letty added, "We were going to scout for Comanches, but Douglas and Stephen want to go look at the alligators at the old Mills place."

"You didn't ask her for the password!" Artie exclaimed, indignantly. "That's not fair! She could be an enemy spy!"

"No, she's a neutral," Letty insisted. "A medical person."

"See?" Retta stuck out her tongue briefly at Artie, who made a face. During this discussion, Douglas and Stephen had made up their minds regarding the new mission for the day.

"The alligators," Douglas said. "Old Man Mills' alligators. Just to settle once and for all that they are really there, like all the stories have it, and that they might be big enough to eat a human body. Or not."

"I dunno why that matters at all," Artie grumbled. He was still miffed at how Retta didn't have to give the password to be invited into the Fort.

Douglas answered, stern and commanding – every bit the leader of their small band. "Because what is true and provable really matters," Douglas insisted. *(For the rest of her life, Letty believed that was her brothers' guiding intellectual principle.)*

Stephen and Douglas planned the incursion into the old Mills place with their customary thoroughness: on foot, leaving pony and bicycles behind, stalking single-file through the clumps of cane and scrub bushes which lined the river to the south of the Fort. The river formed the boundary between the Mills place, and the remains of the Gonzalez rancho, Rincon de los Robles. The Gonzalez acres were lush, well-tended, the pastures green even in summer, dotted with stock tanks hollowed from the earth, and star-scattered with cattle, horses, and even a few goats. In stark contrast, the Mills place seemed deserted. Where once had been cultivated fields and pastures brought forth corn, beans and cotton, and pastured a good few milk cows and their calves – now was all overgrown and worthless. Letty could see this difference, even at a distance as she and Retta and the boys approached the boundary separating the Mills place – several strands of sagging barbed-wire stapled to posts of native cedar, weathered grey and slanting in all directions, or to the trunks of scrub hackberry and cedar trees.

Douglas lifted his right hand, and made a gesture towards Stephen, and then pointed towards a thicket some little distance off. Stephen shouldered his.22 and nodded, slipping away to take up a position on guard. Douglas gestured then towards Artie, who merely looked at him blankly. "You're supposed to be a scout," Douglas hissed through his teeth. "I wanted you to climb up that there hackberry tree and look ahead of the trail."

"Why didn't you just say so?" Artie asked, and Douglas scowled.

"Because we're supposed to be conducting this mission in silence!" He explained, in exasperation and Artie dusted off his hands on the seat of his coveralls, saying,

"OK, then – what am I s'posed to be looking for?"

"Anyone moving about the house or the barn," Douglas still sounded exasperated. "Mrs. Mills, she generally drives to San Antone on a Monday, so likely she won't be round. Look for that ol' Ford truck that she drives, though."

Letty and Retta waited patiently, while Artie shimmied up the hackberry, his bare toes and fingers gripping the trunk and branches rather like a monkey. From where they stood, the girls could see the uppermost parts of the old farmhouse, which commanded a fine view from the summit of a low hill overlooking the river. The place was the picture of neglect, the roof and porches sagging alarmingly. A few shreds of faded paint clung to the upper walls, and the northern roof angles were all furry with moss and lichens growing on the shingles. Heat shimmers rose from the distant county road, and a cloud of dust following an unseen motor vehicle towards the Mills place.

"Holy cats!" Artie exclaimed, in his normal voice.

Douglas, Letty, and Retta all chorused in whispers, "Be quiet! Shusssh! Silence! What did you see! Is Old Man Mills coming towards us?" as Artie slid down the tree as nimbly as he had scrambled up it, and Stephen came from his guard post.

"It's them!" Artie replied, almost incoherent with excitement. "Them! The gangsters in the black Lincoln car, them that tried to stick up the Tip-Top! They're coming along the driveway to the Mills place?" In a burst of enthusiasm, Artie added, "I'll bet they're gonna hide out there! Them an' their moll! Ol' Man Mills, he's a gangster too – from a long way back, ain't he?"

"It stands to reason," Douglas mused, chewing on his lower lip. "Birds of a feather all flock together. But we have to be certain it's really them; those people that Letty saw – before we go and tell your father that they're gangsters. Besides," Douglas added. "It's not as if they did anything wrong, so far. They just looked at the S&L building. Mr. Shaw, he only thought they might try and rob the Tip-Top. They really didn't do anything. There isn't any law 'gainst standing and looking, or for what people might think…"

"They were acting all suspicious," Artie argued. "An' if they really are gangsters, then it might be dangerous to go any closer…"

"We have to be certain it's them – the two men in spiffy suits and the red-haired woman that Letty saw – before we go telling anyone else." Douglas decided. "And it might be dangerous, if they really are gangsters and up to no good at all. So here's what we do. Artie, you and Letty come with me, but Stephen, you and Retta, you stay here, hidden in the bushes. We're gonna walk straight up to the house and ask to speak to Old Man Mills and we're going to keep our eyes peeled for that shiny black Lincoln. If we don't come back this way by the time the sun sinks to that big branch over there, you go straight to Mr. Vaughn and tell him what we did and that we've likely been kidnapped by some bad people at the Mills place."

"What if they catch us," Letty asked, with a shiver. She didn't relish the thought of walking up to the Mills place, derelict and tumble-down, and Artie gulped – game but paling visibly. "What will we say."

"We say that we … we came because we wanted to see the alligators," Douglas announced, with a triumphant grin. "That one of our friends dared us – they said there wasn't any such thing, and we came out to prove him wrong. But we wanted to ask permission, first."

"Would Old Man Mills believe that?" Artie quavered, and Douglas shrugged.

"Prolly. We're kids taking a stupid dare. And we didn't go trespassing; that would be rude. That's got to count for something."

Stephen nodded agreement; so did Retta. They held the strands of wire apart, so that Douglas, Artie and Letty could climb through. In the distance, they heard a car horn honk, several times.

"Remember – wait until the sun drops to the level of that big branch," Douglas said over his shoulder.

"Be careful," Retta replied, and Douglas grinned again.

"Save your bandages for the next time, Retta. We'll be back in good time."

The three walked together, single-file down a narrow track through knee-high dead grass in what once had been a pasture. When the track widened, Letty and moved to walk beside her brother.

"Why didn't you ask Stephen to come with you instead of Artie?" she murmured. "He wanted to come with us. We're the three Musketeers."

"Because Stephen's poppa is a rich man," Douglas replied, in a very low voice, and a feeling like ice-water trickled down Letty's back, as he continued. "Gangsters, Letty. Kidnapping for ransom like the Lindberg baby. If someone told those gangsters that Stephen is a Wyler, who knows what they might try, if he just walked into their hideout and they realized who he is."

"I didn't think of that." Letty admitted. The kidnapping of the Lindberg baby right out of his nursery early that spring, and how the he had been found dead in the woods close by, months afterwards; that had been all over the radio, splashed in the newspaper and the newspapers – even in Texas. "We're McAllisters. Wouldn't we be in as much danger of being kidnapped?"

"We're not anything as rich or important as the Wylers," Douglas replied, confidently. "No one would snatch us for much of a ransom, and as for Artie? They'd pay just for his folks to take him back!"

In further silence, the three climbed over a dilapidated gate at the other end of the overgrown field a gate which opened on a roadway of sorts. This was the track – hardly to be distinguished by calling it a driveway, or even a ranch road – which led to the Mills place. It was merely a pair of tracks beaten into the clay-hard ground, with a strip of grass and weeds growing along the hump in between, and longer weeds and grass growing to either side. There were fresh automobile tracks printed in the soft dust, dust which puffed up under their feet like pale brown talcum powder.

They walked around a bend in the track – that last bend shaded by a pair of oak trees – and the ruined home-place of the Mills farm lay before them. What had once been a garden of cosmos, rose-bushes and hollyhocks was now a wilderness of weeds, broken now and again by thorny and overgrown rose-bush canes. The house looked worse – dilapidated, with window shutters fallen awry from their hinges, once-intricate gingerbread trim ragged, like a mouthful of broken teeth, and a porch roof sagging ominously. The windows gaped – eye-holes in a dark skull. Off to one side, the remains of a barn listed ominously; about one more winter gale from collapsing entirely. There was a brooding silence about the place, broken only by birdsong, and the tinny, faint sound of a radio, somewhere within the house. Yet before that spectacle of rural ruin was parked something entirely apposite; a new jet-black Lincoln touring sedan. The engine creaked and popped, as it cooled: Douglas briefly rested a hand on the hood.

"It's hot," he whispered. "Just got here, I reckon."

"That's the car that I saw in the Square this morning," Letty whispered to her brother, as they stood irresolute at the foot of the ramshackle stairs to the house. "I'm certain. There's not another one like it, in the whole of Luna City."

"What do we do now?" Artie whispered from the other side. He was nervous, shifting from bare foot to bare foot.

Douglas smiled; his own nerves did not entirely belie the confidence with which he spoke. "I'll knock on the door," he replied. And did so – trotting up the decaying steps and rapping smartly on the front door.

The three children waited a response, which came after Douglas knocked again, and called, "Anyone at home? Mr. Mills?"

A step from around the corner of the porch – not the door opening. A young man stood there, coatless, eyeing them suspiciously. His dark hair was parted in the middle, and his ears stuck out like the handles on a sugar bowl. There was a young-old look to him; it was his eyes, Letty thought. Old eyes in a young face, cold eyes, like a rattlesnake deciding whether to strike or not.

"What are you doing here!" he demanded. "What do you want?"

"We came to ask Mr. Mills if we could see the alligators," Douglas replied, just as the door opened, with a creak and a scrape. Douglas stepped back, a little.

"Get the hell out of here," the young man ordered. "Go on, get!"

A woman had followed the young man around the corner of the house; Letty's eyes widened; the red-haired girl. She glanced at the three children, and reached for the man's arm, saying in a soothing voice,

"Clyde, they're only kids. Don't fret so, they must be pals with ol' Charley."

The man opening the door must be Mr. Mills; bent and bearded, his clothes hanging off him like an old suit on a scarecrow. There was something of the same kind of menace emanating from him, just as there was from the young man with cold rattlesnake eyes.

Douglas extended his right hand as if to properly shake hands with Mr. Mills. "I'm Douglas McAllister, sir, and this is my sister, Leticia. I take it that you are Mr. Charley Mills. Leticia and our friend Artie came to ask if we could see the alligators. They're a real curiosity 'round here, and one of our pals didn't believe there was any such thing. We aimed to prove him wrong, so we thought it was only mannerly to come and ask."

"And I'm Artie Vaughn," Artie stepped up to stand next to Douglas, although Letty could see that he was as pale as a freshly-washed sheet, but he spoke up bravely. "Pleased to make your acquaintance, Mr. Mills, sir."

The old man began to wheeze, so heartily that Letty thought he might fall over, clinging to the door as he was. She thought at first that he was coughing, but it was only a fit of laughter as creaky and decrepit as the door itself.

"Mannerly young pups!" Old Mr. Mills shook Douglas' extended hand and then Artie's. "Sure thing, young fella. Go look at the 'gators. They're in the fenced pond, down yonder. Shoot a 'coon or 'possum on the way and throw it in for them. A chicken, iffn' you got any to spare." Old Mr. Mills nodded in an aside to the dangerous younger man. "Don't fret you none, Clyde. These young sprouts are good neighbors of mine."

"Sure," replied the man Clyde, and let the girl take him back around the corner of the porch again.

Letty thought that she ought to put out her own hand, and Old Mr. Mills essayed a bow over it, and brushed the back of her knuckles with a great, smacking kiss. "Especially you, little Miss Leticia."

Letty would, when she was somewhat older, recognize a lubricious leer when she saw one. Now she only resisted the temptation to wipe that wiskery, slobbery kiss off the back of her hand against the seat of her knickerbockers. She stepped back a bit, and put her hand behind her back, grateful that she stood between her smart older brother, and their brave friend Artie, who was brave even though he must be quaking in the boots that he didn't have on his bare and dusty feet.

"If we see anything fitten' for alligator feed," Artie replied, "We will surely feed those critters of yours."

"Thank you, Mr. Mills," Douglas said, and the door creaked closed, leaving the three children alone on the rotted porch. He turned to the both of them, adding. "I guess we'll see the alligators now. And then we'll tell Retta and Stephen that there aren't no gangsters here. They're just friends of Mr. Mills' – come for a visit."

The alligators were there indeed, three of them of only moderate size, languishing around the muddy margins of a large stock pond, a little distant from the ruined farmstead. A stout plank fence surrounded the area around the pond, a structure which appeared to be the only sound thing about the whole place. One alligator dozed on the bank, the other pair lazed, motionless in the shallows, just their eyes and nostrils breaking the surface. Artie wanted to toss a pebble on the nearest gator's back, just to see if it would wake it up, but Douglas vetoed that notion.

"Well," Artie ventured at last. "Now we have seen them, we can say that ol' Mr. Mills's gators are real, and not a yarn to frighten folk with."

"Yes," Letty agreed with a shiver. "Let's go." She did not like the alligators, their muddy pond, the whole decrepit aspect of the Mills place, it's unsavory owner … or his friends.

It was only when Letty and Douglas were several years older, that Letty recognized the dangerous young man with the cold calculating eyes of a rattlesnake, and that pretty red-headed girl who had been Old Charley Mills' visitors on that that summer day.

"So her name is Bonnie," Letty mused, studying the pictures in the Beeville newspaper so closely that the black and white features devolved into a blur of black and grey dots. "I did like the hat she had on, that time."

And So It Begins…

THE FIRST ANNUAL MILLS FARM

INVITATIONAL CHILI CONTEST!

HELD ON SATURDAY, NOV. 17, 2018

AT THE CHUCKWAGON CIRCLE

Cash prize for 1st, 2nd and 3rd place contestants!

To be judged by a panel of celebrity judges, including Alan Lee Mayne, of *Ala Carte With Quartermayne!*

Apply before 1 October

Application can be downloaded from www.millsfarm.com/chili contest

Questions? Send email to events@millsfarm.com

The Wages of Crime

It was Friday at the VFW – guest night, when those in Luna City who had never served in anything resembling a military – were welcome. The VFW was a reconditioned old temporary classroom moved from the grounds of the High School some years ago, to a tree-shaded glade on the banks of the river directly behind the Tip-Top Ice House Gas & Grocery. The tall windows across the back of the old classroom looked out onto a weathered concrete patio set about with heavy wooden picnic tables and benches. This was the venue for many a local celebration, as well as being a long-established male refuge, just as the various church ladies' associations and committees were the female equivalent.

Richard was drawn to sit at one of the tables outside with his closest associates in Luna City – Joe Vaughn, Chris Mayall, and Berto Gonzalez with his cousin Sylvester, dapper as always in a vintage Hawaiian shirt and chino trousers with turn-up cuffs. Chris and Sylvester had been Richards' partner – if not in crime – then in a completely underhanded scheme to sabotage a movie which came to film on location in Luna City some years previous. Since then, Richard had felt considerable camaraderie with them. They had a history together of a daring and slightly underhanded deed done for the best of causes, under the nose of authority, such as the security team at Mills Farm. And of course, Chris had given him refuge several times, not the least when Sammi Colquhoun appeared in Luna City to be married to Doc Wyler's fabulously wealthy son Collin.

The late summer breeze – barely mitigated by the shade of a stand of mighty sycamore trees – rustled the leaves overhead. Some distance along the riverbank, it appeared that work for the day was done on a new riverside landing. A series of Brobdingnagian squared blocks of limestone were apparently being stacked from the riverbank in stair-step fashion, reaching out into shallow water.

"'Lo, Ricardo," Sylvester raised his own beer in greeting, as Richard sat down with a very nice, not-too-over-hopped locally-sourced India Pale Ale. "Admiring the new waterside feature, I see."

"It looks like a staircase for giants," Richard commented, distributing a collegial nod to all, as he sat down with his barely-tasted IPA. "What is it supposed to be, in reality?"

"A launching-ramp for the Mills Farm water-sporting concession," Sylvester replied. "For tubers and kayakers. They start from here, and float down the river, enjoying all the scenic wonders of our little patch of paradise…"

"Might even include the spectacle of the Old Communards, skinny-sipping in the old swimming hole by the Age of Aquarius," Richard pointed out, whereupon Sylvester made gagging sounds.

"Yeah, they're building one on the river-front at Mills Farm, and a third one a bit farther downriver. Just before the bridge on Route 80 that goes towards Helena. Mills Farm is gonna run a regular excursion bus to collect them all."

"It might be nice to float the river," Richard mused. "Without the hazard of running into a stray house or two …"

"You should try it, now and again, Ricardo," Joe Vaughn hoisted his own beer bottle in salute. "Yeah, I agree that your last venture on it in Uncle Harry's boat in a dire emergency might have left ya with some skewed memories of the experience…"

"God – all I recall is the impression that he had a whip in hand, and that if I rowed well, I would live," Richard sank about a third of his own beer. "And then the sobbing women and screaming children."

"But it all came out OK," Joe reassured him. Richard, considering the matter over, at the distance of time involved, concluded that yes, it did. His prep-school experience rowing and sailing had all come to good use, several decades after their acquisition. Now Joe was waxing reminiscent. "Ya handled it all better than I did, with the guy that I was given to ride with, when I first got taken on to the Luna City PD." Joe sighed, deeply. "God help me, I was supposed to be the experienced one. I had this prospective hire to take on my shift, all up and down 123, in the wee hours. New guy; just came out from California. Decided to bail from a tech company in Austin, wanted to get in touch with his inner hippie, come settle in Luna City and tell all the rest of us how we are supposed to be living … anyway. I take the probie on for the midnight shift. As soon as we haul out, I get a call: loose livestock on the highway, from the Wyler place. Some a-hole damaged the perimeter fence, we got …"

"Cattle on the road?" Sylvester ventured. Joe sighed again.

"Nope. We got a couple of Doc Wyler's emu birds wandering around loose. Ever seen an emu? Like an ostrich for size but got an attitude like you wouldn't believe. Aggressive? Those bastards could give lessons to mules and longhorns. Anyway, so I got this probie – a potential new hire along for a ride on shift, see if he has got any game or skills at law-enforcement. We got the call and located Doc Wyler's wandering emus pretty briskly. Came up on them just by the cut-off to the Aquarius. I did say something about that the Wyler Ranch ought to get that stretch of fence repaired … and then I said, just as the emus showed up clear in the spot-light 'Jesus! Do you see the size of those chickens?'"

"And what did he say to that?" Richard inquired, once the roar of laughter from around the table had died down.

Joe grinned, reminiscently. "Nothing much, but he was as white as a ghost, and his eyes went big, looking at those birds, wandering in the headlights. I said, 'Ya know what they say; everything *is* bigger in Texas.' To which he said nothing at all." Joe gave a regretful shrug. "We got back to the station at the end of our shift, he said 'thanks-very-much-I'll-be-in-touch' and that was the last, the very last we ever heard of him. Guess he decided to say in Austin, after all."

"Don't beat yourself up, man," Sylvester consoled him. "The last thing the PD needs around here is an officer who can't tell the difference between an emu and a chicken."

"Shoot, man – that wasn't anywhere near the funniest call we ever drew," Chris chuckled and popped the cap off another beer. "That has to be the time that those two idiots stole Clem Bodie's bass boat."

"Oh, yeah," Joe also chuckled. "'Nacio Gomez and Reuben Sifuentes; Luna City's very own dynamic duo. You remember them, Ricardo? Those two dirtbags who helped Mizz Mason heist twenty million in antique light fixtures."

"Vividly," Richard nodded; the attempted theft of eighteen original, antique Lalique light fixtures from the Cattleman Hotel during the course of extensive renovation work had only been thwarted as a result of casual conversation between himself and Roman Gonzalez.

"You would have thought that the incident to which I refer would have given them both a solid reason to reflect on their career choices, and make an amendment to their lives, but this is 'Nacio and Reuben," Joe looked across the table with a sigh. "You want to tell the story, Chris? You were the first on-scene."

"You tell it better," Chris grinned. "You set up the situation, and I'll fill in the vivid details."

"All right, then. This happened early in the winter; ten years ago, more or less. Now, you know that Clem Bodie is mad for bass fishing, and he had this gorgeous boat – a near to brand-new 18-foot Triton, which was wicked fast. It would be, with a 150 HP outboard engine. Well, that boat sat out on a trailer, round in back of the feed mill, during the working week when Clem wasn't pestering the snot out of the bass in some lake paradise or other. So it was on a mid-week evening that 'Nacio and Reuben were tempted mightily, having looked upon the wine when it was red, the beer when it was flowing, and god knows, whatever else they were pounding down. Or smoking. At about two in the morning 'Nacio drove his old pickup truck around to Bodies…"

"It is a well-established fact that nothing good happens at two in the morning," Richard commented.

"Affirmative, Ricardo," Joe sighed. "So, 'Nacio backed up his truck to Clem's shiny-new bass boat and trailer, and Reuben eased the trailer hitch down over the ball and they took off, going like a bat out of hell, once they got onto CR 81. They were heading east; god only knows what those two numbskulls had in mind for that boat."

"You'd think, if you were embarked on a life of crime, you'd be doing your damndest not to stand out by going 95 miles an hour with a stolen bass boat on a trailer," Sylvester agreed; it seemed that this epic was new to him. "But no one ever said that 'Nacio an' Reuben were the brightest bulbs on the marquee."

"That is probably why they have never had any material success with the criminal lifestyle," Joe agreed with great solemnity. "Such success requires forethought, planning, and conscientious attention to detail. Fortunately for us in the law-enforcement profession, most criminally inclined dirtbags are dumber than a box of hammers, no impulse control, and no grasp of the concept of delayed gratification. It's why we manage to catch so many of them. One of those little details for which Reuben didn't pay any mind was the reality that the ball-hitch on the back of 'Nacio's beater of a pickup was too damn small for the trailer hitch. They went roaring down 81 towards Helena, and just as they came up to where the road crosses Cibolo Creek, the trailer bounces once, twice ... and comes off the ball-hitch. For a few critical moments, however – the trailer continues at roughly the same original speed and trajectory as 'Nacio's pickup."

"We figured out what had happened once the sun came up," Chris picked up the scattered threads of the tale. "I have never seen a more telling demonstration of the concept of stuff in motion continuing to move at speed."

"Newton's first law," Richard contributed sagely, quoting. "*An object at rest stays at rest and an object in motion stays in motion with the same speed and in the same direction unless acted upon by an unbalanced force*. Don't look at me that way, chaps; I had an old-style prep-school education lavished upon me, for which my parents wasted thousands of quid."

"In this case, the unbalanced force was the concrete barriers on either side of the roadway over Cibolo Creek," Chris nodded. "We worked out what happened, when we found the marks on the concrete where the trailer crossed over into the other lane, bashed into it … and the boat itself came loose from the trailer, and continued traveling. At the same speed and in the same direction…"

"At ninety-five miles an hour," Joe inserted. He seemed to be in a rather pedantic mode. "Possibly more. Although it appeared from the skid-marks on the road that 'Nacio hit the brakes when the trailer shook loose from the hitch. His pickup, then going at a speed slightly slower than that of the recently detached trailer and the bass boat on it … was torpedoed by the bass boat. It was a beautiful thing. The boat arrowed straight under the ass-end of 'Nacio's truck. Smashed into it like a bunker-buster. The boat was a loss and 'Nacio's truck was totaled. When we got called out to the scene, the rear wheels were off the deck entirely, and the front bumper was kissing the road. Clem was … irate," Joe added, parenthetically. "He had to write off the boat and the fight with his insurance company over the claim was epic. You wanna pick up the thread now, Chris?"

"Gladly," Chris replied. "The VFD ambulance got called out by the Karnes County sheriff dispatcher. Local good citizen heard two a terrific bangs, then a crunch out on the road with a horn blaring, and called it in; said there had been a massive accident, likely with casualties by the very sound of it on the 81 at the Cibolo Creek bridge, could we render medical assistance as the nearest to the incident. I was on duty with the bus. And there we went. It was the most interesting and awesome spectacle. Yeah – a spectacle. The empty trailer was there, sitting in the other lane, a good few yards along. And there was the bass boat, wedged under the pickup. 'Nacio and Reuben were in shock. They were sitting there in the front seats of 'Nacio's wrecked pickup." Chris sighed, apparently deeply relishing the memory of that call-out. "It was an awesome sight; I shit you not. They were sitting there, in the wrecked pickup, looking out through the windshield, as if they couldn't figure out why this had happened. Eyes as white and big as cue-balls. At least –" Chris added. "They did have their seat-belts fastened. They had that going for them, at least."

"Karma in all it's full, glorious splendor," Joe added. "Getting nailed by the very boat they stole."

"So, what happened to 'Nacio and Reuben, once y'all stopped pointing and laughing?" Sylvester asked.

"Time served in the Karnesville Correctional Center, and a good few stints of dressing in orange jumpsuits and picking up trash from the side of the roads," Joe answered. "Until this last go-round with the light fixtures, I thought they had learned that crime doesn't pay."

"Some people just never learn," Berto announced, demonstrating yet again his sure command of the transparently obvious.

"And thus is my continuing career in law-enforcement guaranteed," Joe stood and stretched. "As well as that of the Luna City Police department in general. Another round, guys? My treat."

Wedding of the Decade!

An Interview with Sammi – Daily Mirror

The wedding of Sammi Colquhoun to international financier Collin Wyler may have been overshadowed in the news by recent royal weddings, but former Page-3 girl and lifestyle guru Sammi was every bit as lavish, as we can report with confidence. We caught up to Sammi in the luxurious apartment in the Canaletto high-rise, overlooking the City, which she shares now with her fabulously wealthy husband, since returning from Texas earlier this summer.

"The wedding itself was marvelous!" Sammi exclaimed, when I asked. "And such a party, with three hundred of our closest and dearest friends for a garden wedding at Collie's old family estate! His mother designed the gardens, years ago, and we exchanged our personal vows in front of a summerhouse covered with climbing Cecile Brunner blossoms. A vision of pink roses – and they set off my wedding dress to perfection. Our photographer and videographer were so pleased with the effect!"

"It sounds perfectly lovely – almost as lovely as an English garden," I said, and Sammi laughed in delight.

"Even better, for there was no chance of a rainy-day ruining everything! Would you believe that in Texas as much as a fortnight might go by in the summer without a single drop of rain? Collie assured me that scheduling a wedding ceremony out of doors would not be in the least hazard of having the weather interfere, and he was so right. Collie is so clever, with his investments and projects, I do believe that he is the most brilliant man in the world. Anyway, it was his notion to be married there, at that quaint old plantation. His father still lives there and runs the ranch, can you believe that – a dear old stick, but such a grump … oh, I'd best not be indiscreet!"

"I see that your wedding party included some other notable personalities," I thought it best to change the subject. "Do you want to tell me something about them?"

"Well, Susannah Wyatt-Gonzales, of course," Sammi enthused. "She was my matron of honor. She is another one of those with bulging brains, like Collie, and she married that simply dishy male model, the Handsome Convict last year. Although he was never a convict," Sammi added hastily. "It was just that he was in costume for some tiresome little theater production and simply everyone leaped to the wrong conclusion. And it was so sweet of Pip Noel-Barrett! He volunteered to be one of the ushers, except that Collie turned him down; Pip and I used to be a pair simply ages ago. Still, he was a perfect lamb, advising me about flowers and decorating the reception venue. At the last moment, he had to bow out, so he wasn't part of my wonderful, fairy-tale day. But another one of my former beaus was there and he made me the most monumental wedding cake, all covered in flowers! It's a matter of pride to me, that I remain on excellent terms with every former companion. Once lovers, always and forever friends! Rich was a master chef, you know – and the cake he made for my special day was magnificent!"

"Rich Hall?" I asked, and Sammi giggled delightfully. "I know that you also used to date Rich Hall, the Bad Boy Chef – didn't he used to be famous?"

"Why yes, but he is mostly retired now. I simply couldn't believe it when Pip told me. Poor Rich has something like anesthesia now – that dreadful condition when you hit your head and simply forget everything in your past. He believes now that he is this person from Barcelona, or whatever. But he did the most splendid cake …"

Custody Dispute

Another day of rewarding work at the Café – Richard set his bike homeward, towards the Age, and what he had begun to think of as home, the little polished-aluminum caravan parked there. It was mid-afternoon on a Thursday. His Kate, his dear sweet Kate, had reported by a cellphone conversation earlier in the day. Her research on a story would take her from Beeville to Karnesville in the late afternoon – might she come by the Age for a supper, and possibly a cuddle?

Even though the cuddle would most likely be with Ozzie, King of Kings and Captain Kitten in his internet guise, rather than himself, Richard assented with happy anticipation. Yes – another splendid supper and sparkling conversation with Kate, his Kate of Kate Hall, his comfortable and affectionate friend, the woman who knew him for all his many faults and appeared to love him anyway. He headed away from the Café, leaving preparations for the next day in the mostly-capable hands of Luc, sometime drummer for a local band most famed for a name which gravitated in many directions from their initials – OPM – and his trained and trusty apprentices… planning in his mind a private, haute-cuisine classical French menu for his Kate, from what he knew to be on hand in the miniscule refrigerator in the Airstream, combined with snippings of herbs and salad greens from the bounty of the raised beds so lovingly-cultivated out in back of the Café. As he pedaled through the tree-shaded outskirts of Luna City towards Route 123, Richard realized that there was no cream in the little caravan refrigerator – bugger! So much for a simple dessert, and for a touch of crème fraiche … hang on, perhaps the Tip-Top might have … yes, indeed. Under the management of Chris Mayall, the crowded and battered old shelves of the Tip-Top Ice House, Gas and Grocery contained an unexpectedly broad variety of grocery items: mostly canned and refrigerated, bottled water and sodas, candy bars and dried beef jerky, crackers … indeed, everything but fresh green vegetables and fruits. A half-pint of cream – Richard veered into the crumbling apron of broken macadam paving which merged almost imperceptibly with the shoulder of Route 123, just before it narrowed again to cross the river on a newly-renovated four-lane bridge.

There was a single car parked in front of the Tip-Top's sagging verandah; not that there was ever much of a crowd in the Tip-Top on weekdays, and certainly not in the parking lot, unless there was a big do at the VFW post – that pink former classroom, in the grove of trees behind the Tip-Top.

"Behave yourself, Ozzie," Richard ordered his feline familiar, who was quite accustomed to an orderly routine: a day of hunting small vermin along the backside of the block of buildings which formed the northern side of Town Square; a short ride in the plastic crate (which had originally been used for gallon jugs of milk) strapped to the rear of Richard's bicycle; a return to the small caravan at the Age, home-sweet-home, a home of comfy soft surfaces; shelter from the dark and cold, and hungry predators who might make a nocturnal meal of a small, brindle one-eyed cat. "Back in a tick – your favorite of the female of our species is coming for a brief visit…"

"Mrrow!" Ozzie replied, butting the top of his brindle head against Richard's careless caress. Richard went in through the swinging door of the Tip-Top, utterly confident that Ozzie would be still in the basket strapped to the back of his mountain bike – like Richard himself, Ozzie was a creature of rigid habit.

There were two other customers in the Tip-Top – paying for gasoline at the cash register. Richard hardly spared them a glance. A couple, about the age of his parents; Chris was ringing up their purchase. He went to the rank of battered refrigerated cases which displayed soft drinks, water, beer and two shelves of dairy products. Yes; a pint of plain cream, the last remaining. Richard snagged it, thinking himself most fortunate and continued mentally planning his supper menu, waiting impatiently for the male half of the couple to finish scrawling a signature on the charge receipt.

"Find everything you were looking for, Ricardo?" Chris grinned in recognition.

"No, alas – your selection of fine burgundies, *foie gras*, and Perigord truffles is painfully limited," Richard answered. "Be a good chap and speak to your manager about this."

"Smart-ass," Chris returned equably and rang up the cream. Richard paid in cash, declined the offer of a plastic bag, citing his concern for over-harvesting of those mighty stands of plastic trees in South America. He could still hear Chris chuckling, as the door swung closed behind him.

To his vague surprise, the couple who had been ahead of him at the Tip-Top still lingered, their attention wholly focused on Richard's bicycle – that trusty fat-tire mountain bike which had been his preferred means of transport, now that hire-cars and chauffeur-driven limousines were out of the question. No – not the bike, he realized as he put the cream in the plastic utility basket bungee-corded to the rear rack – the basket which Ozzie shared uncomplaining with a covered bucket of choice fruit and vegetable scraps intended for the resident chickens at the Age of Aquarius Campground and Goat farm. The man and woman both were staring fixedly at Ozzie, who waited with un-catlike patience and total indifference to the audience for Richard to complete whatever silly human errand had interrupted the commute home.

"I beg your pardon," Richard ventured, and both heads swiveled towards him – the woman was the first to speak.

"What are you doing with my daughter's cat?" she demanded, while the man – obviously her husband half-groaned.

"Marta – there must be a hundred …."

"No!" Marta exclaimed in indignation, "That's Marlene's Mr. Whiskers! I'm certain of it, Fred!"

"Ummm," Richard hated to intervene in what appeared to be a domestic dispute over mistaken cat-identity between Fred and Marta. "I beg to differ, madam – this is my cat. Has been for … over two years, ever since I found him as a stray after the big flood over Memorial Day, behind my place of work. His name is Ozymandias-King of Kings. Ozzie for short. If he is anyone's cat – he is mine, and everyone around here knows it."

"He's Mr. Whiskers!" Marta insisted, a thin edge of hysteria informing the words, like the gold trim on an expensive wedding invitation. "With one blind eye, brindle – and three white whiskers on the left side! That's Marlene's Mr. Whiskers – she nursed him on a bottle, since he was so sickly the PALS office asked her to foster him! There was a litter of three, and they thought he wouldn't survive without care – but he did! Marlene slept with him in her arms that first week, because he needed care around the clock! She sent me the pictures of him!" Marta fumbled in her handbag for a cellphone, brandishing it under Richard's nose. "See – that's my daughter's cat…"

"Careless of her to have misplaced him," Richard remarked, in his most arctic, cut-glass superior British tones, and was interiorly chilled to the bone when Marta burst into incoherent tears, right there on the rickety weathered grey verandah of the Tip-Top.

Ozzie regarded the spectacle with serene feline indifference. Meanwhile, Fred embraced his other domestic half. Over her heaving shoulder, he addressed Richard.

"See … our daughter passed away suddenly. Two years and three months ago, it was. Auto accident, coming home from her job at Christus Spohn in Corpus, on the late shift. We live in New Braunfels, see. A drunk driver t-boned her car and ran away because he had no insurance and no license. She was three days on life support before they told her husband it was no use to go on with it all. I don't think they ever managed to arrest the driver," Fred added, with slight bitterness in his voice. "Greg had to get a job on the oil rigs. He couldn't take on Marlene's pets, you see; keep a place for them to live. The two dogs, and Mr. Whiskers. We were passing this way between Corpus Christi and home, with the dogs and Mr. Whiskers in travel carriers, and a bunch of stuff in a trailer we rented – stuff from Marlene and Greg's place that we were gonna store for him. We stopped right here, at this very place because we needed to gas up, and the dogs needed a whiz break … and somehow in all the fuss, Mr. Whiskers got out of the cat carrier. We called for him. We looked and looked and called for him, but we had the dogs and the trailer, and everyone was afraid that the flood would close the bridge. We had to move on. We …" and Fred swallowed with somewhat of an effort. "We didn't … we hated that we had to go and leave Mr. Whiskers. Came back a couple of times when the flood was past. We thought …"

"We thought that someone must have taken him in," Marta recovered herself. "Someone nice and responsible, who would take care of him the way that Marlene did. And we could find him and get him back. He's so friendly, he would walk right up to anyone at all. He's chipped …"

"Chipped?" Richard looked between Marta, and Ozzie, now regarding the persons who had interrupted his routine with lordly indifference. Richard's hand went, almost involuntarily toward Ozzie's brindled ears, and Ozzie's head rose to meet his caress.

"Mroow!" he demanded, imperiously, as was his habit. Obviously, Ozzie believed that his audience with his worshippers was done. A dish of finest fish-flavored kibble, a cuddle with his favorite human, and an evening of restful slumber at the foot of the bed occupied by his second favorite human were on his personal feline schedule; a schedule far more urgent than the mewlings of these impotent humans.

"He's our daughters' cat," Marta stated obdurately. "Mr. Whiskers. And how he's ours! We can prove it! And we want him returned to us – right this very minute."

***

"What happened then?" Katie demanded, not half an hour later – her fine beryl-colored eyes gleaming with righteous indignation and concern. "And who are these people, anyway? <u>You</u> found Ozzie that night that you fixed that splendid haute-cuisine supper for me. He was hanging out in the hedge between the Café and the

Stein's place. I remember that very clearly, in spite of having too darned many glasses of your landlords' wine that evening."

She and Richard sat out in the brief covered patio space before the Airstream, relishing the calm afternoon, the sun slowly sliding down in the western sky, a bottle of Sefton Grant's priceless white mustang grape wine and two glasses between them. Ozzie was behaving with absolutely kittenish abandon, settled onto Kate's lap, purring with energy and nudging her hand when she stopped stroking his ears and chin. Richard sighed, heavily. In his mind, his call on Kate's affections and those erratic feline attentions of Ozzie were inextricably linked. Gained one, gained the other. Lose one … perhaps lose the other, and perhaps his own grip on a contented life, here serving out caviar cuisine on a canned tuna-fish budget in Luna City. During the ride home from the Tip-Top his resolve to keep Ozzie hardened into adamantine stone. Not having Ozzie would mean not having anything meaningful at all.

"Chris took notice of the fuss – not that he could avoid it, since everyone was pretty overwrought, and he called Joe Vaughn."

"Oh, good!" Kate's pleasant round countenance brightened. "And Joe told them where they could take their custodial demand and shove it sideways? Ozzie is yours! You found him, took care of him, fed him – made him Captain Kitten!? Everybody in Luna City knows that he's been yours, no matter where he came from."

"Well, Joe calmed down the Palmers … that's Marta and Fred. They live in New Braunfels. Is that where that enormous tourist plaza is, where we all met on the way to Marble Falls to cheer on Chris when he competed in that marathon run? Yes, thought so. I couldn't forget a place like that…Amazing the effect that a uniform has on the ordinary middle-class rate-payers. Especially when it's Joe wearing it. His sheer forceful presence ensured a compromise, of sorts."

"Everything is bigger in Texas," Kate agreed, her expression rather smug. "And yes – that's the place. The most palatial and cleanest bathrooms around. Did Joe convince them that Ozzie is yours? Honestly, Joe in official mode is perfectly terrifying."

"No, not entirely," Richard sighed again. "The Palmers insisted that Ozzie had been chipped … that is, some little identifying device inserted into him, registering original ownership. Apparently, any practicing veterinarian possesses a device which can read those chips. Doc Wyler may be the only one in this county who does not utilize such…"

"Well, he's old-school," Kate consoled him. "So old-school, I don't believe that this present century has registered with him at all. Anyway, he doesn't do small animal practice, save as a favor for friends. What compromise did Joe make them agree to?"

"That we should present Ozzie tomorrow at 10 AM tomorrow at a veterinary clinic in Karnesville – myself with Ozzie, and the Palmers; there to wait upon the decision of the thingy-chip-reading device. I have the address and the Palmers secured an appointment and ascertained their willingness to perform such a process. They said they would stay tonight at the Cattleman and meet me in the morning in Karnesville. Kate my darling, I greatly fear that I shall lose Ozymandias." Richard, under the influence of two or three glasses of Sefton Grant's peerless vintage, was moved to unburden himself of his deepest fears. "I don't want that to happen, my dearest Kate, Kate of Kate Hall. Ozzie is more than a pet … I see him as my other self, you know. My familiar, the being in which a good part of my selfish, unworthy soul resides."

"You are rather catlike," Kate agreed. Richard was uncomfortably reminded that his dear keen-eyed Kate had his number down to the thousandth decimal place. "Probably why

Ozzie also adores you. A symbiont soul." She didn't enlarge on this insight any farther, for which Richard was grateful.

"I don't want to give him up," Richard admitted. "But … I might have to. In all honestly, of the chip reveals all…"

"I know," Kate reached out, from the folding patio chair, to clasp Richard's hand. "Sufficient to the day are the evils thereof? Tonight – he is still yours. D'you need a ride to the veterinary clinic tomorrow? I'll take you, of course. I've got to meet with my editor first thing tomorrow, but I'll come to get you at … 9:30. That will give us enough time to get back to Karnesville…"

"Perfect," Richard returned the affectionate clasp. *"Not as perfect as spending the night here, though,"* he near as dammit said out loud. He wished that it could be something more … energetic. Closer. Permanent, even. But this was Kate. Not a fence to go rushing towards. All would happen in good time. "It was tragic, though. Hearing about it from the Palmers. Joe verified, of course. She – their daughter – was a nurse. A very good and dedicated one, from all accounts. Loved by everyone, including our dumb chums, and all her patients and co-workers. Had one of those organ-donor agreements in place. Eyes, heart, lung and kidneys – all went to deserving recipients when they pulled the plug."

"A good life, well-lived," Kate nodded. "But that's another matter entirely. "Her cat has been well-content living with you for … two years?" She sent him one of those beryl-green assessing looks. "Another transplant … just of the other sort. He's as been as good for you, as if he was a heart or a kidney…"

"I know," Richard admitted, although most of this was the mustang grape elixir speaking. Ordinarily, he shied from that embarrassing self-knowledge, much less voicing it. "Good of you to go with me tomorrow, Kate. If worst comes to worst, we might have to give up the Captain Kitten blog…"

"Not necessarily," Kate replied. "I have enough cute pictures of Ozzie in my archives to last into the middle of this century."

"Top up?" Richard extended the jug towards Kate, and when she shook her head, refilled his own glass and confessed. "I'm inordinately fond of the little blighter. He keeps my feet warm on cold nights. Glad to see me when I finish work for the day – and is not so stupidly needy as a dog. I'll be deeply depressed if that chip device proves that he is really theirs."

"We'll sort that out in the morning," Kate replied. During this conversation, Ozzie had curled into a tight ball, wedging his head into the crook of Kate's left elbow. "Let's not dwell on that any more – worrying about it won't change anything, and all that it will do will be to spoil our lovely supper. What are you cooking for me tonight? It smells wonderful…"

"Chicken Marengo," Richard answered. "That is actually the required veal demi-glace reduction that you detect, my dear Kate. I will be preparing it in the original version – chicken breasts with tomatoes, garlic and fresh mushrooms, garnished with fresh prawns, fried eggs and divers fresh herbs. It is legend that Napoleon's personal chef concocted it after a successful battle and a quick whip-round of those delicacies fit for an emperor-general which were available in the near vicinity."

"Sounds delish!" Kate exclaimed, with a warm smile. "Never stop cooking for me, Richard."

"Never," Richard assured her.

He did think, very briefly – that if he lost custody of Ozzie, some of the joy of cooking for Kate and Ozzie would leak out of his life. But Kate had requested that they not speak of that matter any further – and so he resolutely put it out of his mind, lest contemplating that stark loss further spoil the enchantment of an evening of Kate and fine cuisine.

Fall Newsletter

Fall 2018 Newsletter

Luna City Chamber of Commerce

5 North Town Square, Suite 4

Check out our Facebook Page

Luna City fields a team for the first annual Mills Farm Invitational Chili Contest, to be held in November at Mills Farm, as part of their campaign to 'Experience Texas' – a national publicity campaign created to support the expanded program of activities now available at the new Mills Farm extension. Contestants from all across Texas and the US will be competing throughout the day of the event, including a team from our own Luna City Café and Coffee, coached by our own Chef Richard. Lucas Massie III, backed by Robert Walcott and Briana Grant will enter the contest with their own version of the Café's signature wild boar chili. Come on out to Mills Farm on the 17th and support the home team!

An Old Tradition Renewed

The community Christmas Tree will be formally decorated and lighted on the Saturday after Thanksgiving, November 24th at 8 PM, following remarks by the newly-elected mayor of Luna City and various religious leaders. Former Mayor Martin Abernathy made it a project to revive the custom of decorating the tree with ornaments contributed by local families and organizations. This was last done in the 1980ies, when the living cypress tree on the western side of Town Square which previously served as the community Christmas tree fell victim to damage caused by high winds and had to be felled for reasons of safety. The decorations which had been used for nearly half a century were stored in the Cattleman Hotel and rediscovered during extensive renovations over the last year. VPI and Mills Farm are donating a replacement tree, to be planted in place of the original tree.

Upcoming Events

November 6

Election Day, across the nation and in Luna City, where we will cast our ballots for a new mayor and city council. Consult our FaceBook page for a list of local polling places.

November 17

The First Mills Farm Invitational Chili Contest will be held at the Chuckwagon Circle; Judging at 2 PM

November 24

Town Christmas tree lighting, at 2 PM, at the west end of Town Square.

Night at the Opera!

The fall/winter schedule for the Koenig Opera House is available on their website at www.KoenigOpera.com. Our thanks to Sylvester Gonzales and his local small business, the Gonzales Computer Wiz for building the Opera Houses' new website!

Luna City, Texas – Home of the Mighty Fighting Moths

Page 1 of 2

Luna City ISD News

Holiday Food Drive

The Luna City ISD holds their holiday food drive, beginning October 15th. Foodstuffs collected at both the high school and elementary school will be donated to local food banks for distribution to families in need. Please bring shelf-stable, canned, and packaged foodstuffs to containers located in the school foyers. Monetary contributions may be made by check or on-line donation through the LCISD website.

History Weekend – at Rincon de los Robles

The Luna City ISD is sponsoring a sleep-over weekend October 5-8 at Rincon de Los Robles for participating juniors and seniors to participate in an ongoing archeological dig. The project to identify the original adobe foundations of the Rincon de los Robles ranch headquarters house and outbuildings is being directed by Dr. Miranda Ramirez-Gonzalez, of Trinity University's history department. Participating students will learn the rudiments of conducting an archeological dig. Permission slips are available at the main office, Luna City HS, and must be signed and returned no later than September 28th.

Homecoming Queen and Court Elections

Nominations are open for the office of Home-coming queen and the six duchesses of her court. Nominees must be a junior or senior, with a B or better grade average. The Homecoming Queen and her court will preside over the Luna City High School Homecoming game, which will be played on Moths Field on September 30th at 3 PM against the Karnesville Knights. The election of the queen and her court will be held during the week of September 24th, and results announced at a Pep Rally on Friday, September 28th at 3:00.

Community Marketplace

Thanksgiving Is On the Way

Order a pit-smoked whole turkey, turkey breast, or whole boar ham from Pryor's Meats and BBQ before November 14th, for delivery in time for your Thanksgiving feast. Special pricing is available for bulk orders. Please note that free delivery is limited to Karnes County. Deliveries outside Karnes County will involve an additional surcharge

From Chief Vaughn, Luna City PD

The newly-constructed riverfront landings near the Rte 123 bridge over the San Antonio River, at Mills Farm and near Helena will be completed and open for use by mid-September by kayakers, tubers, and small boats on the river. Although the tourist season is winding down with the start of the school year, it still remains warm enough to make water sports attractive.

Drivers are urged to be cautious about school busses and Mills Farm's transport vehicles, all of whom make frequent stops to collect or drop off passengers. Don't be that inconsiderate jerk; you can stand to wait a minute or two.

Luna Café Blue Plate Lunch Special

Tuesday – Burger or Patty-melt
Wednesday – Chicken au Poivre
Thursday – Beef bourguignon
Friday – Sole Florentine
Saturday – Meatloaf
Sunday - Chicken Pot-pie
All selections served with a side of herb rice, parsley-potatoes, salad with Chef Richard's special dressing and dessert of the day

Luna City, Texas – Home of the Mighty Fighting Moths

Page 2 of 2

In the Offices of the Karnesville Weekly Beacon

"Katie!" Acey McClain's fist crashed down on the editorial desk in the prestigious corner office (with a window!) of the *Karnesville Weekly Beacon* – an aging relic of authority nearly as ornate as the White House Presidential Oval Office Resolute Desk, but in considerably worse condition. "What is it that I near now about that Gonzaga Reliant thing? What in heck is a damned three-wheel car with a fiberglass body doing in Luna City? I thought Reliants were a British thing. Is this anything to do with that chef boyfriend of yours from the Café?"

In was a Wednesday morning. The latest issue of the *Beacon* had been put to bed and gone to print Monday afternoon. Tuesday was more or less a day of rest for the regular staff. But Acey, as an old news hound, admitted no rest to his nose for news and neither did his most dedicated young reporter, who early in life had taken Brenda Starr and Hildy Johnson from *His Girl Friday* as her professional role models, thanks to her parents' penchant for old comic books and black and white movies.

"Coming, Chief!" Kate Heisel chirped, gathering up her trusty reporter's notebook from her own desk, out in the high-ceilinged newsroom. That facility – presided over by a stuffed moose head bearing a lugubrious expression and an antique Regulator clock which was usually at least five minutes off – was filled with battered metal government surplus desks and an assortment of chairs of similar origin and vintage. The *Karnesville Weekly Beacon* spared no expense for the comfort of their working staff. That is, it didn't spare a penny more than absolutely required. Only Rita, the receptionist downstairs at the front desk had a decent office chair; a Herman Miller Aeron number, and that was only because her children and grandchildren had bought it for her as a birthday present after having a whip-round among themselves on the occasion of her 60th birthday.

Now Kate settled onto the guest chair in Acey's office and demurely crossed her ankles. "Not my boyfriend, actually," she said. "We're good loyal pals. He's not really *serious* boyfriend materiel. We just have a cat and other obsessions in common."

"The Gonzaga thing," Acey scowled. Kate was not cowed. She knew Acey's temper and mood well of old. He liked doing the irascible boss act. "Explain why I suddenly have a number of old pals – holding down desks at far more prestigious publications than the Karnesville Weekly Beacon – calling me up and demanding information regarding some long-lost Renaissance treasure … which is rumored to have appeared here in Karnes County? Why did you not tell me of this?"

"I did," Kate replied, and studiously licked her pencil point. "Oh … about four months ago. I said that I was following up on it." She took a folded paper out of her notebook. "This is a print-out, isolated from the painting that they found last year in Milan. That new-found da Vinci painting, of a fat-faced young nun contemplating what looks like God's own fancy bottle stopper? Turns out that they … meaning my cousin Mindy and her hot new boyfriend, Xavier Gunnison-Penn … believe that the so-called Gonzaga Reliquary was brought to Karnes County around 1700-something, when the Rincon de los Robles ranch was established. Mindy's own quest is to establish the Rincon home-place as even older than the McAllister house. She wants one of those plaques from the Historical Commission like M.A. Lydecker wants another Oscar for best picture. She's written most of the narrative history already. She's certain that the Rincon Ranch HQ is much older than fifty years and just about everyone agrees with her, but the Historical Commission needs documented proof. Mindy had a bunch of materiel from one of the great-aunts about how the place was renovated in about 1920 or so. Old Don Antonio paid for having a bunch of old adobe walls knocked down, and the rubble carted away in order to enlarge the place and build a better roof for the main house." Kate added, in an academic-sounding aside. "The great-aunts were grateful for the improvement. Indoor plumbing was included in the renovation. They weren't all that keen on household electricity, mind … they were all afraid that it would leak out of the outlets, pool in the corners, and burn the place down if inadvertently ignited. But they adored not having to rely on chamber pots and the outhouse."

"The past is a foreign country," Acey steepled his hands. "And we can't go there again. Not that I would want to, in any case. Not without indoor plumbing. My grandparents had an outhouse at the old family place, and it could get pretty unspeakable in the summer, especially when black widow spiders took up residence under the toilet seat."

"Ewwww," Kate shuddered. "Well … back to the Reliquary. Mindy and her beau are going through the archives at the Rincon; she's looking for proof of age, dated bills for construction, drawings and photographs and stuff to prove absolutely that the original house is two hundred years old, at the very least. He's looking specifically for mention of the Reliquary. There is just a ton of stuff, out in the sheds, and in the attic. Every time they think they have made a dent in it all, they find another set of trunks and strongboxes. Everything has to be unfolded, studied and archived … and it's taken months so far – and they haven't gotten much farther back than 1890. Old Don Antonio and his father, Don Anselmo never threw a bit of paper, a letter or a receipt away … have you ever been out to the Rincon de los Robles, Chief?"

"Can't say I've had the pleasure," Acey grunted.

"It's an interesting old place," Kate flipped to a new page in her notebook. "Pity Don Jaimie has never really taken to opening the place to visitors now and again, like the Lazy W does. And I mean, really, really old, in parts. It reminds me of the Spanish Governor's house in San Antonio. Very thick walls, in the older bits: almost certain to be adobe brick, sheathed in wood paneling on the inside, and siding on the outside – but you can tell because the window embrasures are so thick. The older parts are just used for storage now. The floor tiles are just laid onto dirt in those rooms – very dank and gloomy, not comfortable at all. The floor sort of goes up and down, like the ocean in a flat calm. The house is on on all sorts of levels, too – step up and step down, and then up again. From the outside, it all looks perfectly ordinary: high pitched roof, and two galleries all the way around. The inside is perfectly stuffed with needlepointed this and that, tatted lace edging along all the shelves in the kitchen, and crewel-work embroidery everywhere. Don Jaimie's older sisters did needlework and decorative arts by the bale; he had three of them, you know: Great-Aunts Carmen, Aïda, and Leonora. They're all dead now…" Kate correctly interpreted Acey's raised and interrogative eyebrow. "Their father, Don Antonio was a mad fan of grand opera. He had season tickets for the Houston Opera, most years, back in the day." She continued, "The sisters were like Scarlet O'Hara's mother in *Gone With the Wind* – whose back never touched the back of the chair she sat in, and always, but always had a bit of sewing in her hands. Although I think Tia Aïda branched out into art pottery, and Tia Leonora fiddled with jewelry and metal sculpture after she learned to weld during World War II."

"Every family has a rebel or two," Acey pointed out. "What about the reliquary? Anything found so far?"

"It was pretty definitely there at Rincon during the first years of the Civil War," Kate replied. "But it was hidden at that time – there are references in at least one letter. Maybe more, depending on how much headway Mindy and her hot boyfriend have been able to make. Don Anselmo had gone to Mexico and then to New Orleans to volunteer to serve as an officer in the Union Army, and his father and the rest of the family were afraid of repercussions from the Confederate authorities. The nearest I can come is that old Don Luis-Antonio saw that the Reliquary was hidden away in a safe place, but where? It just never emerged again when the war was over, and Don Anselmo came home to take up management of Rincon de los Robles. It was almost as if it had never been, and everyone soon forgot about it. Even Mindy – and she is a total nut for history, especially family history – she had never heard about it. But Mindy grew up in San Antonio, only came here now and again for family stuff as a kid. Now my cousin Araceli, she grew up in Luna City, and used to be over at Rincon all the time … and she has been swearing that there is something familiar about the Reliquary in the painting. She says that she has seen it somewhere, and she can't shake the feeling that it's associated with Rincon. It's enough to make you think of past lives, and ancestral memory, is what Araceli says."

"Well, keep me posted, doll-face," Acey replied. "Finding the damned thing will make headlines … and big headlines, above the fold, front page, on about every national newspaper that matters."

"Sure will, Chief," Kate closed up her notebook, and rendered her editor a casual salute with her ever-ready Number 2 pencil and took herself back to her own bare-bones, grey metal military surplus desk. Said desk offered her a sumptuous view of a scenic calendar for 2016 and a noticeboard upon which were posted all the notices required by state law in a work setting, concerning employee safety, payday laws, worker compensation, and first aid tips.

Kate didn't mind this an uninspiring view. She spent very little time at her desk and when she did, her attention was dedicated to her laptop.

"Hey," she said to Rita, as she departed the premises. "I'm off to Luna City, I have a friend who needs help and I'm on a big story – but if anyone wants me, I'll be on my cellphone. Give them my number, as long as they give you a solid reason for wanting direct contact and don't sound too freaking insane."

"Not a problem, kiddo" Rita replied, who had been hanging around on the fringes of the small-market news business to have had exposure to the most common indicators of complete insanity and all the various degrees of the human condition. In her time, she had heard everything, including repeat assertions that Bigfoot had constructed a spaceship in the backwoods of the Hill Country in order to emigrate to Mars. "Hey, doesn't it bug you that Acey calls you 'doll-face'? Seems like sexual harassment to me."

"Nah," Kate said, shifting her laptop bag higher on her shoulder. "He's a relic of his time. It's kinda sweet, actually. Makes me think that I am in an old-time movie."

Here Comes the Judge

As of the hour of nine the following morning, he had to contemplate it. To his relief, the Palmers had partaken of the generous breakfast buffet provided for guests at the Cattleman. Or driven to Karnesville already, for some disgusting breakfast fast food take-out: they didn't appear in the Café, anyway, which would have been terribly awkward. The only public notice taken of the impending appointment by any of Richard's customers and friends was made by Joe Vaughn, as the latter filled up his Thermos at the coffee urn.

"Got a ride to Karnesville for the custody battle?" Joe added cream and capped the Thermos.

"I do," Richard stole a glance at the plain industrial analog clock which metered out time in his kitchen. The minute hand hung at three minutes before the hour of nine. "Kate's volunteered. She adores Ozzie – and thinks he should be mine regardless."

"Ah." Joe's eyes were already covered by his sunglasses, so his expression was more than usually unreadable. "Good for her. I'd have offered, if you didn't have a ride. Best of luck, ok? You know you're doing the right thing, Ricardo. Either way it goes, you *know* you've done the right thing. The right thing might be hard, sometimes. The wrong thing is always easy; that's what Miss Letty used to say, when she taught kindergarten. Bear up and do the right thing, even if it's hard. Leastways, you can look at yourself in the mirror, afterwards."

"Right," Richard scowled. "I shall console myself with that lovely thought: you want to cross-stitch it on a framed sampler for me?"

"Naw," Joe replied over his shoulder as he made his escape – nearly colliding with Kate, as she came into the kitchen. "Ask Araceli if her grandma can do that for ya. Morning, Katie! You meaning to tie up Ricardo with a mask and a ball-gag, lead him naked around Town Square with that get-up?"

"I am not!" Kate protested, and Joe escaped, chuckling. Richard nodded to Araceli and Luc – who had already been briefed. It was the height of the morning rush; they both knew that nothing, but this matter of life, death, and the fate of a pet familiar would have taken Richard from the Café on a weekday. "No; it's a leash and harness for Ozzie. I had to borrow from Araceli's uncle across the road. I couldn't arrange a pet carrier on short notice, and the rules say you absolutely must have a pet on restraint or confined for an office visit. He'll be a good boy; I know he will."

Richard nodded in agreement, too depressed for words. *Dammit! Ozzie was his, and had been for years, a boon companion through thick and thin. Why should he give him up to the custody of perfect strangers?* It was simply not fair.

He held this simmering resentment to himself, all the way into Karnesville, after whistling for Ozzie, who appeared with a certain curious feline expression, as if asking why his morning routine was being interrupted. An amiable cat, when Kate was concerned; he submitted graciously to being fitted with the harness and leash.

"Really – he is dog-like, in some respects," Kate observed. "The very best cats often are, you know. When I was growing up, my parents had a Siamese who would come when you called and liked going for walks."

"On a leash?" Richard settled himself into the passenger seat of Kate's late-model VW bug, Ozzie in his lap.

"Oh, yes, of course. And the other odd thing was that Skoshie – that was his name – he would eat anything that he saw us eat. He loved popcorn, cookie dough, canned peaches, and cornflakes. Weird, you know? But if he saw us eating it, he wanted some, too." Kate sighed, deeply. "We had cats after that but none of them were as eccentric as old Skoshie. Only Ozzie comes close." She deftly backed the little VW out of the space in back of the Café, and into the street, taking the short-cut through town. "You know, Richard; you should learn to drive. Surely you can afford a car, and it would let you get out more."

"I do know how to drive," Richard protested. "I just don't *care* to! Bad sense of space around me, when I get behind a wheel. I've bashed repeatedly into things – so many times that my then-employer forcefully requested me to stop getting behind the steering wheel and confiscated my car key. After that, I was always provided with a driver – my agent put it into my contract."

"Curious, that," Kate remarked, and speculated on possible reasons for that condition, and ways to overcome it. Richard listened with half an ear, grateful that she didn't seem to require much of a response from him. Nor did Ozzie, who curled himself into a tight brindle donut and napped for the duration of the fifteen-minute journey to the Karnesville Family Animal Clinic and Grooming. *(Also boarding, doggie day care and regularly-scheduled training dog-training classes.)*

"It's kind of like a cross between a one-stop canine university and full-service spa," Kate remarked cheerily, as she pulled into the parking lot, in front of a tidy brick building, which sprawled for what looked like half a city block on the outskirts of Karnesville; a city which was still Kate's home, and whose various businesses were part of her employer's life-blood. Down at the end and around the corner, an extension of the roof sheltered chain-link fence-enclosed cubicles and cages. Being mid-morning, there were already a dozen automobiles in the parking lot, including the Palmer's sedan.

"We won't have to wait long," Kate observed, in a bracing tone of voice. "Best get it over in one agonizing rip, then a series of painful jerks."

Richard slammed the passenger-side door; Ozzie wriggled to be out of his arms and mewed commandingly.

"I'll take him," Kate offered. "Come to your fairy cat-mother, Ozzie. Don't worry, Richard; he *always* behaves with me."

Richard yielded up the squirming Ozzie. No, this was not going to be easy. The main door to the clinic loomed like the doorway into Tolkien's dark mountain caverns. Slightly ahead of them, a matronly, grey-haired woman with a pair of energetic dachshunds on leads struggled momentarily with their leashes, her keys, an outsized handbag and the heavy door.

"Allow me." Richard sprang ahead, and opened the door for her, whereupon the woman flashed a brilliant and utterly charming smile at him, saying,

"Thank you, young man. I so appreciate the courtesy. Old-fashioned, I know, but so welcome when my hands are full!" The pair of dogs at her feet romped, entangling their leashes as they ran ahead of her; obviously, they had no apprehensions of a visit to the veterinarian – indeed, they barked in a manner most excited, until their owner commanded, "Felix – Oscar! Behave! Thank you again," she added over her shoulder as the excited pair raced into the already-half filled waiting room. Richard sighed, seeing that the Palmers were indeed already present; Marta was already giving him what Araceli had often described as a 'stink-eye' from across the room full of anxious pet-owners and their even more nervously-excited pets; even noisier now that Felix and Oscar, the dachshunds, were adding their own voices to the chorus.

At the receptionists' counter, their owner was already breathlessly presenting herself and her dog familiars for the appointment. She was obviously a regular client.

"Good morning, Carole! I have a grooming appointment for Oscar and Felix."

"Hi, Judge!" The girl behind the counter replied – obviously Carole, as that was what it said on the nametag pinned to her calico-print scrubs *(printed with a pattern of cartoon cats and dogs, Richard noted)*. "They're running a bit late – you don't mind waiting?"

"Not at all," The woman – Judge? A county magistrate? Well – no baggy tweeds, sensible flat-heeled shoes and air of overwhelming middle-class rectitude; this judge wore a plain pair of jeans battening into a pair of western-style boots, and a tunic adorned with folk embroidery – casual good taste for Texas,

Richard had long concluded. The Judge took a seat on one of the hard-plastic chairs, arrayed in the waiting room like troops on parade. Richard, apprehension curdling his blood and digestion, took her place at the reception desk, Kate at his elbow with Ozzie in her arms, and the Palmers hoving up on his other side, like the ghosts of Christmas Past, or a French ship of the line all ready to rake the decks with their cannons. Richard cleared his throat:

"We have an appointment – to have a cat – this cat! To have him scanned for that chip-thing. As a matter of determining ownership. And I have been his owner for some two years, since finding him as a stray," Richard added, in a pathetic attempt to make his case before a bored veterinary clinic receptionist who had doubtless heard many odder things in her time. Carole flashed him an insincere professional smile, just as Marta hissed indignantly,

"Mr. Whiskers was not a stray! He was lost! And now that he is found and proven to be ours, we want him returned to us!"

"Give me a few minutes, sir. Is this Mr. Whiskers?"

"Ozzie," Richard insisted. "Short for Ozymandias-King-of-Kings. And he is mine!"

Carole's insincere professional smile broadened. "You know that cats don't have owners. They have staff. One of the techs will be with you in a moment. Do have a seat; we'll be with you in a moment."

"Sure," Richard answered, and settled into the nearest unoccupied chair, Kate at his side. Wordlessly, she gave Ozzie into his lap, and nodded towards the lady with the dachshunds, who returned the nod, although with a somewhat distracted expression, as if she were trying to remember where she knew Kate from. Ozzie looked searchingly into his face, butted his chest and remarked,

"Mrrroww?" in tones which suggested that he himself was cat-worried that his pleasant routine had already been interrupted and he was none too pleased about it.

Next to them in the row of plastic chairs, Fred Palmer observed, "He does seem fond of you."

"He would be," Richard replied, his voice tight with grief and resentment. "He's been mine for two years now."

"He's Marlene's Mr. Whiskers," Marta insisted, in adamantine determination. "He ought to be with us. She wanted us to have him."

And did she want you to have her heart, liver and lights? Richard thought, and by the grace of god and discretion had the mercy not to say out loud. For that would have sunk any farther appeal, if the judgement of the chip-reader-device went against him.

At his side, Kate whispered, "Didn't you recognize her, Richard? The woman with the dogs, that you opened the door for?"

"Why? Is she a regular at the Café?" He murmured in reply, *sotto voice*, and Kate sighed.

"Is that as far as your public spirit goes? Honestly, I should offer you a civics class, or something. She's the district judge: The Honorable Anita Blake-Silva. Very nice for all of that she's the judge for the entire county."

"So, you're good friends, then," Richard, sunk in depression, had very little emotional space to consider Kate's professional life.

"No, I've just reported on her court for ages," Kate looked exasperated. Ozzie reached out a tentative paw from where he sat in Richard's lap, with a querulous "Mrrrow?" as he patted Kate's hand

"It's all right, Ozzie-kitten," Kate skriched Ozzie's ears, and he subsided again into Richard's lap. Richard contemplated an empty caravan; one empty of Ozzie, should this day's excursion not go well at all, and was startled out of that misery by the woman standing before him. A young woman in the same cartoon dog and cat pattered scrubs, holding some kind of device in her hand, which looked somewhat like one of those early brick-shaped cellphones. The nametag pinned on her scrub tunic read, "Kathy." Kathy was smiling in the assumed-cheerful manner that Richard associated with NHS nurses about to give a painful injection to a small, distrusting child.

"Is this the fur-baby whose' ownership is in question?" she chirped. Richard was so appalled by the twee-ness of Ozzie being called a 'fur-baby' that he was temporarily rendered speechless. Both Kate and Marta chorused an assent, Marta adding an indignant,

"Mr. Whiskers is ours … he was supposed to be ours!"

"Ozzie. His name is Ozzie, short for Ozymandias-King-of-Kings!" Richard recovered his composure sufficiently to insist. Again. "And he has been mine for these last two years!" Richard directed his most hostile glare towards Marta. "I found him in the back alley behind my place of business. If he had anything to complain of in my guardianship, or of his situation thereafter, I certainly never heard a word of it!"

"Umm," replied Kathy uneasily, even as she was briskly running the business end of the chip-sensor device over Ozzie's back and flanks, stem to stern, ventral to dorsal. "Well, sir, cats can't really talk."

"Surely you've met Siamese who could tell you otherwise," Kate assured her. "We had one who did. Skoshie could talk. So can Ozzie. He says *'merrooow'* in so many different tones, it's as if he is really speaking. We understand perfectly what he wants to communicate…"

"He's Mr. Whiskers!" Marta insisted. In Richard's estimation, she was teetering on the thin edge of hysteria.

Fred patted her hand, murmuring, "Now, now, sweetie. We can't be entirely certain, can we?"

"Found it!" Kathy chirped triumphantly, and Richard's heart sank into his trainers, even as Ozzie ventured a small growl at the indignity of having his undersides palpated by a total stranger. "Just give me a moment, people. I have to look at the records now for the registered owner."

She absented herself through a door which obviously gave into the staff office area, behind the counter. Ozzie butted his head again into Richard's hand, and Richard gave him a soothing skritch behind the ears, out of reflex more than anything else.

Across the gap between the rows of chairs set up in the waiting area, the woman with the dachshunds ventured in sympathetic tones, "Oh, dear – a custody dispute. Those are the hardest, I must say. So much love and frustration, especially when either home would be an excellent situation. It is the hardest thing to make a fair decision in the best interests of the child, knowing that someone will be left devastated. It is sometimes a trifle easier when the child is of an age to voice a preference for one party or the other … although sometimes they have been untowardly influenced. I don't suppose that it is any easier when it is a pet … or what is that current phrase? Companion animal. That would be it…"

There was a short pause, when another of the attendants clad in cartoon-animal-patterned scrubs came to take the dachshund pair away into the inner realms of the veterinary practice. After what seemed to Richard to be an age, Kathy the technician returned, still chirpy and smiling.

"Well – good news, folks. The chip in this fur-baby *(Richard winced again)* was registered to Marlene Osborne, with an address in Corpus Christi…"

"I knew it!" Marta exclaimed in triumph, as Richard's heart sank, all the way through his docks and trainers and into the utility linoleum beneath. "He is Marlene's Mr. Whiskers! Now we can take him home, Fred. Is the carrier still out in the car?"

"No," Richard insisted, and he gathered Ozzie to him and Ozzie refrained from squirming away, although he did voice a protesting "Mrroooow!" "Ozzie has been mine for two years. I never saw you in Luna City looking for him in all that time…"

"And there was nothing in the newspaper, either!" Katie added in indignant chorus. "You know, the *Weekly Beacon* will post a free advert for missing or found pets!"

Fred temporized; a most unhappy man in an awkward situation, pleading, "Marta, sweetie, Mr. Whiskers seems real happy with these folks, and he's in good hands…"

"But Marlene …" Marta looked about ready to begin crying again.

"Might I be able to help with a suggestion?" A new voice broke into the disputation; the older lady with the dachshunds. Richard looked up; she was regarding them all with austere sympathy. "It is my sad lot in life to have had a lot of practice when it comes to making decisions of this kind. It's hard, when it's a question of custody pitting one good situation against an equally good one; tragic, even. I always like to talk to the child privately, when I have to decide on custody – given that they are old enough to have thought seriously about who they want to live with."

"And what is your suggestion, Madame Judge?" Richard asked, somewhat bitterly.

"Well, first," Judge Anita Blake-Silva considered them all with dispassionate interest. "If you want to involve me, then I ask that you accept my decision as final. I know that this is not my courtroom, but I can promise you all that I can and will be fair, and make my decision in the best interests of …"

"Mr. Whiskers," Marta cried.

"Ozymandias-King-of-Kings," Richard insisted.

Judge Anita Blake-Silva sighed, a small and resigned sigh. "Will both parties agree to my mediation of this custody dispute then?"

"Yes," Richard yielded, feeling very much as if he had nothing to lose.

"Yes," Fred Palmer agreed, while Marta protested, "I don't see how there could be any question about it at all! Our daughter raised Mr. Whiskers from being a tiny, sick kitten. She bottle-fed him every two hours …"

"A consideration, indeed," the Judge nodded. "Although your daughter, being deceased, really has no voice in this preset situation. Kathy, my dear, is there a room available where we can all confer privately."

"The training room," Kathy the vet-tech still hovered, obviously fascinated by the incipient drama. "As long as it doesn't interfere with the doggie obedience class at 11:00."

"I'm certain we need not take that long," Judge Blake-Silva nodded. "The training room will be perfect. If you all would follow; I know the way. Oscar and Felix came to obedience classes here, for all the good that it did."

Richard gathered up Ozzie in his arms, and followed the Judge, Kate at his elbow, and the Palmers coming after. The training room was at the end of a short corridor, just past where the Judges' two dogs had gone to be bathed, groomed and perfumed; a large room with two ranks of chairs in a circle around a small ring about the size of a children's wading pool, delineated by bright-orange traffic cones.

"If you would all please have a seat," Judge Blake-Silva suggested. "Anywhere – I usually have a bailiff who attends to the traffic direction. And if … the cat; Mr. Whiskers or Ozzie – will permit me to hold him?"

"Yes," Richard yielded up Ozzie with a sigh. "He's very good with women – adores them, unstintingly, in fact."

Ozzie submitted readily to being handed into the arms of the Judge, burying his head into the bosom of the Judges' embroidered tunic. '*The little blighter does prefer women,*' Richard thought to himself, as he, Kate, and the Palmers settled onto chairs, all in a line like birds on an electric line. The Judge smiled slightly and administered a reassuring skritch behind Ozzie's ears.

"He really is a sweetie," Judge Blake-Silva allowed. "Even if I am more a dog person than a cat-person. I can readily see how he has become close to your hearts. To all of your hearts…"

"He was my daughters' cat," Marta Palmer was obdurate. "And she wanted us to have him. In case anything happened to her. She's dead and our son-in-law had to go work on the oil rigs. He told us we could have Mr. Whiskers and the dogs, and so we took them home with us but when we stopped for gas at this dinky dump on 123, he escaped from our car. They said the bridge might close because of flooding, and we had the dogs, so we couldn't stay and look for him …"

"I found him behind my place of business," Richard laid out his cards on the table, flat and with a snap, like an old-time gambler. "The night after the flood. I had no notion of this chip business, and no one recognized him as theirs, that day or two years since."

"He has a name and a career now, as Captain Kitten, the Cooking Cat," Katie weighed in. "He is spoiled and loved! My friend Richard took him in and made him famous. He has a professional career now. Prime-quality food and excellent catnip are his forever, along with the fame…" Kate wrung her hands – Richard had never before in life seen a woman doing what he had only seen described in Victorian novels. "He is such a good cat," Kate added, in a rather hopeless tone of voice. "Richard loves him so much although he would rather die than admit so…"

"Hang on, Katie," Richard protested, more out of form than anything else. "I'm used to the little bugger. The dead mice and all, even…"

"But he was my daughter's cat," Marta was as unyielding as a slab of granite.

"Indeed," Judge Blake-Silva regarded them all, as she administered another comforting scratch to the cat in her arms. "But I will ask; how old is he now? Three years old? Or four? One has to consider such things, you see."

"Marlene took in Mr. Whiskers early in November of 2014," Marta said. "She posted pictures on her personal Facebook page, tracking how he progressed."

"Excellent," Judge Blake-Silva mused, absently caressing Ozzie. "Given that our dear little critters age at a rate of seven to one – that is, seven of their years to one of ours is the rough rule of thumb – the cat in question is now well over twenty-one years of age. Under the laws of this country and county, he is of legal age, and capable of making his own decisions about where he wants to live, and with whom. My ruling in this matter is to let him decide for himself. Will you agree with me on that?"

"I have nothing to lose," Richard added silently, *'Only my cat and my best friend.'*

Fred Palmer looked at his hands for a moment, and then met Marta's accusing gaze.

"I think that's fair, Judge. Marta, sweetheart, Mr. Whiskers never lived with us. He was Marlene's, from the beginning. He's been with this nice young man – this couple – for two years. As far as Mr. Whiskers is concerned, we're as good as strangers. He lost his favorite person in the whole wide world, he prolly doesn't have any clue as to why and how that happened. Then he got taken away from the only home he ever knew, stuffed into a smelly old cage, and got lost in the dark and the rain, and that was our fault, using that rusty pet carrier with a busted latch and not paying proper attention when we stopped for gas after sundown. But he finished up with people who loved him as much as Marlene did … so, go ahead. Let him choose. We'll abide by that, no matter how much it hurts. Go ahead, Judge. Let Mr. Whiskers choose."

"All right then." Judge Blake-Silva nodded, "If you would – make it simpler. If you would each move to a chair, at twelve, three, six and nine … you know, as the clock goes. I will count to ten as soon as you take your places, and then put him down on the floor."

"This is a cat," Richard said, around a lump in his throat that he didn't want to acknowledge. "He's as likely to go wandering around, searching for mice and ignoring us all. What then, Madame Justice?"

"Why then – you all will sit until he gives up on mice, and comes to one of you," The Judge smiled brilliantly. Richard could see how Judge Anita Blake-Silva had handily won a ground-breaking number of elections to political office, as well as being loved and respected all across Karnes County, although those who had their ukase ruled against might justifiably have cause for resentment. "And I will go home with Felix and Oscar, assured in my own mind that Ozzie – or Mr. Whiskers will be one of the happiest and most well-indulged cats in Texas."

"Very well, then." Richard gave a brief squeeze to Kate's hand – which somehow had found its way into his. Kate brushed his cheek with a brief and chaste kiss – not neglecting to return the fond, affectionate squeeze, and went to sit on a chair around the circle at 90 degrees to his right. Fred and Marta took places; Marta directly across from Richard, from whence she favored him with another heaping helping of stink-eye, and Fred went to sit across from Kate.

Judge Anita Blake-Silva counted solemnly to ten, and put Ozzie down on the floor, in the middle of the dog-training rink circle. Richard had barely time for a brief plea to the Episcopalian Trinity, in which he reposed only the barest conventional belief.

Ozzie shot across the floor, a brindle-streak, leaping up into Kate's lap.

"Merroow?" He demanded querulously, in a meow which could be heard across the doggie-training classroom. *Can we go home now, please? Now! Please?!*

Richard let his breath out – only at that moment aware that he had been holding it in.

"The decision is made," Judge Blake-Silva intoned. "And this court is adjourned. I am so sorry for your personal loss," she added, to Marta. "Your daughter was an amazing woman, from all accounts. A friend to all, especially to those who have no voice. She …gave gifts. The gifts of life and love."

Marta opened her mouth, but before she could say a word, Fred spoke up. "We promised to abide by your ruling, Judge, and Mr. Whiskers' choice in the matter. Thank-ye for taking the time and the trouble. Let's head home now, sweetheart, we got a long drive ahead of us." He lingered a little behind his tearful spouse, adding in an undertone to Richard, "I meant what I said. The little guy didn't know us much at all. And I'd have talked Marta around to letting y'all keep him, if he had chosen either of us. But it's better this way, I do believe."

"Thank you," Richard recovered his own voice, nearly drowned in a way of ecstatic relief. "I am quite fond of the little beggar, you see… And … thank you, Your Honor."

"Don't mention it," Judge Blake-Silva tilted her head, already distracted by the sound of energetic barking, out in the waiting area. "It's what we owe to our little furred-friends. Speaking of which, I hear mine calling." With a friendly nod to all, she was gone, leaving the classroom strangely emptier than it would from the departure of anyone else.

"If you want to see how he gets on," Kate held Ozzie very close, while fumbling one-handed into her overcoat pocket. She withdrew a small business card and handed it to Fred. "There's a page on the Weekly Beacon website for Mr. Astor-Hall's cooking show, with Ozzie. He's Captain Kitten in the Kitchen, you see. I post cute pictures of him, all the time. You can check in any time, or send me a message…"

"Thank you," Fred nodded, and followed his wife. Out in the waiting room, Kathy and Carole chorused a farewell, as Richard and Kate passed through. Once outside, Kate handed Ozzie back to Richard.

"Well, that's settled," she observed, with relief. "A good thing I had a packet of Abuelita's finest catnip in my pocket – you know, to solace Ozzie along the way."

"You don't believe in leaving anything to chance, do you?" Richard ventured as the door closed behind them, and they emerged blinking into mid-morning sunshine. Kate shook her head.

"Not when it's someone I care for," she answered. "Come on – let me buy you a burger or something, before I drive you back to Luna City."

The First Texas Cavalry of the Union Army

It is a curious, and perhaps little-known historical oddity outside of Texas itself – that although Texas enthusiastically joined the Confederacy after the election of Abraham Lincoln in 1860 – a substantial number of Texans remained stubbornly Unionist in sympathy. No less a personality than Sam Houston himself refused to take an oath of allegiance to the Confederacy, and thereby removed himself from the office that he held as governor, this after having served for nearly two decades as military general and commander of what military that Texas possessed, president of an independent Texas and as US Senator. There was considerable backing for actually splitting the state between the Union and the Confederacy just as Virginia and West Virginia had done. Alas, Texas was too far removed from the Union as it stood, and those Unionists in Texas were isolated by the sheer distance.

Isolated, perhaps; but not willing to abandon principles by swearing a loyalty oath. Within a few years of bitter fighting in the east, an option of neutrality with regard to the war was taken off the table for fit white men between the age of sixteen and fifty with the initiation of a military draft. Fighting in the East burned through those eager first volunteers from Texas and elsewhere in the south. Those Unionist men inclined to stay at home and mind their own businesses, their crops and herds, taking no interest in the war, instead were brought to the realization that war, in the form of a local draft board and the military needs of the Confederate Army, was interested in them. There were no good options for those Texans who emphatically declined to make a show of serving as Texas state troops, or as local militia volunteers – not when the possibility emerged that such troops could be willy-nilly be reclassified as Confederate Army resources. As a point in fact, there were only two notable Texas units who went to the war in the east or at any rate, out of Texas: the 8th Texas Cavalry, or Terry's Texas Rangers, and Hood's Texas Brigade, which became part of the Army of Northern Virginia and made every battle fought by it save Chancellorsville. *(At war's end there were only about 600 men left, of more than 5,000 who had served in the Texas Brigade.)* Meanwhile, in Texas itself, there were draft riots, hangings, and deserters and draft evaders hiding out wherever they could, including a large party of German dissidents from the Hill Country who made a concerted dash for the border and were caught and massacred by state troops on the Nueces River.

Late in November of 1862, a former judge, officeholder and ant-Secessionist named Edmund Jackson Davis, who had been forced to flee Texas because of those sympathies, was commissioned as colonel and charged with raising a regiment: the First Texas Cavalry, USA. He set up shop in New Orleans, which had been taken by the Union forces in the spring of that year. Eventually, the regiment would recruit nearly two thousand troopers. Davis' regiment would defend New Orleans, putter around in various campaigns without ever seeing much of action, contribute two companies to a fruitless expedition to recapture Galveston, another which would eventually recapture Brownsville, and generally take up much of the following two and a half years of wartime service on patrol and reconnaissance duties. This was probably much more to the taste of his troopers than dodging arrest by the Confederate draft authorities or being forced to swear allegiance to and serve a cause in which they did not in the least believe. It was said of Davis' recruits that they were "… primarily of Mexicans, Germans, and Irishmen."

At the end of the war, when the troopers of the First Texas Cavalry were mustered out and returned home to pick up the threads of civilian life in an impoverished and defeated South, they could comfort themselves knowing that their side had won, and that they were alive, unlike all but a handful of those who had gone east to serve in the Confederate Army.

Edmund J. Davis ended the war as a brigadier general and became the governor of Texas under Reconstruction.

The Great Chili Cook-off

"Hey, Chef, didja hear about the chili cook-off at Mills Farm, the weekend before Thanksgiving?" Robbie Walcott bubbled with youthful enthusiasm – almost his normal emotional condition.

"I have not," Richard replied. "I confess – I have no interest in anything to do with culinary events other than the ones in which I have a direct interest. And my interest in that disgusting chili-pepper burgoo cannot be measured with anything other than an electron microscope with high magnification. I do realize that this is not shared universally – but seriously, I don't care, and can't be made to care."

"But Luc does," Robbie continued slicing potatoes with the professional mandolin, preparing a batch of home-style *pomme frites* for the luncheon special of the day. They would have to soak in a vat of ice-water for the morning, preparing for their apotheosis:

deep-friend and bathed in a sprinkling of selected spices and flavored salt. Richard had decreed such, served with a side of his own gourmet-style spicy ketchup, in an effort to enlighten the diners of Karnes County and environs as to how such simple viands could really taste, in the hands of a master chef. "He wants to enter, Chef. The first prize is two thousand dollars, cash. He wants to buy a diamond engagement ring for Belle," Robbie confided. Richard shuddered.

"He's living dangerously, in that case. Does your dear mother know of his marital intentions?"

"Nope," Robbie shot another potato through the mandolin. "Yeah, I know that Mom will be…"

"Murderous with maternally-protective rage," Richard completed the thought. "You'd better hope that she doesn't find out. I take it that you all are keeping your dear mother from knowing of this plan?"

"Of course," Robbie was all wide-eyed innocence. "I was born at night, Chef, but it wasn't last night. It's just that Luc has figured out that he'll never make anything from being a drummer with OPM …"

"By the way – an errant thought; the initials of the band for which Luc routinely massacres the percussion-line, always remains the same, yet the name of the band itself changes, almost with the phrases of the moon. Is there an explanation for this curious development?"

"Yeah, there is." Robbie picked up another potato and considered it with care. "The band spent a bomb of money on the logo design – OPM. Copyrighted and everything. And for a graphic artist to do a design for them. They had it stenciled on Luc's drum-kit, and on their guitars, even on the squeeze-box. And they each got a tattoo in the same design. Only having spent just about every dollar they had on it all … they are stuck with the initials, but they cannot agree on an ultimate name for the band. That's why it changes so often, you see, Chef."

"Alas, yes," Richard was all weary acceptance. "Interesting concept in establishing a brand, I must say. Where is this orgy of indigestion going to be held, pray tell?"

"That's the best part," Robbie enthused. "At the Mills Farm Chuckwagon Circle. No, not the best part – the very best part is that one of the judges will be Allen Lee Mayne, and it'll be a special edition of *A la Carte With Quartermayne*! Won't it be great to have Allen Lee in town again?"

"My year will be complete," Richard answered, in tones as dry as dust.

Araceli, filling her bountiful coffee carafe at the big urn, looked over her shoulder. "But Chef – you like Allen Lee. He came and helped Patricia and you all make sandwiches in the hurricane emergency. You should sound gladder than that to have him back in town."

"I know that you will be," Richard gave the meats on the grill a quick stir. "You'll resume your shameless flirtation with him, of course."

"Naturally," Araceli grinned. "It's one of the great pleasures in life; flirting with a handsome man just for the fun of it and knowing it will go no farther than playing extravagant compliments to each other. You should try it sometime, Chef."

"Thanks, but I don't swing that way," Richard answered, sourly. "And Kate would be heartbroken, in either case."

"You're not too old a dog to learn a new trick or two, Chef," Araceli topped up the second carafe, of cream from a bottle in the walk-in cooler. She closed the cooler door and added. "You are right, though; Katie would be heartbroken. But that weirdy-beardy

Gunnison-Penn has learned some new tricks. He is out having breakfast with Doctor Mindy and being absolutely lovey-dovey with her."

"Steady on," Richard was alarmed. "I thought there was an injunction against him coming anywhere within fifty feet of either of us, or into the Café!"

Araceli shrugged. "Mindy appealed to Doc Wyler; claimed that he had learned his lesson and was now a completely reformed character. Also, Mindy is sweet on him. They're totally taken up with looking for the Gonzaga Reliquary together."

"Good god," Richard stood stock still, spatula in hand. "Mindy; that short little fireplug of a woman? Academic type; plaid flannel shirts, jeans and work-boots, looks like a caricature of a lezzie? Been in here, a good few times, mostly on weekends? Cousin of yours, although that goes without saying, as two-thirds of Luna City are your kin!"

"Please," Araceli looked pained. "Lesbian. And no, I don't think Mindy was ever a lesbian. She just wasn't interested in sex with men or anyone else. Indifferent, until now. A totally different thing, Chef. It's kind of sweet, actually; Mindy has transformed him. He is all for the honor of the Rincon de los Robles, and its proper place in local history. Although he *would* like to find the Gonzaga Reliquary. So would Mindy, but that is secondary to establishing the Rincon de los Robles' home-place as co-equal to the McAllister house in terms of age. All Mindy wants is to get a historical plaque for the Rincon Ranch home-place."

"Well, they say that every nut has a good screw, somewhere in the world," Richard observed, coarsely.

Araceli scowled. "Honestly, Chef, could you be any more disgusting? Seriously, I've forgiven him for being such a butthole for door-stopping you, all this time ago. You should at least make an effort. He has. By the way Jess is at the regular table, with Martin. They're the last of the breakfast crowd. You should at least go out and say 'hi.'"

"I will do that," Richard said to Araceli's back. The gourmet ketchup was thickening up nicely, under his vigilant attention; a concoction of canned crushed tomatoes, a few red jalapenos and various exotic herbs and spices. He gave it one last stir and took it off the burner to cool. Now to social duties, such as they were. He wiped his hands and went out to the front of the house, observing that the post-breakfast lull had truly descended on the Café, as only the four late breakfast diners were star-scattered at the tables. Jess and her father Martin Abernathy, the current and *(as far as Richard could into the future)* forever mayor of Luna City, sat at the *stammtisch* – the regulars' table. Jess had her usual. Martin was pushing around elements of the Full English, as if he had no appetite at all.

"Where is Little Joe this morning," Richard observed. "Surely he's not starting school? Time does fly, but I did not think it flew that fast."

"No," Jess flashed a weary smile. "He's at Gram and Grumpys' for the morning. Pops and I have medical appointments in Karnesville this morning."

"Nothing serious, I am assured," Richard made a conventional observation: Jess was absolutely blooming, but Martin … Martin looked grey, and tired, as if he had not slept well.

"Routine pre-natal for me," Jess replied, briskly. "Pops has to have an ECG – electro-cardiogram."

"Dicky ticker, eh?" Richard was slightly relieved that Martin was being seen. Martin's laughter was a short bark of amusement.

"Well, that's what my doctor wants to rule out."

"Good luck, then," Richard looked at Martin's plate. "Shall I ask for a to-go-box for the rest of that?"

"Yeah, please," Martin set down his fork, and Richard noted Jess's faint frown. "It's all right, Jessy-Bell. I'll finish it off for lunch. It's time we got moving, anyway."

With a glance and nod from Richard, a hovering Blanca produced a Styrofoam to-go box and took away Martin's plate to transfer the contents: one of the standards that Richard insisted upon, especially for the valued customers.

It was almost too warm now, to sit outside, save when the inside dining area was crowded. On this day, Mindy Ramirez-Gonzales and the peppery, short-tempered Xavier Gunnison-Penn were inside, at the smallest table on the place – the one for two diners, in the farthest corner.

"I came to ask if everything was satisfactory," Richard allowed, with his best professional air.

"*Munfff!*" Mindy nodded emphatically, and swallowed a mouthful of cinnamon roll, the perfection of which was one of Richard's – and the Café's stellar accomplishments. Mindy, or Doctor Miranda Ramirez-Gonzales, was stocky and fortyish; not actually unattractive but skewing more towards in the direction of 'pleasant in appearance and scathingly intelligent' rather than pretty. Not a woman which excited the least romantic interest from Richard, but from the fatuously fond expression on his face, she suited Gunnison-Penn to a tee. "'s perfect. Thanks, Chef."

Gunnison-Penn merely nodded; his mouth was also full.

With slight malice, Richard asked, "How's the search for the Treasure of the Month going, Penn? Any further clues in the Gonzales archives to the whereabouts of the Gonzaga Reliquary?"

"We have actually found several more mentions of the Reliquary, in a trunk of documents from the early 1860ies," Doctor

Mindy replied, as Gunnison-Penn looked to be near choking. She reached across the table, and patted Gunnison-Penn's hand in a soothing, reassuring manner.

"Do tell," Richard urged. He was still a little miffed at how he had been mistakenly door-stopped by Gunnison-Penn and his friends with their lights and cameras, over the matter of the $20 gold piece which Matty – Araceli and Pat's small son had found during the Easter Egg hunt at Mills Farm several years previous. "It will be a remarkable find; the first rich hoard which the Treasure Hunting Man has ever discovered for real."

"Those bastards all conspired against me!" Gunnison-Penn scowled at his plate, from which he had finally masticated and swallowed a bite of full English breakfast, Richard was obscurely pleased to note. Doctor Mindy's comforting hand took Gunnison-Penn's in hers. "But I will show them yet, so help me God, I will!"

"Now – calm down, sweetie," Doctor Mindy said. "You will recall that the letters were unambiguous. They made specific mention of the Reliquary as the treasure of the Family and urged great-great-grandfather Don Luis-Antonio to secure it in safety. It was during the ACW … the American Civil War, you know," she added as an aside to Richard, who murmured,

"Yes, I was cognizant of the fact that other nations had civil wars."

"Yes – well, you see; that it was exceedingly dangerous for Great-great-Grandfather Luis-Antonio to have been in communication with his cousins across the border in Mexico City, since his son and heir, Don Anselmo was an officer in the First Texas Cavalry – in the Union Army, you see. But the Reliquary was of <u>such</u> importance to the Family – that the risk was one which they simply had to take. There is a letter preserved in the archive…." And Doctor Mindy warmed to the subject. "In which Dona Manuela

Diaz y Rivera – the cousin in Mexico City who was the chief correspondent with the Family in this period – thanked Don Luis-Antonio for the water-color sketch by his eldest daughter of the small family chapel in which the Reliquary had been placed, in which it must have been the most notable element, and for his care in securing it's safety…"

"So the Reliquary was proven by this letter, to have been present at Rincon de los Robles in the early 1860ies," Gunnison-Penn, having tucked away and swallowed the last mouthful of his English brekkie. "The water-color in question is not currently one which I have seen …"

"No," Doctor Mindy gave a small sigh. "The other half of this correspondence is gone, perhaps forever; I verified that with a number of phone calls. There was a great deal of war and unrest in subsequent years in Mexico. But that mention is proof positive that the Reliquary was here, present at Rincon, and there were active steps being taken to conceal it. Alas, matters were not very much better here in Texas, even when the war ended. Don Luis-Antonio died late in 1865, just before the war ended. Don Anselmo did not return to Rincon de los Robles for nearly ten years after that, during which the older members of the family had passed away, those of mature years scattered to the four winds, and only those who had been children or perhaps teenagers during the period in question remained."

"So how do you think this Don Luis person hid the Reliquary?" Richard was intrigued, almost in spite of himself, and Doctor Mindy sighed again.

"No one knows," she replied dolefully. "It was a closely-held secret, which is only to be expected – but so closely-held that within a few decades all memory of its existence had been forgotten. I had never heard of any such thing, when I was growing up, and I collected up every scrap and story of the Rincon's history that I could. Until I met Xavie…" and she and Gunnison-Penn exchanged fond smiles, "I had never known that such a treasure had ever existed, much less been kept at Rincon de los Robles."

"Well … happy hunting, then," Richard considered that he had spent as much time as required being social. And that he had heard as much about the previous century or two at Rancho Rincon-whatever as he could comfortably absorb.

When he returned to the kitchen, Luc Massie was just coming in the back door. Luc, painfully thin, tatted to a fair-the-well and coiffed like a mad and colorful species of exotic bird, was the junior cook at the Café, as well as drummer for a local punk band. He was also the requited lover of the unattainable – unattainable if her mother had anything to say about it, which she did and usually in an ear-splitting shriek – and musically-talented Belle Walcott, currently studying at the Julliard School in New York. As Miss Letty noted, Luc was one of those awkward, unsocial children. But he was coming along, as far as the social graces were concerned, and he was a genius-level master of the grill station in the Café's kitchen.

"Hi, Chef," Luc tied on a fresh apron, and swathed his multi-colored mohawk in a hair net. "You want I should help Bree with salad prep now?" Richard felt his own eyebrows rising. Luc actually making an effort to be social, collegial even? He must have been getting coaching from someone …

"Look over the potatoes soaking for *pomme frites* and start mixing the spices to dust the finished servings with," Richard answered. "Then help me roll out a batch for the cinnamon rolls. But you'll be in charge of the fryer and grill today, as that's your métier."

"Great – thanks, Chef." Luc's facial muscles twitched in what might be taken for a smile.

"Tell him about the chili contest," Robbie urged Luc, when no further reaction was produced.

"You know about that?" Luc seemed politely baffled.

"My sister texted me about it last night," Robbie answered. "She said I should be on your team for the contest. And Sylvester said he would do some research for us."

"Yeah, sure," Luc mumbled, sounding baffled still, and unenthused. Robbie continued, with undimmed cheer.

"And Bree, too. It will be awesome! Chef can coach us. Won't you, Chef? We have a whole four months to work up a championship chili recipe, and test it out as a special…"

"Getting ahead of yourself, just a little?" Richard suggested, with a dangerous scowl, and relented, upon seeing Robbie and Bree's good cheer somewhat dimmed at an unduly harsh response.

"Yes, Chef. Sorry, Chef," they chorused.

Bree looked under her brows at Richard, and added, in a rather little-girl voice. "But you will help us? Help Luc win the chili contest, won't you, Chef?"

Richard yielded, most ungraciously. "Of course – I will help you develop a potentially prize-winning recipe, but it must be on my terms, and it must be edible, and not like taking a bite from a lit blow-torch. And we have time to serve it as a special, once I have evolved it. But the actual contest participation is up to the three of you alone. I am allergic to the media spot-light and have no intention of being anywhere that such a spot-light is focused." Richard drew himself up, with a wavering technicolor vision of Henry V terrifying and inspiring his troops. Without realizing that he was doing so, he paced the length of the kitchen, seeing not the familiar stove, and ranks of pot-racks, but the impassive glass eyes of cameras, and the faces of an audience, like so many pale-faced sheep.

"Be it known, here and now that the pressure of preparing the dish on the day of the contest will be brutal," he continued, pounding every word home as if tenderizing a tough cut of meat with the *batticarne.* "Only by intensive practice, and attention to detail can your team prevail. Understand – you won't be working in this kitchen, but in a temporary set-up, alongside dozens of other contestants, also. Plus, the presence of the public and the media with their cameras, swooping in on you, relentlessly. You will have to focus and focus even more intently than you do when you work here."

And you are all so very, very young, Richard added to himself. *A pair of teenage apprentices, and a freaky musician with no social skills whatever. Food contest winners?*

Yeah, if I am behind them. Definitely.

The Three Woman Artists of Rancho Rincon de los Robles

By Dr. Miranda Ramirez-Gonzalez

Submitted to various local and Texas-specific publications and rejected by all of them

The Rancho Rincon de los Robles is situated in Karnes County, on the banks of the San Antonio River some ten miles north-east of Karnesville. It has been home for more than two hundred years to the Gonzales/Gonzalez family who originally were granted a league and a labor by His Majesty King Charles III of Spain, to his loyal servant and subject, Don Diego Manuel Hernando Ruiz y Gonzalez *(or Gonzales)* whose two sons, Augusto and Tomas eventually took up management of a property which in those days, was situated far beyond those bounds of civilization as it was accepted at the time. The family prospered there, until the last quarter of the 19th century, when the eventual heir, Don Anselmo Gonzalez was forced by circumstance to sell three-quarters of the grant to Herbert K. Wyler, who was then established as the largest landholder in the vicinity. However, Don Anselmo was able to hold on to the best-irrigated, and most scenically pleasing acres on the banks of the river, including the venerable home-site, and a grove of noble oak trees at a spot on the river where Luna City would be established at a later date.

His son, Don Antonio continued ranching on the diminished acres of the grant, specializing in pure-bred Merino sheep. He married a distant cousin, Agathe Ruiz-Gonzales, and raised a family in the historic ranch-house; a son, Don Jaimie (who eventually inherited in turn) and three artistically inclined daughters. The three daughters never married, but daringly continued exploring their various chosen arts far beyond the limitations imposed by the expectations of their class and era. Carmen (1899-1933), Aïda (1903-1954), and Leonora (1914-1969) were all named for operatic heroines, as their father was an aficionado of grand opera.

Carmen, the oldest, suffered all of her relatively short life from severe asthma and so did not venture far from home or for an extended period, unlike her younger siblings. Schooled in the traditional domestic arts at the Ursuline Academy in San Antonio, she was trained in needlework and embroidery by the nuns, achieving a mild degree of local fame for her intricate and original designs in all aspects of embroidery, tapestry, and fine lace. Many examples of her fabric artwork adorned the family's historic home on the banks of the San Antonio River, just south of Luna City, most notably in a set of needle-point chair seats in the formal salon. She also designed and oversaw the production of an elaborate series of altar vestments for the parish church of Saints Margaret and Joseph Catholic Church in Luna City, which are still in use for the most formal and traditional church services.

Her younger sister, Aïda was also schooled at the Ursuline Academy, and dabbled in the fine arts, including china-painting, before developing an interest in decorative pottery of the Arts and Crafts movement. Upon matriculation from the Ursuline Academy, Aïda prevailed upon her father to be allowed to attend H. Sophie Newcomb College in New Orleans, which offered an extensive program in the arts to women, including participating in production of art pottery. Aïda continued her art studies through to the post-graduate level and was listed as one of the schools' Art Craftsmen. In 1929, with the failure of the stock market and the start of the

Depression, she had to return home to Luna City, where she taught art and design in the Luna City public schools and continued producing art pottery in her own distinctive style, albeit on a smaller scale than that produced by the Newcomb Pottery.

The youngest sister, Leonora, explored a slightly different and more eccentric artistic path than her sisters, beginning with sculpture, and jewelry-making, in a style which can be described as a kind of found-object Fabergé, incorporating polished stones or beads of ordinary or semi-precious varieties, with simple wire-work settings, or fused-glass jewels or stones set into finely-finished polished hardwoods. Her designs were for items as small as a pair of earrings or a pendant, to belt-clasps and table-top sculptures as much as twenty inches tall. During the Second World War, Leonora took a course offered in welding by the National Youth Administration. Upon successfully completing the course, she worked at the Brown Ship Building Co., in Houston until the war ended. When she returned to the family home in 1945, she continued with larger-scale metal projects, creating ornamental elements such as railings, grilles, gates and fountains. Several of her projects adorn the grounds of Sts. Margaret and Joseph, including a series of Stations of the Cross in the garden between the sanctuary and the parish hall. A wrought-iron fountain by Leonora is situated in the south-east corner of Town Square, opposite the War Memorial.

These three woman artists defied the traditional expectations of their time – and by pursuing their various artistic impulses against the odds, they adorned a larger community in a way which has continued long after their own relatively brief lifetimes.

Parented

On the day that classes began at the Luna City schools, Jess Abernathy walked from the cottage that she shared with Joe, on the outer fringes of Oak Street towards Town Square, wheeling Little Joe in a jogging stroller which seemed to Jess to be about half the size of her little yellow Wrangler. She had an appointment with her father in his office at Abernathy Hardware, at mid-morning. Jess wondered idly what that was about; something to do with running for election again, she assumed. The day was fresh and new and all, still cool with a promise of remaining so for the remainder of the morning. A light breeze rustled the leaves of the oak trees, and the dew, which spangled the grass – some of it mown, and some left to grow long – sparkled in the new sun.

"How come you are so small, but all your stuff takes up so damn much space?" she demanded of her son, who merely showed her his two new teeth in a drool-adorned grin, and took another determined chomp out of the teething aid which Jess had put into the freezer for a short while. Little Joe was about to cut another tooth, and the previous evening, he had managed to walk around the coffee table, to Joe and Jess's rapturous approval. Little Joe had not let go of the coffee table edge, so it could not be said that he was really walking. But Joe was as pleased – ridiculously pleased, as only a father could be, and Jess's heart was warmed. Little Joe was the very image of Big Joe, and all of the other Vaughns that Jess had known from her own childhood: athletic, dark of hair, and eye, strong features, and an incongruous beak of a nose. And magnetically charming, even in embryo.

Now the new embryonic Vaughn briefly squirmed, as if in sympathy, and Jess wondered how on earth this traditional domesticity had ever managed to happen to her: two children, back in Luna City, wheeling a baby stroller along the sidewalk, talking to Little Joe – who couldn't even say much more than 'goo!' and the unborn Vaughnling who was as yet verbally unresponsive. *Barefoot and in the kitchen must be next*, she decided. How on earth did this happen to her? Back when she was a teenager, she was supposed to be either the soigné, polished professional woman, or the champion barrel-racing rodeo queen. It was her best friend, Araceli who was all about being a wife and mother with a dozen children. At the time, Jess thought secretly how that goal of Araceli's would be such a tedious waste. But now and whenever she looked at Little Joe, it wasn't at all a waste. No, it was important, this mingling of her blood and bones and DNA with Joe's – and it was all well-worth doing, having children and raising them successfully. The future belongs to those who show up for it. Or their children.

"In a couple more years, you'll be with them," Jess said out loud to Little Joe and the fetal Vaughnling, "Getting onto that school-bus with all the others. In the end and all-told, you kidlets will only take up about a quarter of my life; the hands-on feeding, diapering, nagging about homework and taking to football practice … it will taper off in about twenty years, and then … well, with luck, I'll have another thirty or forty on this dirtball, and what the heck will I do to occupy myself, then? Probably the same things I did before. Grams flogs Mary Kay to women who want inexpensive makeup. I have no notion of what Mom would have done …" and Jess was diverted into contemplating what her mother, Beth, might have done with her life once, if the fates and metastasizing cancer had not intervened when Jess herself was in the fifth grade. "Not something pointless," Jess assured her offspring. "Although Mom wasn't forceful, like Myrna-Mom-In-Law. It's just that I cannot think of Mom doing anything else than being a Mom. Failure of imagination, I guess."

"Goo!" Exclaimed Little Joe, exuberantly flinging the teething ring from the stroller onto the sidewalk, from where Jess retrieved it with a sigh, regarding her offspring with a severe expression.

"I'm damned as a mother, if I let you have that back," she admonished her son. "God knows what kind of sidewalk germs it has all over it."

Little Joe screwed up his infant features and prepared to howl. Jess wavered for just an instant, before wiping off the slobber-marinated object with a handi-wipe from the comprehensive stock in the gargantuan diaper bag hung on the back of the stroller. She handed the teething ring back to her son. "Don't complain to me, if it tastes like antiseptic," she added, as Little Joe made a moue of distaste. "Consider it as the penalty for throwing it down in the first place."

Upon racking her memory as she paced of the next half a block, Jess recalled that her mother had gone to college, and studied … oh, she had studied French.

"Maybe she would have gone back to school and been a teacher," Jess confided to her offspring; the one paid no attention, as far as she could see, and the other curled contentedly and blessedly now quiescent inside her.

The miracle of life, they called it – a cliché which Jess had never thought about, deeply or in any other fashion, until it happened to her. Children, new and amazingly fragile, impressionable, and yet … resilient. New little people created from the collision of elements within a woman. Mysterious, indeed. No wonder that the ancients worshipped a mother-goddess.

She came out into Town Square, around the side of the old Fire Station. Long ago – even before the far-distant childhood of Gram and Grumpy and Miss Letty, the old Fire Station had housed twin steam-powered water-pumps, side by side behind arched doorways. The pumps were pulled by the firemen themselves. In those years around the turn of the previous century, the VFD held a race on the Fourth of July, and again on Founders Day: which team would be the first around Town Square, hauling a heavy steam pump? There was a large picture hanging on the wall in the Abernathy Hardware office on the mezzanine-level of Jess's great-grandfather Charles Abernathy and his steam pump team, posing in their uniforms and leather helmets in front of the old fire house, on the occasion of Steam Pump #2 winning the race held on the 4th of July, 1901 – all that annotated along the bottom of the print in white letters. Jess always thought that the young Charles Abernathy, with a brilliant and triumphant grin from ear to ear, was the dead spitting image of her father, when he was young.

When the Luna City VFD purchased two motorized pumper trucks in the early 1920ies, the old Fire Station proved to be too small; now the building served as a retail premise on the ground floor, the sliding wooden doors replaced by glass windows and display cases. The quarters on the second floor was now a B&B suite, the upper windows commanded a fine view of Town Square, and the sparkling-new-renewed façade of the Cattleman Hotel. Even as Jess rounded the corner, the Mills Farm excursion bus – a renovated vintage British double-decker adorned with the logo of Mills Farm along the sides – was pulling away from the sidewalk, with a full complement of late holidaymakers inside. As Jess walked past the old Fire Station, she passed that odd little treasure-hunting man who had made such a problem for Rich at the Café not two years before.

"Hi, Penn," she greeted him. "Found any good clues to the golden reliquary lately?"

Not that Jess thought that he had, but Araceli's cousin Mindy insisted that Gunnison-Penn was a reformed character of late, now that he was diverted onto the path of a real, as opposed to a merely legendary treasure. Jess remained skeptical. Penn was such a rude, unprepossessing little man. *Mindy must be purely desperate for male admiration to see him as the perfect knight-errant*, Jess thought.

"I have found a letter," Penn burbled, and Jess resigned herself to listen to him for at least five minutes, until must needs roll the stroller along in order to meet with her father at the appointed time. "A letter from Leonora, the sister of Don Jaimie, written during the war; she made mention of some small scrap-metal and gem-trimmed artifacts which her sister Aïda had found in the ground, while digging an expanded vegetable garden – they called them Victory Gardens, during the war; do you recollect? Leonora wrote with words of the effect; *'Most likely brass and glass, of little intrinsic value, but the enamel plaque of the Blessed Virgin riding on a donkey sounds quite charming. Don't throw them into the scrap-metal drive: I will incorporate them into my next project, when I return home for the christening next month. My best ... et cetera, et cetera...'* It all sounded most a most promising lead in my quest. The Gonzaga Reliquary featured an enamel plaque of the Virgin Mary and Baby Jesus on the flight into Egypt …"

"It sounds fascinating, Penn," Jess said, as Little Joe began to fuss at the lack of movement of the stroller. "Do you have any idea of what Miss Leonora's project was?"

"None at all," Penn sighed in naked discouragement. Jess momentarily felt sorry for him; a pathetic little man who had given his adult life to a fruitless hunt of lost and likely nonexistent treasures in all the wrong places.

"I'm certain you will find it, eventually," Jess said, intending to be bracing. She really felt sorry for Gunnison-Penn. "In the meantime, Mindy is so happy with your help and companionship."

"Is she, really?" and Penn's expression brightened, the exact expression of a thirsty traveler in the desert upon spotting a water hole.

"She is. Her cousin Araceli is my best friend, and Araceli says that Mindy is over the moon with the help you have given her, in researching the history of the Rincon Ranch."

"She's a very clever woman," Penn confided, with what Jess read as a fatuous and fond expression. "And determined. I like that. A good woman, above the price of rubies…"

"For sure," Jess released the brake on the stroller. "Hang in there, Penn – with the treasure and Mindy, and all. Look, I gotta go. Appointment with the Mayor. You understand?"

"Au revoir, Mrs. Vaughn," Penn answered, without any hint of realizing that Jess's withdrawal from the conversation was diplomatic and hasty.

Jess wheeled the stroller away at a pace which left her slightly breathless before she had gone past two more storefronts, whereupon she slowed down for a bit, until she recovered. *Really – how could she have known that the embryonic Vaughnling would cramp her lungs as well as her bladder! She had not noticed that with Little Joe! Gram said it was because she was carrying a girl. Girl babies were always carried high, Gram insisted.*

At the ornate brick storefront which had marked the Abernathy Hardware Emporium for all of the previous century and two decades of the one before that, she maneuvered the stroller through the double-swinging door, to the tune of a gentle silvery chime.

The store was empty, save for a couple of tourists in the back, admiring the array of cast-iron pots and pans stacked in what Grumpy and Gram always called the 'kitchen corner' along with shelves of utilitarian stoneware crocks, jugs and casseroles. Gram – that is, Jess's paternal grandmother – sat behind the cash register desk, leafing through a Mary Kay catalog and making notes on a pad of order forms.

"Hi, Grams," Jess was still slightly breathless. "Dad in the office? He wanted to meet with me this morning. Can I leave Little Joe with you for a moment?"

"You just bring that sweet little darlin' right here," Grams replied, exchanging a brief kiss and embrace with Jess, and a longer embrace of Little Joe, who wriggled with transcendent joy, as his great-grandmother lifted him out from the stroller, and settled him on her lap. Grams – the bountiful provider of treats and affection – was one of Little Joe's most favorite people in all the world. But practically everyone was Little Joe's favorite person in all the world: he admitted not to favor or discrimination. After all, he was only ten months old, and his world was perforce limited.

Jess threaded her way through the aisles of the hardware store – past the tools, past the ancient octagonal spinning tower of small drawers housing screws, nuts and bolts, all neatly labeled, the display of fire irons and BBQ tools. All kinds of interesting and arcane items were neatly arrayed on the farthest shelves, and in the darker corners, many of them antiques in their own right: pump-oil mantle lanterns, replacement vanes for windmills, hand-cranked meat grinders, hinges and latches for iceboxes which had not been manufactured in seventy years. God and Grumpy only knew of what was in the farthest corners of the stock room. Jess climbed the stairway which led up to the office on the mezzanine-level, which space looked out through windows onto the sales floor. Once upon a day, the various cashier stations along the front of the store maintained a system of little cans on a network of pullies and wires, to transfer cash paid straight up to the office for a full accounting and credit. The cashier stations were all gone, but the one – but the system of pullies and wires remained, a spider-web of tiny commercial doings, along the pressed-tin ceiling of Abernathy Hardware. It made it very awkward, trying to move anything tall around on the sales floor. Grumpy insisted on having them remain in place – as he claimed, it was historical and might yet come in handy once again, in the event of an electrical and credit apocalypse which returned commerce to a cash basis, once again.

Jess climbed the stairs – puffing again from exertion, her business laptop in its' case in hand – and found her father in the office, regarding the screen of his laptop computer, all set out on a desk which had the jump on him, seniority-wise by at least three-quarters of a century.

"Hey, Pops," Jess gasped, and Martin sprang from his chair and scooted the office extra-chair towards her.

"Jessy-Belle, you OK?" he asked with such an expression of deep concern that Jess wished that she had not climbed the stairs so quickly.

"I'm fine, Pops. Really. Look, don't you dare get all concerned about me. You are the one who called for this meet. What's up?"

Martin sank back into the office chair – one of those elderly, leather-padded executive-office numbers, which conformed nicely with the vintage of the office itself.

"I'll cut right to the chase, Jessy-Belle. I need to have the heart-valve surgery and soon. That aortic stenosis condition must be dealt with, before it gets any worse. I've started passing out cold, if I move too fast, and it seems like I'm always short of breath. I can't go on this way, I purely can't, and the risk is small. They're gonna do minimally invasive surgery. I checked it all out. Look, it's what the doctor advised. Should be good for at least ten years more, once the surgery is done. Don't look so shocked, Jessy-Bell; you've known about this for a while."

"I don't like hospitals," Jess gave voice to her first stricken reaction. "I never did. Mom died in a hospital. I don't want you to go there. Pops, are you sure?"

"Yeah," Martin answered. "Most people die in bed, Jessy-Belle. You want that I should never go to bed again?"

"Right," Jess sighed, although she was still a little shaken over the prospect of imminent surgery for her only beloved and surviving parent. "So, go for the operation, Pops. You know how much I love you and need you to be around. At least as long as Gram and Grumpy. Little Joe needs you, and so does the kidlet. I had the ultrasound last week – and swear you to absolute secrecy, Pops – a girl. Joe and I are thrilled to bits. I want to name her after

Mom, and Joe's Mom. Elizabeth Myrna Vaughn. How does that sound to you?"

"Like something to live for," Martin answered, honestly relieved. "My lips are sealed about this, Jessy-Belle. Word of honor…"

"What else, Pops?" Jess was suddenly moved to suspicion. Martin was being altogether too agreeable about all this. "You're holding back on me. What else?"

Another deep sigh.

"I'm tired," Martin confessed. "Just … tired. Jessy-Belle, I'm not gonna run for re-election again. Seriously, I need to hand it all off. Clem Bodie is planning to run for mayor, and so is Roberto Gonzales. There are some others, considering a run, as well – but those two have the best chance, I think. I'm glad as heck that someone else is willing to take it all on. A lot of work, you know. A burden I just can't carry on anymore."

"Pops, you've done a lot for Luna City," Jess was a little stunned at first. It seemed to her that Martin had always been the mayor – well, at least since the time she finished college. What was that – four terms? "And now you have a right to give it a rest – especially when you have to have major surgery. That, especially… what else?" Jess added, suspicious that Martin was now looking down at the top of his desk, fiddling with his pen, and the pages of his appointment calendar. "Spill, Pops – what else?"

Martin heaved a deep sigh. "Jessy-Belle, you know I hate to ask this of you, what with your own business, and with Little Joe and the new baby … but I'm going to have to ask you to take over for me in the store, starting next month or so, until the doctor says I am cleared for duty again. Your grandfather is as fit as a flea still, but he's ninety and not getting any younger. We wouldn't dream of handing Abernathy Hardware over to anyone but family."

"Well, yeah, Pops!" Jess was relieved. *That was all?* "Of course, I'll fill in for you. You hardly had to ask."

"I felt obliged," Martin answered. "And it might be for longer than a couple of weeks or months. You still game, Jessy-Belle?"

"Like you have to get a hunting license, Pops," Jess gathered up her computer-bag/briefcase and blew a kiss in Martin's general direction. "Look, I have an appointment with Miss Letty this afternoon, but expect me tomorrow first thing, and we can start going over stuff. Grams can rack up quality time with Little Joe, and I'll stand you lunch at the Café. Don't worry about me, Pops – I can do this, and just have my regular clients come here for business …"

"But when Elizabeth Myrna arrives …" Martin began, and Jess grinned.

"Like Joe says, we'll napalm that bridge when we get to it, Pops. I'll see you in the morning."

Downstairs, she collected her son from his doting great-grandmother, and rolled the jogging stroller out onto the sidewalk. The sun stood nearly overhead, but the trees in the Square whispered of shade, of cool grass. Jess wheeled the stroller across the road, and into that green oasis, the green heart of Luna City. Even the sounds of desultory traffic seemed muffled and distant, hardly louder than the happy shouts from children playing in the elementary school playground. Jess slowed to a leisurely stroll, thinking, evaluating, mentally rescheduling the program of her day, today and for all the days to come.

Of course, she would help manage Abernathy Hardware. Pops needed to take a good long rest. Thinking on that, she was struck by a sudden notion. Of course. She walked on, crossing to the other side of Town Square, opposite the Café. It was lunchtime, and many of the tables were filled with diners. Araceli was taking orders, pen in hand, when Jess crossed the road.

"Hi, Jess! You coming in today for lunch, or just looking? Rich is trying out a new special today; wild boar chili. It's something awesome."

"Just looking," Jess replied. "Maybe tomorrow – save some for Pops and I. Hey, have you got a cellphone number for your Aunt Joanna? And where is she, these days."

"Houston, I think," Araceli replied. "She had a master-class and lecture series there at one of the schools." Araceli fished her own cellphone out of her apron pocket. She thumbed through her contacts list, as Jess brought out her own phone, and copied a new entry into her own contacts list. "Why and wherefore?"

"Pops has to have heart-valve surgery soon," Jess confessed. "And he and Joanna … well, they're close enough that I believe she would want to know."

"You got it, girlfriend." Araceli agreed. "Let me know when, and Abuelita and I will light a candle for him, in the name of St. Raphael the Archangel, and ask for healing. Or maybe St. Thomas More. He's the saint for heart ailments. Two candles then."

"I didn't know that Catholic saints had it down to medical specialties," Jess was momentarily diverted. "I guess it's like doctors. Raphael is the GP and Thomas is the cardiologist." Araceli giggled. And then the patrons at the nearest table made an impatient gesture in her direction – people wandering over from the grand Cattleman. Araceli turned her face away from them and grimaced. Jess read the expression. *Duty calls.* "Thanks, 'Celi. See you tomorrow," she said, over her shoulder.

Another day in Luna City.

The Final Chili Judgement

"Remember," Sylvester Gonzales said, as Richard's assistant cook and two apprentices packed the ice-chests on the Friday afternoon before the chili contest on the following day, "No pepper seeds in the finished chili!"

For some mysterious reason, Sylvester the resident Luna City retro-styled computer nerd, had become part of the Café's chili-construction team, headed by Luc Massie, and coached by Richard. Although Sylvester knew nothing of professional kitchen practice, he did appear to be reasonably knowledgeable about chili-cooking contests, and the requirements for a winning brew. To this end, he had gathered up a compendium of resources to guide Luc, Robbie and Bree hopefully to victory in the lists of chili-dom. Sylvester was very good at research, as Richard had good reason to know;

just that spring he had traced the Cattleman Hotel stolen light fixtures to an auction house in Houston, and done that in a matter of minutes.

"Not a problem, bro," Robbie replied. "At the last minute, we'll blend the flavoring fresh peppers with ice-cubes, and strain the pepper-water on-scene…"

"Omigod!" Bree gasped. "The blender! Did we pack the blender? And the strainer?"

"In the big tub with the cooking gear and the pans," Sylvester brandished his checklist, upon which every single bit of equipment and ingredient had been listed, in excruciating detail. "And the digital scale. Ah … the spice grinder. And the power strip and hundred-foot extension cord."

"On it!" Robbie exclaimed. Richard, lingering by the stove, where he was carefully monitoring the reduction of the stock which would constitute the unctuous liquid in which the meats and spices would be gently simmered upon the morrow, approved the attention to detail.

Yes – I have trained them well. (Although, he appended, in all honesty – there was something to be said for Sylvester's meticulous attention to detail and prowess with logistical detail. Probably had something to do with having been a Marine. Or a computer nerd.)

"How is the stock doing, Chef?" Bree asked, the small electric spice grinder in one hand, and a selection of zip-lock baggies in the other.

"Reducing nicely," Richard answered, and waved his hands over the gently simmering stock pot, wafting the scent of the carefully composed stock towards Bree, who inhaled gratefully.

"Smells wonderful, Chef. It would be boss, just on its' own," Bree said.

"Of course," Richard intended that the condensed stock would contribute no small portion to the final product. Into that stock, he had incorporated every care and culinary stratagem he had ever learned: enamel pot, filtered water, bones and scraps roasted to a rich brown, and the judicious addition of scrupulously cleaned chicken feet, for the collagen which would make the final product rich, thick and savory. He had monitored the stockpot for more than an hour even throughout the morning breakfast rush, laboriously skimming off every particle of froth which bubbled to the surface.

Now, the Café team was engaged in packing for the contest.

"Did you test out the camp-stove?" Sylvester asked, when Robbie returned, panting slightly. The largest tub, with the necessary gear; the cooking pot, the knives and spoons, the cutting board – was already in the trunk of the elderly Volvo sedan. In the morning, the last of the ingredients would be packed in a pair of ice-chests for transport to Mills Farm, including six pounds of carefully minced lean meat – tender wild boar meat, for Richard had decided to explore a new frontier in chili recipes rather than take the more traditional route which led beefwards. The test batches had gone down very well, as a luncheon entrée over the previous month, as Richard refined the technique and adjusted the ingredients, tinkered with the spices and the means of reducing grease to a minimum in the finished dish.

"Affirmative," Robbie answered. "And I made certain the propane bottle is a full one. Is there anything else we might have forgotten, Chef?"

"Not if Sylvester has put it on his checklist," Richard replied. "Now it's all on you chaps and chapess from the moment you check in and start cooking. I'm not an official part of your team. I'd linger purposefully in the vicinity but for having this place to run, but any disasters tomorrow will be yours to resolve."

"We're on it, Chef!" Bree assured him, with a jaunty salute. "Don't worry about a thing. We have it all memorized, down to the second what we should be doing every moment until we turn in the judging cup at 2:00 PM. We know what we're doing."

"I should damn well hope so, by now," Richard answered, with the depressed feeling that now he knew how a mother bird felt, upon observing her nestlings perching on the edge of the nest stretching their wings. He hoped that the first flight would be a resounding success but couldn't help feeling that the flight would a short, one, straight down and with a painful thump at the end of it.

And in the morning, he would only have Bree to help in the kitchen for the Saturday morning breakfast, and himself alone for lunch. But with the chili contest out at Mills Farm, he didn't think there would be much of a house for lunch, not with Mills Farm going all out. He understood that the Country Restaurant would be laying on extra tables, and that there would be food trucks to cater to all those sightseers who had no taste for chili. Sufficient unto the day, he told himself, pedaling home under the stars with Ozzie that evening, having seen off the younger crowd – all excited beyond words, despite the exhaustion of the Café on a Friday night. As he passed by the Spanish-style cottage, just around the corner from Town Square, he noted that there were lights on inside.

"I would reckon that the renovation work is done," he commented to Ozzie. "And that the Lady of the House is now in residence. I expect that she will be at the Café for breakfast any day now." The thought of Jess Vaughn's formidable mother-in-law brought the thought of Jess herself to mind.

I should talk to her about the possibility of hiring another cook, he thought – about his last coherent thought before falling into deep, deep sleep. It would be afternoon before he could scrape some time to come out to Mills Farm to check on his young proteges – maybe Chris could give him a ride? And on that note, he fell asleep.

Chris obliged, of course – Richard settled into the shotgun seat of Chris' little red coupe just after two in the afternoon. According to Sylvester's meticulous schedule, the finished samples of chili were being collected and taken for judging at that hour, and it would take at least an hour and maybe more for the winner to be announced.

"How's it going with the kids?" Chris asked, as the wheels of the red coupe scattered a burst of gravel as it rocketed down the alley in back of the Café.

"I don't know," Richard replied. "I haven't heard a thing." He had half-expected a frantic telephone call or two from the team during the preparation part of the contest, but both the Café's phone and his personal cellie had been quiet. Richard honestly couldn't decide if that were a good thing, or not.

"I got a call from Sylvester, 'bout twenty minutes ago," Chris related, in his best consoling manner. "He says everything's going fine, 'cept could I bring another bag of ice and some bottles of water. It's warmish outside today, even in the shade. They got a good crowd out at Mills Farm today. If you don't mind the walk, I'm gonna go in by the utility gate and park by the Boathouse, ok?"

"Fine," Richard answered. The walk from the 1912 Boathouse to the main complex was a pleasant one, through landscaped grounds along the river – and anything that would help them avoid the crush at the main Mills Farm entrance would be a plus. And it was a nice day; Mills Farm's ground were nearly as lush and green as an English countryside, if a trifle warmer. If it weren't for the daily bicycle commute, Richard would hardly have otherwise spent much time out of doors at all. As it turned out, though, he and Chris didn't need to walk much further than the Boathouse. A quiet crunch of the gravel at their backs and a familiar voice made Richard start uncontrollably.

"Hey, fellas, want a lift?"

"Christ, Benny – you've got to stop sneaking up on a chap like that," Richard exclaimed, and Benny Cordova grinned, unrepentant. He was a slight man with the gift of moving like a ghost even in cowboy boots, the local facility manager at Mills Farm, and mildly famous for being the only Hispanic anywhere about Luna City who was not Gonzales or Gonzalez kin. *(Benny was, in fact, a foreigner from Beeville.)* He was at the wheel of an equally silent electric golf cart, one of those used for transporting larger numbers of people around Mills Farm. There was only one other person in the cart, a slender young woman with long dark hair, and a Mills Farm employee badge on a lanyard around her neck.

"Sure thing, Benny," Chris swung up into a seat, setting down the bag of ice and water at his feet. Richard joined him, and the electric cart set off with a mild lurch, skimming in near silence along the paved pathway towards the expanded main complex of Mills Farm. "Thanks, I was getting tired carrying all that stuff for the Café team. They doin' OK, near as you can tell?"

"We just came out to check on them," Richard explained.

"Time of their lives," Benny grinned over his shoulder, and jerked his chin towards the other passenger in the first-row seat. "You met Miz Royce, guys? Stephanie's our new, full-time publicist. We got enough business now at Mills Farm that Corporate dedicated us our own on-scene publicity expert. Steph, this here is Richard Astor-Hall, but everyone calls him Ricardo, from the Café in town, and Chris Mayall from the Tip-Top."

"Hey," Stephanie leaned around to take Richard's hand for a brief yet energetic handshake. "Love the cinnamon rolls; you're that

English chef-guy? Right. Lew Dubois says you're one of the best around."

"Good man, Dubois," Richard would have said more, but Stephanie Royce's attention had already gone on towards Chris.

"Haven't we already met? I could swear, I know you from someplace," she observed. Richard privately wondered if they weren't related; both lean, whipcord thin, although Stephanie's complexion was several shades paler than Chris' – which was the color of a good cup of Café coffee with lots of cream in it – and she had hazel-grey eyes. Otherwise, Stephanie Royce bore distinct resemblance to the famous bust of the Egyptian Queen Nefertiti.

"Last weekend," Chris snapped his fingers, a look of enlightenment on his face. "In San Marcos, at that marathon run. You came in at third or fourth best time in the women's division."

"Yeah, that's it!" Stephanie's elegant countenance was transformed from severity by a brilliant smile. "I wanted to talk to you, see if you wanted to go out for a drink or something afterwards, but you kinda did a vanishing act."

"Places to go, people to see," Chris waved a careless hand. "Doesn't mean we can't get something now, less'n you're on duty, or something."

"I am," Stephanie acknowledged, with some mild regret. "But I wouldn't say no to a good old root beer float. One of the food trucks here today does ice cream and sodas."

"Awesome," Chris said, and Richard sighed. Chris had a mildly dazzled look on his face.

Looks like a Luna City woman has finally bagged the most elusive bachelor, Richard mused to himself. *Or the second most elusive bachelor, after me.* Out loud, he ventured,

"A good turn-out for today, Benny?"

"Most excellent," Benny replied, and drew the cart to a halt with a flourish in the graveled area above the shallow basin which now housed the Chuckwagon Circle – part of the new Mills Farm extension, which had come to pass through the creative imagination and tireless efforts of Lew Dubois. Lew was almost a legend in Mills Farm's corporate parent, Richard was sure.

"You wanna take this to your team?" Chris handed the heavy insulated bag with the ice and water in it to Richard, hardly waiting for an answer in the affirmative.

"I have to be back at the Café in an hour," Richard said to Chris's back. The latter was already walking away towards the serried ranks of food trucks around the perimeter of the Chuckwagon Circle, arm in arm with Stephanie Royce.

"Sure, man," Chris answered, over his shoulder. "Meet you back at the car."

"Just flag me or one of the other shuttles down, when you need a lift," Benny advised, and Richard sighed. There was a big crowd here, much bigger than he had expected. He directed his steps and shouldered his way toward the enormous open-sided pavilion which had been pitched over the center of the campfire circle to shelter the chili-cooking teams in the event of inclement weather. This part of the new enlarged Mills Farm was an open area, centered on a stone circle surrounded by rustic log benches and presided over by an old-fashioned horse-drawn chuckwagon. The chances of inclement weather were far less likely here than it would have been in England at any time of the year.

When Richard had first arrived in Luna City, Mills Farm had been more of a modest place, for all that it was the second largest employer in the area. A dozen carefully restored and furnished cottages, each individually nestled into its own complex of hedges and garden provided the upscale visitor with every comfort. A larger house provided a range of suites and single rooms – again, surrounded by gardens and lawns. There was the old dance hall building, transported from the Hill Country town where it had peacefully moldered away for a hundred years, offering a small stage for indoor concerts and parties. An outdoor amphitheater had been carved as if by nature into the sloping hillside below the original homestead had once been. A classic red-and-white barn housed the petting zoo, and the 18-hole golf course spread itself out below like a living green velvet coverlet, adorned with ice-white sand traps, sculpted green clumps of trees and water obstacles which reflected the turquoise-blue sky overhead. Closer to the river and beside the specimen garden of native herbs and aromatic lavender, the Country Store and Restaurant raised it's classic standing-seam metal roof, offering what was advertised discretely as the best if not the largest chicken-fried steak in Karnes County – a whopping four pounds, which was free to any diner who could eat all of it, and a monstrous side dish of mashed potatoes and a dozen pieces of toast besides.

It had been the short-lived and grievously misplaced vision of the parent hospitality corporation, Venue Properties International, to transform all this into a water-park, with slides and swimming pools and who knew what else; possibly a salt-water aquarium, for all Richard knew. Fortunately, Lew Dubois had a better notion of how to best provide the upscale rural Texas experience to a wider clientele than previous; offering pony-trekking, kayaking on the river, and hunting excursions. This meant expanding the existing facilities, to which local builder Roman Gonzalez had fallen to with a will. The boathouse and stables were new construction but made to seem as authentically vintage as anything else at Mills Farm. In order to accommodate an increased number of overnight visitors, Lew had negotiated a long-term lease of the venerable Cattleman

Hotel in Luna City itself. So far as Richard knew, it was all working to plan, if the crowds today at the chili contest were any indication.

Although people wearing shirts and aprons printed with chili peppers or boasting hats in the shape of red and yellow chili peppers was an offense against good taste as he conceived it … Richard knew better now than to make any comment.

And besides – there was one of his favorite people in Luna City, his dear Kate of Kate Hall, Miss Kate Heisel; star reporter for the venerable local newspaper, the Karnesville Weekly Beacon, and the one most responsible for restoring custody of Ozzie-cat to him. Her oversized trench coat flapped about her like wings. Kate wore the coat – not for warmth (not needed on a day such as today) but for those deep and generous pockets, which served as a kind of portable office for her notebooks and extra camera gear. And the ever-present packet of luxury catnip from Abuelita Adeliza's garden, which Richard was certain had pushed the levers in Ozzie's tiny but self-serving cat brain into opting for Kate as custodian of himself.

"Hey, you!" she beamed, and offered her cheek up for a chaste and decorous kiss, which he returned in equal measure. "Come to check on your babies? I knew you would. They've just collected the finished chilis … you know that they do this in numbered cups, so that no one can be unduly interested through favoritism. I didn't think you'd want to tear yourself away from the Café on a Saturday …"

"I came with Chris," Richard explained, as Kate tucked her arm into his. "Just for an hour! Only he has gone off with … the woman who has taken his interest. I purely don't know if I am going to get the promised ride back to the Café. He looked pretty ga-ga for her. Stephanie Royce, the publicist for this place."

"Stephanie Royce," Kate mused, and Richard would never confess how much he enjoyed seeing Kate's expression when the mental gears went flip-flipping in her admittedly bulging brain. "Mills Farm's new publicist, now that they rate a local, rather than the VPI main office. Saves me a bit of trouble, trying to get ahold of someone who actually knows something … I believe she is one of Lew Dubois' suggestions … thirtyish, military brat, raised in Europe mostly, dad's a retired general or something. Long retired. Went to college in Texas, got a grand internet presence on her own as a fashion and lifestyle icon, awesome number of followers on the various stages. Plays them like a pro… likely why she got hired in a fit of competence at VPI. So, she is Chris' new crush?" Kate sent him a fond sideways glance and Richards' own heart went flip-flopping in turn.

"I believe," Richard confessed. "They were going off in search of a milkshake together. A first date. It's unbearably quaint. I am afraid that my ride back to town will be forgotten entirely, in the throes of that initial mad passion."

"Never mind," Katie consoled him, as she led him into the vast pavilion which housed the chili cooks. "I can drop you on my way back. Just say the word."

"Drop me – and ruin my incomparable flavor?" Richard replied and Kate giggled.

Inside the pavilion, the air was redolent with the scent of chili-pepper spices and of slow-simmered meats – plus a certain distinct funk of human sweat of the nervous variety.

Kate continued, "The first round of judging is underway, so … everyone is taking a breather."

"*Alea iacta est*," Richard heaved the bag higher on his shoulder and daringly took Kate's hand. "Meaning; the die is cast. Nothing more to do than await developments. The breather appears to be taking the form of tasty adult beverages."

Indeed, most of the contestants, behind their tables and cooling gas stoves seemed to be kicking back with frosty glasses and beer bottles.

"Nothing like a good icy-cold margarita," Kate agreed. "This is the second story of the day for me. I just came from Rincon de los Robles. Doctor Mindy and Mr. Penn are over the moon, with what they found, going through the artifacts found last month in the dig they organized for the high school history students. They were hoping to trace the layout of the original buildings."

"What did they find?" Richard asked, not with any particular interest – save that it had brought Kate out to Luna City on a weekend. He had spotted his people, down at the farthest corner of the pavilion – not that Luc Massie, with his bi-colored mohawk crest of hair was all that hard to miss in a gathering of relatively normal folks. They were all wearing their Luna Café and Coffee aprons and white toques, so as to leave now doubt as to the name of their team.

"It's quite nifty," Kate began, waving across the pavilion at Bree and Robbie, who waved in return. "The line of the original adobe walls, out in back of the present house, underneath the old vegetable gardens. They found a lot of artifacts, too – bits and pieces of pottery and painted tile, a dinged up pewter spoon, hinges and rusty hand-forged nails and the like – all pretty much dated to the late 18th or early 19th century. Mindy's going to have the high school set up a display in the library."

"Sounds depressingly ordinary," Richard sighed. "I have never understood how those archeological types can work up such enthusiasm for all those grotty little bits of broken china and metal scraps."

"In this case," Kate explained, patiently, "It all provides irrefutable proof of the age of the Rincon main ranch establishment, tying the date of construction to at least sixty years before the McAllister house. And there was something more …"

Richard was about to ask what, but at that moment Bree and Robbie bounced from behind their temporary workspace, exclaiming, "Chef! You made it! You would have been so proud! Sylvester says that our chili is in the final round! We're number 42 – I think that means we are lucky, 'cause isn't forty-two supposed to be the answer to everything?"

"That's fantastic!" Kate exclaimed, while Richard shook his head.

"Chris sent you the ice and water that you asked for … I thought all this was supposed to be a secret, until the final winner is announced. The judging cups were marked with a number only…"

"Sylvester went to the top of the hill above the judges table with a hunter's scope," Robbie explained. "He's been watching, and he spotted our number on one of the three cups taken to the final judges!"

"We're in! We're in! We're in!" Bree crowed, nearly dancing with excitement. "I don't know how much longer I can stand this!"

"Patience, my young apprentice," Richard advised, feeling terribly old in the face of such juvenile enthusiasm; why, even Luc seemed to have caught the fever of impatience. Meanwhile, Robbie took the insulated bag from Richard and extracted three bottles of water.

"Thanks, Chef," he said, twisting off the cap of one and downing about half in one gulp. "Nothing quite hits the spot like ice-cold water on a hot day. Y'all better drink up before dehydration kicks in," he added to his teammates. "Dad always says that by the time you're thirsty, you're already dehydrated. And alcoholic beverages," Robbie added with an air of conspicuous virtue, "Are not actually effective – they make it worse. And besides…"

"You're both underage," Kate pointed out, at which Richard shook his head.

"In a sensible country, they figure that if you are old enough to ask for it, you're old enough to drink it."

"But we're not asking for it," Robbie was annoyingly literal-minded. "We've cleaned up our station and put away all our stuff. Let's go over to the judges' table and wait for the announcement of the winner."

It was a jovial gathering in front of the small pavilion which shaded the judge's table, on the far side of the old chuckwagon. Folding chairs were scattered hither and yon on the grass. There was a good crowd – most of them in lamentable tee-shirts and headgear lauding the qualities of chili and chili peppers, and music floated in from a band playing on the terrace by the Dancehall. It was slightly cooler in the shade, where a desultory breeze stirred the leaves of those trees which edged Mills Farm's Chuckwagon Circle grounds. In England, it would have already been too cold and windy, in mid-November for people at an occasion like this to go around coatless and in shirtsleeves. Richard's chili-making team had carried their folding chairs with them and parked them in a bit of shade from the nearest leafy sycamore tree, now turning golden and shedding bits and pieces of itself all over the lawn below. Presently, Sylvester joined them, resplendent in vintage cuffed chino trousers and a vividly-patterned aloha shirt – also equally vintage. He was tucking something which looked at first glance like a large flashlight into the pocket of his chinos.

"Final countdown, gang," he said, as the tension racketed up another notch or two.

At the judging table, Allen Lee Mayne loomed as large as a storm-cloud beside the other two judges. Richard spotted … *oh, horrors!* A film crew with a serious camera, the lens of which was now sweeping across the waiting audience. Richard bent down and readjusted the ties on his shoe for the length of time that he judged that the camera would complete the pass.

"I'm sorry, chaps. I can't be here," he said, as he came up for air. "I'll have to go. Now. Even before they announce the winner. The news media will be all over them … and if it turns out to be you chaps…"

The very thought of that made him queasy, breathless – light-headed, even.

"There's no other media here but me," Kate sounded frustrated in the extreme. "Officially, anyway. Steph told me. Well, some of the chili-heads here have blogs, and Allen Lee has his TV crew but I'm the only capital-M media. I have to stay and cover the winning announcement and interview the winners."

"Yeah, we know – you're a private person," Bree replied.

Robbie echoed her, and Bree continued, "Look, Chef; you can scamper now; we know you're allergic to cameras. I thought you'd want to share the glory, since you did coach us through creating a good chili. But – OK; we've got the rest of that stock in the Café cooler. And the minced meat. How awesome it would be, serving up the prize – or even the final-selection chili tonight for a supper entrée?"

"It would be a wild success," Richard replied. "And I want to leave you to enjoy it, since you did all the work." To be honest, he had never thought that Luc and his scratch team would place at all – and the thought of media interest made him, as his aged Gran used to say, 'Come over all queer.' "Can I count on you all to be back in time to duplicate your championship chili in time for the dinner rush?"

"Well, yeah, Chef," That was Luc – baffled as always when it came to pure human interaction. "Saturday's a big night. A bigger night if the Café team takes first place. Of course, we'll be there."

"I'll get my ride from Chris," Richard whispered to Kate, and kissed her on the cheek, as if she were a mere friend, and not his very dear Kate. "We both have our jobs. Maybe you can stop by the Café later and tell me about what it is the kids found among the potsherds that had everyone so interested."

"Sure thing," Kate replied, also in a whisper, and nearly inaudible, as Allen Lee Mayne stood up, still shuffling some notes in one hand as he stepped up to the microphone stand. "In case I can't … it was a little metal finial-thing. Like from a lamp, and Mr. Penn swears it is gold …"

"What?" Richard hissed, just as Allen Lee tapped the microphone. It sounded like a thump, electrifying the crowd. "Did you say gold?"

Kate's reply was lost in a rising murmur from the audience.

"This thing on? Good! OK, folks – we have a winner! After carefully tasting and considering every entry – and darned good they all were, folks! Texas is sure the place for a darned good bowl of chili! Can I hear an amen?"

Richard, under cover of the whoops and cheers from the audience, hastily pecked Kate's cheek again, made a 'thumbs-up' gesture towards Bree and the rest of the team, and slid back through the crowd as the cameraman made another pass, evidently aiming to immortalize the enthusiasm among. He was at the edge of the crowd, having spotted Chris and Stephanie Royce by a pastel-painted food truck advertising "Scream for the Cream!" in glittery ornate letters.

Well, Chris *had* promised him a ride back to town, Richard told himself. Meanwhile, Allen Lee continued milking the suspense with the expertise of a master.

"We have gone over and over the top three contenders, in this, the first Annual Mills Farm Invitational Chili Contest – and thanks to everyone who participated, and everyone who came out to enjoy this gorgeous day in this beautiful place here at Mills Farm, as well as our sponsors, Venue Properties International, The Food Network and the HEB chain of great groceries."

"Get on with it!" Richard mumbled to himself, as he slunk around the edge of the crowd, aiming for the "Scream for the Cream" truck, where Chris and his potential serious flirtation were alternately sharing spoonfuls of ice cream from each other's plates, and laughing.

"In third place, with a prize of $500 dollars and a five-year pass to Mills Farm's special events," Allen Lee intoned, after a quick consult of his notes. "Entry #6! Put your hands together in a round of applause for Entry #6! A fine-flavored chili with a rich flavor and an excellent after-glow!"

A man in a bright pink guayabera shirt and a straw cowboy hat on his head, whooped and waved the hand that didn't hold an outsized margarita glass – something in a color which almost matched his shirt – in the general direction of Allen Lee. He had a small slip of paper in that hand. He worked his way through the crowd, many of whom slapped him on the shoulders in a congratulatory manner. Allen Lee gave a quick read of the slip of paper and extended the microphone towards the man in the electric pink guayabera.

"You, sir! Entry #6; tell us who you are and what made your chili stand out!"

"Eamon Guthrie, from Beeville!" the contestant exclaimed, in a distinct Irish brogue. "An' before that, County Mayo, in Ireland, the land of great minstrels and tale tellers! 'Tis the flavoring of Guinness finest brown stout in the stock of this chili, I am thinking!"

"Congratulations, Mr. Guthrie!" Allen Lee took back the microphone, as it looked as if Eamon Guthrie was primed to wax poetic and at a length which would play merry hob with the announcing of second and first place winners. "And now to the second place, in the judgement of my distinguished fellow judges; Entry #12! For the second prize of $1000 dollars and another five-year pass to Mills Farm special events! Who here represents the team for Entry#12?"

"Me!" a barely teenaged girl held up another slip of paper, as a small crowd of her peers – all barely teenaged, all in matching polo shirts of dark blue with a small crest over the front pocket, and all shrilling their excitement in ear-splitting soprano. Richard was fairly certain the logo on their shirts was not that of a polo pony. The girl was thoroughly rattled, even Richard could see this from a distance. "Sabrina Morrison. My team is the junior class from St. Scholastica's Catholic High School in Karnesville! Have we really won second place! Oh, gosh! In that case, our cash prize goes to the Karnesville Senior Citizen Food Bank! Thank you so much, Allen Lee – we just love your show to bits! Our secret ingredient is the home-grown ghost peppers that my father grew in our garden…and my mom's own family recipe! And Sister Joan Marie, our coach and art teacher who told us how to enter …" The child was practically incoherent with excitement, all of which was being captured by the video camera, while Allen Lee beamed. Richard could see that excitement among the crowd was raised to a fever-pitch – that excitement cultivated expertly by Allen Lee every bit as carefully as the ghost peppers were in Mr. Morrison's garden. From his vantage point next to Chris and Stephanie, he could see the flash from Kate's camera, and the group of girls in dark blue polo shirts hugging each other in joyous celebration. And if the Café team were one of the final three, and the other two winners had been named, that meant … a bright light seemed to explode in Richard's brain.

Aside from Sylvester, Luc, Robbie and Bree, he was the only one not entirely surprised when Allen Lee held up his hand, commanding silence from the crowd – or if not silence, at least a modicum of relative quiet.

"And finally, placing first, in my opinion and the opinion of my fellow judges – the savoriest, most flavorful chili at this gathering is #42! Number 42! For the grand prize of $2,000 and an all-expenses paid weekend for two at Mills Farm! Who here had # 42!"

"We do!" That was Bree, squealing like the girls from St. Scholastica, waving both hands as Sylvester and Robbie whooped and high-fived each other. "We're the team from Luna Café and Coffee from right here in Luna City!"

Whatever else was said was lost in a roar of acclimation and cheers. Richard caught a glimpse of Luc's face, bearing a mildly baffled expression upon it.

"Good for them!" Chris exclaimed and thumped Richard on the shoulder in an excess of enthusiastic congratulations. "You must be real proud, Ricardo – real proud!"

"I am, and bully for them!" Richard answered. "It's their triumph – and I want them to revel in it. If you don't really mind, I could really use that ride back to town, right about this time."

"Sure thing," Chris agreed easily, although Richard was certain that a shadow of disappointment fell on Stephanie Royce's face. "I gotta see to the Tip-Top anyway. You got my number, Steph? Text me later. We gotta roll, matter of business. C'mon, Ricardo."

A Golden Find at Rincon de los Robles

From the Karnesville Weekly Beacon – by Katherine Heisel, Staff Writer

Last month, Dr. Miranda Gonzalez-Ramirez directed a team of students from Luna City HS in conducting an archeological dig, searching for the original foundations of the Rincon de los Robles main ranch-house and outbuildings, with an eye towards applying for status as a building of historical interest. The Rincon de los Robles was granted by the Spanish king to the family of Don Diego Manuel Hernando Ruiz y Gonzales (or Gonzales) towards the end of the 18th century, and subsequently settled by his two sons, from whom the many Gonzalez and Gonzaleses in Karnes County are descended. Originally constructed of native adobe brick beginning around 1790, the oldest structures became dilapidated by the end of the 19th century. In or about the year 1920, the oldest and most ruinous wing of the original house were pulled down and the area leveled, while the newer portion of the structure, which still dated from around 1850, was renovated and enlarged. At this time plumbing and electricity was installed, and the current wrap-around porch and second-floor galleries were constructed, and a tile roof replaced by a more steeply pitched metal roof.

Over a weekend in early October, the students conducted a series of 'digs' – test trenches dug across where Dr. Gonzalez-Ramirez estimated the outer walls of the house to have been, guided by a series of sketches and watercolors preserved in various family archives. The entire area to the east of the existing house, which at present comprises a small yard planted with citrus trees and the remnant of a WWII-era Victory Garden, was marked off in a grid for excavation. By good luck, one of the trenches intersected a pit used for household trash, dated to the early 19th century, to judge from the artifacts found in it. Those finds included numerous glass and stoneware bottles, pieces of painted china imported from Europe, as well as majolica-styled pottery from Puebla, and fragments of a number of tobacco pipes. The presence of imported china indicates a degree of prosperity, even in the early years of the Gonzalez/Gonzales grant. Other finds included several pewter spoons and forks, and buttons. Another test trench unearthed a corner of a tile floor, decorated in finely painted tiles, possibly from Puebla. A great quantity of animal bones, or portions of bones were found in the trash pit; mostly beef bones, but also goat, sheep, and wild game, hinting at a varied diet in a prosperous household.

A number of metal artifacts were also discovered, either in place in the trash pit, or mixed in soil throughout the dig. All soil removed from the test trenches was painstakingly sifted through screens; from this sifting, the students found dozens of hand-forged iron nails, some with fragments of wood still adhering to them. Doctor Ramirez-Gonzalez is of the opinion that those must be the last remnants of window and door frames from the structures demolished in the 1920s.

However, the most exciting find unearthed in the dig is also one of the smallest: barely two inches long and about the dimension of a woman's little finger – but of gold and finely wrought. It appears to be a finial, perhaps an adornment to a fine dagger, or a ladies' fan or parasol handle. Dr. Ramirez-Gonsalez' fellow researcher, Xavier Gunnison-Penn speculates that it may have been part of the storied "Gonzaga Reliquary", which reportedly was kept at Rincon de los Robles until the period of the American Civil War.

Many of the finds unearthed in the dig will be on permanent display in a special case in the Luna City High School Library.

Shine on, Shine on Harvest Moon

The Café had a line out the door, waiting for tables on the evening after Luc, Robbie and Bree won the chili contest. Even the tables outside were filled, and Araceli was asking couples and singletons if they minded sharing a table with others. No one objected to sharing – as long as it meant a crack at the glorious, prize-winning, famous chili. It turned out that there had been a stringer for one of the TV stations in San Antonio covering the results of the contest. At mid-point in the Café's usual dinner hours, after taking one look at the line of waiting customers outside, and the dining room with every single chair occupied, Richard thought to call Andy Pryor and ask for an emergency resupply of wild boar meat. Which, due to their being no limitation on hunting the critters since they were a pest and a botheration, Andy had a more than plentiful supply on hand. He also took the trouble to run it through his professional-strength coarse-grinder, since Richard and his staff wouldn't have time to carefully mince the meat by hand, as they had for the contest.

"A big night?" Andy obligingly came around in the Pryor Meats & BBQ reefer van to deliver the boar meat and an extra pan of sausage – which was exceedingly generous of him, considering that it was a Saturday, and his own place was doubtless full of hungry customers.

"You've no bloody idea," Richard signed the receipt, "We'll stay open until we're dropping on our feet, I think. Strike while the iron is hot, y'know."

Andy grinned. "Lucky us. As soon as the 'que runs out, we're done. It takes twenty-four hours to do brisket justice in the smoker, and when we're out of what I started the night before, we're done. Close the shutters, lock the door and go home. Good luck, Ricardo. Hold tight and think of the cash register ringing up sales."

"Alas, the card processer doesn't ring," Richard wrangled the first kitchen cart up to the back door. "It just makes a quiet, discrete hum."

"Must not remember the words," Andy replied, slamming the reefer truck door. Richard raised his eyes and addressed heaven, begging for strength as the van ground away in low gear. Yes, he was in for a long and exhausting haul on a Saturday evening, but that was what he had become accustomed to, now that the Cattleman had reopened, and people – all kinds of people, in the main – had begun driving to Luna City on weekends for a nice little day excursion, topped off by a meal at the Cattleman, the Café, or Pryors. It made Saturday evenings a long haul, as Patrick said. Having his team win the chili contest and having it broadcast on all kinds of media made this particular Saturday evening at the Café into an inter-galactic long haul.

He ran the cart into the Café, announcing, "All right – Pryor just brought more of that lovely native Texas wild boar meat. Get to work on it. I hope that none of you have other plans in your social life for this evening. Your soul may belong to God, but for tonight, your asses belong to me."

"Chef, really!" That was Araceli, shadows of weariness under her eyes, and Richard relented. She had been at work since earliest morning – which now to Richard felt like an age ago. And she had Patrick and the children, Angelika and Matty, and a life outside the Café and it's doings.

"Sorry, luv," Richard trundled the cart into the cooler, shut the door and turned to face her, drooping with exhaustion, in her crisp pastel pink waitress dress, and trainers with the matching pink shoelaces. "Clock out and go home, if you want. The line is diminished at least. You didn't need to stay for all of this, since you've been here for fourteen hours now. The B's have got it all under control."

Araceli shook her head. "Biggest Saturday night at the Café in recorded history? Like hell, I would miss this! No, Chef, I'm here until the cows come home. Besides," she added, honestly. "With all these rich out-of-towners? The tips are gonna be just awesome!"

"Your choice," Richard advised, just as the bell on a spring attached to the Café's entrance door chimed again. In turn, Araceli addressed the heavens and sprang into action.

Richard turned to his kitchen, weighing and grinding the spices which extensive research over the previous three months had proved to be the ideal combination. Bree was deftly chopping onions and garlic, her zeal for this prep seemingly unfaded. Mounds of white onions and cream-colored garlic surrounded her on all sides, while Luc tended the two largest kettles, bubbling under the lowest heat that the biggest burners on the vast Wolff stove were capable of.

"Everyone wants chili tonight, don't they, Chef?" Luc observed, exhibiting a perfectly awesome command of the obvious.

"Seems like it," Robbie answered, from where he was working the enormous Hobart mixer, combining the ingredients for cornbread to accompany the chili. Two pans of finished cornbread, nicely crisp around the edges, cooled on the worktable. Half of a third pan was already gone, diminishing even as Richard watched, sliced into uniform squares and borne away by the harried front staff. "Sure hope we don't run out. I guess we'd better start another pot of stock, Chef – We're getting low."

"Emergency supply in the very back of the freezer, double-concentrated," Richard was momentarily distracted by an uptick in the mind hubbub of voices from the dining room, garnished with a decidedly girlish squeal from Araceli. He looked around the corner into the dining room: yes, as big as life and twice as natural, Allen Lee Mayne, with a grin which lit the whole room, and followed by his documentary crew, movie camera and all.

"Girl!" he was giving Araceli a hug, in spite of her having a water carafe in one hand, and her notepad in the other. "They're making you work too hard! When we gonna run away to Los Vegas and get married! Say the word, we can get a charter flight out of Stinson before midnight …"

"Can't be tonight, Allen Lee," Araceli replied, with a becoming show of regret. "We are simply swamped tonight, and I have early mass first thing tomorrow. You and your crew come for some championship chili tonight? We got some places at the *stammtisch*, if you don't mind sharing?"

"You know the way to my heart, girl!" Allen Lee pressed Araceli's hand *(the one with her order notebook in it)* to his heart with a theatrical gesture, yet a faintly repulsed facial expression. "But I'm good for chili, after today – too much of a good thing, you know? I just wanted to see if Ricardo minds the guys shooting some footage of your team at work in the kitchen, and I wanted to look in and say hidee to y'all of my good friends in Luna City!"

"Sure thing," Araceli reclaimed her hand. "Let's check with Chef, 'kay?" She lowered her voice; Allen Lee made a 'cut' gesture to his cameraman and followed her to where Richard lingered in the doorway between the kitchen and the dining room.

"'s agreeable to me," Richard said, in response to Allen Lee's request. "If it's agreeable to my people. And … I'm not interested in being on camera in any way, shape or form. I'm just not here, as was our previous understanding."

"Sure thing, Ricardo," Allen Lee nodded, in acquiescence. "We agreed once before, and that still holds…"

"Good," Richard hesitated. "Look – this is a big thing, especially for Luc and the kids. Don't make them out to be utter twats, but don't give them ideas above themselves. They're good kids – don't open them up for anything they're not prepared for."

"Agreed," Allen Lee nodded, somber as a judge. "We be good, Ricardo. But you do understand … once something is out there, you never really know where it might lead."

"Indeed," Richard agreed with a sigh. He had a vivid recollection of how an inadvertent publicity shot of Romeo Gonzales in costume for his part as an escaping convict for a Luna City Players production had led to all kinds of unexpected developments. "Let me make certain everything is in order, then I'll be out of the way and the camera."

"Ok, sure!" Robbie exclaimed, when Richard explained Allen Lee's request. "Hey, Dad will be back from Dubai by the time the new season of *Ala Carte With Quartermayne* airs! That will be so cool, and Dad will be jazzed! I gotta call Sylvester! He was part of the team, too!"

"On TV?" Luc looked at his shoes and nervously scrubbed at his hands with a towel. "OK, I guess … he really did mean what he told me that day I started here. He said that he expected to come back in a season or two and see me on his show. He said it like he meant it."

"He did," Richard agreed, and added a bit of an exaggeration. "I think he expected great things of you, the day that you started here."

"On TV!" Bree bubbled with incoherent enthusiasm. "Gosh, that's awesome! I'll have to text Mom and Dad to burn a copy to DVD and tell all my old friends to watch! Me on *Ala Carte*! Meryl and Cher will be just green with envy!"

"Right, then," Richard sighed and returned to the dining room, silently added, *'On your heads be it, then.'* To Allen Lee, now kibitzing with various diners and scribbling autographs for them, he murmured, "Right, then – they're ready for you now. And Robbie is going to let Sylvester know. Aafter all, he did manage all the logistics for them. Just don't forget, we're still seating diners!"

"Great!" Allen Lee's pleasure was infectious. "We won't – my guys are good at capturing the moment without interfering with business."

At that moment, the door-chime jingled once more, as the door swung open, admitting some blessedly familiar customers: Araceli's younger brother Berto Gonzales and his cousin Sylvester, accompanying … Heavens forfend, that was their grandmother, Adeliza – tiny, opinionated and the absolute ruler of the whole entangled Gonzales/Gonzalez clan. When she commanded 'jump' the only acceptable reply for a Gonzales/Gonzalez of Luna City was a respectful request for a clarification as to the expected altitude.

She was also Richard's most devoted fan, as the only TV channel she normally watched was The Food Network.

"Just got the call from Robbie," Sylvester explained. "We were on our way over anyway. Abuelita took it into her head to come and congratulate you, and to meet Allen Lee. After listening to me talk about the contest for weeks, she wanted to taste the chili herself."

"Tell your granny that Allen Lee is in the kitchen, interviewing Luc, Robbie and Bree for his show – they were the ones responsible for winning, after all," Richard explained, and Berto translated.

"We'll have to fit y'all in at the *stammtisch*," Araceli warned, eliciting another voluble flood of Spanish from Abuelita Adeliza, who reached up to pull his face towards hers and kiss him once on each cheek. The old dear beamed approval, as Berto and Araceli steered her towards two empty chairs at the *stammtisch*. Sylvester had already vanished kitchenwards with Allan Lee and his cameraman.

"Abuelita says that she is real proud of you," Berto earnestly translated his grandmothers' words. "She says that you're proven to be a real gallant gentleman, giving all the credit an' that to others. She wants you to know that, an' that she is proud of you having come all that way, since you were on TV before you came here. She says, that she could tell you were a bit of a … well, not a real nice person. A good cook, and interesting to watch, but she always had a feeling that it wasn't a good place for you, back then. But now you're doing exactly what Abuelo Jesus would have done, and that's a real good thing. Abuelo Jesus was a fine man," Berto added, with reminiscent affection. "I don't remember him real well, but they say that he was a real good cook, too."

"Thank your Gran," Richard was baffled, and touched, at the same time. "I … might once have had many fans, the world over.

But she is the most loyal and dearest of them to me, and the only one who really matters to me now."

That earned him another set of matched kisses, "Gran thinks you look even more like Abuelo, now that you've grown out your hair," Berto added, while Abuelita Adelizas' beamed approval. Richard himself personally plated her a bowl of chili and square of cornbread and brought it to her with his own hands. It looked like the evening rush on the Café had settled down to a dull roar; a greatly increased number of customers, but at least arriving in regular waves, which allowed them to be seated and served in a timely manner – even if by the time that Richard went out and announced 'last call, ladies and gentlemen', the supernaturally-enthused teenagers Bree and Robbie appeared wilted and weary. It had all been a long day. A very long day.

The last of the disappointed diners wandered off in the direction of the Cattleman, where – if Richard had been informed correctly – there was still some kind of bar buffet available for those customers afflicted with the late evening munchies. He personally turned off the lights, after shooing his staff off to their home and relatively chaste beds – to which he was pretty certain they all were bound. It would have taken a superman to be up to any kind of sexual nonsense after the day which they had all endured and survived.

Ozzie sat in the basket on the back of Richard's bicycle, glaring at Richard with a perfectly fierce expression on his one-eyed feline face. The moon was a few days off from full, casting a chill light on the back of those buildings along the northern side of Town Square.

"Sorry, chum – these things happen," Richard apologized. Ozzie appeared only slightly mollified. "But I would have you know that this one time, I wish that the caravan was parked out in back. I'm trusting that you will ensure that I don't fall asleep on the ride back home…" He swung a leg over the saddle and kicked off. Oddly enough, the cool night air, and the almost-complete full-moon proved to be an energizing stimulant, even on top of the exhaustions of the day. Richard had come to rather relish the quiet, lonely bicycle ride through the darkened town, bathed in pale silvery moonlight and the flickering gold of the old-fashioned streetlamps. A few squares of light showed in the occasional window – but most sober, earnest citizens had long since retired to sleep.

Not the new resident of the Everett house, he noted as he passed the tile-roofed Spanish colonial cottage, which Roman Gonzales and his crew had been renovating over the summer months. Richard slowed the bicycle to a pause. Like Ozzie, he was curious. Light blazed from the curtained windows downstairs, giving an effect rather like that of an elaborate dollhouse, or a well-decorated stage for a domestic drama set in the 1930ies. It had that kind of solid, comfortable look; shelves of leather-bound books, substantial club furniture, a sofa upholstered in cowhide, a brass floor lamp with a bead-fringed silk shade. It reminded him of certain drawing rooms in Bickley, when he was a boy, and taken to visit older friends of his parents'. There were a few lights in the garden as well, illuminating the path leading from sidewalk to front door. In the shadow under a small tree, the tiny spark at the end of a cigarette burned reddish-gold, and the scent of its smoke lingered unseen in the night air. Richard could make out the dim outline of a human form, veiled in the darkness under the tree.

"'Evening," he said to the shadowy form. "Didn't mean to intrude – I was just thinking that your drawing room reminds me of the kind of play where the maid comes out and answers the phone, and tells the caller who everyone is, and what they are doing. And then someone comes in with a tennis racket, or something."

There was a snort of laughter from under the tree. "And halfway through the first act, there is a murder, of course. Most of the furniture came from my family. The Everetts always bought the best-quality and never threw a damn thing away. Never in up-to-the-minute fashion, but never really out of it, my husband used to say."

It was a woman's voice, decidedly authoritative, the kind of woman who does not suffer foolery, or suffer it for very long without making stern corrections to the fool. She moved forward, stepping out of the pool of shadow, to extend a hand toward Richard. "Myrna Vaughn," she added. She had a firm, manly grip.

"Richard Astor-Hall," Richard responded. "And Ozymandius-King-of-Kings … my cat. We're just on our way home. I was taken by the looks of your house, you see."

"You're that Englishman who runs the Café." Myrna Vaughn answered, not sounding very surprised at all. "It was on the news this evening, about the chili contest. My son mentioned you, several times. He said that you were a solid troop. Normally, he is quite sparing with the praise, so consider yourself honored."

"Joe and Jess have always been good friends to me," Richard felt a little of English embarrassment at being complimented. "Almost from the first day that I arrived here."

"Small towns are like that," Myrna nodded, and confessed with a sigh "I imagine I will have to get used to it again. I knew that, when I decided to come back here to live. Joe and Jess tried to talk me out of it, but my mind was made up. A cigarette?" she extended the packet towards Richard, who shook his head.

"Gave it up, years ago," he confessed. "Bad for one's health, they say."

"So they do, and right they are," Myrna replied. "My husband died of lung cancer, even though he quit smoking years ago. I ought to quit, but … Too calming, when one is stressed. I just don't do it in the house. One in the evening, last thing in the day, and that's it."

"Sorry about … your husband," Richard felt distinctly awkward. He had never met the senior Vaughns, aside from Uncle Harry. In fact, until several months ago, he barely knew of their existence.

In the darkness under the tree, he thought Myrna shrugged.

"Everyone dies, eventually," she pointed out. "We had a good few years together. We were happy enough, I suppose, as a marriage goes."

"And now you're back in Luna City," Richard found her unsentimental bluntness rather refreshing, like a splash of ice-water to the face. That kind of brutal honesty had a certain appeal; it reminded him oddly of his Gran, who also spoke her mind and devil take the consequences. He recollected Martin, observing that Myrna didn't possess an ounce of tact: whatever thought came into her mind was coming from her lips a millisecond later. "Better here than anywhere else, I always thought. What do you intend to do with yourself, Mrs. Vaughn – live the life of a lady of leisure?"

"Good heavens," Myrna snorted. "I'd be bored to tears, to sit around all day with nothing to do. No, I'll sort out some project or other, once I get settled into a routine. When one has spent a life taking responsibility, being completely engaged … inactivity is pure torment."

"It is, rather," Richard admitted. As grueling as his days often were at the Café, sometimes a half-day of nothing in particular to do was … daunting. Maddening. Enough to make him want to claw the walls. What was it that Doc Wyler had once observed – he quoted some philosopher or other to the effect that much of mankinds' ills were due to an inability to sit quietly in an empty room and just contemplate something or other. He was overtaken by a mighty yawn and a querulous '*meeeooooow!*' from Ozzie, which plainly meant a demand to cease this pointless yacking and hit the road, metaphorically speaking. "Ooops … my master's voice, Mrs. Vaughn. Sorry – very long day today, as I am certain you can imagine. For the both of us … but tomorrow … I say, we do a very nice breakfast menu at the Café, now. I would admire for you to come and try out the best coffee in Luna City, and my signature full English. Fuel for a full day of … well, whatever you have on your schedule."

"Love the way you pronounce that," Richard could tell that Myrna was smiling. "*Shed-uale.* I will. Dear Jess has been positively lyrical over describing the Café's cinnamon rolls."

"Then we shall see you tomorrow," Richard said. "*à bientôt!* And good night."

"Don't let the bedbugs bite," Myrna returned with a small giggle. "Sorry – it's what my husband used to say. I am certain there are no bedbugs at your place. And I will definitely come and check out the coffee and the cinnamon rolls."

"I will ask Joe to bring you in under restraints, if you are not there by 10:00 AM," Richard said, as he pedaled off, earning a small snicker from Myrna. Once out on the dark back-road which was his favored short-cut to the Age of Aquarius, he commented to his animal familiar. "She seems nice enough – although I suppose that's in small social doses. Well … this all will be interesting."

And that was what it turned out to be. Eventually.

Oh! Christmas Tree!

On the grounds that most of their customers – and certainly all of their employees – had plans for a family Thanksgiving supper, or at least to break bread and carve turkey with friends, Richard only did breakfast and lunch on Thanksgiving Day in the Café. He bid his people to not overeat and return bright and early on Friday and prepare for a busy weekend. He himself was invited to Araceli and Patricks' for Thanksgiving, to which feast he had promised to make something amazing in the way of roast sprouts with a lemon-cream-mustard sauce. He rather thought that Chris and Luc were going to Miss Letty's, and Joe and Jess to Myrna's for Thanksgiving.

Myrna, who had duly appeared in the Café for brunch after the day of the great chili contest, proved to be exactly the kind of woman that Richard assumed to be, during that fatigue-addled, late-night conversation in the dark of her garden. Abrupt, plain-spoken, handsome rather than beautiful, she appeared very much as if she could still play a murderously energetic game of field hockey.

"Truth is, I rather like the older Mrs. Vaughn," Richard confessed, in the aftermath of the ritual feast at Araceli's, where Berto, Sylvester and Patrick were watching a football game on television, while he and Katie helped Araceli set out a range of pies and other post-supper sweets and puddings on the cleared table. "I know – I would hardly have thought she was my cup of tea; one of those bossy, domineering American women … but she's rather endearing, in a blunt kind of way. Not a shred of hypocrisy in her, which is refreshing."

"Yep," Araceli placed a stack of small paper plates next to the pumpkin pie. "Joe said once – that his mom would tell you what you needed to hear, even if you didn't really want to hear it, rather than tell you want you wanted to hear. I hope she can make it easier for Jess, what with the new baby, and Martin having to have heart surgery. Jess now has to help manage Abernathy Hardware, in addition to her own clients."

"I didn't know that," Richard racked his memory. He knew that Martin had not been well for a while. He hadn't run for re-election, and Clem Bodie was now the new mayor of Luna City. "Are you certain?"

"Of course. Aunt Joanna is going to take him on a long ocean cruise, so that he can recover properly. Better than a stint in a nursing home: it's quieter on a luxury liner and the food is a million times better. Nothing like a long, boring ocean cruise for sleeping a lot, which is what Jess says that he needs. They're going to leave after Martin unveils the Town Christmas tree on Friday evening."

"That's going to be awesome," Kate said. "Do you want me to do up the whipped cream, now?"

"No – wait until half-time," Araceli looked into the living room. "The guys are still in a turkey coma."

"What's so special about the Christmas tree?" Richard asked. This would be his fourth year in Luna City: there was a yearly fuss made about formally turning on the lights in the oak trees in Town Square, and the previous year there had been an ornamented tree in front of the Methodist Church."

"There used to be this lovely forty-foot cypress tree at the edge of the Square, just across from the Cattleman," Kate explained. "Shaped perfectly just like you would expect a Christmas tree to be shaped. I think they began decorating and lighting it to celebrate the end of World War II. It was a big thing, for about thirty years. Families and local firms donated a whole bunch of fancy ornaments for the tree – mostly outsized, so that they could really be seen."

"I remember Abuelita and Abuelo Jesus taking us to see the lighting," Araceli agreed. "And people would sing Christmas carols, and hand out candy canes to the children. But the tree got damaged by …. A hurricane coming through when I was about ten years old. The trunk got split by the wind thrashing the branches all around and it was horribly dangerous, so they cut the tree down and put all the decorations in storage."

"It seemed like no one really knew what to do without the tree, so they went on to just light the trees in the Square and leave it at that." Kate picked up the threads of the story. Richard listened, fascinated. "But when they began working to renovate the Cattlemen, they found all the crates of ornaments for the tree, stowed away in the empty rooms. Lew Dubois donated a new tree, to be planted where the old one was – just for the look of the Square from the front windows of the Cattleman, and Martin Abernathy pushed for restarting the tradition of decorating it, just like it was."

"And when are they going to do all this?" Richard asked, and Kate sighed.

"Honestly, don't you read the newsletter – the newspaper, even? Saturday evening, just when it gets dark enough. Formally starting the Christmas season. It will be grand," Kate slivered herself a bit of pumpkin pie. "You want some? I think it's lovely, bringing back a tradition like that. They're going to have a big canvas tarp over the tree, and at the last minute, Martin will pull on a rope to unveil the tree and flip on a switch – and all the lights will come on in the Square at once."

"Something to look forward too," Araceli agreed. Out in the living room, the sports announcer's voice rose to an excited shout, echoed by a groan from the home audience. Richard made a mental note: talk with Luc about the Saturday evening menu for the Café. Anything but turkey…

The excitement was palpable as the late afternoon wore on, the Saturday after Thanksgiving. All during the week of Thanksgiving there had been men with ladders and bucket trucks, busy swathing the oaks in Town Square with strand after strand of fairy lights, wrapped around their massive trunks and wandering off into the heavy branches. The young and vibrantly green cypress tree, planted earlier in spring opposite the main entrance of the Cattleman, had been veiled in canvas, like a sculpture before the grand reveal. Richard looked out from the front of the Café fairly often on Friday and throughout Saturday, as the final touches were added – the ladders and the bucket truck whisked away. The decorated cypress tree stood, robed in canvas, which seemed to glow in the light of the setting sun, as if it were one of those Japanese paper lanterns.

"I think that the rush may slack off a bit, when it comes time to the grand reveal," he said to Araceli, as the hands of the clock in the kitchen crawled slowly towards half-past seven. "If such is the case, let's nip out and take a look – just for five or ten minutes. I know that … well, back in the day, it meant something to you."

"Chef, that's the nicest, most considerate thing you've said," Araceli cooed. "Well, since last Saturday, when you said that it was OK for me to clock out in the middle of the supper rush. But yeah … let's go watch the Christmas tree reveal. Meet you out in front in …" she consulted her wristwatch. "Five minutes. Did I ever say how much the girls and I scored in tips last weekend? I can afford to get a totally awesome Christmas gift for Pat, now. The kids did OK with that chili, you know. I think you ought to put it on the permanent weekly special menu … but that's your decision as head chef, of course," she added hastily.

"That much of a demand?" Richard mused. "Taken into active consideration. Thank you for that input. Will there be sufficient demand, once the original thrill dies off? These things do have a life-cycle, you know."

Araceli considered the question: if anything, she had her thumb on the pulse of the Café. What diners wanted, what they asked for, what they relished – above all, Araceli knew it, down to her very bones. It had been her judgement that the Café's coffee ought to have cream as an option for the coffee – the coffee which Richard insisted be brewed daily from freshly-ground beans.

"I would say yes," she replied. "Replace the meatloaf on the Saturday specials. It's nice meatloaf, and I expect that it's cheap per serving to produce, so don't dump it entirely, but the chili is a draw for now, and the foreseeable future."

"Agreed," Richard nodded. "It's getting to a point when we might consider hiring another cook, if Miss Letty and Doc approve.

That is, if business continues at the pace that it does. And a few more front-of-the-house. Even part-time staff would take some of the pressure off. As it is, I dare not get sick…"

"You scare the biscuits out of any virus that comes around," Araceli agreed.

"I have a remarkably strong constitution," Richard conceded, rather smugly.

Outside in the street, the pace of those strolling past seemed to pick up – as if something were about to happen. Yes, it was; the sun had already slipped below the trees. It was nearly time for the lights in the Square to be turned on.

"Oh, look. There goes Mindy and Xavier," Araceli remarked. "Let's walk with them, Chef."

"And listen to Penn natter on and on about the Gonzaga Reliquary? I'd sooner have my teeth drilled," Richard grumbled. "But all right, if you insist."

"I do," Araceli sighed. "You really have to work on your interpersonal skills, Chef. Think of tolerating Xavier Gunnison-Penn as a useful exercise to that end."

"If you insist," Richard still felt like grumbling, but he followed Araceli out of the Café. They caught up with Mindy and Gunnison-Penn where the pedestrians solidified into a crowd before the façade of the Cattleman. They could move no farther, so thickly had the mass of people congealed. The Luna City PD had blocked off vehicular traffic at either end of Town Square with electric-orange cones. He nodded to Sergeant Milo Grigoryev, leaning casually against the bumper of his patrol SUV, thumbs hooked into his equipment belt.

"'Lo, Ricardo," Sgt. Grigoryev acknowledged him. "Come to see the excitement, then?" Without waiting for a reply, he continued, as his eyes scanned the gathering. Yes, Luna City may have been a small town, and in the main, painfully law-abiding. But that didn't mean that the Luna City PD got by with lounging on their laurels. "Y'know, I'm glad to see this community tree-decorating start up again. My father and mother donated three or four ornaments for the tree back in the day."

"Ours did too," Araceli agreed. "Abuelo Jesus and Don Jaimie – they had Tia Leonora make a whole group of ornaments from metal and glass … and…" Araceli suddenly paused, as if she had just recalled something which had been nagging at her memory for a long time. "Why that's …" she started, and then the crowd hushed, as Martin Abernathy stood up on the back of a bucket truck with a wireless microphone in one hand and the end of a long thin nylon cord in the other. He was brief in his remarks, thanking the crowd for their interest, the management of VPI, specifically Lew Dubois, for replacing the cypress tree, and the families of so many in Luna City who had originally donated tree decorations.

"And now, it is my pleasure, after so many years, to revive our old custom!" Martin gave a good strong pull to the cord, the canvas screen fell, and the lights all over the Square sprang into glorious, sparkling life; a fairyland of illuminated branches, and that single slender green tree, sparkling with jewel-colored ornaments against the green and white. The surf-like murmur of appreciative amazement from the crowd was pierced by a single outcry, as Xavier Gunnison-Penn collapsed to his knees. One hand was pressed to his heart, but he pointed at the tree with the other, crying,

"The Gonzaga Reliquary – it's here! It's been here all the time!"

And then he lay still.

(To be continued – of course!)

Luna City Number 9

Number 9,

Number 9,

Number 9…

Bits, Pieces and Reliquary

"Xavie, sweet-heart! Speak to me!" Mindy Ramirez-Gonzalez begged, kneeling by the collapsed form of Xavier Gunnison-Penn, on the sidewalk in front of the Cattleman Hotel. She was frantic; Xavier Gunnison-Penn, international treasure-hunter extraordinaire, lay unconscious on the sidewalk on the stretch of sidewalk by the narrow façade of the Koenig Opera House. Former mayor Martin Abernathy had just formally unveiled the official Luna City Christmas tree, a good-sized native cypress tree replanted at the edge of Town Square. The branches of this tree, shaped by nature so artfully that the tree looked almost artificial, dripped with flickering golden lights and elaborate ornaments; globes of every size, angels, nut-crackers, outsized candies, and stars – a variety which boggled the imagination of the most Christmas-crazed.

The moment was frozen; gasps of horror from the nearest bystanders, Mayor Abernathy, with the microphone in one hand and the rope which he had pulled to unveil the tree, sized up the situation, and addressed the crowd in calm and resolute tones.

"Is there a doctor or medical professional present? We have what seems to be a medical emergency; a gentleman has collapsed in front of the door to the Koenig Opera House…" With that, he set down the microphone and the rope and was taking out his cellphone, even as Sgt. Milo Grigoryev elbowed his way through the crowd, a thick woolen blanket over his arm. Those nearest Penn and the stricken Mindy Ramirez-Gonzalez had already reacted much as Richard had come to expect: a woman had wadded up her oversized sweater to make a pillow for his head, another woman offered her water bottle, and three more bystanders already had their cellphones out – either calling for additional assistance, or take pictures, Richard wasn't quite certain.

"I've already called EMS," Sgt. Grigoryev informed them, as he unfolded it with a snap and spread it over the recumbent Gunnison-Penn. "They'll be here in a minute or two. Mindy: You gotta calm down, you aren't gonna help your friend here any by getting hysterical."

"I am not getting hysterical!" Mindy declaimed, and began to cry. Sgt. Grigoryev exchanged a look of exasperation with Richard.

"OK, then, you're not hysterical," Sgt. Grigoryev agreed, sounding faintly annoyed. "Does Penn here have a history of heart trouble? Epilepsy? Blackouts?"

"No," Dr. Mindy Ramirez-Gonzalez shook her head. "Xavie is as healthy as a horse … or really, in very good health for a man of his age. I don't know what brought this on! He was saying something about the Gonzaga Reliquary, when he suddenly clutched his chest and collapsed."

"The Reliquary," That was Araceli, staring fixedly at the Christmas tree, with the light of comprehension dawning on her face. "He said it was here, all the time. And it is. It's in the tree."

"Say what?" Now it was Richard and Milo's turn to be baffled.

"The reliquary is there, in bits and pieces made into the Gonzalez family Christmas ornaments," Araceli explained with the patience usually reserved for difficult customers.

At her side, a diffident male voice offered, "Is this the medical emergency? I am a doctor – but my specialty is dermatology. Unless he has a rash or something, I'm not sure I can be of any real help." A bland and slightly balding man of middle age clad in a puffer jacket and jeans had joined the circle around Gunnison-Penn almost unnoticed.

"We have EMS on the way, but thank you for coming forward, Doc," Sgt. Grigoryev replied. "You can get a head start on checking his vitals, or something."

"Oh. Sure." The dermatology doctor knelt and felt along Gunnison-Penn's jaw for the neck pulse. "Seems steady enough. But he ought to have that little patch of eczema on his nose seen to, sometime soon."

The distant wail of the VFD ambulance added a soprano note to the tenor and alto rumbling of the crowd, as Araceli continued.

"Mindy, didn't you write in that monograph of yours, about the great-aunts and Tia Leonora doing metalwork and jewelry … and that she liked using found bits and pieces, like that little gold finial-thingy that you dug up in the old garden. That was what Tia Leonora was on about, when she wrote about using some bits that Tia Aïda found in digging out a Victory Garden during World War II. She made Christmas ornaments out of the broken-up pieces of the Reliquary!"

"It is my understanding that things like that were made in sections?" Richard ventured, and Mindy nodded, her plain features alight with the glow of dawning realization, which made her look almost … well, not pretty, but rather handsome.

"Xavie talked about it; his theory that the Reliquary could be taken apart for transport…"

"And when it was hidden during the Civil War," Araceli nodded. "It was taken apart – and each piece hidden separately…"

"In an adobe wall, in the old house," Mindy was on fire with intellectual insight, seeing the solution to the more than hundred-year old mystery plain writ plain as the directional sign on Town Square commanding a speed limit for motor vehicles of no more than 25 miles per hour. "They hollowed out niches in the wall, then plastered them over … swore the few people who knew to absolute secrecy. Then when the walls were demolished fifty years later, the bits of the reliquary were lost in the rubble, and only found thirty years after that … by Tia Aïda digging to plant more tomatoes and beans. Yes, that's how it all happened, I'm sure!"

"I *knew* something about that reliquary in the painting was familiar, back when I first laid eyes on it," Araceli agreed. "The enamel bit of the Virgin on horseback with the Baby Jesus in her arms. I just *knew* that I had seen that, somewhere before!"

Under the blanket, Xavier Gunnison-Penn moaned softly, and his eyelids fluttered.

"It's here…" his voice was still faint, as if he struggled to speak. Mindy clasped one of his nerveless hands between hers, just as the VFW ambulance pulled around the corner. The crowd scattered, obediently making way for it, as Sgt. Grigoryev waved his arms over his head, directing the ambulance to the precise scene of the emergency.

"We know, darling Xavie, we know," Mindy replied. "All the pieces of the reliquary are up in the Christmas tree. Don't you worry; I'll see them to a safe place."

"The picture …" Gunnison-Penn fumbled with his other hand in his coat pocket. "The picture … I have made … diagrams all the elements … see them secured, Miranda!"

Meanwhile, Chris Mayall and his current volunteer medic trainee emerged from the ambulance; the trainee agog with excitement at having a for-real call-out, and Chris as imperturbable as ever.

"Yo, Ricardo," he drawled, setting down the immense first aid bag, and hunkering down on his heels. "I take my eye off y'all for a single minute, and then all kinds of hell breaks loose. What's with ol' Gunny-Penn here? Hey, man; we're here for you now. Tell me what happened."

Chris Mayall, unflappable former Navy medic and manager of the Tip-Top Icehouse, Gas and Grocery had the most casually reassuring presence of anyone whom Richard had ever known; he assessed Gunnison Penn's vital signs with far more confidence than the doctor dermatologist had shown, and simultaneously had Mindy Ramirez-Gonzalez regarding him with eyes in which a look of worshipful hope mingled with abiding trust.

"He saw the Christmas tree unveiled," Mindy replied. "And then he just collapsed. I think he had a heart attack!"

"I'll leave it to the doctor at the Karnesville Med-Center to decide on that," Chris tucked away his stethoscope. "Hey, look, Gunny-Penn; I think you'll be OK, but you should go for a wild ride in the magic VFD bus, and get a second opinion."

"The reliquary!" Gunnison-Penn gasped, and his hand clamped on Chris's wrist. "It's here – and it must be saved! For posterity! Promise me, it will be preserved, Miranda! Take this …" and he fumbled with his coat-front, just as Chris' assistant man-handled the wheeled stretcher out of the back of the ambulance and brought it around to park, right where Gunnison-Penn lay.

"Sorted, Gunny-Penn," Chris replied, just as Mindy took the folded paper from his hand, clasping both to her heart. "OK – let your friends see to this … thing, and the Med-Center make certain you ain't gonna drop dead, stone cold. 'Kay? Oh, Hi, Steph, Katie – sorry, can't talk now. On the job."

There stood Kate Heisel, Richard's … something or other; also reporter for the Karnesville Daily Beacon, beloved of Richard's cat, Ozzie, and – not to put too plain a point on it, beloved of Richard himself, although he would probably prefer to have his fingernails pulled out rather than say so, baldly and in public. With her was the elegant Stephanie Royce, the on-scene publicist for the renewed Mills Farm. Thirtyish and mixed-race, Stephanie looked like the portrait bust of Queen Nefertiti come to life; Richard had good reason to think that Chris and Stephanie were, as the elderly Miss Letty McAllister would have expressed it – an item, due to their devotion to running marathons and their standing as relative racial outsiders to Luna City, where two-thirds of the residents were Hispanic, surnamed Gonzalez/Gonzales and had been there for nearly 300 years, and the other third were lately-arrived (as with the establishment of the city itself) Anglo and only for about half that. As in local parlance – Anglo-Saxon Protestants of no color other than slightly sunburned. Now, Stephanie nodded, her public-affairs oriented mind obviously already running ahead of the unfortunate event at what should have been a public-affairs coup for the newly expanded Mills Farm. Mindy seemed torn equally between devotion to man and retrieving the shards of the Gonzaga Reliquary. Araceli solved the conundrum for her, by taking Gunnison Penn's paper from her hand.

"Look, Mindy. Go with Xavie, or follow the ambulance in your car. Katie and I will round up all the bits and pieces that we can find on the tree. I'm sure Mr. Abernathy will let us use the bucket-truck, and the Chamber of Commerce will let us put them in the old bank vault."

"Good idea. You realize how valuable this will be, once all the bits and bobs are cleaned up and reassembled?" Richard murmured. "A genuine Cellini artifact and once painted by da Vinci ... The Tower of London might be a better bet for security, once word gets out."

All parties to this quiet observation now bore identical expressions of horror; horror almost immediately replaced with quiet calculation as those hearers processed and mentally gamed out a solution.

"I think we had better embargo word of this, until security can be organized," Stephanie Royce was the first to speak, as she shot a significant look at Kate, who waxed mildly indignant.

"People have a right to know," Kate pointed out. "But the *Beacon* goes to press on Monday, so y'all have until then."

Meanwhile, Xavier Gunnison Penn had been hoisted onto the rolling stretcher by Chris and his assistant, with the aid of Sgt. Grigoryev and the passing dermatologist.

"I'll be with you, Xavie!" Mindy promised, as their hands reluctantly parted. "I'll be with you – right behind the ambulance!"

"But the Reliquary!" Xavier Gunnison-Penn protested, as his formidable bulk was swallowed up in the maw of the VFD ambulance.

"It's a Gonzalez thing," Araceli called, her face perfectly adamantine with determination. "A family thing, and we Gonzalezes never let go of a family thing. Not the last of our lands;

and not the Gonzaga Reliquary. Our promise on it, Mindy. Xavie, too. Don't worry!"

The ambulance pulled away slowly, the lingering crowd in Town Square making way for it, as it rounded the corner and picked up speed. Only then did the siren activate, a diminishing wail in the distance.

"Get your car and go," Araceli commanded her cousin Mindy. "You'll want to be there, to look after your studly treasure-hunting dude, OK? Don't worry, Katie and I will see to the bits and pieces, and we'll text you when they're all rounded up."

"All right," Doctor Ramirez-Gonzalez yielded to the force of Araceli's personality, honed by years of dealing with difficult Café customers. Against this irresistible force, the challenge of a classroom of college students was barely a bump in the path towards getting what a Gonzalez/Gonzales wanted and/or promised. *(Mostly to defeat their enemies, drive them before, and listen to the laments of their cis-gender significant others.*) "Take care of it, 'Celi – the family depends on you!"

"I have never let the family down yet!" Araceli asserted in her most authoritative voice, and she turned towards Richard. "Look, Ricardo – I've got some stuff to clean up here. Be back in the Café in time to deal with the rush. But I have to get this Reliquary sorted – kay? Give me twenty minutes!"

"I am certain that it will be sorted, down to the last little tiny peg and jewel," Richard assured her. He was not entirely certain that she heard him, as she plunged through the crowd around the bucket truck, heading towards Martin Abernathy, who was at the center of an interested group of tourists and locals – including his Kate, his lovely, beryl-eyed Kate, who already had her camera deployed. No – nothing of the rest of this was his affair and interest. Best return to the Café, and to all that which was.

In the Offices of the Karnesville Weekly Beacon

"Kate! Kate! Get in here and tell me why the heck I have fielded calls all morning from the AP, UPI, the *London Times*, *Archeology Today*, and some rude as hell asshole from New York!" Acey McClain, part-owner and managing editor (as well as every other editor) bellowed from his more or less private corner office on the second floor of the building which had served for almost a century and a quarter as the headquarters of the *Karnesville Weekly Beacon* – which at the time of its' founding, had been a daily, serving Karnes County as far as Falls City to the north and Kenedy to the south. Now the local small-town newspaper struggled bravely against the economic tide, borne up by small-town concerns, crime, and gossip about strictly small-town doings, a large part of which were reported in both the print version and in the Karnesville

Beacon blog (*Your Beacon on What's Happening in Karnes County!)* which was run by Kate Heisel, the Beacon's ace reporter, photographer, and social media maven. Kate, who patterned herself professionally after Brenda Starr and Hildy Johnson as played by Rosalind Russel in the movie *His Girl Friday*, collected up her slim reporters' notebook from her desk, and went to report to her irascible boss. Acey, long retired from active and notable crime beats in much more prestigious venues than the *Weekly Beacon*, retained an interest in national news, not to mention professional and personal contacts in a wide variety of national news and media organizations. It should be admitted that most of those contacts, like Acey himself, were well past the age of collecting Social Security.

"Good morning, Boss!" Kate chirped, settling herself in the lone guest chair which stood, like a prisoner about to be executed by firing squad before the battered late-19th century splendors of the editor's desk. *(Said desk looked like a down-market version of the White House Oval Office Resolute desk, without the secret compartment, or being wrought from the timbers of a British warship.)* "It was a glorious event in Luna City! They've found the Gonzaga Reliquary! Or most of the relevant bits and pieces. Was the rude guy from the *New York Times*? Yeah, that would figure; they're <u>always</u> rude when they are forced by circumstance to deal with us hicks from the sticks. The Brits are usually so much more superficially polite. Richard says it's because..."

"Focus, Kate," Acey commanded. "What's all this about the Gonzaga-thingus?"

Kate heaved a deep and theatric sigh. "That Renaissance relic which was supposedly painted by Leonardo da Vinci in a rediscovered masterpiece found when they renovated a moldy convent in Milan a couple of years ago. God's own ornamental bottle stopper in a portrait of a fat-faced nun who looks like my

Aunt Conchita when she was younger. Supposed to be an ancestress of ours. After being painted, it vanished for about three hundred years before turning up as elements of some Christmas decorations on the Luna City public Christmas tree…"

Acey pressed his fingers against his forehead. Yes, he vaguely recalled hearing about this, at least six months and two-score of hangovers ago, while Kate smoothed the skirt of her modest tailored suit over her knees and continued. "It turned out that the Gonzaga Reliquary in the painting – they claim that it was the creation of Benevento Cellini, but the serious art historians do have doubts because of the spotty provenance. The long and short of it …"

"Please, Kate, favor me with the *Readers' Digest* version," Acey interjected and Kate consulted her notebook.

"OK, the short version is that the original reliquary was returned to the family – the Gonzagas – when their darling daughter was kicked out of the convent for insufficient devotion to the ideals of chastity and reverence. She and her son," Kate snickered, a rather lewd snicker, "Returned to those ancestral acres in northern Spain. A couple of hundred years later, her descendants, or members of that family immigrated to Mexico and took up a land grant in what would in the fullness of time and history become the Rancho Los Robles, on the banks of the San Antonio River. Even before there was a Karnes County, or a Texas," Kate added, with a certain amount of modest pride, "The Gonzaleses and Gonzalezes were here, with their rancho. My cousin Mindy has proved that, beyond any shadow of a doubt – but that's another story entirely. You have my notes on that, in the email that I sent you last week … erm. And it was the front page of the November 5th issue," Kate added helpfully. "But for the reliquary itself; it was disassembled for hiding during the Civil War, and those parts variously concealed in the walls of the old adobe wing of the Rancho de los Robles house.

Only a few people must have known of this – maybe three or four? Yeah, they were paranoid as heck about security back in the day, and who the heck could blame them? Don Luis-Antonio's only son and heir Don Anselmo was serving with the Union, and Texas was part of the Confederacy…"

"Comment would have been made," Acey nodded. "At the very least. And possibly a capital sentence imposed for spying and counterrevolutionary sympathies. So they hid the high-value stuff. Understandable, considering the times."

"And then," Kate took a deep breath. "That handful of people who knew the secret of where they hid it … they died, or went off to greener pastures, even before Don Anselmo returned after the war. The story among the family is that he got delayed by a passionate and doomed romance with a married opera singer in Mexico City for about half a decade. By that time, everyone forgot about the whereabouts of the Reliquary, or even that it existed at all. Don Anselmo's son, Don Antonio – you remember him? He fought the last personal duel in the streets of Luna City with a Maldonado! There's a plaque on Town Square where that happened, back in the early Twenties, sometime. Anyway, Don Antonio had the old adobe walls knocked down, turned into rubble about a hundred years ago, when he wanted to renovate the old ranch headquarters house. The rubble – it was only adobe mud brick, after all … got plowed into a what became a Victory Garden during the Second World War. Don Antonio's artistic sister Leonora took the found bits and pieces and made them into ornaments for a Christmas tree … oh, in about 1945 or '46. She had a thing for making jewelry and other ornaments out of bits of this and that. My Cousin Araceli is pretty certain that she saw them on the Christmas tree at the Rincon de los Robles home place when she was a kid … and at some point Great-Aunt Leonora's ornaments were donated to the City to use on the Town

Square Christmas Tree. They were pretty awful looking," Kate admitted honestly. "Not one of Great-Aunt Leonora's finer artistic accomplishments, to be strictly truthful. I think I could do better with a hot-glue gun and a sweep through Hobby Lobby's marked-down section the week after Christmas. Anyway, at the instant when the civic Luna City Christmas Tree was formally unveiled last week, Cousin Araceli, and Cousin Mindy's hot international treasure-hunting boyfriend both recognized the bits from the Gonzaga Reliquary. Mostly the enamel plaque of the Virgin and Child riding on St. Gigobertus' horse; a plaque surrounded by a nimbus of diamonds set in a corona of silver-gilt. Cousin Mindy's BFF practically collapsed when he spotted them. He's OK; just a bad case of indigestion, compounded with extreme emotion. Gunnison-Penn is given to emotion when it comes to his treasure quests. This one is for the history books, since he has actually found one of those treasures that he set out looking for." Kate consulted her notebook once again, thumbing through the pages for so many minutes that Acey began to tap his fingers impatiently against the battered and scarred top of the editorial desk.

"Ah, here it is – yes, I'll send you the link. I got close-ups of every element as Cousin Araceli retrieved them from the Christmas tree …" Kate sighed, sounding disconsolate. "Don't get your hopes up, or at least – don't encourage your buddies in old media to get their hopes up. Whatever artistic element and value in the reliquary derived from the great Cellini has been pretty well wrecked … and not just from getting buried for fifty years and then welded into Christmas ornaments."

"Oh?" Acey sat back in his battered leather-upholstered chair, and steepled his hands, as he eyed his best reporter. "And the value of these bits and pieces remaining?"

"Well," Kate sounded as if she were temporizing. Excusing, even. "The gold and enamel bits are real enough. But just about all the so-called diamonds and precious stones set in the bits remaining … are glass fakes. Oh, there were a couple of them which were real," she added hastily. "But Mindy thinks that the Reliquary must have been seen as a portable bank account … hit a couple of bad patches, civic unrest, the necessity of skipping old haunts because of politics … and swap out a diamond or two for gold, sell on the down-low market for cash in hand, and swap in a glass gem through the same means. The tooth of St. Gigibertus' horse didn't feature in the Christmas ornaments – although Mindy believes she found it in the dig last month, along with a couple of shards of heavy-duty glass in a cylindrical shape. It was a puzzle for her; the horse tooth all by itself, without any other remains of horse bones in the trench. The bits of crystal glass fitted into a perfect cylinder of the right size. Well, now it all comes clear," Kate added, parenthetically. "The guesses that archeologists have to make about what they find … Mindy said something about a book called *Motel of the Mysteries*. A kind of in-joke for archeologists, I guess."

"The bottom line, Kate," Acey looked as if his hangover was especially intense. "The very bottom line, if you please. What's with the bits and pieces of the reliquary and where are they now?"

"In the hands of an artistic expert and restorer recommended by Georg Stein, who runs the western-relic bookstore on Town Square," Kate closed up her notebook. "An expert friend of an expert friend of another expert friend, as it were. Great Uncle Jaimie is still pretty strict with the budget, although there may be a bit of a tangle ongoing over who exactly owns the bits and pieces. Depends on the wording of the donation to the city, Were the decorations for the Town Christmas tree a loan on the part of the families who provided them, or a donation? I expect that I will have to venture another deep dive into the *Beacon* archives to make certain," Kate added. "That, and into the city council archives."

"Put on a dust mask when you do," Acey advised, with an air of heavy foreboding. "The crap and mold in the air, and on the old archives. The basement is a toxic environment, for certain."

"I'll do that," Kate promised with a sigh.

Her boss regarded her with an expression of concern. "What's the matter, dollface? Personal stuff?"

"Yeah," Kate admitted, with another deep sigh. "Don't want to burden you with it, since it is my personal biz, which ideally should have nothing to do with work stuff … but Christmas. I committed with Mom to bring Richard to our Christmas dinner. Months ago. He's … umm – sort of my boyfriend, I guess. I like him lots, Acey. When he is cut, I bleed."

"Sounds serious," Acey commented, somewhat warily. Deep emotional commitment worried him, especially when it concerned his employees. "He doesn't exhibit serial murder tendencies, does he? In that case, I'd have to call in law enforcement."

"Don't worry, Chief!" Kate replied. "If that were the case, I would have called in law enforcement at the very first. The chief of the Luna City PD is married to a good friend. That's not what the problem is. Mom just texted me that Grandpa Fritz Heisel will be there, too."

"And this would be a problem in what way?" Acey ventured.

"Because," Kate replied, with an air of tolerance. "Poppa Fritz hates the English, root and branch. He damned near got shot as a spy by them during World War Two – twice!"

"I can see," Acey replied, after a long moment of thought. "That might lead a reasonable man to be a little bit sour. The Germans were indiscriminately blitzing English cities, sinking

English shipping – not to mention chasing them out of France. It's been a while since then, Kate."

"The trouble is that Poppa Fritz was serving as a US Army paratroop with the 507th Paratroop Infantry Regiment at the time. He is still pretty pissed about the whole shot-as-a-spy thing," She took up her notebook, and added, "And he's still mad about the room-temp beer."

"Oh. My." Acey said to the door, as Kate departed the editorial corner office. "Yes. I do understand why he might still be holding a teensy bit of a grudge, Kate."

Programme for "A Christmas Carol"

Charles Dickens' A Christmas Carol

A Seasonal Diversion
Presented by the Luna City Players
Friday and Saturday Evenings at 7:00 – Sunday Matinee 12:00
In the Koenig Opera House – December 2019

Cast

Scrooge...Benjamin Cordova
Marley.. Orlando Biggs
Ghost of Christmas Past .... Caroline Brodie Mills
Mr. Fezziwig ....Dwight Garrett
Mrs. Fezziwig .... Annise Stein
Young Scrooge .... Bodie Madison
Fan Scrooge .... Linda Brodie
Belle .... Catherine Mills
Bob Cratchit .... Anthony Gonzales
Mrs. Cratchit .... Marisol Gonzales
Martha Cratchit .... Linda Brodie
Tiny Tim .... Mateo Gonzales
Ghost of Christmas Present...................................Bill Weitzman
Frederick Scrooge .... Bodie Madison
Mariah Scrooge .... Araceli Gonzales-Gonzalez
Ghost of Christmas Future ....Isabelle Walcott
Boy Sent For Goose .... Anson Pryor

Carolers, Guests, Dancers: The Complete Company of the Luna City Players

Direction, Lighting and Set Design ...... Patricia Pryor

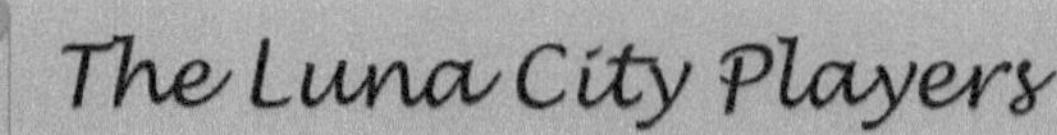

The Odd Couples

"Do you know, I saw the funniest thing, last night – coming away from the office after putting the edition to bed," Kate remarked. "It was nearly nine o'clock and I went to The Original Market BBQ for some take-out, and I saw the oddest couple – Myrna Vaughn and Ignacio Gomez, sitting together at a table together, looking like they were the best of friends."

"What!?" Richard was mildly appalled; not that Kate would know Ignacio Gomez by sight – she was, after all, the *Weekly Beacon's* crack news reporter and social media expert – but that half of Luna City's notoriously incompetent team of criminal geniuses was associating on near-to-intimate terms with the mother of Luna City's chief of police. "You must have been mistaken, Kate! Myrna Vaughn's of the country gentry, the widow of a highly-respected man – and I'd venture to say that she is far too intelligent for the likes of the dumbest criminal in the county. I've met her – got a mind like a steel trap with sharpened spikes all the way around. Why would she be associating with a numbskull like 'Nacio Gomez? Romantically or otherwise? Perhaps it was only someone who looked like him…"

"No such luck, Richard," Kate reached over to top up her wineglass from the contents of the chilled carafe of red which sat on the tiny table within the Airstream. Ozzie lounged in her lap and meowed a faint protest at having his slumber briefly disturbed. "I went over to the table to say hi, and she introduced him to me. 'My friend Mr. Gomez,' she said. 'We just came from a meeting and stopped for a bite to eat, since the Café will be closed by the time that we drive back to Luna City.' We chatted for a bit … they certainly didn't look like a romantic couple. In fact, 'Nacio seemed kind of squirmy, like he was a bit embarrassed…" Kate soothed Ozzie with a gentle scritch to the back of his ears. "I can't think of what kind of meeting they would have been at," she added. "There's a regular lecture at the community center for the Karnesville Historical society – but that's on the first Monday, not the third, I thought. Maybe they changed it at the last minute, because of the holidays. Choir practice for St. Scholastica's parish … there's an AA meeting at the library every Monday evening, and then the Aggie Alums have a quarterly get-together pot-luck."

"I think the Historical Association must have been the draw," Richard ventured. "I cannot imagine that the college association would have attracted either party. Mrs. Vaughn-the-Senior is very much that kind of woman – drawn like a moth to community matters, and even more if she can command a leadership role in them. 'Nacio Gomez … he is supposed to have done some excellent reconstructive woodwork in the Cattleman as part of the refit. Roman Gonzalez said that he can do very fine work, but most of the time he is too damn lazy to live up to potential. It sounds like that is the story of his life," Richard added, giving a last stir to the savory concoction of an authentic *beef bourguignonne* over which he had been laboring for all afternoon on the tiny gas-powered cooktop in the old Airstream. "Are you hungry, my dear Kate? Supper will be ready momentarily."

"Ravenous!" Kate twinkled at him, and they conversed on other more interesting topics, while the sun went down in glorious technicolor and mellow golden lantern-light bloomed in the twilight at the glorious straw castle which crowned the hill opposite. Richard dished up savory bowls of beef bourguignonne, topped with a round of crisp-baked puff-paste, and set aside a small portion of the tenderest beef for Ozzie, all so that he and Kate could eat theirs in peace, without having Ozzie insinuate himself onto whatever lap and steal from their very plates. All was serene in his world – a supper with his Kate, Ozzie scarfing his share and later asleep in gluttonous satisfaction in the middle of the bed. Richard completely forgot about Myrna Vaughn and 'Nacio Gomez reportedly having a tête-à-tête in the Karnesville Original BBQ … until the following week.

On a fair January morning, the rising sun comfortably banishing the winter chill from that sheltered corner of Town Square, Richard saw another oddly assorted pair from inside the Café. He could hardly believe the evidence of his own eyes. Miss Letty McAllister, the oldest resident of Luna City, a woman of stern and inviolate rectitude, a pillar of the Methodist Ladies, past and honored president of the Luna City Historical Association, the only woman in Karnes County who still invariably wore gloves and a hat whenever she left her house *(a historic, limestone-build residence further ornamented with a state historical marker, which sat across Route 123 from the Tip-Top Icehouse, Gas and Grocery,)* sitting at one of the Café's sidewalk tables with Reuben Sifuentes! Reuben Sifuentes, a rotund Jeff to 'Nacio Gomez' Mutt and his customary partner in spectacularly inept crime – at a table with Miss Letty? Miss Letty, who would probably sit at the left hand of the Deity when her time came to ascent to a higher world, clearly on amiable social terms with the other half of Luna City's own dynamic criminal duo? Richard wondered if he should make mention of it to Chris Mayall, who lived in the second-floor bachelor apartment over the garage at the McAllister house. Chris kept a watchful yet unobtrusive guard on Miss Letty. Somehow, in the mists of the previous decade, Chris had become an odd kind of surrogate grandson, or perhaps a very special kind of Red Cross rehabilitation project for Miss Letty.

Yes, Richard decided. *I'm certain that he loves the old dear, and she looks after him ... a word to the wise should be sufficient. At the coffee-and-donuts after the weekly training session the day after tomottow. Yes – that should be the right time and place.*

Training sessions at the Luna City Volunteer Fire Department were a two-hour long affair at the firehouse on Wednesday evenings, most often a combination of lecture, demonstration and exercise. Richard, had volunteered for the VFD after the original Age of Aquarius main structure had burned to the ground after a mishap with the fire in a free-burning and authentic American Indian sweat lodge. *(The old building had been a substantial, yet dark and smelly home-build yurt, dating from the establishment of the commune in the Summer of Love.)* Richard could be brought to admit *(usually after a drink or so at the VFW on guest night)* that his wholly uncharacteristic bout of civic responsibility was because he was fond of the Grants, and of Luna City generally, and did not wish to witness another such catastrophe.

The VFD was one of those Luna City community things and participating in it was the activity most personally congenial for him. Richard felt no inclination towards joining in historical reenactor activities, was not a military veteran or a hippy, and possessed no religious convictions sufficiently strong enough to compel him towards regular attendance at any of Luna City's notable congregations on Sunday mornings, or any other time at that. The Café had to be open, meals served – even if, and especially if – on Sunday morning. The volunteer fire department and guest night at the VFW allowed him to give back to a community which he had chosen to join, for good or ill.

The lecture that Wednesday was fairly relaxed; to do with the various expanded properties at Mills Farm, for which the VFD was responsible, helmed by the new local media relations authority for Mills Farm; Chris's girlfriend, Stephanie Royce. A very nice and informative 3-D map of each new building was provided by Sylvester Gonzalez, and projected onto the large whiteboard in the VFD training classroom for the edification of the VFD who might yet have to put out fires in them. The elegant and competent Miss Royce was available to answer searching questions regarding construction, lay-out and amenities such as the exact location of the nearest hydrant or retention pond on the Mills Farm property.

"I approve of your new light o' love," Richard murmured, as he and Chris lined up at the table for coffee, and to scoff some of the fresh cinnamon rolls, contributed to this civic occasion by the Café. "She's a keeper. But look … I have a worry about Miss Letty to convey to you. I've been wondering, since I saw her at the Café, meeting with Reuben Sifuentes, half of our local team of incompetent and gullible crooks. They got suckered into helping that awful Mason woman into stealing from their worksite, to the tune of twenty million dollars' worth of antique light fixtures…"

"Miss Letty is inclined to charitable consideration," Chris murmured, a suddenly hostile expression taking over his features.

"But that a-hole? He visits her three or four times a week. I see them, sitting out on the porch, of an afternoon. Ricardo, I do not have a good feeling about all this. Miss Letty, she is as shrewd as the day is long, but she's getting up there in years… I can't sit by and see that scumbag take advantage."

"Miss Letty wouldn't be an easy pushover," That was Jess Abernathy-Vaughn, in the line behind Chris, and having overheard that bit of conversation. In spite of bulging considerably with advanced pregnancy, Jess still attended weekly VFD training – her condition excusing her from anything the least bit physically strenuous. "Sorry, guys, didn't mean to stick my oar in. I do her financials. She's still got every marble of her original issue. There is no possible way that Reuben Sifuentes could con Miss Letty out of a single solitary thin dime. Not with some sob story and certainly not by pitching romantic woo – she's in her nineties, for heavens' sake, and he's young enough to be her grandson. Great grandson, even. I believe that she must have heard every hard-luck story ever written by the time she was my age."

"No, probably not," Chris agreed, with a somewhat strained smile. "But I will keep a close eye on Miss Letty, anyway. That Reuben character is just too skeevy for words; he and that pal of his, Ignacio."

"Who is hanging around socially with your mother-in-law," Richard informed Jess, having remembered that bit of interesting social gossip from Kate. Ah, the joys of living in a small town. "Kate saw them in Karnesville last week, having supper together. After a meeting, they told her. But the association is … dubious, in my own humble opinion."

"Yeah," Jess replied, suddenly alert. "Mine, too. I'll ask Joe about that, and he can check with their parole officer. Law enforcement privilege, you know. Myrna-Mom is not exactly immune to a hard-luck story, and I doubt that either one of our Dubious Duo could con her out of anything, but there's always temptation. 'Nacio and Reuben can resist anything but that, especially as an alternative to hard work."

"So sayeth Roman Gonzalez," Richard agreed. He had discovered the downside to involvement in community, having a casual observation taken with utter sincerity. From there, unforeseen results unfoldedwith the inevitability of Indiana Jones fleeing the path of an enormous stone ball in an ancient Mayan tomb rolling down upon him. "Seriously," Richard added. "I mentioned the light fixtures to Roman … and the next thing I know, the Dubious Duo and the obnoxious Mason woman are charged with crimes and subsequently enjugged. Honestly, I hope there is nothing sinister involved in their friendships with a pair of respectable ladies…"

"Trust but verify," Jess agreed with a cynical chuckle.

"Sorted, Ricardo," Chris added – and Richard considered the matter of unsuitable friendships and attachments handed on to those who being now alerted, would see that everything would be sorted, tickety-boo. No longer his concern.

* * *

Jess Abernathy-Vaughn drove home slowly, through the early-spring twilight; it was only a matter of three blocks, which she would have easily walked, but for the exhaustion at the end of a long day of work and the additional physical burden of Babe-to-Be-Plus. And because Joe had insisted that she not overexert herself, and Jess knew that her husband's concern for her was totally real, and not to be lightly set aside. It was much less trouble to drive her little yellow Jeep Wrangler, than to take part in another extended discussion about how pregnancy was not more than a temporary disability, and that she was totally fit and up to whatever challenge. She was tired. More than tired – bone-deep exhausted and slightly nauseated. She parked the Wrangler in back of the tidy small cottage on Oak Street and let herself in through the back door. The screen door of the back porch fell closed behind her, and as soon as she came in through the kitchen, Joe called from the front room.

"Hey, Babe … come take a load off. Little Joe had his bedtime story and is already in dreamland. Mom came by and dropped off dinner. Salisbury steak and onion gravy, with mashed potatoes and green beans."

"Oh, good. I'm starving." Jess tossed her enormous handbag-cum-briefcase in the direction of the antique coatrack next to the door and collapsed next to her husband on the overstuffed sectional sofa which took up most of the front room. Yeah, the damn thing was a serious interior decorator *faux pas*; a huge late 20th century object in a smallish room from the early century, a room which cried out aesthetically for something Craftsman-style, blocky, square, and small, with simple woodwork and minimal padding. On this occasion, as on others after a hard day – and with pregnancy, all days were hard – Jess was grateful for the comfort afforded. Aesthetic appeal could go hang until after Little Joe and his sisters were grown.

Joe dropped a brief kiss on her forehead. "OK, Babe – your wish is my command. Just put your feet up for a moment and let us enjoy some connubial bliss and togetherness for a couple of minutes."

"Feed me, husband dear," Jess whimpered. "I starve. The girls starve. I might begin to eat you… If I don't throw up, first."

"Promises, promises," Joe replied, and eased himself up off the sectional. Jess noted, through her misery, that he walked stiffly. His knees were giving him heck again. Hot wraps and Motrin, definitely.

She focused her attention briefly on the television screen; a foreign series on streaming video, with subtitles. Lots of desert and explosions were involved, along with the subtitles. She had no interest, especially not after Joe returned with a tray, set it in front of her, and switched the television channel to some channel featuring vistas of scenery and cute animals. "What was that you were watching?" she asked, stifling another surge of nausea, as she took up a fork. One of the weird effects – now she got nauseous when hungry. The only cure was to push through the gag reflex and start eating.

"Turkish series about their spec ops," Joe replied, more terse than usual. "I like it. They have actors that look like regular grunts and normal people. And happy endings not guaranteed."

"Your kind of life," Jess replied, and Joe grunted by way of reply.

"Your supper is served," he settled gingerly next to her on the sectional. She noted the special care with which he settled his knees on the divan. "Bon appetite. Shall we now have some quality married time?"

"If I can stay awake long enough for it," Jess replied, and leaned her head against his shoulder. Those first bites of chopped steak, generously moistened with rich brown gravy miraculously took effect. Now her supper looked appetizing. "Between you and the cute critters. Your mom does miracles with ground beef, you know."

"A splash of marsala in the gravy," Joe explained. "Red wine – that's Mom's miracle secret ingredient. By the way, there was a postcard from your Dad in the mail this afternoon. Mailed from Bali, about three weeks ago."

"Dad's old-school," Jess sighed. "He will do emails, but texting is a bridge too far. How's he doing?"

"He and Joanna won a rumba contest," Joe reported, as Jess settled herself against his shoulder with a small sigh of contented relief. "And toured a historic Hindu temple complex. He wrote – *Don't Worry, Didn't Overdo It.* Where are they going next?"

"Singapore, and then Australia," Jess contentedly forked in some more steak, followed by creamy mashed potatoes, and a quantity of restful silence during which Jess relished the sheer comforting presence of her husband. He was there, strong and indomitable, fearlessly standing guard on that wall. Nothing bad could ever happen, with Joe out there on the wall. "Speaking of parents … did you know that your Mom is hanging out with 'Nacio Gomez? Katie Heisel saw them last week, eating supper at that BBQ place in Karnesville, and told Ricardo. Ricardo is a bit freaked, and so is Chris, because Reuben Sifuentes is having regular meetups with Miss Letty … and you know what those two are like. Chris and Ricardo are worried about what they are up to. I told them I would ask you about it. Can you check with their parole officer, or something?"

"I can," Joe mused, thoughtfully. "But I just don't know about Miss Letty, Babe. She's old school in her way; always been about charity for the worthy cause, although I do wonder that she can see ol' Reuben as deserving. As for Mom, she hired 'Nacio to do some specialty carpentry repair in the house. Bookshelf for all of my Dad's old books that he treasured, something that will blend in with all the other built-ins. Mom wants it to fit in with the historic woodwork. A dirtbag 'Nacio might be, but when he puts his mind to it, he does really fine carpentry. Or so says Roman. Can't figure why they'd be going to Karnesville for BBQ, though. Maybe I should talk to Mom … she's only just come back to town, prolly isn't up to speed on what goes down on the Weekly Beacon police blotter…"

"Talk to her, yeah," Jess agreed. She had been working over her plate with increasing energy and enthusiasm as the hunger-nausea eased, and the animals in the nature series romped in the gorgeous scenery. "But …"

"Yeah, Babe?"

"Don't tell her about the twins, just yet."

"Why not?" Joe asked, sounding completely reasonable.

"Because she'll practically move in with us," Jess confessed with another sigh. "And I just don't want to cope with Myrna-Mom, twenty-four seven. I like your mom. Might even love her, given enough space and time for reflection. But she is a bit overwhelming and once she knows that I – that is, we – are having twins? No, please. Let it all be a surprise to everyone. Promise onna stack of Bibles, Joe. Don't tell her. Or anyone. I haven't even let word to Dad. He'd bag the round-the world-tour and come flying home if he had any idea about us expecting twins. Let it be our secret, for as long as we can keep it."

"Agreed," and Joe took the tray – with the amazingly clean plate – off to the kitchen. "Mom <u>can</u> be overwhelming. Great to have in your corner, but, yeah. Babe, it's understood. But know this: if your OB is right and you have to go on total bed rest for the last couple of months, I'll <u>have</u> to say something by way of explanation. To Mom, your Dad, and your grand-rents, and all your clients, too. Just saying. Want dessert? Mom brought apple crumble. It was great."

"A small helping, please," Jess replied. "As for the total bed rest thing? Napalm that bridge when we come to it. I'll think of something. My OB has advised it. Something."

"Your wish is my command, Babe," Joe called from the kitchen, over the sound of the dishwasher humming through its' slow cycle. "Want some cream on top? You're eating for three, now."

"Indulge me," Jess replied, and stretched out luxuriously on the sectional, having been feasted and satiated. "And whatever you hear about our less-than-dynamic criminal duo – tell me, so that I can tell Richard and Chris. They're worried."

"Will do, Babe." Joe returned from the tiny old-fashioned kitchen with a small plate of dessert – apple crumble in a puddle of cream, with a spoon laid temptingly on one side.

"Bliss," Jess sighed, and scooched closer to Joe as he settled onto the sectional again.

Another good evening; married life in Luna City.

* * *

Friday evening was guest night at the VFW post; now that Richard had a full complement of staff at the Café, he was able to partake regularly of guest privilege at what was about the main (if not entirely exclusively so) male refuge in Luna City. Curiously enough for the restaurant trade, Friday evenings at the Café were a rather quiet evening, well within Luc Massie's ability to cope. Richard had come to believe that this was because of Pryor's BBQ drawing most local diners of a Friday evening. And ever since the Cattleman Hotel had reopened under Mills Farm management as their alternate hospitality venue, their splendid dining room was the restaurant of choice for anyone, local or not, wanting to make an event of a Friday night supper date.

"I should be eaten up with resentment over this," he lamented to Jess in a recent session, after this interesting anomaly had been noted and thoroughly discussed. "Losing out on a premier restaurant evening, to a BBQ stand and a corporate façade, but strangely enough, I can't work up the energy."

And Jess had laid a comforting hand on his. "Look, the Café is the solid venue of choice for breakfast and lunch – same as it always was. And Saturdays are looking good. Not spectacular, but good. You know, I would look at the prospects for take-out, of an evening throughout the working week. It's still a chore to cook supper, after a long day on the job. No one wants to dress up to go to the Cattleman or eat smoked BBQ every night of the week – although, honestly, there are serious fans for that. I've been running the figures with Araceli, and local delivery of ready-to-eat cooked suppers would be something that might draw some interest. Mankind cannot live on pizza delivery, six nights a week, as much as some of them might like, or even casseroles from their mother. Maybe I can talk Doc into hiring another waiter or waitress who can handle deliveries. Think of it as a local niche market, which you can fill."

"I hope so," Richard had replied on that occasion. "Resting on previous laurels is a recipe for doom, in the restaurant trade. Always onward and upward, that's the ticket…"

Now, Richard sat with Chris and Joe, at one of the random arrays of tables in the VFW. It was too cold and windy to sit outdoors, under the leafless sycamore trees which edged the San Antonio River, as it lapped on the fringes of Luna City, and those last few out-skirting commercial establishments. The chat with Jess reminded Richard of the Café and of how Miss Letty had once again met with Reuben Sifuentes, that very morning. Oh, the aged grand lady of the Luna City manor had sat at the farthest outside table with Reuben – aggravatingly out of earshot of Richard or anyone else who might have monitored their topic of conversation.

"I saw Miss Letty this morning at the Cafe with Reuben of Unblessed Memory," Richard said, as he partook of his first drink of the evening. "And it recalled to me, Chris; what is the deal with her, and the larger half of our unholy criminal duo? You said that you would ask her why she was spending time with half of our local low-life duo. Should we be worried on Miss Letty's behalf?"

"No," Chris sank half of his own beer in one prolonged gulp. "No, there is no reason at all. Miss Letty is just doing her thing. As she has always done. She saw … I dunno, a need that everyone else was skipping past. And you have to swear to secrecy. She told me, on that account. Miss Letty knew that y'all might be worried," Chris added. "Don't let it go any farther than this table."

"What's the story, then?" Joe squinted into the middle distance, out to where the bare sycamores sketched a black outline against the pale and ice-blue sky.

"She's teaching Reuben to read," Chris replied.

Richard sank another drought of his own beer. "Strewth. That sod is illiterate? Well, stone the crows. I thought he was just a determinedly criminal a-hole."

"God is my witness," Chris looked at them all, stone serious. "Reuben got passed through the public schools where he grew up, until he dropped out – he for sure can't read; dyslexic, seriously far-sighted and needing glasses, and no one ever noticed or gave two sh*ts. It didn't happen in Luna City, by the way. Someone like Miss Letty would have spotted it, for sure. Nope," Chris sunk a long draft of his own drink of choice. "He couldn't read much more than his own name, until Miss Letty began working with him. How f**ked up is that, a kid could make it through the schools in this country and not be able to read a f**king word?"

"Depends on how good a BS artist he was," Joe nodded, not at all shocked or surprised. "All kinds of reasons, Chris my man. Ol'

Reuben was good at gaming the system. School to some guys …" Joe sat back in his chair and regarded them all, in a meditative mood. "Is just something that they want out of, in the worst way. And they get out – in the worst way. They say what they think that they have to say to get out of something that they don't have any interest in, and never realize the long-term implications. Like not being able to read… stuff. Yeah, met some of those in the Army. At least, they were able to read enough to get through the ASVAB and satisfy the recruiter. They were at best maybe at the comic-book level; small words, nothing over two syllables." Joe heaved a great sigh and looked into the depts of his almost-empty beer. "Well, that accounts for Miss Letty's social life among the dirtbag element. OK, who's turn is it to buy? I gotta drive to Victoria tomorrow. An outpatient appointment at the VA. So it's all sorted with our local dirtbags? Good. See ya later, guys. Glad we got that resolved. See ya tomorrow."

Only later did Richard wonder why Joe had never mentioned his mother's cozy tête-à-tête at that BBQ place in Karnesville.

The Return of Clovis

It came not upon a midnight clear, but a fortnight before Christmas, that word of the return of Clovis Walcott (Colonel, US Army Retired) arrived in the Café.

This intelligence arrived through the medium of Colonel Walcott's youngest son, Robbie, allowing in his usual artless manner, as he arrived for his usual Saturday morning shift,

"Hey, Dad is coming home! The Dubai job is done and dusted, he said. He called from Atlanta last night. Got a meeting with some possible clients there, but he's coming home in time for Christmas."

"I suppose that Mrs. Walcott is thrilled beyond words," Richard observed, biting his tongue on his next impulse, to suggest that Sook Walcott, the most ferocious tiger mother in several counties, was looking forward to serving as a sort of bedroom sausage roll, now that her husband was on his way home.

"She is," Robbie replied, appearing now somewhat mildly anxious, as he tied on his clean kitchen apron. "Oh, hey – Luc? Dad wants to speak to you. About your intentions towards Belle, I think. He sounded kinda serious." Robbie sent a look towards Luc Massie, who was industriously scraping the grill station, after the breakfast rush and didn't seem to have heard a word.

Luc – thin, tattooed to a fair-thee-well, body-modified with studs and round metal ear-plugs through which Richard could have passed a thumb, topped with a multi-colored Mohawk crest of hair – hardly reacted at all. Luc was, as Miss Letty McAllister allowed, one of those odd children who had never quite gotten the hang of comfortable social interaction with others of their species. A genius at the grill, whose command of the sauté station was above peer and beyond reproach, Luc also doubled as the drummer for a desperately unsuccessful local alt-rock band known as OPM. Which initials stood for anything and everything which began with the letters O, P, and M, since the band members couldn't agree on an exact definition. Still, having invested in a logo incorporating those letters, and all gotten tats alike – they were pretty well stuck with those letters and logo.

Now Brianna Grant, the other teenage apprentice, who was finishing the last of those garnishes required for luncheon service, heaved a deep sigh. "Luc!" she repeated. "Didn't you hear what Robbie just said? Belle's dad will want to speak to you. You know – if you want to work the sex-magic with her. When and if she comes back from New York. You'd better think of something to say, when he asks you if you do. And something to say to her, if you don't."

Luc finally glanced up from the grill. He appeared – to Richard's view – to be comprehensively rattled at having a human-reaction problem presented to him.

"What?"

Brianna sighed theatrically. "Luc – Belle's dad is back in town. Belle; you know, you love her, et cetera, et cetera? Her dad will want to know if you are serious about doing the sex-magic with her, or anything more intense. I know – you need to think about this all, before you formulate an answer…"

"I do," Luc replied, although no one in the Café's kitchen was entirely certain of to which question his answer was a reply.

"My advice to you, Mr. Massie," Richard cut into the conversation, as it was obviously a distraction to all of his staff, "Is to take one long and searching look at young Belle's maternal parent. Decide if you wish to be romantically-allied to a woman with her very same qualities in thirty years. As the twig inclines, so will the mature tree, given enough time."

Luc stared at Richard, completely baffled. Richard gave up on talking sense to him.

"I mean no criticism of your mother, Robbie; merely a statement of the realities to be recognized when embarking on a long-term relationship."

"Mom is a firecracker," Robbie acknowledged with a sigh and a shrug. "And she was pretty upset when she caught Belle an' Luc kissing in the boathouse."

"Upset? Upset is as masterful a bit of understatement as I have ever heard from an Englishman," Richard shuddered, remembering the epic diatribe following upon that unfortunate encounter. Sook Walcott had not just chastised her offspring, at length and top decibels, but had taken the time and trouble over the following days to lecture Luc *(from the street below the windows of the bare-bones flat that he rented from Miss Letty).* She also had harassed Richard himself at the tiny vintage Airstream caravan at the Age of Aquarius Campground and Goat Farm. Until Doc Wyler, the owner of the Café and much else of real (estate) value around Luna City, had called a halt to Sook's maternal warpath, there was little peace to be had among the stately oaks and Beaux Arts-era facades of Luna City for those who had the ill-luck to be on the periphery of the most ill-judged mésalliance since Abelard and Heloise.

In the spirit of the seaman in charge of the last lifeboat to leave the Titanic, Richard inquired of Robbie, the Walcott's fortunately even-tempered youngest son, "I know how your dear mama feels about all this. Any indication that your father will be more reasonable? Or if not that, at least considerably less operatically-unhinged about the matter?"

"I dunno," Robbie confessed, with an expression of honest bafflement on his features; features which merged the four-square and ruggedly handsome bones of his father with the sloe-dark eyes, epicanthic fold and pale olive complexion of his mother, who was alleged to have descended from old Korean nobility. "Dad didn't say much, when Mom vented to him over the phone about Belle last night. All he said this time was that he wanted to have a serious talk with this Luc, as soon as possible when he got back home."

"I expect that your father was hard-put to get in a word edgewise," Richard still wondered how on earth Clovis Walcott; an otherwise genial and even-tempered man, managed to endure marriage to the tempest of temperament that was Sook. Perhaps – perish the thought – Clovis privately enjoyed the drama.

It was therefore no great surprise, three or four days later, when Clovis Walcott appeared; mid-morning, after the rush to serve breakfast and before the rush to organize for lunch. Doubtless the good colonel had consulted with Robbie; a touch of professional consideration which Richard greatly appreciated. The dining room was all but empty; Beatriz and Blanca were attending to the last of the morning crowd, when Clovis walked through the door, heralded by the silvery jingling of the old-fashioned shop bell attached to it.

Richard, as was suitable for a manager of what he hoped would be the top-line purveyor of excellent cuisine in a charming, historically-significant location, appeared in the dining room – although he was drying his hands on a towel strategically tucked into his waistband as he did so.

"Colonel Walcott – welcome home! So happy to have you back again, among us! Robbie let it slip that you would return soon … a good lad, and a hard worker as well…"

"Glad to be home as well, Ricardo!" Clovis gave every indication that this was purely true, in that he shook Richard's hand with enthusiasm and brotherly affection. "Might you have one or two of your cinnamon rolls to spare and a cup of that magnificent coffee as well? I'd like to have a word with your cook, Mr. Massie," Clovis added, as he took a seat at the big table set before the picture window at the Café – the regulars' table, or as the Stein's called it, 'the stammtisch.'

"Robbie was good enough to tell me that you would want a quiet word with Luc, seeing that Miss Walcott is somewhat serious about their romantic affections. If you like – the two of you can go out in back," Richard offered, and Clovis shook his head.

"No, the stammtisch will do nicely and the conversation won't take but a moment. Just ask Mr. Massie if he will spare a few moments out of his busy day. There are some things that we have to get straight."

Clovis Walcott's face bore a stern expression upon it; Richard hoped devotedly that he would, after all this brief conversation was done, still have a junior cook available to deal with the lunchtime grill orders.

"I hope that he doesn't take very long with Luc," he ventured to Araceli in a low voice as he passed the cash register desk. "Or leave much of a mess. Blood on the stammtisch will be hard to explain to lunch customers."

"And leave us short of a cook," Araceli murmured in reply. "But I wouldn't worry, Chef – Clovis is actually an old softy. Most often he lets Sook be the bad cop; I think they have it down to a science."

"Just keep an eye on them both," Richard advised over his shoulder as he stepped into the kitchen to tell Luc that doom was upon him. "Come and get me if it looks like the conversation is going sideways, or the daggers are coming out."

Oddly enough, Luc himself did not seem terribly apprehensive. He took off his apron, and the food-handling gloves which he was wearing while slicing meats and cold cuts for the lunch rush, and ran his fingers through his wildly colored mohawk, while mumbling,

"Five minutes, Chef. That's all. Mr. W. is O.G. – original gangster; best kind. It's Miz W. who threw all kinna shade on us."

"Fine. I think," Richard replied, with heavy sarcasm and in some doubt of what Luc had actually said. "Five minutes. Send up a smoke signal if you need help."

"S'not a problem, Chef," With that unconvincing statement, Luc slouched his way into the dining area and towards the stammtisch. As no obvious nuclear cloud erupted when he joined Clovis Walcott there, Richard withdrew into the kitchen, but towering curiosity drove him forth again within minutes. No; still no giant eruption of fatherly authority, or rapidly spreading pool of gore. In fact, it all appeared most civilized, decorous, even. Araceli lurked silently at the cash desk, her feet shod in thick-soled trainers tied with pink laces which matched her uniform of the day. She seemed to be inventorying the contents of the cash desk and fussing over precisely rearranging the contents; Richard was certain that was just cover for her remaining in the dining room.

"What have they been talking about?" Richard hissed; Araceli replied without looking up.

"I have not been eavesdropping, Chef – that would be rude. But Luc did say something like – 'That's chill, Mr. W – you played the bass?' That's odd. It's almost as if Clovis was in a band himself, and Luc was really impressed. It must have been ages ago, though; I'd never heard anything about it."

"Our good colonel had a misspent youth?" Richard marveled. "I'll be damned; who would have thought it?"

"Shhsss!" Araceli made an elaborate show of breaking open a coil of quarters and emptying them into the cash register drawer. Not very much put down, Richard lowered his voice.

"Well, it's not like Luc is the answer to every maiden's prayer – and certainly not the prayers of her father. Dare I assume that Clovis is making nice, and not secretly planning to have some underworld types scare him into leaving town?"

"I don't think so," Araceli replied. "And it looks like they're done."

So they were; Luc and Clovis both stood and shook hands with every indication of amiable and mutual respect.

"You outta come and jam with us sometime," Luc offered, rather shyly, and Clovis smiled.

"I might, at that, son." Which sounded promising for Belle and Luc as a couple, until Richard recalled that Clovis routinely addressed all younger men as 'son.' Still, it didn't look as if Clovis was planning to have his daughter's unseemly swain disposed of in some extra-legal way. Which Richard would not have put past him; the Colonel possessed a large personal arsenal, had friends with large personal arsenals, and a wider circle of friends who possessed acres of relatively uncultivated land and heavy earth-moving equipment.

As Luc passed Richard, standing by the cash desk, Luc averred,

"Hey – Chef. Mr. W. and I are OK. We agree about Belle. Did you know that Mr. W. played in a band, once? Ever so chill…" and Luc wafted back into the kitchen, while Araceli and Richard exchanged looks of open-mouthed astonishment.

Meanwhile, from the stammtisch Clovis Walcott ventured, "Hey, can I get a top-up on the coffee, or is it too late for breakfast? I've been missing the Café's good brew for six months, and I want to relish the experience again."

"Sure thing," Araceli shoved the cash drawer closed, hissing to Richard. "I'll take care of it. Look, you go talk to Clovis; he looks like he wants to unload. Remember, being a good listener is part of our good customer service. Besides, if he decides to run Luc out of town, we'll have to find and hire another cook or two, and they might be even nuttier than he is!"

"Point taken," Richard admitted, with a sigh. As eccentric as Luc might be, especially for an ill-timed romance with the gifted daughter of a Luna City power couple – he was an excellent cook and a reliable employee. "Bring me a cup, too – might as well make it look chummy."

"Might I join you?" He ventured to Clovis, who smiled and replied,

"Your place, your rules. Damn, but I missed the Café while I was in Dubai!"

"I imagine your family is glad to have you back," Richard ventured into the potentially choppy conversational waters. "Especially Mrs. Walcott. She … errr … was…" Richard searched desperately for the most tactful way to describe Sook Walcott's epic and near-week-long tantrum upon discovering that Belle and Luc were much, much more than just good friends. "Most distraught. Over the relationship between your daughter and Luc. He is an odd sort. And he will pursue that professional career with his band. If I have a daughter, I would be quite concerned at her relationship with a chap like Luc. No mistake, really – he's a grand cook, I trust him in the kitchen implicitly *(well, sort of, Richard added in his silent inner voice)* but as a prospective son-in-law? I mean – he plays in this grotty little weekend band in bars for beer money from the patrons and little more. Now, if he would apply himself in the kitchen … but still; while it's a solid career track, there's little chance of a princely income from practicing it."

Clovis regarded Richard silently over his coffee. Richard continued, wondering if he was doing this right at all. "It strikes me that … really, you are being quite superhumanly tolerant, regarding his romantic attachment to Miss Walcott. It's not that I want to poke my nose into your family dynamic," Richard added hastily. "It's just that I am rather oddly *in loco parentis* to Luc. I cannot for the life of me see why you yourself are tolerating the relationship."

There, he had done it – gone a bit too far in laying out his concerns on the table. But to his relief, Clovis Walcott grinned.

"Ah; two things, Ricardo. I played in a band, too, back in the day. Another grotty little garage band, a really noisy one. A couple of years in high school, and then in college." Clovis sighed, reminiscently. "About the purest fun I had in life to that date. Well, there <u>was</u> blowing stuff up as an Army engineer. And as for the other; there was this dog."

"A dog?" Richard goggled. No, he had not expected this. "What has a dog to do with Luc? And your daughter?"

At that moment, Araceli appeared, with her bounteous carafe, and pitcher of cream, and a tray with two plates upon it – another cinnamon roll on one, and a piece of toast and some scrambled eggs on the other. She put the cinnamon roll in front of Clovis, the toast and egg in front of Richard, and silently poured out the coffee. When she had whisked herself off on silent feet, Clovis added the contents of a sugar packet to his. The spoon clinking against the side of his coffee cup as he stirred was momentarily the only sound. Richard applied himself to his breakfast and had his plate half-cleared before Clovis was even half-way into his story.

"The dog," Clovis looked into the distance, as if meditating. "The dog that we got when Jerry and Belle were kids; Jerry was about eight at the time, Belle three and a half. Robbie hadn't been born at that point. We took a luxury vacation in Morocco; I was working on a project in Spain, and it was just a hop, skip and jump from there. The political situation had pretty much settled down, and this was before 9-11, of course. We stayed in this spectacular old place on the beach in Casablanca, in the historic part of town, and the kids loved it. The beach, mostly – and going to the old market. Well, this one day, we were walking along the street in the old district, and we saw some local boys with a dog. Didn't realize it at first, until the dog began yelping in pain; the local kids were tormenting the dog. You know – Islamic countries, they don't really like dogs much. Breaks your heart to see how they get mistreated there. Here's this poor, wretched little half-grown hound-dog, with ribs sticking out, covered with mange and oozing sores. Well, you know my boy Jerry, and how he hates to see anyone being picked on and hurting. He grabbed the sunshade that My Little Bride was carrying, and he went to waling on those boys like a whirlwind of fury, beating them off that dog. They weren't much bigger than him, being skinny, dirty street kids, but there were more of them; Jerry didn't hesitate for a minute." Clovis added, with an air of fatherly pride. "Belle was on his heels, screeching like a banshee. There was a policeman came up just then. I suppose that we might have all gotten into trouble, being that we were foreigners and all, but the doorman from our hotel came out, and he and the policeman began shouting at each other, while the street kids scattered, and Jerry picked up that poor little hound, and is saying to me, 'Dad, it's hurt and bleeding – can you do anything?' while Belle is hanging onto him and the dog, crying her eyes out, saying 'Poor, poor puppy!' and that dog is licking her hands." Clovis gave a frustrated and reminiscent sigh. "You ever have kids, Ricardo? You'll soon find out that all they have to do to talk you into anything is to cry."

"I would have thought Mrs. Walcott would be made of sterner stuff," Richard said, and Clovis chuckled.

"You would have thought so, but My Little Bride does have this streak of sympathy for anyone or anything reduced to living in the gutters. Me? I had half a mind just to let the damned dog go, once the kids tormenting it had gone off. You never saw such a wretched critter in your life: big patches of mange, scrapes and sores – hell, I think the street kids had been putting lit cigarettes against its belly, there were all these little round burns. Tail was crooked – been broken; One ear ragged and scabbed over. And Jerry is looking at me, cuddling that poor thing to him…"

"You yielded, of course." Richard ventured, and Clovis nodded.

"Of course. The hotel management were not enthused, but My Little Bride flashed her credit card, and the doorman sent for a veterinarian, while the kids ran a bathtub full of warm water and gave the dog a bath. Heck, probably the first time the wretched dog ever <u>had</u> a bath. Handled it pretty well, or maybe it was just stunned by the soap and water." Clovis chuckled in fond reminiscence. "To cut that part of the story short, the veterinarian made a house-call, did what was necessary, and when we left Morocco, the dog went with us. Oh, son, you can't even begin to imagine the border inspection paperwork, bringing that dog with us. I think Doc Wyler called up his congressman, thank god! Back to the dog, though; We named him Tongy, from Korean for mongrel or mutt – *ttong-gae*. When the Spanish job was done, we came back to Luna City to settle in one place, and finally build My Little Bride's dream house – start the kids in school – all that good stuff. I just put up with Tongy, because he was the kid's pet. I didn't think he was much of a dog, but he was devoted to the kids. I don't think that dog spent a night on the floor; he was on Jerry's bed or Belle's. And when Robbie was born, and we brought him home – there he was again, pattering about the crib, and whining whenever the baby cried."

"Like Nana the dog, in Peter Pan," Richard said, becoming intrigued, in spite of himself. "But I don't see why …"

"I would change my mind about Tongy?" Clovis smiled. He reached around to dig his wallet out of his back trouser pocket. "There's another story, if you have the patience. This is my favorite picture of Tongy and the kids. My Little Bride has the big version on the bedroom dresser in a fancy frame."

Clovis was just old school enough that he kept an old-style leather wallet with a sheaf of pictures in it; he flipped through the plastic sleeves, until he came to one in particular, which he held out for Richard to survey. This picture was a carefully composed studio portrait in somewhat faded colors; three children and a handsome light-brown dog with the clean short coat of a hound of no particular breed. The youngest child, a boy toddler, sat with his arm around the dog's neck. A girl child, just barely recognizable as

Belle, aged eight or so, knelt beside the smaller boy, and the oldest child – yes, that was Jerry Walcott – perched on a low stool, his arms wrapped around his knees. The photographer knew his business; all the children appeared relaxed, mildly cheerful, but the dog was alert, ears pricked forward.

"He looks like a good dog," Richard remarked, and Clovis folded away the wallet. "And the kids all look as if they adored him. What happened, that you changed your mind about him?"

"It happened on one of those days, when they had just started work on the house," Clovis folded away his wallet and replaced it in his trouser pocket. "Roman's guys had graded the driveway to the top of the hill and began bulldozing and leveling off the house site. One Sunday, before they were ready to start pouring foundations, we decided to go out there and have a picnic, look over the site, get an idea of what the view would be like … spend the afternoon looking around, getting an idea of what to do about landscaping. We wanted to keep some of the bigger trees, and maybe carve out some terraces for garden levels below the house. I called Roman, asked if he would join us for a while, so he could get an idea of what we were thinking; advise me if it were doable. Sunday afternoon, Conchita had a church meeting, so Roman has his daughter and niece with him; you know, Blanca and Beatriz. A bit of good fun for the girls, they were all in the Second Grade together with Belle. So, we get out to the property, on one of those gorgeous spring afternoons; comfortable out in the sun, cool in the shade, the wildflowers are in bloom, the big redbud trees where we wanted to establish the front gate, they're all blooming as well. The kids all went off with Tongy to explore the hillside after lunch, while Roman and I walk around, working out how to carve out the terraces." Clovis paused to bite into his cinnamon roll and continued. "We could hear the kids around the side of the hill,

Tongy barking now and then. There was a ledge of rock, like stair-steps halfway down the hill and little natural seep of water for a couple of weeks after it rains. I think the kids wanted to see if the seep was still running. Anyway, after a while, Roman and I hear Tongy barking – serious barking, not play-barking … and the girls were shrieking. You know – not playing, but genuinely distressed. Jerry came running up the deer path between the low brush. I didn't know what to think," Clovis shook his head. "Jerry could hardly speak for breathing hard. 'Come quick, Daddy! Tongy snapped at the girls and made like he was going to bite Belle! He's in the middle of the path, growling at us, if we try and go down to the rocks and the spring under it! Oh, my god, I think – that dog has gone rabid-mad. If we have to put him down the kids are never gonna forgive me!"

"So, what happened then?" Richard asked. "In all these sad tales, the dog usually dies. Is that what happened?"

"Not exactly," Clovis chuckled, a short and humorless chuckle. "Not then, anyway, although Roman was carrying. Just as a precaution. The coyotes can get bold, and those wild hogs are vicious bastards. We both went running down the path with Jerry. Yes, the girls were all bunched up, just short of that rock outcrop, with Tongy in the path downhill from them, barking to beat the band. He was," Clovis meditated on that memory, "acting like a herding dog, which is what Roman said to me as soon as we saw what was going on; it was almost as if he were trying to get the girls away, run them back up the path. Which is the reason I didn't order Roman to shoot him in the head as a danger to the kids. Tongy kept doing this darting thing, as if he wanted to chase the kids back up the trail." Clovis looked into the distance, staring at his long-ago memory of that scene.

Richard saw an opening, as the conversational silence dragged on. "So, what happened then? Was that when the dog died?"

"No, of course not," Clovis refreshed himself with another bite of the cinnamon roll. "Tongy lived almost to nineteen. Tough as old Army boots, as dogs go. A good old dog. We gave him a grand send-off when the time came. Dinner of rare steak, a trip to the ocean, Jerry came home to give him that last petting and hug. Canine lymphoma was what the veterinarian diagnosed. Doc Wyler came to the house for the final …" Richard could have sworn that Clovis appeared absolutely tearful, or at least, considerably less stoic, at speaking that last.

But Clovis continued. "Anyway, going back to that day; Roman and I came running down the path with Jerry. The girls were crying, Tongy barking … and Roman listens carefully and then looks at me. 'There's something down by the rocks; Clovis. I'm gonna check it out," he says, and he takes out this old Colt from under his vest that he got from his grandfather – I swear, that thing must be an antique by now, but it's a .45, so Roman meant business. He's used to shit out in the countryside, so I let him go at it; I wasn't carrying that day. What the hell, Ricardo, this was supposed to be our home, once it's built! I stay with the kids. As soon as Roman goes down the path toward the stone outcrop, Tongy stops carrying on so much, but he stays in the path, watching Roman go down towards the rocks, covering his six…"

"Like a good dog," Richard said. He had not that much experience with dogs, although he knew all the old verities; dogs were loyal, obedient, self-sacrificing … all of that. For himself, he liked cats better; but dogs were the better part of animal-kind, having thrown in their lot with humans so long ago, beyond the reach of historical documentation.

"A good dog," Clovis echoed. He took a steadying gulp of coffee and continued with the tale. "A very good dog. Roman vanishes round the bend in that little deer-path. The girls calm down and Tongy comes to stand next to Jerry and me – but watchfully. His ears are just pricked forward. Two, then three shots from the point where Roman walked down to the rock ledges. Tongy flinches a bit, the girls begin to whimper again. Then Roman appears around the bend in the trail through the scrub. 'You would not believe,' he says then. 'Colonel, you got the most humongous nest of rattlesnakes that I've seen at that rock ledge. I got three of the biggest." Clovis Walcott looked into the far mirror of memory for a long moment, and Richard held his peace; he was picturing the children – so small, innocent, defenseless – all romping down that path on the hill, heedless of the danger posed by poisonous snakes. Large, venomous snakes, with savage fangs. And there was the dog, their inarticulate, stalwart guardian, doing his loyal canine best to keep them safe. The mongrel rescued from a Moroccan street; mangy, starving, abused. Clovis continued, after that long moment.

"We took the kids back up to the top of the hill, away from those rocks. Of course, Roman didn't need to explain about how snakes prefer the bare rocks, warmed by the sun, when the nights have been cold, but Christ on a crutch, the biggest of the three was as large around the body as my arm, and there were a whole passel of smaller ones – and their venom is just as deadly, even more so, since they haven't expended as much. It made my blood run cold, thinking of how the kids could have blundered in and surprised them into striking at them or Tongy. These days, snakebites aren't guaranteed to be fatal, but … yeah, there's that one in a hundred." Clovis' jaw hardened. "Not my kids. Nor Roman's either. Or our dog – and a snakebite to a dog…"

"*There is sorrow enough in the natural way,*" Richard was given to quote, out of the vast store of poetry which his Gran had loved. (She had a whole tiny animal graveyard at the foot of her garden, with tiny stones and all, among the cosmos and petunias.) "*From men and women to fill our day; And when we are certain of sorrow in store? Why do we always arrange for more? Brothers and sisters, I bid you beware – of giving your heart to a dog to tear!*"

"Ah – Kipling," Clovis acknowledged with a sad smile. "A man of words, yeah? Well, that was it. That's why I'll give your freaky assistant cook a measure of tolerance when it comes to Belle, in spite of what My Little Bride thinks. I didn't think much of Tongy at the first – but he was there, with the last full measure of devotion, all where it counted. Luc's a pretty repellant piece of work, but that's what I thought of Tongy at first. Call it the benefit of the doubt, Ricardo. I'm old enough to have learned that lesson. And don't worry about My Little Bride," Clovis added. "She's a fiery-tempered woman, when it comes to our kids, especially Belle – but I'll talk her around."

"I'm sure that you will," Richard answered, and got up from the stammtisch with a feeling of relief. Mostly that he would still have an assistant cook, and that the father of that assistant cook's inamorata wouldn't be going all 'bring me the head of Afredo Garcia' on the poor drum-playing sod.

He did remind himself to open a can of salmon for Ozzie that evening, a special treat, for no reason in particular. A man might well give his heart for a dog to tear, or even for a cat to nibble at, delicately.

Christmas at Home With the Heisels

"Are you sure that Ozzie will be OK?" Kate asked, as she wheeled her little VW bug down the disgracefully rutted drive between the Age of Aquarius Campground and Goat Farm and Route 123. "I mean, we could have taken him with us, or left him in the trailer…"

Richard sighed. "Absolutely not, Kate of my heart. Your parents don't know me, let alone my cat. And if we left him behind, he would have pissed in the bed, through fury at having been left behind, and locked up for all of a day. Ozzie is a social cat, although I am not entirely sure of the beings that he chooses to be social with … after all, the mice must be absolutely narked at being stalked and hunted. Bree promised that she would take care of him and ensure that he was properly amused and diverted until tomorrow morning; she insists that Ozzie would relish a slumber-party at the Straw Castle, and absolutely promised that she would keep the Grants' other cats from beating up on him. He adores her as much as he adores you, since she saves out the juicy fish scraps for him, when we prep the Friday luncheon entree. Although she claims that he cheats at Monopoly something awful…"

"You're chattering, Rich," Kate shot him a sideways look from those amazing blue-green eyes; eyes the exact color and sparkle of very fine beryl jewels. "You're not nervous about meeting Mom and Dad, are you?"

"Yes," Richard confessed with another and even deeper sigh. "Paralyzed with terror, actually. I don't suppose that we could turn around and spend Christmas here … you know, I could fix you a splendid dinner, with a lovely little *bûche de Nöel* made from scratch, and we could open each other's gifts…"

"Nope, sorry," Kate replied, heartlessly, as she waited for a very large tanker lorry to pass on 123 northbound towards San Antonio, raising a cloud of grit as it blew past the unpaved and little-marked road from the Age. "You committed when I asked you about this two months ago, and every single time since then that I asked to reconfirm. Mom and Dad are expecting you to show … we've been dating for what – two years now? You simply must bite the bullet and show up with me for a traditional Griswald family Christmas gathering. Everyone is expecting to meet my nice English boyfriend. You promised that authentic English Christmas pudding with the flaming brandy for the dessert table, don't forget."

"Griswald?" Rich was utterly confounded. "What fresh hell might this be, Kate? Not that I have any intention of balking at the jumps – but what?"

"Christmas movie, about overdoing Christmas," Kate explained, and the tiny engine of the Bug roared obligingly as she stomped on the accelerator. "No, sweetie – you'll be fine. You've hung out often enough with Joe and Jess, and Araceli and Pat on Sunday afternoons; you'll be able to get along with Dad, and my big brother Matt, my other brothers, and Cousin Lester the shrink, if they want to talk about football. Especially if they want to talk about football; real football, not that soccer! Mom will be sweet – she thinks the world of you already, since she tried out that white-bean and garlic on pita chip dip at Thanksgiving, and everyone couldn't get enough of it. No, the 'rents will be cool. It's ...."

There was a long and heavily pregnant pause, nearly long enough to birth a litter of kittens. Richard thought it might be due to Kate's adamantine concentration on overtaking an enormous and ponderously slow articulated lorry, which had inconveniently decided to take up a lane and a half. Richard, his heart in his mouth, kept heroic silence. He could never entirely become comfortable with the insouciant manner in which Kate drove; a manner more befitting a some reckless movie daredevil intent on leaping over gaps in highways and abruptly raised drawbridges than a woman at the wheel of a VW Bug.

He didn't want to distract her. Not for a moment. When the Bug's little engine settled down to a steady purr, as the car slid into a position ahead of the enormous lorry, Richard recovered his voice.

"You said 'it's', Kate of my heart. As if there was an individual exception to a happy reception of my own self at your familial Christmas gathering. You'd better spill. You know how very much I hate unpleasant surprises. Such incidents are ... unsettling."

Another beat and a pause, as Kate cast a glance in the rear-view mirror.

"All right, then Rich. Poppa Fritz – my grandfather, Dad's dad – is coming to Christmas dinner. His girlfriend Hazel busted him out of the assisted-living place where he lives. No, not really busted, like she smuggled him out in a basket of laundry, or a sheet rope over the wall. She's a visiting nurse and social worker, which is how they met. She got him out totally legit. You'd like Hazel – she's …"

"Kate," Richard cleared his throat in a meaningful manner. "I care nothing for your grandfathers' social life among the geriatrics."

"Please," Kate replied, smartly. "Hazel is half his age. She likes him lots; says he's the most interesting and original guy she knows. But Poppa Fritz … it's going to be awkward, and I should have told you as soon as Mom texted me that he would be there, too."

"And?" Richard held his breath and his patience, as Kate zipped around another vehicle – this one a pickup truck piled high with two worn sofas and a large mattress, all inexpertly bungy-corded together. As soon as Kate eased the Bug into the fast lane, she confessed. Or something that sounded like a confession.

"Poppa Fritz is … a real character. He was born and raised on a little ranch way north-west of Boerne; you know that town up the highway from San Antonio that's pronounced 'Bernie'? Well, yeah – Poppa Fritz went to high school there. But he grew up speaking German; his first language. You know, there's heaps of people in the Hill Country who are ethnically a hundred and ten percent German, and there's ever so many of them. Enough that the Hill Country was basically German speaking – schools, churches, newspapers and everything, until … well, never mind about that. Poppa Fritz – Dad's father, to make it clear…"

"You're babbling again, Kate of my heart," Richard interjected.

"Am I? Sorry," Kate sounded honestly rattled, for nearly the first time in their acquaintance. Richard found this endearing; he held his tongue and waited patiently for Kate to elaborate. Which she did, as soon as she had negotiated another pass by a pickup truck – this one held what looked like a chest of drawers and a mass of dining-room chairs. "Well, he's 93, and kind of autocratic. He was in the war, you see. World War Two; he was in the paratroops, although he fibbed about his age initially, just to enlist in the Army after Pearl Harbor. He jumped on D-Day, although he never really talked about that to anyone but Matt…"

"What did he talk about, Kate of my heart," Richard ventured after a few moments, while Kate's little Bug bored down the featureless highway toward Karnesville, unimpeded by any other traffic.

"Mostly how he and three of his buddies broke out of their camp in England and went drinking in a local pub in the nearest town." Kate had her eyes resolutely on the highway, a single-mindedness of which Richard fully approved. "They didn't officially have liberty to leave camp. They went for a drink or two, and Poppa Fritz got arrested by the Home Guard and the local constable. They thought he was an escaped German prisoner of war. It was a bit embarrassing, as they were all in uniform. American uniform."

"Why would that have been a problem?" Richard demanded, in some indignation. "Our coppers aren't idiots even now, and they certainly weren't seventy years ago, even allowing for wartime paranoia."

"Because Poppa Fritz had a German accent, when he spoke English," Kate confessed. "He still does. And seriously – at the age of eighteen or so he looked like the perfect Hitler Youth recruiting poster. The brutal Hun personified from central casting in one of those old black and white war movies. Dad has a book at home with a picture of Poppa Fritz and his paratroop buddies as they were forming up the night before D-Day. Yeah; I'd have wondered, myself, American uniform or no."

"What happened, then?" Richard was honestly intrigued. His Gran had maundered over her memories of being a Land Girl at that time; more of the fun she had with her friends, not so much of the brutal agricultural labor which that wartime situation had involved.

"Their commander got …" Kate considered her phrasing with care. "Informed. Because of the ruckus when the local constable tried to arrest Poppa, and his pals took exception. To hear Poppa tell it, there was a lot of busted-up furniture and some bloody noses. The result was that everyone in his unit got confined to camp for a month as punishment, and the feelings were pretty bad all the way round, because nobody could go out drinking. The locals were pissed because Poppa Fritz and his buddies wrecked the pub and the constable and a couple of Home Guard volunteers were injured in the fracas. Later on, in France in the middle of the push back against the Germans, Poppa Fritz got separated from his unit, and when some British forces picked him up, they were all about shooting him as a German spy in US uniform." Kate sighed. "The way that Poppa Fritz tells it, he was about five minutes from being stood up against a wall and offered a last cigarette. He is still <u>very</u> angry about it all."

"The prospect of being shot at dawn does concentrate the mind wonderfully," Richard observed. "Kate, of Kate Hall, will there be sufficient other guests present that I may tactfully avoid close conversation with your formidable and justifiably resentful grandfather?"

"Most likely," Kate replied. "I mean, you won't have to sit next to him, or anything. There'll be my Mom and Dad, of course, and my brothers; Matt and Cherry and their kids, Pete and Marsha and theirs … Alan and Brenda with the baby – it's his first Christmas. My little bro Ken and his girlfriend. Then Cousin Lester and Marian, and I don't know which of their kids are coming, Bill

Weitzman from the University – you know him, right? He's one of the Luna City Players; and he dressed up as Marie Antoinette when the Karnes Company Rangers absolutely destroyed that stupid zombie movie? You remember?"

"That moment is branded irreversibly on my memory," Richard confessed, for it certainly was – the moment when a brawling band of cross-dressers came over the sunrise-lit ridge and charged downhill into the ranks of visibly-rotting zombie Mexican soldiers, to the detriment of the biggest movie moment ever to be filmed in or around Luna City.

Kate snickered. "Yeah, that moment lives on in infamy for Bill. He claims that his obituary, decades from now, will make note of his appearance in that awful movie. Anyway, between the family, and whatever friends who are at loose ends at Christmas … you should be able to avoid Poppa Fritz. Except that I'm Mom and Dad's only girl-child. Simply <u>everyone</u> will be wanting to check you out and make certain that you are good enough for their little Katie. No, you cannot go and hide out in the kitchen. Mom will simply not permit that until the main supper prep is done, and you put the final touches on the flaming Christmas pudding. Are you really going to pour flaming brandy over all?"

"Yes, I am," Richard answered. "And prepare the custard sauce … say, I won't be allowed in the kitchen until that moment?"

Kate took no apparent notion of his desperation. "No," she replied, heartlessly – especially heartlessly to Richard. "You simply have to meet my immediate kinfolk, Rich. They love me, you love me! And I … umm, rather love you. Time to move out of your comfort zone, Rich. Time to grapple with the human race. You know, those others of your kind? You are human, after all; or so we have always assumed…"

"I'm a time lord from Gallifrey," Richard returned, solid in his insistence, whereupon Kate favored him with a brief and heart-warming smile, and signaled a turn off Route 123, onto a side-road. Yes, they were almost to Karnesville. His doom was nearly upon him.

Kate drove through the scattered outskirts of Karnesville, which looked much like the scattering of streets where Luna City unraveled out to the pastures and thickets of countryside. The paved streets were lined with shallow ditches; no sidewalks that Richard could see. The houses were mostly the same undistinguished early to mid-twentieth century bungalows, now and again interspersed with older two or three-story mansard-roofed frame houses adorned with slightly worn fretwork.

The Heisel residence proved to be one of those larger, older ones, further ornamented with a wide veranda which wrapped around the left front corner. It sat square in the middle of a sweep of lawn, a lawn which was slightly the worse for winter wear, attended by a huddle of trees which had lost most of their leaves, raising bare and skeletal branches to the sky. Nine or ten automobiles, pick-up trucks and SUVs sat parked along the street nearest this house: a random but generally well-kept assortment. The day was shirt-sleeve comfortable, and the faint sounds of Christmas music floated out of opened windows, along with the murmur of genial conversation.

Kate slammed the driver-side door closed, as Richard fetched out the two fabric market bags from the back seat – one of them clinked, faintly.

"All ready to meet the dragon, my gentle knight Sir Richard?" Kate asked, with determined good cheer.

"As I'll ever be," he replied. *All for Kate ... really, how awful could her family be, aside from a geriatric veteran with an abiding grudge? Just because one member of a family was ... er ... difficult, it didn't argue that all the rest would be. Look at the Walcotts.* On that hopeful thought, he followed Kate towards the house – somewhat cheered as she reached for his hand. She didn't bother with ringing the doorbell or knocking. Unless she struck the panels with a sledgehammer Richard thought it likely that no one inside would have heard over the music, the rumble of voices, laughter, and the faint thread of a cartoon sound-track,. Kate just opened the door and walked in, towing Richard and his burden of market bags behind her, like the tail on an unresisting kite.

"Katie!" exclaimed the nearest and first person to notice their presence, and only after the door closed with a thump behind them, for the room immediately inside the Heisel manse was as crowded as a stand-up cocktail party in an old move. "Merry Christmas, kiddo – 'zat the boyfriend? Hey, welcome to the Heisel bear-pit, guy." That person embraced Kate while holding a Shiner beer bottle at arms-length in one hand; a broad-shouldered and capably fit-looking man of fortyish or so. He had the same dark hair as Kate, and the same brilliant smile. He wore a dark polo shirt with "Karnesville Fire & Rescue" embroidered over the pocket where the polo pony normally went.

"My big brother, Matt," Kate performed the introductions. "Matt, this is Richard."

"Oh, hey, you're the Café guy," Matt Heisel enthused and crushed Richard's hand with a welcoming grip. "The kids are gonna want to meet ya! They love Captain Kitten in the Kitchen! The kids don't miss an episode."

"Where's Mom and Dad?" Kate interjected, as Matt beamed approvingly at Richard.

"Where they usually are on Christmas afternoon. Mom's in the kitchen with Cherry and Marsha, agonizing over the turkey gravy, and Dad's out in back with Pete and Lester, supervising the brisket … say, Rich – they're all gonna meet you. Fortify first with a tasty adult beverage?"

"Yes, please," Richard clung to that as a drowning man clutches a life-ring. "A gin and tonic if it isn't too much. I brought some wine from Sefton Grant's little enterprise, by the way – and some brandy for the Christmas pudding…"

"I'll take that, sweetie," Kate murmured, as she relieved Richard of the two bags, and dropped a brief kiss on his cheek. "Don't worry, I'll pass on your instructions about boiling the pudding again to Mom, and Matt promised me that he'll take care of you – but you are not to set foot in the kitchen until it's time to do the custard sauce…"

"Don't worry, Li'l Sis," Matt answered with a broad grin. "I'll see that no one waterboards him." He added, in a slightly lower voice, "Joe Vaughn says your Brit boy-toy is solid, and that's good enough for me. And that his coffee is the bomb!"

"He is not my boy-toy!" Kate protested, and her brother grinned even more broadly. Yes, there was some interesting sibling-needling going on, a country to which Rich was entirely foreign, being an only child. Kate's expression magically changed to pleading. "And don't you dare hurt him or let anyone else hurt him. I want him undamaged and he's mine, you louse!"

"Sure, Li'l Sis," Matt returned with an air of indulgence, and added to Rich in an undertone. "She's never forgiven me for taking the head off her baby-doll to show her how the wetsy-diaper thing worked; she was in tears for a week." Then Kate was gone, leaving Richard feeling adrift in a sea of Heisels. Well, Kate was OK with leaving him in her oldest brother's social custody. For some unfathomable reason, Matt Heisel was in his corner.

The room was furnished with shabby comfortable furniture; armchairs and sofas with various tables squeezed between them. There was a comfortable feel to the room, a feeling which Richard had always associated with 19th century spaces, of walls papered with Morris wallpaper, interspersed by moderately ornate cornices, chair-rails and fireplace mantels. Otherwise it was also filled with … Heisels and friends, or so Rich assumed – and to his mild astonishment, most of them were playing board games like Scrabble and Monopoly, although there was a fast-moving game of Chinese Checkers going on over in the bay window, and some of the younger set were intensely bent over a game involving multi-sided dice and lists of … something or other.

There was only a brief pause in the level of conversation and laughter when Matt waved his arm and called out, "Hey, everybody, Kate and Richard are here!" Everyone but one of the Chinese Checker players looked up, murmuring a brief welcome before returning attention to their game. That exception swiftly tracked a marble the width of the board and scowled at his opponent. He was an elderly man with brush-cut grey hair, the oldest in the room. Richard assumed that this must be Poppa Fritz, from the expression of poisonous dislike that he shot in Richard's direction. "Don't bother to get up, anyone! Richard brought us a real old-fashioned English Christmas pudding," Matt continued. In a lower voice, he added to Richard. "Get you that drink now? Fortify yourself before meeting Dad?"

"If it's not any trouble," Richard replied. "And thank you. I did not know that it was an American tradition to play games, instead of watching football or something on the telly at Christmas."

"Heisel family tradition," Matt grinned. "From time immemorial. The kids are in the den, watching Christmas cartoons. Ours will wanna ask a million questions; don't say that I didn't warn ya. They'll be sorry you didn't bring Captain Kitten. C'mon, we got the bar set up in the dining room."

Matt led the way into the adjoining room, which proved to be every bit as comfortably set up, even if there was a slight air of disuse about it. An ornate Victorian sideboard towered over a pair of tables set with china, silver and glass, like the Matterhorn looming over the Alpine valley below. On the sideboards' main surface, an array of bottles, glasses, a covered ice bucket and implements were arrayed in perfect formation; the dignity of it all somewhat spoiled by a Styrofoam cooler on the floor next to it. The cooler proved to be full of more ice and cans of soft drinks and mixers. Matt capably poured a measure of gin into a tall glass, filled the rest with tonic water and ice, and added a quarter of lime to the top. Then he drew out another bottled beer and popped the crimped cap with one of the handy nickel-plated and obviously expensive bar tools laid out on the sideboard.

"So, how did you come to start dating Katie?" Matt inquired as he handed over the tall glass. Richard regarded it skeptically; the largest gin and tonic he had ever seen mixed for him.

"We met," Richard steadied himself with a sip; the gin was so strong he hit back an urge gasp and cough. "Ummm … it was a social event a couple of years ago that Kate was covering for the *Beacon*. We talked very briefly. And then it turned out that we had mutual friends; Araceli and Pat Gonzalez began inviting me over to their place on Sunday afternoons. Araceli works at the Café, you know. I was there with them at Mills Farm when their little boy found the Mills Treasure gold piece. It sort of grew from there, you see. Joe and Jess Vaughn are also mutual friends …"

"Good old Joe," Matt Heisel chuckled fondly. "Never played against him; he was only a freshman when I played for the Knights, but the fun we had chewing over old times when we ran into each other in this dive in Fayetteville. We keep in touch now, you know? Army, me – Airborne all the way! I'm in the Karnesville FD now and we still run into each other at veteran things."

"Amazing," Richard murmured.

Matt chuckled. "No, not so much. Texas is one big small town, cunningly disguised as a humongous state. Hey, look – come out to the back and meet Dad. But I gotta tell you a couple of things; things that you and I ought to have clear between us. Come out on the porch and siddown." Matt led Richard out through the long French door which seemingly led to the deep and substantial porch, set with comfortable wicker chairs and a substantial swing padded with tropical-print cushions and throw pillows. He took a seat on the swing and regarded Richard with a look freighted with menace and meaning. Richard quailed and wished that he had insisted on taking on Poppa Fritz first. *How much trouble could a geriatric former paratrooper be?*

Now Matt continued, after a swig of his beer. "First off, Rich; I know about the flood rescue thing at Mills Farm a couple of years ago. You went out with Joe's Uncle Harry to rescue that family…"

"Bastard," Richard remarked with feeling. He took a seat on the nearest wicker chair, as gingerly as if it had been wired for electricity and gathered his thoughts as Matt chuckled again. "I wanted it all to be … bloody discrete. I didn't want any credit! I was drafted under protest into that particular sodding enterprise by an old-age pensioner with a rotten bad attitude, in a cockleshell old tin boat with a wonky engine and it was only through the greatest good luck that we had any success at all in rescuing that family!"

"Yeah, that's what Cousin Hernando said," Matt covered the top of his beer, as a puff of strongly scented BBQ smoke blew over them, a smoke of rich burning woods, as if a sacrifice to the gods. "But you went out anyway. And I know that Poppa Fritz already is prejudiced against you – that English … err, that flaming asshole, he calls you. He's convinced you're gay in spite of all celebrity reportage to the contrary."

"What!?" Richard almost choked on a mouthful of gin and tonic, flummoxed beyond all coherence.

Matt shrugged, in reply. "I did some internet searches on your name; both of them, when Katie messaged that she was going out for a supper date with you. What are big brothers for, if they can't also appeal to a county sheriff pal to run a wants and warrants search on potential dates? Now, Poppa Fritz has his reasons for not being all-in for you, but they are seventy-year-old reasons, so I seriously wouldn't pay them any mind. I don't think that the family will, in any case. But on the grounds of what you did for that family, and because Katie likes you, and Joe thinks you're solid; you're OK in my book. You and Katie … she could sure as hell do worse in this world." Matt shot a particularly piercing look in Richard's direction. "So, I'm OK with you and my li'l sis doing whatever it is you have going on. Consider that I've got your back, unless and until you show yourself to be one of the biggest a-holes in the Western World. Make my little sister cry for any reason, and you'll be dealing with me, the minute I hear about it."

"I have no intention of ever making Kate cry," Richard recovered his voice, his temper, and his composure. "And as a matter of fact, you made her cry yourself, when you decapitated her doll! I take serious exception to anyone who makes Kate cry!"

"She was three and I was fourteen!" Matt replied, momentarily indignant. "But I see your point. And I accept that your intentions are honorable towards Katie. We're good. You ready to meet Dad, now? He's been supervising the brisket since last night. It's another Heisel tradition – turkey as well as hickory-smoked brisket for

Christmas dinner. Dad uses an old family recipe, and when he married Mom, they sort of had to combine traditions."

"I've become inordinately fond of smoked brisket since taking up residence in Texas," Richard felt his mouth begin to water. Perhaps … just perhaps he might have a chance, a wispy ghost of a chance of enjoying himself at this holiday gathering. "Lead on, then."

At the end of the verandah, a pair of sagging wooden steps led down to ground level, and a path of flagstones set into the winter-bleached short grass staggered around to the back like the footsteps of a particularly clumsy giant. A matched pair of concrete stripes ended at a garage of the old-fashioned detached sort. It was rather like the old stable and garage with the living quarters upstairs which sat around the back of Miss Letty's house. Only this one didn't actually incorporate an upstairs apartment. Instead it boasted an open-sided arbor on one side, with the woodwork twined throughout with bare grapevines, the largest branches of which were the thickness of a man's arm. Before this venerable and somewhat ramshackle structure stood massive, soot-blackened metal barbeque/smoker on wheels, sending a thin trickle of delightfully scented smoke skywards. A dozen folding patio chairs were scattered around, as if a storm had blown in and left them in place. A stocky man with a long BBQ fork in one hand, and a beer bottle in the other hovered over this soot-stained behemoth. Richard could not see much family resemblance to Matt and Kate, really. Mr. Heisel senior was a middle-aged cove, with indeterminately fair hair fading into white and sparse, covered by a red ballcap tilted back: "Make Cotton Great Again" was the motto embroidered along the front of it.

"Hey, Pops, how's the brisket coming?" Matt drawled and gestured with his own beer bottle. "Need another one? I've brought Katie's boyfriend out to meetcha."

"Getting there," Mr. Heisel replied. "This one's OK," and from the way that he eyed Rich, somewhat skeptically, he wasn't passing judgment on anything but the beer. "But you can go tell your Mom, about another half hour. Lemme have a private conversation with Mr. Hall, OK?"

"Sure, Pop," Matt replied, and in the next moment, Kate's brother vanished into the house by a back door. There was nothing much to say, and Richard waited, with shredding patience, for Mr. Heisel to assume the conversational lead. The silence lengthened, as Mr. Heisel opened the BBQ cover, fussed over the contents within – which looked to be coming along nicely, to judge by the entrancing scent of slow-roasted meats, slathered with the contents of a small cast-iron pot, also on the griddle. Richard couldn't stand any more silence.

"I'd say from my weekly experience at the Gonzalezes – that the brisket is indeed coming along nicely. How do you do, sir – Richard Astor-Hall. We … that is … Kate, your daughter and I ... we have been … umm … seeing each other. Keeping company. Something like that. Which does not involve sex … Oh, Christ…" Richard took a deep gulp of the insanely-potent G&T. "I have the utmost respect for Kate, sir … I would not presume…" Richard took a second gulp, just to armor himself against the pain and possibility of being driven from the premises and festivities by repeated blows from hot BBQ tools.

"That's good," Mr. Heisel replied, judiciously. "You're a cook yourself? Katie said something about that, a while ago. How do you prefer your BBQ, then?"

"Slow-cooked, Texas style," Richard answered. "As that is the mode to which I have been primarily exposed. I remain agnostic regarding the meat involved, although I find I am inclined towards beef. But pork ribs are appetizing, given if they are sufficiently meaty to be worth the trouble. I have tasted pit-roasted whole pig which I felt was the food of the gods…"

"Completely different technique," Mr. Heisel chided him.

Richard recovered now that the topic of conversation was on familiar ground. "I am not wedded to any particular method," he declaimed. "I appreciate any and all techniques peculiar to the culinary arts and consider none of them beneath consideration. It has been an enlightenment to me, as I was trained in the strict French tradition of the culinary arts."

"Oh, France," Mr. Heisel shrugged, dismissively. "Got their good points, I reckon. But barbeque is a whole 'nother art in itself."

"Do tell," Richard urged, mostly as a means of keeping the conversation limping along, but Mr. Heisel's somewhat lugubrious expression brightened at those words. "I am always fascinated by such matters."

Mr. Heisel sipped from his beer, consulted his watch. "Are you, indeed?"

"Cooking is my life," Richard assured him.

Mr. Heisel grinned, a fleeing and rather shy grin. "Mine too, in a strictly amateur way. My great-great grandfather was supposed to have invented barbeque, back in the day. He and his father had a butcher-shop in New Braunfels; that was one of the German towns, when there was not much in the way of refrigeration for stuff that didn't sell during the day. The family story has it that Great-great-grandfather Bernhard Heisel thought of putting the unsellable bits on a rack in the family smokehouse and selling them as something cooked and ready-to-eat the next day. Or maybe the day after…"

Richard cleared his throat. "I'm pretty certain that other local butchers had the same problem and the same solution. The 19th century was one pretty much deprived of large-scale refrigeration technology."

Mr. Heisel beamed. "But you see – in the summer, Texas was hot! Day and night hot, even in the Hill Country! No such thing as a cool room for unsold meats, not in quantities as a commercial butcher had to sell. Can you imagine the smell, as meats began to putrefy in the summer? And the economic loss. Time is money, cut meat is money. No, I am certain that other butchers had the same notion. But Great-great-grandfather Bernard had a local friend with an interest in processing local chili-peppers for out-of-season sales. They say that the friend made a fortune from it, eventually, once he moved to San Antone. But before he ever came up with that formula, he mixed a special mix for Bernard to rub on the leftover meats for the smokehouse … and so the craze was born right then and there for spiced beef and pork, smoked or slow-roasted. There is no way to prove it in the record books," Mr. Heisel added hastily. "Just family stories … and our secret recipe."

"Might I ask…" Richard began.

Mr. Heisel favored him with a slow and mischievous wink. "You may not. It's a family secret. Marry our little girl, and I'll write it down and give it to you as a wedding gift, but not a day before. Understand?"

"Perfectly," Richard agreed. "It sounds … but don't assume that I am being ungallant – perfectly reasonable. Miss Heisel – Kate – is a marvelous woman. A brilliant, talented, far-seeing woman. I fear that I am not now worthy of her or will ever be truly worthy. I have been…" Richard gulped and plunged, as if into icy water. "A right bastard where women in my past have been concerned. Inconsiderate, self-centered. The intelligent ones among them effed off as soon as that became obvious to them, I am afraid. So, I can never be wholly convinced that I might be able to make her happy for more than the moment, or the evening. It's my own personal failing…" Richard was wondering, even as he spoke, how powerful was that gin & tonic, and had Matt somehow sneaked a powerful, alcohol-based truth serum into it? He couldn't ever recall having been that honest with someone unless it was Kate herself.

"Well, that's all right, then," Mr. Heisel returned, comfortable in receipt of a painful confession, like a priest who has heard everything in his time in the confessional and remained completely bomb-proof. "Have a seat, Rich – take a load off your feet. You respect and appreciate her, so that's how it stands. No one is perfect, you know. Not any of my kids are perfect, so don't beat yourself up because you think you don't measure up to our Katie. Even Matt was an asshole teenager, until he joined the Army and straightened out." Mr. Heisel took a seat on the nearest of the folding chairs: Richard followed suit, discretion warning him to shut the heck up and hear what the father of his Kate – his lovely, sensible, intelligent Kate – was about to say.

"You can grow out of being an asshole," Mr. Heisel confided. "Matt did. He was your typical smart-mouthed, shaggy-haired, know-it-all teenager. Lazed around the house, spent the nights hanging out with worthless friends, worked at nothing much when he got out of high school and got fired frequently. The Missus and I worried about him, which is something to wonder at now, seeing as how he turned out. He wasn't like our Katie…" Mr. Heisel's expression warmed. "Katie was a love; never gave us a moment of worry, not even when she decided that she wanted to be a reporter and work for a big-city newspaper. 'Katie,' I said then, and she was only fifteen or so – 'that's a recipe for professional disaster. You'll be living at home or in some cold-water dump, forever and ever, never make a living enough to have your own nice place' … but she made it all work. You've got a good girl in Katie. She'll never let you down or sell you out."

"She has proved that, several times over," Richard confessed, reflecting on the many times that Kate – his adorable, stalwart Kate – could have shopped him to the tabloids, or even to her own employer, the little regional weekly newspaper. Damn if that chair wasn't comfortable, the drink satisfying, or the general conversation inviting of confidences.

"But Matt," Mr. Heisel continued. "We really despaired. Until he took it into his head to talk to an Army recruiter. Maybe Dad – you know, my own Dad – Poppa Fritz? Maybe he put a bee in Matt's bonnet. Matt went off to basic training, and he was a changed kid after that; changed in a good way. We went to his graduation parade at Fort Sill." Mr. Heisel took a long draft of his own beer, and meditatively regarded the column of smoke rising from his BBQ stove. "Made a long road trip of it, with Poppa Fritz, Katie, and the younger boys. We couldn't hardly recognize Matt; he was that changed. Tanned and fit, clean and respectful. Poppa Fritz went up to Matt's drill instructor, shook hands and tried to give him a fifty-dollar bill. 'What for?' said the drill instructor; he was that baffled. Poppa Fritz said, 'Gratitude – my grandson has a haircut and a job, and he just called me 'sir', that's what for!'" Mr. Heisel chuckled, reminiscently, and shot a shrewd, sideways glance toward Richard. "Matt and I, we talked about it a couple of times, long afterwards. Matt said that it was like waking up; suddenly he realized what he was headed for in the rest of his life, and he realized that he didn't want to be that shiftless, meth-addled loser, living in a trailer park with a toothless girlfriend. I think it happened the first time his drill instructor got blunt with him. It's never too late to grow up, if you've a serious mind to do it, and conditions are aligned in your favor."

"Your faith in me is touching," Richard blurted, although he winced at the mention of living in a trailer park. He lived in an Airstream at the Age of Aquarius Campground and Goat farm, and rather liked that life. "So is Kate's … I swear, I have no notion of why she puts up with me at all."

"For your cooking," Kate herself replied, having come up unseen from the back of the house. Richard jumped from a recumbent position in the lawn chair, unspilled drink in hand, as Kate added, with a smile. "Don't sell yourself short, sweetie; you have other fine qualities. Mom says it's OK for you to check on your pudding, now that the turkey is out of the oven and resting. How's the brisket doing, Pops?"

"Another fifteen minutes," Mr. Heisel replied.

"Timing is everything," Kate tucked her hand into Richard's elbow. "Come and check on your pudding and meet Mom. But you absolutely <u>cannot</u> hide out in your favorite comfort zone for the rest of Christmas."

"Why not?" Richard grumbled, as Kate steered him up the back steps of the old house, and across a covered porch which seemed to serve as a kind of catch-all for garden furniture brought in for the winter. "I like my comfort zone. I'm safe there, because I am the absolute king of the place."

"You need to develop a social life," Kate replied. "Because life is so ever much more amusing with one and Cousin Lester would say that you needed to recalibrate."

"I've been adjusting and recalibrating for months," Richard still felt inclined to grumble in protest, as Kate opened the back door. "Sundays with Araceli and Pat and the rest. Monday with you. Wednesday training at the VFD, Friday at the VFW for happy hour.

What more could you want of me?" She brushed his cheek with a brief kiss, as light and brief as a butterfly alighting.

"You have, love," she pointed out. "But it's like exercise; once you start, you have to keep upping the level. Christmas with the Heisels is the next level."

"Thank you, very much," Richard barely breathed, still feeling quite sour over how he had been dragooned into all this. But still – for Kate and her ongoing affection and trust, he would endure much, much worse. Not that he would ever confess it – because he was certain that she would serve him up a heaping helping of much, much worse. All in the service of upping the level, naturally.

The kitchen of the old house was a suitably roomy one, only a little damaged by a faddish redecoration some four or five decades previous, which left the place cursed with a massive gas stove and a refrigerator unit, both enameled an unfortunate shade of slime green. This big old-fashioned room was dominated by a central island-cum-worktable-and-cutting board. Something enormous in a tub-sized roasting pan, tented with half an acre of aluminum foil dominated the worktable, attended and surrounded with an array of covered serving dishes and vast serving platters. But for the relative size of the room, and the revolting color of the large appliances, Richard was reminded irresistibly of his Grans' comfortable cottage kitchen, even to the open shelves of a monumental dresser, filled with a random assortment of china, and an old-fashioned coffee grinder.

There was but a single person in the room. A comfortably plump lady of certain years; dark hair and with the same amazing blue-green eyes as Kate, fussing over a steaming kettle on the stove. Kate's mother, Richard surmised at once; confirmed when Kate announced,

"Mom, this is Richard. How is the steamed pudding doing?"

The comfortably plump lady wiped her hands on the kitchen towel tucked into the apron waistband and beamed warmly at Richard. "Richard – how lovely to meet you in person, finally! Kate has told me so much about you, I think that we know you very well already!" Kate's mother enfolded him in an exuberant and familial embrace. "There you are – your first Heisel family Christmas! How brave of you! But you know that this whole family thing is a blending of traditions! Food – everything good and welcome, and enough leftovers to feed the family for at least a week. Kate gave me strict instructions for your pudding, you see … Katie, dear – will you tell the girls that we can dish up the sides, now? Tell everyone to wrap up their games, supper will be served in ten minutes as soon as the brisket is off the fire and the turkey is rested…"

Ah, Richard told himself, as he returned the embrace; *Mother Heisel is the social butterfly of the family. And Kate will be like her, in about three or four decades. I can live with that. I can live with her – as if I needed any further reassurance.*

Meanwhile, Kate's mother chattered cheerfully away. "I didn't know what to expect from a Christmas pudding! I have only read about them in novels. And you pour flaming brandy over them to serve? How very peculiar! Oh, custard sauce! Kate said that you would want to prepare that yourself, but that there was hardly any secret to it. Still, though – you brought your own double-boiler and whisk!"

"It's a matter of being comfortable with my own tools," Richard answered. "I'd have brought my own stove, if it were possible."

Mrs. Heisel erupted in the most charming giggles. "Oh, I know! Whenever we travel to visit the other children, I must bring my own pillow and comforter! Nothing else will do, in the least.

Will the custard sauce take much time? I suppose when we pause for seconds, then you can go and prepare it. All in the timing, I know. Katie says that you are terribly strict about timing; only to be expected, considering the constraints of a restaurant. Ten minutes too late, and a dish is absolutely ruined, ten minutes too early, and it's barely warm…"

At that very moment, Kate's father came in from the back, the old-fashioned screen door falling closed with a clatter. He held an enormous aluminum pan in his oven-mitted hands, similarly tented with more aluminum foil.

"The brisket is done!" Mrs. Heisel exclaimed cheerily and welcomed the alternate main course with a fond kiss on the cheek of the bearer of it. "Katie has gone to tell everyone that supper is served … oh, you did meet Richard? Katie's beau – I hope that you had a nice talk; he's such a nice young man, and with a useful profession? I did tell you about how Katie set him up with the Captain Kitten in the Kitchen. Such useful recipes, and such a dear little cat! His pet and companion, you know. Although it's not actually his cat, doing the recipes…"

"I know, dear," Mr. Heisel dropped the pan on the vast central table, just as the interior door opened and closed; a gaggle of women burst through it – a spectacle at which Richard would have quailed, save that the hindmost was his Kate.

"We're almost ready!" chirped the nearest of them, as she brushed past Mrs. Heisel. "Hi, I'm Susan – Matt's my guy! Our kids love your podcast! You gonna do something next week about doing something with turkey leftovers?"

"I might," Richard conceded warily, as the female kitchen brigade swarmed the center table; one of the younger women began emptying hot water from the assortment of covered dishes which had been staged there – to warm the dishes, of course. He approved of this most heartily. Meanwhile, Mr. Heisel was transferring a massive chunk of savory smoked brisket to the butcherblock tabletop and deftly transforming it into luscious, savory-juice-dripping slices. "Although," he added, "I might come up with some notions for leftover brisket, as well."

Mr. Heisel sent him a sharp glance, as sharp as the knife with which he was performing brisket-dissection. "There's never any leftovers for my brisket, though. Turkey, yes – my brisket, no."

"I stand corrected," Richard acknowledged, judging that a spirit of humility might best be his refuge. "What about the turkey, then?"

"Poppa Fritz carves that at the head of the table," Kate assured him. "He's a whiz with that electric carving knife, and he never misses a chance to show off with it. The assisted living place won't let him carve any more, ever since he threatened the assistant director with the knife. And it wasn't even plugged in at the time!"

"Best laugh I have had in years," added the comfortably middle-aged lady with suspiciously lemon-yellow hair done up in a medium poof, as she plated a vat of … orange vegetables into one of the heated serving dishes. "They confiscated that knife before he could carve up the Easter ham a couple years ago. Fritzi was really pissed about that. He thinks that the staff at the Residence all are all out to get him on holidays, but I talked him down." She nodded companionably towards Richard. "Hazel Gordon. Pleased to meetcha, Rich; Fritzi bent my ear all about you on the way down, but don't worry. He's at the head of the table, and you're way down at the end, with Katie and the elder grandkids. Consider it a graduation from the kiddie table, OK? Hafta say, I really liked that bean dip thing at Thanksgiving." Hazel added, almost inconsequentially.

"I'll show you where to sit, then," Kate tucked her hand into Richard's elbow, in a most confidant manner, and gently pulled him away from the scene of an abundance of holiday entrees and sides being plated.

"I wanted to pick out the platter to serve the pudding on," Richard complained, and Kate replied.

"You can do that when you set up the custard sauce. Mom will put the eggs on the side to come up to room temp, and the bottle of cream as well." She gave his arm a comforting squeeze. "Don't worry. Mom has your back in the kitchen, and Hazel and Dad between them will wrangle Poppa Fritz into behaving himself." In the brief passage between the old-fashioned kitchen, and the dining room, Kate went in tiptoes and brushed his cheek with a brief, butterfly-light kiss. "Try and enjoy this, 'kay? A meal which you didn't slave throughout the day to produce. Remember what it was like to eat a meal you didn't cook?"

"Of course, I do," Richard grumbled. "And most of the time, it was inedible, ghastly slop. That's why I trained as a chef; so that I would never have to eat ghastly, boarding-school slop or fast-food garbage-onna-bun ever again."

"Not at Mom and Pop's," Kate rewarded him with another fleeting kiss. "And especially not for Christmas dinner, with all the family gathered. So, OK, Cherry has always done that ghastly green bean casserole, but she is Matt's wife, so we accommodate for the sake of tradition, and some of the family even like it. You don't have to take a bite of it – there'll be plenty of other sides. … but honestly – all the rest is as good as ever you cooked in the Café, or for Carême. Just be appreciative of Mom's turkey and Dad's brisket. Be good for me, please. And don't deliberately provoke Poppa Fritz!"

"I won't," Richard hissed. "Promise on my word as a gentleman."

"Thanks, love," Kate beamed. "And Cherry is adventurous. She fixes her green bean casserole with cream of celery soup, rather than the customary cream of mushroom!"

"Cutting-edge innovation in the kitchen," Richard grumped, and Kate giggled. She drew him into the dining room, miraculously set now with fine china, gleaming silverware, and cut-crystal which glittered like ice under sunshine. Centerpieces adorned the table, glorious silver stemmed bowls, arranged with seasonal fruit; small pumpkins, glossy red pomegranates and small tangerines, ears of jewel-colored corn, and vases crammed full of stems of holly – or something which looked like holly – all red berries and green spiky leaves. Richard stood amazed. "Christ, it looks like a set for a production of *A Christmas Carol* – the party feast scene."

"We Heisels don't do anything by halves," Kate replied, somewhat smugly. "And that's where the kids sit."

The wide dividing doors which separated the dining room from the front parlor had been drawn aside, making a single large room. The gaming tables arrayed in the parlor had also been drawn together and dressed in white linen, with similar holly-filled centerpieces, yet set with plates, glasses and tableware of a slightly less value quality – to Richard, it looked like ordinary melamine, plain tableware and glasses.

"Not certain that I wholly approve of this," Richard murmured. "How are the barbarian young to be civilized, save by the example of their elders?"

"Our barbarian young are usually more interested in eating and going back to watch the rest of the movie before dessert is served," Kate sighed. "Myself, I couldn't <u>wait</u> to move to the adult table – Thanksgiving of the year that I was a junior in high school. I wrote about it for *The Scholar* – that's the student magazine at St. Scholastica's. Brother Gerald liked that essay so much that he put it on the front page. I was so thrilled. My first cover story! That's when I broke it to Mom and Dad that I wanted to major in journalism when I went to college … we're sitting here, opposite Alan and Brenda – that's my youngest brother and his wife. Matt and Cherry are sitting next to Mom and Dad and Hazel at the other end – all the better to distract Poppa Fritz, I guess."

"An excellent plan," Richard approved. Anything which kept him far – as far as could be possible in a dining room – from a geriatric with an ancient and abiding grudge and armed with an electric carving knife.

Now the door to the dining room opened; Mrs. Heisel entered trundling what looked like an old-fashioned bar cart, upon which sat the enormous turkey on a platter, followed by the other women of the female kitchen brigade, all bearing covered dishes and platters.

"Chow down!" Matt Heisel bellowed, somewhat inelegantly from the hallway, as all those dishes were transferred with efficiency to the table, and the sideboard. Richard imagined that he could hear the boards whimper slightly, if not an outright groan under the heavy and delicious-smelling weight of turkey, brisket, mashed potatoes, bread and sausage stuffing, sweet-potato souffle, two gravy boats of rich brown gravy, a medley of braised sprouts … and other dishes whose contents were covered and left to be a gourmand's surprise. A small rush of footsteps in the hallway, and the lesser table rapidly filled with every age of the immature species from a pair of five-year-olds perched on booster seats, all the way up to a handful of gangling teenagers. Richard, steered by Kate's comfortable hand on his elbow, took a chair close to the bottom of the table, flanked by and across from a handful of slightly-older than teenage youths, boys and girls alike; the family resemblance bearing true enough across the generations for at least three of them.

"Matt's oldest, Frankie and Margaret," Kate enlightened him in a whisper, "And Bill Weizman's son – he has custody this year, I guess – and I don't know, if friend or kin. Mom and Dad collect strays."

"Consider me warned," Richard murmured in reply, as everyone took their seats, in a grand and noisy shuffle of chairs and feet scraping on the floor. At the head of the table, Mr. Heisel cleared his throat.

"For the blessing, please," he ventured, sounding rather tentative at first. "A silence, and bow your heads… for this bountiful meal and the company of our family and friends, and those blessings and gifts showered upon us all … may we give thanks to our Lord and Creator… good food, good friends, good God, let's eat!"

"Amen!" chorused the multitude at the tables among a ripple of laughter, and the clatter and traffic of dishes passing, with the buzzing obbligato provided by the electric carving knife. Grandpa Fritz began skillfully disassembling the gargantuan roast turkey and slicing even cuts of pale breast and darker leg meat.

"I like your father," Richard murmured, under the cover of those pleasant murmur. "He doesn't stand on ceremony. I imagine that everyone is hungry, after a hard afternoon of board games…"

"Shut up, you!" Kate murmured back. "And pass the platters. Dad went for the long blessing, this year."

"Pass to the left around the table, I know," Richard said, as the first of a veritable avalanche of serving dishes began processing around the two tables, promising that bounty of good things, promised in the blessing to be showered on all.

And it all promised to be good, Richard realized almost at once, as every passed dish paused in the temporary space between his and Kate's place settings; a bit of salad, served out with silver tongs onto the small plates arrayed to the left of the main plate and silverware. Baked yams, crusted with brown sugar and toasted pecans; roasted sprouts with slivers of red onion and chunks of sausage; the historic green-bean casserole *(of which he took only a small spoonful, to be courteous)*; a garnish of stewed spiced pears and raisins and several glass dishes full of cranberry compote *(which he made room for on the salad plate)*; creamy mashed potatoes; a scoop of richly fragrant bread and sausage stuffing; and then came the turkey, attended lovingly by a boat of gravy; the platter of smoked brisket … all too much for words, and almost more than an ordinary dinner plate could bear. Biscuits, bread rolls and hot cornbread were also offered, piled up in a number of baskets set about the table, … a bounty indeed. Richard noted that most of the breads were swathed in crisply-ironed cloth napkins, and with a warmed flat disc of unglazed pottery at the bottom of the basket. This warmed his sense of presentation and utility, almost as much as they warmed the rolls, biscuits and crumbly-cut squares of cornbread

The traditional English Christmas dinner had nothing on an American Thanksgiving, Richard realized. He was hungry, more than hungry. He had last eaten eight hours previously; a couple of slices of toast with butter and cup of tea. Mere memories now. And it was all going well: Mr. and Mrs. Heisel and Matt had received him hospitably, and with every indication of affectionate regard. So all was well … perhaps there was a chance of making a sort of peace with the grudge-bearing O.A.P. with the brush-cut hair at the head of the table, still regarding Richard with baleful resentment over the semi-stripped turkey carcass.

The Christmas pudding … that ought to do it, Richard thought. The crowning achievement and a gesture of peace to Kate's irascible old grandfather. Bring it to the head of the table, all spectacularly wreathed in blue flames generated from a puddle of brandy… yes. That would be the ticket. His gesture of good faith. He ate – and it was a marvelous meal, all told, all the while considering how some of the dishes could be translated and offered at the Café … why had no one ever told him about traditional American Thanksgiving cooking? Aside from the unfortunately commercial aspects, about which every one of his previous acquaintance had sniggered in a superior fashion, usually making some jest about nasty cheap TV suppers.

And he had not had to cook a single dish of what was on offer, arrayed around the Heisel's groaning board. He searched for Kate's hand, under cover of the tablecloth, found it and gave a comforting squeeze, which was returned, even as she smiled at him sideways.

"So … how did you train that cat to cook, sir?" earnestly inquired the teenager sitting opposite, after the procession of dishes had completed their circuit of the table, returning to their resting places as everyone got down to the serious eating. "We can't even get ours to 'fetch'. Is there some kind of secret to training a cat?"

"Video-editing," Richard answered. Kate squeezed his hand again, and he realized that he had sounded rather waspish and impatient. Kate was in a warning mode. "Seriously," Richard continued, carefully modulating his tone of voice. "It's all a bit of video magic. Our cat isn't really cooking … Katie just snaps pictures of him posing with all the tools and then she edits that footage together with … scenes of my staff posing with that silly cat-head thing…"

"Cool," the teenager answered. "I want to get into that kind thing… is there some kind of course you can take?"

"Self-education," Kate replied, before Richard – utterly flummoxed – could formulate a sensible reply. He devoted himself to his plate, savoring every bite; tasting, analyzing, considering, while Kate enlightened the younger generation. He lost himself in visualization of how the most sublime dishes at the Heisel table could be translated and incorporated into the regular menu at the Café, only coming up to the surface of table conversation when Kate nudged him, and murmured,

"OK, while everyone who wants them is getting second and third servings. This is your best time to use Mom's kitchen for the custard sauce…"

"On it, my most beloved Kate of Kate Hall," Richard replied, in the same low voice. He raised Kate's hand, still held in his, and kissed it, ere they parted.

"Do me proud, lover," Kate answered, and Richard took the memory of those blue-green and jewel-tinted eyes into the kitchen, where he was soon joined by Kate's mother and a double-boiler, with the bottom pan of water already simmering.

It was a positive bliss to be alone – well, nearly alone – in a comfortable old-fashioned kitchen, industriously stirring a concoction of egg-yolks, heavy cream, milk, sugar infused with a whole vanilla bean in the smaller pot, suspended over the bubbling lower pan, until the custard sauce was thick enough to coat a cold spoon, with a fine-mesh sieve and the serving pitcher at hand. Mrs. Heisel watched as she tended to the resupply of serving platters, borne into and away from the massive island by relays of the younger of the Clan Heisel. Nothing interrupted his thoughts, communing as they were with the spirit of Carême and every one of the minor culinary gods. Richard was inordinately pleased by this; Kate did not hector him when he cooked for her, only asked the occasional leading question and took down his responses. He also had a smaller saucepan on the 'warm' hob, a saucepan full of good brandy. *Yes, this would be a notable culinary experience in the House of Heisel*! He assured himself, silently.

At last, when the custard sauce had thickened sufficiently and been strained and decanted into the pitcher, he turned to Mrs. Heisel and asked, "Is everyone ready for dessert – the *piece de resistance*?"

"Piece of resistance?" Mrs. Heisel appeared totally baffled. "OK … sure. I think everyone is as full of turkey and such as they are going to be. Honestly, though – don't take offense if not everyone wants much dessert at first. They tend to nibble at it, for the several hours of the football game."

"I don't mind," Richard said, although obscurely he did. But as long as he could present the flaming Christmas pudding at the head table – that would make up for everything! Now came the moment of unveiling, as the custard sauce was decanted and strained into the small pitcher. Unbidden, Mrs. Heisel brought the deep-rimmed plate in which the Christmas pudding was to be served, as Richard undid the saturated towel which covered the top of the pudding basin – a gift sent through Amazon UK from his eccentric Aunt Moira. "A match, please?" he commanded, as he reached for the pan of warmed brandy. "Oh, perfect!" he added, as Mrs. Heisel handed him a small, long-necked barbeque lighter. It flicked a bit of flame on first trigger, and the pan of brandy flamed up, in sullen blue flames, dancing over the warmed brandy like spirits in ballet over a black lake. Richard decanted the brandy and the flames over the dark mound of pudding, where they continued their willow-the-wisp dance.

"Now!" he commanded. "Before the alcohol burns off!"

"It looks wonderful!" Mrs. Heisel sounded dubious. That didn't bother Richard in the least. This was the moment of triumph, his moment of supremely impressing Kate's family, even the irascible, Brit-hating old grandfather. He took up the dish with the flaming pudding, Mrs. Heisel the pitcher of warm custard sauce, and she followed him at his elbow as they returned to the dining room.

Richard was aware of all the beaming, anticipatory faces orienting in his direction, like sunflowers turning to follow the sun, the rustle of appreciative sounds. Only Poppa Fritz scowled balefully, as Richard negotiated the narrow passage along the crowded dining room table.

Within an arms-reach of the table head, where the platter of stripped turkey bones had been whisked away, disaster struck, as it always did, clear out of a calm blue sky.

Richard approached the table head, preparing to lower the platter with the flaming pudding centered upon it. *Careful, careful*, he told himself. *Gently does it!*

Cherry Heisel, seated at Poppa Fritz' right hand rose abruptly from her chair, exclaiming, "Oh, Matt – I have to take a picture of this! Isn't it wonderful! It's just like a movie!" Cellphone in hand, she stepped to the side.

Richard carefully lowered the platter of pudding, wreathed in flickering blue flames to the table, and somewhere to his right and out of sight, he was aware of a flash of light … and then a clatter and a muffled squeak of annoyance.

"Oh, darn, I dropped it – I hope the screen isn't broken!" That was Cherry Heisel.

Richard hardly dared to breath; now, before the flames died – the pudding, as a peace offering to the resentful Heisel patriarch. Mission nearly accomplished, the pudding flaming to perfection, redolent with the fumes of good brandy, spices and preserved fruit, about to be delivered. He was aware of a scuffle below table level, assumed that Cherry must be reaching between chair legs to retrieve her phone. And then, something below table level bumped against him, fatally jostling his elbow.

"I'm so sorry!" Cherry cried.

"Damn and blast!" Richard exclaimed as well, for one end of the dish dropped with a crash from his hand, sending a tide of flaming brandy onto the tablecloth and into the lap of Poppa Fritz.

Poppa Fritz shot up from his chair with a roar like that of an enraged sea lion, thundering Germanic curses to a chorus of dismayed exclamations; Odin declaiming from his throne in Valhalla, accompanied by shrieking Valkyries. The pudding rolled across the table, trailed by dying blue flames, straight towards Hazel Gordon, who recaptured it neatly, crying, "I got it! "even as Poppa Fritz grabbed the electric carving knife in one hand and beat at the brandy flames with another.

"That's the third damn time those Limey bastards have tried to kill me!" Poppa Fritz swung the buzzing knife at Richard, and that end of the table devolved into a maelstrom of exclamations and cries of anguish, chair legs being violently pushed backwards.

Richard, in backing away from the threat of that knife, blundered into Mrs. Heisel, who amid all the sound and fury managed to keep hold of the pitcher of custard sauce. The knife, buzzing like a hive of angry bees, slashed perilously close to Richard's face – and he couldn't back up any farther, for the crush of bodies behind him in the crowded dining room. Then the knife miraculously fell silent; Mr. Heisel had the electric plug in his hand. Matt caught up a can of mineral water from the sideboard where the drink fixings had been laid out and poured the lot on the dying blue flames.

Richard cleared his throat. "The pudding is served," he said, into the sudden quiet. "Although in the good old English tradition, the presentation involves a bit less inadvertent arson, assault and battery."

Much later that evening, on the way back to Luna City, Kate broke into Richard's brooding silence. "I think it went pretty well," she ventured. "Honestly, much better than I had expected. Except for dropping the pudding. And it wasn't your fault, everyone said so. Cherry just caught her foot on the corner of the dining room rug. You needn't sulk, Richard. It was just Poppa Fritz and his old grudge."

"I'm not sulking," Richard answered. "I'm just depressed over the disaster with the pudding. And your grandfather. I wanted to make a good impression on your family. Especially your grandfather."

"It wasn't your fault," Kate said again. "Honestly, I don't think you could ever have made a good impression on Poppa Fritz. Not the first time, anyway. It took time for him to nourish the grudge, it'll take a bit of time for him to get over it – once he really gets to know you."

Richard sighed. "I suppose it was a good thing that Ms. Gordon made him take his pills. And your father and Matt finally got him to admit that I hadn't deliberately dropped the plate with the pudding. Small steps, I suppose."

"Baby steps, lover," Kate agreed, comfortably. She signaled a lane change, and upon swooping ahead of a lumbering pickup truck towing a horse trailer *(who the heck was taking horses anywhere on Christmas day?)* began to laugh.

"That is that about?" Richard demanded. "What's so funny?"

"It will become a family legend for the ages," Kate replied. "Right up there with the time that Mom forgot the sugar in the pumpkin pie … or the year that the dogs got to the brisket, or the year that one of the cousins upchucked at the kid's table." She twinkled a brief sideways smile at Richard. "Believe me, as Christmas dinner disasters go – this one was fairly mild. We could eat the pudding afterwards! And …"

"What?" Richard felt only slightly comforted, and Kate flashed another smile at him.

"The pudding was magnificent! You'll have to fix it again next year, you know."

Ah. There would be a next year, at home with the Heisels. And that contended Richard enormously.

Winter 2018 Newsletter

Winter 2018 Newsletter

Luna City Chamber of Commerce

5 North Town Square, Suite 4

Check out our Facebook Page

For the first time in the history of Mills Farm, the yearly Christmas Bazaar will be open in the Ballroom of the Cattleman Hotel, throughout the weekend of November 30-December 1, from 10:00-5:00 daily. Over 70 vendors will have tables at this event, selling handmade and unique gift items, boutique apparel, home-goods, jewelry, and gourmet foods. Bring your children for pictures with Santa and his assistant elves on Saturday and Sunday afternoons from 1:00 until 4:00

Richard's Christmas Plum Pudding

Richard at the Luna Café and Coffee shares his recipe for traditional English Plum Pudding, as outlined in *Mrs. Beeton's Book of Household Management*. Combine: 1 ½ pound of raisins cut in half, ½ pound each of currants and thinly sliced mixed peel, all chopped with ¾ pound each of fine fresh breadcrumbs, and grated suet. Mix with 8 beaten eggs and ¼ cup of brandy. Dough will be fairly stiff: press into a buttered pudding mold, tie a dishtowel or cloth dusted with flour over it, and place in a large kettle or double boiler filled to below the level of the pudding mold with boiling water. Steam or boil pudding for five or six hours, adding more water as required. This pudding is always prepared in advance of Christmas. On the day it is to be served, boil again for two hours. Unmold, garnish with a sprig of holly and pour ½ cup of warmed brandy over. Light the brandy and serve with wine or custard sauce.

Upcoming Events

November 30

Mills Farm Christmas Bazaar opens at 10:00 AM in the Ballroom of the Cattleman Hotel.

December 7

Luna City VFD fund-raising pancake breakfast at the firehouse from 8-11. Profits will go towards purchase of the latest in turn-out gear.

December 21

Christmas on the Square, with the annual torchlight Christmas Parade commencing at 7:00.

Charles Dickens' *A Christmas Story*

The Luna City Players present *A Christmas Story* every Friday and Saturday evening at 7:00 and a matinee at 12:00 noon on Sundays throughout December at the Koenig Opera House!

Tickets may be purchased through the LCP website, or at the box office half an hour before performances.

Luna City, Texas – Home of the Mighty Fighting Moths

Page 1 of 2

Luna City ISD News

Holiday Food Drive

The Luna City ISD holds their holiday food drive, beginning October 15th. Foodstuffs collected at both the high school and elementary school will be donated to local food banks for distribution to families in need. Please bring shelf-stable, canned, and packaged foodstuffs to containers located in the school foyers. Monetary contributions may be made by check or on-line donation through the LCISD website.

Madrigal Choir and Band Rehearsal

The High School madrigal choir and marching band will hold rehearsals for the annual Luna City Town Square Christmas every Tuesday and Thursday afternoon from October 23rd. Participants in the band and madrigal choir must attend at least one rehearsal weekly in order to participate in the Christmas concert.

Fall LCISD Book Sale

The yearly LCISD Book Sale will be held in the auditorium of the Luna City Elementary School Thursday-Saturday, November 8-10. All paperback books .50, all hardbound books $1.00. Or for $15, purchase a LCISD reusable grocery bag and fill it with as many books as can be fitted inside. Cash, personal checks and credit cards can be accepted. Book donations for the sale will be accepted at the LCISD front office until the week of the sale.

Volunteers will be on hand during the sale to carry heavy purchases to your car.

Community Marketplace

For Your Thanksgiving and Christmas Dinners!

Order a pit-smoked whole turkey, turkey breast, side of ribs, standing roast or boar ham from Pryor's Meats and BBQ before November 14th, for delivery in time for your Thanksgiving feast. Special pricing is available for bulk orders. Please note that free delivery is limited to Karnes County. Deliveries outside Karnes County will involve an additional surcharge

From Chief Vaughn, Luna City PD

There is now increased tourist traffic on side roads and Rt. 123 between Luna City and the newly reopened Cattleman Hotel, and Mills Farm, especially on weekends and whenever special events at either location are scheduled. Please be considerate and careful of wandering automotive idiots who couldn't find their own backsides with a compass and a topo map. Remember, Luna City is all about hospitality and courtesy.

Luna Café Fall Blue Plate Lunch Specials

Tuesday – Salisbury Steak w/Onion gravy and mashed potatoes
Wednesday – Turkey Sandwich w/green peppers and a side of *Pomme Frite*
Thursday – Roast Ham w/Sweet Potato and fruit Confit
Friday – Authentic English Fish and Chips
Saturday – Spaghetti Bolognese w/Garlic bread
Sunday – Shepherds' Pie
All selections served with a green salad dressed with Chef Richard's special dressing and include dessert of the day

Luna City, Texas – Home of the Mighty Fighting Moths

Page 2 of 2

The Chapel

"So, have they sorted out what to do with that benighted bloody reliquary?" Richard demanded on a Monday in mid-January when frost had rendered the dead grass on the verges to the consistency and crunchiness of corn flakes. Kate had come to share an evening in the caravan, as the sun set in layers of orange and bronze, behind the black-pen strokes of the veil of trees to the west. The old Airstream was a cozy cocoon of light and warmth, in the deserted caravan park which was the Age of Aquarius Campground (and Goat Farm) for most of the calendar year, natural disasters along the coast notwithstanding.

Kate reclined against the banquette, having kicked off her sensible low-heeled pumps with a slight groan; an odalisque lounging along the comfortable length of the padded sofa-bench at the kitchen/dining area of the Airstream. She had brought some extra-strong fresh catnip for Ozzie, who was now blissed out of his tiny cat-mind, sprawled on the hand-hooked rug in the bedroom end of the tiny metal-clad caravan. Richard tried to imagine what Ozzie might be dreaming of. World domination and three-story-tall granite statues of noble cats in the Egyptian style, lined up in ranks in front of a temple precinct, in which an Ozzie-priest of high cat-rank, clad in cloth of gold and notable jewelry presided over a ritual sacrifice of mice, brought on catnip-adorned trays of silver and gold by devotees to the shrine … Richard wrenched his mind away from that mental vision, and back to the bouillabaisse under the final stages of preparation. Supper for Kate, his Kate! demanded his complete attention as well as her reply.

"It's the treasure of our family … a fill-up, please? I'm wiped."

"Minx," Richard reached across the tiny table and topped up her wine glass with another hit of Sefton's peerless white local vintage. "Are you hoping to seduce me, if I get you drunk?"

"You can never get me drunk," Kate's amazing, beryl-blue/green eyes twinkled at him. "I have the hardest head in Karnes County. I grew up drinking Poppa Fritz's home-brewed ale. Thinned with sparking water, early on. Consider me inoculated." She sipped from her glass and continued. "What is happening with the Gonzaga Reliquary, or what there is left of it after a couple of centuries of hard use and the family treating it as a kind of portable checking account is that Great Uncle Jaime is going to fund a small chapel on the home ranch to house it. He says that it is the treasure of the family, so it's going to stay with the family. Father Bernardo did make a pitch for adding it to the sanctuary at St. Antony and Margaret, but Great Uncle Jaime is stubborn that way. Family stuff stays with the family, end of discussion. He's talked to Uncle Jesus at the garage, and Roman about building a small chapel at the rancho. Father Bernardo says that he will ask the auxiliary bishop if he would come for the consecration. Araceli's brother Berto is going to design it as part of his senior engineering project…"

"I hope he isn't going to go all tinfoil and odd shapes," Richard turned his attention to the preparation of the richly garlicky rouille to go with. "I'm not strictly a person of religion, but it just doesn't put one into the proper frame of mind, sitting in one of those modern monstrosities, with clear glass windows and a minimalist altar-piece and pulpit …just all right angles and no ritual, bells, smells and stained glass parables. If it's theater, it has to put one in the proper mood…"

"You're a traditionalist, sweetie," Kate grinned at him. "An agnostic religious traditionalist. Berto is already champing at the bit – especially as he can repurpose a lot of salvage from a deconsecrated church in Beeville, which Uncle Roman thoughtfully set aside for something like this project. It gives Berto extra points on the sustainability scale for his class. He reckons that he can get an A for this project, and all props for reuse, recycle, and re-purposing," Kate added with an air of conspicuous virtue. "Uncle Roman has already poured the foundation, and the walls start going up at the beginning of the month. You'll be amused no end by this part. When it's completed and consecrated, Cousin Mindy wants to marry her dearest Xavie, at the chapel, before the Reliquary which brought them together…"

"Good God!" Richard had just taken a sip from his own glass of Sefton's peerless mustang grape elixir – the white, to go with the fish. It went down the wrong way, and he coughed. "Oh, Christ, Katie, you might have warned me. Has your cousin entirely lost her mind? A career academic, mad is the operating assumption, but really? Marrying that tosser Gunnison-Penn, the mad treasure-hunting enthusiast? It will not turn out well," Richard prophesied balefully, between coughing. "Mark my words; it will not turn out well!"

"Relax, lover; she has tenure, and a generous retirement plan," Kate replied, comfortably assured. "Are you all right, sweetie?"

"Just went down the wrong way," Richard coughed some more, while Kate continued.

"Tenure – Gosh, that must be nice! And she loves him. Which has boggled those members of the family who have assumed for years that she is a lesbian. No, she just adores looking for odd bits of history, to the exclusion of practically everything else, to include a viable love-life. And he does, too – until now. Isn't it always said that a successful marriage is founded on mutual enthusiasms? They both adore looking for treasure. And the Reliquary is the one thing that they have found together."

"It's the <u>only</u> thing they have found together," Richard observed, sourly. He had gotten over the spasm of coughing. "It's an inarguable fact that Gunnison-Penn has never found any of that long list of missing treasures that he has gone searching for and fallen flat-footed, after every damn one of them. Until coming here his record was unsullied by any hint of success."

"But Mindy loves him," Kate answered, serenely assured. "And honestly, I think she will keep him from his madder ventures. They're a perfect pair. Speaking of relationships and mutual enthusiasms – which one do we have in common? Besides the circumstance that you love to cook and I love to eat what you prepare?"

"We have Ozzie," Richard answered, considerably rattled by that question. *Yes, what did he and Kate have in common, as regards culinary enthusiasms?* "We have… well, we have Luna City in common. My quest to bring an appreciation for the finer elements of classical French cuisine. We have friends…."

"Yes, we do," Kate twinkled at him, completely assured and confident. "And that bouillabaisse smells absolutely amazing!"

Honestly, Richard mused, as he combined soggy breadcrumbs with garlic, olive oil and certain spices; no wonder he had been an absolute tool in the hands of women. They were perpetually three jumps ahead of him, in the chessboard of life: Kate, Jess, Miss Letty, Araceli, Patricia Pryor, even the faithless Sammi, and the commanding Myrna Vaughn. He might as well just surrender to his fate.

The next that Richard heard of the prospective chapel was a bare fortnight later, as the morning rush died down at the Café. There at the regular's large stammtisch, the table which sat before the large picture window of the Café, which gave on an unparalleled view of Town Square and the faultlessly-preserved late Victorian facades of the various enterprises which lined it – there sat Berto Gonzales, head bent down over a sheaf of drawings on large paper rolls. Berto was partnered at the stammtisch by his cousin-uncle-kin Roman, the construction boss of anything going in that part of Karnes County, and – most unexpectedly – the slightly-skeevy 'Nacio Gomez, he of the woodworking talents and suspect friendship with Chief Vaughn's redoubtable female parent.

With them sat another man, an elderly gentleman in battered work clothing of the kind that Richard recognized as the fashion favored by men who worked the local ranches. In his previous life, he might have dismissed that older man as a semi-retired navvy and passed over without notice or comment. But Richard had been in Luna City sufficiently long enough to note the beautifully-ornamented leather cowboy boots, the chased silver belt-buckle and tie clasp, not to mention the antique pocket watch, reposing in the elderly gentleman's vest pocket, at the end of a heavy silver chain and toggle. The elderly gentleman withdrew that watch and consulted it briefly.

"Hi, Rich," Berto looked up from the stack of drawings. "This is Great-Uncle Don Jaimie. He don't come to town very often; you might not have met him before. He owns the family ranch, the Rincon de los Robles. I'm designing the chapel for him – the chapel to house the Reliquary. You wanna take a look at tell me what you think?"

"Honored," Richard exchanged a courtly nod with the elderly gentleman. "And I can spare a few moments. Would you require more coffee?"

"I'm good," Don Jaimie responded, absently, still surveying the topmost layer of architectural renderings. Richard slid into an empty chair at the stammtisch and wordlessly surveyed Berto's collection. "Berto, *hijito* – tell me again, how the walls are to be ornamented on the inside. This is not to be like a grand cathedral, only a simple country chapel."

"We have the six leaded glass windows," Berto unrolled another length of paper. Richard saw, to unspoken relief, that Berto had come up with a modest, traditional-style chapel, a kind of home-made early Norman, with thick plain walls and restfully unornamented woodwork. "See – the four long stained-glass windows, and the two small rose windows in seeded glass. Two each of the colored class on each side, and the rose windows in the gable ends. See … the rising sun and the setting sun will shine into the rose windows, morning and afternoon. It's gonna look so neat! An' Reuben is gonna paint a mural across the end wall above the altar, where the Reliquary is gonna be kept. You know," Berto regarded his cousin-uncle and great-uncle with the most solemn earnestness. "He really is good. He did a preliminary sketch; Joseph and Mary and Baby Jesus on their way to Egypt; but the scenery in the background will be all Texas. Live oak trees, an' wildflowers on the ground, the river at their feet which they are about to cross – is just as it is by Luna City. True Texas, where the Reliquary belongs."

"As it is fitting for the great treasure of our family," Don Jaime rumbled, approvingly.

"We got a dozen pews salvaged from that reno," Roman enthused, "Which we can cut-down and refinish to better fit the chapel. It's only gonna be a small place, after all. And some fine old aged oak planks, usta be part of a paneled study in an old house in Alamo Heights; 'Nacio's just itching to get his hands on that wood, aren't ya, 'Nacio? Build the altar from that lovely wood, an' sturdy shutters for the windows…"

Thus appealed to, 'Nacio Gomez appeared to shrink back in his seat and attempt to efface himself. Though that could have been because Myrna Vaughn just walked into the Café, attended by the silvery musical tinkle from the bell on a spring attached to the door, and by Jess Abernathy-Vaughn. Jess was wheeling the Brobdingnagian baby carriage which contained her offspring – that small and tender shoot on the Vaughn-Abernathy family tree. Young Joe, almost a year old and was already scowling in a manner which reminded Richard most piercingly of Joe Senior, handing out dire warnings and citations for excessive speed along that section of Rte. 123 which abutted Luna City. Jess, Myrna and the infant spawn settled on the small table on the other side of the Café's dining room. Out of the corner of his eye, Richard noted that Araceli was already attending upon them.

"It's gonna be a total work of art, Uncle Jaime," Berto affirmed, his eyes alight with creative fervor. "From floor to ceiling, an' wall to wall! I'm so gonna send pictures to Amy. She's my girl, you know."

"Another architecture student?" Roman ventured, as he signaled for Araceli to produce the bill for his best all-fried British breakfast, the last remains of which were congealing on the plate before him.

"Nah. She's at Cal-Tech, majoring in physics," Beto began rolling up the vast sheaf of drawings for the chapel project. "She's really bright, you know. Uncle Roman, what's your timeline on all this?"

"We poured the foundation three weeks ago," Roman consulted the battered pocket calendar on the table before him. "So the guys can start putting up the conblock walls by the end of next week. The roof beams are ready to go, the outer roof skin is gonna be standing-seam metal … sure I can't talk you into tile, Don Jaime?"

"I wanted more of a traditional ranch-building look in the design," Berto explained.

Don Jaimie replied, "Costs almost $15 a square foot for that old-fashioned tile; metal roof is half that, even at the kinship rate you're giving me; and I'm not made of money, *hijito*."

"But Reuben an' 'Nacio are doing the woodwork an' the fresco painting as a donation, so you are saving a bundle on that," Roman pointed out. Obviously, he was more in favor of the old-fashioned mellow Spanish tile as a roofing material.

"That is a matter between them and Our Father," Don Jaimie rumbled. "I put no price on an act of penitence for past transgressions."

At that, 'Nacio Gomez looked down at the plans on the tabletop, the very picture of penitence. "Our offering," he mumbled, indistinctly. "Mine and Reuben's. To God, for forgiveness for our many sins. And for the Family … to honor the Reliquary;

contemplating it brought us to… well, we saw the error of our ways."

Richard felt his eyebrows raise, almost to his hairline. Reuben and Ignacio, the undynamic criminal duo of Luna City, suddenly getting that old-time religion? Well, as the school chaplain was apt to remark, God did work in mysterious ways, his wonders to perform. Although he did speculate that perhaps Miss Letty teaching the near-illiterate Reuben to read must have had something to do with a change of heart. But had happened to 'Nacio, to bring him into awareness and a sense of community responsibility? Richard couldn't wait to find out. Eventually he would; everyone came to Richard and the Café.

"It's appreciated, 'Nacio," Roman acknowledged solemnly. "And we know you'll do fantastic work with the wood … specialty carpentry is your God-given gift, when you pay attention to actually showing up for work, clean, shaved, and sober."

"I know," 'Nacio was the very picture of the repentant sinner. "I been working on that, a day at a time."

At that moment, Myrna Vaughn passed by the stammtisch, carrying her grandson and his immense diaper bag in the direction of the ladies' lavatory. She was obviously giving Jess a break when it came to swap out a soiled diaper for a clean one.

"Mr. Gomez," she said, as she paused by the table. "Do you need a ride to the meeting on Thursday, or are you set?"

"I'm set, Mrs. V," 'Nacio Gomez replied, with every evidence of cheerful amity. "I got the truck fixed, since I been racking up the hours at work. See you there."

"Sure thing, Mr. Gomez," Myrna Vaughn passed on, with a casual nod of her head, and 'Nacio added, by way of explanation,

"I been going to AA. You know – Alcoholics Anonymous. We meet every Thursday, to encourage each other, ya know; Miz V.

suggested it, a couple months ago. I'm going on six months sober. You gotta take it a day at a time, she said … an' they say you really have to choose bein' sober, every day."

Richard was boggled; not that he should have been. From what he had heard – especially about the karmic denouement when 'Nacio and Reuben took it into their head following upon a night of drinking to steal Clem Bodie's brand new bass boat – the undynamic duo had been notorious around Luna City when it came to alcohol-fueled and usually unlawful antics.

"Good advice, 'Nacio," Roman nodded judicially. "I always said the first step to dealing with a problem is to admit that you have a problem in the first place."

"A lot of my problems came out of that ol' six-pack," 'Nacio agreed. "But I can't be blaming it all on the six-pack. Miz V. had the right of it – she told me that I was too easy distracted from what was really my talent." He looked at them all, with utmost earnest. "She's a smart woman, Miz V. She figured out her problem early. Most of us have to hit bottom in a lot of ways, before we can fight our way out."

"Good to hear, *hijito*," Don Jaime put aside his coffee cup and the plate upon which a few lonely crumbs of cinnamon roll lingered. "Berto, I like the plans for the inside. Let me know when the next phase begins."

"Sure thing, Uncle Jaime," Berto gathered up his long scroll of drawings and plans. He beamed at them all impartially. "Don't you love it when a good plan comes all together?"

"The hand of God, *hijito*," Don Jaimie replied. "Who knows when a sparrow falls."

"I'll call you when my guys are ready to start the walls," Roman had also scoffed the last of his English fry-up, and also rose from his chair. "Let's get cracking, 'Nacio – that client in Karnesville won't want to wait another day. See ya, Ricardo."

Richard nodded, as they all three abandoned that end of the stammtisch, and the ever-attentive Beatriz swooped in to clear away the debris. And that was a small mystery solved – the odd association of Myrna Vaughn and 'Nacio Gomez; not romantic at all. Richard reminded himself to tell Katie. Not romantic at all … just responsible.

The Legend of the Hanging Tree

"I think the branch on that big oak at the corner of the square looks dead," Roman the builder remarked one bright spring morning, as brilliant sunshine flooded into the Café. The oaks in the square, which gave an air of nobility and the atmosphere of a green forest glade to Town Square, were covered in the green of new foliage and dusty springs of blossoms, which shed a kind of bright yellow dust the length and breadth of the heart of Luna City. All but a single barren branch; a branch the thickness of a man's body, and which stretched out some twenty feet above the paved promenade opposite the front window of the Café. Roman continued. "I better tell the Mayor, get the work crew out to take out that branch, before it falls and kills somebody."

"Do, please," Miss Letty agreed. "I have noted several woodpeckers in that tree, and they prefer dead wood, of course. The oak wood can be salvaged, and sawn into planks," she added, thoughtfully. “It’s a historic tree, you know. They called it the ‘Hanging Tree,’ back in the day.”

“Was it, indeed, Miss Letty?” Richard was fascinated. He hovered around the stammtisch now that the morning rush was winding down, attending on his most valued regular customers. “I never knew that …”

“Well, the historical marker is around on the other side of the tree,” Miss Letty added sugar to her second coffee, sounding especially acerbic. “You cannot see it from here, I suppose. But that is the tree from which Old Charley Mills was nearly lynched in 1926.”

“I knew that,” Clovis Walcott gestured for the hovering Araceli to add a refill to his own coffee cup. “Local history, of course. But I’ve never really heard the full tale. I suppose that you know of it, Miss Letty – as president emeritus of the Luna City Historical Society.”

“Better than that,” Miss Letty took a dainty bite from her just-from-the-oven cinnamon roll. “I was there and witnessed what happened, although much of the aftermath as well as the contributing events were kept from me at the time. I was only a child of six or so,” she added hastily. “Shopping with my dear mother on that morning. The Wild West Emporium next door used to be a dry goods store. Mother wanted to purchase a length of calico for a new apron, and a spool of thread. And a quantity of fine linen for a dress for me. For my seventh birthday, you know. She had a nice pattern from the Simplicity Company. Mother had ordered it from Sears. We were going to pick out some nice fabric there, and then go shopping for the weekly groceries at Dunsmores’ Grocery; it was where that real estate office is now in the narrow building next to Abernathy Hardware. In my young days, it was the general store. Luna City had one, you know; we didn’t need to travel all the way to Karnesville to buy groceries. Mr. Dunsmore was a fine-looking man, who always gave me a piece of peppermint candy. I liked him. His wife Eloise was much younger than he was. She came from the East – she was the first woman in Luna City to have her hair bobbed, and wear skirts above her knee. Mother thought she was fast – and wore too much lipstick and powder for a properly married woman," Miss Letty added, in mildly-arctic disapproval. "Mrs. Dunsmore was even said to have rouged her knees."

"The scandal of it all," Richard commented, privately thinking that the senior Mrs. McAllister sounded like a perfectly dismal, po-faced old trout.

"It was a small town," Miss Letty didn't distain the obvious. "Mother was raised with the understanding that it was unsuitable for a lady to improve upon nature with anything more drastic than papier poudre. She thought Eloise Dunsmore's free and easy ways made it most difficult for the Dunsmore's daughter, Susan. Susan was eleven. She helped her parents in the store, after school. We were not close enough in age to be friends, and by the time I was older, Susan Dunsmore had been sent back east to her mothers' kinfolk because of the scandal, even though the Reverend Rowbottom's family had taken her in after the arrests. They wanted to keep her with theirs', you see, since she knew and trusted them. The Governor, Mrs. Ferguson, issued Mr. Dunsmore a pardon after he was put in prison for running an illicit saloon, But the scandal when it all came out! Poor Susan: memories are long in small towns," Miss Letty added apologetically. "Especially when it comes to affairs of the romantic sort."

Clovis Walcott snorted. "Not long enough, Miss Letty. I've never heard of this, and I've read Dr. McAllister's history so often the pages in my copy are ragged."

"My brother did hit the relevant points," Mis Letty agreed. "That Charley Mills was nearly hanged by a mob, from the Hanging Tree in Town Square, after being accused of molesting Susan Dunsmore in her bedroom at two in the morning. He was such a disgraceful character that practically anything might be believed of him. But it was a very complicated matter, and many relevant facts didn't come out until well after my brother had written his history. Douglas was Susan's age, you see. They were friends and my brother was always sentimental about his friends. And it may have been the one single time in history," Miss Letty added thoughtfully, "That Charley Mills was actually quite … well, not innocent, exactly. But blameless. Blameless in the matter of which he was accused on that occasion. It was all made clear when Phillip Vaughn found his father-in-law's unpublished memoir and donated it to the Historical Society. That would have been in 1990, or so, five years after the centenary celebrations and the publishing of my brother's history of the town. Alistair Magill was the chief of police in Luna City for many years. He had …" Miss Letty reflected, while Roman, Richard and Clovis attended breathlessly, "The most imposing mustache. It really was a monument, that mustache. Chief Magill was a notable monument in himself; he most resembled Victor McLaglen – an actor of the time, you young people would hardly know of him. Chief Magill was a Scot, originally – from Fife, I believe. He boxed professionally, in his youth, being billed as the "Fife Bomber." He was promoted from constable to sergeant of the police force after knocking out an obstreperous prisoner with a single blow. That kind of skill was appreciated among law-enforcement circles, back in the day," Miss Letty added, with a slight air of apology. "He became so popular and efficient in that role, that he was eventually commissioned as chief of police by the City Council – and remained in that office for three decades. On

Founders' Day, he wore a kilt and played the bagpipes as part of the observations. My father respected him enormously. Father was the mayor of Luna City at that time, you see. For Douglas and I, there could have been no higher testament to his worth. His only daughter married Frank Vaughn, who had a small property near Beeville, foreclosed in the first year of the Great Depression. That is how the Vaughn family came to Luna City and inherited a role in local enforcement of the law. Frank Vaughn was hired as a patrolman, because of his father-in-law's influence, you see. Sometimes nepotism is not a harmful thing."

"But the hanging mob, Miss Letty," Clovis Walcott urged, while Richard meditated on the odd turn of events which led a Scot from Fife named Magill to become the long-serving and much respected senior law enforcement officer in Luna City. "How did that come to involve a respectable merchant of the town and a socially non-conforming spouse? I take it that having received a pardon from the office of Ma Ferguson he had been unjustly imprisoned for violating the laws prohibiting alcohol consumption?" Clovis Walcott, as a practicing open-air historian specializing in 19th century Americana, was perhaps even more thoroughly steeped in the Victorian ideal of social conduct than Miss Letty, Richard mused privately.

"As it happens," Miss Letty replied, every inch the stern Methodist church lady, "He was not unjustly charged and condemned. Mr. Dunsmore was operating an illicit saloon – a speakeasy, as they termed such an enterprise then. A secret subterranean storeroom behind the grocery, with a triple-barred door opening into the alleyway behind. I believe the Steins now use that room as a wine cellar. It came as a surprise to everyone save those who knew of and patronized that establishment. It seemed from what I overheard when my parents talked of it, that the men of town were indulgent regarding Mr. Dunsmore's speakeasy. It was only when three drummers – traveling salesmen, as they called them back then – were poisoned by bad alcohol that Chief Magill was forced to take action. This is a long story, gentleman. Are you certain you wish to hear it?"

"I've got nothing but time this morning," Clovis Walcott gestured for another a fill-up of his coffee. "So, I'd admire to hear the full story, Miss Letty."

"I don't," Roman added, "But I'd like to hear it anyway. And if I have to rush away in half an hour, I can always ask Great Uncle Jaimie for what he might know. He was around then… And what he doesn't remember, Cousin Mindy can find out."

"Indeed," Miss Letty nodded magisterially. "Jaimie Gonzales is about the same age that I am, but his family hardly ever came to town at that time. They kept themselves to themselves, back in the day: Spanish nobility, you know."

"That, and a lynch mob coming for them, on the off-chance of some criminal outrage being blamed on some poor idiot Tejano," Roman nodded, in cynical agreement.

Miss Letty sighed. "In a way, the presence of Charley Mills served as a kind of social lightening-rod. Any notable criminal goings-on happening in Luna City were blamed on him, or on the Newton gang. His presence and his well-known record of criminality and anti-social behavior served to keep the social peace in very sad times, as curious as that might seem."

"I do want to hear the full story, Miss Letty," Richard insisted. "Although … I have only forty minutes before I must go and oversee preparations for lunch."

"Very well," Miss Letty agreed, with a regretful expression. "Although the full story may take much, much longer."

From the Archives

From the Karnesville Daily Beacon issue of March 5, 1926 – A Fatal Poisoning Among the Traveling Fraternity!

Three traveling drummers were discovered dangerously ill or dying in their rooms at the Cattleman Hotel in Luna City this Monday just past. Identified through their personal effects and the hotel registry, the deceased are Mr. Arthur Montgomery of Dallas, Texas, (aged 27) and Mr. James McArdle (aged 25) of Tulsa, Oklahoma. They were employed by several respectable commercial enterprises and were traveling through the region seeking business on behalf of their employers. A third drummer, Mr. Dennis Charlton, (aged 30) of New Orleans, Louisiana remains desperately ill in the Karnesville Regional Hospital. Doctors attending on him fear that he may lose his sight, if he recovers at all. Interviewed briefly by investigating authorities, Mr. Charlton insisted that nothing had been out of the ordinary in his visit to Luna City, where he had been received by regular clients among the commercial enterprises there, including representatives from Abernathy Hardware, and Dunsmore Groceries and Sundries.

***

From the Karnesville Daily Beacon, March 9, 1926 – An Update on Fatal Poisoning at the Cattleman Hotel, Luna City

Mr. Dennis Charlton, a traveling salesman for the California Perfume Company, stricken by a mysterious and dangerous ailment last week, perished of that condition at the Karnesville Regional Hospital this day past. Two other traveling drummers had previously been discovered dead in their rooms by the staff of the Cattleman Hotel in Luna City this previous week, as reported in our story on Page 1 of our March 5 issue. An investigation into the circumstances of this sad affair is ongoing, according to Chief of Police in Luna City, Alistair Magill.

***

From the evidence file pertaining to investigation of case #26-3-005: item 4

A handwritten note found in the possession of the accused C. E. Mills when taken into custody by the arresting officer at 3:24 AM, 15 March 1926. *(Not actually in his possession, but in his trouser pocket – note by AM)*

Dearest – come to me tonight. Mr. D in K'ville. The window will be unlatched. Love, E

The Mills Lynching

From an untitled and unpublished memoir by former chief of police, Luna City, Alistair Duncan Magill, found among his private papers by his family, after his death from natural causes at the age of 98 in February 1987. Chapter 47 – The Deaths of Three Drummers

The matter began as part of an entirely separate case; that of the three traveling salesmen, discovered by the staff of the Cattleman Hotel to be dead or near-death in their rooms on the morning of March 3. Simple case, you say. Three adventurous young fellows on the road; of course, they went out drinking of an evening, and the liquor they had the ill-fortune to consume that evening was adulterated with wood-grain alcohol. Nasty stuff; deadly as a matter of fact. Never was a strict dry, myself; always of the opinion that a real man could and ought to exert control over his baser urges and I never said no to a drop of the good creature, even during Prohibition. Only a weak namby-pamby would look to a higher authority to control it for him. But enforcement of the Volstead Act was the law of the land and I was sworn to uphold the law, no matter what my own private feelings in the matter. As for Prohibition in Luna City, as long as there was no harm done to any, save perhaps a thunderous headache the next morning for those who had over-imbibed, my fellows and I kept the law as sensibly as it could be and looked the other way as often as we could in good conscious and in accordance with our oath.

There was but one serious bootlegger in the vicinity; Charles Everett Mills. His general criminality was a well-known matter, and a thorn in my side as well as that of many others. Mills, as scabrous a villain as I ever encountered, none the less had the wit and purse sufficient to employ an excellent and creative lawyer – Newsome by name. Gabriel Newsome. Had an office and partnership in Karnesville: Newsome, Porter & Daws. Never saw a whisker of Porter and Daws; between you and I and the gatepost, I shouldn't be surprised to learn that they were imaginary, indeed. It was a matter of growing resentment among those residents in Luna City who had cause and clear evidence sufficient to bring criminal charges against Charley Mills as well as the persistence to follow through with charges, regularly had those charges dismissed by the judge in Karnesville.

"Look, you," I said to Mr. Newsome, sometime late in 1925, as I recollect now after many years. This was after another charge against Charley Mills was dismissed, following Newsome, Esq.'s eloquent defense of the character of the defendant along with a subtle impugnment of the character and eyesight of those testifying witnesses – those few brave enough to come to Karnesville and testify. The jury's verdict went for Charley Mills, of course. I believe that they were all foreigners from Karnesville and farther afield. "This can't go on. Your client is a menace. Too many local people know what he is, indeed."

"That may be," the rascal replied, impertinent, as he gathered together his paper briefs. "But his money is good, and I endeavor to give full value for it. Are you intending to intimidate me, Chief Magill? My hours are flexible; I may complain to the judge about this, if you persist."

"Consider it a word of professional warning," I replied, considerably irked.

Indeed, there was little that I could do, and I was full annoyed at having my good advice spurned so. For Mr. Mills was indeed walking a thin line, for all that his lawyer could keep him from a conviction and a long term in the county jail. My reading of local temper was acute, as were those of my constables. Charles E. Mills had offended against too many law-abiding citizens; openly flouted the law, in matters other than the bootlegging of spirits. Indeed, it was my sense that this was the least of his offenses against the laws of God and man.

If he had only kept himself to his distilling and distribution enterprise, most in Luna City would cheerfully have looked the other way. Our Lord was one who relished the taste of good wine and saw it as a pleasure available to all in celebration. Indeed, the Miracle at Cana attests to that inclination, and in that, my good friend the Reverend Rowbottom of the First Methodist Church of Luna City agreed privily with me, although most in his congregation did not. Father Antoine of Sts. Margaret and Stephen also agreed, citing the same scriptural accounts. Father Antoine was a Papist of the stern old school and the Reverend Rowbottom was unusually broadminded for a hard-shell Methodist … aye, but that is neither here nor there.

My sergeant and chief investigator at the time of these developments was John Drury; a trusty man who had been a Texas Ranger with Captain McNelly's border company before he needed to shave – a bare boy of sixteen then and only because his father had also been a Ranger and recommended his son to Captain McNelly. Now it was near half-a-century on; still, John Drury was a canny man and a trusty one, too. Not half-bad a marksman, either; a widower now, and his three sons long grown and seeking their own lives, so his life and full attention was devoted to the law. He was near to the age of seventy at this time but appeared as fit and vital as a man half that span of years. If the city budget could afford his salary, and he was willing to work for it, who was I to object? When I was told by Mayor McAllister in a midday phone call to my home that the third drummer died in hospital, I called Drury into my office for a consultation as soon as I returned from my repast. Mayor McAllister was of the mind that we could all sort it out without much fuss and he had expressed his complete confidence in my department.

"So, what think you, John?" I asked, for we were familiar enough to use our first names, when it was a matter of us in private, although John Drury usually preferred to address me by a customary rank of a leader in a Ranger company. He shook his head.

"A curious thing, Captain. There's many a tale told about Charley Mills, but never a one that he makes bad likker. Not the slightest whisper. A rogue, a bad and wicked man, not to be trusted within reach of any honest man's money, any portable property of value, or the virtue of his wife and daughter, but I've never heard anything about his whiskey being bad to drink. Not even in these parlous times."

"Neither have I," said I in reply. "I dare say that I have sampled enough of it, in the time that I have been living here and taken no ill at all. Even before the Volstead Act was signed into law."

"I would say the same and had no concern," John Drury answered. He looked thoughtful, as if he were considering much. "Until the matter of those three unfortunate lads. Mills supplies Dunsmore's little speakeasy exclusively, I am certain of it. There's been no illicit deliveries that I can see. An outsider to Luna City would be remarked upon, especially if they were thought to be bootleggers from outside Karnes County. Even disguised as groceries … no, Captain. It's irregular, as near as I can see. Rogues go to a pattern, unless they are very, very clever. It's to my mind that Charley Mills is not all that clever."

"Clever enough to pay a good lawyer," I pointed out, "And keep him on retainer. It irks me, John, knowing that Mills lives like an old robber baron, among his castle ruins, abusing and robbing the peasantry as he feels the urge, and no one might touch him, legally."

John Drury was already shaking his head. "There is that, Captain. Above all, Mills is an indolent, lazy bastard. He's not given to the spirit of invention in his criminality… but his common-law wife …"

"Mrs. Mills, or Miss Carolina de San Pedro," I said. "A woman of such obvious aristocratic qualities, and she must be less than half the old reprobates' age! One does wonder how the old goat managed to attract her, or why she remains with him for longer than five minutes."

"Indeed, Captain," John Drury nodded agreement. "High-bred Mex, in my experience as proud as Lucifer. Usually claim to be Spanish of the pure blood, *limpieza de sangre* as they used to say. A common-law marriage, as I have heard, based merely on cohabitation for seven years or more. Now, if Mrs. Mills is looking to expand the local market by trading on the Mills reputation and cutting corners … When did she become part of the Mills ménage?

About ten years back, if I recall. A refugee from political violence in Mexico, as her family was on the losing side of the Huerta-Carranza revolutionary brangle. She slipped over the border and went to ground in the nearest handy refuge, having no other useful skill than offering her hand in marriage."

"When is there ever not political violence in Mexico?" I replied. "It's like the border wars between England and Scotland, you ken; raids, refugees from the losing side going back and forth across the border, fomenting resistance and rebellion against whomever. In my home country it eventually became a wholesome outdoor sport."

"Texas has become your element, Captain!" John Drury grinned with unalloyed delight. "The ground is familiar to you in theory, which is a useful guide to practice, when used carefully." His countenance sobered. "I think that we should interview the so-called Mrs. Mills. Something has changed drastically within their operation. We should know what it was, if she will be honest…"

"When have we ever known one of the criminal fraternities to be honest?" I said.

John Drury chuckled. "When it's their living at stake, Chief. Their nuts in a vice, or Old Casuse standing them up in the saddle of his horse, under a tree with a sturdy branch and a noose around their neck. Sing like canaries, they do. Guaranteed."

"We can't go to that limit, John," I said, although I do not deny that I relished a mental image of doing so to Charley Mills.

So we got in my car, and drove out to the Mills place, to interview Mrs. Mills as was she called. It was a mild day, with spring just beginning to shyly come on, new green leaves on the trees and swarms of pink primrose and yellow daisies, the grass in the meadows beside the road to the south of town. The prettiest time of the year, so I have always thought. The Highlands in my youth may have been more glorious for scenery two or three days out of the month, but the incessant dreary rain for the other twenty-seven or twenty-eight was enough to drive a man to drink, or to travel to any place with nicer weather. We hummed along the road at a goodish clip; can't recollect if Route 123 had been paved with macadam by that time, or if it were still only graveled.

The turn-off road to the Mills place was barely marked; a sagging gate with a faded and hand painted "No Trespassing!" board hung from it. John Drury got out to tug the gate all the way open, and wrestle it closed after I had driven through. He resumed his place in the passenger seat with a sigh.

"The Mills place was the pride of Karnes County, back when I first settled here. A beautiful, well-run showplace; a pretty painted house, manicured pastures, fat and contented stock. Now, I swear, the only fat contented stock are Charley's pet alligators. It's a tragedy, Captain, that such a fine, hard-working man and wife as James and Jane Mills should have been blessed with a lazy, worthless piece of work like Charley for a son and heir! The three Graces, they called the daughters; each one as lovely a girl who ever turned heads in the street! They went to finishing school in San Antonio, you know. Every imaginable womanly accomplishment between them, and then Charley … a disappointment in every possible aspect!"

"Cruel it is, John," I said, for it seemed that John had been fondly attached to the Mills family, especially the girls, and of a proper age to have courted several of them, but with little success, as he was a man of no great property himself. He looked out though the windscreen of the Ford, a bleak expression upon his countenance, as the Ford bumped at a careful speed, down the rutted lane which led through the neglected acres of the Mills Place; pastures and fields now well-overgrown with cane and mesquite.

The prospect of the main house and the outbuildings presented a picture of even more ruin and neglect. A climbing rose with small blood-red blossoms straggled up along one side of what once had been a trim little cottage, lavishly adorned with fret-sawed wooden lace. The porch sagged, dangerously, and the white paint which once must have been renewed every decade or so, under the blast of a pitiless Texas summer sun, was peeling and chipped away on the south-facing walls. The rose should have been pruned many seasons since. Many windows boasted broken panes, filled in with squares of cardboard, tin and other such trash. It was a sad prospect and I felt something of John Drury's sorrow; a goodly inheritance gone to rack and ruin, under the rule of a careless and dissolute keeper.

The only thing in the Mills demesne which appeared to be whole and in excellent repair and condition was the green Ford panel truck which sat around the side of the house, before the grey weathered barn of unpainted planks. This barn leaned precipitously towards south-east, in an unsettling manner, which suggested that the next vicious Blue Norther would bring the whole edifice down in a tumble of planks. The panel truck was brand new. *Charley Mills' bootlegging operation must be prospering.* I conveyed that thought silently to John Drury by a significant glance towards it and a raised eyebrow. He nodded in agreement. There was a woman, just coming out from that barn, a slender young woman wearing unwomanly trousers, lugging a heavy crate in her hands. A crate of bottles from the clinking sound that they made when she settled in the back of the panel truck. Then she sauntered boldly to meet us.

"Mrs. Mills," said I, courteously; for of course, we wished to cultivate this woman, not frighten her into uncooperative defiance. "Might we have a moment of your time?"

"Chief Magill," she nodded, warily. "And Sergeant Drury. Good morning. To what do I owe the pleasure of your company?"

Mrs. Mills had a pleasing voice, with only the slightest of accents. She spoke like a lady of noble station, and without any trace of nervousness in her manner or expression. Carolina de San Pedro Mills was then about thirty, I would have judged. She wore her plain shirt and unladylike trousers with the air of a woman modeling them for a fashion magazine, or perhaps a poster advertising a moving picture. She was not one of those who had bobbed her hair in the current fashion, but wore it long, smooth and dark, knotted at the back of her head. I fancied that she would have favored one of those tall Spanish combs with a length of fine lace draped over it, and perhaps a pair of clicky-castanets to go with. As fair of complexion as any Englishwoman, she also had arresting eyes – eyes of a peculiar blue-green color, the same blue-green shade of the shallow waters off the Holy Isle of Iona, blue-green water on a strand of beach the color of fine white sugar. Whatever might have led a woman of such quality to a marital alliance with a villain like Charley Mills was a mystery even more profound than the mystery which had led John Drury and I to this place in the beginning.

"Tis a matter of investigating murder in a lesser degree, a courtesy that I would remember, in the event of any future investigation from outside my office."

"Murder?" At that she appeared distinctly shaken. "How can that be?"

"It is a matter of tainted alcohol," I said, after waiting for John Drury to speak. "That which poisoned the three travelling drummers. They drank at Dunsmore's speakeasy, the evening before they were stricken – no, it is a matter of record and the witnesses are reliable and have made sworn statements…"

A bit of an exaggeration, I will admit to these pages – but all may be fair in love, war, and criminal investigations. John Drury nodded in solemn affirmation

"You know about Dunsmore?" she asked, warily. "But of course. I have heard there is nothing happening in Luna City of which you do not know."

"Flattery, lass, will get you nowhere," I replied, although I was pleased. A reputation for omniscience was a useful thing, I had long since known, although I was no more gifted with particular insight than any other human with skills for good observation and logical deduction. "Of course, I know about Dunsmore – 'tis an open secret. Look, lass; I care nothing for whether gentlemen drink among company or alone, as long as they conduct themselves fittingly and don't take from wages that would feed their little children to drink themselves silly every night after work. But I care very much that someone tainted the alcohol at Dunsmore's with poisonous wood-alcohol. So too does Mayor McAllister. I wish for insight into why this might have been done, if it were deliberate and not merely an accident. If deliberate, then I wish to know to whose' advantage the painful death of good customers might have been, so that they may be rightfully charged with contributing to cases of wrongful death. Mr. Mills has long been the source of much in the way of spirituous liquors in this vicinity. Would you wish that the great clumsy feet of investigators from the Bureau of Prohibition come trampling into Luna City, interfering with our business, and harming those who have never given harm to anyone? Ours is a delicate spiderweb, Mrs. Mills. Outsiders will not take the care that I will; the care which Mayor McAllister desires me to exercise in this matter. What you say to Sergeant Drury and myself will be kept in confidence, so we urge you to be candid, for the good of us all.

You do not wish to be repatriated as a criminal foreigner back to Mexico, I would take it."

A misstep. She regarded us with a level gaze. "No, for I am legally married to Mr. Mills and this was recorded before witnesses in the office of the Justice of the Peace in Brownsville in 1915. You can send for the records if you wish. A wife cannot be made to testify against her husband."

"Aye, then, for such is the law," I made a tactful withdrawal in the military sense. "And 'tis a law that I am sworn to uphold, Mrs. Mills. I beg you not to make upholding it difficult for us all. You would swear on anything you hold in reverence, that the liquor provided to Mr. Dunsmere's place of business was sound, not tampered or adulterated with wood-alcohol or any other such substance? That it was so, when it passed from your hands into Mr. Dunsmore's or those of his agents."

"Who took possession of the delivery on Thursday last to Dunsmore's grocery?" John Drury pressed, with the adept timing of an actor with a cue. "That, and the previous shipment? My information is that such is consigned weekly, as he cannot stock very much at a time, and the consignment is near-consumed at the end of the week before the next delivery?"

"Mrs. Dunsmore, sometimes," Carolina Mills regarded me slantwise, from those amazing blue-green eyes, all the more startling for being fringed by ink-dark lashes. "Humiliating; to make deliveries after dark or in the early morning, after arranging a time with that painted man-hungry *puta*. But last week, it was Ambrosiano. Ambrosiano Gonzales. Most usually, Mrs. or Mr. Dunsmore took delivery. Ambrosiano only came to work for them in January. He is a very poor relation of Don Antonio, of the Rancho Rincon and there is no work for him there. He took employment, working in the grocery. Shifting heavy boxes and running errands. He also is fleeing la Revolucion," Carolina Mills added. "Because he is a good Catholic and a believer."

"God save us, they've got yet another internal war going on," John Drury commented, *sotto voice*, and I said, rather loudly,

"And this was your usual delivery of …"

"Mixed goods," Carolina Mills replied. "Bourbon whiskey, brandy, apple-jack from our enterprise – all the good stuff…" that last term came rather awkwardly from her lips. Not her native speech, I judged, but that of her so-called-husband. "All pure, all un-tainted. I … that is, we – we have a reputation for superlative quality. I would not spoil that, not for anything. Neither would Mr. Mills. A matter of pride. Not to cheat. Here," she went to the back of the Ford, where the box which she had just carried to it reposed on the bed. "Pick a bottle. Pick two at random. Take them away and test them. I vow that if they are tainted and poisonous, then come and put your bracelets on my wrists," And she held up her hands, close together in a splendid gesture. "And then do with me what you will. For I will swear to you on our Holy Mother – that our liquor is pure and of the highest quality imaginable."

"I will, and thank you for your cooperation," I said, as I took two bottles at random out of the open crate in the Ford. "I believe that we are done here, Sergeant Drury. My thanks for your information, Mrs. Mills. We shall test this in our laboratory. Do not attempt to leave the area, or if needs must, let us know."

We took our leave, with courtesy, although I did wonder where Charley Mills was and what he was doing, and why his place should be the spectacle of disrepair and neglect. Yet, there was that almost new Ford panel truck for Mrs. Mills to drive. And one more thing…

"John," I said, when he climbed back into the passenger seat, after wrestling the ramshackle gate of the Mills place back into position. "Did it not seem to you that there is a deep animus between Mrs. Mills and Mrs. Dunsmore? 'That painted man-hungry whore' is not a term of endearment. I would know the reason for this, as it might have a bearing on this case."

"*Cherchez la femme*, Captain," John Drury replied. "Or rather – look for the women and ask them."

"True," I mused. "Women will know. If you wish to know anything which has a bearing on a woman, especially in a town such as this, or when I was growing up in Fife, 'twas best to ask other women. For a woman will talk to her friends, and her friends will talk to their friends. I was going to Mayor McAllister's house this evening, to brief him on what we have found so far. I regret that Mrs. Magill and I regularly attend St. Dunstans' in Karnesville, so that we are not affiliated with any of the religious circles in Luna City. Early on, I thought it best, a sense of detachment, ye'll see, between social attachments and professional distance. Mrs. McAllister's Methodist ladies sewing circle is likely to be meeting. The Dunsmores are Methodists, I take it?"

"Unenthusiastic," John Drury agreed. "Of the Christmas and Easter, weddings and funeral variety of Christian. As for Mrs. Mills, being from Mexico…"

"Likely a Papist," I agreed. "And not striking me as excessively devout, either. But still … is there not something going on at the St. Margaret and Anthony parish hall this very afternoon? A tea reception for a new junior priest, I think 'twas said. Since you speak Spanish…"

"Of course," John Drury looked out through the windshield of my car, a watchful expression on his face. Nothing more was said. This was why I liked working with the man; his mind coursed swiftly over the same tracks as my own, so little needed to be said.

Spring Newsletter

Spring 2019 Newsletter

Luna City Chamber of Commerce

5 North Town Square, Suite 4

Check out our Facebook Page

Join us at the Mills Farm 1912 Boathouse on Saturday, March 31 for our annual Easter Egg hunt! Grounds open at 10:00, and the hunt for eggs in the riverside garden begins at 11:00 followed by a gourmet picnic luncheon. Tickets for the egg hunt and a specialty picnic basket lunch will be on sale at the front desk of the Cattleman Hotel and at the Mills Farm Country Restaurant. (Kosher and vegan options for this lunch are available. Each basket serves 4.)

The Café's Own Prize-Winning Chili

4 large Maui or Vidalia onions, 2 cups celery, diced, 2 T minced garlic, l each green, red, yellow Bell pepper, 1 poblano, 2 sweet banana, 4 jalapeno, 4 serrano and 1 ripe habanero pepper, all peppers seeded and diced. 6 Lbs boar loin, cubed, 1 gal. boar stock, 1 each #10 can crushed tomatoes and tomato puree, (additional tomato paste if needed), 2 each 16oz cans dark red and light red kidney beans, cannellini, red, pinto and navy beans. ½ cup chili powder, 1 t ground cumin 1 T each cayenne pepper, smoked paprika, crushed red pepper flakes, ground black pepper, 2 T sea salt, 1 large bay leaf, 1t Yucatan Sunshine hot sauce. Additional salt, black pepper, garlic powder, onion powder, and chili powder to season meat.
6 strips bacon, diced, 6 strips bacon, diced, 1/4 C olive oil (x2) 1/2 stick butter (x2)

In large sauté pan, cook diced bacon until crisp, add 1/2 stick butter and 1/4 C olive oil, add vegetables, cook until onions are translucent. Set aside. Put tomatoes, spices, and 1/2 gallon of boar stock in a 5-gallon stockpot, bring to slow boil, reduce to simmer. Add cooked vegetables.
Open and drain canned beans. In another large sauté pan, melt 1/2 stick butter, add 1/4 C olive oil. Season meat and brown, add 1/2-gallon boar stock, bring to boil and simmer for 15 minutes. Add meat and beans to stockpot. Bring to slow boil, reduce heat. Simmer for 3 hours, adding tomato paste if needed to thicken. Makes approximately 5 gallons.

Upcoming Events

December 31

Welcome the New Year in with a dance on Town Square! Music provided by Los Maldonados, with fireworks at midnight!

March 5

Luna City VFD fund-raising pancake breakfast at the firehouse from 8-11. Profits will go towards purchase of the latest in turn-out gear.

April 21

An ecumenical Easter sunrise service will be held beginning at 5:30 AM at the new riverside landing on the San Antonio River.

The Luna City Players

The Luna City Players announce try-outs for those wishing to join as new members on Saturday, February 9 at 4:00 PM in the Koenig Opera House. Prospective members should be prepared to perform a five-minute monolog, either of their own creation or from a well-known classic.

Luna City, Texas – Home of the Mighty Fighting Moths

Page 1 of 2

Luna City ISD News

School Lunch Program

Parents of students participating in the LCISD's school lunch program are reminded that payment for school lunches is due by the tenth of every month. Families undergoing economic hardship and having difficulty paying my apply for relief at the ISD main office, in the Luna City Elementary school building on Town Square. Please bring one form of picture ID if applying for this program.

Driver Training Permission Slips

Parents of sophomore and junior students participating in LCISD's Driver Education program must have permission forms signed by parent or legal guardian, in addition to passing the exam on rules of the road, before being allowed to participate in the 'behind the wheel' portion of the program.

Senior Spring Break Trip

Seniors of Class of '19 must have permission slips signed by parent/legal guardian turned into the LCHS main office by March 15th, and all fees paid in order to participate in the Spring Break road trip to Galveston on March 22. The excursion bus departs at 4:00 PM from the high school parking lot and returns on the 31st. Students will stay in the Raddison Country Inn & Suites, four per room, and will enjoy days at the beach, plus guided tours of the Moody Mansion & Gardens, Haunted Galveston, and a sightseeing tour of the harbor.

Community Marketplace

For the Clients of Jessica Abernathy-Vaughn, CPA

For the foreseeable future, MS Abernathy-Vaughn will no longer be able to make on-site visits to clients but has set up an office on the second floor of Abernathy Hardware. Clients are asked to call to make appointments, weekdays and Saturdays from 9-4. MS Abernathy-Vaughn apologizes for the inconvenience caused, but there is simply no other way for her to continue as formerly, due to personal and family considerations.

From Chief Vaughn, Luna City PD

The young, reckless and bored are reminded that informal drag racing on Rte 123, or various deserted backroads adjacent to the Wyler Ranch is strictly forbidden by local, county and state laws. The movie series "Fast and Furious" is not a documentary.

Luna Café Spring Blue Plate Lunch Specials

Tuesday – Patty Melt with *Pomme Frite*
Wednesday – Fried Chicken w/ Biscuit and Gravy
Thursday – Breaded Pork Chop with Root Vegetables
Friday – Salad Niçoise & Cheddar/Potato Soup
Saturday – Pasta Primavera w/ Garlic Toast
Sunday – Pot Roast

All selections served with a green salad dressed with Chef Richard's special dressing and include dessert of the day.

Luna City, Texas – Home of the Mighty Fighting Moths

Page 2 of 2

Cherchez la Femme

It needs to be said, that I liked Mayor McAllister; a sober and responsible man, the son of the architect who had been so much a part of the founding of Luna City. It was no fault of the original McAllister that the railway intended to bring regional prominence and wealth to the place had never come through, instead being constructed through Karnesville, some fifteen miles distant. McAllister and his family lived in a stone house at the edge of town, a house older than town by some four decades. It was an oft-repeated witticism that in Scotland a hundred miles was a graidly long distance and a hundred years only yesterday, whereas the opposite was true of Texas. I let John Drury off at the Catholic parish hall, where a scattering of automobiles, bicycles and a few buggies stood, with horses in harness moodily exploring the contents of their nosebags. Such was the time; the twentieth century arrived in this part of Texas in a leisurely manner.

"We'll consult in the morning," I said, "Unless you discover something of such import that it cannot wait until then."

"Will do, Captain," and he sketched a casual salute, and strolled towards the parish hall. Meanwhile, I turned the corner and drove along to the main road again, to where the McAllister house sat among extensive gardens, and where I hoped to find the Methodist ladies at their sewing circle. Fortunate for my investigation the same assortment of automobiles, bicycles and buggies or wagons with horses standing in harness lined up along the roadside before the McAllister garden. A boring life it must be, indeed, for a horse. I found a place to park the Ford and walked through the gardens to the house.

It was then early spring; the prettiest time of the year in Texas. The hydrangea bushes were in full and glorious bloom. A bed of daffodils nodded their yellow heads over the sun-kissed bed. The grass lawn had put out a brave new growth; someone had mown it, so that the fragrance of cut grass vied with the perfume of cascades of purple laurel, on the small tree next to the walkway. Sweet green grass, and the grape-pop odor of mountain laurel brings to me the memory of that day.

Mayor McAllister answered my pull at the doorbell. He was wearing carpet-slippers, and his cravat was loosed. He had a glass of lemonade in his hand, and his wee daughter at his side.

"I did not expect you so early, Chief Magill," he said, in mild surprise, "But come in, come in. Join me in my study. Letty, darling, will you bring another glass of lemonade for our guest?"

I followed him to the small study at the back of the house; a comfortable dark room adorned with many bookshelves and framed renderings of the designs for various grand buildings in Luna City, a bare handful of which had actually been constructed. We settled into that pair of comfortably shabby leather-upholstered chairs before the small fireplace, which had warmed that room in winter, when the chill settled into the bones of the stone.

I replied, "I had intended to brief you on our finding so far, but then it came to me that the Methodist church ladies have their sewing circle every Wednesday. If I were curious about a marked dislike between two women whose husbands are neck-deep in this whole sordid matter, then perhaps Sergeant Drury and I should talk to those ladies who move in the same circles."

Ed McAllister grinned. "Save you, Chief – a stroke of genius. What doesn't come to the attention of the gossip circle probably isn't worth knowing. So," and his genial expression sobered in an instant. "The two women involved since their husbands are under suspicion?"

"Carolina Mills. Her man is the chief and sole producer of illicit alcohol in Luna City. Mrs. Eloise Dunsmore is the wife of the proprietor of the sole illegal saloon in this place, the speakeasy in the cellar of Dunsmore's grocery store. Yet the two of those women appear to be at odds."

"Mrs. Dunsmore talks of herself, all the time," said Letty McAllister, who had appeared in the study like an owl-eyed sprite. "She never asks about anyone else. Only talks about herself."

"Letty, sugar, children are to be seen and not heard," Ed McAllister gently reproved his daughter, who set a tall glass of lemonade, clinking with chunks of ice, on the table at my elbow."

"She does, Papa," Letty replied, looking at me with grave regard. An odd child, I thought. One might believe stories of the fae, replacing human children with one of their own. The girl had sober eyes, calm and judgmental. Curiously adult. "And her parents are awful to her."

"Letty, that's enough," Ed McAllister reproved his daughter again. "Go see if your mother and the other ladies want anything. Chief Magill and I have important matters to discuss."

"Yes, Papa," Letty obeyed, not seeming to feel a sting of reprimand. When the study door closed, Ed McAllister looked straight at me.

"All right, then; what have you found so far?"

"Not much," I admitted ruefully. "Although 'tis certain that the alcohol came from the Mills place. We talked to Mrs. Mills, not half an hour ago, and she confessed plain that Mills supplies the Dunsmore speakeasy through regular deliveries to the back of the grocery. I canna think they have another supplier, unless they make deliveries at midnight, and drop them down the chimney, like Saint Nicholas. She is a woman who strikes us as proud of her enterprise, and not willing to poison good and regular customers in the pursuit of short-term gain. She swore on the most holy that their liquor is sound, indeed. Even provided us with a pair of bottles – bottles of our random choosing – to prove it. I'll send them for analysis in Karnesville in the morning."

"So, we can tentatively rule out an outside bootlegger," Ed McAllister settled back into his armchair. He looked like a man doing his own interior calculations. "And yet the tainted booze came from somewhere."

"We rule out nothing, absolutely," I replied. "There is a slight probability of a single small shipment of tainted alcohol from other than the Mills place. But Sergeant Drury and I think it unlikely that another bootlegger has made deliveries to Dunsmore."

"Perhaps the three drummers procured their own bottle from somewhere else, prior to drinking at the Dunsmore establishment … and it was that bottle which was fatally tainted."

"A most perspicuous suggestion," I acknowledged. "But, the one survivor was questioned on that account, and insisted that he and his fellows had not partaken of any spirits save that which they purchased and consumed on Saturday night at the speakeasy. He could have omitted to mention the truth of it, but it has been my experience that men on their deathbed are inclined to be truthful, having little or nothing else to lose by confessing the truth. It remains that if Mills is the sole provider to the Dunsmore speakeasy, and poisoned alcohol was consumed there, then someone in the establishment there poisoned the alcohol after it arrived. There is no more narrow way to slice this, Mayor McAllister. As the third possibility, we must carefully consider the Dunsmores and their employees. The circle of suspects narrows to a bare handful: Mr. and Mrs. Dunsmore, and the man who works in the store … and I presume in the speakeasy itself; Ambrosiano Gonzalez. All had access, none can be eliminated from suspicion, if you are given to a logical sense of the matter. Sgt. Drury and I must know; what are the resentments and tensions within that small circle? There must be some, for she is so very much younger than he. And had those tensions boiled over? For answers to that, I must speak to the ladies."

"You must indeed," Mayor McAllister replied, with a mischievous grin. "And so you will; and commend your soul to our Creator before you do, for you may well require His aid on that expedition."

Mayor McAllister conducted me personally to the pleasant parlor in which the ladies' sewing circle were at work; an old-fashioned chamber which opened through tall French doors onto a generous verandah. This additional open-air space was furnished with comfortable wicker chairs and small tables overlooked a most pleasing aspect of the gardens and green lawn. Lush green ferns and colorful pink and red fuchsias in hangers were suspended in hanging baskets from the eaves and from brackets on the supporting columns. A full pitcher of lemonade, clinking with chunks of ice, sat in pride of place on an embroidered cloth on a small table, attended by an array of tall glasses, and plates of cake and biscuits. Ed McAllister rapped briefly on the doorjamb; all converse instantly ceased when the ladies within raised their eyes towards us.

"Muriel, my dear," he addressed his wife, whose lap overflowed with a small tablecloth on which she was inflicting a border of ornate crochet-work in an unfortunate shade of acid green. "Chief Magill has come to me with a most peculiar request. In his investigation of the unfortunate deaths of the three drummers at the Cattleman last week, it seems that he and Sergeant Drury seek information on … well, I'll leave it to the Chief to explain precisely that information which he seeks."

Well, that was blunt enough, I thought to meself.

"Consider yourself thrown to the lions," Mayor McAllister added, sotto voice. "Send Letty to me, when you wish liberation from their den."

"You are a hard man, Mayor," I whispered. Upon which Mayor McAllister grinned like a boy and left me to my wit and own devices, in a parlor full of women; their eyes upon me reminded me of nothing so much as a box of fish.

Mrs. McAllister was the saving of me, in this regard. She set aside her crochet hook and the ball of acid-green heavy thread. "How may we be of assistance to you then, Chief Magill? Would you like a glass of lemonade? Letty, dear – pour a glass of lemonade for the man, he must be parched."

"No, I have already partaken," I replied. Little Miss Letty was sitting, owl-eyed and obedient on a small chair at her mothers' elbow. "Thank you for the consideration Mrs. McAllister. The question is …" and here I was stumbling for a wee moment, until Mrs. McAllister saved me.

"You are wondering about Mrs. Dunsmore," She observed. "It is her husband who runs the speakeasy. And she is fast. Too loose and easy with other men than her husband. It pains me to say so," she added, with what appeared to be a sincere air of regret. "Married women have always taken comfort and support from the friendship of other married women. Our sorority is a great comfort to us all, when there are these rocky patches. Mrs. Dunsmore's path is all rocky patches, and mostly of her own making, I daresay. She wishes no degree of friendship with other women, a friendship which might smooth over those patches."

The Dunsmore woman had been tried, I sensed – and found wanting. Now to find out the full reason of "why."

"I am, indeed, Ma'am," I replied. "And I would relish a bite of … is that Dundee cake that I see? Yes, I would relish a sliver of that."

"I learned to make it from a Scots friend of mine, when we were nursing together in France." That was Doris Rowbottom, the wife of the Methodist minister. The Rowbottoms lived in a small house across the road from the Dunsmores. Mrs. Rowbottom, contra a popular literary imagining of the wife of a small-town Methodist minister, was a tall and elegant women, and verra intelligent; she had taught science and chemistry in a high school in Victoria before her marriage, and volunteered as a nurse in the late War. Nae good would ever come of assuming that the wife of a minister would be an obedient and unlettered slave to her husband and master – especially in a parish such as Luna City, a place remarkably free from the sort of Babbittry so often assumed to be prevalent in small towns.

Beaming, Mrs. Rowbottom served me up a generous slice adorned with carefully placed almonds, and very good it was, indeed. I complimented Mrs. Rowbottom after sampling a small bite and then another.

"So," I made a casual transition, as I thought it, from judging the baked goods among the ladies' social circle, to what I really wished to discuss. I set aside the small plate now empty of cake and took out my notebook and pencil. "Thank you for the cake, ladies." I met their eyes again, wondering if this was a bootless errand after all.

"Now, returning to my purpose. It seems that Mrs. Dunsmore and Mrs. Mills, whose' men are in a profitable business arrangement between them, are not fond friends; they are antagonistic, indeed. Any insight into this would be welcomed as part of our investigation into the unfortunate deaths at the Cattleman. You see, ladies; this is a matter of civic interest and pride. We cannot simply allow murder by deliberate poisoning to be set aside out of embarrassment. There is …"

"A skunk in the outhouse," Mrs. McAllister said, bluntly. "And that can't be permitted. Shoo the skunk to another shelter or endure the pestilential stench."

Well, that was frank; indeed. Mrs. Dunsmore an unwanted, odiferous creature? Or was it murder which Mrs. McAllister meant by the comparison.

Mrs. McAllister continued, continuing to crochet without looking at her work. "It is in my mind that Eloise Dunsmore is a kind of fortune-hunter. Noooo, I am reluctant to judge another of our sex so harshly, but it remains that she is. I was there in the grocery, when Mrs. Mills came to pay the account, driving that new green Ford van. She had a gold bracelet set with bands of diamonds and sapphires, which Eloise Dunsmore was remarking upon as I waited my turn. 'So lovely,' says she to Mrs. Mills. 'Was that a present for Christmas, then?' and Mrs. Mills said, very terse, 'No, it was by way of apologizing to me.' And Eloise Dunsmore made as if she wished to get in a dig, but wanted it veiled; she made as if to admire the bracelet, saying, 'Such fine work, the diamonds and sapphires do look so very real, don't they?' At that, Mrs. Mills bristled like a cat, and said, 'They are real, it came from Neiman's in Dallas.' Eloise Dunsmore made a face like she had bitten into a sour lemon. 'Do tell,' says she, 'By that, your husband must be doing very well at his enterprise.' 'Our enterprise,' snaps Mrs. Mills, and she counts out the bills and slaps them on the counter. 'Our enterprise, and this is his apology for trying to cheat me out of my proper share of it!' She turns on her heel and marches out of the store, whereupon Eloise Dunsmore looks at me, all indignant, and says, 'Well, really! And all this time, everyone thought old Mills was just scraping by! Gold bracelets from Dallas, indeed! Whoever would have thought it, Mrs. McAllister?'"

A gold bracelet adorned with gems – I made a careful note without interrupting. Curious indeed.

Meanwhile, Mrs. McAllister continued in full spate. "And Eloise Dunsmore says to me, 'Did you think it real, Mrs. McAllister? She said to me. 'There have been many stories about Old Mills,' I said. 'Which stories are common knowledge among those who were brought up here. They say that in his youth, he was a member of a notorious gang of robbers, and a treasure of gold bars and coin is hidden somewhere on his place. But that is only a story. If it were true, any sensible body would think he would have taken better care of the property!' 'That may be so, Mrs. McAllister,' she said to me, 'But what if he is really a rich man?' That was said as if she were thinking aloud, with no notice of me, standing there. It was such a calculating expression on her face,"

Mrs. Mayor McAllister added, and the ladies in the room with her all nodded in agreement. "And then she said something to me about Mrs. Mills flouncing around flaunting a bracelet which was obviously set with cheap paste stones. Really, it was no interest to me what that woman got as a gift from that old scoundrel of a husband."

"It is not money itself, which is supposed to be a sin, but the excessive love of money," Doris Rowbottom remarked, thoughtfully. "Money is a paltry thing in itself, a simple tool like a hammer or a chisel. But when someone takes as their object of worship? No good will come of that." She regarded me with sad comprehension. "Eloise, I fear, is obsessed with money and materiel things."

"You are neighbors, I take it," I hinted, inviting further confidence from a woman who lived in the house across the street from the Dunsmores. If my knowledge of the ladies' powers of observation, she might very well reveal some insight into the conduct of my suspects. "What do you know, or have good reason to suspect of them? I shall be discrete of whatever you reveal to me," I added, as Mrs. Rowbottom looked down on the embroidery in her lap. "Please, ladies, a promise on my honor as a gentleman. What you tell me shall remain in this room. But anything you say to me which might, even peripherally, have a bearing on this matter and might assist myself and Sgt. Drury in solving this matter. I beg of you to be frank. Lives may depend on your words."

"Very well, then," Doris Rowbottom sighed. "I do not like to gossip. It is a common refuge for the bored and malicious, the customary habit of evil tongues. The harm that unconsidered words might do is very well known to us both. My husband and I have often discussed this issue, as he is in the profession of ministering to souls in torment. I do believe that the Dunsmores' marriage is not a happy one."

There was a rustle of agreement from the other ladies. Mrs. Rowbottom continued, if heartened by that. "From what I have observed from across the road – not that I am a confidant of either of the parties – but both are equally unhappy and equally inclined to stray…"

"Is there evidence you have for that?" I asked, and Doris Rowbottom sighed again.

"Well you see," she replied, rather apologetically. "Poor little Susan has brown eyes. Both Eloise and Mr. Dunsmore have blue or blue-gray eyes. It is one of those scientifically-proven things, beyond all shadow of doubt – that two blue-eyed parents simply cannot give birth naturally to a brown-eyed child. It goes against everything known about genetics, you see, Chief Magill."

"Oh, dear," I said.

This bore serious consideration. Meanwhile, Doris Rowbottom continued, still with the slight air of apology. "And she is the sweetest child, in any case. So polite and intelligent."

"She is a friend of our son's," Mrs. McAllister put in, a most particularly grim expression on her pleasant and angular countenance. "She often comes after school to play with Douglas and Letty, and their other friends. Very often at suppertime, she is still there. I asked once, if she was going to go home for supper, but she said that all that she had for supper commonly would be some bread and cheese, or something cold in the icebox left for her, because her parents were both working and wouldn't be home until midnight or later. On such days, I set an extra place for supper, without making any comment."

Ah, I thought to meself; I ken how Mrs. Dunsmore has made her name mud among the good Methodist church ladies. She takes no care of her offspring. As if she has left the nestling to grow up in the care of others. There is a species of bird, I have heard, who routinely makes a point of laying their eggs in the nests of other birds – and the proprietors of that nest then make every heroic effort for the interloper nestling, sometimes to the detriment of their own offspring. That is what Mrs. Dunsmore has done; left her nestling to the care of other nests. And the women know this and condemn her for it. I made a note to meself – to take special notice of my own dear nestlings, those which I had at that time with Mrs. McGill and to make especial gestures to her, especially on the moment of my arriving home that very evening. But enough of this; I wished for the insight of the good ladies into the resentment between to women, who were to all intents and purposes, engaged in an illicit enterprise, an enterprise in which their husbands were in, to the neck and above.

"I also have looked in on poor little Susan, now and again," Doris Rowbottom continued, with the same faint air of apology. "The doors in Luna City residences are never locked, you know. Their house is only across the road from ours. I think she has had a touch of the grippe. She had a temperature, three days ago. I brought out our own thermometer to be certain. I spoke to Eloise in passing, the following day when I went to the grocery. She made a face of concern and promised me that she would take care to have Susan sleep in her bedroom where she could most carefully tend to her. And I said that perhaps Mr. Dunsmore might object and …" Doris Rowbottom looked down upon her own needlework; a beaded purse, I think, although it was only half-completed. "And that was when I perceived that their marriage is not altogether a happy one. They keep separate bedrooms. Have for some months, or so Eloise intimated to me. It is … not a good indicator of a good marriage, keeping separate bedrooms."

"Although I have heard that among the aristocratic class in Europe, that custom is very much the thing," I said, heartily. "As well as turning a blind eye to nocturnal traffic in the corridor," I added, whereupon all of the ladies regard me with puzzled or blank expressions.

"Their ways in that foreign place are a puzzle," Muriel McAllister discarded several centuries of aristocratic marital misconduct with a dismissive gesture. "They have their customs and we have ours. Proper married folk here in Luna City share the same bed. Warmth in the winter and all that. The Dunsmores can keep to whatever custom and practice that suits them. I am sure that I care nothing for it, as long as they don't inflict their odd notions on the rest of us."

"So … indade, the Dunsmore marriage is not one of the properly companionate variety," I concluded. "They share little care for their child, but more interest in their mutually-held commercial enterprise. I see. In your judgment, ladies; are their affections of an intimate nature directed elsewhere? And focused upon whom? Any such observances and speculation will be held strictly in confidence. I assure you ladies most sincerely …"

"Letty, dear," Mrs. McAllister spoke first, and to her small daughter, sitting attentively at her feet. "Would you go and fetch us more lemonade from the kitchen. You may have to squeeze more lemons, if there is not another pitcher in the icebox."

"Yes, Mother," the dear little tyke replied obediently. I had the sense that Mrs. McAllister did not wish her little pitcher to exercise big ears. As soon as the door had closed on that small back, Mrs. McAllister exchanged a slight nod with Doris Rowbottom.

"Tell what you have observed, Dorie. It's a matter of life and death, I am certain. You had reason to believe…"

"That Eloise Dunsmore is conducting an affair with Mr. Mills," Doris Rowbottom confessed, with an air of reluctance. "On many nights – late nights, when my dear husband was at a meeting with the parish council, or on an errand to administer succor to one of our congregation, I left the porch light on for him. And when hearing the sound of an automobile engine, I would look out of our bedroom window, hoping that it was him returning."

"The Reverend Rowbottom's Hudson makes a very distinctive sound," Muriel McAllister put in, by way of explanation. "Mr. Gonzalez at the garage thinks that it may need more frequent adjusting."

"I would put on my dressing-gown and look out the window." Doris Rowbottom continued. "And most often it would be his car, but then, it was frequently the Mills' Ford! Parked quite blatantly on the street in front of the Dunsmore house. For hours," she added, with mild indignation. "I cannot imagine what Eloise must be thinking! Conducting a blatant liaison with that scoundrel! And she a respectable married woman, with a position! What does she see in him, anyway?"

"I cannot presume to follow the thinking of a woman," I admitted, somewhat cravenly, for I hoped to eventually plumb the depths of the sewing circle's insights into the depravity of small-town scandals. "An advantage of some sort, I would think. Or perhaps some kind of revenge upon her husband."

No one would think Charley Mills the beau ideal as the male object of illicit affairs went. Although, upon thoughtful consideration; with competent barbering, more frequent baths and perhaps a new suit, he might not present so ill-favored a swain as all that, for a man of his age.

A Mystery Indeed

Again … this bore consideration. I wondered if John Drury would return from his adventure among the ladies at St. Margaret and Anthony with an equally heavy freight of leads, gleaned from the gossip exchanged … but now, Mrs. McAllister was speaking.

"He is from one of the old original families in Texas," she was saying, in a meditative manner. "Although in many of these old family trees, there are unfortunate branches. Every family has their black sheep. The Taylors, for example. No one can claim that John Wesley Hardin was a particular ornament to that family."

"Indade," I murmured, encouraging the conversation to continue along those lines which I desired, for the purpose of investigation. I made a mental note to consult with John Drury. John Wesley Hardin and the Taylor clan? Indeed, Texas feuds bore a most amazing resemblance to the ancient border feuds of my native land.

"He has very nice blue eyes," One of the younger women contributed, somewhat bashfully noting Charley Mills' appeal to the female. "He can sometimes be obliged to spare a most wonderous and flattering compliment. And his voice; like roughened velvet," she added blushing as pink as a primrose and fell into an abashed silence, upon receiving a disapproving look from Mrs. McAllister

But Mrs. Rowbottom nodded in agreement. "I can see how women of a certain nature might be susceptible to flirtatious advances. The attraction of a charming rogue, you see. I saw it often, while serving as a nurse in the late War. Sometimes, the soldiers were quite shameless in pressing their attentions. I began to think that a charming manner and a flattering tongue were more than sufficient in making up for an unprepossessing appearance."

"Indeed," A bolder among the younger ladies put in, with a giggle. "A man can be as handsome as a Greek god, but if he has no more wit and conversation of a tailor's dummy, you may as well prop him up in a corner and admire at a distance."

There was a general buzz of humorous agreement to that, and certain ladies gave testament with vivid and somewhat unflattering reminiscences concerning the romantic inadequacies of men who had courted them, back in the days when they were woo-worthy. With an eye on the doorway, expecting at any moment that little Letty might return, I recalled the gathering to my original purpose.

"So, Mrs. Dunsmore seems to have begun a romantic affair with Charley Mills," I said, clearing my throat and tapping my pencil impatiently upon my notebook. "Might any of you have any notion of when this affair commenced? And what his attraction to her might be?"

"I believe Eloise Dunsmore believes him to be a rich man, contrary to all appearances," Mrs. McAllister ventured. "She was envious of that jeweled gold bracelet of Mrs. Mills – indeed, she could not stop talking of it. I am certain that was when she set her cap for him."

There was a rustle of agreement at this – and I made a note, while a colloquy among the ladies emerged, only broken when little Letty returned, with another pitcher of lemonade.

"Bring us some more ice, dear," her mother suggested, and Letty set the pitcher down on the table laden with refreshments and obediently trotted away. When the child was out of sight, Muriel McAllister looked at me. "I would guess," she said. "That the affair began within a week or so of my conversation at the grocery. After Eloise cast aspersions on the quality of Mrs. Mills' bracelet. This would have been … about mid-January, I think. I was considering the purchase of some fine cake flour for my son's birthday cake, and he was born late in that month."

"That is about right," Doris Rowbottom agreed. "Then was about the time that I noted the Mills' Ford van appearing at night. February, at the earliest. And consistently every week or so then, up until the present."

I made a note of this and underlined it twice for future reference; there might be something of significance in an affair between Mrs. Dunsmore and Charley Mills. What if Carolina San Pedro Mills was of a subtly jealous nature? How would she react to her husband straying afar from the marital bed on a regular occasion? Again; a matter to consider. How angry would a hot-blooded woman of the old Mexican nobility be, with a husband straying – if not from her bed, from their established business arrangement? In what manner might she retaliate against him? A matter to seriously discuss with John Drury, who I hoped would have uncovered as profitable an investigatory vein among the ladies of the Catholic parish as I had among the Methodist sewing circle.

"So, are they properly married? The Mills couple, I mean," I ventured. "Legally in the eyes of the state? Would the gift of a new Ford van, and an expensive diamond and sapphire bracelet around the beginning of this year meant as a peace offering, perhaps – after a bitter falling out?"

"I would have no idea of the state of the Mills marriage, as neither of them are among our social circle," Muriel McAllister returned, just as little Letty returned, bearing a basin of small chips of ice. The child returned to her seat at the side of her mothers' chair and watched me with interested anticipation.

One of the other ladies ventured a supposition in a most tentative manner from the far corner of the McAllister parlor, stabbing a needle into her cross-stitch sampler. She was Mrs. Clara Bodie, a very new member of the sewing circle, whose junior status among the ladies was offset by the prosperity of her husband. He ran owned and ran the feed mill, supplying all manner of good cattle fodder to the district.

"Nathalie might know. Nathalie Everett. She's Nathalie Corson now, since she married. Her mother was a friend of my mother, but Nathalie took up work in Karnesville, working in an office as secretary and typist, since she learned to take shorthand dictation and type. She worked in a legal office; Newsome, Porter & Daws. She used to come back to Luna City to visit her mother, but since Mrs. Everett passed away last summer …" Young Mrs. Bodie blushed and ducked her head over her embroidery. "I have not seen her in months. But you might want to talk to Nathalie. She gave her notice when she got engaged, but she would know something for certain, since Mr. Newsome was Old Charley's lawyer."

"Oh, was she now?" I felt a thrill of satisfaction pass through me, possibly akin to that felt by the inimitable Sherlock Holmes when a promising lead to a solution in a case unfolded before him. And the potential informant which the young and tentative Mrs. Bodie had suggested to me no longer worked for the odious Newsome, and the possibly imaginary Porter & Daws! Excellent; she might freely discuss the legal doings involving Mr. Mills, without engaging the litigious interest of Counsel Newsome! "Mrs. Corson is her name, now? Might I trouble you for her address in Karnesville?" I had my pencil at the ready.

"I don't have my address book with me," Mrs. Bodie sounded so regretful. "And I cannot recall it without written aid. But she and her husband have a telephone. If you call and ask the directory in Karnesville, surely, they will know it."

"I thank you, ladies," I said, making a note of that last name, feeling unexpectedly heartened at the information gleaned through an attentive hour – that and the Dundee cake, which was a culinary delight unlooked for, in a Texas desert. "You have been most helpful and can count on my undying gratitude. If we unravel this sad mystery to its very core as I expect that we shall – you all have been of inestimable value in this, our investigation."

I set the small plate aside, empty of all but a few crumbs of very excellent cake, stowed away my pencil and notebook, and made a gentlemanly exit from the parlor.

In the hallway, though, I was shortstopped by Ed McAllister, who murmured, conspiratorially, "You escape with an unharmed pelt, Chief. My compliments on your survival. Did you glean from this what you had hoped?"

He escorted me towards the front door and awaited my reply.

"I have, indeed, Mayor. A good measure, pressed down, shaken together and running over. I hope to have this matter resolved very shortly, given the insights gleaned from your good lady's circle. Now, I must see what Sgt. Drury has gained from the other circle of women. I am in the expectation that his mission has been equally fruitful."

"Petticoat government," Mayor McAllister closed the front door behind us, and we looked out together, across the blooming grounds of the McAllister house, to where the county road slashed across the landscape in a veil of dust. "It might be that the Wyler brothers wish to talk to you regarding this sad affair."

I bit back my first unbridled reaction. The Wyler brothers were joint heirs to the vast ranch which took up a good stretch of Karnes County to the east, north and south of Luna City. I honestly did not wish to speak to them at this time, not before writing up my notes and consulting with John Drury. What could they have to do with the case at hand? Albert Wyler was a stout and trustworthy chap, but his younger brother Tom was a rake and a wastrel. Still, they were not half the b*stards which they might have turned out, knowing what their father had been. Fortunately, at the time of which I speak, the old b*stard, Herbert K. Wyler, late Captain in the equally late Army of the Confederate States of America was a quarter of a century dead. He considered himself the lord and master of Karnes County and half the remainder of creation. As I understand it, he was also the man chiefly responsible for Luna City not having the railway come through – the result of an almighty tantrum regarding his young daughter eloping with a handsome railway engineer. Well good luck for her, but unfortunate for the town, I had always thought.

"They may call upon me in my office at the police station, at any time of their convenience," I replied, for I would be damned if I would go to them. I was no poor tenant summoned to the laird's house, directed to enter by the servant's back door and wait their pleasure with my cap in hand. Rich men they might be, indeed, but I was no man's errand boy, least of all theirs. "It was not a matter of particular urgency, in your judgement?"

"No; more a matter of sketching in the background to this matter." Mayor McAllister tipped me a knowing wink. "It seems that Thomas Wyler is a frequenter of the illicit establishment and has never taken any ill from the experience. I'll let Albert and Thomas know," Mayor McAllister replied, most genially; seeming to think I was being quite reasonable, considering our office and responsibilities within Luna City.

"I shall expect them to call upon me in the mid-morning," I replied. "For it is now almost suppertime and I would like to have a word to Sergeant Drury first."

"Good man," Mayor McAllister replied, and offered a cordial smile as he closed the door after me.

"I endeavor to give satisfaction in the discharge of my professional responsibilities," I murmured to myself as I walked through the McAllister garden, on the way back to my vehicle. Late afternoon it was, the warmest time of the day. I drove to my home – as it was then almost six of the clock. I kissed my dear Amanda, and our little children; thus it was that at the end of the day, I was given time with my dear family. What had John Drury discovered in his time with the ladies of the Catholic parish? That I determined could wait until the following day.

The Mystery Deepens

John Drury waited for me in my office on the following morning. The Luna City Police Department was then housed in a four-square stone building a block from Town Square, a building once strongly built with bars on the windows but was in a calamitous state of disrepair at the time of this case. I could have kicked through any of the doors without expending very much effort at all. Although the window-bars appeared sturdy enough at first glance, the mortar holding them in place was well-rotted, and the bars themselves were mere rust garnished with many layers of paint. This building also housed the jail, although prisoners were not held there often, commonly being transported to Karnesville if being held for longer than a few days. My office overlooked the stables in back of the Cattleman Hotel. It was a relatively pleasant place to work, albeit rather cramped, and the recent hasty electrification of the building itself left much to be desired. *(This building was later replaced by a larger, more modern structure long after I retired.)*

"Well?" I asked, as John Drury settled into a chair and took out his own little notebook. "What were you able to find out from the ladies of the Catholic parish?"

"That Mrs. Mills is the object of pity rather than condemnation among them," John replied. "They care nothing for the matter of bootlegging or maintaining the Dunsmore speakeasy. For a certainty, many of them make wine or near-beer for household consumption. As for Mrs. Mills, they are sorry, sorry that she is married to that *vieja cabra* they called him, that old goat. Even if he gives her generous gifts. He has bought her, and they are sorry at the shame of it all to a good Catholic woman."

"Old goat indeed," I said. "Who is having an affair with Mrs. Dunsmore. Such was the intelligence which I gleaned from conversation with the Methodist ladies, specifically Mrs. Rowbottom."

John Drury's eyebrows lifted nearly to his hairline. "Indeed. There is no question of that?"

"The Rowbottoms live opposite the Dunsmore house. Mrs. Rowbottom has excellent eyesight, no imagination that I could detect, and a splendid view from the upper floor of the front of the Dunsmore place. In front of which the Mills van was parked for hours on many a late night and early morning. It is the opinion of the assembled informants whom I interviewed yesterday, that Mrs. Dunsmore initiated the liaison, believing him to be a man of wealth."

"A gold-digger, for certain!" John Drury gave a cynical chuckle. "And if Old Mills isn't the very beau ideal! Well, hold your nose, woman, lay back and think of mink coats, diamond bracelets and expensive suppers at the Ritz!"

"Don't be vulgar, Mr. Drury," I replied, and John Drury chuckled again.

"What can Old Mills be getting out of it, but a free romp for his Nebuchadnezzar in the Dunsmore woman's garden?"

"She had best hope that Mr. Dunsmore never catches wind of what his wife and his business partner are getting up to," I predicted, and John Drury replied,

"You might be wrong on that, Captain. From what the Catholic ladies reported, Mrs. Mills is complaining to them of how Mr. Dunsmore has been making calf-eyes at her for the last two months."

"You can't be serious!" I exclaimed. "Mrs. Dunsmore being bedded by Mills for two or three months, while her husband launches romantic overtures to Carolina Mills! How did this mystery become a nickelodeon farce, with everyone bouncing in and out of everyone elses' beds, willy-nilly? And what might it have to do with the poisoning of the three drummers?"

"I have no idea, Captain," John Drury first appeared amused, and then sobered. "Yet. But as I said at the start; *cherchez la femme*. Jealousy is a powerful motivation for murder."

"*Cherchez la homme* too, it appears," I said, as the sound of a powerful automobile engine floated through my open office window, and then abruptly cut off, as that automobile seemed from the auditory evidence to have pulled in and parked before our offices. I stood up and went to look out the window. "Oh, good. I was told that the Wyler lads wanted to meet with me. Mayor McAllister assured me that they had intelligence to share in the matter of the Dunsmore speakeasy."

'Lads' a term which I used rather casually, in referencing the Wyler sons. Albert was at that time my own age, and Thomas nearly fifteen years younger. But it is ever thus. Those scions of a giant among us always appear somewhat the lessor, when compared to their sire, estimable men in their own right as they might otherwise be.

The two; Albert and Thomas were showed to my office by the duty sergeant. Albert appeared completely composed, even displaying some signs of being amused by the whole matter. Thomas seemed ill at ease, if I read the signs aright. From the alert expression on the countenance of John Drury, I wondered if my ever-vigilant sergeant had some other suspicions.

"I take it that you are familiar with the Dunsmore illicit saloon, in the cellar of the grocery," I said, as the Wyler brothers settled into the comfortably padded guest chairs in front of my desk. John Drury had absented himself to another chair; a small straight one, set unobtrusively in the corner of my office. "No, do not bother with denial. I am aware of that sub-rosa enterprise, for as long as it has been established, and the Volstead Act signed, sealed and delivered by fools who took no care for the consequences of a well-meant piece of legislature. Frankly, I had little interest in the whole matter, until there were deaths come from it all. Your purpose in coming into my office on this beautiful spring morning?"

"I might have some insight into the matter," Tom Wyler replied. "My brother insisted that I share what I know with you. I will confess to being rather more familiar with Dunsmore's juice-joint than Al, since he is the responsible married man," With a grand flourish, he extended his wrists, as if inviting manacles to be snapped on to them, much as Carolina Mills had. Tom Wyler was like that; a handsome rake of a man, given to flamboyant gestures and manners, and quite the dandy when it came to sporting fine-cut suits and gaudy cravats; a cake-eater, as the old phrase had it. "You may put me under arrest, if you like, for frequenting the only joint in the county where one can get a decent drink!"

"Don't act the fool, Tommy," Albert Wyler looked exasperated. "You were the one who heard Dunsmore and his missus arguing. You kept on about seeing Mrs. Dunsmore resealing bottles on the evening that those three drummers were poisoned. You thought that you might have witnessed a preparation for murder." He looked directly at me. "It was at my urging that he come talk to you, Chief. There's some things that we can't let slide, and deliberate murder is one of them."

"Right," Tom Wyler heaved a sad sigh, and ran his fingers through his immaculately barbered hair, somewhat mussing the careful arrangement. "I … have a young friend. He works at Dunsmores … in the grocery, and in the evening at the juice-joint. Not exactly a friend, though: I dearly wish that he was. Divinely handsome, would you believe, but has hardly a word to spare for anyone, let alone poor little me. He waits on the customers, while Dunsmore tends bar, after Mrs. Dunsmore ankles for the evening."

"Ambrosiano Gonzalez," John Drury put in, from his corner, and Tom Wyler nodded. I might almost have thought he was blushing like a girl.

"That's him. Well, I've been a regular since Dunsmore opened his little social club round at the back of the grocery. Which is what we call it, those of us who go to see the man about a dog on a regular basis. Anyway. On this particular evening, I was … dammit it, feeling particularly lonely, so I went over and let myself in. Yes," Tom smirked just the tiniest bit. "I have a key to the place as a cherished and regular customer. None of this *'knock a special knock at the door, eye-balled through the grate and asked for a password,'* not for a Wyler. So, I let myself in. I could hear voices coming from the storeroom behind the bar. Thought nothing of it, at the first. I sat myself down in my usual chair, in the corner farthest from the door, and waited for one of them to take notice. I didn't pay any mind at first," Tom Wyler added, with a shudder. "But they sounded so angry. Dunsmore and the missus. Don't care for that sort of unpleasantness, myself."

In the corner, John Drury's lips moved; something short, derisive and silent. I frowned, and Tom Wyler must have thought I meant the frown for him.

"It's not my biz-wah, you see," he continued plaintively. "And I don't recall the exact words. Save that she was angry at him for tomcatting on the down-low with Mrs. Mills and he was even more angry with her for over-friendliness with Old Mills himself. Really, I almost regretted the impulse that brought me there, that evening. As it was, extremely harsh words were exchanged by Dunsmore and his ball-and-chain in equal proportion, and by the sound of breakage, a couple of thrown glasses or empty bottles as well. Dunsmore went storming out of the place, shouting over his shoulder at her that she could go to hell or back to her sister in St. Louis, wherever she pleased."

"Did he take any notice of you?" I asked.

Tom Wyler shook his head. "No, he did not even look in my direction. Just pulled his hat over his eyes and ankled up the stairs and out the door at speed. I felt a bit hurt at being so ignored. After a decent interval – say, about five minutes, I went to the bar. From where I stood, I could look into the back room through the door behind the bar. There I saw Mrs. Dunsmore, with two bottles in front of her, emptying the contents of a third bottle into them through a funnel. The look on her face!" Tom Wyler shuddered, theatrically. "A perfect Medea! Hate and vengefulness in every line! It quite gave me the shudders, I tell you."

Did Tom Wyler do anything non-theatrically? I wondered. *And did his sensible brother Albert finally snap through exasperation with the drama and order his sibling to come clean with us, just to get some peace and quiet about it all?*

"And then," Tom Wyler continued, still aiming for maximum dramatic effect, "After she re-corked the two bottles with a cork press, she looked up, catching my eye through the doorway. 'Mr. Wyler, sir,' said she, always the perfect doll, 'Do you want a drink? What would be your pleasure, then?' And I replied, 'I think that I have changed my mind. I will go have a lemon-sarsaparilla at the ice cream parlor and call it a day.'" I did. The look on her face when she didn't think anyone noted, just gave me the cold grue. Quite killed any appetite I might have had for whatever was in those bottles and any of the others. So I tipped my tile to her and went as though the hounds of Hell were at my back, and I haven't returned since. It was that very evening that those three drummers came and consumed tainted liquor and went to sing in the choir eternal. Honestly," he added in plaintive tones, "I like a decent drink and the company of beautiful young fellows who also like a decent drink, but the prospect of dying in agony is just not worth it all!"

"Best get your whiskey straight from Charley Mills, and have done with it," Albert Wyler commented. "Drink at home, Tommy. That's always been my advice."

"You're such a milk-toast, Al," Tom Wyler grumbled.

Albert Wyler replied, "Yes, but at least I'm not sweating over how narrowly I escaped drinking poisoned giggle-juice, am I?" He turned to me, saying, "Do you need anything more of us, Chief Magill?"

"Can you recollect anything about that third bottle? The one which Mrs. Dunsmore was decanting into the first two?" I asked. "Were there any markings on it, that you noted?"

"No, none at all," Tom Wyler answered. "Plain clear glass, I think the label was in orange print, but too small for me to read it – and the fluid within also clear. There was a distinct smell, though; of alcohol, extraordinarily strong. I could smell it all across the bar, and from the next room."

"Booze hound," Albert noted cheerfully, and his brother scowled, but only briefly.

"I relish life, Al," Tom replied, in plaintive tones. "And every and all the experiences that life has to offer. What can be wrong with that, drinking experience from the overflowing cup?"

"You don't get out alive," Albert replied. "Whether you live adventurously or not. Come along, Tommy; are you quite finished with questions, Chief?"

"I am," I replied, and Tom protested in a minor voice as his brother steered him towards the door, "Well, no one does, Al. Why not have some amusement while awaiting the halo and harp, then?"

When they had departed, and the sound of a powerful auto engine died in the distance towards the palatial front gate of the Wyler place, John Drury and I looked at each other.

"*Cherchez la femme*," John Drury remarked, after a brief silence. "Should I bring her in for questioning, Captain?"

"I did nae think I would have to make an order out of it," I said. John Drury grinned mirthlessly, like a wolf, snapped his notebook closed and departed my office with a purposeful air.

I did not sit in on his interview with Mrs. Dunsmore. The management of the department required my attention for the rest of that morning. I could hear her indignant screeching from several rooms away, as John Drury conducted his questioning. I could hear his voice, measured and low, too low to hear what he was saying. It seemed to be an inconclusive interview; she flounced past the half-open door of my office, the heels of her shoes tapping indignantly on the old wooden floor. She made no reply to the duty sergeant who greeted her cordially as she went past his desk, other than to let the front door fall closed behind her, the thump of it putting an emphatic period. In a moment, John Drury tapped upon the doorjamb of my office.

"Well?" I asked, as he sank into the nearest chair. "What did she have to say?"

"Noting of relevance or courtesy," he replied. "Not that I expected much but flat denials from the woman. She claims that she was merely topping up two half-empty bottles from a third, and that is all that Tom Wyler saw."

"What of the empty bottle?" I probed, as John Drury opened his little notebook.

"Into a box intended to be returned to the Mills place for re-use; a box collected at some point early in the week after the deaths. If there was something special about that bottle, if it was clearly marked with a label printed in orange ink, it could have been methyl alcohol."

"And clearly marked as a poison, not for human consumption," I agreed with a sigh. "We should ask if any has been purchased lately at Abernathy's by either of the Dunsmores or their hired man."

"I'm going over there right now," John Drury closed his little notebook. "Are you finished with the quarterly budget request for the town council, Captain?"

"Nearly," I confessed. As the saying was then – and still is – the job is not finished until the paperwork is done, signed, witnessed and filed accordingly. "But this case niggles at me, John. I want it sorted, as soon as is possible. Tomorrow, I'm driving myself down to Karnesville to interview a Mrs. Courson, who may have relevant knowledge of Old Charley Mills' business affairs.

She worked in the office of his lawyer but left when she married. I am hoping that she will be forthright with me, regarding those matters and the validity of the Mills marriage."

"A wife cannot be compelled to testify against her husband," John Drury nodded in agreement. "Even a common-law wife, assuming that to be the case. If they are not truly married, or if she has reason to believe him to be unfaithful, that is a wedge which we may use to good effect in resolving this case."

"Any tool which comes to hand, John," I said, as the sound of another powerful auto engine floated into my office from the street below. I looked out of my window. "And we have another visitor, it appears. I am thinking that this must have a bearing on our most immediate case."

"Other than a couple of townies pestering the cows in the pasture, trying to tip them over?" John Drury grinned. "Who is it, Captain? Are they coming to confess all, just to get it off their chest? As if this job has ever been easy!"

"It appears to be Don Antonio, of the Rancho Encino! This is a rare turn-out. Would you entertain a bet on whom he has with him?"

"No," John Drury put up his hands in mock-despair. "Bet against the Fife Bomber? Not on your life or mine, Captain!"

I told him what I thought of that, quite rudely, so my remark on that occasion will not be recorded by my pen. Then I said, "He has Ambrosiano Gonzalez with him' that Mexican lad who works in the grocery, and at the speak-easy. I would venture at a guess that this is to do with the Dunsmore matter."

"I suppose I can put off the visit to Abernathy's until later," John Drury now looked over my shoulder, down at the street below. "We'd have wanted to speak to him next, anyway. It looks like Don

Antonio has saved us the trouble. Do you think young Ambrosiano is guilty in any part?"

"No," I replied, as the main door to the station opened and closed below, and the voice of the booking sergeant floated up the staircase to us. "I would judge an excess of caution on his part, and the wit to bring an ally of standing and substance with him, and not his employer, either. If he is an observant lad, and more intelligent than they give him credit for being, he must already suspect them, as proprietors of the speak in the cellar. And if he was at work in the grocery store today, he will know that we have already interviewed Eloise Dunsmore."

"Well, then," John Drury opened his little notebook, and took up his seat on the discreet straight chair in the corner. "Let us see what he has come to tell us, Captain. He doesn't speak much English, or so I have gathered. Shall I question him directly in Spanish, or just make note of what he and Don Antonio say, if they assume that neither of us is fluent in the lingo?"

I considered, as I heard footsteps on the stairway, and a quiet rap on the doorjamb from one of the young city constables.

"Chief, you have visitors, requesting a conversation with you," said a very young city policeman, who had the onerous duty of running messages for the desk sergeant, since we were still training him. Nice young chap, been a soldier in Russia practically from the moment he had finished with wearing diapers. In whose army we didn't inquire, although I was fairly certain he wasn't a Red; otherwise we wouldn't have taken him on the strength. I liked his punctilious respect for authority. "Sir Antonin Gonzalez and Gospodin Gonzalez. They say that they have important information for you, regarding the nasty matter at the illegal saloon,"

"Thank you, Constable Grigoryev," said I. "Show them in. We have a murder most vile to investigate, and these gentlemen may hold the key. I'll let them talk, John – in whatever language – and you will listen and take notes."

"Fly on the wall, Captain," John nodded.

***

In a moment, Constable Grigoryev again rapped smartly at the doorjamb. "Sir Gonzalez, Gospodin Gonzalez, for your attention, sah!"

Constable Grigoryev opened the door, and ceremoniously gestured in the two men who had accompanied him up the stairway. Dearie me, oh, dearie me: I sighed. The constable-in-training had gotten the gist of ceremony in presentation to authority, but he had not quite gotten the hang of dialing it down a degree or so, in accordance with local custom. For Luna City was a place which didn't go much in for that sort of thing. Still, I thought it likely that Don Antonio Gonzalez appreciated the deference, for everyone said that he and his family were descended from the old Spanish nobility, as proud as Lucifer. He owned what was left of the original land grant given to his ancestor for service to the Spanish crown; indeed, Luna City was built on land which Don Antonio had donated for the founding of the town, back when it had been expected that the San Antonio and Aransas Pass Railroad would pass through, and situate the town as the queen city of Karnes County and all of South Texas north of the Valley of the Rio Grande.

At the time of this visit to my office Don Antonio was a fine-looking man of sixty or so, as straight-backed as a soldier, with a head of white hair, and a flowing mustache, although his eyebrows were still as dark as ink. As always when he came to town, he wore elegant black suits of a vaguely foreign cut. A high-collared starched white shirt with an old-fashioned string tie, a heavy antique revolver at his hip and a soft-sided leather portfolio in one hand completed the ensemble. The fashions of this modern century were merely a distasteful rumor to Don Antonio. He had a notoriously hot temper to match the imperious manner, and some six or seven years before, had challenged a local tough to a duel on the sidewalk in front of the ice cream parlor on Town Square. A forceful man, he countenanced no slights by anyone. He nodded briefly at Constable Grigoryev in the manner of a king acknowledging the bow of a minor courtier, and then at me, as Constable Grigoryev closed the door after himself.

"Good afternoon, Chief Magill," he said, without preamble, carefully setting down the soft leather portfolio next to the chairs before my desk. He spoke English like a native of that tongue, although more formally than was customary among most residents of Karnes County. "I have a matter of grave importance to discuss with you, regarding the matter of the poisoned alcohol at Dunsmore's grocery. A matter of justice, and as it involves my young nephew here, I thought it best to consult with you." He nodded brusquely towards the younger man, lingering hesitantly at his elbow. "Sit, Ambrosiano! There will be no harm come to you, since you provide the evidence." That last was spoken in soft Spanish – yes, I knew sufficient of that tongue to grasp the gist of his remarks in that language. From the corner of my office, where John Drury sat with his pencil and notebook at the ready, he nodded towards me, an almost imperceptible nod.

"We are grateful for your assistance in getting to the bottom of this sad affair," I replied, equal in courtesy. "We have ascertained that at least two bottles of alcohol served in the Dunsmore's illicit saloon were deliberately contaminated with methyl spirits, although we are not at liberty to reveal who we suspect, or the name of the witness who gave cause to suspect them, I am entirely open to hearing from your … nephew is it? Of course."

I sat back in my chair, assuming an air of detached interest. No, I did not believe that Ambrosiano was truly a nephew of Don Antonio. A very distant connection, though; of that I was certain. What would the lad have to say? Ambrosiano was merely a kinsman of some remote degree to the great laird of the Encino ranch, Don Antonio Gonzalez who held the loyalty of just about all of that surname, who had very rightfully come to ensure that his young kinsman was heard fairly. Don Antonio was determined that his kinsman received consideration and courtesy in the pursuit of justice; a concept of which I approved. Such is the way that it was among the clans, or so I had been always told.

The two of them remained silent for a long moment, during which I surveyed the lad; considerably more than a lad, I must confess. It was more his tentative manner which deluded observers into thinking, mistakenly, that he was very much younger than his apparent age, which I judged to be in his third decade, or close enough to it. If he had any assurance about him; even a tenth portion of what Don Antonio displayed, I would have considered him a Lothario. If he had put his back and other parts into that enjoyable enterprise, he could have seduced every single woman in Luna City, or perhaps even Karnes County. Ambrosiano Gonzalez was undeniably handsome and well-formed, blessed by the gods who dispense these things. I thought to meself that he looked like the reigning cinema heartthrob among the ladies at the time, Rudolph Valentino. The resemblance would have added to his romantic appeal, no doubt about it. But at this moment Ambrosiano had no hint of assurance about him, more's the pity. Uncertain though he was, like Valentino himself, he had already won considerable of the susceptible and available *(and even unavailable)* female hearts to his considerable masculine charms. Don Antonio spoke first, giving a brief nudge to his kinsman.

"The youngest son of my second cousin's sisters' family, from Mexico City," Don Antonio announced. "Meant for the priesthood, but alas, he cannot read well enough to be admitted to Holy Vows. His older brothers are all handsome in the eyes of those who regard them; intelligent as well. His sisters are all the most beautiful and pleasing of women …"

"But the runt of the litter," I commented, and Don Antonio's eyes flashed, momentarily indignant.

"Ambrosiano is a good boy," he replied. "And honest, modest and moral! It is not his fault that he is the youngest and least of his family. He is not careless in his duties, nor a murderer. His honor," Don Antonio said, in the most meaningful manner, as he twitched his coat aside from the pistol at his hip, "And the honor of my family are a matter that I would defend in blood."

"We take your concern for your family to our heart," I replied, noting how Ambrosiano flinched at the mention of blood and the implied threat. "But what we are after is the truth of this matter. Speak truth, and pursue justice, even if the heavens fall; I am your ally in this pursuit of justice, Sir Antonio. What did your nephew see, regarding the poisoning at the Dunsmore's illicit saloon?"

A short colloquy in the Spanish language ensued, during which I saw that John Drury made notes.

"He does not consider Senor Dunsmore with trust or favor," Don Antonio replied. "And even less his wife. He thinks Senora Dunsmore is a whore; a woman of negotiable virtue, and that Dunsmore is a brutal and selfish man. And he does not trust either of them to any degree, but he must work to eat. So he runs errands for them, little though he or I like it."

"Did he run an errand to Abernathys' or elsewhere, to purchase a bottle of wood alcohol at any time in the last week or so," I asked, looking briefly to John Drury, who nodded very briefly in approval.

Ambrosiano brightened. "*Si, dos botellos,*" he replied, before embarking on a spate of rapid Spanish too quick for me to follow, although from the speed with which John Drury's pencil raced across the page of his notebook, my sergeant detective was taking in every word. When Ambrosiano finished, he glanced towards his uncle, who obligingly translated.

"He says yes. Senor Dunsmore sent him next door to the *ferretería,* last Thursday for two bottles of wood alcohol to burn in a little spirit stove. Ambrosiano delivered the bottles to Dunsmore's house. He says that in the early mornings, Senor Dunsmore wishes to make coffee for himself without the bother and time wasted in putting wood in the big stove. On Monday morning, Ambrosiano found one of those bottles behind the grocery, in a box for empty glass bottles to be returned to Senor Mills. He thought it curious, after hearing of the dead drummers at the Cattleman, whom he had served the very night before! Ambrosiano began to wonder. How had the bottle come to be emptied so fast? And who had brought it from the house where he had delivered it and left it among the glass bottles behind the grocery?" Don Antonio reached down and unfastened the latches on the soft-sided briefcase. He brought out a square bottle of clear glass, a bottle adorned with a buff-colored label with bright orange printing on it. The skull and crossbones, and the word "Poison" stood out in larger print, although a corner of the label was torn away. Indeed, the bottle looked as if it had been sitting for a good while on a shelf at Abernathy's. Don Antonio set it on my desk with a flourish. "My nephew pondered long regarding these questions. This then, is the very bottle! Being certain that there was evil afoot, he took it, and sought my council!"

In the corner, John Drury sighed and murmured. "There'll be no chance of getting good fingerprints off it now, I think, Captain."

"Is Ambrosiano absolutely certain that this is one of the bottles that he bought last week?" I ventured. "How can he be so very certain? If it comes to a trial, he will have to swear so, in a court of law, and that may be perilous, seeing that his testimony might convict a respectable Anglo of the town."

Another colloquy in rapid-fire Spanish between Ambrosiano and Don Antonio. John Drury's pencil raced across his notebook page.

"My nephew says that those bottles which he bought for Senor Dunsmore last Thursday were the last two remaining of that brand on the shelves and had been there for some time. See; Senor Abernathy marked the original price in pencil, then crossed it out and wrote a lower price. And the label is torn at the corner. He will swear on the Bible in your courts, on the Shrine of the Virgin of Guadalupe, or anything else which you value, that this is one of the bottles which he bought last Thursday and Senor Abernathy must assuredly swear the same. Ambrosiano is a good Catholic. He will not lie over this or any other matter. He was going to be a priest, but … well, since he cannot read the Holy Offices properly."

"Ahh. I see," I replied, and I did see the various pitfalls which might be put in the way of investigating and prosecuting this case. Mainly that one of the key witnesses at this point was a Mexican who did not speak English. I took heart. Charlie Abernathy would stand fast and fearless and there might always be the chance that other witnesses would be discovered; those willing to testify … but I was getting ahead of myself. Now I said, to Don Antonio, with every courtesy due a local laird and power in the land,

"And will you want me to write out a receipt for this bit of evidence, noting how this bottle came into the possession of the police. For I swear to you honestly that this is a key piece of evidence. By it, we will be able to follow the trail to the perpetrators of this awful deed…"

"So I do hope," Don Antonio stood, gathering his valise and his nephew to himself with a commanding gesture; obviously calculating his grand operatic exit. "I will… your pen and your receipt, if you would be so kind. Your sergeant has been making excellent notes of what my nephew and I have said during this interview. Will you be so good as to enter them into any official record which you make of this matter? Thank you, Chief Magill; I recognize an honest man in a wasteland of fools and mountebanks. Please call upon me at the Rancho if you should require any further testimony in this matter."

He and his nephew departed the office, and John Drury and I looked at each other.

"You'll want to file all of this with the notes on this case," I said, as the door downstairs opened and closed, to the cordial comment of Constable Grigoryev. "I believe that this case is close to being sorted."

"I'll follow up with Charles Abernathy and his clerks, confirming that this is the very bottle which came from Abernathy's," John Drury replied. "Not so much urgency now that we know where it came from. The case is sorted, solved and convicted … or we hope, Captain."

"I'll drive down to Karnesville in the morning," I answered. "To talk to Mrs. Courson and tie up any loose ends with regard to Mills … there's an itching in my thumbs, John."

The Arrest of Charley Mills

And what a Hurley-burley I found at the station when I arrived the next morning, bright and early to brief and be briefed by John Drury and the on-duty constables! There was a small sullen gathering of men, hardly more than half-a-dozen at the top of the narrow street which led to the station; a red-faced and indignant Jed Dunsmore among them. All made dagger-eyes at me, as I parked the Ford and walked briskly up the steps to the police station.

"What is the grocery-man doing outside the police station at this hour of the morning, instead of opening his place of business?" I demanded, as I came in through the battered wooden front door, in the near-to-crumbling stone front of the police station. I regarded the sad façade of the place with disfavor every morning, and every fiscal year my campaign for a larger portion of the budget allocated for the police station was renewed with greater urgency.

"Kapitan-Leader Mcgill, sah!" Constable Grigoryev rendered a crisp salute from the duty-sergeant's desk. "Good morning, sah! I have no idea, sah! Although doubtless the mob is angered by the presence of the prisoner, sah!"

"Constable," I conceded with a weary acknowledgement a half-salute rendered in Constable Grigoryev's direction. "You need not address me as sir quite so slavishly. I work for a living. Address me as 'Chief' if you would be so kind. This will be easier on all of our nerves, I daresay."

"Sah! Chief…" Grigoryev appeared baffled but obliging. "What are your orders, s – chief?"

"A prisoner," I replied. "We have a prisoner. And an incipient mob? I do wish that I might be kept informed regarding these things at the earliest. The telephone is a simply marvelous modern invention, and I possess one at home. I could have been informed."

"We did not think it all that urgent," John Drury spoke in apologetic tones, from his desk in a corner of the main floor, on the other side of the barrier which divided the working segment of the squad room from the public side. "The prisoner is Charley Mills."

"Yet once again," I commented with asperity. Mills was a frequent and usually brief guest at the Luna City jail, or alternately at the Karnesville county prison. Really, the old sod ought to have his own towel, supper service, and regular cell, since he was arrested so often. "What is the old reprobate charged with now?"

"Molestation of a child," John Drury replied, with a grim expression upon his countenance, an expression which exactly mirrored those on the faces of the men outside. "Charley Mills climbed through the bedroom window of the Dunsmore place at 2:45 in the morning, took off his clothing and got into bed … where he embraced Susan Dunsmore, who had been sleeping in her parents' bed, as she was suffering from a mild case of the grippe. Being startled …"

Here, Constable Grigoryev made a sotto-voice comment, which I ignored, and John Drury continued. "The child screamed in hysterical fear and could not stop screaming."

"Quite naturally," I said. "Charley Mills in a state of nature is a repugnant picture to contemplate, even at a distance and at second-hand report." I was overwhelmed with a sense of disgust, and here I had been in the matter of enforcing the law for twenty years, at that point. Of all the varied offenses against the laws of God and Man perpetrated by the odious Charley Mills, I assumed that this was the single standard of civilized behavior left unviolated by him "Where is little Susan now? Is she being tended carefully by those who should be her natural protectors. I see that her father is outside, so obviously he does not feel a need to reassure his child."

"S—Chief," Constable Grigoryev sounded slightly less formal. Good, the lad was learning. "She was taken to the house across the road. To the residence of the *svyashchennik*, the heretic protestant Rowbottom. She knows them, and they are affectionate towards her. Her mother …" Grigoryev added what sounded like a curse in his natal language, to which I chose not to pay attention.

"Not a heretic, Grigoryev," I pointed out, "But a good Methodist."

"Heretics in the eyes of the One True Church," Grigoryev insisted, stoutly. "But she is well, and I have taken her statement, and that of her mother, the *schlyukha* – that slut from the grocery…"

I agreed with Constable Grigoryev, and I was certain that the ladies of the Methodist congregation would likewise agree, although they might not use terms so apparently blunt. However, my office as a senior officer of the law in Luna City prohibited me from open partiality. "The child is safe and sheltered? And where might her mother be, now that the accused miscreant has been apprehended in the very vile act?"

"Opening the store," John Drury answered, with an expression on his countenance which would likely have soured milk. "While Dunsmore himself goes about, complaining to his cronies and the town layabouts. I like not the temper in the streets, Captain."

"We have our duties, John," I replied. "I will drive to Karnesville, as I had originally scheduled. We cannot allow a mob to rule our streets or cause us to vary from our scheduled tasks."

"Indeed, Captain," John Drury grinned, a grim and crooked grin over the top of his desk and the ancient typewriter on which he was writing up his notes for the record. "One riot, one Ranger. We'll manage. I'll only go as far as Abernathys' – the clerk who sold those two bottles of wood-alcohol to Ambrosiano Gonzalez was away having a tooth filled when I called yesterday, and I want to confirm the sale with him."

"I'll expect none but the best effort," I replied. "I suppose that I should go and have a word with Mr. Mills. I imagine that his lawyer has already been called for."

"Mr. Newsome has been called, and a message left for him at his office," John Drury replied.

I sighed deeply. "Ah. I will arrange for that tarnished miscreant to be transported to the Karnes County prison – for his own security, of course. But I will have some words with him, first, before I depart."

"You're the boss, Captain," John Drury bent over his cantankerous keyboard and I went through the door into the portion of building which held the cells. On this morning, there was only a single resident. I confess that I took an unworthy degree of pleasure at seeing him clad in the black and white striped trousers and shirt of convict garb. He shot up from the comfortless bunk in the single barred cell like a puppet whose strings have been jerked by an inept puppeteer.

"Good morning, Mr. Mills," I said; courtesy is always worthwhile, but usually wasted on a creature like Charley Mills. "And are you enjoying your stay with us? Was your breakfast to your taste? We have meals supplied to the jail by the kitchen of the Cattleman, you know. And the manager will want to know …"

"Get me my lawyer!" he demanded, red-faced with fury. An interesting contrast to his white hair and unkempt straggling beard. "I demand to consult with my lawyer at once! This is a put-up job! She tricked me, that …" and he described Eloise Dunsmore in the same obscene terms as Constable Grigoryev had, and at considerable length in English, so that I understood them readily enough.

"Control yourself, Mr. Mills," I advised; deliberately reasonable I was, knowing that it would infuriate him even more. He was a man I didn't mind goading, knowing that with insensate fury comes an unforced loosening of the tongue. Perhaps a useful clue or two into the matter of the poisoning at Dunsmore's speak might slip out, unbidden. "You insult a respectable lady of this town … of sorts. And you are accused of molesting an innocent maiden of a most tender age. It astonishes me to see that you have been caught red-handed in the commission of such a crime; attempting intercourse with a child! Tsk, tsk, Mr. Mills. I had always thought you above that particular charge."

"With a child!" Mr. Mills raged, quite insane with fury, and gripping the bars between us so tightly that his knuckles and finger-joints stood out white, as white as his face was red. "I don't like children – don't even like my own, damn you!" and he ripped off another long string of obscenities regarding the morals of Mrs.

Dunsmore. He shook the bars in helpless fury and concluded his diatribe with an observance that she lacked the creative talents of an apprentice whore. He shouldn't even have bothered with her lamentable bed skills but for the opportunity to cadge a better deal for his alcohol with the Dunsmore speakeasy by carrying on with Mrs. Dunsmore. Mills' diatribe was otherwise tedious, and predictable. He concluded it with another demand to see his lawyer. I reassured him on that matter and took myself out of the jail portion of our establishment.

"Did he say anything incriminating?" John Drury asked, as I went through the office.

I retrieved my hat from the rack by the front door and replied, "This small nugget: he hoped to get a better deal for the distilling business by bedding Eloise Dunsmore. Other than that; he hates children, and Eloise Dunsmore is the most lamentably unskilled tart in all of Karnes County. I'm off to interview the Courson woman. I'll speak with the sheriff about transferring custody of Mr. Mills to the county. Aye well, it will make it easier for his lawyer to consult with him, won't it, now?"

"Wish the sheriff joy of him," John Drury replied. He rolled up the document in his typewriter, removed it and set the original and the two flimsies aside. "I'll have my notes from the Gonzalez interview on your desk by the afternoon, Captain."

"Thank you, Sgt. Drury," I replied. As I got into my Ford, I noticed that the group of angry men had gotten larger by the addition of half-a-dozen more. But I was not worried; they were across and at the end of the lane, and I assumed that they would not have the nerve or organization to make any trouble for the Luna City Police Department.

In that assumption, I was near-fatally mistaken. But that is for the next chapter.

Miss Letty Deposes

"So," Letty McAllister drew a deep breath, and looked around at the enthralled listeners at the stammtisch. "It came about to the morning after Charley Mills was arrested – this was several days after the deaths by alcohol poisoning of three traveling salesmen." Roman Gonzalez, Clovis Walcott and Richard had been joined by the Steins. Richard knew that he really ought to be back in his kitchen, overseeing those preparations for luncheon service, but he was absolutely confident in his supremely competent staff. *(For hadn't he trained them over the last few years in the most exacting form of classical French kitchen management? Why, indeed he had, and therefore they could do without his eye on them for another twenty minutes.)*

He admitted to being completely fascinated by Miss Letty's tale of how Charley Mills – bootlegger, legendary bank robber and all-around career blot on the civic escutcheon – escaped being hung from the branch of the big oak tree across from the Café. The story had more twists and turns than a season of *Eastenders*; Richard could hardly wait for the denouement. Miss Letty continued, while all at the table hung on her words.

"Mother intended to purchase material for my birthday dress at the drapers', in the store building where Stein's is now." She sighed, reminiscently. "Mother used to love shopping for material there. She was a marvelous seamstress – most women had to be, in that day. Only the very rich bought dresses ready-made, like Eleanor Wyler – that was Stephen's mother – and hers came from Nieman's in Houston. Mother had bought a pattern from the Sears Roebuck catalogue, and she had promised me that I might pick out the materiel. Then we would go to Dunsmores' for the weekly shopping, and she would cut out the dress that very afternoon. There was an odd feeling in the air that morning. I cannot quite describe it; a feeling like a thunderstorm about to blow in. An electric feeling in the air…"

"The sky turning dark, and the air looking kind of greenish," Clovis Walcott nodded. "Even though there is nothing happening at the moment."

"Exactly," Miss Letty nodded. "But there was nothing like that, as Mother and I walked into town from the house. Father had already taken the motor and gone to his office. There was nothing that really alarmed me until we arrived at the drapers' at about mid-morning. There was some shouting going on; shouting that seemed to come from the street behind the Cattleman Hotel. But then we were inside the drapers' place of business and could not hear much of the street noise. Mr. Milhouse, was his name, if I recall correctly. It was all a perfectly ordinary call on his establishment, until he looked out of the window and said, in the most urgent tones, 'Mrs. McAllister, you should take the child and go home through the back way at once! She ought not to see this!' And Mother replied,

'Indeed – and what is this happening?' Mother was quite outraged at being ordered thus. Mother disliked authority being exercised on her behalf, as if she wasn't capable of exercising it herself. And I was quite torn between two patterns of linen fabric.

'There was talk all this morning, of how Dunsmore and his friends were going to bust Charley Mills out of jail! Now it looks as if they've done it, and not going to waste any time until they hang him from the big oak tree in the square, just as they said they would!" Mr. Milhouse exclaimed, as he locked and barred his front door. "Go home, Mrs. McAllister, out through the back way!" and Mother replied, in considerable indignation, 'No, that cannot be! He has never been convicted of a hanging offense and what has he been charged with, anyway? And who is in charge here? The mob or Chief Magill? This is insupportable, Mr. Milhouse! I must call my husband at once! Where is your telephone!?'" Miss Letty shook her head, in awe. "Mother was adamant. Charley Mills was a disgrace, a blot on the civic landscape – but a public lynching? Without the benefit of a proper trial? That was not to be countenanced. Mother went to the telephone in Mr. Milhouse's office, and he went with her, wringing his hands and telling her over and over again that she ought to leave, this was nothing for the eyes of women and children to see. I confess … I was rather curious about the whole matter," Miss Letty confessed, with a diffident smile. "And while Mother and Mr. Milhouse were in the office, I went to the front window. I was only six years old, going on seven and the whole matter interested me in a purely intellectual manner. I didn't see the affair as being quite real, you see. It was to me rather like the motion pictures. Things happened, and I watched them, at a kind of remove."

"What did you see, Miss Letty?" Clovis Walcott asked. If Richard could judge aright, Clovis was more than fascinated.

"Everything," Miss Letty confessed, "From the window of Milhouse's Drapery. I saw them lead Mr. Mills by his bound hands all around the Square. He was tied at the end of a rope from the bumper of someone's pickup truck. He was stumbling and staggering, blood flowing from his brow, soaking into his prisoner's stripes of black and white. The blood showed most vividly against the white stripes and matting in his hair and all down his face. He was shouting back at the men tormenting him. I could not hear the words, through the plate glass window. A most horrible sight. It created in me then a horror regarding public violence, of a mass crowd tormenting a chosen scapegoat, even should that scapegoat be rightfully prosecuted. Later on, when I saw pictures in the newspaper, and the newsreels in the cinema of Nazis persecuting and tormenting random Jews, I was already set against such. Funny, how the injustices one observes and condemns as a child become a lasting influence."

"Head wounds always bleed like a sum-bitch," Clovis Walcott remarked. "I deduce that the bastard survived the experience? How did that come about, Miss Letty?"

Miss Letty looked into the distance beyond the front window to the Café, into the green depths of Town Square, and the even farther distance of eighty years and more.

"They pulled him at the bumper of the pick-up truck to the sidewalk under the that very tree. They went all around the square at least once, so it was a good-sized mob for Luna City; I think fifty or more. They already had a noose around his neck; they boosted him into the back of the truck, although he fought viciously against them, like a scared wildcat, until several men clubbed him almost senseless. Two or three men were in the back of the pickup truck, holding him upright as they tightened the noose, and threw the loose end of it over that branch."

"Needs a good long sudden drop and a careful bit of calculation to hang a man efficiently," Clovis Walcott remarked. "Otherwise, he'd just dangle there, strangling slowly. Not a good clean execution, Miss Letty. What happened then?"

Richard knew very well that Clovis was rather the expert in all aspects of the 19th century. It figured that he would know minutia like the best way to administer death via the rope. Miss Letty also appeared to know that; Richard didn't want to know how she might know of it.

"There was then this most miraculous appearance," Miss Letty continued. "Honestly, it was better than anything Douglas and I had ever seen in the Saturday cinema. The single most courageous deed that I had ever witnessed personally in my lifetime or would ever see again. Four men appeared at the edge of the mob, and by some means, I think by their force of character and courage, made their way through, to the foot of the Hanging Tree, where the other end of the rope was already being made fast. The Wyler brothers, Sergeant Drury, and the Reverend Rowbottom. Unlike the Wylers and Sergeant Drury, The Reverend Rowbottom was unarmed. He was the man who climbed up into the bed of the truck of the mob and began to speak. I verily believe that the Spirit of Tongues descended on the Reverend, for he spoke in so loudly a voice that even Mother and I, and Mr. Milhouse could hear, from the front of the shop. 'What have you done?' He cried, in a voice that could be heard to the edge of town. He was an almighty eloquent preacher, when the spirit took him. 'What have you done, what are you about to do; that you can countenance the murder of a man without a rightful trial, and a hearing under oath – regardless of the crime of which he has been accused? We are a people of law, of rightful justice! You are about to trample over that law, that law which is what we hold most dear to our hearts, as a civilized body! Why?

Because you have been inflamed to insensate fury by mere accusations! Accusations so inflammatory that they have overcome your good sense and reason! Good citizens of Luna City, be recalled to reasoned justice! This man is accused of a most vile crime but stay your vengeful anger and reconsider! I beg you to reconsider, in the name of Jesus our Savior and our judge before the Most High! How did he come to be accused, and by whose' testimony? Ah – by the word of a man who has whipped up the mob to fury!' And the Reverend Rowbottom pointed to Mr. Dunsmore, pointing his finger directly at him, as he continued, 'This man, who has done unlawful business with Charley Mills, in providing the demon alcohol to his illicit saloon – this is a man who has been trying to seduce Charley Mills' wife! This man, whose <u>own</u> wife has been regularly fornicating with the accused, a wife who regularly invited this accused man to the Dunsmore house under cover of night to continue their fornication'… Really, at that age, I had no notion of what the Reverend Rowbottom meant by that word," Miss Letty observed, with an air of serene detachment. "I had no idea, other than it meant a kind of petting. And that confused me at the time. I thought that petting had to do with showing affection to animals."

"Sounds like the good Rev had the right idea, in that case," Richard observed, and Miss Letty shot him a severe and quelling look. "About affection to animals, I meant. This Mills character, he was a bit of an animal, right? A tiger when it came to bed-sports, amiright?"

Both Roman Gonzalez and Clovis Walcott snorted in stifled laughter, and Miss Letty regarded them both with arctic displeasure.

"I have no idea," she replied. "But the Reverend Rowbottom went on, and on; pointing at this man or that among the mob, naming and shaming them for their own sins, and for each one he gave chapter and verse. As he spoke, the mob shriveled. Men in it looked down at their feet and were ashamed. Of course, it helped that The Wyler brothers and Sergeant Drury stood there, as stalwart as a Rock of Gibraltar, their coats swept aside from their side arms. I thought that Thomas Wyler appeared rather nervous, at first, but his brother *(that would be Doctor Wyler's father, you know)* he had a pump-action Winchester shotgun slung over his shoulder. Albert Wyler was known to be a rather quiet man, but not one to pick any kind of quarrel with. He had been a Rough Rider volunteer trooper when he was a young man, and idolized Teddy Roosevelt, who in turn was said to have thought the world of him. But the Reverend Rowbottom carried the day."

"The day that he socked it to the Harper Valley PTA," Clovis Walcott remarked. Roman Gonzalez snickered, while Richard and the Steins looked at each other, baffled.

Miss Letty continued, undismayed. "And when three-quarters of that crowd had melted away, shamed like puppies smacked across the nose for piddling on the parlor carpet, my father appeared from his office on the other side of the square, and Chief Magill's Ford careened into town square, followed by an ambulance! The ambulance was from the Karnesville County Hospital. Chief Magill drove most recklessly into the edge of the crowd. The rest of it scattered, as Chief Magill emerged from his car. He went to the Reverend Rowbottom, to Sergeant Drury and the Wyler brothers and my father and spoke to them, briefly. In that moment, the lynch mob died away." Miss Letty shook her head. "Evaporated; the whole dangerous mob. And all that was left of it was Charley Mills, looking like the body of a run-over animal at the side of the road. The ambulance attendant and Sgt. Drury lifted him down from the tail of the pickup truck onto a stretcher. My father put away his revolver and stood surveying what was left of the mob, who appeared to discover that they had urgent business elsewhere to attend to. And there – it was all over. Not the murder investigation, though," Miss Letty added. "But it was a lesson to me, and one brought home at an early age; there is no substitute for intelligent courage in the face of an ignorant mob, roused to deliberate fury. And substantial firepower," she added, almost irreverently. "As a back-up, of course. The ambulance primarily was for Constable Grigoryev. He was the grandfather of our current police sergeant, you see."

"Another family enterprise upheld," Richard acknowledged. It seemed that he was getting quite the hang of matters genealogical in Luna City, for Miss Letty nodded in austere agreement.

"He was injured when the initial mob stormed the jail. A broken jaw and a couple of other bone fractures, as well as a severe concussion. He was unconscious for days, but he recovered eventually. The mob took Charley Mills only after Constable Grigoryev was overwhelmed, and the police station all but destroyed. There was no help which could get to him in time, you see, as the police department was very small in those years; just the Chief, Sgt. Drury and six constables, spread over three shifts. The city budget was quite parsimonious."

"So, what happened then?" Roman asked, deeply fascinated. Outside the Café's window, another Gonzalez Construction truck pulled in next to his own vehicle, and the passenger of it waved impatiently. "Make it quick, I gotta chapel roof to finish. Who did they finally figure out poisoned the booze that killed the three traveling salesmen?"

"Oh, that was Eloise Dunsmore, of course," Miss Letty replied.

Resolution

From the untitled and unpublished memoir of Alistair Magill, long-time chief of police in Luna City: Chapter 48 – The Dunsmore Matter and Resolution

The resentful presence of Dunsmore and his handful of angry friends hardly bothered me, as I departed Luna City on that fateful morning. There were many places in Texas and across the South *(and North as well, let it be admitted)* where it was a simple enough matter in those times to whistle up a violent mob, full of resentment regarding action or non-action on the part of lawful authority with regard to the fate of a man accused of a most heinous crime. But my town was not one of them. In my years spent to that date in Luna City, I had established our small police force as a fair and even-handed adjudicator of the law, among residents of every color and persuasion. I had the backing and support of all-important local powers, Mayor McAllister, Albert Wyler, Don Antonio, among them. I had the permanent enmity of Charley Mills, however. Since he was presently locked up in the dilapidated stone building which served as our police headquarters, *(Replaced not long after these calamitous events)* I assumed that I could safely venture to Karnesville, to continue the investigation. John Drury and my department had all things safely in hand. Although the parlous condition of the Luna City jail which served as our base of operations was an ongoing matter for mild concern, I had left the place in the direct charge of Constable Grigoryev, who was one of those nail-the-banner-to-the flagpole do-or-die-fellows, and John Drury, the most formidable man of my acquaintance. I steered the Ford towards Karnesville, then and still the county seat.

It was a pleasant drive; nothing to occupy my thoughts or distract my attention from the road unspooling before me, as it led through pastures and farmland, with ploughed fields already coming up green in neat rows of corduroy, interspersed with stands of dark green scrub oaks. The sky was a clear pale blue, dotted with small clouds which resembled handfuls of clean-washed wool. I thought about the case; now complicated by the arrest of Charley Mills. I was fairly certain that he had not expected to find Susan Dunsmore in that bed – of course, it was her parent's bed, and had not Doris Rowbottom – who was a nurse in the Great War – expiated to me on how the child had been suffering from the seasonal grippe? Her mother had promised Mrs. Rowbottom that she would be put to bed in her parents' bedroom, so that she might be taken care of … A sudden thought as I negotiated a curve in the road, a few miles short of Karnesville and the shock of that realization nearly took me across the center and into the path of a lumbering removal van.

What if Mrs. Dunsmore had deliberately engineered the whole matter? Sent a note to her lover, encouraging him to come into her bedroom in the wee hours of morning, assuming he had an assignation with her and instead, her poor little daughter, sleeping blissfully in the parental bed, was subjected to those foul embraces? What kind of woman, what kind of mother would do such a vile, unnatural thing? Had she hoped to provoke her husband into a fury against Charley Mills? I had, until that moment, been of a neutral mind, regarding Eloise Dunsmore, as befitted an impartial investigator and representative of the law. But this was clearly unnatural. The Dunsmore marriage was not a happy one; and I recollected the observation of Doris Rowbottom, regarding the parentage of a brown-eyed child by a pair of blue-eyed parents.

I would have to review the notes of the constable who had arrested Charley Mills in the Dunsmore place. Dunsmore put on a pretense of care for the child which he called his daughter, but did he, really feel any paternal affection at all? Was his ire more directed at his wife? And why might he make gestures of affection towards Mrs. Mills, if Carolina de san Pedro was indeed legitimately Mrs. Mills? Was she or was she not legally married to the man? Was there a double-cross in the making, between these men and their wives, complicated by a marital double-cross? Honestly, I would need to sit with John Drury in my office and map out this tangled web on the chalkboard. What, if any, was the involvement of the Adonis of Luna City, Ambrosiano Gonzalez, other than his undoubted male beauty, aside from having the wit to save out the incriminating bottle of wood spirit, likely used to poison two bottles of alcohol in Dunsmore's speak? These questions and others diverted my mind, as I drove to Karnesville.

In the interests of my investigation, I intended to visit Mrs. Corson first, having previously called on the telephone to arrange such an interview. She and her husband had taken up residence in a tidy small bungalow on the outskirts of Karnesville; a newly built place, fresh with paint and the lingering scent of cut lumber, as well as a garden which had only begun to be planted. She proved to be a woman in her late twenties, who welcomed me into her tidy parlor and offered me tea or coffee as I preferred, and a plate of small biscuits and cut squares of lemon pound cake.

"I should not indulge, but for acknowledging and appreciating your hospitality," I said, carefully choosing the smallest biscuit and a small morsel of cake. "I know that you have a household to attend to, and the care of an infant. I appreciate your assistance in providing information." I had noticed the pram parked in on the front porch, out of the weather, and the fact that Mrs. Corson had faint shadows under her eyes, which hinted at interrupted sleep, but those eyes still displayed intelligence; I assumed she had been a most satisfactory legal secretary. "I am conducting inquiries into…"

"The poisoning of those three poor men in Luna City," Mrs. Corson nodded. "Geraldine Bodie telephoned a few days ago and told me that she had referred you to me, as I might know something of Charlie Mills' doings. Chief Magill – there are things that I might not reveal, as a matter of professional confidentiality. Mr. Newsome was generous to work for, and I would not want to say anything which would reflect badly on him. It would be terribly awkward if I might have to testify in court."

"I do not see the likelihood of that arising," I replied. "I am only seeking information of a general sort, required to build an understanding of the personalities involved. Mrs. Bodie intimated that you might be able to provide such an understanding. We … that is, my sergeant and I have wondered if Mr. and Mrs. Mills are legally married – and if there was some potential for a divorce in the offing. There appeared to be some serious marital discord, early this year."

"About that," Mrs. Corson nodded, and gestured towards the teapot. "Another cup, Chief Magill? No … this happened during my last week at the office. I had already given notice, since I was …" She blushed, faintly, and yet with a smidgeon of pride. "…far along in the family way, and of course I could not work, did not want to work, although Mr. Newsome was quite agreeable to employing a married woman. I knew how all the files were ordered; no matter how long ago the case, I could lay hands on the file in a moment and recall all the relevant details. He claimed that I was a secretarial pearl above all price. Perhaps I might go back to working for him when the baby is in school. Only part-time, of course. Family, you see. But in answer to your question; yes, Mr. and Mrs. Mills were legitimately and legally married. Mr. Newsome retained a copy of the marriage documents in his files. From a JP in Brownsville, if I remember correctly."

"I am certain that you do," I said, having experience of the long administrative memories of certain women. For myself, I wished that the Luna City Police Department budget allowed us to hire such a woman possessing that set of exacting skills. It would make mine and John Drury's daily tasks so much easier. Mrs. Corson nodded and poured herself another cup of tea.

"Of course," she replied – not immodest, merely acknowledging the truth of the situation. She was the all-powerful goddess of the files and office management. "And there was a bad patch in their marriage, shortly after Christmas, if I remember. The truth of it is, as I have observed from distance, Mr. Mills is not good husband materiel. Poor woman: I certainly wouldn't have picked him to be my life partner," she added with a brief shudder. "But they have a business in common. That wretched alcohol business: she is the master of the craft of distilling, the expert producer, and he just rakes in the cash, through his contacts with the illicit retail providers of the vile stuff. It seemed that he had been detected by Mrs. Mills attempting to cut her out of her rightful share of the profits from that disgusting trade. She had him dead to rights. The discussion in Mr. Newsome's office was private," she added with a shudder. "Yet quite violent, as words and threats went. It was also very loud, which is why I knew of it. Mr. Mills was most intemperate. I overheard the conversation, as I was attempting give some last words of encouragement to my replacement." Mrs. Corson sadly shook her head. "Poor girl; she was distraught, expecting an even tenor of office conduct in working for Mr. Newsome. I don't know if she ever returned to the office," Mrs. Corson added, almost irreverently. "But that was none of my concern, Chief Magill. It was my last day, and I had already cleared out my desk. From what I can recall, Mr. Newsome advised in the most strenuous terms that Mr. Mills to make peace with his wife. I can only assume that Mr. Mills eventually agreed. At least, Mr. Mills stopped shouting."

"I think that he did indeed follow that advice, perhaps reluctantly," I said. I recalled the incident of the gift of a gold, diamond, and sapphire bracelet from Nieman's, and the splendid new Ford van. Yes, Charley Mills had made a peace through generous gifts with his legal wife, however temporary that peace might prove to be. "Tell me, Mrs. Corson' do you believe that Charley Mills is a rich man? Mrs. Dunsmore, who appears to have been conducting an affair with him certainly believed so. Do you share that estimation?" I thought it a ridiculous question on second thought, considering that the man commonly appeared to be no better clad and barbered than a common tramp, and his home property was the very picture of ruin and neglect. Still, he must have been getting renumeration from the illicit manufacture of alcohol. Mrs. Corson regarded me thoughtfully.

"I began to believe so," she replied, with care. "For he paid Mr. Newsome's bills, which were not insubstantial, promptly and without a quibble. He was wealthier – far wealthier – than he appeared at first or even second glance. As to what was the source of that wealth, I cannot think it was from the property."

"I do not believe so either," I agreed, and Mrs. Corson nodded.

"I would assume that he was profiting greatly in the illicit provision of alcohol, or that he did have source of income gleaned from long-ago crimes. I have heard the rumors," Mrs. Corson added, "That he was the last survivor of the Bent Cactus Gang and had all the gains from their final robbery. There was a huge fortune in gold ingots and coin hidden somewhere about his place. I do not credit this, as Mr. Newsome's invoices were always paid in paper notes. Although," Mrs. Corson mused thoughtfully, "I suppose he could have had some means of exchanging gold for currency, so that our curiosity and that of our bank would not be excited. Yes, I do believe that he was a wealthy man, eccentric and," she shuddered slightly, "crude though his appearance and conduct might have been. He was a man of wealth. I am most certain of that."

"Although most lacking in gentlemanly charm," I said, closing my notebook. "Thank you for your time," I added, as the thin wail of a cross and hungry infant echoed from a room within the house, and Mrs. Corson sprang up from her chair. "I think that I hear your child. We are done, and I have no further questions. I will see myself out."

"Thank you, Chief Magill," she replied in some distraction. "I take it that you need nothing more… would you like to take some cake with you? I baked it special, in anticipation of this interview…"

"It was very good," I said, honestly. "And if it would be no trouble for yourself, and you can spare it, I will take some cake to share with the good fellows of the Luna City police department."

"Of course," she sent me a distracted smile, and wrapped up a generous portion of cake, all the while with her ears and attention bent on the impatient cry from the inner room. "Mama is coming!" she said, several times, as she showed me out with my napkin full of cake and notebook similarly full of notes. "Mr. Mills was not without appeal," she added, distractedly. "He has the most soulful blue eyes, and such a way of paying compliments. I can believe that he might readily have seduced your Mrs. Dunsmore. He did have a kind of rough charm, when he cared to exercise it."

Supplied with both cake and insight, I proceeded to the Karnes County offices on Wall Street, intending to see to the transfer of Charley Mills to their custody. Really, I would be glad to have our hands free of him, and distant from Luna City. He was an incubus, a disruptive element to the tenor of quiet in our – in my city – and I would be glad to see him handed off to practically any other authority. But the moment I came in, and announced myself and my stated purpose, the desk sergeant looked at me in horror.

"There's been an emergency," he said. "Sgt. Drury has called and left messages for you: a mob assailed your police station, overwhelmed the duty officer and took the prisoner out to be hanged!"

"When was this!?" I demanded; all other thoughts being instantly driven from my mind.

Mind you, in my innermost heart, I wouldn't have minded if Mills, the lord of criminality in Luna City were once and for all permanently disposed of. But not by unlawful means, not at the hands of a rampaging mob. I stood for the law, as much as any honest man of Scots blood could, and for a mob to form and take decisive action against Drury and I regarding a prisoner? No, that was not to be endured.

"About twenty minutes since the first call. Your constables has been gravely injured in the fracas," the desk sergeant added. "There's an ambulance on the way, even now."

"I will endeavor to catch up," I replied, replacing my hat on my head. I think in my alarm I may have abandoned Mrs. Corson's gift of cake. But the sheriff's department could make good use of it, anyway. I had an emergency to attend upon and pushed my trusty Ford in making all speed in the drive to Luna City, all the while reproaching myself for having paid little mind to the incipient mob forming. Not the first mistake I had ever made, in a career devoted to the law, but certainly the most galling. I came into the alley behind the Cattleman where the police station stood. The evidence was already there that my fortress of law had been overrun and conquered by a superior force. The main double door was made of stout oak planks reinforced by iron straps and hinges. Now it was smashed to splinters, each side hanging uselessly from those hinges. The rusted metal bars over the ground-floor windows all hung askew, the glass behind them smashed. A figure tenderly swathed in bandages and blankets was being taken on a stretcher by the ambulance attendants, down those scarred limestone steps, who appeared to have arrived only a few minutes in advance. It could be none other than Constable Grigoryev, barely recognizable, for the bandages and bruises. Within seconds, another ambulance spun around the corner and pulled to a halt behind the first. I signaled the stretcher-bearers to halt.

"This is my man," I said. "He was left in charge of the station and our prisoner, after Sgt. Drury. What is his condition?" I added in a lower voice, in case the constable was sensible.

"I'm not a doctor," replied the attendant at the head of the stretcher. "But he's still breathing and conscious, so that's promising. If you wish to speak to him, keep it short. It's a goodish way to the hospital and he has a concussion, if I'm any judge."

"Thank you," I replied, looking down on poor Grigoryev's battered figure and bloody countenance. "Lad, you did well," I said, helplessly. "The prisoner was ours to keep, for the judgment of the law to do it's work. It is no crime to have been overwhelmed by superior numbers. Indeed, it is more noble to have fought against the odds…"

"Thank you, Kapitan-Leader … Chief!" Although I could scarcely credit it, Grigoryev raised one feeble hand from the stretcher to clasp mine. "Those *…ublyudki* … I stood fast, Chief – until I was overwhelmed by numbers. *Mne zhal'* … my apologies *…o bozhe, chto bol'no!"* he added.

"You did very well, Constable," I replied. "And have no fear – we will wait for your return to duty. Your job is secure; take as long as you need to recover."

"*Blagodaryu vas*!" he replied, fervently "Thank you …" and then his eyes rolled up in his head, and he wandered off into a state of merciful oblivion, either from his injury, or whatever sedative the ambulancemen might have administered – which they should not have done, seeing that our good Constable Grigoryev did appear to have a concussion, at the very least.

"And who might the other ambulance be for," I asked, as more stretchers began emerging from the battered shell of what had been my police headquarters, to be loaded into the back of the second ambulance – not with the same solicitous care taken of Constable Grigoryev that I could observe.

"Who are these other chaps?" I asked, as first one stretcher came out the door to be loaded in the waiting second ambulance.

"We only had the two men on duty, and one is gone to the scene of the incident..."

"Ah," replied the man at the head of the stretcher, whom I judged to be the driver. "This would be for the five or six rioters beaten in the fight by your constable. He's certainly a game one in good knock-down drag-out!"

"I expect nothing but the best from my officers and men," I answered, and my thoughts turned immediately to the matter of Charley Mills, and the mob in Town Square intent on hanging him. Now that my stout good constable was being tended to, I considered my next duty to be that of seeing to the mob and Charley Mills – although, I would not have wept more than a tear or two if I had arrived too late. But from the sound of the crowd gathering in Town Square, I had not. There was the rumble of a crowd, an unhappy crowd by the sound of it, emanating from that direction. If they had already managed to hang the old b**tard, I was fairly certain there would be nothing but a certain guilty silence from that direction, as well as a limp and unprotesting body hanging by the neck from the biggest oak tree in Town Square. I leaped behind the wheel of my trusty Ford and careened down the alleyway between the Cattleman and the building next to it, wishing that I had remembered to bring my revolver. Carrying such openly was beneath my dignity as the Chief, for I was of the belief that this was no longer the Wild West. I was in the habit of depending on the authority of my office ... and too late, feared that such authority might have appreciated back-up of the high-caliber variety.

Too late for such regrets. I came out into Town Square and sized up the situation in an instant. There was a crowd around a pick-up truck drawn to that side of the road directly beneath the largest tree on Town Square; a tree with an enormous branch extending over the avenue bounding the square. I braked the Ford in front of the ornate storefront where Mr. Milhouse the draper had his place of business. I could see the small pale face of a child watching with intense interest from that window, little Miss Letty, the mayor's daughter. *Why had her mother not taken her home?* I wondered, in a moment of distraction. This was as close as I could get to the crowd. I set the brake and sprang out.

Charley Mills stood in the back of that truck, a noose drawn tight about his neck, the other end of that rope secured over that branch. The old b**tard still was alive, although drenched in a flood of crimson gore from a wound to his head. But the crowd seemed to be losing interest; they stood sullen and diminishing by ones and twos, for the Reverend Rowbottom stood next to Charley Mills in the truck bed, supporting his drooping figure with one arm while he pointed at one and yet another of the remaining mob, orating like a veritable stentor. The Wyler brothers stood side by side, on the street below the impromptu gallows, shoulders square, their defiant gaze roving here and there. With them stood John Drury, leaning against the tailgate of the pickup truck, smoking a cigarette as if he had all the time in the world, waiting for the end of a spectacle which bored him unutterably, but which he was obliged to attend upon. The four of them stood tall; the Wyler brothers, well-heeled as befitted the local lairds, John Drury with his air of casual indifference, and the Reverent Rowbottom, as commanding as if he were in his own pulpit on a Sunday morning. That quartet of brave men had turned command of the diminishing mob against those who had originally whistled it up. I speak as one who escaped death by a whisker during the blockade of Ladysmith during the war in South Africa – this was the closest-run thing that I had ever seen in my life.

Now, as I approached the shriveling mob across the Square, I could see Mayor McAllister himself, hurrying through from his place of work in the building which housed the administrative offices of Luna City. Not before time, I thought, and then chastised myself for incivility. I had not been on hand when this outrage began, so how could I rightfully criticize the mayor himself? There were but a handful of the sullen mob remaining when Mayor McAllister and I arrived from separate directions. The grocer, Mr. Dunsmore was among them, red-faced with thwarted fury, his usually neat garments and apron disarrayed and dirtied from the fight at my police station.

"What is the meaning of this?" I roared, and the last remaining handful of die-hard lynchists blanched and fled, leaving Dunsmore standing along.

John Drury threw away the remnant of his gasper and remarked sotto voice, "A day late and a dollar short, Captain. The Reverend has got the mob settled, through publicly chastising them for their many … many personal sins."

"I see, and not before time," I replied.

Mr. Dunsmore grasped the sides of his coat and demanded loudly, but in a not entirely confident voice. "I demand justice! This man debauched my wife, attempted to molest my innocent young daughter…"

"And justice you will have," I replied warmly. "In good time, and before a proper jury. Take the man down, John. There is an ambulance loading up by the police station, doubtless they will have room for one more. As for you, Dunsmore," I rounded on him, as the Reverend Rowbottom and Tom Wyler assisted the near-fainting Charley Mills down from the tail of the truck. "I have excellent reason for believing that your wife was debauched with her enthusiastic cooperation in the matter, and that Charley Mills was let into your house, intending to find her asleep in your bed. Not your daughter, poor innocent little tyke. What says it about your wife, that she deliberately engineered that little scene, hey? Perhaps in revenge for your clumsy attempts to seduce Mrs. Mills! Your wife is a fine piece of work, no doubt, but encouraging a mob called up by an outraged husband in order to murder her lover?"

Overhearing this, Charley Mills, semi-conscious and gore-covered, straightened and growled some wholly ungentlemanly, yet accurate observations on the character of Eloise Dunsmore.

"That **** **** **** framed me!" he snarled. "***** ****! And a lousy lay, into the bargain, Dunsmore! You have my sympathies for marrying the w***e in the first place! At least my wife has skills in the distillery, if not in the bedroom!"

"Mr. Mills!" protested the Reverend Rowbottom. "You speak of ladies!"

Charley Mills spat contemptuously. His lack of gratitude towards the good reverend was unspeakably bad manners, considering that the man's courage and presence of mind had saved him from a painful fate, but that was typical of him. "You'll hear from my lawyer!" he added, in my direction, as John Drury cuffed him, advised him to keep a civil tongue in his head, and led him away. I turned to face Dunsmore and brought out my own set of handcuffs. At least, I had the presence of mind to have stowed them in the recesses of my coat pockets.

"Put out your hands," I said. "You are under arrest; first for maintaining an illegal drinking establishment, and secondly for inciting a mob."

"What … this is an outrage!" he fumed at length for some minutes, while I sighed and turned to the Reverent Rowbottom. "I would trouble you and the Mrs. to have a care for little Susan," I confessed, with a heavy heart. "For I shall have to arrest Mrs. Dunsmore on a charge of murder, and the poor little bairn will need someone to look after her."

"Murder?" The Reverend Rowbottom absolutely goggled at me. "She … but … Eloise Rowbottom … for murder? How can you know…"

"Circumstances and at least one eye-witness." I looked towards the Wyler brothers, and Tom nodded, although he did shoot an anxious glance at his brother before he did so. Stout fellow, I had to admit. In this dire circumstance, he had the nerve, even if he was a bit of a nancy. But as long as he kept his amours discrete and harmed no one beneath the age of legal consent … well, we could overlook all that. He wasn't doing it in the road, frightening the horses and obstructing traffic. "Come along quietly, Dunsmore. I suppose that your man Gonzalez can manage the grocery, unless you have someone else in mind. You are nicked and doing time. Not quite as much time as your wife might be bound for but count on the grocery being under different management for a bit."

***

"And that was the end of it," Miss Letty concluded, to a rapt audience, which now included most of the lingering patrons for late breakfast at the Café, and Bree and Araceli. Bree stood with a tray of fresh-baked cinnamon buns, and Araceli with her coffee carafe in one hand, and the pitcher of dairy cream in the other. "Both the Dunsmores were arrested; tried and convicted on the charges brought against them, although Mr. Dunsmore was pardoned after a year or so by the Governor. Mrs. Ferguson, you see. A sensible woman, who disapproved of Prohibition, generally. Eloise Dunsmore was convicted of murder, though. It was an awful scandal at the time, of course. And the grocery remained open for a while. Dunsmore sold the place to another man who maintained the business until it closed, at the end of the War, what with the competition from bigger newer grocery stores in Karnesville. So much has changed, since I was a child!" Miss Letty sighed and took a bite from the fresh cinnamon bun. "So much of it to be lamented, although this good pastry at the Café is not one of them! Thank you, Richard."

"Constable Grigoryev!" Clovis demanded. "Was he related to …?"

"Grandfather to our own Sergeant," Miss Letty swallowed, and regarded the remainder of her cinnamon bun with favor. "He recovered from those injuries incurred in defending the police station against the mob. In time, he became Chief of Police in Luna City for some years, upon Chief Magill's retirement. There is the most remarkable family resemblance. I recall my dear father remarking on it, after seeing a newsreel to do with Russia and their leadership. It seems that Chief Grigoryev's mother, or maybe it was her grandmother, was a wild and rebellious hoyden in her young days. They were from Georgia. Not OUR Georgia, you see." Miss Letty added helpfully. "The OTHER Georgia. Constable Grigoryev's mother, or perhaps his grandmother, had a very bad boyfriend when she was a teenager. The boyfriend was a criminal and revolutionary, which was very embarrassing for them when she had his baby; Chief Grigoryev, or his father. The family hushed it up, of course, ensured that she married someone respectable, even before the war began."

"He didn't go by the nick of Joe Steel, did he? That bad boyfriend?" Clovis Walcott asked, with a faintly ironic smile.

Miss Letty replied, "I wouldn't know, Colonel. I may be old, but not that old. This all happened in Russia before the Red Revolution anyway."

"What of the little girl, Susan Dunsmore?" Araceli asked, hovering with her carafes. "I don't ever remember Abuelita mentioning her, and I thought I had heard all of her stories of when she was growing up."

"Adeliza Gonzales is about five years younger than I am and would have been an infant or barely a toddler at the time," Miss Letty answered, regretfully. "It wasn't something that she would have known about. Poor little Susan. She was with the Rowbottom family for about six months, while the trials were going on. Near an orphan, as it turned out. Eloise Dunsmore's older sister was married to a very respectable and well-to-do factory owner in St. Louis, if I recall, and she was sent to them, as her closest and most responsible relatives. I believe that she took their family surname, since the scandal of her mother being a murderess and her father a criminal would have made her life in elementary school nearly unbearable. Children can be so cruel, you know, until they are trained out of it by responsible adults. At any rate, she never returned to Luna City although my brother Douglas kept up a pen-friendship with her for many years."

"What about Charley Mills and his distilling business?" Roman belatedly gathered up his thermos of Café-brewed coffee. His workmen were waving impatiently from where they had parked in front of the Café. "Tell me quick, we gotta foundation near Runge to pour…"

"For all intents and purposes, he became almost a recluse after the almost-hanging," Miss Letty replied. "He rarely came to town. I believe he was much less inclined to venture into dealing in illegality. Although I am certain he hosted other criminal outlaws at his homestead for a brief time, for the sake of old times remembered. Clyde Barrow and Bonnie Parker were sheltered there for a time. I saw those two there myself, when my brother, myself, and Artie Vaughn, went adventuring there, some years later. But that is a different tale. I imagine that Charley Mills was mortally frightened, after being taken out of the police station by a mob of local men. Carolina Mills kept on with the business, all through Prohibition and even after repeal. It is my impression as a child, backed up decades later by my brothers' research when he wrote our volume of local history – that Charley Mills was mentally scarred by the whole matter. Any sensible person would be, or at least, anyone with a finely developed sense of self-preservation. He was hardly ever seen in town after that. He died, six or seven years after being attacked by the lynch mob. Natural causes said the county coroner, which came as a mild surprise to almost everyone acquainted with his character and reputation. His widow immediately married Ambrosiano Gonzales which shocked practically no one," Miss Letty added, with a reminiscent sigh. "He was the most purely handsome man of any race in Luna City and one of the most morally-upright. Even I could see that, at an early age. They say that he might have been a priest, but that he was one of those odd children who cannot make sense of letters. Dyslexia is the proper term they have for it now." Miss Letty sighed deeply and finished off the last of her cinnamon roll in several dainty bites. "You would need to ask Miss Heisel about the rest of that family history, Richard. Carolina San Pedro and Ambrosiano Gonzales went to Canada; she was extraordinarily talented at the distilling business. She was hired by the Hiram Walker firm and did so very well for them that she was very comfortable in life thereafter. She and Ambrosiano Gonzales lived happily on a palatial country estate near Windsor and between them had a half-dozen extraordinarily handsome children."

"And my Kate would know of all this?" Richard asked, as all the other listeners at the stammtisch bolted what was left of their breakfast and absented the Café, having listened attentively and to the dislocation of their daily schedule to Miss Letty's once-in-a-lifetime and first-hand disquisition on a matter known only to them in cast letters on a metal historical marker on the far side of the largest oak tree in Town Square.

"She's one of their great-grandchildren," Miss Letty answered. "The Gonzalez and Gonzales children regularly return to Luna City, and to the historic rancho. It's rather like salmon returning to the spawning grounds. Only rather more civilized, I think."

Going to the Chapel, Gonna Get Married

"Chef," Araceli reported halfway through the mid-morning, just as the breakfast rush was dying down. "Someone wants to talk to you."

"That circumstance does not necessarily mean that I want to talk to them," Richard snarled. He had just finished scraping down the grill and was not in the mood for casual conversation at the front of the house. "Who are they, anyway? And what do they want? Oughtn't I just tell them to feck off …"

Araceli heaved a deep and exaggerated sigh.

"No, Chef," She assumed her most patient voice and attitude. "They're customers. And catering customers, for one. They want to hire you to cater their wedding reception. Be nice and polite to them. Make the effort, Chef."

"Well, that's all right, then," Richard assumed a brighter aspect. "The usual venue? At the Cattleman, I assume?"

"No," Araceli had her most stern expression, before which the strongest and most cantankerous customers of either sex were known to quail, even Doc Wyler. "It's a special location. The Gonzales Rancho Encino de los Robles. It's for Cousin Mindy and Gunnison Penn. They've decided to tie the knot in the new Chapel, once it has been blessed by the Bishop. And he is going to perform the wedding ceremony."

"Well, as long as His Right Reverendship is in the neighborhood, may as kill two ecclesiastical birds with a single stone," Richard shed his dirty apron for a clean one, and tossed the desperately smeared one towards the wheeled bin in the back entry dedicated for used linins. "I appreciate the efficiency. Your cousin the eminent, and tenured dedicated academic is going to tie her fortune and tenure to an entity who is on record as a treasure-hunter who has never, ever found a treasure. Good career move, I must say."

"No," Araceli replied smartly, as she refilled the coffee carafe, and scooped up a clean mug. "He has found a treasure, the Gonzalez Reliquary. Or what they both are convinced ..."

"Are the unproven and sadly battered remains of what might possibly be golden and gem-trimmed reliquary, originally from the mitts of Cellini and painted by the genius da Vinci," Richard recited wearily, strictly in the line of complete historical accuracy. Gunnison Penn, famed international hunter of legendary treasure troves, was renown at least as much for a combative and litigious nature, as for never really having found anything which made a spectacular note in treasure-hunting circles. Still, he was famed for being famed – and as far as Richard could see, for not very much at all, rather like a Kardashian. Not that he would have said so to the presumably happy couple, as he collected up his large three-ring catering notebook, the smaller notebooks of wedding cakes, and followed Araceli to the front of the house, to where Xavier Gunnison-Penn sat with Dr. Mindy Gonzales at a small table off to the side. The 'Couples Table' Richard always privately termed it. The table which had been the venue for his and Kate's multi-course meal in the classic high-French tradition, the evening during which he had come to a kind of romantic rapprochement with Kate, and a short time later with Ozymandias, the King of King of cats.

"Araceli tells me that you wish to engage my services," Richard took up a chair from another table and taking a seat upon it, opened the discussion, feeling that he had nothing to lose but time. And he really did wish to return to his kitchen. "For a wedding…"

"Oh, yes," Dr. Mindy already had Gunnison-Penn's hand in hers. "A cake, of course. Araceli says that you do lovely bride cakes. And a catered buffet reception at the Rancho. Uncle Jaimie is going to host it there, and give me away, since my father has moved on…"

"My sympathies," Richard ventured. Everyone had long insisted that one must say something of the sort, upon being informed of that kind of personal loss. "It must be a grief to you that he cannot be there on such a momentous day…"

"Oh, no, Papa isn't dead," Dr. Mindy hastily assured him. "He has just moved on … to a condo in Costa Rica with his boyfriend. He sent me his best wishes, by the way, and a lovely generous gift card." She sent her soon-to-be-husband a beatific smile. "Honestly, I am going to cash it in and spend it on my wedding. I'll post the pictures on Papa's FB feed, so that he and Rodrigo can be there in spirit."

"Er … umm," Richard brought himself to mumble, in what he hoped was an encouraging manner. The form and function of a modern family sometimes baffled him, entirely. "Well … I brought my portfolio of wedding cakes. How many guests might we be expecting?"

"Three or four hundred," Araceli still hovered, for which Richard was grateful. "Possibly more. Practically every Gonzales in Karnes County will come, and you know how we all are about RSVPs. Even if you put in little post-paid cards in the invitation."

"It will be splendid," Dr. Mindy, starry-eyed with happiness, looked quite handsome. "Tio Jaime promised a whole roast beef, done the traditional way, so that is all taken care of … just the additional side dishes, you see. Really, I leave it all to your best judgement, Ricardo. About the cake …"

Richard handed her the small portfolio. "Do you have any preference as to flavor of the cake itself?"

"*Dulce de leche*, of course," Dr. Mindy replied promptly, as she leafed through the portfolio, coming to the page with graduated tiers of square layers, adorned with plaques of colored sugar-paste, depicting scenes of the Wyler ranch, which design Richard had originated earlier in the year. "I like that one – only scenes of the Rincon de los Robles … and a topper of the Reliquary …"

"Replicated in gold-colored sugar paste and molded blue sugar gems…" Richard mused, feeling his creative senses tickled and stir to life. He loved this kind of challenge, to build something magnificent, yet tasty, although he was in two minds about *dulce de leche*, as canned sweetened condensed milk figured highly among the ingredients. Every fiber of his traditional, French-trained soul rebelled against something so industrial and artificial.

"Could you?" Dr. Mindy breathed, almost worshipfully. "That would be so meaningful, to both of us. And to Tio Jaimie, since the chapel is going to be sanctified, just before our ceremony. But my sweetie has a special request. Xavie, your turn."

Xavier Gunnison-Penn, the love of Dr. Mindy's academic and romantic life, cleared his throat. He was a stout and bearded chap of some six decades, although still quite fit and tanned from leading an adventurous life, mostly on the track of spurious treasures. This life-long trek had mostly been without result, although Gunnison-Penn had managed to eke out a living from writing up those adventures. Said adventures alternated with occasional successful suits for defamation of character in obscure courts of law whose' judges didn't know any better, and an occasional term of prison in certain third-world countries. He had, so far, spent only short stints in durance vile, owing his subsequent liberty to the tireless efforts of the Canadian foreign office – heroism and devotion to duty which left Richard amazed and wondering why they bothered. On reflection, even Canadians valued matters of principle and national pride, Richard supposed. Now Gunnison-Penn regarded Richard over the table, and the opened book of proposed wedding cakes.

"I'd like you to be my best man," he said, bluntly.

Richard stared at him in absolute shock. His first and almost overwhelming impulse was to scream, "No!" and "Hell, No!" followed by a shouted and obscenity-freighted deposition as to why he had refused such an honor. Fortunately, that impulse was instantly overwhelmed by the second – which was this was the Café, Gunnison-Penn and Dr. Mindy were paying customers, and Araceli still lurked at his elbow with a carafe of very hot coffee in one hand.

"I am honored that you would consider me for this," Richard belatedly allowed. He hoped that after all, he did not sound ungracious. Gunnison-Penn was a touchy and litigious man. "But really – have you no other friends in the locality who can step up and perform those duties?"

Gunnison-Penn shifted uncomfortably in the café chair.

"I really don't have all that many local friends," He confessed. "I did ask Mindy's younger brother but he refused absolutely. He said that he was no good at public speaking, and the address by the best man at the reception was not something he felt equal to performing. That and organizing a bachelor do, on the night before. Although he did volunteer to be an usher."

"What about …" Richard cast through his mind for anyone else *anyone else!* who might look fondly enough on Gunnison-Penn to perform the brief social duty of being at the groom's side in the initial marital hustings. "What about Sefton Grant? He should know you well enough, since you first settled in at the Age of Aquarius."

Gunnison-Penn was already shaking his head, dolefully. "Mrs. Grant is still exceedingly angry over the set-to at the Age. In a fit of … unguided temper and in the midst of a ruckus, I struck her pet llama. Completely without malice – you know, you were there! I have pled for forgiveness and understanding, but Mrs. Grant remains adamant and unyielding. She does wear the trousers," Gunnison-Penn added with an uneasy chuckle. "That is … when the Grants do wear trousers!"

"I have noted that, regarding Mrs. Grant," Richard admitted, feeling a degree of sympathy. Sefton Grant adored his sweetly unreasonable spouse, who had a decades-long passion going for every New Age-ism imaginable, including nudism, aroma therapy, spiritualism, Tarot-card reading, Druid-rituals and nature-worship.

"The thing is," Gunnison-Penn continued, "Our situation does not require all that much of a best man. Hold the ring and present it at the correct time after the exchange of vows and make a nice little speech at the reception. Surely that does not take much of your time. I'd really rather forgo a bachelor party in any case."

"Visitor night at the VFW on the Friday night before will have to suffice," Richard agreed. "I don't have time to do parties. But I can see my way clear to stand for you as a witness, and say a few kind words for you both at the reception, but since I must oversee the catering… Well, as I'll be there anyway."

"Thank you, Richard," the bride-and-groom to be chorused, their plain and middle-aged faces alight and almost attractive with happiness and gratitude.

"I'll work up some figures based on what I judge to be appropriate for the main course and let you know before I bring the contract for you to sign," Richard rose from the table, feeling that there was not much more to be said. "Look over my lists and let me know if you have any particular preferences."

"Tomorrow, then," Dr. Mindy replied, a woman who already knew her own mind and didn't like wasting time.

"That went well," Araceli confessed, as soon as they both were returned to the sanctuary of Richard's kitchen, for once empty of all but themselves. The junior staff seemed to have taken the opportunity for a quick break, out in the back. "I was always afraid that Mindy would be the most awful bridezilla the world has ever known, after putting off marrying for so many years." She sent a very purposeful look through narrowed eyes at Richard. "Now, on the other hand, I'm absolutely certain that Kate wouldn't go nuts when it came to marrying. She's always said that she is one for being married in a Mexican cotton embroidered dress, barefoot in a meadow of bluebonnets while a string trio plays Vivaldi, and everyone has a nice picnic afterwards. The wedding is just a day, a day to celebrate among friends, not an open invitation to a mass nervous breakdown." There was a certain meaning in her look, one which Richard rightfully interpreted, especially when Araceli continued, "You've ever considered proposing to Katie? I'm almost certain she would say yes, although I don't know about sharing the trailer with you. Katie has lots of books, and you barely have any shelf-space for them, out at the Age."

Richard, on the spur of the moment, decided upon complete frankness, admitting, "I have considered that option, now and again."

"What's holding you back, then?" Araceli lowered her voice, to barely audible over the hum of the industrial dishwasher which Beatrice, the junior waitress, had loaded and set to cycle through before joining her fellows on break.

Richard decided that he might well be honest with the person who was his oldest and truest ally and friend in Luna City. "The absolute conviction that I am not worthy of Kate. I remain what I always have been. An unbearable, self-centered and inconsiderate shit. She's a fine and worthy woman, admirable in every possible way; about the only one such that I have known since I was in short trousers. I am afraid that I would cause her deep unhappiness … and believe me, Araceli! I have caused enough women unhappiness to know the signs, especially after having several table lamps and a small Henry Moore bronze sculpture shied at my head. I don't want to run that risk with Kate!"

"Wow," Araceli replied. "I never heard about that one."

"I paid a bomb to keep it out of the tabs," Richard admitted, with somewhat of a shamed face. "It was a private fight with Sammi. No need for anyone else to get involved. The thing is … frankly, I adore Kate, mostly because she seems to believe that I am a better and more worthy person. In spite of nearly immolating her aged grandparent last Christmas with a flaming plum pudding."

"That one I heard about," Araceli grinned. "But OK; it wasn't deliberate. It wasn't?" she added, and Richard chuckled sourly.

"No, it was totally accidental. Everyone who was present, which includes just about all of the Clan Heisel and witness said so, solo and chorus. But you see …" and Richard took the deepest breath of his life, feeling that he was about to dive into deep and cold waters in being honest out loud where anyone could hear. "I do love Kate. I love Ozzie, and I cannot bear the thought of losing either from my life. I can't endure the risk, you see."

"I see," and it reassured Richard that Araceli sounded understanding, completely so. "Look, you're in a vulnerable place…"

"Please don't use amateur psychobabble on me," Richard snapped, and immediately relented, as Araceli replied,

"Seriously? Psychobabble? I think I must have heard more heartfelt confessions with this pot of coffee in my hand than just about any analyst in Karnes County, and given out just as much good and effective advice as any of them. Pull up your big-boy pants, do your job, be honest, not a pathetic BS-artist. Be an adult, Ricardo. Seriously! Try it out – you might like it. And it even might make your life easier, even if it seems hard at first." Araceli set down the ever-threatening hot carafe and regarded Richard with exasperated affection. "Go ahead – bring up the subject of marriage with Katie, in your own sweet time, but I'm about ninety-five percent certain that she'll say yes to a straight-forward proposal. Just give it some thought and don't let the opportunity slide."

"I will."

Curiously, Richard felt at ease with the concept and the possibility, even relieved that Araceli had brought it up. "You're a brick, Araceli. In the event she says 'yes' and we carry through with it, can you be my Best … well, Best Person? Carry the ring, make a speech and all that? You're practically my best friend in this place. Would you?"

Araceli giggled. "Actually, I think Chris would be a better choice for Best Man. Tell you what, Ricardo: when you and Kate set a date, let me act as your big sister and organize everything for you. Deal?"

"Deal," Richard acknowledged, feeling now even more relieved. "Yes, Chris would stand up with me; a scholar and a gentleman, and a damn-fine judge of … whatever. Thank you, Araceli. You know, it's rather refreshing. I was an only child … it's nice to have an older sister and think that I'm part of a larger family."

"You are, Ricardo," Araceli collected up the coffee carafe and cream jug again. "You are."

Alone in the quiet of the kitchen, something fell into place, a quiet certainty, a feeling of peace and assurance.

"I will ask her," Richard said aloud. "I'll ask Kate if she wants to get married to me. Monday, the first time that we are alone together. I will for certain ask her."

To be continued ... of course!

www.ingramcontent.com/pod-product-compliance
Lightning Source LLC
Chambersburg PA
CBHW032252020726
47495CB00001B/70

9780989782173